KILLOE

In 1858, Texas was getting crowded, so Dan Killoe, his father and family, their friends and their cattle, headed west to find new, untouched land.

All they had to do was beat off the bushwhackers who wanted to steal their cattle, slip by the Comanches, who would lift their scalps, outsmart the Comancheros—and then hold the land they settled on.

This is the story of violent men in a violent time—men who had one simple rule: keep what's yours—cattle, horses, land, women—and KILL TO KEEP IT!!

Also by Louis L'Amour

HOW THE WEST WAS WON
THE STRONG SHALL LIVE
BENDIGO SHAFTER
THE IRON MARSHAL
FAIR BLOWS THE WIND
TO THE FAR BLUE MOUNTAINS
WESTWARD THE TIDE
MAN FROM BROKEN HILLS
RIVERS WEST
SACKETT'S LAND
LANDO
RADIGAN
THE LONELY MEN
DOWN THE LONG HILLS
THE EMPTY LAND
TREASURE MOUNTAIN
THE DAYBREAKERS
RIDE THE DARK TRAIL
SACKETT
THE KEYLOCK MAN
KIOWA TRAIL
THE HIGH GRADERS
HANGING WOMAN CREEK
MOJAVE CROSSING

THE FIRST FAST DRAW
GUNS OF THE TIMBERLAND
GALLOWAY
MUSTANG MAN
DARK CANYON
THE BROKEN GUN
THE SKYLINERS
KILRONE
YONDERING
THE WARRIOR'S PATH
THE WAR PARTY
THE BURNING HILLS
MATAGORDA
THE SILVER CANYON
OVER ON THE DRY SIDE
RIDER OF THE LOST CREEK
LONELY ON THE MOUNTAIN
MILO TALON
HIGH LONESOME
CALLAGHEN
TUCKER
THE FERGUSON RIFLE
WHERE THE LONG GRASS BLOWS

and published by Corgi Books

Louis L'Amour

Killoe

CORGI BOOKS
A DIVISION OF TRANSWORLD PUBLISHERS LTD

KILLOE
A CORGI BOOK 0 552 08386 0

First publication in Great Britain

PRINTING HISTORY
Corgi edition published 1962
Corgi edition reissued 1970
Corgi edition reprinted 1972
Corgi edition reprinted 1974
Corgi edition reprinted 1977
Corgi edition reprinted 1982

Corgi Books are published by Transworld Publishers Ltd.,
Century House, 61-63 Uxbridge Road,
Ealing, London, W5 5SA.
Made and printed in Great Britain by
Hunt Barnard Printing, Aylesbury, Bucks.

Chapter One

Pa came down to the breaks along the Cowhouse where I was rousting out some steers that had taken to the brush because of the heel-flies.

"Come up to the house, boy. Tap has come home and he is talking of the western lands."

So I gathered my rope to a coil and slung it on the pommel of my saddle, and stepping up to the leather, I followed Pa up through the trees and out on the open grass.

Folks were standing in the breezeway of our Texas house, and others were grouped around in bunches, listening to Tap Henry or talking among themselves.

It was not a new thing, for there had been argument and discussion going on for weeks. We all knew that something must be done, and westward the land was empty.

Tap Henry was a tall man of twenty-seven or -eight and we had been boys together, although he was a good six to seven years older than me. A hard, reckless man with a taste for wild country and wilder living, he was a top hand in any man's outfit, and a good man with a gun.

You couldn't miss Tap Henry. He was well over six feet tall and weighed a compact one hundred and ninety. He wore a freshly laundered blue shield-style shirt with a row of buttons down each side, shotgun chaps, and Spanish boots with big California spurs.

He still packed that pearl-handled six-shooter he had

taken off a man he had killed, and he was handsome as ever in that hard, flashy way of his. He was our friend and, in a sense, he was my brother.

Our eyes met across the heads of the others as I rode up, and his were cold and measuring. It was a look I had seen in his eyes before, but never directed at me. It was the way he looked when he saw a possible antagonist. Recognition came suddenly to his eyes.

"Danny! Dan, boy!" He strode through the crowd that had gathered to hear his talk of the lands to the west, and thrust out a hand. "Well, I'll be forever damned! You've grown up!"

Stepping down from the saddle, I met his grip with one of my own, remembering how Tap prided himself on his strength. For a moment I matched him, grip for grip, then let him have the better of it, for he was a proud man and I liked him, and I had nothing to prove.

It surprised me that we stood eye to eye, for he had always seemed very tall, and I believe it surprised him too.

Almost involuntarily, his eyes dropped to my belt, but I was wearing no gun. My rifle was in my saddle-boot and my knife was in its sheath.

"We're going west, Danny!" His hand on my shoulder, we walked back to where Pa now stood with Aaron Stark and Tim Foley. "I've scouted the land, and there is grass enough, and more!"

Pa glanced curiously from one to the other of us, and from the shadow of the breezeway Zebony Lambert watched us, a strange light in his green eyes. Zeb's long brown hair lay about his shoulders, as carefully combed as a woman's, his eyes level and hard under the flat brim of his Spanish hat.

Zebony Lambert was my friend, but I do not think he had many friends, for he was a solitary, self-keeping sort of man little given to talk. Of medium height, his extraordinarily broad shoulders made him seem shorter, and they were well set off by the short Spanish jacket he wore, and the buckskin, bell-bottomed breeches.

Lambert and Tap had never met until now, and it

2

worried me a little, for both were strong men, and Tap was inclined toward arrogance.

"Is it true, then?" I asked Pa. "Is it decided?"

"Aye . . . we're going west, Dan."

Tim Foley was our neighbor who ran a few cows of his own, but occasionally worked for us. A square-built man with a square, honest face. "And high time," he said, "for there is little grass and we have those about us who like us not at all."

"How far is it, then?"

"Six hundred miles or less. Right across Texas and into New Mexico. If we do not go on, it will be less."

Pa looked at me. More and more he was paying mind to my judgment, and listening to what I had to say. He was still the boss . . . I knew that and he knew it, but he had respect for my judgment, which had grown since he had been leaving the cattle business to me.

"How many head, Dan? What can we muster?" Pa put the question and I caught a surprised look from Tap, for he remembered me as a boy, and a boy only.

"Fifteen hundred at least, and I'd say a bit more than that. Tim will have a good three hundred head under his own brand, and Aaron nearly as many. When all are rounded up and the breaks swept clean, I would say close to three thousand head."

"It is a big herd, and we will be short of men," Pa commented thoughtfully.

"There will be three wagons, and the horse herd," I added.

"Wagons?" Tap objected. "I hadn't planned on wagons."

"We have our families," Tim said, "and there are tools we must take."

There began a discussion of what to take, of trail problems and men, and I leaned against the corral rail, listening without paying much attention. In every such venture there is always more talk than is necessary, with everybody having his say, but I knew that when all was said, much of it would be left to me, and I would do as seemed best to me.

3

There is no point in such endless discussion, except that men become familiar with their problems. Long ago, when the first discussion of such a move began, I had also begun thinking of it, and had made some plans I thought necessary. Lambert, a thoughtful man, had contributed a few pointed and common-sense suggestions.

We could muster barely a dozen men, far too few for the task that lay ahead. Once the herd was trail-broke, four to five men might keep it moving without much trouble, but until then it would be a fight. Some of these old mossyhorns had grown up there on the Cowhouse and they had no wish to leave home.

There would be the usual human problems too, even though the people who would be accompanying our move would all be known to us. And once away from the settlements, there would be Comanches.

It was a risk, a big risk. We were chancing everything. We might have fought it out where we were, but Pa was no hand for a fight, although he had courage enough for two men, and had seen his share of fighting in the Mexican War and with Indians. He had grown up in the Five Counties and knew what feuding meant. It was Tap who had suggested going west, and Pa fell in with it.

But there was risk connected with everything, and we were hard men bred to a hard life in a hard land, and the lives that we lived were lonely, yet rich with the voice of our singing, and with tales told of an evening by the campfire.

What pleasures we had were created by ourselves or born of the land, our clothing was made by our own hands, our houses and corrals, also. Those who rode beside us knew the measure of our strength as we knew theirs, and each knew the courage of the other.

In that country a man saddled his own broncs and fought his own battles, and the measure of his manhood was that he did what needed to be done, and did it well, and without shirking.

Me? I, Dan Killoe, was born in a claim cabin on Cowhouse Creek with the roar of buffalo guns filling the room as Pa and my Uncle Fred beat off an Indian attack. I let out my first yell in a room filled with gunsmoke, and when Ma died I was nursed by a Mexican woman whose father died fighting with the Texans at the Alamo.

When I was six, Pa met Tap's Ma on a trip to Fort Worth, and married her, bringing her west to live with us, and they brought Tap along.

She was a pretty woman, as I recall, and good enough to us boys, but she wasn't cut out for frontier life, and finally she cut and run with some no-account drifter, leaving Tap to live with us.

Tap always pulled his weight, and more. He took to cow country like he was born to it, and we got along. He was thirteen and doing a man's work and proud of it, for the difference between a man and a boy is the willingness to do a man's work and take a man's responsibility.

Being older than me, he was always the leader, no matter what we were doing, and a few times when we had a chance to attend school, he took up for me when I might have taken a beating from bigger boys.

When Tap pulled out the first time he was seventeen and I was a bit more than ten. He was gone most of a year, working for some outfit over in the Big Thicket.

The next time I saw him he was wearing a pistol, and we heard rumors he had killed a man over near Caddo Lake.

When he was at home he worked like all get-out, but he soon had the name of being a good man to let alone. Pa said nothing much to him, only dropping a comment now and then, and Tap always listened, or seemed to. But he was gone most of the time after that, and each time he came back he was bigger, tougher, and more sure of himself.

It had been three years since we had last seen Tap, but now he was back, and at the right time, too. Trouble was building along the Cowhouse and neighbors were crowding in, and it was time we moved west and laid claim to land.

We would be leaving mighty little on the Cowhouse. When Pa moved into the country a body couldn't live there at all without neighbors and they bunched up for protection. Some died and some were killed, some drifted and some sold out, but the country changed and the people, and now it was building into a fight for range.

Some of the newcomers had no cattle, and from time to time they would kill a beef of ours. Pa was no one to keep a man's youngsters from food, so he allowed it. The trouble was, they turned from killing a beef for food to driving them off and selling them, and trouble was cropping up.

A couple of times I'd caught men with our brand on some steers they were driving, and I drove them back, but twice shots had been fired at me.

The old crop that worked hard and fought hard for their homes were gone. This new lot seemed to figure they could live off what we had worked for, and it was developing into trouble. What we wanted was land that belonged to us—land with boundaries and lines drawn plain and clear; but due to the way everybody had started out on the Cowhouse, that wasn't true here.

There was talk of moving west, and then Tap rode in, fresh from that country.

Pa was a farmer at heart, more interested in crops than cattle, and of late I'd taken to running the cattle business.

"It is a bad trip, I'll not lie about that," Tap was saying. "But the time of year is right, and if we start soon there will be grass and water."

"And when we get there?" Foley asked.

"The best grass you ever saw, and water too. We can stop on the Pecos in New Mexico, or we can go on to Colorado."

"What would you suggest?" Foley was a shrewd man, and he was keeping a close watch on Tap as he questioned him.

"The Pecos country. Near Bosque Redondo."

Karen Foley came to stand beside me, her eyes watching Tap. "Isn't he exciting?" she said. "I'm glad he will be with us."

For the first time I felt a twinge of jealousy, but it

6

was a small twinge, for I liked and admired Tap Henry myself, and I knew what she meant.

Tap was different. He had come riding back into our lives wearing better clothes than we could afford, riding a fine chestnut gelding with a beautifully hand-tooled saddle, the first one I had ever seen. Moreover, he carried himself with a kind of style.

He had a hard, sure way about him and he walked and moved with an assurance we did not have. You felt there was no uncertainty about Tap Henry, that he knew what he wanted and knew how to get it. Only faintly, and with a twinge of guilt, did I think that perhaps he cared too little for the feelings or interests of others. Nevertheless, I could think of no better man on a trip of the kind we were planning.

Karen was another thing, for Karen and I had been walking out together, talking a little, and a couple of times we had taken rides together. We had no understanding or anything like it, but she was the prettiest girl anywhere around, and for a girl out on the Texas plains she got herself up mighty well.

She was the oldest of Tim Foley's three children. The other two were boys, fourteen and ten.

It was plain she was taken by Tap Henry, and one thing I knew about Tap was that he was no man to take lightly where women were concerned. He had a way with them, and they took to him.

Pa turned around. "Come over here, Dan. We want your advice."

Tap laughed as I walked up, and clapped a hand on my shoulder in that way he had. "What's the matter, Killoe? You taking advice from kids now?"

"Dan knows more about cattle than anybody I ever knew," Pa said quietly, "and this won't be his first trail drive."

"You?" Tap was surprised. "A trail drive?"

"Uh-huh. I took a herd through Baxter Springs last year. Took them through to Illinois and sold them."

"Baxter Springs?" Tap chuckled. "Lost half your herd,

I'll bet. I know that crowd around Baxter Springs."

"They didn't cut Dan's herd," Foley said, "and they didn't turn him aside. Dan took them on through and sold out for a good price."

"Good!" Tap squeezed my shoulder. "We'll make a team, won't we, boy? Man, it's good to be back!"

He glanced over toward the corral where Karen was standing. All of a sudden he said, "Well, you understand what's needed here. When you are ready for the trail, I'll take over."

He walked away from us and went over to where Karen stood by the rail. Tim Foley glanced after him, but his face revealed nothing. Nevertheless, I knew Tim well enough to know he disapproved.

Foley turned and went into the house and the others drifted away, leaving Pa and me standing there together.

"Well," Pa said, "Tap's back. What do you think of him?"

"We're lucky to have him. He knows the water-holes, and he's a good hand. Believe me, Pa, before this drive is over we'll need every man."

"Yes, that we will." He seemed about to say something more, but he did not.

Pa was a canny man and not given to unnecessary talk, and I knew that if he had something on his mind he would say it soon enough. Something was bothering him, however, but all he said a minute later was, "Do you remember Elsie?"

Elsie Henry had been Tap's mother, and I did remember her. She was the only mother I'd ever had, but somehow she never seemed like a mother . . . more like somebody who came to stay for a while and then went away. Yet she was good to Tap and me and, looking back on it, I knew she had done a lot of thinking before she broke loose and ran off.

"Yes, I remember her."

"She wasn't cut out for this life. She should not have come west."

"I often wondered why she did. She was a pretty

8

woman with a taste for pretty clothes and fancy living. Seems to me she would have been happier back east."

"Character," Pa said, "is the thing, whether it's horses, dogs, or men. Or women, for that matter."

He walked off without saying anything more, and I took my horse to the corral and stripped off the outfit and hung it up. All the time I was thinking of what Pa had said, and wondering what lay back of it. Pa had a way of saying things that left a lot unsaid, and I was wondering just how far he wanted that comment to go.

But with the trip coming up, there was very little time for thinking of that. Or of anything else.

It was spring . . . hot and dry. There had been some good winter rains, and there should be water along the trail to Horsehead Crossing on the Pecos.

Squatting on my heels near the corral, I gave thought to that. Karen and Tap had wandered off somewhere, but right now I was thinking about horses. We would need a cavvy of fifty or sixty head, and with all the horses we could round up between us, including those belonging to Tim Foley and Aaron Stark, we would be short about twenty head.

Two of the wagons needed working on and there was harness to mend. Also, we must get a lot of lead for bullets, and cast enough at least to get us started in case of Comanche trouble. And we would need some additional barrels for carrying water.

Zebony Lambert strolled over and dropped to his heels beside me. He was smoking tobacco wrapped in paper, a habit some of the Texans were picking up from the Mexicans. Most of us smoked cigars, when we smoked.

"So that's Tap Henry."

He spoke in a peculiarly flat tone, and I glanced around at him. When Zeb spoke in that voice I knew he was either unimpressed or disapproving, and I wanted them to like each other.

"We spent a lot of time together as boys, Zeb. He's my half brother, stepbrother . . . whatever they call it."

"Heard that."

9

"When his Ma ran off, Pa let him stay on. Treated him like another son."

Zeb looked across the yard to where Tap was laughing and talking with Karen.

"Did he ever see his mother again?"

"No. Not that I know of."

"He fancies that gun, doesn't he?"

"That he does . . . and he's good with it, too."

Zeb finished his cigarette, then pushed it into the dirt. "If you need help," he said, "I stand ready. You'll need more horses."

"You see any wild stuff?"

"Over on the Leon River. You want to try for them?" Zeb was the best wild-horse hunter anywhere around. The trouble was there there was so little time. If we wanted to travel when there was water to be found we should be starting now. We should have started two weeks ago.

Zebony Lambert never worked for any man. Often he would pitch in and help out, and he was a top hand, but he would never take pay. Nobody understood that about him, but nobody asked questions in Texas. A man's business and his notions were his own private affair.

"Maybe we can swap with Tom Sandy. There's a lot of young stuff down in the breaks, too young for a trail herd."

"He'll throw in with you if you ask him."

"Sandy?" I could not believe it. "He's got him a good outfit. Why should he move?"

"Rose."

Well, that made a kind of sense. Still, any man who would leave a place like he had for Rose would leave any other place for her, and would in the end wind up with nothing. Rose was a mighty pretty woman and she kept a good house, but she couldn't keep her eyes off other men. Worst of all, she had what it took to keep their eyes on her, and she knew it.

"She'll get somebody killed."

"She'll get Tom killed."

Zeb got up. "I'll ride by about sunup. Help you with

that young stuff." He paused. "I'll bring the dogs."

Zebony Lambert had worked cattle over in the Big Thicket and had a bunch of the best cattle-working dogs a man ever did see, and in brush country a dog is worth three cowhands.

He went to his horse and stepped into the saddle. I never tired of watching him do it. The way he went into the leather was so smooth, so effortless, that you just couldn't believe it. Zeb had worked with me a lot, and I never knew a better coordinated man, or one who handled himself with greater ease.

He walked his horse around the corral so he would not have to pass Tap Henry, and just as he turned the horse Tap looked up.

It was plain to him that Lambert was deliberately avoiding him, for around the corral was the long way. Tap laid his eyes on Zeb and watched him ride off, stepping around Karen to keep his eyes on him.

The smell of cooking came from the house, where Mrs. Foley was starting supper.

Karen and Tap were talking when I approached the house. He was talking low and in a mighty persuasive tone, and she was laughing and shaking her head, but I could see she was taken with him, and it got under my skin. After all, Karen was my girl—or so everybody sort of figured.

Tap looked up. "You know, Karen, I can't believe Danny's grown up. He used to follow me around like a sucking calf."

She laughed, and I felt my face getting red. "I didn't follow you everywhere, Tap," I replied. "I didn't follow you over the Brazos that time."

He looked like I'd slapped him across the mouth, but before he could say something mean, Karen put a hand on his sleeve. "You two are old friends . . . even brothers. Now, don't you go and get into any argument."

"You're right, Karen," I said, and walked by them into the house.

Mrs. Foley glanced up when I came in, and then her

eyes went past me to Tap and Karen. "Your brother is quite handsome," she said, and the way she said it carried more meaning than the words themselves.

For three days then we worked sunup to sundown, with Tap Henry, Zeb Lambert, and Aaron Stark working the breaks for young stuff. Pa rode over to have a talk with Tom Sandy about a swap, and Tim Foley worked on the wagons, with his boys to help.

Lambert's dogs did the work of a dozen hands in getting those steers out of the brush and out of the overhang caves along the Cowhouse which gave the creek its name.

Jim Poor, Ben Cole, and Ira Tilton returned from delivering a small herd to San Antonio and fell in with us, and the work began to move faster.

Every time I had the chance I asked Tap questions about that route west. The one drive I'd made, the one up through Kansas and Missouri into Illinois, had taught me a good deal about cattle, but that was a sight better country than what we were heading into now.

The corn grinding was one of the biggest jobs, and the steadiest. We had a cornmill fixed to a post and two cranks on it. That mill would hold something around a peck of corn, but the corn had to go through two grindings to be right for bread-baking. We ground it once, then tightened the mill and ran it through again, grinding it still finer.

We wanted as much corn ground as possible before the trip started, for we might not be able to use the grinder on the road without more trouble than we could afford. Between grinding the corn and jerking beef, there was work a-plenty for everyone.

None of us, back in those days, wore store-bought clothes. It was homespun or buckskin, and for the most part the men dressed their own skins and made their own clothes, with fringe on the sleeves and pants legs to drain the rain off faster. Eastern folks usually thought that fringe was purely ornamental, which was not true.

For homespun clothes of either cotton or wool, the stuff was carded and spun by hand, and if it was cotton, the seeds were picked out by hand. Every man made his own moccasins or boots, repaired what tools or weapons he had, and in some cases made them from the raw material.

Down among the trees along the Cowhouse the air was stifling. It was a twisty creek, with the high banks under which the cattle took shelter, and it was hot, hard work, with scarcely room to build a loop.

A big brindle steer cut out of the trees ahead of me, and went through them, running like a deer, with me and that steeldust gelding right after him. Ducking a heavy branch that would have torn my head off, I took a smaller one smack across the face, making my eyes water. The steer lunged into a six-foot wall of brush and that steeldust right after him. Head down, I went through, feeling the branches and thorns tearing at my chaps. The steer broke into the open and I took after him, built a loop, and dropped it over his horns.

That old steeldust sat right back on his haunches and we busted that steer tail-over-teakettle and laid him down hard. He came up fighting. He was big, standing over sixteen hands . . . and he was mad . . . and he weighed an easy eighteen hundred.

He put his head down and came for me and that steel-dust, but that bronc of mine turned on a dime and we busted Mr. Steer right back into the dust again.

He got up, dazed but glaring around, ready for a fight with anything on earth, but before he could locate a target I started off through the brush at a dead run and when that rope jerked him by the horns he had no choice but to come after us.

Once out in the open again and close to the herd, I shook loose my loop and hazed him into the herd.

It was heat, dust, sweat, charging horses, fighting steers, and man-killing labor. One by one we worked them out of the brush and up onto the plain where they could be bunched. Except for a few cantakerous old mossyhorns, they were usually content as long as they were with others of their kind in the herd.

That tough old brindle tried to make it back to the

brush, back to his home on the Cowhouse, but we busted him often enough to make a believer of him.

Tap, like I said, was a top hand. He fell into the routine and worked as hard as any of us.

We rolled out of our soogans before there was light in the sky, and when the first gray showed we were heading for the brush. We wore down three or four horses a day, but there are no replacements for the men on a cow outfit.

Breakfast was usually beef and beans, the same as lunch, or sometimes if the women were in the notion, we had griddle cakes and sorghum . . . corn squeezings, we called it.

Morning of the third day broke with a lowering gray sky, but we didn't see that until later. We had two days of brutal labor behind us, and more stretching ahead. Usually, I slept inside. Pa and me occupied one side of the Texas, Tim Foley and his family the other side; but with Stark's wife and kids, we gave up our beds to them and slept outside with the hands.

Rolling out of my soogan that third morning, it took me only a minute to put on my hat—a cowhand always puts on his hat first—and then my boots and buckskin pants.

The women had been up and we could hear dishes a-rattling around inside. Tap crawled out of his blankets and walked to the well, where he hauled up a bucket of water and washed. I followed him. He looked sour and mean, like he always did come daybreak. With me it was otherwise—I always felt great in the morning, but I had sense enough to keep still about it.

We went up to the house and Mrs. Foley and Karen filled our plates. That morning it was a healthy slab of beef and a big plate of beans and some fried onions.

Like always, I had my bridle with me and I stuck the bit under my jacket to warm it up a mite. Of a frosty morning I usually warmed it over a fire enough to make it easy for a horse to take, and while it wasn't too cold this morning, I wanted that bronc of mine to be in a good mood.

14

Not that he would be . . . or ever was.

We sat on the steps or squatted around on the ground against the wall, eating in silence. Karen came out with the big pot and refilled our cups, and took a mite longer over Tap's cup.

None of us was talking very much, but Zebony moved over beside me when he had finished eating and began to make one of those cigarettes of his.

"You been over to the Leon?"

"No."

"You and me . . . we take a *pasear* over there. What do you say?"

"There's plenty of work right here," I said. "I don't see—"

"I do," Tap interrupted. "I know what he means."

Zeb touched a delicate tongue-tip to his thin paper. "Do you think," he said to me, "they will let you drive your cattle away?"

"They belong to us."

"Sure—there are mighty few that don't. Those others . . . the newcomers . . . they have no cattle, and they have been living on yours. By now they know you are planning a drive, and are cleaning out the breaks."

"So?"

"Dan, what's got into you?" Tap asked irritably. "They'll rustle every steer they can, and fight you for the others. How many men have we got?"

"Now? Nine or ten."

"And how many of them? There must be thirty."

"Closer to forty," Zeb said. "There's tracks over on the Leon. They are bunching your cows faster than you are, and driving them north into the wild country."

"I reckon we'd best go after them," I said.

Tap got up. "I reckon we had," he said dryly. "And if you ever carried a short gun, you'd better carry one when you go after them."

It made sense. This lot who had squatted around us had brought nothing into the country except some beat-up horses and wagon outfits. Not more than two or three had so much as a milk cow . . . and they had been getting

15

fat on our beef, eating it, which Pa never minded much, and even selling it. And not one of them had done a tap of work. They had come over from the east and south somewhere—a bedraggled bunch of poor whites and the like.

That did not make them easy. Some of that outfit had come down from Missouri and Arkansas, and some were from the Five Counties, where there had been fighting for years. Pa was easy-going and generous, and they had spotted it right off.

"Don't tell Pa," I said. "He's no hand with a gun."

Tap glanced at me briefly as if to say, "And I suppose you are?" But I paid him no mind.

Tim Foley saw us bunched up and he walked over. That man never missed a thing. He minded his own affairs, but he kept an ear to the ground. "You boys be careful," was all he said.

The sun was staining the sky with rose when we moved out from the place. As we rode away, I told Ben Cole to keep the rest of them in the bottoms of the Cowhouse and to keep busy. They knew something was up, but they offered no comment, and we trailed it off to the west, then swung north.

"You know who it is?" I asked Zeb.

"That Holt outfit, Mack, Billy, and Webb—all that crowd who ride with them."

Tough men, and mean men. Dirty, unshaven, thieves and killers all of them. A time or two I'd seen them around.

"Webb," I commented, "is left-handed."

Tap looked around at me. "Now that," he said, "is a good thing to know."

"Carries his gun on the right side, butt first, and he draws with either hand."

We picked up their trail in a coulee near the Leon River and we took it easy. They were driving some twenty head, and there were two men. Following the trail was no trick, because they had made no attempt to hide it. In fact, they seemed to be inviting trouble, and realiz-

16

ing how the odds figured out, they might have had that in mind.

We walked our horses up every slope and looked around before we crossed the ridges or hills. We kept to low ground when we could and just managed to keep the trail in sight.

If we moved our cattle out of this country the rest of that ragtag and bobtail would have to move out or starve to death. Cattle were plentiful in most parts of Texas and it wasn't until later that folks began to watch their beef. For a long time, when a man needed beef he went out and killed one, just as he had buffalo, and nobody paid it no mind.

In those days cattle were good for their hides and tallow, and there was no other market. A few drives had been made to Louisiana, to Shreveport, and over into Alabama, but cattle were a drug on the market. However, this far west the wild cattle had begun to thin out, and fewer were to be found.

This was the frontier, and west of us there was nothing but wide, unsettled country. In those days the settler furthest west in Texas was a farmer who was about four miles west of Fort Belknap, and that was away off north of us, and a little west.

Cattle liked the country further east or along the river bottoms where the grass was thick. Zeb Lambert told me he had seen a few over on the Colorado, west of us, but they were strays that had somehow found their way there. Nobody lived in that country.

The coolness remained in the morning, clouds were heavy, and there was a dampness as of coming rain. Despite the work we had to do, we hoped for it. Rain in this country meant not only water in the water-holes and basins, but it meant grass on the range. In a few days our lives would depend on both.

Zeb Lambert pulled up. "Dan," he said, "look here."

We both stopped and looked at the trail. Two riders had come in from the east and joined the two we were trailing. The grass was pushed down by their horses' hoofs

17

and had not straightened up—they could have joined them only minutes before.

Tap Henry looked at those tracks. "It could be accident," he said.

"What do you mean?" I asked him.

"Or it could be that somebody told them we were riding this way."

Zebony said nothing, but he started building himself one of those cigarettes he set so much store by.

"Who would do a thing like that?" I asked. "None of our crowd."

"When you've lived as long as me," Tap said shortly, "you won't trust anybody. We were following two men . . . now two more come in out of nowhere."

We rode on, more cautiously now. Tap was too suspicious. None of our folks would carry word to that bunch of no-account squatters. Yet there were four of them now, and only three of us. We did not mind the odds, but it set a man to thinking. If they were tipped off that we were moving against them there might be more of them coming.

Tap suddenly turned his head and saw Zeb cutting off over the rise.

"Now what's got into him?" he demanded.

"He'll be hunting sign. Zeb could track a coon over the cap-rock in the dark of the moon."

"Will he stand?"

"He'll stand. He's a fighter, Tap. You never saw a better."

Tap looked after him, but made no comment. Tap was riding tall in the saddle this morning, head up and alert, ready for trouble. And Tap Henry was a man who had seen trouble. There had been times before he left us when he had to face up to a difficulty, and no telling how many times since then.

Suddenly, we smelled smoke.

Almost at the same moment we saw our cattle. There must have been three hundred head bunched there, and four men were sitting around the fire. Only one of them got to his feet as we approached.

"Watch it, Tap," I said, "there's more of them."

The hollow where they were was long, maybe a quarter of a mile, and there were willows and cottonwood along the creek, and here and there some mesquite. Those willows shielded the creek from view. No telling what else they might hide.

The remuda was staked out close by. My eyes went to the staked-out horses. "Tap," I said, "five of those horses are showing sweat."

Webb Holt was there, and Bud Caldwell, and a long, lean man named Tuttle. The fourth man had a shock of uncombed blond hair that curled over his shirt collar, and a chin that somehow did not quite track with his face. He had a sour, mean look about him.

"Those cows are showing our brand," I said mildly. "We're taking them back."

"Are you now?" Webb Holt asked insolently.

"And we're serving notice. No more beef—not even one."

"You folks come it mighty big around here," Webb commented. "Where'd you get the right to all these cattle? They run loose until you came along."

"Not here they didn't. There were no cattle here until my father drove them in, and the rest came by natural increase. Since then we've ridden herd on them, nursed them, dragged them out of bogs, and fought the heel-flies and varmints.

"You folks came in here with nothing and you've made no attempt to get anything. We'd see no man go hungry, least of all when he has young ones, so we've let you have beef to eat. Now you're stealing."

"Do tell?" Holt tucked his thumbs behind his belt. "Well, let me tell you something. You folks want to leave out of here, you can. But you're taking no cows."

"If you're counting on that man back in the brush," I said, "you'd best forget him. He won't be able to help you none."

Holt's eyes flickered, and Bud Caldwell touched his tongue to his lips. The blond man never turned a hair. He kept looking at Tap Henry like he'd seen him some place before.

"I don't know what you're figuring on," I said, "but in your place I'd just saddle up and ride out. And what other cattle of ours you have, I'd drive back."

"Now why would we do that?" Holt asked, recovering some of his confidence. "We got the cows. You got nothing. You haven't even got the men."

"The kind we've got," Tap said, "we don't need many."

Holt's eyes shifted. "I don't know you," he said.

Tap jerked his head. "I'm Dan's stepbrother, you might say, and I've got a shooting interest in that stock."

"I know him," the blond man said suddenly. "That's Tap Henry. I knew him over on the Neuces."

"So?"

"He's a gunfighter, Webb."

Webb Holt centered his attention on Tap. He was wary now. Bud Caldwell moved a little to one side, spreading them out. My Paterson revolving rifle lay across my saddle, my hand across the action, and as he moved, I let the muzzle follow him . . . it seemed to make him nervous.

Tap kept his eyes on Holt. We knew there was a man out there in the brush, but we—at least I did—depended on Zeb to take care of him. It was a lot of depending, yet a man can do only so much, and we had four men there in front of us.

"You're going to have a choice to make," Tap said, "any minute now. If you make the right choice, you live."

Webb Holt's tongue touched his lips. He knew he was looking right down the muzzle of Tap's gun, and if Tap was faster then he was, Webb was dead. I had let my horse back up a mite so I could keep both Bud and that blond man under my eyes.

"You can catch up your horses and ride out," I said. "You can start any time you're of a mind to."

Suddenly Zebony Lambert was standing on the edge of the brush. "You boys can open the ball any time you

20

like," he said. "There's nobody out there in the brush to worry about."

You could see them start to sweat. It was three to four now, and my rifle was laid right on one of them. Bud was a tough enough man, but he wasn't going to play the hero. Not on this fine spring morning. Until a few minutes ago he had been complaining the weather was mighty miserable; now any kind of a morning was a fine morning.

"You kill that man?" Holt demanded.

"He didn't make an issue of it," Zeb replied.

Nobody said anything for about a minute, and it was a long minute. Then I stepped my horse up, holding that rifle muzzle on Caldwell.

"Case you're interested," I said, casually, "this here is a Paterson revolving rifle and she shoots five shots . . . .56 caliber."

"Webb . . . ?" Bud Caldwell was kind of nervous. That Paterson was pointed right at his stomach and the range was less than twenty feet.

"All right," Webb Holt replied, "we can wait. We got forty men, and we want these cows. You folks take 'em along now—you won't keep them."

"Webb?" Tap's voice had an edge to it that raised the hair on the back of my neck. "You and me, Webb. Those others are out of it."

"Now see here!" Webb Holt's face was touched with pallor.

"Forty, you said." Tap was very quiet. "I say thirty-nine, Webb. Just thirty-nine."

Bud Caldwell reached for the sky with both hands and the thin man backed up so fast he fell over a log and he just lay there, his arms outspread.

The blond man stood solid where he was. "He called it," he said loudly. "It's them two."

Webb Holt stood with his feet spread, his right side toward Tap Henry. His gun butt was on his right hip, the butt end to the fore and canted a mite.

"Look," he said, "we don't need to—" He grabbed iron and Tap shot him twice through the chest.

21

"Lucky you warned me about that left hand," Tap said. "I might have made a mistake."

We rounded up those cattle and drove them home, and nobody said anything, at any time.

Me, I was thinking about those other thirty-nine men, and most particularly about Holt's two brothers.

It was time we pulled out, and pulled out fast.

Chapter Two

We were there when the country was young and wild, and we knew the smell of gunsmoke and buffalo-chip fires. Some were there because they chose the free, wild way, and some were born to it, and knew no other.

To live with danger was a way of life, but we did not think of it as danger, merely as part of all that we must face in the natural order of living. There was no bravado in our carrying of guns, for a man could no more live without a gun in the Texas of the 1850's than he could live without a horse, or without food.

We learned to live like the Indians, for the Indians had been there first and knew the way of the land. We could not look to anyone for help, we must help ourselves; we could not look to anyone for food, we must find our food and prepare it ourselves.

Now there was no more time. Westward the land was open, westward lay our hopes, westward was our refuge. Those were years when half the world grew up with the knowledge that if everything went wrong they could always go west, and the West was foremost in the thinking of all men. It was the answer to unemployment, to bankruptcy, to adventure, to loneliness, to the broken-hearted. It was everybody's promised land.

We pointed the cattle west into the empty land, and the brindle steer took the lead. He had no idea where he was going, but he intended to be the first one there. Three thousand five hundred head of mixed stuff, with Tap Henry and Pa away out there in front, leading the herd.

The wagons took the flank on the side away from the dust. Tim Foley's boy was driving a wagon, and his wife drove another. Aaron Stark's wife was driving a third, and Frank Kelsey was driving Tom Sandy's big wagon.

Tom and Rose Sandy were coming with us. Zeb Lambert had been right about Sandy, for when he heard of our move he promptly closed a deal on an offer for his ranch, sold all his stock but the remuda and some three hundred head of selected breeding stock, and threw in with us.

He brought two hands with him. Kelsey had been with him ever since Tom Sandy had come to Texas riding a sore-backed mule, and the other hand was Zeno Yearly, a tall Tennessean.

Tilton, Cole, and Poor rode one flank, and two of Pa's other hands, Milo Dodge and Freeman Squires, the other.

We had been making our gather before Tap Henry returned, so getting on the road was no problem. Above all, speed was essential. Now that we had determined to leave, there was no sense in delaying and awaiting an attack, if it came.

We started before sunup, and those first few miles we kept them moving at a trot. We hoped that if we could keep them busy thinking about keeping up they would have less time to worry about where they were going.

We had two scouts out, Tim Foley away on the left, and Aaron Stark to the north, watching for any of the Holt crowd.

Zebony Lambert and me, we ate the dust of the drag, hazing the stragglers back into the herd, changing the minds of any that took a notion to bolt and run for their old home on the Cowhouse.

We made camp fifteen miles out that first night, bedding them down on about six acres in a bottom where the grass was good and there was water from a small stream that flowed toward the Leon River.

Ben Cole and Jim Poor took the first guard, riding around the herd in opposite directions. The rest of us headed for the chuck wagon where the women folks had prepared a meal.

From now on, the routine would vary little unless we headed into trouble. We would be lucky to make more than fifteen miles a day with the herd, and most of the time it would be closer to twelve. We were short of horses, having about five horses per man, when a drive of that kind could use anywhere up to eight or nine per man.

A herd of that size would spread out for a mile along a stream when watering, and when bunched for the night would browse a good bit; when actually bedded down they would use a good six acres. After they had fed they would sleep, and about midnight, as if by some secret order, they would rise, stretch, usually browse a little, and finally go back to sleep. Maybe a couple of hours later they would get up again, stretch, and then go back to sleep. Some of them might browse a mite during that second stretch. But by dawn they were all up and ready to move. In ordinary weather two men could keep guard over that many cattle. If there was a storm brewing it might take every hand.

Going to the fire with my cup and a tin plate in my hand, I could hear Ben Cole singing them to sleep. Singing was not just a way of keeping himself company; partly it was that the sound of a human voice—most cowpunchers sounded somewhat less than human when they sang—had a quieting effect. Also, it served notice to the cattle that the shadow they saw out there was a man, and therefore all right.

Karen filled my plate and cup. "You riding all right, Karen?"

She nodded, and her eyes went beyond me to where Tap was sitting. "He's a good man," I said dryly.

Her chin came up defensively. "I like him." Then she added, "After all, he is your brother."

Taking my grub, I walked over and dropped to the ground where Tap was sitting. "How you coming, kid?" he asked.

After that we ate in silence, and I expect all of us were thinking about what lay behind us as much as about what lay ahead. There were long, dry miles before us, but the

25

season was early, and our chances were good. At least as far as Horsehead Crossing on the Pecos.

When I had cleaned the Patterson, I turned in and stretched out. Nothing better than turning in after a hard day's work. I slept a little away from the rest of them so I could listen better, never wanting anything to come between me and the night.

The clouds had drifted off and the sky was clear. Somewhere over on the bluffs a coyote was talking it up, and from time to time a bird called in the night.

Next thing I knew a hand was shaking me and it was Ira Tilton. He and Stark had relieved Ben Cole and Jim Poor on first guard.

Rolling out, I put my hat on and slid into my boots. Tilton still stood there, chewing tobacco. He started to say something, then turned and walked off toward the fire, which was burned down to coals.

Hitching my chaps, I took the Patterson and went to the fire. Tap, who was sharing my night guard, was already squatting there, cupping his hands around the warm cup, and sipping coffee. He glanced up at me, but said nothing, and neither did I.

Tom Sandy had taken on the job of wrangling horses, and he was up and had a *grulla* caught up for me. Of a right, a hand usually caught up his own mounts, but Tom was not sleeping much these days. Seemed to me Tom should worry less and spend more time in bed, with problems like his.

The night was cold. Glancing at the Dipper, I saw it was after three in the morning. I swallowed another belt of black, scalding coffee and went over to that *grulla* and stepped into the saddle.

He unwound in a tight circle, crow-hopped a few times, and then we started off for the herd, both of us feeling better for the workout.

Tilton had little to say. "Quiet," he said, "quiet so far," and he rode off.

He was a puzzling man in a lot of ways. He had worked for us upwards of three years and I knew him hardly

26

better than when he first came. Not that that was unusual. Folks those days said little about their personal affairs, and many a man in Texas had come there because the climate was not healthy where he came from.

In Texas you did not ask questions about a man's past—that was his business. A man was judged by what he was and how he did what there was to do, and if he had been in trouble elsewhere, nobody paid it any mind. And that went for the law, too, where there was law. The law left you alone, no matter how badly you might be wanted elsewhere, so long as you stayed out of trouble where you were.

As far as that goes, there were several men working for Pa who might have had shady pasts, but they did their work and rode for the brand, and we expected nothing else.

That coyote off on the ridge was talking to the stars. And he was a coyote, too, not an Indian. Once you've heard them both, a body can tell the difference. Only a human voice echoes to any extent, and next to the human the coyote or wolf, but an owl or a quail will not echo at all.

Off across the herd I could hear Tap singing low. He had a good voice, and he was singing "Brennan on the Moor," an old song from the old country about an Irish highwayman. Circling wide, I drew up and listened.

The coyote was still . . . listening to Tap, most likely . . . the stars were bright. There was no other sound, only the rustling of the water in the stream nearby.

A big steer stood up and stretched, then another and another. A faint breeze stirred and the big steer lifted his head sharply. Now, a man who trusts to his own hearing only is a fool . . . you learn not only to look and listen, but to watch the reactions of animals and of birds, for they will often tell you things you would never sense otherwise.

Something was moving out there. That steer faced around, walking a step or two toward the north. My Patterson lifted a mite and I eased back on the hammer. The click was loud in the night, and that big steer flipped an ear at me, but kept his eyes where they were.

Tap was across the herd from me, but he was coming around, walking his horse. The herd was uneasy, so, risking revealing myself to whatever was out there, I commenced talking to them, speaking low and confidently, working my horse in nearer to them.

And I walked my horse toward the trouble.

The big steer kind of ducked his head, and I could almost see his nostrils flare as he moved up a step. He was full of fight, but his attitude puzzled me.

Cattle did not like the smell of Indians, and were apt to get skittish if they came around . . . maybe it was the wild smell, or the use of skins so many of them wore, but the herd did not act like they would if Indians were out there.

They would not get excited if a white man was approaching, nor were they as nervous as if it was a bear or a cat. In those days grizzlies often were found down on the plains in Texas, in the Edwards Plateau country, and there were a good many lions around.

Walking that *grulla* ahead, I eased my rifle forward in my hand, then listened.

The big steer had kept abreast of me. He was not frightened, but full of fight. Nevertheless, he liked the company.

And then I heard it.

Straining my ears into the darkness at the edge of the bottom where the cattle were, I heard a faint dragging sound.

It stopped, but after several minutes it began again.

Suddenly, Tap was beside me. "What is it, Dan?" he whispered close to my ear.

"Something dragging. Cover me, Tap. I'm going into the brush for a look."

He caught the reins of my *grulla* when I passed them to him. "Careful, kid. Might be an Indian."

On cat feet, I went into the brush. All my life I'd lived in wild country, and this was second nature to me. Over

28

the years I'd become like any cat, and could move in the night and through the brush making no sound.

A few feet, and then I listened again. Squatting down, I peered under the brush, but it was too dark to see anything. And then I heard that faint dragging sound again, and a panting . . . a gasping for breath.

Lifting the Patterson, I put the muzzle on the spot and spoke in a low, conversational voice. "You're covered with a five-shot Patterson. If you're in trouble, tell me. Start anything and you get all five shots."

There was a sort of grunt, almost as if somebody tried to speak and couldn't, and then there was no more sound at all.

I eased through the brush and found a long sort of aisle among the willows. There was a faint gray light there, for it was getting on to four o'clock, and lying on the grass was something black.

"Speak up," I said, just loud enough.

No reply. Suddenly there was a faint stirring beside me and a low growl. It was one of Zeb Lambert's dogs.

"Careful, boy." I whispered it to him, but he was going forward, sniffing and whining.

It was no animal, I knew that. Cautiously I went forward, and suddenly I stood over a dim figure. It was a man, and he was badly hurt.

"Tap?" I called, keeping my voice down. "It's a man, and he's in bad shape!"

"I'll get Milo," he said quickly.

Milo Dodge was a cowhand who'd had a good bit of experience with wounds and such, and one of the best men in any kind of sickness or injury that I'd ever known. On the frontier we were mighty scarce on doctors. In fact, here I was pushing twenty-three and I'd never even seen one, although there was one down to Austin, and I think they had a doctor or two in San Antonio. When sickness came, or wounds, we naturally cared for our own, and had nowhere else to turn.

Seemed like only a minute or two until Milo and Tap were back there, and meanwhile I'd put together a mite of fire to give us light.

The injured man was a Mexican, a slim, handsome man with a fine black mustache, but you never did see a man more torn up than he was. His fancy shirt and jacket were soaked with blood and his pants all the way to his knees were covered with blood and soaked with it. He'd dragged himself a long distance, you could see that, but he had a knife in his hand, gripped so hard we couldn't get it loose.

Milo indicated the ripped and torn sleeves of the wounded man's jacket. "Wolves been at him." He pointed at the lacerated condition of the man's wrists. "He fought them with the knife. Must have had one hell of a time."

"I'll get back to the cattle," Tap said. "You help Milo. Free Squires is out at the herd."

The Mexican stirred and muttered as we cut away his bloody clothing. As we examined him, the story became clear.

Somewhere, several days ago, he had been shot and had fallen from his horse. Obviously his horse had stampeded with him and dragged him at a dead run over the rough country. Somehow the Mexican had held onto his gun long enough to shoot his horse . . . which was one reason guns were carried, for a man never knew when he might be thrown from one of the half-broken wild horses.

Then he had probably started to crawl, and the wolves had smelled blood and had come after him. He must have used up what ammunition he had, and sometime later they had grown brave enough to rush in on him and he had fought them off with a knife.

"He wants to live," Milo said dryly; "this one really put up a fight."

"I wonder who shot him?"

Milo glanced at me. "I was wondering about that. My bet is that he came from the west."

We heated water and bathed his wounds and his body. The bullet wound and the drag wounds were several days old and some of them were festering. The teeth marks had all come later.

The bullet had gone all the way through him and was

pressed against the skin of his back. Milo made a slit with his Bowie knife and took the bullet out. Then he made a poultice of ground maize and bound it on both bullet holes.

It was broad daylight by the time the wounds were dressed, and one of the wagons had pulled alongside to receive the wounded man.

We were the last to move out, for the cattle had already started, and the wagons had all gone but the one into which we loaded the Mexican, bedding him down in the wagon on a mattress Tim Foley had found he could spare.

The day was clear and bright. The cattle had moved off at a good pace with only a few of them striving to turn back.

Lingering behind, I watched them trail off, and then rode my horse up to the highest bluff and looked off across the country. As far as I could see, the grass moved lightly under the wind, and there was nothing else. In the distance a black object moved out of a draw and started into the plain, then another followed . . . buffalo.

Searching the plain, I thought I could see the track that must have been made by the Mexican, for grass that is damp does not immediately straighten up when pressed down, and this track had been made, in part at least, during the night.

Holding the Patterson rifle in my right hand, I rode down the slope and scouted the vague track I had seen. Even when I was on the ground and close to the track, it was scarcely visible, nevertheless I found it.

There was blood on the grass.

As I walked the horse along, I saw so much mute evidence of the man's courage that I felt hatred swell within me for whoever had done this to him. Yet I knew that there were many men in Texas, some of them close to me, who believed any Indian or Mexican was fair game.

Whoever the man was, he had come a long way, and he had come with courage, and for that I had only respect. Courage and bravery are words too often used, too

31

little considered. It is one thing to speak them, another thing to live them. It is never easy to face hardship, suffering, pain, and torture. It is always easier to die, simply to give up, to surrender and let the pain die with you. To fight is to keep pain alive, even to intensify it. And this requires a kind of courage for which I had only admiration.

And that Mexican, crawling alone and in darkness, had come a long way, and against fearful odds. I thought of him out there in the darkness, stalked by wolves, close to death, yet fighting back, stabbing, thrusting, fighting with the knife clutched desperately in his fist. This was a man I wanted for a friend, for of his kind there were too few.

Dipping into the coulee, I rode my horse up the other side and followed the herd.

What was it that drove the man on? Was it simply the will to live? To survive in spite of everything? Or was there some other reason? Was it hatred of those who had shot him from the saddle? The desire to live and seek revenge? Or something else?

When I rejoined the herd Pa was working the drag with Zeb.

"Milo says he's in bad shape," Pa said. "Did you see anything?"

"Only that he crawled a long way last night," I said.

The cattle were strung out in a long column, all of half a mile from point to drag. Moving up behind them with Pa, we started bunching them a little more, but keeping them at a good pace. What we wanted now was distance between us and the Cowhouse; and also the faster we got into dry country, the better.

Yet they were settling down, and fewer of them were trying to make a break for their home on the Cowhouse. Nor was there any sign of the Holt crowd or any of that renegade bunch. When nightfall came we had another fifteen miles behind us, and we bedded them down in the shelter of a bluff near the Colorado.

Through dust and rain we made our way westward, and by night the cattle grazed on the short-grass plains and watered from the Colorado River of Texas. Each day with the sun's rising we were in the saddle, and we did not stop until shadows were falling across the land.

The rains were few. Brief showers that served only to settle the dust, but left no pools along the way. The river water ran slack, and Tap's face was drawn with worry when he saw it, but he said nothing, and neither did Pa.

But we had staked everything on this westward move, and all of us knew what lay ahead, and we had all heard of the eighty miles of dry country across which we must take the herd.

It was a hard, grueling business. Alkali dust whitened our faces, dusted over our clothing and our horses. Sweat streaked furrows through the dust, turning our faces into weird masks. Throughout the day the children dropped from the slow-moving wagons to gather buffalo chips for the nighttime fires. These were carried in a hammock of cowhide slung beneath each wagon.

Our trek had taken us north further than we might need to go, because we wished to strike a known trail sooner, a trail where the difficulties, being known, could be calculated upon and planned for.

We reached that trail below Fort Phantom Hill, and turned south and west again.

We were followed . . . we saw their dust by day, sensed the restlessness of our horses by night, and we knew they were near.

We did not know whether they were Comanches prowling to steal ponies and take scalps, or whether they were the renegades from the banks of the Brazos and the Cowhouse.

Tap Henry killed a buffalo, and the meat was a welcome thing. Later he killed an antelope, and reported Indian sign. The further we went, the wilder the country became. We were striking for Horsehead Crossing on the Pecos, used by the Comanches on their raids into Mexico. Named, it was said, for the skulls of the horses that died there after the wild runs up out of Mexico.

Occasionally we found tracks. The old idea that an Indian always rode an unshod horse and a white man a shod one did not hold true, for Indians often stole shod horses from ranches, and the white man often enough rode an unshod pony.

Cracked mud in the bottom of water-holes worried us. The river still had water, but it ran shallow. There had been few rains and this was spring—what would it be like in a few weeks more with the sun baking the land?

There was almost a feeling of doom hanging over us that quieted our songs and stilled our voices. The herd was our all. On this move we had staked our futures, perhaps our lives.

Off in the front was Tap, usually riding with Pa, guiding our way through the wild, dry country. At night we heard the wolves. By day occasionally we saw them slinking along, watching for a chance to pull down a calf.

We carried our guns across our saddle-bows, and we rode high in the saddle, ready for trouble. Tempers grew short; we avoided each other, each man guarding himself against the hot words that could come too easily under the circumstances.

Karen ignored me. Before Tap returned we had walked out together, danced together, gone riding together. Now I hardly saw her; every moment she could spare she was with Tap.

On this day she was driving the Foley wagon and, breaking away from the herd, I rode over to her. She kept her eyes on the road ahead.

"I haven't seen much of you lately," I said.

Her chin went up. "I've been busy."

"I noticed that."

"I don't belong to you. I don't have to answer to you."

"No, ma'am, you surely don't. And Tap's a good man. One of the best."

She turned and looked right straight at me. "I am going to marry him."

Marry *Tap?* Somehow I couldn't see it. Tap was a drifting man . . . or that was how I thought of him.

"Didn't take you long to make up your mind," I commented. "You haven't known him a week."

"That's neither here nor there." Her temper flared suddenly. "He's a man! A *real* man! That's more than most people can say! He's more of a man than you'll ever be!"

There did not seem reason to be mad about it, except that she was expecting criticism and was all wound up for it.

"Maybe," I agreed. "Tap's a good man," I said again, "no question about it. Of course, it depends on what makes a man. If I was a woman I'd give a lot of thought to that. Now, Tap is a man's man . . . he's strong, he's regular, he does his work."

"So?"

"He's like a lot of men, he doesn't like to stay hitched. I don't think he will change."

"You'll see." But her tone was less positive, and I wondered if she had given it any thought at all. Many a time when a girl gets herself involved with romance she is so busy being in love she doesn't realize what it can lead to. They are all in a rosy sort of glow until suddenly they find out the man they love was great to be in love with, but hell to be married to.

Well, I just drifted off, feeling a sort of ache inside me, and angry with myself for it. Seems to me folks are foolish about other people. Karen and I had walked out together, and folks had come to think of her as my girl, but as a matter of fact, we were scarcely more than good friends. Only now that it seemed I'd lost her, I was sore about it. Not that I could ever claim I'd had a serious thought about her, or her about me.

Moving over to the drag, I hazed a laggard steer back into the bunch, and ate dust in silence, feeling mean as a grizzly with a sore tooth.

Yet through it all there was a thread of sanity, and I knew that while there had been nothing between Karen and me but conversation, Tap was all wrong for her. Karen and me had known each other quite a spell, and she knew the others around. Tap Henry was different: he was a stranger who came riding into camp with a fancy outfit and a lot of stories. It was no wonder she was finding something in him that she had been looking for.

Truth to tell, all folks dream, old and young, and they

picture in their minds the girl or man they would like to love and marry. They dream great dreams and most of them settle for much less. Many a time a man and wife lie sleeping in the same bed, dreaming dreams that are miles apart and have nothing in common.

Only Tap Henry was a drifter—yet maybe not. Maybe Karen was the answer to his dream, too, and maybe he was going to settle down. It seemed unlikely, but it was none of my business.

Milo Dodge rode back to the drag. "Talked to that Spanish man. He wants to see you."

"Me?"

"You found him. You fetched us to him."

"Where's he from?"

"He won't say. Except he kept asking me about a man with a spider scar on his cheek, a big, dark man with a deep indentation in his cheek and little scars radiating out from it, like a spider's legs."

We made camp on Antelope Creek where the water was clear and sweet. Large oaks and pecan trees grew along the banks, and the place we found to locate was a big open meadow of some thirty or forty acres. The cattle scattered along the creek to drink, then wandered back into the meadow to feed.

Pa came back to where I was sitting my horse in the shade of a big pecan. "Good country," he said. "It tempts a man."

"It does," I said, "and it might be a good thing to hold up here another day and let the cattle fatten up and drink their fill. From now on, according to Tap, the country gets drier and drier."

Tap rode up to join us, and Zeb Lambert followed. The wagons were bunching in a rough circle near the bank of the stream. A faint breeze stirred the leaves of the trees. Tap glanced across the Concho at the bluffs beyond the river. Close to where we sat, the Antelope joined the Concho, and the Concho itself pointed our way west.

"I don't like those bluffs," Tap commented, "but we're as safe here as anywhere, I guess."

Pa told him what we were thinking, and he agreed We couldn't have chosen a better place to stop, for we had some shelter here from any wind that might blow up, there was good water, and there was grass. The youngsters were already rousing around in the leaves and finding a few pecans left over from the previous fall.

Switching saddles to a line-back dun, I rode over to the wagon where the Mexican was riding. He was propped up a little, and he had some color in his face.

"I'm Dan Killoe," I said.

He held out a slender brown hand and smiled; his teeth were very white. *"Gracias, amigo.* You have save my life, I think. I could go no further."

"You'd crawled a fair piece. I don't see how you did it."

He shrugged. "It was water I needed, and a place to hide." He grew serious. *"Señor,* I must warn you. By sheltering me you will make the enemy . . . even many enemies."

"A man who makes tracks in this world makes enemies also," I said. "I figure a few more won't matter."

"These are very bad . . . *malo.* They are the Comancheroes."

"I've heard of them. Some of your people who trade with the Comanches, is that it?"

"Si . . . and we do not approve, *señor.* They found me in their country and they shot at me. I escaped, and they pursued . . . I killed one Comanchero, and one Comanche. Then they hit me. I fell, they caught me with a rope and dragged me. I got out my knife and cut the rope and I took that man's horse from him and rode . . . they pursued again. My horse was killed, but they did not catch me."

This Mexican was something of a man. In my mind's eye I could see that drag and that chase. The only way he could get that horse was to kill its rider, and after that horse was killed he had dragged himself a far piece.

"You rest easy," I told him. "Comanchero or Comanche, nobody is going to bother you."

37

"They will come for me." He hitched himself to a better position. "You give me a horse and I shall ride. There is no need to risk."

"Let them come." I got down on the ground. "The Good Book says that man is born to trouble. Well, I don't figure on going against the Bible. What trouble comes, we will handle as we can, but nobody in my family ever drove a wounded man from his door, and we aren't about to."

That line-back dun was a running horse. He was also a horse with bottom. Leaving off the work that had to be done, I started for the Concho, and Zeb Lambert fell in alongside me.

This was Indian country, and we were expecting them. We scouted along the river for some distance, mainly hunting tracks, or signs of travel, but we found none.

Across the river we skirted the foot of the bluffs, found a faint trail up, and climbed to the top.

The wind was free up there, and a man could see for a long distance. We sat our horses, looking over the country. Zeb's brown hair blew in the wind when he turned his head to look.

The country away from the river was barren, and promised little. But no matter how we searched the country around we saw no movement, nor any tracks. Finally we circled back to camp.

They were out there somewhere, we were sure of it. But where?

The fires were ablaze when we rode in, and there was the good smell of coffee and of steaks broiling. Ben Cole and Freeman Squires had taken the first guard and were already with the cattle.

The herd was still feeding, relishing the fine, rich grass of the meadow. A few head had returned to the creek to drink again. Somewhere out on the plains a quail called.

Tap Henry came over to where I stood with Pa. "We'd best double the guard tonight," he said. "I've got a feeling."

"We've been lucky so far. The way I see it," Pa said, "that outfit back on the Brazos decided to let us get far enough out so they can blame it on Comanches."

Tap looked around at me. "Who's your Mexican friend?"

"He had trouble with the Comancheros. Says the man after him had a spider scar on his cheek."

Tap gave me an odd look. "Maybe we'd better give him the horse," he said, and then he got up and walked away.

"Now, what's the matter with him?" Pa asked.

It was unlike Tap to say such a thing, or to shy from trouble with anybody. "He must know something we don't," I said. "I'm getting curious about that man with the scar."

We ate, and I caught myself a little shut-eye, spreading my soogan under a pecan tree and lying half awake, half asleep, listening to the bustle around the camp.

All too soon, Zebony came to call me. He was pulling on his boots and, sitting there beside me, he said, "It's quiet out there . . . too quiet. You better come loaded for bear."

Milo Dodge was at the fire, and so was Aaron Stark. They were drinking coffee, and Stark had his Sharps repeater beside him.

Stamping my feet into my boots, I walked over to the fire. Once I had got to sleep I'd slept sound . . . so sound it worried me, for I did not like to get into the habit of sleeping so soundly I could not be awakened by the slightest move.

The coffee was strong, and hot as hell. Pa came to the fire and handed me a cold biscuit, which I ate with my coffee.

"You boys be careful, now. I never knew Tap to be jumpy, but he surely is tonight."

Tom Sandy had the line-back dun ready for me, and when I stepped into the saddle I glanced over at Tap's bed. The bed was there, but Tap was not.

"You seen Tap?"

Tom turned away. "No, I haven't!" he said, almost snapping the words at me.

Once we were away from the firelight, the night was dark, for the area was partly shielded by the bluffs and the trees. We rode out together, the four of us, scattering to places about the herd.

At such a time all the little noises of the night become intensely clear, and sounds which one has always known are suddenly strange and mysterious. But the ears of men accustomed to the wilderness and the nighttime silences and sounds choose from among the many small noises those which are a warning.

A bird rustling among the leaves, a small animal in the grass, a branch rubbing against another, the grunts and gasps and breathing of the cattle, the click of horns accidentally touching—all these are familiar.

We scattered out, circled, and then fell into pairs. As always, I rode with Zebony.

It was very still. Some of the usual noises we did not hear, and this in itself warned us that something was out there, for the small animals and birds become apprehensive at strange movements among them.

"What do you think, Zeb?"

"They'll try to get close."

Milo Dodge and Stark rode up from the other side. "Milo," I whispered, "Zeb and me, we're going to move out into the edge of the trees. We'll try to meet them before they get to us."

"All right," he said, and watched when I pointed out where we would be.

We never got the chance. There was one brief instant of warning, a rushing in the grass, and then they came with the black loom of the bluff behind them so that we could catch no outline at which to shoot.

They came charging, but in silence, and then the first shot was fired.

It was my shot, fired blindly into the blackness, as much as a warning to the camp as anything.

There was an instant burst of firing in reply, and I

40

heard a heavy fall somewhere near me, and the grunt of a man hitting the ground. A spot of white . . . a man riding a paint horse showed, and I fired again.

The horse swerved sharply and then we were all firing. The surprise had been mutual. They came unexpectedly from the night, but they charged when all four of us were almost together, and our fire smashed them back, caused them to swerve. Shouting and yelling, they bore down on the herd.

The cattle lunged to their feet and stampeded down the valley and away from camp.

Catching the momentary outline of a man against the sky, I fired again, and then again. Hastily I reloaded and started after them. But as suddenly as it had happened, it was over. The attackers were gone and the herd was gone.

Zeb came riding up out of the night. "Dan! *Dan?*"

"Yeah . . . somebody's down."

There was a rush of horsemen from camp, and Pa yelled out, "Dan? Are you all right?"

Zeno Yearling spoke from nearby. "Here he is. I think it's Aaron."

Pa struck a light. Aaron was down, all right. He was shot through the chest and he was dead.

"They'll pay for this," Pa said. "By the Lord Harry, they'll pay!"

We circled warily, hunting for other men who were down. We found two of theirs. One was a man named Streeter, a hanger-on who had drifted to the Cowhouse country from over on the Neuces after trouble with the Rangers. The other man we had seen around, but did not know.

"Two for one," Tap said.

"Two, hell!" Pa exploded. "I wouldn't swap Stark for ten of them! He was a good man."

"We'll wait until daylight," I said, "then go hunting."

We rode back to camp with Aaron across a saddle. Nobody was feeling very good about it, and I didn't envy Pa, who would have to tell his widow.

There was no talking around the fire. Picking up some sticks, I built the flames up. We checked around, but nobody else had been hurt.

"Two doesn't seem right," Zeb said. "I know we hit more of them. They came right at us, close range."

Karen and Mrs. Foley were at the fire, making coffee. Taking the Patterson, I cleaned it carefully, checked the loads, and reloaded. Then I went out and looked the line-back dun over to see if he'd picked up any scratches. He looked fit and ready, and I knew him for a tough little horse.

The day broke slowly, a gray morning with a black line of trees that slowly took on shape and became distinct. With the first light, we saddled up again.

Tim Foley, despite his arguments, was forced to stay behind with the wagons, and Frank Kelsey stayed with him.

"You'd better stay, Tom," Pa said. "We've lost one married man already."

"Be damned if I will!" Sandy replied testily. He hesitated. "We should leave another man. Suppose they come back?"

"Free"—Pa looked over at Squires—"you stay. You stood guard last night."

"Now, look here!" Squires protested.

"As a favor," Pa said. "Will you stay?"

Freeman Squires shrugged and walked away. The rest of us mounted up and moved out.

The trail was broad enough, for they had followed the herd into the night, and the herd had taken off into the broad, empty lands to the south.

This was Lipan country, but the Lipans, of late, had been friendly to the white man.

We rode swiftly into the growing light, a tight bunch of armed horsemen, grim-faced and bitter with the loss of Aaron Stark and our cattle. No longer were we simply hard-working, hard-riding men, no longer quiet men intent on our own affairs. For riding after lawless men was not simply for revenge or recovery of property; it was necessary if there was to be law, and here there was no law except what right-thinking men made for themselves.

The brown grass of autumn caught the golden light of morning, and the dark lines of trees that marked the Concho fell behind. Our group loosened, spread out a little to see the tracks better. Among the many cattle tracks we searched for those of riders.

Away off on the flank, I suddenly came upon the tracks of a lone rider whose mount had a magnificent stride. Drawing up, I checked those tracks again.

It was a big horse—far larger and with a better gait than our cow ponies—and it carried a light burden, for the tracks indicated the weight upon the horse must be small.

The tracks came from the northwest, which did not fit with those we followed, unless they were being joined by some scout sent on ahead. Yet why would such a scout be sent? And who among the renegades who followed the Holts could possibly have such a horse?

The tracks had been made the night before, or late the previous afternoon, and I followed them, but kept my own party in sight.

Suddenly the tracks veered sharply west, and I drew rein, looking in that direction.

There was a clump of black on the prairie . . . mesquite? Cautiously, rifle ready, I walked the dun toward it. The size grew . . . it was a clump of trees and brush almost filling a hollow in the plain.

The edge broke sharply off in a ledge of rock, and the tops of the trees barely lifted above its edge. The tracks I followed led to the edge and disappeared into the copse. Warily, I followed.

Then I heard running water, a trickle of water falling into a pool. A wind stirred the leaves, then was still.

My horse, ears pricked, walked into a narrow trail where my stirrups brushed the leaves on either side. After some thirty yards of this, there was a sudden hollow under the arching branches of the live oaks, and an open space some fifty feet in diameter, a pool a dozen feet across, and a magnificent black horse that whinnied gently and pricked his ears at my dun. There was coffee on a fire, and bacon frying, and then a voice spoke, "Stand where you are, señor, or I shall put a bullet where your breakfast is."

My hands lifted cautiously. There was no mistaking the ominous click of the cocking gun . . . but the voice was a woman's voice.

Chapter Three

She was young and she was lovely, and the sun caught and entangled itself in the spun red-gold of her hair, but the rifle in her hands was rock-steady, its muzzle an unwinking black eye that looked at my belt buckle.

A flat-crowned Spanish hat lay upon her shoulders, held by the chin strap which had slipped down about her throat. She was dressed in beautifully tanned buckskin, the skirt was divided for easy riding—the first I had seen, although I'd heard of them before this.

"Who are you? Why are you following me?"

"Unless you're one of the cow thieves that ran off our herd last night, I wasn't following you until I came across your tracks out there."

The rifle did not waver, nor did her eyes. "Who are you? Where do you come from?"

As she talked, I was getting an idea. Maybe a wild one, but an idea.

"The name is Dan Killoe, and we're from over on the Cowhouse. We're driving to New Mexico. Maybe to Colorado. We're hunting new range."

"You spoke of cow thieves."

"They ran our herd off last night. The way we figure, it's a passel of thieves from back on the Cowhouse. If we leave the country with our stock, they've all got to go to work."

She watched me with cool, violet eyes. Yet it seemed to me she was buying my story.

"You must have heard the cattle go by a couple of

hours back," I added. "Now may I put my hands down?"

"Put them down. Just be careful what you do with them."

Carefully, I lowered them to the horn of the saddle. Then I glanced around. "Seems to me you're a long way from home," I said, "and you a woman alone."

"I am not alone," she said grimly. "I have this." She gestured meaningfully with her rifle.

"That's a mighty fine horse you've got there. Fact is"— I pushed my hat back on my head—"that's one reason I followed you. I wanted to see that horse."

She lowered her rifle just a little. "Have some coffee?" she suggested. "It will boil away."

Gratefully, I swung down. "I'd like a cup. Then I'll have to follow after the others and lend a hand. I figure in about an hour we're going to have us a scrap with those thieves."

My own cup hung to my saddle-horn and I helped myself and looked again at her. Never in all my born days had I seen a girl as pretty as that.

"Now," I said, "I've got an idea. You wouldn't be looking for somebody, would you?"

She glanced at me quickly. "Why do you ask that?"

"Wondered." I took a swallow of hot coffee. "Do you know anything about the Comancheros?"

Oh, I'd hit pay dirt all right, that was plain enough from the way she reacted. "I know about them," she said.

"We picked up a maverick a while back, and he was in mighty bad shape. He had been shot and he had been dragged, and the Comancheros had done it."

"He's alive? He's all right?"

"Friend of yours?"

"Where is he? I am going to him."

"He's in bad shape, so you take it easy. We found him out in the brush, and the wolves had been at him. He'd fought them off, but he was chewed up some." I swallowed the last of the coffee and rinsed my cup at the stream. "He's got nerve enough for three men. How he ever crawled so far, I'll never know."

46

She gathered her meager gear. "I am going to him. Where is your camp?"

"Ma'am, that boy is in bad shape and, like I said, he had some rough treatment. I don't know you, and for all I do know you might be one of his enemies."

"I am his adopted sister. After my father was killed, his family took me into their home."

It was time I was getting on, for I'd already lost too much time, and the Kaybar outfit was riding into trouble. "You ride careful when you get to camp. They are expecting trouble, and you might collect a bullet before they see you.

"You ride north from here. The camp is on the Antelope near where it empties into the Middle Concho. Tell them Dan Killoe sent you."

Mounting up, I rode up to the plain and swung south. Keeping to low ground, I rode swiftly along, coming up only occasionally to look for the trail of torn earth where the Kaybar crew had passed.

They had been moving slowly, so I figured to overtake them before they ran into trouble. But I was almost too late.

When I finally saw them they were fanned out, riding toward a bluff. The country beyond that bluff stretched out for miles, and I could catch glimpses of it. Suddenly, just as I slowed down so as not to rush among them, the grass stirred between them and me and a man reared up, rifle in hand.

Intent upon making a kill, he did not notice me, and my horse made little sound with his hoofbeats on the plain's turf. Not wishing to stampede their horses by rushing among them, the dun was walking at a slow pace when the man rose from the brush.

He came up with his rifle and lifted it, taking a careful sight on Tap, and I slapped the spurs to the dun. I was not a rider who used his spurs, and the startled dun gave one tremendous leap and then broke into a dead run.

The ambusher heard the sound of hoofs too late, and even as he brought the rifle into position to fire, he must have heard that rushing sound. It could not have been loud, for the turf was not hard and there was short grass, but he turned quickly, suddenly, but I was fairly on top of him and he had no chance. I fired that Patterson of mine like you'd fire a pistol, gripping it with one hand and holding it low down close to my thigh.

He was slammed back by that .56-caliber bullet as though struck by an axe, and then I was over and past him and riding up to join the others.

As if on order, they all broke into a run, and when I reached the ridge they had been mounting, I saw the camp that lay below.

At least two dozen men were lying about, and my shot must have startled them, for they evidently had jumped up and started for their guns, those who didn't have them alongside.

There were several men with the herd, and my first shot went for the nearest guard. It was a good shot, for he left the saddle and tumbled in a heap, and then we ripped into that camp.

We were outnumbered two to one, but our coming was a complete surprise and we made the attack good. I saw Tap wheel his horse and come back through a second time, blasting with a six-shooter. Then he tucked that one away and started blasting with a second one, and unless I missed my guess, Tap would be carrying at least two more.

In those days of cap-and-ball pistols many a man when fighting Indians—and some outlaws too—carried as many as six pistols into action because of the time it took to reload. And some carried extra cylinders that could be placed fully loaded into the pistol.

A big man with a red beard and red hair all over his chest jumped at me, swinging a rifle that must have been empty. The dun hit him with a shoulder and knocked him head over heels into the fire.

He let out an awful yell and bounded out of that fire with his pants smoking, and sticks and coals were scattered all over the place.

We swept on through camp and started those cattle

high-tailing it back to the north, and if we picked up a few mustangs in the process, we weren't taking time to sort them out, even if we'd been a mind to.

We got off scot-free.

Ben Cole had a bullet burn alongside his neck, and he grumbled all the way back to the Concho about it. Fact is, it must have smarted something fierce, with sweat getting into it, and all. But you'd have thought he had a broken knee or a cracked skull, the way he took on.

Zeno Yearly rode back alongside me. He was a long-legged man with a long face, and he didn't look like he could move fast enough to catch a turtle in a barley field. However, out there when the fighting was going on, I'd noticed he was a busy, busy man.

Tap fell back beside me. "Where'd you drop off to?" he asked. "I figured you'd taken out, running."

"Had to stop back there to talk to a girl," I said carelessly. "She offered me coffee, so I stopped by."

He looked at me, grinning. "Boy, any girl you find out in this country, you can have!"

"Prettiest girl you ever did see," I commented, "and she'll be back at camp when we get there."

"You're funnin'!" He stared at me, trying to make out what I was getting at. The idea that the girl actually existed he wouldn't consider for a moment, and in his place I wouldn't have believed it either.

"Too bad you're getting married," I said. "Puts you out of the running."

His face flushed. "Who said I was getting married?" he demanded belligerently.

"Why, Karen. She allowed as how you two were looking for a meeting house."

His face flushed a deeper red under the brown. "Nothing to that," he protested. "Nothing to that, nothing at all."

"She seemed mighty positive," I said, "and you know how folks out here are, when it comes to trifling with a good woman. Tim Foley is a mighty handy man with a shotgun, Tap. I'd ride careful, if I were you."

He grinned. He was recovering himself now. "Now,

49

don't you worry, boy. Nobody ever caught old Tap in a bind like that. Karen's a fine girl . . . but *marriage?* I ain't the marrying kind."

Whether it was what I'd said or something else, I can't say, but that night I noticed Karen sitting by herself, and she wasn't liking it, not one bit.

The red-headed girl was there, and she was the center of quite a bit of fuss by the women folks. Most of the men hung back. She was so beautiful it made them tongue-tied, not that any of them, unless it was Tap, would have won any prizes in an elocution contest.

Me, I hadn't anything to say to her. She was the prettiest girl I'd ever seen, and to ride out there by herself took a lot more nerve than most men would have, riding right through the heart of Comanche country, like that.

Two or three times she looked over at me, but I paid her no mind. Most of the time she spent talking to the Mexican or fixing grub for him.

Karen's face was pale and her lips were thin. I'd never noticed how sharp and angular her face could get until that night, and I knew she was mad, mad clean through. Tap, he just sat and joked with the men, and when he got up Karen would have cut him off from the bunch, but he stepped into the saddle and rode out to the herd.

Tom Sandy came up to the fire for more coffee, and for the first time I saw he was wearing a six-shooter. He favored a rifle, as I do, but tonight he was packing a gun. Rose was at the fire, too. A dark, pretty woman with a lot of woman where it mattered, and a way of making a man notice. She had those big dark eyes, and any time she looked at an attractive man those eyes carried a challenge or an invitation. Or something that could be taken that way. Believe me, she was no woman to have around a cow outfit.

Sandy looked across the fire at her a few times, and he looked mean as an old razor-back boar.

Rose dished up some beans and beef for Tom and brought them to him, and then she turned to me. "Dan, can I help you to something?"

50

I looked up at her and she was smiling at me, and I swallowed a couple of times. "Thank you, ma'am. I would like some more of those *frijoles*."

She went to the fire for them, giving her hips that extra movement as she walked away, and Tom Sandy was staring at me with a mean look in his eye.

"Hot," I said, running a finger around my shirt collar.

"I hadn't noticed," he said.

Pa came over and dropped down beside me. "Tap figures we'd better get on the road right away in the morning, before daybreak. What do you think?"

"Good idea," I said.

Tom Sandy walked off, and Pa looked at me. "Dan, you aren't walking out with Rose Sandy, are you?"

"Are you crazy?"

"Somebody is. Tom knows it and he's mad. If he finds out, there'll be a killling."

"Don't look at me. If I was planning to start something like that, she wouldn't be the one."

At sunup we were well down the trail and moving steadily westward. Away from the stream the land was dry and desolate, and showed little grass. It was a warning of what lay ahead.

So far we had done well. Despite the driving off of our cattle and our recovery of them, we seemed to have lost none, and we had gained by half a dozen horses that had been driven off with the cattle when we recovered them.

We saw little game. There were the usual prairie dogs and jackass rabbits, and when we camped that night Zeno caught us a mess of catfish which offered a change of diet.

Out on the plains away from the river there was prickly pear, greasewood, and sage brush, but mighty little else. Here and there in a bottom or at a creek crossing we found a few acres of grama, and we took time out to let the cattle eat. It was a scary thing to think of the long marches ahead of us with grass growing less and less.

We all knew about the eighty miles of dry march ahead

of us, but we preferred not to think of it. Each night we filled our barrels to have as much water as we could for the day to come. But all of us knew there might be a time when there would be no water, not even for ourselves and our horses.

We nooned at a pool, shallow but quite extensive, but when we left, it was only a patch of muddy earth churned by the feet of our cattle.

While there, I went up to the Mexican's wagon to see how he was . . . or at least, that's what I told myself.

When I spoke, the redhead drew back the curtain, and her smile was something to see. "Oh, please come in! Miguel has been telling me how it was you who found him."

"Just happened to be first," I said, embarrassed.

"If you had not found me," Miguel said, "I should now be dead. That I know. Nobody else had come to see what lay out there, even if they heard me."

"Your name is Dan Killoe?" she asked. "I am Conchita McCrae. My father was Scotch-Irish, my mother a Mexican."

"You had nerve," I said. "You must have ridden for days."

"There was no one else. Miguel's father is dead, and there is only our mother . . . his mother. She is very old, and she worried about her son."

Well, maybe so, but it took nerve for a girl—or a man for that matter—to ride into Comanche country alone. Or even to drive through it, as we were. She had a fast horse, but that isn't too much help when the Comanche knows the country and is a master at ambuscade. There was very little about hunting or fighting that the Indian did not know, and what he did not know, he learned fast.

Conchita McCrae stood tall in my estimation, and I liked the way she looked straight into your eyes and stood firmly on her small feet. That was more of a woman than I had ever seen before.

"The Comancheros," Miguel said, "I do not approve of what they do. They are some of my people who trade

52

with the Comanche, and it is a profitable trade, but they sell the rifles with which to kill, and they kill our people, and yours also."

He paused to catch his breath, and then said, speaking more slowly, "They believed I was spying when I was only hunting wild horses, for they knew me as one who did not approve. I had hoped to avoid trouble with them, but there are men among the Comancheros who are worse than the Comanches themselves."

"The man with the scar?"

The skin around his eyes seemed to draw back. "He is the worst of them. He is Felipe Soto. You know of him?"

I knew of him. He was a gunfighter and a killer. It was said he had killed more than twenty men in hand-to-hand battles with knife or gun. How many he had killed in fights of other kinds, no man could guess.

In a few short years the man had become a legend, although so far as I knew he had appeared east of the Pecos on only one occasion. He had crossed the Rio Grande from Matamoras and killed a man in Brownsville.

He was an outlaw, but he was protected by many of his own people, and among them he had been guilty of no crimes. A big man, he was widely feared, and even men who might have faced him with some chance of winning did not care to take the risk such a meeting would involve.

"Where did they find you?"

"Ah! There is the trouble, *amigo!* They find me just as I have come upon their . . . shall we say, rendezvous? It is a word you know?

"There is a canyon to the north, a great long, high-walled canyon, and in the bottom there is rich, green grass. They were there . . . the Comanches and the Comancheros. This place I have seen is a secret place, but I had heard of it. It is is the Palo Duro Canyon."

"They will follow him, Mr. Killoe," Conchita said. "They will not let him live now. The Comancheros are men of evil. If they do not find him now, they will come searching for him when he is home again."

"What they do then is no business of mine," I said, "but we won't let him be taken from us. I promise you that."

There was a movement behind me. "Don't make any promises you can't keep."

It was Tap Henry. His features were hard, and there was a kind of harsh impatience in his eyes that I had seen there before this.

"I'll keep the promise, Tap," I replied quietly. "I have made the promise, and it will stick."

"You'll listen to me," Tap replied shortly. "You don't know what you are walking into."

"I have made my promise. I shall keep it."

"Like hell you will!" Tap's tone was cold. "Look, kid, you don't know what you're saying."

He paused, taking a cigar from his pocket. "We've got enough to do, getting our cattle west, without borrowing trouble."

"Please," Miguel had risen to one elbow, "I wish no trouble. If you will loan me a horse, we can go."

"Lie down, señor," I said. "You are my guest, and here you will stay."

"Whose leading this outfit, you or me?"

"I thought Pa was," I said dryly. "When it comes to that, we're both working for him."

His face stiffened a little. "Well, we'll see what Pa has to say, then!" he said sarcastically.

We walked together toward where Pa stood by the fire. Zeb Lambert was there, squatting on his heels, and Zeno Yearly was there too. Ira Tilton had come in from his guard for coffee and I saw his eyes go quickly to Tap Henry.

"Pa," Tap said, "the kid here has promised those Mexicans that they can have our protection all the way into New Mexico. Now, we know the Comancheros are hunting them, and that means trouble! They can muster fifty, maybe a hundred white men and more Comanches, and we're in no shape to stand up to that kind of a crowd. I say we let them shift for themselves."

54

Zeno glanced up at Tap, but his long horse-face revealed nothing.

Pa glanced at me. "What do you say about this, Dan?"

"I told them they were our guests, and they were safe with us."

Pa looked at Tap. "What's wrong with that?"

Tap's face darkened, and his eyes were cold. "Pa, you don't know what you're saying. Neither you nor the cattle nor any of us will get through if that outfit tackles us! I heard that Mex say he knew where their hide-out was, and that's the best-kept secret in this part of the country. They dasn't let him live."

"We will try to see that he does," Pa said quietly.

Pa was a square-faced man with carefully combed gray hair and a trimmed gray mustache. No matter how bad times got or how busy we were, Pa was always shaved, his hair was always trimmed. And I do not recall ever seeing Pa lean on anything—he always stood on his own two feet.

He looked steadily at Tap now. "I am surprised, Tap. You should know that I would never leave a man—least of all a man and a woman—out here on the plains alone. If we have to fight to protect them, then we shall have to fight."

Tap Henry stared at him with sullen eyes. "Pa, you can't do that. These folks are nothing to you. They are—"

"We took them in. They needed help. So long as I live, they will have it from me. I have never turned a man from my door, and I never shall."

Tap Henry drew a deep breath. "Pa . . ." He was almost pleading. "These Comancheros . . . they're worse than Comanches. Believe me, I know—"

"How do you know, Tap?" Pa asked mildly.

Tap shut up and turned sharply away. That he believed us all to be a pack of fools was obvious, and maybe he was right. Pa was not a man who ever preached to anyone, least of all to his boys, but he had taught us always to stand on principle. I say taught us, but it was mostly example. A man always knew where Pa Killoe stood on any question, and no nonsense about it.

Not that we had any doubts about the trouble we were in. The plains were alive with Comanches, and the Comancheros were as bad, if not worse, and Tap was right—they would be hunting Miguel.

An idea that was sheer inspiration came to me of a sudden. More than likely they already believed Miguel to be dead, but suppose they wanted to see the body before they believed?

"Pa . . . I think we should bury him. Miguel, I mean."

Pa glanced around at me; and Conchita, who had come down from the wagon, stood stock-still, listening. "We should bury him right here," I said, "and put a marker over the grave."

Zeno Yearly walked over to the wagon and took a shovel from the straps that bound it to the wagon-side where it would be handy. Without any further talk, he walked off to one side and stuck the spade into the ground. Getting another shovel, I joined him.

We dug the grave four feet deep, then dropped in a layer of big rocks, then another. If they were curious enough to open the grave they might not be curious enough to lift out all those rocks. We filled in the dirt and put up a marker.

"Name?" Yearly asked.

"No," I said, "we don't want them to think he talked. Just make it: *Unknown Mexican Died on This Spot April 16, 1858.*"

After a short nooning, we rolled our wagons again, and the herd moved on.

Tap had nothing to say, but he was short-tempered as a rattlesnake in the blind, which is the way they refer to a snake when he is shedding his skin. At that time a rattler won't rattle—he simply strikes at anything that moves.

But Tap was wary. He rode far out much of the time, scanning the hills. The word got around, of course, and most of the hands went out fully armed and loaded for bear. We kept the herd moving late, and five miles further on we crossed the South Fork, sometimes called the

Boiling Concho. This was real water—deep, clear, and quite rapid in some places, and the herd spread out along the banks for water while we hunted a place to ford it.

Tap found the spot he was looking for—a ledge of rock under the water that gave sure footing for the cattle and was wide enough to take two wagons abreast. We crossed over, moving them slow, and started across some flat country dotted with mesquite and occasional live oak. The grass was good. We crossed Dove Creek, filled with rushes, and pushed on to Good Spring Creek.

The water was clear and cold, the grass good, and there was plenty of wood and buffalo chips. It was coming on to dark when we rounded the cattle into position and circled our few wagons.

Zeno Yearly got out his tackle and threw a bait into the creek. By the time the sun was gone he had six black bass, all of them good. Those fish were so hungry and so unfamiliar with fishhooks that they could scarcely wait to grab.

The fish tasted good. Nobody was saying anything, but our grub wasn't holding up like we had hoped. We had figured to kill more game, and we just hadn't seen any, and we didn't want to kill a steer because we would need all we had. Aside from the steers, we were depending on the rest for breeding stock.

Nobody talked very much, and we ate quickly and turned in for a rest. Ben Cole and Zeno Yearly took the first guard, but Tap Henry was awake, too. He smoked near the fire for a while, then got up and walked out beyond the wagons. He was still standing out there alone when I dropped off to sleep.

Tom Sandy woke me. He looked thinner, and he was rough waking me. I got out of my blankets into the cool night and put on my hat, then my boots. Tom had walked off to the fire without saying anything, but he looked mean and bitter.

Zebony was at the fire, and he glanced up at me. "Did you see Tom?"

"I saw him."

"Trouble's riding that man. Something's chewing on him."

Glancing over at Tap's bed, I saw him there, sleeping. We mounted up and rode by and out to the herd. We were relieving Kelsey and Squires.

"Quiet," Kelsey said.

They rode off toward the fire and Zebony started away. From where I sat by the edge of the herd I could see Tom Sandy huddled in his blankets near the wagon. My eyes strayed to Tap's bed, but somehow it did not seem occupied. Bushes obscured it somewhat, however, and it was none of my affair.

Slowly, I started around the herd. I was riding a big roan horse that was hard-riding but powerful, and for his size, quite fast.

My mind went suddenly to the blond gunman who had accompanied Webb Holt on the day Tap killed him. That man worried me. He had taken the whole affair too calmly, and I had a feeling we would see more of him. And Bud Caldwell, too, for that matter.

It was almost an hour later and the cattle had gotten to their feet for a stretch, and some had begun to graze a little, when suddenly a big longhorn's head came up sharply. Looking where he looked, I saw only the blackness of a patch of live oak.

With the Patterson ready in my hand, I walked the roan toward the trees. Trust a longhorn to spot trouble, for although they were considered domestic cattle, actually they were wild things, reacting like wild things, and most of them lived wild all their lives.

Suddenly, from the corner of my eye, I saw movement in the blackness, and caught a gleam of light on a gun barrel.

Somebody else was searching that patch of woods, somebody from our camp. Stepping the roan around a patch of brush, I took him into the darkness. He was curious, and he could sense danger as any mustang would, so he stepped light and easy.

There was a stir of movement, a low murmur of voices and then a woman's soft laugh.

An instant there, I stopped. I could feel the flush climb up my neck, for I knew what I would find in there . . . and in the same instant I knew who that other man was.

Instantly, I pushed the roan through the brush. It crackled, and I saw the man across the small clearing lift his rifle. Slapping spurs to the roan, I leaped him ahead and struck up the gun before it could be fired. Grasping the barrel, I wrenched it from the hands of the startled man.

There was a gasp of alarm, and then a cool voice said, "Turn him loose, boy. If he wants to come hunting me, give him his chance."

"Give me the rifle, Dan." It was Tom Sandy. Only he was not the easy-going man I had known back on the Cowhouse. This was a cold, dangerous man.

"Give me the rifle," Sandy persisted. "I shall show him what comes to wife-stealers and thieves."

"Let him have it," Tap said coolly.

Instead I laid my rifle on Tap. "You turn around, Tap, and you walk back to the herd. If you make a move toward that gun, I'll kill you."

"Are you crossing me?" He was incredulous, but there was anger in him, too.

"We will have no killing on this outfit. We've trouble enough without fighting among ourselves." I saw Tom Sandy ease a hand toward his shirt front where I knew he carried a pistol. "Don't try it, Tom. That goes for you, too."

There was silence, and in the silence I saw Rose Sandy standing against a tree trunk, staring at the scene in fascinated horror.

Others were coming. "Turn around, Tom, and walk back to camp. We're going to settle this, here and now. You, too, Rose."

She looked up at me. "Me?" Her voice trembled. "What—?"

"Go along with him."

Tap Henry stood watching me as they walked away. "You'll interfere once too often, boy. I'll forget we grew up together."

"Don't ever do it, Tap. I like you, and you're my brother. But if you ever draw a gun on me, I'll kill you."

The late moon lit the clearing with a pale, mysterious light. He stood facing me, his eyes pinpoints of light in the shadow of his hat brim.

"Look, you damned fool, do you know who you're talking to? Have you lost your wits?"

"No, Tap, and what I said goes as it lays. Don't trust your gun against me, Tap, because I'm better than you are. I don't want to prove it . . . I don't set store over being called a gunfighter like you do. It's a name I don't want, but I've seen you shoot, Tap, and I can outshoot you any day in the week."

He turned abruptly and walked back to camp. Pa was up, and so were the others—Tim Foley and his wife, Karen, her face pinched and tight, and all of us gathering around.

"Free," I said to Squires, "ride out and take my place, will you? We've got a matter to settle."

Pa was standing across the fire in his shirtsleeves, and Pa was a man who set store by proper dress. Never a day but what he wore a stiff collar and a necktie.

Tap walked in, a grin on his hard face, and when he looked across at Tom Sandy his eyes were taunting. Tom refused to meet his gaze.

Rose came up to the fire, holding her head up and trying to put an impudent look on her face and not quite managing it.

Pa wasted no time. He asked questions and he got answers. Tap Henry had been meeting Rose out on the edge of camp. Several times Tom Sandy had managed to see them interrupted, hoping Rose would give up or that Tap would.

Karen stood there listening, her eyes on the ground. I knew it must hurt to hear all this, but I could have told her about Tap. As men go he was a good man among men, but he was a man who drew no lines when it came to women. He liked them anywhere and he took them where he found them and left them right there. There would have been no use in my telling Karen more than I had . . . she would believe what she wanted to believe.

Worst of all, I'd admired Tap. We'd been boys together and he had taught me a good deal, but we were a team on this cow outfit, and we had to pull together if we were going to make it through what lay ahead. And every man-jack on the drive knew that Tap Henry was our insurance. Tap had been over the trail, and none of us had. Tap knew the country we were heading toward, and nobody else among us did.

Tap was a leader, and he was a top hand, and right now he was figuring this was a big joke. The trouble was, Tap didn't really know Pa.

Tom Sandy had heard Rose get out of the wagon, and he knew that Tap was gone from his bed, so he followed Rose. If it hadn't been for that old longhorn spotting something in the brush, Sandy would have unquestionably killed one of them, and maybe both. He would have shot Tap where he found him. He said as much, and he said it cold turkey.

Tap was watching Sandy as he talked, and I thought that Tap respected him for the first time. It was something Tap could understand.

"What have you to say for yourself?" Pa asked Tap.

Tap Henry shrugged. "What can I say? He told it straight enough. We were talking"—Tap grinned meaningly—"and that was all."

Pa glanced over at Rose. "We're not going to ask you anything, Rose. What lies between you and your husband is your business. Only this: if anything like this happens again, you leave the drive . . . no matter where we are. Tom can go or stay, as he likes."

Pa turned his attention back to Tap. His face was cold. "One thing I never tolerate on my drives is a trouble-maker. You've caused trouble, Tap, and likely you'd cause more. I doubt if you and Tom could make it to the Pecos without a killing, and I won't have that, nor have my men taking sides."

He paused, and knowing Pa and how much he cared for Tap, I knew how much it cost him. "You can have six days' grub, Tap, and a full canteen. You've got your own horse. I want you out of camp within the hour."

Tap would not believe it. He was stunned, you could see that. He stood there staring at Pa like Pa had struck him.

"We can't have a man on our drive, which is a family affair, who would create trouble with another man's wife," Pa said, and he turned abruptly and walked back to our wagon.

Everybody turned away then, and after a minute Tap walked to the wagon and began sorting out what little gear he had.

"Sorry, Tap," I said.

He turned sharp around. "Go to hell," he said coldly. "You're no brother of mine."

He shouldered his gear and walked to his horse to saddle up. Ira Tilton got up and walked over to him, and talked to him for a minute, then came back and sat down. And then Tap got into the saddle and rode off.

Day was breaking, and we yoked up the wagons and started the herd. The river became muddy and shallow. We let the cattle take their time, feeding as they went, but the grass was sparse and of no account.

We had been short-handed when we started west, and since then we had buried Aaron Stark and lost Tap Henry. It wasn't until the wagons were rolling that we found we had lost somebody else.

Karen was gone.

She had slipped off, saddled her pony, and had taken off after Tap.

Ma Foley was in tears and Tim looked mighty grim, but we had all seen Tap ride off alone, and so far as anybody knew he had not talked to Karen in days. But it was plain enough that she had followed him off, and a more fool thing I couldn't imagine.

Pa fell back to the drag. "Son, you and Zeb take out and scout for water. I doubt if we will have much this side of the Pecos. There's Mustang Ponds up ahead, but Tap didn't say much about them."

We moved out ahead, but the land promised little. The stream dwindled away, falling after only a few miles to a mere trickle, then scattered pools. Out on the plains there was a little mesquite, all of it scrubby and low-growing. The few pools of water we saw were too small to water the herd.

The coolness of the day vanished and the sun became hot. Pausing on a rise where there should have been a breeze, we found none. I mopped my neck and looked over at Zebony.

"We may wish we had Tap before this is over."

He nodded. "Pa was right, though."

At last we found a pool. It was water lying in a deep hole in the river, left behind when the upper stream began to dry out, or else it was the result of some sudden, local shower.

"What do you think, Zeb?"

"Enough." He stared off into the distance. "Maybe the last this side of Horsehead." He turned to me. "Dan, that Pecos water is alkali. The river isn't so bad, but any pools around it will kill cattle. We've got to hold them off it."

Suddenly he drew up. On the dusty earth before him were the tracks of half a dozen unshod ponies, and they were headed south. The tracks could be no more than a few hours old.

"As if we hadn't trouble enough," Zeb commented. He squinted his eyes at the distance where the sun danced and the atmosphere shimmered.

Nothing . . .

"I wonder what became of Tap?"

"I've been wondering if that Foley girl caught up with him," Zeb said. "It was a fool thing for her to do." He glanced around at me. "Everybody thought you were shining up to her."

"We talked some . . . nothing to it."

We rode on. Sweat streaked our horses' sides and ran down under our shirts in rivulets. The stifling hot dust lifted at each step the horses took, and we squinted our eyes against the sun and looked off down over the vast empty expanse opening before us.

"If the women weren't along . . ." I said.

We had come a full day's drive ahead of the herd, and there was water back there, water for a day and a night, perhaps a little more, but ahead of us there was no sign of water and it was a long drive to Horsehead Crossing.

"We'll lose stock." Zeb lit a cigarette. "We'll lose a-plenty, unless somewhere out there, there's water."

"If there is, it will be alkali. In the pools it will be thick, and bad enough to kill cattle."

Removing my hat to wipe the hatband, I felt the sun like a fire atop my skull—and I carry a head of hair, too.

Once, dipping into a hollow, we found some grass. It was grama, dead now and dry, but our horses tugged at it and seemed pleased enough.

From the rim of the hollow we looked again into the distance toward Horsehead.

"Do you suppose there's another way to drive?" I asked.

Zeb shrugged. "It ain't likely." He pointed. "Now, what do you think of that?"

In the near distance, where the road cut through a gap in the hills, buzzards circled. There were only two or three of them.

"First living thing we've seen in hours," Zeb commented. "They must have found something."

"If they found anything out there," I said, "it's dead, all right."

We walked on, both of us shucking our firearms. I held the Patterson with light fingers, careful to avoid the barrel, which was hot enough to burn.

The first thing we saw was a dead horse. It had been dead all of a day, but no buzzards had been at it yet. The brand on the shoulder was a Rocking H, the Holt brand.

Topping out on the rise, we looked into a little arroyo

64

beside the trail. Zebony flinched, and looked around at me, his face gray and sick, and Zeb was a tough man. My horse did not want to move up beside his, but I urged it on.

The stench was frightful, and the sight we looked upon, even worse. In the bottom of that arroyo lay scattered men and horses . . . at first glimpse I couldn't tell how many.

The men were dead, stripped of clothing, and horribly mutilated. That some of the men had been alive when left by the Comanches was obvious, for there were evidences of crawling, blind crawling, like animals seeking some shelter, any shelter.

We walked our horses into the arroyo of death, and looked around. Never had I seen such a grim and bloody sight. What had happened was plain enough. This was some of the outfit that had followed us from the Cowhouse—some of the bunch that had stolen our cattle, and from whom we had recovered the herd.

They must have circled around and gotten ahead of us and settled down here to ambush us when they were attacked. Obviously, they had been expecting nothing. They would have known they were far ahead of us, and they had built fires and settled down to prepare a meal. The ashes of the fires remained and there were a few pots scattered about. There were, as we counted, eleven dead men here.

What of the others? Had they been elsewhere? Or had some of them been made prisoners by the Indians?

Hastily, we rode up out of the arroyo, and then we got down and pulled out rocks and one way and another caved in the edge of the arroyo on the bodies to partly cover them.

"Wolves won't bother them," Zeb commented. "We haven't seen any wolves in the past couple of days."

"Nothing for them to feed on but snakes. According to Tap Henry, this country is alive with them."

We turned away from the arroyo, both of us feeling sick to the stomach. They had been our enemies, but no man wishes that kind of fate on anyone, and a Comanche with time on his hands can think of a lot of ways for a man to take time to die.

Circling the scene of the ambush, we found the trail of the departing Indians. There must have been at least forty in the band—the number could only be surmised, but it was at least that large.

Their tracks indicated they were going off toward the north, and it was unlikely they would attempt to remain in the vicinity, because of the scarcity of water. But they must have crossed this terrain many times, and might know of water of which we knew nothing. Judging from the arid lands around us, though, it was doubtful.

We had started back toward the herd when we saw those other tracks. We came upon them suddenly, the tracks of two horses.

"Well, she caught up with him," Zeb commented, indicating one set of tracks. "That's Tap's paint . . . and those other tracks belong to that little *grulla* Karen rode off. I'd know those tracks anywhere."

They had come this way . . . after the massacre in the arroyo, and they were headed due west. Before them lay the eighty miles or so to Horsehead Crossing . . . had Karen taken any water? They would need it.

We camped that night by the deep pool in the river bed —the last water of which we knew.

Chapter Four

The deep pool was gone. Where the water had been was now a patch of trampled mud, slowly drying under the morning sun.

"All right, Dan," Pa said to me, "I'm no cattleman, and I have the brains to know it. You take the drive. I don't need to tell you what it means to all of us."

"There's eighty miles, or close to it, between here and Horsehead." I was speaking to them all. "But as we get close to the Pecos we may come up to some pools of water. I'll have to ride ahead, or somebody will, and spot those pools before the cattle can get wind of them, and then we'll have to keep the herd up-wind of that water.

"It's death if they drink it. Water in the pools is full of concentrated alkali, and they wouldn't have a chance.

"This is a mixed herd, the toughest kind of all to drive. From now on, anything that can't keep up will have to be left behind—any calves born on the drive must be killed.

"You know the best day we've had was about fifteen, sixteen miles. On this drive we will have to do better than that, and without water.

"The first night out, we will go into camp late and we'll start early. From that time on every man-jack of you will be riding most of the day and night."

"I can ride." Conchita McCrae stood on the edge of the group. "I've worked cattle since I was a child. We want to pull our weight, and Miguel isn't up to it yet."

"We can use you," I replied, "and thanks."

Nobody said anything for a few minutes, and finally it

was Tim Foley who spoke. "There's no water for eighty miles? What about the Mustang Pools?"

"We don't know, but we can't count on them. Maybe there is water there, but we will have to think like there wasn't."

Pa shrugged. "Well, we have been expecting it. Nobody can say we weren't warned. What we had best do is fill all the barrels, jars, everything that will hold water, and we had best be as sparing of it as we can."

Zebony led off, his long brown hair blowing in the wind, and after him came the brindle steer, still pointing his nose into God knows where, and then the herd.

Ben Cole and Milo Dodge rode the flanks; and behind them, Freeman Squires and Zeno Yearly.

Turning, I walked my horse back to where Tim Foley was getting ready to mount the seat of his wagon. His wife sat up there, her eyes fastened on distance.

"Everything all right, Tim?"

He turned around slowly. "No . . . and you know it isn't. Karen's gone, and you could have kept her, Dan."

"Me?" It was not at all what I'd expected from him. "Tim, she wouldn't have stayed for me. Nor for anyone, I guess."

"We figured you two were going to marry," Tim said. "We counted on it. I never did like that no-account Tap Henry."

"Tap's a good man, and there was no talk of marriage between Karen and me. We talked some, but there weren't any other young folks around . . . just the two of us. And she fell hard for Tap."

"He'll ruin her. That is, if she isn't lying dead out there already."

"She's with him. We found their tracks. She caught up to him and they are riding west together."

This was no time to tell them about the massacre. I had told Pa, and some of the boys knew, because I wanted them to look sharp . . . but it might only worry the women folks.

If I had a wife now, well, I'd tell her such things. A man does wrong to spare women folks, because they can stand

68

up to trouble as well as any man, and a man has no right to keep trouble from them, but this was Tim Foley's wife and Aaron Stark's widow, and there was Rose Sandy.

The wagons rolled, their heavy wheels rocked and rolled down into the gully and out on the other side, and we moved the cattle westward. Dust lifted from the line of their march, and the rising sun lit points of brightness on their thousands of horns. Somebody out along the line started up a song, and somebody else took it up, and glad I was to hear them, for they needed what courage they had for the long march that was ahead.

The cattle lowed and called, the dust grew thicker, and we moved on into the morning. Sweat streaked their sides, but we moved them on. Every mile was a victory, every mile a mile nearer water. But I knew there were cattle in this herd that would be dead long before we came to water, and there were horses that would die, and perhaps men, too.

The way west was hard, and it took hard men to travel that way, but it was the way they knew, the way they had chosen. Driving increases thirst, and the sun came hot into the morning sky, and grew hotter with the passing of the hours. The dust mounted.

Twice I switched horses before the morning was over. Working beside Jim Poor, I handled the drag, with Pa off in front with Zebony Lambert.

And when at last the cool of night came, we kept them moving steadily westward until at last we camped. We had made sixteen miles, a long drive. Yet I think there was a horror within us all at what lay ahead, and Conchita looked at me with wonder in her eyes. I knew what she was thinking.

We were mad . . . mad to try this thing.

We cooked a small meal and ate. We made coffee and drank, and the cattle were restless for water and did not lie down for a long time. But at last they did.

The burden was mine now. Carefully, I looked at the men, studying their faces, trying to estimate the limit of their strength.

It was late when I turned in at last, and I was the first

awake, rolling my blankets and saddling the dun. Zeno Yearly was squatted by the fire when I came up to it.

He gestured at the pot. "Fresh made. He'p yourself."

Filling my cup, I squatted opposite him. "I ain't a talking man," Zeno commented, out of nowhere, "so I've said nothing about this. Especial, as Tap is your brother."

Swallowing coffee, I looked at him, but I said nothing.

"This here range Tap located—how come that grass ain't been settled?"

"Open country. Nobody around, I reckon."

"Don't you be mistook. That there range was settled and in use before you were born."

Well, I couldn't believe it. Tap had told about that range out there, free for the taking. Yet Zeno was not a talking man, and I had never known him to say anything but what proved true.

"Tap found it for us," I protested. "He left a man to guard it."

"Tolan Banks?"

"You know him?"

"I should smile. That's a mean man, a mighty mean man. I heard Tap call his name, and I said nothing because I'm not a gun-fighting man and wanted no part of Tap unless he brought it to me. That Tolan Banks is a cow-thief and an outlaw."

So there it lay. We were headed west across some godawful country, running risk of life and limb, thinking we were bound for fresh and open range, and now I found that range belonged to somebody else and we would be running into a full-scale range war when we arrived.

They say trouble doesn't come singly, and surely that was true of ours. So I drank coffee and gave thought to it, but the thinking came to nothing. For all I could see was that we were committed, and we would arrive faced with a fight—and us with starving, thirsty cattle, and folks that would be starved also.

"Zeno, you keep this under your hat. This is something I've got to study about. Seems to me, Tap should have known better."

Zeno he put down his coffee and filled his pipe. He

was speaking low, for fear we would be overheard. "Meaning no offense, but it seems to me that Tap Henry is a self-thinking man. I mean, he would think of himself first. Now, suppose he wanted that land, but had no cattle? To claim land in this country you have to use it . . . you have to run cows on it.

"So what better could he do, knowing you folks were discontented and talking the West? I think you will ride into a full-fledged range war, and you'll be on the side of Tolan Banks . . . which puts you in a bad light."

"It isn't a good thought," I said. "I don't know this Tolan Banks."

"Like I say, he's a mean man. He will fight with any sort of weapon, any way you choose, and he's killed a lot of men. Some folks say he was one of that Bald Knob crowd, up there in Missouri. On that I couldn't say, and it seemed to me his voice sounded like Georgia to me."

We moved our herd on the trail, and they were mean. They had nothing to drink, and had not had anything the night before, nor was there water in sight.

We moved them out before the light and walked them forward, moving them steadily. And this day we worked harder than ever before. Now that water was gone, these cow-critters began thinking back to the Cowhouse or the Middle Concho, and they had no notion of going on into this dry country. First one and then another would try to turn back.

Again, I worked the drag. Nobody was going to say that because I was in charge that I was shirking my job. At noontime we found a sort of bluff and there was shade along it for a good half-mile. We moved the herd into that shade and stopped, lying up through the hot hours.

Miguel was sitting up when I went to the wagon. "I shall be able to ride soon," he said, "and I shall help."

Glancing out, I could see nobody close by. "Miguel," I said, "we are heading for land in New Mexico."

"*Si,* this I know."

"Do you know the Mimbres Valley?"

"*Si.*" Miguel's face had grown still, and he watched me with careful attention.

71

"Is it claimed land?"

Miguel hesitated. "*Si* . . . most of it. But there is trouble there. However, the valley is long—perhaps it is not the place of which I speak."

"And Lake Valley?"

"*Si* . . . I know it. There is much trouble there, from the Apache . . . but from white men also, and from our own people, for some of them are bad, like Felipe Soto."

"Do you think we will have trouble there? We were told the range was open. It is not open, then?"

"No . . , and you will have much trouble." Miguel paused. "Señor, I regret . . . I wish I could ride. I know how hard it is for you."

"Have you been over this road?"

"No . . . I came from the north. I was trying to escape, and then when hurt I tried for water on the Concho."

As it grew toward evening, we started the herd once more, and Conchita was in the saddle at once, and riding her big horse. Surprisingly enough, it proved a good cutting horse, and it was needed.

Now every rider was needed. The herd slowed and tried to turn aside or turn back, but we worked, keeping them moving, pointing westward into the starlit night. At last we stopped, but the cattle would not settle down. They bawled continuously, and finally I gave up.

"Pa, let's move them. They aren't going to rest, so they might as well walk."

Once again we started, and we sagged from weariness. The men around me were bone-tired, their eyes hollow, but we pushed them on. And the white dust lifted from the parched plain, strangling, stifling, thick.

When the morning came there was no rest, no surcease. The sun rose like a ball of flame, crimson and dark, and the air was still. No slightest breeze stirred the air, which lay heavily upon us, so that our breathing required effort. And now the cattle wanted to stop, they wanted even to die, but we urged them on.

Here and there one fell out, but they had to be left. The horses slowed, and stopped, starting again with a great effort.

At the nooning the ribs of the cattle stood out, and their eyes were wild. The brindle steer stared about for something to attack, and the weary ponies had scarcely the agility to move out of the way.

We made coffee, and the riders came back to the fire one by one, almost falling from their horses, red-eyed with weariness. Yet there was no complaint. Conchita was there, her eyes great dark hollows, but she smiled at me, and shook her head when I suggested she had done enough.

Foley came to me. "Dan," he said, "we're all in. The horses, I mean. We just made it here."

"All right . . . let's load everything into two wagons."

Miguel hitched himself to the tail-gate of the wagon. "I can ride," he said. "I prefer to ride."

Nor would he listen to anything I said, and in truth it was a help to have him on horseback, although he would be hard put to take care of himself, without trying to help us. The goods, which had thinned down owing to our eating into the supplies, were loaded into two wagons, and the team of the abandoned wagon was divided between the other two.

The bitter dust rose in clouds from the feet of the cattle, the sun was a copper flame in a brassy sky, the distance danced with heat waves and mirage. The cattle grew wearier and wearier with each succeeding mile; they lagged and had to be driven on, slapped with coiled riatas and forced back into the herd.

Here and there an aging cow fell out of the herd, collapsed, and died. Our throats burned with thirst and inhaled dust, and our shouts mingled with the anguished bawling of the thirsty cattle. And there was no respite. We pushed on and on, finding no convenient place to stop until hours past noon.

We stopped then, and a few of the cattle fell to the ground, and one horse died. The sky was a ceiling of flame, sweat streaked our bodies and made strange signs on the dusty flanks of the cattle.

As the suffering of the cattle increased, the tempers of the men shortened. Here and there I lent a hand, moving twice as much as any other hand, working desperately, the alkali dust prickling my skin, my eyes squinted against sun and trickling sweat.

It was brutal work, and yet through it all Conchita was busy. She did as much as any hand, and asked no favors. At times I even saw Miguel hazing some steer into line.

Wild-eyed steers plunged and fought, sometimes staggering and falling, but we pushed them on, and then I began moving out ahead of the herd, scouting for the poisonous water-holes of which I had been warned by Tap Henry.

A thousand times I wished he had been with us, a thousand times I wished for an extra hand. For three days we did not sleep. We gulped coffee, climbed back into the saddle, rode half blind with sweat and dust, fighting the cattle into line, forcing them to move, for their only chance of survival lay in moving and getting them to water.

The brindle steer stayed in the lead. He pushed on grimly, taking on a fierce, relentless personality of his own, as though he sensed our desperation and our need for help.

And every day the sun blazed down, and long into the night we pushed them on.

Cattle dropped out, stood with wide-spread legs and hanging heads beside the trail. How many had we lost? How many horses worked to a frazzle?

We lost all idea of time, for the cattle were almost impossible to handle, and we fought them desperately through the heat and the dust.

Pushing on alone, I found the Mustang Ponds, but they were merely shallow basins of cracked dry mud, rapidly turning to dust. There had been no water here in months. It was the same with the Flatrock Holes, and there was nothing else this side the river, except far and away to the northwest what were known as the Wild Cherry Holes . . . but they were off our route, and of uncertain nature.

Staring into the heat waves, it came upon me to wonder that I was here. What is it that moves a man west? I had given no thought to such a thing, although the loneliness of the far plains and the wide sky around move a man to wonder.

We had to come west or be crowded. As for the Holt crowd, we could have fought them better there than on the road. Was not this move something else? Maybe we just naturally wanted to go west, to open new country.

There have always been wandering men, but western men were all wandering men. Many a time I've seen a man pull out and leave good grass and a built house to try his luck elsewhere.

Twice I came upon alkali ponds, the water thick with the white alkali, thicker than thick soup, enough to kill any animal that drank from it.

I pushed on, and topped out on a rise and saw before me the far dark thread of growth along the Pecos. My horse stretched his neck yearningly toward the far-off stream, but I got down and rinsed my handkerchief twice in his mouth after soaking it from my canteen. Then we turned back.

We turned back, the dun and myself, and we had only some sixteen or seventeen miles to go to reach the herd.

It was a sickening sight, a dread and awful sight to see them coming. From a conical hill beside the trail I watched them.

Pa was off in front, still sitting straight in his saddle, although I knew the weariness, the exhaustion that was in him. Behind him, maybe twenty feet, and leading the herd by a good fifty yards, was that brindle steer.

And then Jim Poor and Ben Cole, pinching the lead steers together to keep them pointed down the trail.

Over all hovered a dense cloud of white dust. Alkali covered them like snow. It covered the herd, the riders, their horses . . . it covered the wagons too.

Back along the line I could see cattle, maybe a dozen within the range of my eyes. Two were down, several were standing, one looked about to fall.

But they were coming on, and I walked the dun down the steep slope to meet them.

"Pa, we'll take the best of them and head for the river. I dislike to split the herd, but if we can get some of them to water, we can save them."

Most of them were willing to stand when we stopped, but we cut out the best of them, the ones with the most stuff left, and, with Pa leading off, four of the boys started hustling them toward Horsehead on the Pecos.

The day faded in a haze of rose and gold, great red arrows shot through the sky, piercing the clouds that dripped pinkish blood on the clouds below. The vast brown-gray emptiness of the plain took on a strange enchantment, and clouds piled in weird formations, huge towers of cumulus reaching far, far into the heavens.

Many a time I had heard talk of such things, the kinds of clouds and the winds of the world, and I knew the wonder of it. But no evening had I seen like that last evening before Horsehead, no vaster sky or wider plain, no more strange enchantment of color in the sky, and on the plains too.

Pulling up alongside the wagons, I told Mrs. Foley, "Keep it rolling. No stops this side of Horsehead!"

She nodded grimly, and drove on, shouting at the tired horses. Frank Kelsey mopped the sweat from his face and grinned at me. "Hell, ain't it, boy? I never seen the like!"

"Keep rolling!" I said, and rode back to where Miguel was coming along, with Conchita holding him on his horse. "You, too," I said. "Pay no attention to the herd. If you can, go on to the river."

The crimson and gold faded from the sky, the blues became deeper. There was a dull purple along the far-off hills, and a faint purplish tone to the very air, it seemed. We moved the remaining cattle into the darkening day, into the slow-coming night.

Under the soft glory of the skies, they moved in a slow-plodding stream, heads down, tongues lolling and dusty. They moved like drunken things, drunken with exhaustion, dying on their feet of thirst, but moving west.

The riders sagged wearily in their saddles, their eyes

red-rimmed with exhaustion, but westward we moved. The shrill yells were gone, even the bawling of the cattle had ceased, and they plodded on through the utter stillness of the evening.

A heifer dropped back, and I circled and slapped her with the coiled rope. She scarcely flinched, and only after the dun nipped at her did she move, trancelike and staggering. More cattle had fallen. Twice I stopped to pour a little from my canteen into the mouths of fallen cows . . . both of them got up. Some of the others would be revived by the cool night air and would come on because they knew nowhere else to go.

And then the breeze lifted, bringing with it the smell of the river.

Heads came up, they started to walk faster, then to trot, and of a sudden they burst into a head-long run, a wild stampede toward the water that lay ahead. Some fell, but they struggled up and continued on.

There was the hoofs' brief thunder, then silence, and the smell of dust.

Alone I rode the drag of a herd long gone. Alone, in the gathering night. And there was no sound then but the steady *clop-clop* of the dun's hard hoofs upon the baked ground, and the lingering smell of the dust.

The stars were out when I came up to the Pecos, and there our wagons were, and our fire.

When the dun stopped, its legs were trembling. I stepped down heavily and leaned for a moment against the horse, and then I slowly stripped the saddle and bridle from him and turned him loose to roll, which was all the care most mustangs wanted or would accept.

Zebony came in to the fire. "They've drunk, and we're holding them back from the river."

"Good . . . no water until daybreak." Sitting down near the fire I took the Patterson from its scabbard and began to clean it. No matter what, that Patterson had to be in shape.

"I want a four-man guard on those cattle," I said, "and one man staked out away from camp, to listen. This is an Indian crossing too. The Comanches used it

77

long before any white man came into this country, and they still use it."

Mrs. Stark brought me a cup of coffee. "Drink this," she said. "You've earned it."

It was coffee, all right, laced with a shot of Irish, and it set me up somewhat. So I finished cleaning my rifle, then went to the wagon and dug out my duffel-bag. From it I took my two pistols. One I belted on, the other I shoved down behind my belt with the butt right behind my vest.

When I came back to the fire, Pa was there. He looked at that gun on my hip, but he said nothing at all. Tom Sandy looked around at me. "Never knew you to wear a hand-gun," he said, "you expecting trouble?"

"You're tired, Tom," I said, "but you get mighty little sleep tonight. I want all the barrels filled now."

"Now?" Tom stared at me. "You crazy? Everybody is dead-tired. Why, you couldn't—"

"Yes, I can. You get busy—every barrel full before we sleep."

And they filled them, too.

It was past one o'clock in the morning when I finally stretched out, slowly straightening my stiff muscles, trying to let the tenseness out of my body, but it was several minutes before I could sort of let myself go . . . and then I slept.

The first thing I heard when I awoke was the water, the wonderful, wonderful sound of water. Even the Pecos, as treacherous a stream as ever was . . . but it was water. The sky was faintly gray. I had been asleep almost two hours, judging by the Big Dipper. Rolling over, I sat up and put on my hat. Everything was still.

I pulled on my boots, belted on my gun, and walked over to the fire.

What I had believed to be trees and brush along the line of the Pecos was actually the shadow cast by the high bank. The river at this point was destitute of anything like trees or shrubs. The only growth along it was a thin line of rushes. It lay at the bottom of a trough that was from six to ten feet deep. The river itself was

78

about a hundred feet wide and no more than four feet deep at the deepest point. The plain above was of thin, sandy soil, and there was only a sparse growth of greasewood, dwarf mesquite, and occasional clumps of bear grass.

Zebony came up to the fire and sat his horse while drinking a cup of coffee. It was quiet . . . mighty quiet.

The cattle, still exhausted, were bedded down and content to rest, although occasionally one of them would start for the river and had to be headed back

"You going to lay up here?"

"No."

Tim Foley looked around at me. Tim was a good man, but sometimes he thought I was too young for my job. Me, I've never seen that years made a man smart, for simply getting older doesn't mean much unless a man learns something meanwhile.

"We're going to finish crossing, and then go up stream a few miles." I gestured around me at the row of skulls marking the crossing, and at the crossing itself. "We don't want to run into Comanches."

Zeb started to turn his horse and stopped. "Dan . . . !"

Something in his voice spun me around. A party of riders were coming toward us. Near as I could make out, there were six or seven.

"You wearing a gun, Tim?"

"I am."

"I'm holdin' one." That would be Zeno Yearly.

Behind me there was a stirring in the camp. I glanced across the river where the herd was lying. Four men would be over there . . . but what about the fifth man who was staked out? Had he seen these riders? Or had they found him first?

Conchita was suddenly close by, standing half concealed by a wagon wheel.

My eyes fastened on the man in the lead. He rode a powerful bay horse, and he was a huge man. This, I knew at once, was Felipe Soto.

He rode up to the edge of camp and I saw him look carefully around. I do not know how much he saw, for we looked like a sleeping camp, except for the three of us standing there. Foley was across the fire from them, and Zeb on his horse some twenty feet off to one side. I was in the middle, and intended it that way.

My Patterson lay on the rolled-up blankets of my bed about a dozen feet off.

"I look for Miguel Sandoval," the big man said. "Turn him over to me, and you will have no trouble."

Taking an easy step forward, I took the play away from him. "What do you mean, no trouble? Mister, if you want anybody from this outfit you've got to take them. As for trouble, we're asking for all you've got."

He looked at me with careful attention, and I knew he was trying to figure how much was loud talk and how much was real trouble.

"Look, señor, I think you do not understand." He gestured behind him. "I have many men . . . these are but a few. You have women here, and do not want trouble."

"You keep mentioning that," I said quietly, "but we're as ready as you are. We've had a mean drive, and we're all feeling pretty sore, so if you want to buy yourself a package of grief, you just dig in your spurs and hang on."

His men started to fan out and Zebony spoke up. "Stand! You boys stand where you are or I'll open the ball," he said coolly. "If there's to be shooting we want you all bunched up."

Soto had not taken his eyes from me, and I do not know if he had intended to kill me, but I know I was ready. Whatever notion he had, he changed his mind in a hurry, and it was Zeno Yearly who changed it for him.

"You take the big one, Dan," Zeno said conversationally. "I want the man on his right."

Soto's eyes did not leave mine, but I saw his lips tighten under the black mustache. They had not seen Zeno, and even I was not sure exactly where he was. They could see three of us . . . how many more were there?

There was no use losing a good thing, so I played the

80

hand out. "Zeno," I said, "you've gone and spoiled a good thing. Between you and the boys on the river bank, I figured to collect some scalps."

Soto did not like it. In fact, he did not like it even a little. He did not know whether there was anybody on the river bank or not, nor did he like what he would have to do to find out.

He knew there must be men with the cattle, and that, had they seen him coming or been warned in time, they might easily be sheltered by the high bank and waiting to cut Soto and his men to doll rags.

"I regret, señor"—Soto smiled stiffly—"the shortness of our visit. When we come again there will be more of us . . . and some friends of ours, the Comanches. You would do well to drive Miguel Sandoval from your camp."

"There was a grave back yonder," I said, "of a Mexican we found and buried."

Soto smiled again. "A good trick . . . only we turned back and opened the grave. There was no body."

He turned his horse and walked it slowly away from camp, but we knew he would come back, and we knew we were in trouble.

"All right," I said. "A quick breakfast and then we move out."

During the night several steers and a cow had managed to make the river, and rejoined the herd. There was no time to estimate the loss of cattle on the drive, although obviously several hundred head were gone.

We pushed on, keeping up a steady move, pausing only at noon to water in the Pecos, whose route we were following. One or more of us trailed well behind or on the hills to right or left, scouting for the enemy.

The earth was incredibly dry and was covered over vast areas with a white, saline substance left from the alkali in the area. Wherever there had been water standing, the ground was white, as if from snow.

Pa fell back and rode beside me. "We're outnumbered, Dan," he said. "They'll come with fifty or sixty men."

We saw not a living thing. Here and there were dead cattle, dried to mere bones and hide, untorn by wolves, which showed us that not even those animals would try to exist in such a place. By nightfall there was no grass to be found, so we brought the wagons together on a low knoll, with the cattle behind it.

There was a forest of prickly pear, which cattle will eat, and which is moist enough so they need little water. Half a dozen of us went out and singed the spines from bunches of pear with torches, and it was a pretty sight to see the torches moving over the darkening plain. But the cattle fed.

With daybreak, the wind rose and the sky was filled with dust, and clouds of dust billowed along the ground, filling the air and driving against the face with stinging force. The sun became a ball of red, then was obscured, and the cattle moved out with the wind behind them, herded along the course of the Pecos, but far enough off to avoid its twistings and turnings.

By nightfall the dust storm had died down, but the air was unnaturally cold. Under the lee of a knoll the wagons drew up and a fire was built.

Zebony rode in and stepped down from his horse. Ma Foley and Mrs. Stark were working over a meal. There was little food left, but a few of the faltering cattle had been killed, and some of the beef was prepared. The flour was almost all gone, and no molasses was left.

Zeno Yearly came up and joined us. There was a stubble of beard on his lean jaws, and his big sad eyes surveyed us with melancholy. "Reminded me of a time up on the Canadian when I was headed for Colorado. We ran into a dust storm so thick we could look up betwixt us and the sun and see the prairie dogs diggin' their holes."

Squatting by the fire, I stared into the flames, and I was doing some thinking. Pa was relying on me, with Tap gone, and I hadn't much hope of doing much. The herd was all we had, and the herd was in bad shape. We had a fight facing us whenever Felipe Soto and his Comancheros caught up with us, and we were short-handed.

We had lost several hundred head and could not afford to lose more. And from what Conchita and Miguel said, we were heading into a country where we might find more trouble than we wanted.

We were almost out of grub, and there was no use hunting. Whatever game there had been around here had drifted out, and all we could do was keep driving ahead.

Our horses had come out of it better than most, for many a herd crossing the Horsehead had wound up with most of the hands walking, their horses either dead or stolen by Indians. About all a man could do was go on; but I had found that many a problem is settled if a man just keeps a-going.

It wasn't in me to sell Felipe Soto short. He was a tough man, and he would come back. They did not want any talk of Comancheros or of the Palo Duro Canyon to get around . . . there already was opposition enough from the New Mexicans themselves.

"We'll push on the herd," I told Zebony. "We should reach the Delaware soon."

It was amazing how the water and the short rest had perked up the cattle. There had been little grass, but the prickly pear had done wonders for them, and they moved out willingly enough. It was as if they, too, believed the worst of the trip was past. Knowing something of the country that lay before us, I was not so sure.

We closed up the herd and kept the wagons close on the flank. Zeno Yearly and Freeman Squires fell back to bring up the rear and do the scouting. Pa led off, and part of the time was far out ahead of us, scouting for ambush or tracks. The rest of us kept the herd closed up and we moved ahead at a steady gait.

Toyah Creek, when we reached it, was only a sandy wash, so we went through and pushed on. As we traveled, we gathered the wood we found where wagons had broken down and been abandoned, for there was nothing along the trail for fuel but buffalo chips and occasional mesquite, most of which had to be dug out of the ground to find anything worth burning.

The coolness disappeared and again it became incredibly hot. The heat rising from the herd itself, close-packed as it was, was almost unbearable.

Conchita rode over to join me.

"We have talked, Miguel and I," she said. "You protected us, or we should have been killed."

"It was little enough."

"We did not expect it. Miguel . . . he did not expect to be helped, because he is a Mexican."

"Might make a difference to some folks, not to us. When we first came into this country—I mean when Pa first came—he would never have made out but for help from Mexican neighbors."

"We have talked of you, and there is a place we know —it is a very good place. There is danger from Indians, but there is danger everywhere from them."

"Where is this place?"

"We will show you. It lies upon a route used by the *padres* long ago. By traders also. But there is water, there is good grass, and I think you can settle there without trouble."

"Where will you go?"

"To my home. To Miguel's mother and his wife."

"He did not mention a wife. I thought maybe . . . Miguel and you . . ."

"No, señor. He is married. We are grown up in the same house, but we are friends only. He has been a very good brother to me, señor."

"Like Tap and me," I said. "We got along pretty good."

All through the day we rode together, talking of this thing and that. The cattle moved steadily. By nightfall we had twelve miles behind us.

There was a chance the dust storm might have wiped out miles of our tracks, and that might help a little. But in the arid lands men are tied to water, and they must go where water is, and so their trails can be found even if lost.

Ira Tilton was out on the north flank of the drive as we neared the last stop we would make along the Pecos. From that point we would cut loose and drive across country toward Delaware Creek.

Toward sundown he shot an antelope and brought it

84

into camp. It was mighty little meat for such a crowd of folks, but we were glad to get it.

We were of no mind to kill any of our breeding stock which we needed to start over again, and the steers we needed to sell to the Army or somebody to get money for flour and necessaries to tide us over the first year. We were poor folks, when it came to that, with nothing but our cattle and our bodily strength for capital.

That night when the firelight danced on the weathered faces of the cowhands, we sat close around the fire and we sang the songs we knew, and told stories, and yarned. There was a weariness on us, but we were leaving the Pecos, and no cowhand ever liked the Pecos for long.

Firelight made the wagon shadows flicker. Ma Foley came and sat with us, and the firelight lit the gold of Conchita's hair to flame, to a red-gold flame that caught the light as she moved her head.

Rose Sandy came to the fire, too, sitting close to Tom, and very quiet. But I do not think there was censure among us for what she had done, for nobody knew better than we that the flesh was weak.

Pa was there, listening or talking quietly, his fine-cut features looking younger than he was.

"We will find a place," he said, "and we will settle. We will make of the Kaybar a brand we can be proud of."

There was hope in all of us, but fear too. Standing up at last, I looked at Conchita and she rose too, and we walked back from the fire together. Miguel stood by his wagon, and when we passed him, he said, *"Vaya con Dios."*

Freeman Squires shook me out of a sleep and I sat up and groped for my hat. It was still . . . the stars were gone and there were clouds and a feeling of dampness in the air. Stamping into my boots, I picked up my gun and slung the belt around me, then tucked the other behind my belt.

Then I reached for the Patterson, and as I did so

there was a piercing yell far out on the plains, and then a whole chorus of wild Comanche yells and the pound of hoofs.

The cattle came up with a single lunge and broke into a wild stampede. I saw Free Squires riding like mad to cut them off, saw his horse stumble and go down and the wave of charging, wild-eyed cattle charge over him.

And then I was on one knee and shooting.

A Comanche jumped his horse into camp and my first shot took him from the saddle. I saw Pa roll out of bed and fire a shotgun from a sitting position.

In an instant the night was laced with a red pattern of gunfire, streaks of flame stabbing the darkness in the roar of shooting.

Zebony Lambert ran from the shelter of a wagon, blazing away with a six-shooter. I saw an Indian try to ride him down and Zeb grabbed the Indian and swung up behind him and they went careering off into the night, fighting on the horse's back.

A big man leaped past me on a gray horse—it was the blond man who had been with Webb Holt when he was killed.

A horse struck me with his shoulder and knocked me rolling, a bullet spat dirt into my mouth as it struck in front of me.

Again I started to get up and I saw Pa firing from his knee. There was blood on his face, but he was shooting as calmly as if in a shooting gallery. Ben Cole was down, all sprawled out on the ground, and I saw Jim Poor rise suddenly from the ground and run to a new position, with bullets all around him.

Suddenly I saw Bud Caldwell charge into camp, swing broadside, and throw down on Pa. I flipped a six-shooter and shot him through the chest. The bullet hit him dead center and he was knocked back in the saddle and the horse cut into a run. Turning on my heel I fired again from the hip and Bud Caldwell fell on his face in the dirt and turned slowly over.

And as it had started, it ended, suddenly and in stillness.

The wagontop on one of the wagons was in flames, so I grabbed a bucket of water and sloshed it over the flames, and then jumped up and ripped the canvas from the frame and hurled it to the ground. A bullet clipped the wagon near me and I dropped again and lay still on the ground.

Our herd was gone. Freeman Squires was surely dead, and it looked like Ben Cole was, too.

Nothing moved. Lying still in the darkness, I fed shells into my six-shooter and tried to locate the Patterson.

Somewhere out in the darkness I heard a low moan, and then there was silence. The smell of dust was in my nostrils, an ache in my bones; the gun butt felt good against my palm. Behind me I could hear the faint rustle of water among the thin reeds along the bank, but nothing else moved.

They were out there yet, I knew that, and to move was to die.

What had happened to Conchita? To Ma Foley? Where was Pa?

In the distance, thunder rumbled . . . the night was vastly empty, and vastly still. A cool wind blew a quick, sharp gust through the camp, scattering some of the fire, rolling a cup along the ground.

With infinite care, I got a hand flat on the ground and eased myself up and back, away from the firelight. After a moment of waiting I repeated the move.

Thunder rolled . . . there was a jagged streak of lightning, and then the rain came. It came with a rush, great sheets of rain flung hard against the dusty soil, dampening it, soaking it all in one smashing onslaught.

When the lightning flared again, I saw my father lying with his eyes wide to the sky, and then the lightning was gone, and there was only the rumble of thunder and the rush of rain falling.

Chapter Five

In a stumbling run I left the place where I lay and ran to my father's side.

He was dead. He had been shot twice through the body and had bled terribly.

Taking the rifle that lay beside him, I leaped up and ran to the nearest wagon and took shelter beneath it. If any of the others lived, I did not know, but my father was dead, our cattle gone, our hopes destroyed, and within me, suddenly and for the first time, I knew hatred.

Under the wagon, in partial shelter, I tried to think ahead. What would Soto and his men do? All my instincts told me to get away, as far away as possible before the morning came, for unless I was much mistaken, they would come to loot the wagons.

How many others were dead? And did any lie out there now, too grievously wounded to escape? If so, I must find them. Knowing the Comanche, I could leave no man who had worked with us to fall helpless into their hands.

Carefully, I wiped my guns dry. The Patterson still lay out there somewhere, but I had my father's breech-loading Sharps. The shotgun he had also had must still be lying out there.

The storm did not abate. The rain poured down and the Pecos was rising. It was a cloudburst, or something close to it, and the more I considered it the more I began to believe that my enemies might have fled for shelter, if they knew of any. Or perhaps they had gone off after our cattle, for without doubt they would take the herd.

Suddenly, in the wagon above me, there was a faint stir of movement. Then thunder rumbled in the distance, and lightning flashed, and on the edge of the river bank, not twenty yards off, stood two bedraggled figures. I knew them at once.

Tim Foley and his wife!

They lived, at least. And who was in the wagon? One of us, I was sure . . . yet could I be sure? Perhaps it was some Comanche who had started to loot the wagon.

Carefully, I eased out from under the wagon. The rain struck me like a blow, the force of the driven rain lashing viciously at my face. It would be completely dark within the wagon, and I would be framed against the lightning, but I must know. The Foleys were coming, and they must not walk into a trap.

One foot I put on a horizontal spoke of the wheel, and, holding to the edge of the wagon with my left hand, I swung myself suddenly up and into the wagon.

There was a startled gasp.

"Conchita?"

"*Dan!* Oh, Dan! You're *alive!*"

"More or less. Are you all right?"

"Of course, but this man is hurt. He has been shot."

Risking a shot myself, I struck a light. It was Zeno Yearly, and there was a graze along his skull and a crease along the top of his shoulder. Evidently the bullet had struck him when he was lying down in the wagon, and grazing the side of his skull, it had burned his shoulder. He had bled freely, but nothing more.

The rain continued without letup, and through the roar of the rain on the canvas wagon cover we heard the splash of footsteps, and then Ma Foley and Tim climbed into the wagon.

Zeno sat up, holding his head and staring around him.

"It's safe, I think, to light a candle," I said. "They have gone or they would have shot when I struck the match."

When a candle was lighted I rummaged in the wagon for ammunition.

"Here," Tim Foley said, holding out the Patterson, "I found it back there."

Taking the gun, I passed the Sharps over to him, and began cleaning the Patterson, wiping the rain and mud from it, and removing the charges.

"Are we all that's left?" Ma Foley asked plaintively. "Are they all gone?"

"Pa's dead, and I saw Squires go down ahead of the stampede. I saw Ben Cole fall."

"Jim Poor got down under the bank. I think he was unhurt then, if the river didn't get him."

Huddled together, we waited for the morning, and the rain continued to fall. At least, there would be water. We must find and kill a steer, if we could find a stray. And somehow we must get to the Rio Grande, or to the Copper Mines.

For we had been left without food. What had not been destroyed in the brief fire in the other wagon was undoubtedly damaged by the rain, although I hoped the damage would be slight. And there had been little enough, in any event.

Our remuda was gone, the horses stolen or scattered, and the chances of catching any of them was slight indeed. The trek that now lay before us would in many ways be one of the worst that anyone could imagine, and we had women along.

The responsibility was mine. These were our people, men who worked for us, and my father was dead. In such a case, even with the herd gone, I could not, dared not surrender leadership. Now, more than ever, we needed a strong hand to guide us out of this desert and to some place where we might get food and horses to ride.

Fear sat deep within me, for I had encountered nothing like this before, and I feared failure, and failure now meant death . . . at least, for the weakest among us.

All the night long, the rain fell. The Pecos was running bank-full, and so would be the arroyos leading to it. Our way west was barred now by one more obstacle, but, once the sun came out, the arroyos would not run for long, and their sandy basins, long dry, would drink up the water left behind. Only in the *tinajas,* the natural rock cisterns, would there be water.

The sun rose behind a blanket of lowering gray cloud, and the rain settled down to a steady downpour, with little lightning, and thunder whimpering among the canyons of the far-off Guadalupes.

Stiffly, I got to my feet and slid to the ground. Donning my slicker, I looked carefully around.

The earth was dark with rain, the ground where the camp stood was churned into mud, and wherever I looked the sky was heavy with rain clouds that lay low above the gray hills. The Pecos rushed by—dark, swirling waters that seemed to have lost their reddish tinge. Crossing the camp, I picked up Pa's body and carried it to shelter under the wagon, then began to look around.

On the edge of camp I found Bud Caldwell . . . he was dead. Another man, unknown to me, but obviously a Comanchero, lay dead near the river bank.

Ignoring their bodies, I gathered the body of Ben Cole in my arms and carried him to where Pa lay.

We desperately needed horses, but there were none in sight. There was a dead horse and a saddle lying not too far away and, walking to them, I took the saddle from the horse, tugging the girth from beneath it. The horse lay upon soft mud, and the girth came out without too much trouble. Then I removed the bridle and carried them to the wagon.

Tim Foley got down from the wagon. "Tim," I said, "you and Mrs. Foley can help. Go through both wagons and sort out all the food you can find that's still good. Also, collect all the canteens, bedding, and whatever there is in the way of ammunition and weapons."

He nodded, looking around grimly. "They ruined us, Dan. They ruined us."

"Don't you believe it. We're going to make it through to the Copper Mines, and then we'll see. If you find Pa's papers, account books and the like, you put them aside for me."

Zeno Yearly got down from the wagon also. He looked wan and sick, but he glanced at me with a droll smile. "We got us a long walk, Dan. You much on walking?"

Together we hunted around. There was no sign of Jim Poor, but he might have been drowned or swept away by the river.

The one thing none of us was talking about was the kids. Tim's two boys and Stark's children. Nobody had seen a sign of them since the attack, yet I had seen them bedded down and asleep when I was awakened to go out for my night guard.

Zeno and me walked slowly up along the bank of the river. Whatever tracks there had been were washed out. It was unbelievable that they could all have survived, but the fact that we saw no bodies gave us hope.

Zeno and I spread out, and suddenly he gave a call. He was standing looking down at or into something. When I got over there, I saw that he was standing on the edge of some limestone sinks.

The earth had caved in or sunk in several places that were thirty feet or more in diameter. Looking across the hole where Zeno stood, we could see the dark opening of a cave.

Zeno called out and, surprisingly, there was an answering call. Out of a cave under the very edge where we stood came Milo Dodge.

"Heard you talkin'," he said. "You all right?"

"You seen the youngsters?"

"They're here with me, all dry and safe. Emma Stark is here, too."

Slowly, they climbed out of the cave and showed themselves. Milo climbed up to where we were.

"Frank Kelsey's dead. He lived through the night, died about daybreak. He caught two damned bad ones, low down and mean . . . right through the belly."

"Pa's dead," I said, "and Ben Cole."

"Emma Stark got the youngsters out when the first attack hit, and I'd seen this place, so I hustled them over here. I got in a couple of good shots, and missed one that I wished had hit."

"What do you mean?" He had a look in his eyes that puzzled me.

"Ira Tilton," Dodge said. "He was with them. When they came riding in he was alongside Bud Caldwell. I took a shot at him."

"Remember the fight Tap had with Webb Holt? If Ira was with them, that explains how those other men showed up so unexpectedly. He must have warned them."

"I'll make it my business," Milo said coldly. "I want that man."

"You'll have to get to him before I do," Zeno said. "I never liked him."

Slowly we gathered together, and it was a pitiful bunch we made.

Tim Foley, Milo Dodge, Zeno Yearly, and me . . . three women, five children. Foley's boys were fourteen and ten . . . Emma Stark's youngsters were a girl thirteen, and two boys, one nine, one a baby.

"First off," I said, "we'd better move into that cave, Milo. The women and youngsters can hide there while we hunt horses. I can't believe they were all driven off, and I think we should have a look around. Some of those horses may come back to camp."

We stripped the wagons of what was left that we could use, and took only the simplest of gear. We moved our beds and cooking utensils down there, and what little food was left, and we moved our ammunition too.

Zeno and I started out in one direction, each of us with a rope. Milo and Tim started out the other way. Unluckily the storm had left no tracks, but we had agreed not to go far, to keep a wary eye out for Comanches, and if we found nothing within a few miles, to return.

Zeno and me climbed a long, muddy slope to the top of the rounded-off ridge. The country was scattered with soapweed, prickly bear, and mesquite. Far off, we saw something that might be a horse, or maybe a steer—at that distance, we couldn't make it out.

"There's another!" Zeno picked it out with his finger. "Let's go!"

We started off, walking in the direction of the animal we had seen, and when we had gone scarcely half a mile we could make it out to be a steer. It was Old Brindle, our lead steer.

"You ever ride a steer, Dan?"

"When I was a youngster—sure. I don't think anybody could ride Old Brindle, though."

"Maybe," Zeno looked at him with speculative eyes. "Toward the end there, he was getting mighty friendly. Acted as though he and us were handling that herd together. Let's go get him."

Well, we walked along toward him, and pretty soon he sighted us. We saw his big head come up—his horns were eight feet from tip to tip—and then he walked out toward us, dipping his horns a little as if ready for battle. A man on the ground is usually fair game for any steer, although they will rarely attack a man on horseback.

He came toward us and I spoke to him, and he watched us, his eyes big and round, his head up. Turning away, I started toward that other animal. "Come on, boy!" I said. "You're with us."

And you know something? That big old steer fell in behind us like a big dog, and he walked right along, stopping when we stopped, moving when we moved.

"He might stand for a pack," I said, "and if he did, it would take a load off us."

"We can try."

And then we had a real break.

Rounding the clump of mesquite that lay between us and the other animal we had seen, we saw it. Standing there in a sort of hollow was that line-back dun of mine, and with him were two other horses from the remuda. One was a bay pony, the other a paint.

I called out to the dun, and he shied off, but I shook out a loop. He ducked and trotted around, but when the loop dropped over his head he stood still, and I think he was glad to be caught. Horses and dogs thrive better in the vicinity of men, and they know it. Moreover, they are sociable animals, and like nothing better than to be around men and to be talked to.

Rigging a hackamore from some piggin strings, I

94

mounted up, and soon had caught the paint. Zeno was packing the bridle I'd found on Bud Caldwell's dead horse—if it was his—and he was soon riding the second horse. The third one was more shy, but he seemed to want to stay with the other horses, and when we started back toward camp he followed along and pretty soon Zeno dabbed a loop on him.

Foley and Dodge returned empty-handed. They had seen fresh tracks, however, made since the rain, of both cattle and horses.

We camped that night in the cave, and made a sparing supper of the remnants of some salt pork and beans.

"This cave goes away back," Foley commented. "Looks like the whole country's undermined with it. I used to live in a limestone country in Kentucky, and believe me, caves like this can run for miles."

At daybreak we loaded what gear we had and moved out. The youngsters and the women were to take turns riding, and surprisingly enough, Old Brindle seemed pleased with his pack. That cantankerous old mossyhorn was full of surprises, but he had gotten used to folks, and he liked being around them. Not that Conchita and the youngsters hadn't helped by feeding him chunks of biscuit or corn pone touched with molasses.

We made a sorry outfit, but we started off. The bodies of Pa and the others were buried in a row, and what little we could find of Freeman Squires.

There was no sign of Zebony Lambert, of Jim Poor or the Sandys.

The last I'd seen of Zeb he had jumped on a horse behind a Comanche and gone riding away into the night, fighting with him. Maybe he was a prisoner, and maybe he got off scot-free. Anyway, we had found no other bodies, though in hunting horses we had looked around a good bit.

We kept going, and by nightfall came up to a place in the bend of Delaware Creek. There had been a big encampment here at some time in the past, and there was a lot of wood lying about, and one busted-down wagon from which two wheels had been taken.

The grass was the best we had seen in weeks, and there were a couple of clumps of mesquite of fair size.

About sundown Zeno killed an antelope, and we had antelope steaks for supper. It was the first good meal we had since leaving the Pecos.

We took turns standing guard, for we figured we weren't finished with the Comancheros, and wanted to be ready for them. It was nigh on to midnight when I heard a horse coming. He was coming right along, but when he got somewhere out there in the darkness, he stopped.

My dun whinnied, and he answered, and came closer. It was Conchita's big horse.

Shaking her awake, I explained, and she got up quickly and went to the edge of the firelight, calling him. He came right up to her and started to nuzzle her hand as if looking for corn or sugar or something. He was wearing a saddle and bridle of Spanish style, with a high cantle and too much tree for my taste. There was a good rifle in the scabbard, and the saddle-bags were evidently packed full.

Conchita opened the saddle-bags. There were a couple of small packets of ammunition and a buckskin sack containing some gold pieces.

She handed this to me. "We can use that," she said.

Nothing had been said about Miguel, but I could see by the stillness of her face and a tightness around her eyes that she was trying to maintain her composure. His body had not been found, and nobody could recall seeing him after the first burst of fighting.

Obviously, the big horse had been captured along with the rest of the stock, but he had thrown his rider at some later time and returned to us.

"No man had ridden him," Conchita explained. "He would have watched for his chance to throw any rider but myself, or perhaps some other woman."

We moved westward, and the clouds withdrew and the sun came out. Heat returned to the plains . . . the grass grew sparser again, there was little fuel. We men walked . . . and we saw no Indians.

On the third day we killed an ox we found on the

desert. Obviously left behind by some wagon train passing through, perhaps long before, he had fattened on mesquite beans. We killed and butchered the ox, and that night we dined on good beef and cut much of the remainder into strips to smoke over the fire.

In the distance we could see the tower of Guadalupe Mountain shouldering against the sky.

Surprisingly, we made better time than with the herd and wagons. On the first day after finding Conchita's horse we put sixteen miles behind us, but we made dry camp that night.

Morning came and we were moving out before dawn, with Zeno and myself off in the lead. The women and youngsters on the horses came in between, and Tim Foley brought up the rear with Milo Dodge.

The desert shimmered with heat waves, and on the open plain weird dust-devils danced. A chaparral cock appeared from out of nowhere and ran along beside us. Everywhere we passed what had been pools from the rain, now dried up, the earth cracked and turning to dust. Our canteens were nearly empty, and there was no food left but the strips of dried, smoked beef.

The soil was hard and gravelly; there were frequent limestone outcroppings, and low hills. Westward was the beckoning finger of Guadalupe Mountain. Toward dusk we made camp in a little valley where the grazing was good. There were a few trees here, and three springs, one of them smelling strongly of sulphur and a soda spring, but the third was pure, cold water.

Foley helped his wife from the saddle, and for a moment they stood together, her arms clinging to his. Her naturally florid features were burned even redder by the sun and wind, but she was pale beneath the color, and he led her carefully to a place under a tree, where she sat down.

The children scattered to gather wood and cow chips for a fire, and Zeno led the horses into the shelter of the trees.

Tim Foley walked over to where I stood talking to Zeno Yearly. "My old woman's about had it, Dan. She's done up. If she don't get some food and proper rest soon, we won't have her with us long."

"You're looking kind of long in the tooth yourself, Tim," I said, "but you're right. Seems like we'd better get some meat before we pull out of here."

"This is Apache country," Milo Dodge said, "so keep an eye out."

It was finally settled that I would go alone, and the other three would remain behind to keep a sharp lookout. Foley's boy was provided with a rifle, for he was fourteen and coming on to manhood, and they settled down to guard the women folks and the horses.

Wearing my two pistols, with the Patterson fully loaded, I walked out. Twice I saw rattlers, but I left them alone.

The evening was still. The desert was gathering shadows in the low places, and the distant mountains were taking on the soft mauve and purple of evening. Somewhere out on the desert a quail called . . . and after a minute, there was an answer. These were the blue quail, which rarely fly, but run swiftly along the ground. They were small, scarcely larger than a pigeon.

Twice I paused, and with piggin strings, the short strips of rawhide carried by a cowhand for tying the legs of a calf, I rigged several snares where I had seen rabbit tracks.

But I found no game. Toward dusk I did get a shot at a quail, and killed it. Returning home, I had only the quail to show. At daybreak I checked my traps and found I'd caught a large jackass rabbit. What meat there was on him was divided among the women and children.

So we started on at the break of dawn. The Guadalupe Peak loomed higher than ever, and the long range that stretched out to the north from behind it seemed dark and ominous. Tim Foley, who was the oldest of us all, fell down twice that day. Each time he got up slowly, carefully, and came on.

We camped that night after making only a few miles, in a small grove of live oak and pines, with the mountain looming over us.

Tim Foley dropped to the ground, exhausted, and it was Milo and Zeno who stripped the saddles from the horses and helped the women down. Taking my Patterson, I walked out at once.

To tell you the truth, I was scared. We men had gone a whole day without food, and during the past four or five days had been on mighty short rations. Tim was older than we were, and had lived a life in the saddle, but it was still a good long trek to the Copper Mines for all of us.

Nobody had much to keep them going, and if I did not scare up food of some kind we were not going much further.

Several times I saw deer droppings, but all were old, and I saw no deer, nor any recent tracks. Because this was Apache country, I did not wish to shoot unless I was sure of a kill.

It was very still. Sweat trickled down my chest under my shirt. The sky overhead was very blue, and the clouds had gone. For some reason my nerves were suddenly on edge, yet I had heard nothing, seen nothing. Carefully, I edged forward.

Far overhead a lone buzzard circled lazily against the blue. The vague trail I followed now had carried me over a thousand feet above the tiny valley where our camp lay concealed. Drying my hands on my shirt, I started forward again. Suddenly, on the edge of a cliff some fifty yards away, I saw a bighorn sheep.

He was a big fellow, and he was watching something below him. His big horns curved around and forward, and he had the color of a deer, or close to it, and the same sort of hair. It was the first bighorn I had seen.

Carefully, leaning my shoulder against the cliff, I lifted the Patterson and took a careful sight on a point just back of his neck. I was trying for a spine shot, hoping to stop him where he was. Shot through the heart, he might disappear into the rocks and be lost. Deer will often run half a mile after a heart shot and the bighorn might do even more, and this was a rugged country.

But even as I laid the sights on the point where I wished

the bullet to strike, the poise and attention of the sheep worried me. Lowering the rifle, I eased forward a step further, and looked down into the rugged country below.

The first thing I saw was a cow . . . it was a white-faced longhorn cow, and then behind it came another and another, and they were our cows. And then a man stepped from the brush. It was Jim Poor!

Holding still, I watched them slowly come from a draw onto the open mountainside, at least thirty head of cattle, some cows, some young stuff, and a few old steers, and behind them walked two men, and a woman who rode their one horse.

Catching myself just as I started to call out, I looked again at the bighorn. He had drawn back and turned away from me, and he was ready to get out of there, and fast. Lifting the Patterson, I caught my sight again, and squeezed off the shot.

The bighorn leaped straight up and landed with his legs spread out. He started to go forward and I steadied the rifle for another shot. Just as I was about to fire, his knees buckled and he fell forward on one shoulder and lay still.

Glancing into the basin below, I saw no one. Only the cattle, standing now with their heads up, staring, nostrils distended. Grinning, I lowered my rifle and, knowing how a voice can carry in that still air, I called out.

"You boys scared of something? A body'd think you all stepped on a hot rock!"

"Dan? Dan Killoe?" That was Zeb's voice.

"If it ain't," I yelled back, "then Pa fed me for a long time for nothing!"

They came out in the open then, and I saw that the woman on the horse was Rose Sandy, and the men were Zeb Lambert, Jim Poor, and Miguel. And then another came from the brush, and it was Tom Sandy!

I let out a whoop and started to go down the mountain, then remembered that sheep.

"Jim! Come on up here! I've killed me a bighorn!"

He clambered up the slope. "You're a better butcher

than I am, Jim, so skin him out and I'll talk to those boys and then come on up and help you pack it in."

The horse on which Rose was riding was the one Zebony had taken from that Indian he rode off behind. He had been well outside the circle of the fighting before his battle with the Comanche ended, and by the time he started back the rain was pouring down and the fighting was about over.

The country was covered with Comanches and Comancheros, so he had found a place where a notch cut into the river bank and concealed himself there with the horse. He had put in a wet and miserable night, but at daybreak he saw some cattle to the south and started around to gather them, and then he met Rose and Tom Sandy.

Miguel was with them, and in bad shape. He had been captured by the Indians, had killed his captors and escaped, but had been wounded again. These, though, were merely flesh wounds, and he had recovered quickly in the succeeding days.

Banding together, they had rounded up what strays they could find and started off to the northwest, heading toward a limestone sink Miguel knew of. There they had found water and some friendly Lipans, who traded some corn and seeds they had gathered for a steer.

Twenty miles west they had come upon Jim Poor. He was standing beside a horse with a broken leg . . . he had ducked to the shelter of the river bank, but caught a horse whose owner had been shot, and when the shooting died down, believing everyone in the camp was dead, he had started west alone.

Nine days later we reached El Paso, a small town of one-story adobe houses, most of it lying on the Mexican side of the river. On the north side of the river there were several groups of settlements, the largest being Coon's Rancho and Magoffinsville, the two being about a mile and a half apart. There was a third settlement, about a mile from Magoffinsville, around another ranch.

Zebony came to me after we had found shelter and

had our small herd, once more led by Old Brindle, gathered in a pasture near the town.

"Dan, what are we going to do?"

"What we started to do," I said. "At least, I am. I'm going on, and I'm going to find us an outfit, and I'm going to use what cattle we have to start a ranch."

"And then?"

"Why, then I'm going hunting. I'm going hunting for a man with a spider scar, a man named Felipe Soto."

Pausing for a second, I considered the situation. Around me I had a lot of good folks, and they had come west trusting to work for my father and myself, and it was up to me to see they made out. Yet there was scarcely more than fifty dollars among the lot of us, and cattle that we dearly needed. And to go on, we must have horses, gear, and supplies of all kinds.

Ahead of us lay miles of Apache country, and where we would settle would probably be Apache country too. Being a slow man to anger, the rage against Soto and his Comancheros had been building up in me, and I feared it.

There was in me a quality I had never trusted. A quiet sort of man, and scarcely twenty-three, I liked to work hard and enjoyed the pleasure of company, yet deep within me there was a kind of fury that scared me. Often I'd had to fight it down, and I did not want the name of being a dangerous man—that is for very young boys to want, or older men who have never grown up. Yet it was in me, though few of those about me knew it.

Pa knew—he had been with me that time in San Antonio; and Zebony knew, for he had been with me in Laredo.

And now I could feel it mounting. Pa was dead, cut down in the prime of life, and there were the others, good men all. They were men who rode for the brand, who gave their lives because of their loyalty and sense of rightness.

Within me I could feel the dull fury growing, something I had felt before. It would mount and mount until

102

I no longer thought clearly, but thought only of what must be done. When those furies were on me there was no fear in me, nor was there reason, or anything but the driving urge to seek out my enemies.

My senses became super-sharp, my heart seemed to slow its beat, my breath seemed slower, I walked with careful step and looked with different eyes. At such times I would become utterly ruthless, completely relentless. And I did not like it.

It was the main reason that I rarely wore a hand-gun. Several times the only thing that had saved me was the fact that I carried no gun and could not do what I wished. Twice in my life I had felt these terrible furies come over me, and each time it left me shaken, and swearing it must not happen again.

Now there were other things to consider. We must find horses, a wagon, and the necessary supplies for the rest of our trip. Our herd was pitifully small, but it could grow. We had two young bulls and about twenty head of cows, mostly young stuff. The rest were steers, and a source of immediate profit, even if their present value might be small.

Some of the people at Magoffinsville preferred to call their town Franklin. Others were already calling the town on the American side El Paso del Norte, but most still referred to the three towns by their separate names. At Magoffinsville I tied the line-back dun at the rail in front of James Wiley Magoffin's place and went in. Zebony Lambert and Zeno Yearling were with me.

Magoffin was a Kentuckian who had come to the area thirteen or fourteen years earlier and had built a home. Then he erected stores and warehouses around a square and went into business.

When I walked through that door, I knew there was little that was respectable in my appearance. My razor had been among the things lost in the attack, and I had not shaved in days. My hat was a beat-up black, flat-crowned, flat-brimmed item with a bullet hole through the crown. I wore a worn, fringed buckskin shirt and shotgun chaps, also fringed. My boots were Spanish style, but worn and down at heel. The two men with me looked little better.

"Mr. Magoffin," I said, "the Comancheros took my herd. We're the Kaybar brand, moving west from the Cowhouse to new range northwest of here, and we're broke. We came into town with only our women and children riding, and the rest of us afoot."

He looked at me thoughtfully. "What do you want?"

"A dozen horses, one wagon, supplies for seventeen people for two weeks."

His eyes were steady on me, then he glanced at Zebony and Zeno Yearly.

"Women, you say?"

"Yes, sir. The wives of two of my men, the widow of one, and there's five children, and a single girl. She's from New Mexico."

"Mind if I ask her name?"

"Conchita McCrae."

He glanced over my shoulder toward the door, and I felt the hackles rise slowly on the back of my neck. Turning slowly, I saw Felipe Soto standing there, three of his men behind him.

My fist balled and I swung.

He had expected anything but that. Words . . . perhaps followed by gunplay, but the Texan or New Mexican rarely resorted to his fists. It was not, in those days, considered a gentleman's way of settling disputes, while a gun was.

My blow caught him flush on the jaw. Being six feet two inches tall, I was only a little shorter than he was, but half my life I'd been working swinging an axe, or wrestling steers or broncs, and I was work-hardened and tough. He did not stagger, he simply dropped.

Before the others could move, Zebony covered them with a pistol and backed them up.

Reaching down, I grabbed Soto by the shirt front and lifted him bodily to his feet, slamming him back against the counter. He struck at me, and I slipped inside of the blow and smashed a wicked blow to his belly and then swung to his chin.

He fought back, wildly, desperately, and he was a huge man and strong, but there was no give in me that day, only a cold burning fury that made me ignore his blows. He knocked me down . . . twice, I think. Getting up, I spread my legs wide and began to swing, and I was catching him often. I drove him back, knocked him through the doors into the street, and went after him. He got up and I smashed a wild swing to his face, then stabbed a wicked left to the mouth, and swung on his chin with both fists.

He was hitting me, but I felt none of it. All I wanted was to hit him again. A blow smashed his nose, another split a lip through to the teeth. Blood was pouring from a cut eye, but I could not stop. Backing him against the hitch-rail I swung on his face, chopping it to a bloody mess.

And no one stopped me. Zeno had a six-shooter out now, too, and they kept them off.

Soto went down and tried to stay down, but I would not let him. I propped him up and hammered on him with both fists until his face was just raw meat. He fell down, and grabbed at the muddy earth as if to cling to it with all his might.

He was thoroughly beaten, and Magoffin stepped forward and caught by arm. "Enough!" he said. "You'll kill the man!"

My hands were swollen and bloody. Staggering, I stepped back, shaking Magoffin's hand from my shoulder.

Soto lay in the mud, his huge body shaking with retching sobs.

"Tell him," I said to the Soto men, "that if I see him again—anywhere at all—I'll kill him.

"And tell him, too," I added, "that I want my herd, three thousand head of cattle, most of it breeding stock, delivered to me at Bosque Redondo within thirty days.

"That will include sixty head of saddle stock, also driven off. They will be delivered to me or I shall hunt him down and beat him to death!"

With that, I turned and staggered against the door post, then walked back into the store. Magoffin, after a glance at Soto, followed me inside. Zebony and Zeno stood watching the Soto men pick up their battered leader and half drag, half carry him away.

"That was Felipe Soto?" Magoffin asked me curiously. "I have heard of him."

"That was him," I replied. My breath was still coming in gasps and my heart was pounding. "I should have killed him."

"What you did was worse. You destroyed him." He hesitated. "Now tell me again. What was it you needed?"

"You must remember," I said, "I have only fifty dollars in money."

"Keep it—your credit is good with me. You have something else—you have what is needed to make good in this country."

Conchita turned pale when she saw me, and well she might, for in the excitement of the fight I had scarcely felt the blows I received, and they had been a good many. One eye was swollen almost shut, and there was a deep cut on the other cheekbone. My lip was puffed up, one ear was swollen, and my hands had swollen to twice their normal size from the fearful pounding I had given him.

"Oh, your poor face!" she gasped. Then at once she was all efficiency. "You come here. I'll fix that, and your hands too!"

She poured hot water into a basin with some salts, and while she bathed my face ever so gently, my swollen hands soaked in the hot water.

It seemed strange, having a woman fuss over me that way, and it was the first time it had happened since one time as a youngster when Tap's mother had taken care of me after I'd been bucked from a bad horse.

That started me thinking of Tap, and wondering what had become of him, and of Karen.

The Foleys never talked of her around the camp, and what they said among themselves I had no idea. She had

106

taken on more than she was equipped to handle when she followed after Tap, and it worried me.

Everybody was feeling better around camp because Zebony and Zeno had told them about the deal I had made with Magoffin. Not that it was so unusual in those times, for a man's word was his bond, and no amount of signatures on paper would mean a thing if his word was not good. Thousands of head of cattle were bought or sold on a man's word, often with no count made when the money was paid over. Because of that, a man would stand for no nonsense where his word was concerned. A man might be a thief, a card cheat, and a murderer, and still live in the West; but if his word was no good or he was a coward, he could neither live there or do business with anyone there.

"You reckon that Soto will return your cattle?" Tim Foley asked skeptically.

"If he doesn't, I'll go get them. I have told him where he stands, and I shall not fail to carry out my promise."

"What if he takes to that canyon?"

"Then I shall follow him there."

We had a camp outside of Magoffinsville. It was a pretty place, with arching trees over the camp and a stream running near, and the Rio Grande not far off. It was a beautiful valley with mountains to the north and west, and there seemed to be grapes growing everywhere, the first I'd ever seen cultivated.

We sat around the fire until late, singing the old songs and talking, spinning yarns we had heard, and planning for the future. And Conchita sat close beside me, and I began to feel as I never had before. It was a different feeling because for the first time I knew I wanted a girl . . . wanted her for always, and I had no words to speak what I thought.

Soon we would be on the trail again, moving north and west into the new lands. Somewhere up there was Tap Henry, and I would be seeing him again . . . what would be our relationship, now that Pa was dead?

Tap had respected Pa . . . I did not think he had such respect for me. He was too accustomed to thinking of me as a youngster, yet whatever we planned, Tap could have a share in it if he would do his part to make our plans work out.

I got up and walked out to where the horses were, and stood there alone in the night, looking at the stars and thinking.

Magoffin would supply us with what we needed, but the debt was mine to pay. We had few cattle to start with, and such a small herd would make a living for nobody. Whatever happened, I had to have the herd they had stolen, or the same number of cattle from elsewhere.

If Felipe Soto did not bring the cattle to me, I was going after them, even to Palo Duro Canyon itself.

Conchita came up to where I stood. "Are you worried, Dan?"

"They came with me," I gestured back toward the people at the fire; "they trusted my father and me. I must not fail them."

"You won't."

"It will be hard."

"I know it will, Dan, but if you will let me, I want to help."

Chapter Six

We came up the valley of the Mimbres River in the summer of fifty-eight, a handful of men with a handful of cattle and one wagon loaded down with supplies.

We put Cooke's Spring behind us and trailed up the Mimbres with the Black Range to the east, and on the west the wilderness of the Mogollons. We rode with our rifles across our saddle-bows, riding through the heart of Apache country, and we came at last to our Promised Land.

The Plains of St. Augustine, a vast inland sea of grass, surrounded by mountains, made the finest range we had ever seen, with nothing in sight but a few scattered herds of antelope or wild horses.

Our camp was made in the lee of a cliff close by a spring, with a bat cave in the rocks above us. We turned our cattle upon the long grass, and set to work to build a pole corral to hold our saddle stock.

Cutting poles in the mountains, we came upon both bear sign and deer sign. Zeno Yearly stopped in his cutting of poles. "It is a fair land, Dan, but I've heard tell this is an Indian trail, so we'd best get set for trouble."

"We're building a fort when we have the corral, but first we must protect our saddle stock."

The fort was not so much to look at, not at first. We made a V of our wagons, pointing it toward the open valley, and we made a pile of the poles for the corral along one side, and threw up a mound of earth on the other side, with the cliff behind us. Though it was not much of a fort, it was a position that could be defended.

Three days later we had our Texas house built, with the Foleys occupying one side and the Stark family the other. We had also put up most of a bunkhouse, and had our cattle fattening on the long grass. We had scouted the country around, killed a couple of deer and a mountain lion we caught stalking a heifer from our herd.

We were settling in, making a home of the place, but it was time I made a move.

News was beginning to filter through to us. There was trouble down in the Mimbres Valley—a shooting or two, and the name we heard was that of Tolan Banks, the man Tap Henry had mentioned.

And then one day they came riding up the valley, Banks and Tap, and a third man with them. It was the blond man who had ridden with Caldwell.

Tap was riding a grudge, I could see that. He rode up and looked around. "What the hell is the idea? I thought you were going to settle down in the Mimbres with us?"

"Before we talk about anything else," I said, "you tell that man"—I indicated the blond man—"to start riding out of here. If he comes around again, I'll kill him."

"He's a friend of mine," Tap replied. "Forget him."

"Like hell I will. He was one of those who ran off our cattle. He was in the attack on us when Pa was killed."

Tap's face tightened. "I heard about that. I couldn't believe it."

Zebony was standing by the corral, and Milo Dodge was in the door of the Texas with Jim Poor.

"You tell that man to leave, Tap."

His face stiffened. "By God, kid, you don't tell me what to do. I'll—"

My eyes held them all, but mostly the blond man. "You," I said, "start riding. And keep riding. When I see you again, I start shooting."

The man touched his tongue to his lips. "You think you—"

I shot him out of his saddle.

110

A moment there had been silence, and then I was holding a gun with a slow twist of smoke rising from the muzzle, and the blond man was on the ground.

Whatever Tolan Banks might have done he did not do, for Zebony was holding a rifle in his hands, and so was Milo.

"Tap," I said, "you pick that man up and ride out of here. You're welcome any time, but when you come, don't come with a murdering renegade like him."

My bullet had gone a little high, and the man was shot through the shoulder, but from the look of it, he was badly hurt.

Tap Henry sat very still on his horse, and there was a strange look in his eyes. It was as if he was seeing me for the first time.

"I'll come back, Dan. I'll come back looking for you. Nobody talks to me like this."

"You're my brother, Tap, by raising if not by blood. I want no trouble with you, but when you start traipsing around with men who have atacked us, it is time to ask where your loyalty lies."

"You'll be seeing me too," Banks said.

My eyes swung to him. "I was wondering when you were going to put your ante into this game," I said, "and I'm ready any time you are."

He sat his horse, smiling at me. "Not now . . . not right now. You've too many guns against me."

"Ride out of here then."

Banks turned his horse and Tap got down to help the wounded man into the saddle. Jim Poor came down to help him.

"You come back when you want, Tap. But come alone or with Karen, and come friendly."

"Where is Karen?" Tim Foley demanded.

"She's in Socorro," Tap said sullenly. "She's all right."

Foley held a shotgun. "Are you two married?"

Tap glanced at him bleakly. "You're damned right," he said. "What do you think I am?"

"Take care of her," Foley said. "I'm no gunfighter, but this shotgun doesn't care who it shoots."

Tap rode away, leading the renegade, who was swearing in a high, plaintive voice.

There I stood, in the sun of a bright day, watching them ride off down the valley. There went Tap, who had been my hero as a youngster, and there went the last of whatever family I had, and I watched him go and was lonely.

Ours was a hard land, and it took hard men to ride it and live it, and the rules had to be laid down so all could read, and the lines drawn.

Tap Henry was different. It seemed to me Tap was rootless, and being rootless he had never quite decided where he stood, on the side of the angels or against them. Well, today should force him to a decision. He knew where I stood.

If that blond man had been trying to sneak a gun on me, I was not sure . . . nor did I much care. He had been there when my father was killed, and was as guilty as if he himself had fired the shot—and he might have.

One thing I had learned. It saves a lot of argument and trouble, and perhaps mistakes leading to greater violence, if folks know exactly where you stand. We came to a raw and lonely land, a land without law, without courts, and with no help in time of danger. There were men who wished the land to remain lawless, for there were always those who were unable to abide by the rules of society; and there were others who wanted schools, churches, and market days, who wanted homes, warm and friendly. Now I had taken my stand . . . I had drawn a line that no man could mistake.

After they had gone, nobody had any comment to make. The work picked up where it had ceased, and went on as it always must; for birth, death, and the day-to-day matters of living never cease. There are meals to be prepared, cattle to be cared for, meat to be butchered, fences to be built, wood to be cut. For while man cannot live by bread alone, he must have the bread before other things can become real. Civilization is born of leisure, and leisure can come only after the crop has been harvested.

In our hearts we knew that, for lonely men are considering men, given to thought to fill the empty hours of the lives they live.

Yet now the time had come to ride eastward, to be sure that we recovered our herd. I doubted if it had yet been sold, and while my warning to Soto might cause him to deliver the herd, I doubted that it would. Even if he wanted it so—which I doubted—there were others involved.

"Tim," I said, "I'm riding after the herd. I'm leaving you in charge. Jim Poor and Tom Sandy will stay with you—and Miguel."

"I go with you, Dan." Miguel looked up from the *riata* he had been mending. "It is better so. Soto, he has many friends, and we are a people who protect our own. If you go among them, a stranger, all will be against you, even if they lift no hand.

"If I go with you to tell what Soto has done, and that you are good people, your enemies will be only the Comancheros." He smiled. "And I think they are enough for trouble."

There was no arguing with him, for I knew what he said to be the truth. The Spanish-Americans of Texas and New Mexico were clannish, as they had a right to be, and I would be a stranger among them, and a *gringo*. They would know nothing of the facts of my case—whether I was a true man or false. In such a case they would either ignore me or actively work against me.

And then Conchita declared herself. She, too, was coming. She had much to do. She must go to Socorro. There were things to buy . . . In the end, she won the argument, and she came with us.

Zebony, Zeno Yearly, Milo Dodge, Miguel, and myself made up the group. It was a small enough party for what we had to do.

Socorro was a sleepy village on the Rio Grande, built on the site of a pueblo. A mission had been established there as early as 1628, but during the Pueblo revolt the people had fled south and established a village of the

113

same name on the Rio Grande, returning in 1817 to re-establish the village. All this Conchita told me as we rode toward the village from the west.

Though we were a small number, we were veterans at the sort of trouble that lay before us. Growing up on the frontier in Texas is never easy, and Zebony had killed his first Kiowa when he was thirteen. He had spent a week dodging Comanches even before that, and had seen his family killed.

Zeno Yearly had come west from Kentucky and Tennessee, where he had lived at various places along the Natchez Trace and in the mountains. Most of his life he had lived by hunting. Milo Dodge had been a Texas Ranger with Walker, and had served as a boy in the army during the War with Mexico.

We rode into Socorro, a tight, tough little band. And there we would buy supplies and start east, for we had far to go to reach the land of the Comanchero.

It was cool in the little *cantina* where we went to drink and to listen. Conchita was in the store, and her brother had disappeared somewhere among the flat-roofed adobe houses.

We four went into the *cantina* and ordered the wine of the country, for they were raising grapes and making wine at Socorro, as at El Paso and elsewhere. There were old apple trees here, too, planted long ago by the friars, or so it was said.

Zebony put his hat on the table and combed out his long brown hair, hair fine as a woman's and as beautiful. Yearly watched him, touching his long mustache from time to time.

There was a stillness within us, a waiting. Each knew what lay beyond this place. For out there was a wild and lonely land where the Apaches roamed, and beyond that, where we were going, the Comanche—great horsemen and great fighters, and we were few, going into a harsh land where many enemies awaited us. But this was what we had to do, and not one of us would draw back.

The wine was good, and after a while the owner brought

114

us each a huge bowl of *frijoles,* a stack of *tortillas,* and some eggs scrambled with peppers and onions.

Miguel came in, standing inside the door until his eyes became accustomed to the dimmer light, and then he crossed to our table and sat down. Leaning toward us, his eyes very bright, he said, "It is well that we came here, for my friends tell me something very interesting."

We looked at him, and waited. Miguel took out his *cigarito* and put it between his lips.

"Soto is not at Palo Duro . . . he is on the Tularosa."

"That's east of here, ain't it?" Zeno asked.

"It is a place—a very small place which I think will get no larger because of the Apache—a place called Las Placitas. It is near Fort Stanton, where there are soldiers."

He lighted his *cigarito.* "It is tell to me that Soto brings his cattle there to sell to the soldiers."

"I didn't know there was a fort over there," Dodge said. "Stanton, you say? There was a Captain Stanton killed there a few years back."

"*Si*, it is name for him. The fort was built . . . 1855, I think. So these people come to the Rio Bonito and they begin a settlement, but I think the Apache will run them out."

"Soto is there?"

"*Si* . . . with many men. And a large herd of cattle and some horses."

"Why, then," I said, looking around the table, "that is where we will go."

We walked out on the boardwalk and stood there together, four men looking up and down the street, and knowing that trouble might come to us at any time.

And then I saw Karen.

Or rather, Milo Dodge saw her. "Dan . . . look."

She was coming toward us, and I thought she looked older, older by years, and she looked thinner, too. As always, she was neat, and when she saw us she almost stopped; then, chin up, she came on.

"Karen . . . Mrs. Henry," I said, "it is good to see you again."

115

"How do you do?" We might have been strangers. She spoke and started to pass on. "Your folks are still with us. Tap knows where we are, and they would like to see you."

She had gone past us a step when she stopped and turned slowly around. "I do not think you like my husband," she said.

"Whenever you folks feel like coming home," I said, "there's a place for you. Pa left no will, and though he sent Tap away, that makes no difference. If Tap wants to come back, it will be share and share alike."

"Thank you."

She started away, then stopped again. Maybe it was something in our manner, maybe it was just the way we were armed, for each one of us was carrying a rifle, and each had two or more pistols.

"Where . . . what are you doing?"

"We're going after our cattle, Karen," I said. "Felipe Soto has them over at Las Placitas."

"But . . . there's so many of them! You won't have a chance! Why, there must be twenty men with him—or even twice that many."

"Yes, ma'am, we know that, but they're our cattle."

That was how we felt about it. They were our cattle, so we must go after them, and thieves must not be permitted to escape the consequences of their deeds. We had a land to build, we had peace to bring to the land, and for a few years now we would have to bring it with a gun. To the violent, violence is the only argument they understand. Justice they understand, but only when it is administered from strength.

Before the sun was over the eastern mountains we were miles upon our way. We crossed some desert, we crossed the lava flows, and we came up through the live oak and the pines to the mountains and the Rio Bonito. We followed it along toward the cluster of adobes and shacks along the stream.

There were scarcely half a dozen, and a few tents, a few tipis. We spread out as we came into the town, and beyond the town we could see the herd. There were some

116

men on horseback where the cattle were, and some of them wore plumed helmets and blue uniforms. That would be the cavalry.

We rode our horses down there, and we saw men come into the street behind us and look after us. A couple of them started to follow.

"One thing," I said, "this here's my fight. If anybody comes in that ain't asked, you boys do what you've a mind to . . . but I will do the talking and if it is man to man, I'll do the shooting."

They understood that, but I wanted it on the line so they could read the brand of my action.

Felipe Soto was there, and when I saw who was with him I felt something turn cold inside of me. Tolan Banks was there, and Tap Henry.

There were eight or nine of them, and four or five Army men inspecting that beef.

Walking my horse up to them, I saw Banks speak suddenly, and Soto turned sharply around.

I did not take my eyes from Banks and Soto. "Captain," I said, "these are stolen cattle, stolen from me. The brands have been altered, but skin any beef here and you will find a K Bar brand before it was changed."

"I am buying beef," the Captain replied coolly, "not fighting over it, or sitting as a court in judgment of ownership." He turned his horse. "When you have decided whose beef it is, I shall be in Las Placitas."

He turned his horse and, followed by his brother officers and a couple of sergeants, he started away.

My eyes sought them out, man by man. On each man I directed my attention, and on each I let my eyes rest for a minute. I wanted each man to believe that he was marked.

"Well, Soto, you did not deliver the beef. I have come for it."

"Dan—!" It was Tap. "Dan, for God's sake!"

"Tap," I said, "you'd better decide where you stand before the shooting starts. Riding the fence can give a man a mighty sore crotch, and you've been on it long enough."

"Now, wait!"

"To hell with that, Henry!" Tolan Banks yelled suddenly. "You're with us or against us! Stand aside and let me kill that Killoe whelp!"

What I did, they did not expect. For years Tap and me had practiced shooting on the run, shooting while riding at a dead run, like the mountain men did, and I slapped spurs to that line-back dun and he jumped right into the middle of them.

They outnumbered us, so as I jumped into them I jumped shooting.

It looked like a damned fool trick, but it was not. They had been sitting there as we came up and no doubt everyone of them had picked a target. They had us cold and we had them the same way, and in about a split second a lot of men were going to die.

Starting off with a cold hand that way, a man can shoot accurately, and I would be losing men. So I jumped my horse into their group, which forced them all to move, and each had to swing to get on his target again.

My Patterson was across my saddle, and as I jumped I shot. My bullet missed Soto and knocked a man behind him sidewise in the saddle, and then I was in among them. One more shot left the Patterson before it was knocked from my grip, but I had already come out with a draw with my left hand from my belt.

Soto swung on me and his gun blasted almost in my face. Knocking his gun up, I shot and saw him jump back in the saddle like he'd been struck with a whip. He shot at me again but I had gone past him and he turned fast, but his big horse was no match for that dun, who could turn on a quarter and give you twenty cents change. The dun wheeled and we both shot and my bullet hit him right below the nose.

He swung around and fell back out of the saddle, kicking his foot loose from the stirrup at the last minute. He started up, gun in hand, blood flowing from his face in a stream. But I went in on a dead run, holding my six-shooter low and blasting it into him. I saw the dust jump from his shirt twice as I went into him, and then he went down under the dun's hoofs and I wheeled around in time to see Tap Henry facing Tolan Banks.

"I'm with them, Tolan! That's my brother!"

"To hell with you!" Banks pistol swung down in a dead aim on Tap's chest and Tap triggered his gun charging, as I had.

Banks left his saddle and hit the ground and rolled over, all flattened out. He made one heave as if he was trying to get up, and then he lay still.

The gray dust lifted and slowly swirled and settled, and the riderless horses trotted off and stood with their stirrups dangling and their heads up, and men lay on the ground.

Yearly was down, and Zeb was gripping a bloody arm, his face gray.

Four of them were down, and I knew my jump into them had given us the break we needed, for my boys had been sitting still taking dead aim.

The Army came riding up. One of the men rode right to Zebony. "Here! Let me see that arm! I'm a surgeon!"

We rode around, looking at the men on the ground. Felipe Soto was dead, and of the others only one man was alive.

Among the dead was Ira Tilton. I had never even seen him in the brief encounter, nor did I know whose bullet had put him down, but he had died an ugly death.

By the look of it the slug had been one of large caliber and it must have hit the pommel of the saddle or something, because the wound looked like a ricochet. It had ripped across the belly, and he had died hard, a death I would wish for no man.

I turned to the officer as he rode up. "Captain, that man was Felipe Soto." I indicated the sprawled body of the big Comanchero. "He has been selling rifles to the Indians for years. His own people will tell you of it."

"I am buying cattle," the Captain replied, "and personal feuds are not a part of my business. However, I do know of Soto, but did not realize that was who it was."

He glanced at me. "My name is Hyde. It is a pleasure to know you, sir. That was a nice bit of action."

Zebony picked up my Patterson from the ground and handed it to me. "You'd better see the Doc. You're bleeding."

"I'm all right. I just—" Glancing down, I saw there was blood on the skirt of my saddle, and my left leg was sopping with it.

"You!" the surgeon said. "Get down here!"

It was Tap who caught me when I started to get down and almost fell. He steadied me with an arm to a place under a tree, and he pulled my shirt off.

A bullet had gone through my side right above my hipbone, but the doctor merely glanced at it. "You've lost a lot of blood, but it's only a flesh wound."

Hearing a pound of hoofs, I looked around in time to see Conchita throw herself from her horse and come to me. The doctor looked at her, then at me. "If she can't make you well," he said dryly, "nothing can."

Zeno was going to be all right. He had caught two slugs, and he was in bad shape, but he was going to pull through. Tap Henry told me that some time later, for about the time that Conchita arrived everything faded out. I had started to speak, and then everything blurred. The next thing I knew it was hours later and I was in bed at the Fort.

"Are the cattle all right?"

"Sold 'em," Tap said, "all but a couple of hundred head of breeding stock."

"Looks like I'll be here for a while," I said, "so you'd better take the boys and start for home with that herd."

"Dan." Tap hesitated, as embarrassed as I'd ever seen him. "I've been a fool. I'm . . . well, I never intended for the herd to go to Bosque Redondo. Banks and me wanted to use it to grab land on the Mimbres."

"I guessed it was something like that."

He looked at me for several minutes. "Dan, I'm going to let Karen ride back with the boys. I'll wait here until you can ride, and we'll go home together."

"Sure," I said, "that's the way Pa always wanted it."

120

LONELY ON THE MOUNTAIN by LOUIS L'AMOUR

The Sackett Brothers didn't know exactly what kind of trouble Cousin Logan had got himself into but they knew he needed beef cattle badly. So William Tell Sackett, Tyrel, Orrin and Cap Trountree rode north to the wild country – pushing 1100 head of fat steers across the wide Dakota plains towards the mountains of far western Canada. Past Sioux, past Logan's treacherous enemies, through trails no cattle had ever crossed, the Sacketts drove on. Because the Sacketts stick together – and when you step on the toes of one Sackett, they all come running!

0 552 11668 8 – 95p

THE WHIP AND THE WARLANCE by J.T. EDSON

Having thwarted one scheme to invade Canada from the USA, Belle Boyd, the Rebel Spy, and the Remittance Kid were hunting the leaders of the plot, who had escaped and were plotting another attempt. To help them, they called upon a young lady called Miss Martha Jane Canary – better known as Calamity Jane ... Belle, Calamity and the Kid made a good team, but they knew they would need all their fighting skills when the showdown came. For they leLoup Garou and the Jan-Dark, the legendary warrior maid with the warlance who, it had long been promised, would come to rally all the Indian nations and drive the white man from Canada.

0 552 10964 9 – 65p

A SELECTED LIST OF CORGI WESTERNS

WHILE EVERY EFFORT IS MADE TO KEEP PRICES LOW, IT IS SOMETIMES NECESSARY TO INCREASE PRICES AT SHORT NOTICE. CORGI BOOKS RESERVE THE RIGHT TO SHOW AND CHARGE NEW RETAIL PRICES ON COVERS WHICH MAY DIFFER FROM THOSE ADVERTISED IN THE TEXT OR ELSEWHERE.

THE PRICES SHOWN BELOW WERE CORRECT AT THE TIME OF GOING TO PRESS (DECEMBER '81)

J.T. EDSON
☐ 07900 6	MCGRAW'S INHERITANCE No. 17	95p
☐ 07992 8	THE DEVIL GUN No. 21	65p
☐ 10964 0	THE WHIP AND THE WARLANCE	65p
☐ 11224 0	THE GENTLE GIANT No. 89	75p
☐ 09607 5	THE QUEST FOR BOWIE'S BLADE No. 75	95p
☐ 08065 9	GUN WIZARD No. 32	95p

LOUIS L'AMOUR
☐ 11668 8	LONELY ON THE MOUNTAIN	95p
☐ 11618 1	THE WARRIOR'S PATH	95p
☐ 11561 4	YONDERING	95p
☐ 11838 9	MILO TALON	95p

OLIVER STRANGE
☐ 11440 5	SUDDEN TAKES THE TRAIL	85p
☐ 11797 8	SUDDEN	95p
☐ 11795 1	SUDDEN: MARSHAL OF LAWLESS	95p

JOHN J. MCLAGLEN
☐ 10789 1	HERNE THE HUNTER 1: WHITE DEATH	60p
☐ 11585 1	HERNE THE HUNTER 15: TILL DEATH	85p
☐ 10526 0	HERNE THE HUNTER 5: APACHE SQUAW	65p

JAMES W. MARVIN
☐ 11218 6	CROW 2: WORSE THAN DEATH	75p
☐ 11858 3	CROW 6: THE SISTER	95p

All these books are available at your bookshop or newsagent, or can be ordered direct from the publisher. Just tick the titles you want and fill in the form below.

CORGI BOOKS, Cash Sales Department, P.O. Box 11, Falmouth, Cornwall.

Please send cheque or postal order, no currency.

Please allow cost of book(s) plus the following for postage and packing.

U.K. CUSTOMERS. 40p for the first book, 18p for the second book and 13p for each additional book ordered, to a maximum charge of £1.49.

B.F.P.O. and EIRE. Please allow 40p for the first book, 18p for the second book plus 13p per copy for the next three books, thereafter 7p per book.

OVERSEAS CUSTOMERS. Please allow 60p for the first book plus 18p per copy for each additional book.

NAME (block letters) ....

ADDRESS ....

(DECEMBER '81) ....

Who's Who
in Northern Ireland
2004

Fourth Edition

Inglewood Books

Published by Inglewood Books
Overtoun, Mauchline, Ayrshire KA5 5SY
01290 559055

Copyright Inglewood Books 2004

ISBN 0 9546631-1-X

Printed in Great Britain by
Antony Rowe Ltd., Chippenham

Foreword

Welcome to the fourth edition of Who's Who in Northern Ireland. The books contains biographies of prominent people in the life of Northern Ireland including figures of interest and influence in politics, public service, the law, the churches, education, business and finance, the arts and media, voluntary and professional organisations.

The third edition has been comprehensively corrected and revised and many new entries have been introduced.

Each entry in Who's Who in Northern Ireland typically contains details of professional career and personal background based on information supplied by respondents themselves. As a guide to using the book and the abbreviations used, this is how most entries appear:

Name; Honours; Degrees, Diplomas, Affiliations; Present Post; Date of Birth (abbreviated to b. in each entry); Marriage and Children (s. and d. are abbreviations for sons and daughters); Education (abbreviated to Educ. in each entry); Summary of Professional Career; Voluntary Offices and Membership of Societies; Publications; Recreations; Address (h. and b. are abbreviations for home and business) and Telephone Number.

Great care has been taken to ensure that information presented is accurate and as up to date as possible. However it is inevitable that some circumstances will have changed while the book has been in preparation. Our thanks to everyone who completed questionnaires or revised existing entries. This ensures the highest standards of accuracy in the information presented.

The Editor
February 2004

CONTENTS

Page 6
THE DIRECTORY
A classified guide to organisations in Northern Ireland

Page 21
WHO'S WHO SECTION
An A-Z of prominent people in Northern Ireland

BUSINESS AND INDUSTRY

BOMBARDIER AEROSPACE
SHORT BROTHERS PLC
Airport Road
Belfast BT3 9DZ

BOMBARDIER
AEROSPACE

Tel: 02890 458444
Fax: 02890 733399
website: www.Bombardier.com
Contact: Michael Ryan, Vice-President and General Manager, Aerospace
            Alec McRitchie, Director, Communications and Public Affairs

BOMBARDIER AEROSPACE is Northern Ireland's largest private sector employer with 5,600 employees in the province. It is a centre of excellence for the design and manufacture of fuselages and engine nacelle systems, and for processes such as advanced composites and metal bonding.

DCL GROUP
2 Donegall Square East
Belfast BT1 5HB

Tel: 028 9033 9949
Fax: 028 9033 9959
e-mail: info@dclmedia.com
website: www.dclmedia.com
Contact: Tom Kelly, Managing Director, DCL Public Relations
            Pauline McGreevy, Managing Director, DCL Event Management
            Paul McErlean, Senior Client Director
            Carlton Baxter, Senior Client Director

Formerly Drury Communications, **DCL GROUP** is the leading corporate communications and public affairs consultancy in Northern Ireland and includes specialist services DCL Event Management and dclmedia.com, a new media and internet consultancy.

Winners of the PRCA All Ireland Best Corporate Communications campaign, DCL Public Relations advises leading companies and Government on a range of strategic business, political and public relations issues. The DCL Group employs 15 staff.

Our Business is Knowledge.

MILLWARD BROWN ULSTER LTD
115 University Street
Belfast BT7 1HP

Tel: 02890 231060
Fax: 02890 243887
e-mail: enquiries@ums-research.com
Contact: Richard Moore, Managing Director
           Catherine Toner, Research Director
           Stephen Young, Director
           Alan Lobo, Director

MILLWARD BROWN provides a comprehensive market and social research service in Northern Ireland and the Republic of Ireland. Over 30 years experience is allied to a thorough understanding of social, cultural, and economic conditions.

CHARITABLE AND VOLUNTARY

CITIZENS ADVICE
11 Upper Crescent
Belfast BT7 1NT

Tel: 02890 231120
Fax: 02890 236522
website: www.citizensadvice.co.uk
Contact: Derek Alcorn, Chief Executive

CITIZENS ADVICE is the largest advice charity in Northern Ireland working against poverty, and meeting the information and advice needs of some 200,000 people per year, 53 per cent of CAB enquiries relate to social security. Within the UK, Citizens Advice in Northern Ireland has pioneered the development of electronic information and advice, and administers a wide area network across Northern Ireland. The system uses broadband to connect each local office to all the others and to the regional office via a single central server which holds all case records. Computers are used in interview rooms with clients, information is updated by phone, and laptop computers are used for home visits. The Association is building on this work with the development of specialist databases for frontline advisers, the continuing development of its web site, the use of standard specifications across the network, and the use of specialist software for money advice and benefit calculations.

THE HONOURABLE THE IRISH SOCIETY
Cutts House
54 Castleroe Road
Coleraine
Co. Londonderry BT51 3RL

Tel: 028 703 44796
Fax: 028 705 6527
e-mail: joy@irishsoc.freeserve.co.uk
website: http://irishsociety.infm.ulst.co.uk
Contact: Edward Montgomery, Society's Representative (Ireland)

THE HONOURABLE THE IRISH SOCIETY is a charitable organisation operating in Co. Londonderry, which links The City of London to The County of Londonderry. The Society is governed by a body of Trustees drawn from the Corporation of London, as laid down under its 17th century Royal Charter. It owns fishing rights on the Lower Bann and other rivers in the County, together with property in Londonderry and Coleraine, and uses the income from these assets to assist a wide range of charitable projects within County Londonderry, especially in the educational, voluntary and community sectors.

COMMUNITY RELATIONS

COMMUNITY RELATIONS COUNCIL
6 Murray Street
Belfast BT1 6DN

Tel: 02890 227500
Fax: 02890 227551
e-mail: info@community-relations.org.uk
website: http://www.community-relations.org.uk
Contact: Dr. Duncan Morrow, Chief Executive Officer
            Ray Mullan, Director of Communications
            John Fitzsimons, Administrator

The **COMMUNITY RELATIONS COUNCIL,** formed in 1990 as a registered charity, performs a leading role in addressing communal divisions in Northern Ireland. The council provides advice and financial support for community relations and cultural diversity projects in the voluntary and community sector. It also works with people of influence in a wide range of public and business sector institutions in order to help them recognise the effects on their work of communal divisions and to develop appropriate community relations policies and practices in response.

CONSERVATION

THE NATIONAL TRUST (NORTHERN IRELAND REGION)
Rowallane
Saintfield
Ballynahinch
Co Down BT24 7LH

THE NATIONAL TRUST

Tel: 02890 510721
Fax: 02890 511242
Contact: Ruth Laird, Director
           Patrick Casement, Regional Chairman
           Kathy Bruce, Customer Services Manager

THE NATIONAL TRUST for Places of Historic Interest and Natural Beauty is a conservation charity which owns, conserves and provides public access to some of the finest coast and countryside in Northern Ireland, as well as historic houses, fine gardens and industrial archaeology. These properties include the Giant's Causeway, a World Heritage Site; Slieve Donard; the Crown Liquor Saloon, one of the finest examples of a high Victorian public house in existence; Patterson's Spade Mill, the last working water-powered spade mill in the British Isles; and the magnificent house and gardens at Mount Stewart. The Trust is completely independent of Government and relies heavily on membership subscriptions, donations, and income from its shops and tea rooms for its funding.

EDUCATION

COUNCIL FOR THE CURRICULUM, EXAMINATIONS AND ASSESSMENT (CCEA)
29 Clarendon Road
Belfast BT1 3BG

Rewarding Learning

Tel: 02890 261200
Fax: 02890 261234
e-mail: info@ccea.org.uk
website: http://www.ccea.org.uk
Contact: Dr Alan Lennon, Chairman
           Mr Gavin Boyd, Chief Executive

The role of **CCEA** is to: keep all aspects of the curriculum, examinations and assessment under review; advise the Department of Education in Northern Ireland (DE); publish and disseminate curriculum, examinations and assessment materials; conduct and award certificates for examinations; conduct the moderation of relevant examinations and assessments; ensure that standards of the relevant examinations and assessments are recognised and maintained; conduct and mark the transfer tests; develop and produce teaching support materials; carry out other activities as directed by the Department of Education. CCEA also has a regulatory role in relation to standards in all general and vocational GCSE and GCE examinations offered in Northern Ireland.

NORTHERN IRELAND COUNCIL FOR INTEGRATED EDUCATION (NICIE)
44 University Street
Belfast
BT7 1HB

NORTHERN IRELAND COUNCIL FOR
INTEGRATED EDUCATION

Tel: 028 90236200
Fax: 028 90236237
e-mail: info@nicie.org.uk
Contact: Michael Wardlow, Chief Executive Officer, Tel: 02890 236200
             Yasmin Jeffery, Public Relations Officer, Tel: 02890 725772

THE NORTHERN IRELAND COUNCIL FOR INTEGRATED EDUCATION (NICIE)
is an organisation working to support the growth and development of Integrated Education in
Northern Ireland

Established in 1987, NICIE is a voluntary body that acts as a central forum and umbrella
organisation for integrated schools and groups or individuals that are interested in Integrated
Education. It works with parent groups to start new schools, supports existing integrated
schools and helps schools seeking to become integrated through the transformation process.

The key principle underpinning Integrated Education is that the schools bring together, pupils,
staff and governors, in roughly equal numbers, from both Protestant and Catholic traditions,
as well as those of other faiths or with no religious tradition.

There are currently 63 integrated schools, educating over 15,000 pupils in 29 Primaries, 18
Colleges and 17 Nurseries.

ULSTER TEACHERS' UNION
94 Malone Road
Belfast BT9 5HP

Tel: 02890 662216
Fax: 02890 663055
e-mail: office@utu.edu
Contact: Mr R Calvin, General Secretary
             Ms A E Hall-Callaghan, Assistant General Secretary
             Mr L Love, Field Officer
             Mr M Graves, Field Officer
             Mrs K M Taylor, Executive Officer

The **ULSTER TEACHERS' UNION** is now one of the largest and strongest organisations
of teachers in Northern Ireland. Recognised teachers of all types, irrespective of rank or sex,
belong to this comprehensive Union and enjoy its protection, benefits and services.

The UTU is a live, flexible organisation constantly adapting to the changes of our education
system and having special departments to cater for the interests of Primary, Secondary,
Nursery, Special Education and Young Teachers.

UNION THEOLOGICAL COLLEGE
108 Botanic Avenue
Belfast BT7 1JT

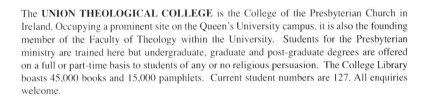

Tel: 02890-205080
Fax: 02890-580040
e-mail: admin@union.ac.uk
Contact: Professor J. P. Taylor, Principal [e-mail: jp.taylor@union.ac.uk]
Professor L. S. Kirkpatrick, Secretary [e-mail:ls.kirkpatrick@union.ac.uk]

The **UNION THEOLOGICAL COLLEGE** is the College of the Presbyterian Church in Ireland. Occupying a prominent site on the Queen's University campus, it is also the founding member of the Faculty of Theology within the University.   Students for the Presbyterian ministry are trained here but undergraduate, graduate and post-graduate degrees are offered on a full or part-time basis to students of any or no religious persuasion. The College Library boasts 45,000 books and 15,000 pamphlets. Current student numbers are 127. All enquiries welcome.

FINANCE

ULSTER BANK LTD
Group Head Office
11-16 Donegall Square East
Belfast BT1 5UB

Tel: 028 9027 6000
Fax: 028 9027 5507
Contact: Dr. Alan Gillespie, Chairman
Martin Wilson, Group Chief Executive
Tony McArdle, Chief Executive, Retail Banking

ULSTER BANK, a member of the Royal Bank of Scotland Group, is a leading provider of financial services in both Northern Ireland and Republic of Ireland. The Bank's activities are handled by two main customer facing business divisions - Ulster Bank Corporate Banking and Financial Markets, assisted by the Manufacturing, Central Services and Finance support functions.

Serving our large and mid-corporate and Institutional customers Corporate Banking and Financial Markets has responsibility for Business Banking as well as wholesale market activities. These include NCB Stockbrokers and Treasury operations together with activities in the International Financial Services Centre (IFSC) in Dublin.

Serving our personal and small business customers Retail Banking has responsibility for all the Branch Banking, Wealth Management and Direct Banking activities of the Group.

GOVERNMENT

LISBURN CITY COUNCIL
Lagan Valley Island
The Island
Lisburn
BT27 4RL

Tel: 028 9250 9250
Fax: 028 9250 9288
e-mail: enquiries@lisburn.gov.uk
website: www.lisburncity.gov.uk
Contact: Mr Norman Davidson, Chief Executive
          Mrs Claire Bethel, Marketing Manager

LISBURN CITY COUNCIL is Northern Ireland's newest City, covering the second largest Council area in the Province stretching from Glenavy and Dundrod in the north to Dromara and Hillsborough in the south and from Drumbo in the east of Moira and Aghalee in the west.

Representing over 108,000 residents, the City is home to some of the finest facilities to be found anywhere including the Council's award-winning Flagship Lagan Valley Island, the Island Arts Centre and one of Northern Ireland's most comprehensive sport and leisure facilities, the Lagan Valley Leisure Plex.

The City itself continues to experience unprecedented growth. Northern Ireland's only designated Regional Centre is situated at Sprucefield within the City. Such rapid developments are matched with a commitment to maintain and regenerate important heritage sites within the City. Major projects such as the Historic Quarter, the regeneration of the River Lagan and the many community projects undertaken are just some examples of Lisburn City's commitment to be Lisburn, a city for everyone.

NORTHERN IRELAND AUDIT OFFICE
106 University Street
Belfast BT7 1EU

Tel: 02890 251000
Fax: 02890 251051
e-mail: auditoffice@nics.gov.uk
Contact: J M Dowdall, Comptroller and Auditor General (Tel.: 02890 251130)
          J H Savage, Personnel Director (Tel.: 02890 251119)

The primary aim of the **NORTHERN IRELAND AUDIT OFFICE** (NIAO) is to provide independent assurance, information and advice to the Northern Ireland Assembly.

1.   On the proper accounting for Northern Ireland Departmental and certain other public expenditure, revenue, assets and liabilities (Financial Audit);
2.   About economy, efficiency and effectiveness in the use of resources (Value for Money Audit).

To achieve this aim, NIAO applies auditing standards based closely on those of NAO (its GB equivalent) and broadly similar to those applied within the auditing profession.

NORTHERN IRELAND OMBUDSMAN
Progressive House
33 Wellington Place
Belfast BT1 6HN

Tel: 028 9023 3821
Fax: 028 9023 4912
e-mail: ombudsman@ni-ombudsman.org.uk
website: www.ni-ombudsman.org.uk
Contact: Mr Tom Frawley - Ombudsman
             Mr Lindsay Rainey - Office Manager

THE NORTHERN IRELAND OMBUDSMAN is a popular name for two offices: the Assembly Ombudsman for Northern Ireland; and the Northern Ireland Commissioner for Complaints. The Ombudsman deals with complaints from people who believe they have suffered injustice as a result of maladministration by Northern Ireland government departments and their agencies; public bodies in Northern Ireland; and the Health and Personal Social Services in Northern Ireland. The term "Maladministration" is not defined in the Ombudsman's legislation but is generally taken to mean poor administration or the wrong application of rules.

The Ombudsman is completely independent of the Northern Ireland Assembly, the Northern Ireland Executive, and of the government departments and public bodies which he can investigate. All complaints made to the Ombudsman are treated in the strictest confidence. The Ombudsman provides a FREE service.

HEALTH

CANCER RESEARCH N. IRELAND
Unit 1, The Pavilions
22a Kinnegar Drive
Holywood BT18 9JQ

Tel: 02890 427766
Fax: 02890 421822
e-mail: customerservices@cancer.org.uk
website: www.cancerresearchuk.org
Contact: Barbara Blundell, Community Fundraising Manager

CANCER RESEARCH N. IRELAND is part of Cancer Research UK, the world's largest independent cancer research organisation, dedicated to curing cancer by understanding its causes and investigating how best to prevent and treat it.

With a team of 3000 scientists and doctors, we are currently funding vital research in Northern Ireland at Queen's University Belfast, Belfast City Hospital and the University of Ulster at Jordanstown.

One in three of us will develop cancer at some point in our lives. Cancer Research N. Ireland offers help and advice for those affected, their families and carers, through its free website and our cancer information nurses provide a confidential telephone helpline for anyone with questions about cancer - freephone 0800 (CANCER) 226237.

Our science is funded almost entirely through public donations, so if you would like to help, please give us a ring.

Everyone benefits from our work and everyone can help fund it.

THE LEPROSY MISSION (NORTHERN IRELAND)
Leprosy House
44 Ulsterville Avenue
Belfast BT9 7AQ

Tel: 02890 381937
Fax: 02890 381842
e-mail: info@tlm-ni.org
website: www.tlm-ni.org
Contact: Colin Ferguson, Executive Director
            Tom Robinson, Deputy Director
            Sam Smith, Development Officer

THE LEPROSY MISSION or **TLM** is an international, interdenominational Missionary Society founded by an Irishman in 1874. It exists to join in partnership with people affected by leprosy; sharing resources so that their physical, social, psychological and spiritual needs are met. We are motivated by the example of Jesus and his special love for the poor and marginalised. The Leprosy Mission is a member of the International Federation of Anti-Leprosy Associations.

HOUSING

NORTHERN IRELAND FEDERATION OF HOUSING ASSOCIATIONS
38 Hill Street
Belfast BT1 2LB

Tel: 028 9023 0446
Fax: 028 9023 8057
e-mail: info@nifha.org
website: www.nifha.org
Contact: Christopher Williamson, Director
           The Communications Officer

NIFHA is the umbrella body for housing associations in Northern Ireland. Its purpose is to enhance the ability of housing associations to improve the social well-being of people in Northern Ireland. Our small team does this by representing, promoting, training and supporting our members in the work that they do.

The Northern Ireland Federation of Housing Associations (NIFHA) represents 44 independent voluntary organisations, which benefit the community by providing affordable accommodation and related housing services to those in greatest housing need. Taken together, our members manage more than 27,500 dwellings and build over 1000 each year. Over the last twenty-five years the associations have undertaken a range of projects to respond to the needs of a diverse society and this way of working continues today.

In its role as a membership organisation NIFHA articulates the views of the housing association movement in Northern Ireland.

NORTHERN IRELAND HOUSING EXECUTIVE
The Housing Centre
2 Adelaide Street
Belfast BT2 8GB

**Housing
Executive**

Tel: 02890 240588
Fax: 02890 318715
e-mail: info@nihe.gov.uk
website: www.nihe.gov.uk
Contact: Mr S McDowell, Chairman
            Mr P McIntyre, Chief Executive
            Mrs I McGrath, Head of Information

The **NORTHERN IRELAND HOUSING EXECUTIVE** is Northern Ireland's strategic regional housing authority. It owns and manages 116,000 properties and has an annual budget of £540m.

Its key aims are to:

- assess housing needs, ensure that housing programmes are targeted at those individuals and areas in greatest need and are delivered in accordance with the principles of "Best Value"; develop strategies to influence the wider housing market, and work with others to foster urban and rural renewal;

-manage the Executive's stock in an effective and efficient manner, in accord with obligations under the Citizen's and Tenant's Charters and promote best practice throughout the social rented sector.

Our business is:

- Meeting housing need

- Tackling homelessness

- Improving housing conditions across the residential sector

- Managing housing benefit - £330m annually

- Implementing urban and rural regeneration strategies

- Addressing fuel poverty and improving energy efficiency

- Delivering value for money, business excellence and innovation.

LEGAL

KENNEDYS
64-66 Upper Church Lane
Belfast BT1 4QL

Kennedys
Legal advice in black and white

Tel: 02890 240067
Fax: 02890 315557
e-mail: mailbox@kennedys-law.co.uk
website: www.kennedys-law.com
Contact: Seán Craig, Partner [e-mail: s.craig@kennedys-law.com]
            R. Graeme Moore, Assistant Solicitor [e-mail: g.moore@kennedys-law.com]
            Chris Ritchie, Partner [e-mail: c.ritchie@kennedys-law.com]

An associated office of **KENNEDYS,** London, one of the leading litigation firms in the country. The firm is primarily known as insurance litigation practice and the Belfast office has a direct link into the London Insurance Market, handling disputed claims in Northern Ireland. Kennedys is also recognised for its skills in the non-contentious commercial field, particularly within the insurance, construction and transport industries. Legal services offered to companies in Northern Ireland include: Insurance Litigation; Company/Commercial; Construction (contentious and non-contentious); Medical Negligence; Banking; Employment; Commercial Property; Transportation/Railway Law; Defamation.

LIBRARIES

LINEN HALL LIBRARY
17 Donegall Square North
Belfast BT1 5GB

Tel: 028 9032 1707
Fax: 028 9043 8586
e-mail: info@linenhall.com
website: www.linenhall.com
Contact: John Gray, Librarian
            John Killen, Deputy Librarian
            Gerry Healey, Irish Studies Librarian

linen hall
library
established 1788

Established in 1788, the **LINEN HALL LIBRARY** is a centre for excellence with particular strengths in Irish and local history. Special collections include the NI Political Collection and the Genealogy Collection. With over 4000 members it is both a subscription Library and open to all for research purposes. Daily newspapers, current periodicals and coffee shop. Limited edition reproduction prints and maps for sale. Conference facilities available. The Library has an illustrious profile as a centre of cultural and creative life. It offers a tradition of excellence reflected in a varied programme of events ranging from exhibitions, theatre and music, to readings and lectures. E-commerce facility available for buying membership, gifts and publications online. Open 6 days a week.

PHARMACEUTICALS

NORBROOK LABORATORIES LIMITED
Station Works
Clough Road
Newry
Co Down BT35 6JP

Tel: 028302 64435
Fax: 028302 61721
Contact: Dr. Edward Haughey, Chairman (Tel.: 028302 64435 ext. 2225)
             Mr Martin Murdock, Financial Director (Tel.: 028302 64435 ext. 5270)

NORBROOK LABORATORIES is one of the world's largest producers of veterinary pharmaceuticals. It is also a producer of medical sterile injectable products and it has a large pharmaceutical synthesis facility for antibiotics and steroids. It is a major producer of Oxytetracycline Dihydrate injectable grade; Ampicillin; Amoxycillin, both sterile and non-sterile; Cloxacillin, both sterile and non-sterile; flu Cloxacillin, both sterile and non-sterile. It is also a major producer of Flunixin. It is licensed by both the European Community and the United States FDA for Production.

PROFESSIONAL AND TRADE ORGANISATIONS

EQUALITY COMMISSION FOR NORTHERN IRELAND
Equality House
7-9 Shaftesbury Square
Belfast
BT2 7DP

Tel: 028 90 500 600
Fax: 028 90 331 544
Textphone: 028 90 500 589
e-mail: information@equalityni.org
website: www.equalityni.org

THE EQUALITY COMMISSION combats discrimination and promotes equality of opportunity through advice, promotion and enforcement.

Anti-discrimination legislation gives us powers covering sex discrimination and equal pay, racial discrimination, disability discrimination, and discrimination on the grounds of religious belief, political opinion and, in employment and training and sexual orientation. The public sector's duty to promote equality of opportunity which we oversee, includes the additional grounds of marital status, caring responsibilities and age.

We have been given a wide range of powers and responsibilities including:

- advising and assisting complaints

- investigation and enforcement

- information, education and promotion

- overseeing the public sector's statutory duty to take equality into account in its work

- research

- awarding grants for promotional and education work

- reviewing the equality legislation.

The Equality Commission was established in 1999, bringing together the staff and responsibilities of four previous equality bodies.

RELIGION

SANDES SOLDIERS' AND AIRMEN'S CENTRES
30a Belmont Road
Belfast BT4 2AN

Tel: 02890 500250
Fax: 02890 652592
e-mail: sandes1869@btconnect.com
Contact: Sandra A. Stamps, Executive Director
            Alex Courtney, Chairman
            James Brewster, Finance Manager

The aim of the **SANDES SOLDIERS' AND AIRMEN'S CENTRES** is to lead servicemen and servicewomen and their families to trust in Christ for salvation; to build up believers to Christian maturity; and to offer friendship in the warmth of a Christian home-from-home.

SLAVIC GOSPEL ASSOCIATION (UK)
37a The Goffs
Eastbourne
East Sussex BN21 1HF

Tel: 01323 725583
Fax: 01323 739724
e-mail: office@sga.org.uk
Contact: William Smylie, General Director (Tel: 01455 631647, e-mail:
william.smylie@saga.org.uk)
Derek Maxwell, Field Director (Tel: 028 9261 1874, e-mail:
derek.maxwell@sga.org.uk)
Brian McFarland, Communications Co-ordinator (Tel: 028 3887 0025, e-mail:
brian.mcfarland@sga.org.uk)

The **SLAVIC GOSPEL ASSOCIATION (UK)** is an interdenominational, conservative
evangelical Missionary Agency formed in 1950. Our aim is to: "serve the Church in Central
and Eastern Europe by assisting it to become fully equipped to fulfil the great commission of
Jesus Christ, particularly amongst its own peoples."
SGA (UK) seeks to accomplish its aim and calling through 5 core activities:
1. Biblical Leadership Training
2. Leadership Support
3. Biblical Student Support
4. Bible and Literature Projects
5. Crisis Response.

SPORT

NORTHERN IRELAND SPORTS FORUM
House of Sport
Upper Malone Road
Belfast BT9 5LA

Tel: 02890 383825
Fax: 02890 682757
Contact: K M McLean, Secretary (Tel: 02890 401727 home)
K G Nixon, Chairman (Tel: 02890 424059 home)

The **NORTHERN IRELAND SPORTS FORUM** is a voluntary association whose
membership consists of Governing Bodies of Sport, other organisations and individuals with
an interest in sport and physical recreation. It was constituted and registered as a limited
company with charitable status in 1974. The Forum aims to be the independent, democratic
voice of sport and represent the interests of voluntary sport to the government, Sports Council
and other agencies. The Executive Committee, elected every two years, meets to consider
matters of common interest and to discharge the Forum's advocacy, communication and
consultative roles on behalf of the voluntary sector.

YOUTH

THE DUKE OF EDINBURGH'S AWARD
28 Wellington Park
Belfast BT9 6DL

Tel: 028 9050 9550/1/2
Fax: 028 9050 9555
e-mail: nireland@theaward.org
Contact: Eric Rainey MBE, Secretary for Northern Ireland
           Evelyn Waring, Northern Ireland Award Scene Magazine
           Sylvia Hamilton, Gold Award Presentations
           Rosemary Laird, Silver Award Presentations
           Valerie Pitman, Young People at Risk
           Colin Henderson, Expeditions and International Exchanges

The **DUKE OF EDINBURGH'S AWARD** is a comprehensive programme of practical, cultural and adventurous activities for all young people aged between 14 and 25. There are 3 levels: Bronze; Silver and Gold, each has an increasing degree of commitment. To gain an Award participants must complete four sections: Expedition; Skills; Physical Recreation; Service and an additional Residential Project at Gold level. Participants can develop existing interests or try something new. Whatever they choose to do for their Award, they can find enjoyment, excitement and satisfaction.

A

Abercorn, Duke of (James Hamilton), KG. Lord-Lieutenant, Co Tyrone since 1987; b. 4.7.34; m., Anastasia Alexandra; 2s.; 1d. Educ. Eton College, Royal College of Agriculture, Cirencester. Joined HM Army, 1952: Lieutenant, Grenadier Guards; Ulster Unionist Member of Parliament (Fermanagh and Tyrone), 1964 - 70; Director, Northern Bank Ltd, 1970 - 97; Chairman Laganside Development Corporation, 1989 - 96; Director, Northern Ireland Industrial Development Board, 1982 - 87. Member: Council of Europe, 1968 - 70; European Economic and Social Committee, 1973 - 78. President, Royal UK Beneficent Association since 1979; Patron, Royal Ulster Agricultural Society, 1990 - 96; Trustee, Winston Churchill Memorial Trust since 1991; High Sheriff, Co Tyrone, 1970. Hon. LLB, Queen's University, Belfast, 1997; Director, Intertrade Ireland, 1999; Trustee, Omagh Trust, 1998.

Acheson, Peter Newton, MA, DL. Retired Solicitor; b. 21.4.38, Belfast; m., Hilary Joan McMaster; 1s.; 3d. Educ. Elm Park School, Armagh; Merchiston Castle School, Edinburgh; Brasenose College, Oxford. Director, David Acheson Ltd, Linen Manufacturer, 1960 - 70. Ronald Rosser and Co, Solicitors, 1974 - 98. Recreations: boating. Address: (h.) Castlecaulfield, Dungannon, Co Tyrone, BT70 3NY; T.- 028 8776 1223. e-mail: pnacheson@yahoo.com

Adams, Clare, MB, BCh, FRCPsych. Consultant Psychiatrist in Psychotherapy, South and East Belfast Trust, since 1993, b. 26.4.46, Coleraine. Educ. Coleraine High School; Queen's University of Belfast. Senior Lecturer in Mental Health, Queen's University, Belfast, 1980-2000; clinical specialties: eating disorders and psycho-dynamic psychotherapy. Founder Member: NI Institute of Human Relations, Universities Psychotherapy Association; UKCP registered psychotherapist. Address: (b.) Department of Psychotherapy, Woodstock Lodge, 1, Woodstock Link, Belfast BT6 8DD. T.-028 90737531.

Adams, Gerard (Gerry), MP Sinn Féin Member of Parliament (Belfast West) since 1997; President, Sinn Féin since 1983; Member (West Belfast), Sinn Fein, Northern Ireland Assembly since 1998; b. 6.10.48; m., Colette McCardle; 1s. Educ. St Mary's Christian Brothers School, Belfast. Interned, 1971 and 1973, released, 1976; Member, Northern Ireland Assembly, 1982; Vice President, Sinn Féin, 1978 - 83; MP (Belfast West), 1983 - 92. Thorr Award, Switzerland, 1995. Publications: 6 books including 3 volumes of autobiography, most recently, Before the Dawn, 1996; An Irish Journal 2000; A Quest for Peace, 2001. Address: (b.) Sinn Féin, 55 Falls Road, Belfast, BT12 4PD.

Adams, Dr. Richard W. Chief Executive, Forensic Science Northern Ireland. Address: (b.) 151 Belfast Road, Carrickfergus, BT38 8PL; T.- 028 90361888. e-mail: forensic.science@fsni.gov.uk

Adams, Robert Edward Stephen, BSc (Econ), MHSM. Head of Corporate Services, Eastern Health and Social Services Board, since 1993; b. 21.5.51, Belfast. Educ. Coleraine Academical Institution; Newry High School; Queen's University, Belfast. Strategic Planning Team, Northern Health and Social Services Board, 1973-75; Eastern Health and Social Services Board, from 1975 in a range of posts. Recreations: travel; walking; DIY; voluntary community and church activities. Address: (b.) EHSSB, Champion House, 12-22 Linenhall Street, Belfast, BT2 8BS; T.- 028 90553731; Fax: 028 90553681. e-mail: sadams@ehssb.n-i.nhs.uk

Adamson, Dr. Ian, OBE, MB, BCh, BAO, DCH, MFCH, FRIPH. Member (East Belfast), Ulster Unionist Party, Northern Ireland Assembly since 1998; Community Medical Officer, North and West Belfast Trust; Former Lord Mayor of Belfast; b. 28.6.44, Bangor, Co Down; m., Kerry Carson. Educ. Bangor Grammar School; Queen's University, Belfast. Registrar in Paediatrics, Royal Belfast Hospital for Sick Children/Belfast City Hospital/Ulster Hospital, Dundonald; Specialist Community Child Health and Travel Medicine. Founding Chairman: Somme Association, 1989; Ulster-Scots Language Society, 1992; Founding Secretary, Farset Youth and Community Development Ltd, 1982; Founding Member: Cultural Traditions Group of the CRC; The Ultach Trust; First Rector, Ulster-Scots Academy, 1994. Publications: The Cruthin, 1974; Bangor - Light of the World, 1975; The Battle of Moira, 1980; The Identity of Ulster, 1982; The Ulster People, 1991; 1690, William and the Boyne, 1995; Dalaradia, Kingdom of the Cruthin, 1998. Councillor, Belfast City Council since 1989; Lord Mayor of Belfast, 1996; Serving Brother, Order of St John of Jerusalem, 1998; President, Belfast Civic Trust, 2001. Recreations: reading; oil painting; languages. Address: (b.) Members Room, City Hall, Belfast, BT1 5GS;T.- 02890-421005.

Adgey, Professor Agnes Anne Jennifer, CBE, MD, FRCP, FRCPI, FACC, FESC. Consultant Cardiologist, Royal Victoria Hospital, Belfast since 1971; Hon. Professor, Cardiology, Queen's University, Belfast since 1991. Educ. Regent House, Newtownards; Queen's University, Belfast. Royal Victoria Hospital, Belfast: Junior House Officer, 1964 - 65; Senior House Officer/Registrar, 1965 - 67; Research Fellow, Cardiology, Presbyterian Medical Centre, San Francisco, 1967 - 68; Senior Registrar, Cardiology, Royal Victoria Hospital, Belfast, 1968 - 71. Publications: co-author of two books and author of over 200 articles on cardiology. Recreations: classical music. Address: (b.) Regional Medical Cardiology

Centre, Royal Victoria Hospital, Belfast, BT12 6BA; T.- 02890-894975.

Agnew, William Alexander Fraser, MIOB, AMIET. Member (South Belfast), United Unionist Assembly Party, Northern Ireland Assembly, 1998-2003; Cultural Co-ordinator, Farset Youth and Community Development Ltd; b. 16.8.42, Belfast; m., Lila; 1s. Educ. Ballyclare High School; University of Ulster at Jordanstown; Belfast Technical College; College of Business Studies. Architectural Draughtsman and Company Director until 1990; Part-time Sports Journalist; Presently following a career in history: one of the foremost authorities on the Orange Order; Presenter, History Programmes, Community Radio; Lectures include, The Battle of Diamond; The Industrial Revolution; Glorious Revolution; History of Unionism. Chairman, Ulster Young Unionist Council, 1970; Member, Northern Ireland Assembly, 1982; Councillor, Newtownabbey Borough Council since 1980; Mayor, Newtownabbey, 1990 - 91. Chairman, Ulster Tourist Development Association; Chairman, Newtownabbey Borough Council's Culture and Tourism Committee. Publications: numerous pamphlets on aspects of Ireland's history. Recreations: soccer coaching to children (qualified coach); 5-a-side football; golf. Address: (h.) 1 Knockview Crescent, Newtownabbey, BT36 6UD; (b.) Newtownabbey Council Offices, 1 The Square, Ballyclare, Co Antrim.

Alcock, Professor Antony Evelyn, BA, MA, PhD. Professor of European Studies, University of Ulster at Coleraine; b. 12.9.36, Valetta, Malta; m., Mary Catherine Wedgewood; 1s.; 2d. Educ. Harrow School; McGill University, Montreal, Canada; Stanford University, California, USA; Institute of International Studies, Geneva, Switzerland. National Service, Commissioned, Seaforth Highlanders, 1955 - 57; Translator, OECD, Paris, 1963; Historian, International Labour Organisation, Geneva, 1968 - 70; International Civil Servant, International Labour Organisation, 1970 - 71; International Civil Servant, Unitar, New York, 1971 - 72; International Civil Servant, European Economic and Social Committee, Brussels, 1973 - 74; Senior Lecturer/Professor, New University of Ulster since 1974, Professor Emeritus, 2001. Member, Ulster Society Executive since 1986 (President 1995-2000); Chair, British Cultural Studies, since 2001; Member, Ulster Unionist Party Executive, 1991 - 96; Chair, Ulster Unionist European Committee, 1995; Ulster Unionist member, Northern Ireland Forum for Political dialogue, 1996 - 98; Member, Ulster Unionist Party Talks team, 1998, British Irish Agreement. Publications: History of the South Tyrol Question, 1970; History of the International Labour Organisation, 1971; Südtirol Seit Dem Paket, 1982; Understanding Ulster, 1994; A Short History of Europe, 1998; A History of the Protection of Regional Cultural Minorities in Europe, 2000. Recreations: Bridge (Northern Ireland international and inter-provincial); chess;

squash; gardening. Address: (h.) White Lodge, 9 Roselick Road, Portstewart, BT55 7PP; T.- 02870-832450. e-mail: ae.alcock@ulster.ac.uk

Alcorn, Charles Derek, BSS, MSc. Chief Executive, Northern Ireland Association of Citizen Advice Bureaux since 1988; b. 15.4.49, Belfast; m., Clare Elizabeth Dornan; 2s. Educ. Royal Belfast Academical Institution; Trinity College, Dublin; University of Edinburgh; University of Ulster. VSO, Solomon Islands, 1967 - 68; Community Worker, Strathclyde Social Work Department, 1973 - 75; Community Services Officer, Belfast City Council, 1976 - 79; Head of Information/Editor Scope Magazine, Northern Ireland Council for Voluntary Action, 1979 - 87; Associate Lecturer: Open University, 1988 - 96; Federal Executive Institute, Virginia, USA, 1996. Chair, Friends of the Earth (Belfast), 1978; Founder Member, Chair Community Technical Aid, (NI), 1984. Publication: The Elusive Boundary, State and Voluntary Sector, 1997. Address: (b.) 11 Upper Crescent, Belfast BT7 1NT; T.-02890-231120.

Alderdice, Rev. David, MA, BD. Senior Minister, Wellington Street, Presbyterian Church; b. 19.6.29, Co Armagh; m., Annie Margaret Helena Shields; 2s.; 2d. Educ. Shaftesbury House, Belfast; Magee University College; Trinity College, Dublin; Edinburgh University; Assembly's College, Belfast. Assistant Minister: Prestonfield, Edinburgh; Nelson Memorial, Belfast; Wallyford, Musselburgh, Scotland; Strand, Belfast; Minister: Donacloney Presbyterian Church, Co Armagh; Westbourne Presbyterian Church, Belfast; Wellington Street Presbyterian Church, Ballymena. Recreations: gardening; Address: (h.) Aganlane Lodge, 124 Glenariff Road, Parkmore, Ballymena, Co Antrim, BT44 0QX; T.- 028 2175 697.

Alderdice, David King, OBE, MA (Oxon), MB, BCh, BAO, MRCPI. Belfast City Councillor since 1997; Lord Mayor, Belfast, 1998 - 99; Consultant Dermatologist, since 2002; m., Dr. Fiona Alderdice; 1s.; 2d. Educ. Ballymena Academy; Queen's University, Belfast (Medicine); Manchester College, Oxford, (PPE). Medicine, Queen's University, Belfast, 1989; Junior and Senior House Officer, 1989 - 92; Studying for BA, 1992 - 94; MRCPI, 1996; Fellowship from Ulster Hospital, Dundonald, researching the genetics of portwine stains, 1997 - 98. Economy Spokesperson (Alliance Party of Northern Ireland), since 2002. Awarded OBE, 1999. Recreations: squash racquets; jazz. Address: (h.) c/o Members' Room, Belfast City Hall, Belfast BT1 5GS. T.-07714-670462.
e-mail: alderdice@btopenworld.com

Alderdice, Lord, Rt. Hon. John Thomas Alderdice, MB, BCh, BAO, FRCPsych. Leader, Alliance Party, 1987 - 98; Speaker, Northern Ireland Assembly, 1998-2003; Member for East Belfast, Northern Ireland Assembly, 1998-2003;

Consultant Psychiatrist in Psychotherapy, Department of Psychotherapy since 1983; Hon. Lecturer in Psychotherapy, Queen's University, Belfast, 1990 - 1999; b. 28.3.55; m., Joan Hill; 2s; 1d. Educ. Ballymena Academy; Queen's University, Belfast. Specialist Senior Registrar, Psychotherapy, 1983 - 87; Appointed Ireland's first Consultant Psychotherapist, Eastern Health and Social Services Board, 1988; Established Department of Psychotherapy and Masters Degree course, 1988; Executive Medical Director, South and East Belfast Health and Social Services Trust, 1993 - 97; Founder Director, Northern Ireland Institute of Human Relations, 1990 - 95; Regional Tutor, Psychotherapy, Royal College of Psychiatrists, 1988 - 97. Held a series of offices, Alliance Party of Northern Ireland, 1978-98, including Convener of Policy, Vice-Chairman and Party Leader; Belfast City Councillor, 1989 - 97; Led Alliance Delegation, Inter Party Talks, 1991 - 98; Leader, Alliance Delegation, Forum for Peace and Reconciliation, 1994 - 96; Leader,Alliance Group, Northern Ireland Forum 1996 - 98. Member, Central Council, European Liberal Democratic and Reform Party, 1987-2003 (Treasurer, 1995 - 99); Vice-President ELDR, 1999-2003; Vice-President, Liberal International, 1991 - 99; Chairman, Human Rights Committee of Liberal International since 1999; Deputy President, Liberal International, since 2000. Elevated to House of Lords, 1996. Member: Belfast Education and Library Board, 1993 - 97; Board of Trustees, Ulster Museum, 1993 - 97; Commonwealth Parliamentary Association since 1996. Patron of several charitable bodies concerned with mental health and national and international conflict resolution. Member: British Medical Association; Association for Psychoanalytic Psychotherapy; Member and Founder, Irish Forum for Psychoanalytic Psychotherapy; Fellow: Royal College of Psychiatrists; Ulster Medical Society; Hon. Fellow, Royal College of Physicians, Ireland, 1997. Elder, Presbyterian Church in Ireland; W Averell Harriman Award for Democracy, 1998; J F Kennedy Profiles in Courage Award, 1998; Silver Medal of Peruvian Congress, 1999; Medal of Honour, College of Medicine, Peru, 1999, Galloway Medal, NSF (NI), 1987. Hon. Professor, University of San Marcos, Lima, Peru, 1999; Hon. Member, Peruvian Psychiatric Association, 2000; Hon. Fellow, Royal College of Psychiatrists, 2001; Hon. Member, British Psychoanalytical Society, 2001; Knight Commander of the Order of Francis I (KCFO), 2002; Member of the International Thornton Commission for Northern Ireland, since 2003. Recreations: reading; music; gastronomy. Address: (h.) 55 Knock Road, Belfast, BT5 6LB; T.- 02890-793097.

Alexander, Dr. Desmond. Director of Christian Training, The Magee Institute for Christian Training, since 1999. Address: (b.) 108 Botanic Avenue, Belfast. T.-028 9020 5080.

Alexander, Kyle, MSc, MRTPI. Chief Executive, Laganside Corporation, since 2002; b. 22.12.52, Coleraine; m., Audrey; 1 s.; 1 d. Educ. Coleraine Academical Institution; Queen's University Belfast. Involved in Urban Regeneration and Development in Belfast for over 25 years with experience in both private and public sectors - Building Design Partnership, Housing Executive; Laganside Corporation, since 1991: previously Director of Development. Member of: Board of Investment Belfast, Salzburg Congress on Urban Planning and Development, 'Cabernet', EU Network on Brownfield Regeneration. Address: (b.) Laganside Corporation, 15 Clarendon Road, Belfast BT1 3BG.

Alexander, Moira, MBE, BA, DipEd, Froebel. Chairman, Southern Education and Library Board; Former Principal, Fair Hill Primary School, Kinallen; b. Scotland; m., E Alexander. Educ. Denny High School; Open University; Jordanhill College, Glasgow. Teacher: Banton Primary School, Scotland; Longroft Primary School, Scotland; Drumbo Primary School; Harmony Hill Primary School; Dromore Central Primary School; Principal: Carnew Primary School; Kinallen Primary School, Fairhill Primary School; Chairman, Southern Education and Library Board; Past President, Ulster Teacher's Union. Recreations: handicrafts; flower arranging. Address: (h.) 'Shiloh', 197 Ballynahinch Road, Dromore, Co Down; T.-(h.) 028 97532104. e-mail: mambe@tiscali.co.uk

Alexander, Prof. Nicholas Simon, BA, MA, MPhil, DPhil. University of Ulster: Professor of Services Management, since 2000, Head of School: Business, Retail and Financial Services, since 2001; b. 7.4.60, Cardiff, Wales; m., Myfanwy; 6 d. Educ. King's College, Taunton, Somerset; University of Wales Aberystwyth; York University; University of Ulster. University of Wales, Cardiff; University of Edinburgh; University of Surrey; University of Ulster; Bournemouth University; University of Ulster. Publications: The Emergence of Modern Retailing: 1750-1950, 1999; International Retailing, 1997; Values and the Environment, 1995; Retail Employment, 1995; Retail Marketing, 1995; Retail Structure, 1995; Internationalisation of Retailing, 1995. Recreations: history and sport. Address: (b.) School of Business, Retail and Financial Services, University of Ulster, Coleraine. T.- 02870 324166.

Alford, Rev. William Laird, BA. Methodist Minister; b. 2.12.27, Sligo, Ireland; m., Muriel Constance Poole; 3s. Educ. Dundalk Grammar School; Bishop Foy School, Waterford, Ireland; Edgehill Theological College, Belfast; Open University. Royal Bank of Ireland, 1947 - 60; Studying for the Ministry, 1960 - 63; Ordained, 1963; Minister: Limavady, 1963 - 67; Greencastle, Belfast, 1967 - 71; Carrickfergus, 1971 - 78; Lisburn, 1978 - 84; Belfast South, 1984 - 92; Chairman, Belfast District, 1986 - 92; Armagh

City, 1992 - 96; Retired 1996. Publications: Sermons published in The Times Book of Best Sermons, 1995 and 1996. Recreations: golf; boating. Address: (h.) 19 Kernaghan Park, Anahilt, Co Down, BT26 6DF; T.- 028-9263 8917.

Allamby, Les, BA (Hons), IPLS. Director, Law Centre; b. 26.10.58, Epsom, Surrey; partner, Hazel Gordon; 1s.; 1d. Educ. Oakham School, Rutland; Durham University; Queen's University, Belfast. Law Centre, Northern Ireland since 1982, previously, Casework Volunteer; Casework Manager. Legal Services Commissioner, since 2003; Member, Lord Chancellor's Legal Aid Advisory Committee, 1998-2003; Standing Advisory Commission of Human Rights 1998; Election Monitor, Bosnia, 1996 and 1997 and 1998; under Organisation for Security and Co-operation in Europe, EU monitor for elections in Pakistan, 2002, worked for Lawyers for Human Rights in South Africa, 1993; National Addiction Research Centre, Bombay, India, 1991; Chair, Standards Committee for Social Security, 1999. Publications: Dying of Cold - cold related ill health in Northern Ireland; The Social Fund - Deserving/Undeserving Poor (with E Evason and R Woods); Debt - An Emergency Situation?; Debt Handbook (with M Walls). Recreations: walking; reading. Address: (b.) Law Centre, Northern Ireland, 124 Donegall Street, Belfast, BT1 2GY; T.- 02890-244401.
e-mail: les.allamby@lawcentreni.org

Allan, William Roderick Sinclair, BSc, BArch, DipProMan, DipCons, RIBA, RIAI. Principal/Managing Director, Allan Associates Architects Ltd since 1991; b. 20.1.53, Dublin; m., Catherine Ann Walls; 1 d.; 1 s. Educ. Portora Royal School; University of Wales. Architect, Northern Ireland Housing Executive, 1978 - 80; Architect, Paddy Rooney Associates, 1980 - 82; M A Doherty and Associates: Architect, 1982 - 83; Partner, 1983 - 87; Principal, 1987 - 91. M A Doherty changed name to Allan Associates (now Allan Associates Architects Ltd since 1997). President, European Surfing Federation, 1988 - 92; Vice-President, European Surfing Federation, 1985 - 92, President since 1999; Chairperson, Irish Surfing Association since 1985. Recreations: surfing; skiing; snowboarding; tennis; squash; golf. Address: (b.) 55 Tempo Road, Enniskillen, Co Fermanagh BT74 6HR. T.-028 66 323500.
e-mail: roci@allanarc.com

Allen, Very Rev. David Henry (Harry), MA, BD, DD. Retired Minister; Former Moderator, Presbyterian Church in Ireland; retired 1998; b. 10.6.33, Portadown; m., Florence Watson; 2s. Educ. Edenderry P E School; Portadown Technical College; Shaftsbury Tutorial College, Belfast; Magee University College, Londonderry; Trinity College, Dublin; New College, Edinburgh University; Magee Theological College; Assembly's College, Belfast. Assistant Minister, Dundonald Presbyterian Church, 1958 - 61; Minister: Main Street Garvagh Presbyterian

Church, 1961 - 79; Killaig Presbyterian Church (with Garvagh), 1975 - 79; New Row Coleraine Presbyterian Church, 1979 - 98. Clerk, Coleraine Presbytery, 1972 - 85; Moderator, Coleraine Presbytery, 1966 - 67; Moderator, Synod of Ballymena and Coleraine, 1983 - 84; Moderator, General Assembly of Presbyterian Church in Ireland, 1996 - 97. Publications: Short History, Main Street, Garvagh; various articles and sermons in magazines. Recreations: walking; fishing; photography; reading. Address: (h.)32c Coleraine Road, Garvagh, Co Londonderry, BT51 5HP; T.- 028 295-57800.

Allen, Prof. James Moorehead, BSc, PhD, CBiol, FIBiol. Pro-Vice-Chancellor, University of Ulster, since 2000; b. 25.11.51, Coleraine; m., Anne; 1 s.; 2 d. Educ. Foyle College, Londonderry; Queen's University Belfast. Lecturer: Ulster Polytechnic, 1977-84, University of Ulster, 1984-88, Senior Lecturer, 1989-91, Director, Biomedical Sciences Research Centre, 1991-93, Reader, from 1993, Head, Research Graduate School, 1995-97, Personal Chair in Physiology, 1995, 1997-2000, Dean, Faculty of Social and Health Sciences, 2000. Member: Physiological Society, British Pharmacological Society; Fellow: Institute of Biology, Royal Academy of Medicine in Ireland. Over 250 scientific publications. Address: (b.) University of Ulster, Magee Campus, Londonderry BT48 7JL. T.-028 71 375261.
e-mail: jm.allen@ulst.ac.uk

Allen, John A (Jack), OBE, Freeman of the City of London. Treasurer, Ulster Unionist Party since 1989; Head of Administration, Ulster Unionist Assembly Party, Stormont, 1998-2002, Acting Chief Executive, Dec. 2000-03; Former Mayor of Londonderry; b. 5.1.41, Londonderry; m., Elizabeth McLaughlin; 1s.; 1d. Educ. Cathedral Primary School, Londonderry. Owned and managed bar/restaurant in Londonderry and other retail interests, 1960 - 90. Councillor, Londonderry Corporation, 1966 - 69; Councillor, Londonderry City Council, 1973 - 81; Mayor, Londonderry, 1974 - 75; Member, Londonderry Harbour Commission, 1974 - 86; Member, Northern Ireland Assembly, 1982 - 86 (Ulster Unionist Party Chief Whip; Chairman: Assembly's Devolution Committee; Economic Development Committee); Member, Northern Ireland Housing Association 1976 - 92 (Chairman, 1982 - 92); Chairman, Oaklee Housing Association, 1992-2002; Member, Ulster Unionist Party since 1960 (Chairman, 1985 - 89), Chairman, Finance Committee, since 2002; Member, Ulster Unionist Talks Team, 1991 - 92 and 1996 - 98; Member, Foyle Carlingford Commission, since Dec. 1999. Awarded Freedom of City of London, 1976; OBE, 1995. Recreations: travel; dining. Address: (h.) 'Avonmore', Clooney Park East, Londonderry, BT47 1JZ; T.- 01504-342400.

Allsop, Professor Nigel William Henry, BSc, MICE, CEng. Visiting Professor, Queen's University Belfast since 1997; b. 2.4.51, Salisbury,

Wilts. Educ. Wellington College, Crowthorne, Berks; University of Surrey. Scientific Officer, Hydraulic Research Station, 1969 - 74; Surrey University, 1974 - 77; Engineer, Hydraulic Research, Wallingford, 1977 - 84; Manager, Coastal Structures, HR Wallingford since 1984; Part-time Professor (associate), University of Sheffield since 1994. Chairman, Institution of Civil Engineers Breakwater Conference. Publications: numerous papers and book chapters on breakwater and coastal engineering. Recreations: gardening; circuit driving; examining coastal engineering in winter. Address: (b.) c/o HR Wallingford, Howbery Park, Wallingford, OX10 8BA.
e-mail: w.allsop@hrwallingford.co.uk

Anderson, Rev. Brian Babbington, BTh (Hons). Methodist Minister, Glenburn Methodist Church; Superintendent Minister, South Derry Mission; b. 26.10.62, Belfast; m., Lesley; 1d. Educ. Orangefield High School; Queen's University, Belfast. Insurance claims settler; Loss adjuster; Methodist minister. Recreations: football; golf; reading. Address: (h.) 7 Upper Knockbreda Road, Belfast, BT6 9QH; T.- 02890-803769.

Anderson, Prof. Roger Sproule, BSc, MPhil, PhD, MCOptom, FAAO. Professor of Vision Science, University of Ulster at Coleraine, since 2000; b. 28.1.65, Belfast; m., Mary Patricia; 1 s.; 2 d. Educ. Kilkeel High School; University of Wales, Cardiff. Pre-Registration Optometrist, Moorfields Eye Hospital, London, 1986-87; Private Practitioner and Hospital Optometrist, Bristol Eye Hospital, 1987-90; Research Assistant, Indiana University, School of Optometry, 1990-94; Research Fellow, Dept. of Ophthalmology, University of Edinburgh,1994-95; Senior Lecturer in Optometry, University of Ulster at Coleraine, 1995-2000. Member of: Council, General Optical Council, Advisory Board, Medical Research Council, Royal Institution; Fellow, Royal Academy of Medicine in Ireland. Recreations: church activities; reading. Address: (b.) School of Biomedical Sciences, University of Ulster at Coleraine, Northern Ireland. T.-028 7032 4891.

Anderson, Walter Harold, FInst FF (BIFA). Chairman, Ireland Freight Services Group of Companies; b. 19.2.38; m., Hilary de Lacy; 2d. Past Chairman, NI Branch, Institute of Freight Forwarders; Fellow, Institute of Freight Forwarders (BIFA); Member, Institute of Export; Member, Institute of Directors. National and International Certificate of Professional Competance. Recreations: rugby; golf; family; wines. Address: (b.) Ireland Freight Services Group of Companies, IFS Logistics Park, Seven Mile Straight, Antrim, Co Antrim, BT41 4QE; T.- 028 9446 4211.

Andrew, Professor Malcolm Ross, MA, DPhil, DLit, FEA. Professor, English Language and Literature, Queen's University, Belfast since 1985; b. 27.1.45, Paddock Wood, Kent; m., Lena M

Andrew; 1s.; 1d. Educ. Perse School, Cambridge; St Catharine's College, Cambridge; Simon Fraser University, Canada; University of York. Assistant English Master, Haileybury College, Hertford, 1973 - 74; Lecturer/Senior Lecturer, English, University of East Anglia, Norwich, 1974 - 85; Head of Department/Director, School of English, 1986 - 92; Dean Faculty of Arts, 1992 - 96; Provost of Humanities, 1993 - 98; Pro-Vice-Chancellor, 1998-2002. Canada Council Doctoral Fellowship, 1969 - 72; Member: Humanities Research Board, British Academy 1997 - 98; Arts and Humanities Research Board, 1998-2000. Publications: On the Properties of Things, Book VII, 1975; Poems of the Pearl Manuscript (with R Waldron), 1978; The Gawain-Poet: An Annotated Bibliography, 1979; Two Early Renaissance Bird Poems, 1984; Critical Essays on Chaucer's Canterbury Tales, 1991; Variorum Chaucer, the General Prologue (with C Moorman and D Ransom), 1993; Geoffrey Chaucer, The Canterbury Tales (ed with A C Cawley), 1996; Geoffrey Chaucer: Comic and Bawdy Tales (ed with A C Cawley), 1997; Geoffrey Chaucer: Three Tales About Marriage (ed with A C Cawley), 1998; Geoffrey Chaucer: Three Tales of Love and Chivalry (ed with A.C. Cawley), 2000. Recreations: art; music; architecture. Address: (b.) School of English, Queen's University, Belfast, Belfast BT7 1NN; T.- 028 9027-3317. e-mail: m.andrew@qub.ac.uk

Andrews, Rev. Joseph John, BA (Hons), Dip Th. Minister, Ballee Presbyterian Church; Clerk of Presbytery of Ballymena; Clerk of Synod of Ballymena and Coleraine. Educ. Coleraine Academical Institution; University of Ulster; Queen's University, Belfast; Union Theological College. Assistant Minister, Wellington Street Ballymena Presbyterian Church; Minister, Loughall and Tartaraghan Presbyterian Churches. Address: (h.) Ballee Manse, 1 Forthill Park, Ballymena, BT42 2HL.

Andrews, Margaret Mary, BSc (Hons). Headmistress, Victoria College, Belfast since 1993; b. 24.6.49, Belfast; m., Ronald; 1s.; 1d. Educ. St Dominics High School, Belfast; Queen's University, Belfast. Victoria College: Vice-Principal, 1987 - 89; Deputy Head, 1989 - 93. Member, Board of Curators, Queen's University, Belfast, Member of Senate, since 1996. Recreations: gardening; walking. Address: (b.) Cranmore Park, Belfast; T.-02890 661506.

Andrews, Dr. William John, MB, BCh, BAO, DCH, MD, FRCP (Lond), FRCP (I), FRCP (Ed), JP. Consultant Physician, United Hospitals; b. 22.7.49, Belfast; m., Muriel Jane Jack; 3s.; 1d. Educ. Campbell College; Queen's University, Belfast; University of Texas at Dallas. Junior Doctor, Eastern Health and Social Services Board, 1973 - 80; Senior Medical Tutor, Belfast City Hospital, 1980 - 81; Postdoctoral Fellow, University of Texas/Visiting Scientist, National Institutes of Health, USA, 1981 - 82; Consultant, General Medicine, Diabetes, and Endocrinology,

Northern Health and Social Services Board, 1982; Medical Director, Whiteabbey Hospital, 1990 - 94; Clinical Director, United Hospitals, 1994 - 97. Honorary Senior Lecturer in Internal Medicine, Queen's University Belfast, 1990. Publications: numerous papers on gut hormones, insulin resistance and clinical medicine; Chapter in Diabetes, 1991. Recreations: golf; horses (district commissioner, East Antrim pony club); cricket; rugby. Address: (h.) Ruthmount, 64 Hillhead Road, Ballycarry, BT38 9JF; T.- 02893-373386. e-mail: andrewsjohn442@aol.com

Andrew-Steer, Elizabeth Joanne. Retired Personnel Director, Andrew of Hillsborough; b. 25.4.40, Belfast; m., 1. Cliff Steer; 2. Colin Andrew; 2s.; 1d. Educ. Friends' School, Lisburn; Miss Dunne's Business College. Royal British Legion Women's Section: Northern Ireland Representative on Central Committee, London, 1989 - 93; Northern Ireland Area Chairman, 1989 - 93; Vice-Chairman, 1986 - 89, 1991-; Welfare Visitor since 1991; Holder, National Golden Award; Vice-President, The Not Forgotten Association, (NI), since 1993; Member, Council for the War Memorial Building 1986-2002; Joint Services Committee since 1992; Ladies League Member, The Royal Belfast Hospital for Sick Childen 1979-2002. Publications: A Legion of Recipes, 1992. Recreations: hand and machine knitting; gardening; sailing. Club: The Reform Club Belfast. Address: (h.) 19a Ballynahinch Street, Hillsborough, Co Down, BT26 6AW; T.- 01846-682616.

Anglesea, Martyn, BA, MLitt. Keeper, Fine Art, Ulster Museum, Belfast since 1994; b. 7.6.47, Mold, Flintshire; m., Josephine Conlon. Educ. Alun Grammar School, Mold; Leeds University; Edinburgh University. Voluntary Assistant, Grosvenor Museum, Chester, 1971; Research Assistant, Department of Art, Ulster Museum, 1972; Curator of Prints and Drawings, Ulster Museum, 1981; Visiting Fellow, Yale Center for British Art, 1987; Chairman, Association of Irish Art Historians, 1987 - 91; Chairman, Irish Museums Association, 1993 - 95. Publications: Richard Dunscombe Parker's Birds of Ireland, 1983; numerous articles, reviews and exhibition catalogues including, Kenneth Shoesmith, 1977; The Royal Ulster Academy, Centennial History, 1981; Andrew Nicholl's Views of the Antrim Coast, 1982. Recreations: sporadic painting; printmaking; ceramics; cooking. Address: (b.) Division of Fine and Applied Art, Ulster Museum, Botanic Gardens, Belfast BT9 5AB; T.- 01232-383000. e-mail: <martyn.anglesea.um@nics.gov.uk>

Antrim, Earl of, Alexander Randal Mark, Dip Fine Art; FRSA. Consultant Conservator (Paintings); b. 3.2.35, London; m., Elizabeth Hannah; 1s.; 3d. Educ. Downside; Christ Church, Oxford; Ruskin School of Art. Painting Conservator, Ulster Museum, 1969 - 71; Tate Gallery: Painting Conservator, 1965 - 75; Keeper

of Conservation, 1975 - 95; Head of Collection Services, 1990 - 95. Director, Ulster Television, 1982-2000; Member, Executive Committee, City and Guilds of London Art School since 1983; Prime Warden, Fishmongers Co., 1995 - 96; Director: Antrim Estates Company; Northern Salmon Company, Chairman, since 2000. Exhibitions of paintings in Belfast and London. Publications: numerous articles in conservation journals. Recreations: veteran and vintage cars. Address: (h.) Deerpark Cottage, 3 Castle Lane, Glenarm, Co Antrim, BT44 0BQ; T.- 01574-841514.

Archer, Professor Desmond Brian, OBE, MB (Hons), FRCS, FRCOPHTH, FMedSci. Professor Emeritus, Ophthalmology, Queen's University Belfast, 1972-2001; Honorary Consultant Ophthalmic Surgeon, Royal Victoria Hospital, Belfast; b. 21.10.35, Belfast; m., Amelia Stephanie Wright; 2s.; 2d. Educ. Methodist College, Belfast; Queen's University, Belfast. Junior Doctor, Royal Victoria Hospital/Benn and Ophthalmic Hospitals, Belfast, 1959 - 62; Resident Ophthalmic Surgeon, Westminster Hospital and Moorfields Eye Hospital, London, 1963 - 68; Assistant Professor of Ophthalmology, University of Chicago, USA, 1968 - 72; Deputy Dean, Faculty of Medicine, Queen's University, Belfast; Founder, Fellow of the Academy of Medical Sciences, 1998. OBE 1999. Publications: over 200 publications on ophthalmology and vision science; national/international lectureships including the Doyne, Sir Stuart Duke-Elder and Bowman Lectures; textbooks on hereditary, retinal and choroidal diseases. Recreations: golf; travel; music; gardening. Address: (b.) Department of Ophthalmology, Eye and Ear Clinic, Royal Victoria Hospital, Grosvenor Road, Belfast, BT12 6BA; T.- 02890-346278.

Armit, Ian, MA, PhD, FSA, FSA (Scot), MIFA. Senior Lecturer in Archaeology, Queen's University Belfast, since 1999; b. 7.11.63, Falkirk, Scotland. Educ. Larbert High School; University of Edinburgh. Manager of The Centre for Field Archaeology, University of Edinburgh, 1990-92; Inspector of Ancient Monuments, Historic Scotland, 1992-99. Publications include: Beyond The Brochs (Ed), 1990; The Archaeology of Skye and The Western Isles, 1996; Celtic Scotland, 1997; Scotland's Hidden History, 1998; Towers in the North, 2003. Address: (b.) School of Archaeology and Palaeoecology, Queen's University Belfast, University Road, Belfast.

Armitage, Pauline Alderman. Member (East Londonderry), Ulster Unionist Party, Northern Ireland Assembly, 1998-2003; Member of The Health Social Services and Public Safety Committee and Public Accounts Committee, Stormont; elected to Coleraine Borough Council, 1985; Mayor for two terms, 1995 and 1997; member of the Board of The Northern Ireland Housing Executive, 1996-98; Vice President, Queen's University Young Unionist Association;

Member of the Equality Group, Coleraine Borough Council. Address: (b.) Parliament Buildings, Stormont, Belfast, BT4 3ST; T.-02890-520700.

Armstrong, Rev. Douglas, MA. Retired Minister; b. 3.3.33, Belfast; m., Eileen Chambers Martin; 3s.; 1d. Educ. St Marks School, Belfast; Belfast College of Technology; Magee University College, Londonderry; Trinity College, Dublin; Assembly's College, Belfast. Minister: Balteagh Presbyterian Church, Limavady, 1960 - 66; Strand Presbyterian Church, 1966 - 72; Superintendent, Irish Mission of the Presbyterian Church in Ireland, 1972 - 73; Minister, Greenisland Presbyterian Church, 1973 - 98. Moderator, Synod of Ballymena and Coleraine, 1995. Publications: History of the Greenisland Presbyterian Church, The First Fifty Years, 1934 - 84; Rev. Sinclare Kelburn 1754-1802 Preacher, Pastor, Patriot. Recreation: golf. Address: (h.)15 Downshire Drive, Carrickfergus, BT38 7LF; T.-02893-362108.

Armstrong, Gillian Alexandra, BA, DPhil, PGCUT, MIFST. Lecturer, University of Ulster at Jordanstown, since 1997; b. 18.11.71, Ballymena; m., John Johnston. Educ. Cambridge House Girls Grammar School; University of Ulster at Jordanstown. Lecturer in Marketing within Faculty of Business and Management (research area includes food marketing and food product development). Address: (b.) School of Marketing, Entrepreneurship and Strategy, University of Ulster, Shore Road, Newtownabbey, Co. Antrim. T.-028 90366472.

Armstrong, Henry Napier, BA, DL. Retired Farmer; b. 28.2.36, Nairobi, Kenya; m., Rosemarie White; 2s.; 1d. Educ. Elm Park, Killylea; Winchester; Trinity College, Cambridge; Inns of Court Law School. Barrister, Inner Temple, 1962; Advocate, High Court Kenya, 1963 - 78; Advocate, Tanganyika, 1967; Editor, East African Law Reports, 1964 - 66. Member, Northern Ireland Dairy Quota Tribunal, 1984; Chairman, Ulster Farmers Union, Legal Committee, 1993 - 96; Member, Armagh City and District Partnership Board, 1997-2001; Member, Central Board, Charles Sheils Charity. Certificate of Merit, Royal Agricultural College, Cirencester, 1978; 2nd All Africa 505 Championships, 1970. Recreation: sailing. Address: (h.) 67 Fellows Hall Road, Killylea, Co Armagh, BT60 4LU; T.- 02837-568606.

Armstrong, Maureen, BA (Hons). Assistant Director, Arts and Community, Antrim Borough Council, since 1997; m., Ivan Armstrong; 2s.; 1d. Educ. St Mary's High School, Bulawayo, Zimbabwe; Queen's University, Belfast. Teacher and Lecturer, 1970-78; Local Government Arts Officer: North Down Borugh Council; Ards Borough Council; Antrim Borough Council, 1983 - 97. Recreations: music. Address: (b.) Development and Leisure Dept., The Steeple, Antrim, BT41 1BJ; T.- 02894-463113.

Armstrong, Sir Patrick (John), Kt, CBE, BA, Dip Econ Pol Sci, Dip Soc Stud, Cert App Soc Stud, JP. Former Chairman, Police Authority for Northern Ireland; b. 16.9.27, Omagh. Co Tyrone; m., Agnes Carson; 2s.; 2d. Educ. Christian Brothers Grammar School, Belfast; Ruskin College, Oxford; Queen's University, Belfast; University of Newcastle-upon-Tyne. Factory Worker, 1947 - 57; Student, 1957 - 63; Social Worker, 1963 - 65; Senior/Principal Social Worker, 1965 - 66; Deputy County Welfare Officer, 1966 - 71; Chief Welfare Officer, 1971 - 73; Deputy Chief Inspector of Social Services for Northern Ireland, 1973 - 83; Chief Inspector of Social Services for Northern Ireland, 1983 - 89; Police Authority for Northern Ireland: Vice Chairman, 1994-96, Chairman, 1996-2001. Recreations: reading; walking; cycling.

Armstrong, Stella Catherine, BA (Hons), Cert Ed, AMIPD. Manager, NICOD Training Services, Eastern Health and Social Services Board since 1995; b. 22.11.66, Belfast. Educ. Richmond Lodge School; University of Ulster. Social and Life Skills Tutor, NICOD, 1989 - 91; Training Services Manager, ORTUS, 1991 - 94; Manager, Datalink, South Eastern Education and Library Board, 1994 - 95. Recreations: amateur drama; reading; travel. Address: (b.) NICOD Training Service, 1a Upper Lisburn Road, Belfast, BT10 0GW; T.- 02890-612424.

Armstrong, William. Member (Mid Ulster), Ulster Unionist Party, Northern Ireland Assembly, since 1998; b. 21.6.43, Coagh, Co Londonderry; m., Glynis; 2 s.; 2 d. Educ. Cookstown Secondary School. Farmer, since 1958; Vice-Chairman, Stewartstown Development Association; Treasurer, East Tyrone Ulster Unionist Party; Treasurer, Mid Ulster Ulster Unionist Party; Delegate, Ulster Unionist Council; Director, Cookstown & Western Shores Area Network; Member, committees in Northern Ireland Assembly. Recreation: genealogy. Address: (b.) Parliament Buildings, Stormont, Belfast BT4 3ST; T.-028 90520305. e-mail: mla@billyarmstrong.co.uk web: http://www.billyarmstrong.co.uk

Armstrong, William Alan Oliver, BA, PGCE, DASE. Headmaster, Inchmarlo Preparatory School since 1992; b. 26.6.54, Omagh, Co Fermanagh; m., Patricia Phyllis McCaughey; 3d. Educ. Portora Royal School; London University. Cabin Hill Preparatory School: Assistant Master/House Master/Vice Master, 1977 - 92. Recreations: golf; cricket; cycling; walking; reading; caravanning. Address: (b.) Inchmarlo Preparatory School, 51 Cranmore Park, Belfast, BT9 6JR; T.- 02890-381454. e-mail: armstrong@inchmarlo.belfast.ni.sch.uk

Armstrong, Rev. William John. Minister, Antrim Free Presbyterian Church since 1999; b. 11.10.57, Ballymena; m., Alison Margaret; 1s.; 2d. Educ. Ballymena High School; Whitefield College of the

Bible.   Livestock auctioneer until 1991, left to study for the church; Minister, Tullyvalen Free Presbyterian Church, 1995 - 99.   Recreations: reading; computers; keep fit; sport.   Address: (h) 11 Oldtown Road, Kells, Ballymena, BT42 3NL. e-mail: j.armstrong@btinternet.com

Arthur, Professor Paul.   Professor of Politics, University of Ulster; Senior Fellow, US Institute of Peace, 1997 - 98; b. 22.3.45, Derry; m., Margaret Porter; 1s.; 2d. Educ.   St Columb's College, Derry; Queen's University, Belfast.   Lecturer/Principal Lecturer, Ulster Polytechnic, 1974 - 84; Senior Lecturer/ Professor, University of Ulster since 1986.   Member, Independent Inquiry chaired by Lord Kilbrandon, 1984.   Judge, Ewart-Biggs Memorial Literary Prize since 1986.   Executive Member, British Irish Association, 1985 - 92 and since 1997; Northern Ireland Representative, British American Project, 1986; Member, Northern Ireland Community Relations Council, 1990 - 94; Senior Research Fellow, United States Institute of Peace, Washington DC, 1997-98; Advisory Board member, Project on Justice in Times of Peace, (Harvard University) since 1995.   Weekly columnist, The Irish Times, 1988 - 90; regular broadcaster. Publications: co-author, author and editor of five books including Special Relationships. Britain, Ireland and the Northern Ireland problem, 2001. Recreations: swimming; cooking; reading. Address: (b.) University of Ulster, Magee Campus, Derry BT48 7JL.

Aston, Irene Isabella, BSc (Geol) Queen's. Director of Planning and Governance Services, University of Ulster, since 2000; b. 21.9.55, Ballymena; m., Alan. Educ. Cambridge House, Ballymena;   Queen's   University   Belfast. Management Services Officer, Belfast City Council, 1978-85; University of Ulster: Senior Administrative Officer, Planning, 1985-96, Senior Planning Officer, 1996-2000. Recreations: sailing; music (trad. and classical); racket sports; walking. Address: (b.) University of Ulster, Cromore Road, Coleraine, Co. Londonderry BT52 1SA. e-mail: ii.aston@ulster.ac.uk

Atkinson, Professor A Brew, DSc MD FRCP FRCPI.   Consultant Physician, Royal Victoria Hospital, Belfast since 1980; Hon. Professor of Endocrinology, Queen's University Belfast, since 1993; b. 9.10.48; m., Hilary; 4s. Educ.   Royal Belfast   Academical   Institution;   Queen's University, Belfast.   Clinical Scientist, Medical Research Council, Glasgow, 1978 - 80; MRC Travelling   Fellowship/Fogarty   International Fellow,   Vanderbilt   University,   Nashville Tennessee, USA, 1980.   Publications: numerous papers, books and chapters in endocrinology, particularly   pituitary   and   adrenal   diseases, hypertension and diabetes.   Recreations: running; rugby spectator; golf.   Address: (b.) Regional Centre for Endocrinology and Diabetes (Metabolic Unit), Royal Victoria Hospital, Belfast, BT12 6BA.

Atkinson, Professor Ronald, BSc PhD, FInstP, CPhys, SNIEEE.   Professor in Physics, Queen's University, Belfast since 1998;   b. 25.1.48, Blackburn, Lancs; m., Kathleen Dorothy; 1s.; 1d. Educ.   Billinge   Grammar   School;   Salford University.   Lecturer in Physics, Queen's University, Belfast; Senior Lecturer, Queen's University, Belfast, 1993 - 96; Reader in Physics, Queen's University, Belfast, 1996 - 98. Fellow of the Institute of Physics since 1997; Member of the Institute of Learning and Teaching in Higher Education. Recreations: gardening; watercolour painting. Address: (h.) 6 School Road, Millisle, Newtownards, Co. Down BT22 2DZ. e-mail: ron.atkinson@qub.ac.uk

Atkinson, Ronald James, MD, FRCS, FRCOG, ILIM. Senior Lecturer, Oncology, Queen's University, Belfast; Consultant in Oncology, Belfast City Hospital since 1980; b. 8.9.45, Northern Ireland; m. Dr. Pamela Gawley; 2d. Educ.   Bangor   Grammar   School;   Queen's University, Belfast.   House Officer, Belfast City Hospital, 1971 - 72; Training in Obstetrics and Gynaecology, 1972 - 76; First Cancer Research Fellow (NI), 1976 - 78; Training in Medical Oncology, 1978 - 80; Acting Head, Department of Oncology, Queen's University, Belfast, 1993 - 96; currently involved in teaching, research and patient care. Publications: in journals on gynaecological cancer especially ovarian. Recreations: gardening; skiing.   Address: (b.)   Oncology Department, University Floor, Belfast City Hospital, Lisburn Road, Belfast, BT9 7AB. e-mail: r.j.atkinson@qub.ac.uk

Auld, Rev. McConnell, MA, FRGS, FMA. Former Mayor, North Down; b. Holywood, Co Down.   Educ.   Sullivan Upper School; Royal Academy; Trinity College Dublin; Princeton, New Jersey, USA; Union Theological College, Belfast. Through Captain, US Army Far East Tour, 1953; Inducted,   Parish   of   Goodwood,   Adelaide, Australia,   1955;   Founder   Member/Lecturer, American Youth Foundation, 1957 - 74; Senior House Master/Head of Divinity, Royal Belfast Academical Institution, 1958 - 88.   Council Member, Save the Children Fund, 1962 - 88; Councillor, North Down Borough Council, 1973 - 88 (Deputy Mayor and Mayor, North Down, 1980 - 84); Member: University of Ulster Court, 1977 - 88; Countryside Commission, 1984 - 89; Chair, Friends of Holywood Library since 1992; Member, Presbytery of Ards General Assembly since 1954; Millennium   Awards   Fellowship,   2003;   Travel Scholarship   to   Australia   and   USA,   2003. Publications: various articles and research for media and periodicals; Letters to a Causeway Coast Millhouse, 2004; Forgotten Houses of Holywood, 2003; Holywood Then and Now, 2002. Recreations: sailing; world sea travel; oil and water colour painting; local history lecturing; heritage   hikes;   gardening;   various   charities. Address: Martello Corner, Holywood, BT18 9BD; T.- 01232-423145; The Braddan, Port Braddan, Bushmills, BT57 8TA; T.- 01265-731254.

Austin, Wendy. Presenter Good Morning Ulster; b. 19.11.51, Belfast; divorced; 1s.; 2d. Educ. Victoria College, Belfast. East Antrim Times/Belfast Telegraph, 1973 - 76; Downtown Radio, 1976; Reporter, BBC Northern Ireland, 1976 - 80; Presenter, BBC Northern Ireland since 1981, television programmes include: Children in Need; Scene Around Six; Inside Ulster; Open House; Campaign Questions; The DIY Show; radio programmes include: Morning Extra; PM, Woman's Hour, Radio 4, The Exchange, R4; 5 Live Breakfast; Pioneers and Presidents; The Thin Green Line; Good Morning Ulster. Chairman, Spirit of Enniskillen Trust, Patron, Northern Ireland Children's Hospice Appeal; Patron, NIPPA. Recreations: walking; cooking; travel; driving children around. Address: (b.) BBC Broadcasting House, Ormeau Avenue, Belfast, BT2 8HQ; T.- 02890-338664.

B

Bach, The Reverend John Edward Goulden, JP, BA, Dip Theol. Chaplain and Lecturer in Criminology, University of Ulster; Freelance Journalist and Broadcaster; b. 26.8.40, London; Great Nephew of Mrs Pankhurst; m. The Reverend Frances Mary Bach; 1s.; 1d. Educ. Stowe and University of Durham (where President of the Union, and successively Jenkyns and Evans Scholar). Assistant Master (Mathematics), Arnold House School, London, 1959 - 61; Probation Officer, County of London Sessions, 1961 - 63; ESU Debating Tour of USA (with Michael Horowitz QC), 1967; Consultant, National Council of Churches, New York, 1967-68; Lecturer, Social Sciences, Extra-Mural Department, University of Durham, 1968; Minor Canon, Bradford Cathedral, 1969-73. Council, Association of JP's; Member of the Lord Chancellor's Juvenile Lay Panel and of the Editorial Panel of the Centre for Voluntary Action Studies, University of Ulster; Vacation Chaplain in various Swiss resorts and on P & O cruises; Former President, Church of Ireland Clergy Refresher Course. Former Chairmanships include Board of Visitors, HM Prison Maze; Senior Common Room, University of Ulster at Coleraine; Board of Governors, Mill Strand Integrated School. Publications: "Why the University, but not the Gas Works at Coleraine Needs a Chaplain" (New Divinity, 1974); "Is the Ulster Crisis Religious" (Heaven and Earth, ed. Linzey and Wexler, 1986); "Me, I'm a Citizen of the World, Like" (Cool Britannia, 1999); over 500 articles in Ulster News Letter, Belfast Telegraph, Sunday Times and other publications. Presenter, Bach on Friday, Bach on Thursday (Radio Foyle), and The Bach View (Radio Ulster); contributor, Any Questions? and many other programmes. Guest lecturer/preacher at about 40 UK universities. Recreations: travelling (including on skis); thinking on (but no about) feet; after dinner speaking. Address: (h.) 70 Hopefield Avenue, Portrush, Co. Antrim BT56 8HE. T.-028 70823348.

Bailey, Christopher M. C., BA, MLitt. Director, Northern Ireland Museums Council; b., 11.5.57, Dublin; m., Frances; 1s,; 1d. Educ. Portora Royal School; Trinity College, Dublin. Lecturer, History of Art and Design; Director, Crescent Arts Centre, Belfast; Arts and Heritage Manager, Belfast City Council. Recreations: gardening; riding. Address: (h.) 108 Glenavy Road, Lisburn BT28 3XD; T.- 028 92648388.

Bailey, Professor Mark E. Director, Armagh Observatory; b. 1952. Address: (b.) College Hill, Armagh, BT61 9DG; T.- 028 3752 2928.
e-mail: meb@arm.ac.uk

Bailie, Roy E., OBE. Chairman, W & G Baird (Holdings) Ltd; Non-Executive Chairman, Northern Ireland Tourist Board; b. 2.6.43, Belfast; m., Paddy; 2s.; 1d. Educ. Belfast High School; Queen's University, Belfast; Harvard Graduate Business School. Began career in the printing industry, MSO Ltd (now part of W & G Baird Group of Companies); Led management buy-out of W & G Baird Ltd, from BPC, 1977. Director: W & G Baird Ltd; Graphic Plates Ltd; Greystone Books Ltd; MSO Ltd; Biddles Ltd, Guildford; Biddles (Bookbinders) Ltd, Kings Lynn; Blackstaff Press Ltd; The Thanet Press Ltd; Corporate Document Services Ltd; Non Executive Director, Bank of Ireland; Ulster Television. Member, British Printing Industries Federation (Past Chairman, North Western Region, Vice President, 1998; President, 1999; Chairman CBI (NI), 1992-94; Appointed, Bank of England Court of Directors since 1998; Trustee, Re-Solv. Recreations: sailing; walking. Address: (h.) 60 Ballymena Road, Doagh, Ballyclare, Co Antrim, BT39 0QR; T.- 02894 466107.

Bain, Professor Sir George Sayers, BA (Hon), MA, DPhil. President and Vice-Chancellor, Queen's University Belfast since 1998; b. 24.2.39; m., 1. Carol Lynn Ogden White (marr. diss. 1987) 1s,; 1d.; m., 2. Frances Gwynneth Rigby. Educ. University of Manitoba; Oxford University. Lecturer in Economics, University of Manitoba, 1962 - 63; Research Fellow, Nuffield College, Oxford, 1966 - 69; Frank Thomas Professor of Industrial Relations, UMIST, 1969 - 70; University of Warwick: Deputy Director, 1970 - 74; Director, SSRC Industrial Relations Unit, 1974 - 81; Pressed Steel Fisher Professor of Industrial Relations, 1979 - 89; Chairman, School of Industrial and Business Studies, 1983 - 89. Principal, London Business School, 1989 - 97. Secretary, British Universities Industrial Relations Association, 1971 - 74; Member: Mechanical Engineering Economic Development Committee, NEDO, 1974 - 76; Committee of Inquiry on Industrial Democracy, Department of Trade, 1975 - 76; Council: ESRC, 1986 - 91; National Forum for Management Education and Development, 1987 - 90; Chairman, Council of University Management Schools, 1987 - 90; European Foundation for Management Development: Member, Board of Trustees, 1990 - 96; Vice-President, 1991 - 95. Member, International Affairs Committee, 1990 - 92; Director, American Assembly of Collegiate Schools of Business, 1992 - 94; Council member: Foundation for Management Education, 1991 - 95; IMgt (formerly BIM), 1991 - 93; Member: International Council American Management Association, 1993 - 95; Senior Salaries Review Body, 1993 - 96; Foundation for Canadian Studies in the UK, 1993-2001; Executive Committee, Co-operation Ireland GB, 1997 (Deputy Chairman, 1996 - 97); Board, Co-operation Ireland since 1998; Board of Directors, Graduate Management Admission Council, 1996 - 97; Scotch-Irish Trust, since 1999; Chairman: Food Sector Working Group, NEDO, 1991 - 92; Low Pay Commission 1997-2002; Northern Ireland Memorial Fund, 1998-2002; Conference of University Rectors in

Ireland, 2000-01; Work and Parents Task Force, DTI, 2001; Pensions Policy Institute, since 2002; Independent Review of the Fire Service, ODPM, 2002; Association of Commonwealth Universities, 2002-03. President: Involvement and Participation Association, since 2002; Director: Blackwell Publishers Ltd, 1990 - 97; The Economist Group, 1992-2001; Canada Life Group (UK) Ltd since 1994; Canada Life Assurance Company, 1996-2003; Electra Investment Trust Plc since 1998; Bombardier Aerospace Shorts Brothers Plc since 1998; Navan at Armagh, 1999-2003; Northern Ireland Science Park Foundation, since 1999; Northern Ireland Advisory Board, Bank of Ireland, 2000-02. FRSA, 1987; CIMgt, 1991; Hon. DBA De Montfort, 1994; Fellow British Academy of Management, 1994; Hon. LLD, National University of Ireland, 1998; University of Guelph, 1999; University College of Cape Breton, 1999; Manitoba, 2003; Warwick, 2003; Academician, Academy of Learned Societies for the Social Sciences, 2000; Hon. Doctor of Letters, Ulster, 2002; New Brunswick, 2003. Honorary Fellow, Nuffield College, Oxford, 2002. Publications: several books on industrial relations, and contributions to learned journals. Recreations: reading; genealogy; family history; western riding. Address: (b.) Queen's University Belfast, Belfast BT7 1NN;T.- 028-90-335134.

Baker, Mary Josephine, RGN, ENT Cert. Councillor, Cookstown District Council since 1997; Member of Northern Health and Social Services Council, since 1997; b. 14.3.36, Loup, Magherafelt; m., Emmet Baker; 2s.; 1d. Educ. St Mary's Grammar School, Magherafelt. Student Nurse, Belfast City Hospital, 1954 - 58; Staff Nurse: City Hospital, Belfast, 1958 - 62 and 1963 - 64; Royal National Ear Nose and Throat Hospital, London, 1962 - 63; Royal Victoria Hospital, Belfast, 1964 - 66; Ulster Hospital, Dundonald, 1967 - 77; Mid Ulster Hospital, 1977 - 94; retired, 1994. Recreations: gardening; reading; walking; competitions; crosswords. Address: (h.) 3 Rogully Road, Loup, Magherafelt, Co Derry. BT45 7TR; T.- 01648-418429.

Ballard, Linda-May, BA, BPhil, MPhil. Executive and Policy Officer, National Museums and Galleries of Northern Ireland, Ulster Museum, since 2001; b. Belfast; m., Ronald D Ballard; 1d. Educ. Masonic Girls' School; Methodist College; University of Ulster; University of York. Research Post, Collection and Publication, Oral Narrative, Ulster Folk and Transport Museum, 1985; Curator of Textiles, Ulster Folk and Transport Museum, 1985-2001. Regular Broadcaster and Lecturer throughout the United Kingdom, Europe and the United States. Publications: Ulster Needlework, The Continuing Tradition, 1989; Tying the Knot, 1991; Forgetting Frolic, 1998; numerous articles on subjects relating to folklife, ethnography, textiles and costume. Recreations: chess; reading; music; travel. Address: (b.) Office of the Chief Executive, National Museums and Galleries of

Northern Ireland, Ulster Museum, Botanic Gardens, Belfast 9. T.-028 90 383000.

Ballentine, Rev. Thomas Crawford, BD, MPhil, PhD, DipScot, CGIA, FTC, DipIIM, ECDL. Senior Minister of Grange Presbyterian Church; Minister of Craigmore Presbyterian Church; Part-time Lecturer, North East Institute of Further Education; Senior Chaplain, Braid Valley Hospital, Ballymena; b. 1.7.37; m., Marion Chalmers Sanderson; 2s.; 2d. Educ. Ballymena Academy; Scottish College of Textiles; Edinburgh University; Leeds University. Oldgreen Woolen Mills, Ballymena: Junior Executive; Production Manager; Mill Manager and Training Executive; Scottish College of Textiles, Lecturer, Textile Technology; Lecturer, Management Studies; Minister, Ruthwell, Cummertrees and Mouswald churches, Dumfrieshire/Custodian, Ruthwell Cross. Past President, N. Ireland Hospital Chaplains' Association. Bronze medal and Woolmen's prize, Leeds University; Prizeman of the Year and Dr Rupert Judge Award, Geneva College. Publications: New Life in Christ; The Epistle to the Romans; The Book of Malachi; Epistle of Jude. Recreations: indoor bowls; gardening; walking. Address: (h.) 4 Ashbourne Manor, Old Park Road, Ballymena, Co Antrim, BT42 1BF; T.-028 25 630838.

Bambrick, Rodney Stuart, BA, LTCL. President, Ulster Society of Organists and Choirmasters; b. 1.3.27, Belfast. Educ. Bangor Grammar School; Queen's University, Belfast. Head, History Department, Gransha High School, Bangor until 1986. Currently Organist, Queen's Parade Methodist Church, Bangor. Member, North Down Arts Advisory Panel. Recreations: music; travel; photography; books. Address: (b.) 1b Beverley Hills, Bangor, BT20 4NA; T.-028 9146 5222.

Bamford, Prof. David Richard, BA, MSc, CertEd, AAPSW, CQSW. Professor of Social Work, University of Ulster, since 1995; Chairman, Northern Ireland Association for Mental Health, since 2000; Hon. Professor, University of Transylvania, Romania, since 2001; Chairperson, Review of Mental Health Policy and Legislation, N. Ireland, 2002; b. 11.12.45, Belfast; m., Heather; 1 s.; 2 d. Educ. Annadale Grammar School, Belfast; Trinity College, Dublin; University of Leeds. Social Worker, Belfast, 1968-75; University of Ulster: Senior Lecturer in Social Work, 1975-80, Principal Lecturer in Social Work, 1980-89, Head of Department of Social Work, 1989-95, Head of School, Applied Social Studies, since 2001. Chair, CRUSE Bereavement Care, Belfast; Chair, Romanian Partnership Committee (NI); Member: Alliance Party of N. Ireland, since April 1970, Irish Cricket Union, Ulster Reform Club; Elder, Presbyterian Church in Ireland; Member: Gordon Lightfoot Internet Fan Club, UK Association of Professors of Social Work; External Examiner for Social Work at: Exeter University, Robert Gordon University, Kingston University,

University of North London; Member, Management Board, Institute for Ulster-Scots Studies. Publications: author of 5 books and numerous journal publications. Recreations: sport; music; history; theology. Address: (h) 9 Gowan Heights, Drumbeg Road, Belfast BT17 9LZ. T.- 02890 603752. e-mail: dr.bamford@ulst.ac.uk

Bannerman, Rev. Denis, BD, MTh, MSc. Minister, Greystone Road Presbyterian Church, Antrim since 1994; b. 29.6.46, Newtownards; m., Hendra; 2d. Educ. Comber High School; Queen's University, Belfast; University of Ulster at Coleraine; Union Theological College, Belfast. Assistant Minister, Mersey Street, Presbyterian Church, Belfast, 1981 - 84; Minister, Glenarm and Cairnalbana Presbyterian Church, 1984 - 94. Chairman, Irish Council of European Christian Mission, 1995 - 99. Recreations: swimming; photography; caravanning; information technology. Address: (h.) 2 Brantwood Gardens, Antrim; T.- 028 9446 2844. e-mail: dbannerman@presbyterianireland.org

Barbour, David Donaldson, MSc, HNC. Divisional Manager, NIAS Trust since 1995/Ulster Unionist Party Councillor, Coleraine Borough Council; b. 29.5.42, Limavady; m., Margaret Elizabeth McDowell; 2s. Educ. Limavady Technical School; University of Ulster at Jordanstown and Coleraine. Heavy Machinery Apprentice, 1958 - 64; Hospital porter/Ambulance Driver, 1964 - 67; Transport Driver/Ambulance Driver, 1967 - 71; Ambulance Driver, 1971 - 83; Ambulance Station Officer, 1983 - 91; Assistant Chief Ambulance Officer, 1991 - 1995. Governor, Coleraine College, since 2001; Governor, Culcrow Primary School; Ambulance Divisional Officer, since 1995; Board Member of North Eastern Education and Library Board, since 2001. Recreations: home and extended family. Address: (h.) 44 Carthall Road, Coleraine, BT51 3PQ; T.- 028 70343288; (b.) 028 70344486.

Barker, David, DipAD.ATC, HON.RE. Reader in Printmaking, University of Ulster; Hon. Professor, LuXun Academy of Fine Arts since 1997; Hon. Professor, China National Academy, 2002; b. 11.1.45, Dorchester; m., Catherine Grover; 1s.; 2d. Educ. Clapham College, London; University of London, Goldsmiths' College. Diploma in Art and Design, 1966; Art Teachers Certificate, 1967; Editorial Board, Printmaking Today, 1993. Hon. Fellow, Royal Society of Painters/Printmakers, 1995. Publications: An English-Chinese Glossary of Printmaking Terms, 1995; Chinese Art Academies Printmaking Exhibition, 1993; The Woodcuts of Zheng Shuang, 1999; 30 years of the printmaking workshop, 2001; Yoko Omomi - recent prints, 2001; Japanese Woodcut Prints, 2001. Recreation: swimming. Address: (b.) University of Ulster, York Street, Belfast, BT15 1ED. T.-028 90 267284.

Barnett, Professor Richard Robert, BSc, PhD. Pro Vice Chancellor (Teaching and Learning),

University of Ulster, since 2000; b. 17.10.52, Huntingdon, England. Educ. St Ivo School, St Ives; The Abbey School, Ramsey; University of Salford. Lecturer in Economics: University of Salford, 1977 - 78, University of York, 1978 - 90; Vivienne Stewart Visiting Fellow, University of Cambridge, 1987; Visiting Professor, Queen's University, Ontario, Canada, 1989 - 90; Professor of Public Finance and Management, University of Ulster, since 2000, Head, School of Public Policy, Economics and Law, 1994, Dean, Faculty of Business and Management, 1994-2000. Non-Executive Director, United Hospitals Health and Social Services Trust since 1996. Publications: over 80 articles in academic journals and chapters in edited books. Member, Editorial Board, Government and Policy. Recreations: theatre; reading; motor sport. Address: (b.) University of Ulster, Shore Road, Newtownabbey, Co Antrim BT37 0QB; T.- 028 9036 6848.

Barrow, Andrew James, LLB. Senior Partner, Travers Smith Braithwaite (NI), since 1996; b. 17.5.54, St Pancras, London; m., Helen Elizabeth; 3s.; 1d. Educ. King's School, Canterbury; Nottingham University. Joined Travers Smith Braithwaite, 1976; Articled Clerk, 1976 - 78; Solicitor, 1978 - 83; Partner, Travers Smith Braithwaite, since 1983. Recreations: family; golf. Address: (b.) 10 Snow Hill, London, ECIA 2AL. e-mail: andrew.barrow@traverssmith.com

Barry, Edward Norman, CB. Retired former Under Secretary, Northern Ireland Office, 1979 - 81; Former Hon Treasurer, Irish Football Association Ltd; b. 22.2.20, Belfast; m., Inez Anna Elliott; 1s.; 2d. Educ. Bangor Grammar School. Ministry of Finance: Establishment Division, 1940 - 51; Works Division, 1951 - 60; Treasury Division, 1960 - 67; Establishment Officer, 1967 - 72; Assistant Secretary, Ministry of Home Affairs, 1972 - 74; Assistant Secretary, Northern Ireland Office, 1974 - 79. Member, Probation Board for Northern Ireland, 1982 - 88 (Deputy Chairman, 1988). Recreations: golf; football; gardening. Address: (h.) 40 Sydenham Avenue, Belfast, BT4 2DR; T.- 028 90655918.

Basheer, Professor Muhammed Paliakarakadu Assen, BSc, MSc, PhD, CEng, MIE MCS. Chair, Structural Materials, Queen's University, Belfast since 1999; b. 9.2.59, Tiruvalla, Kerala, India; m., Lulu Basheer; 1s.; 1d. Educ. St Behnan's High School, Kerala; University of Kerala; University of Calicut; Queen's University, Belfast. Assistant Engineer, Public Health Department, Kerala, 1981 - 82; Lecturer, Kerala, 1982 - 87; Queen's University, Belfast: Research Student, 1987 - 90; Research Associate, 1991 - 92; Lecturer, 1993 - 96; Senior Lecturer, 1996 - 98; Reader, 1998 - 99. Young Scientist Award, Government of Kerela, 1991; ACI/James Instruments Award, 1991 and 1999. Recreations: driving in the countryside; listening to classical music; social outings. Address: (b.) School of Civil Engineering, Queen's University, Belfast, BT7 1NN; T.- 02890-274026.

Baxter, Rev. Albert Arthur Priestly, BSc, BD. Minister, 1st Portglenone Presbyterian Church since 1985; b. 15.10.56, Downpatrick. Educ. Down High School, Downpatrick; Queen's University, Belfast; Union Theological College, Belfast.   Assistant Minister, Ballyclare Presbyterian Church, 1982 - 85.   PCI Ireland Outreach Teams Organiser, 1990 - 95; Scripture Union Camp Leader, 1983 - 97. Recreations: tour-coach driver.   Address: (h.) 16 Townhill Road, Portglenone, Co Antrim, BT44 8AD; T.- 028 2582 1345. e-mail: abaxter@presbyterianireland.org

Baxter, John Lawson, DL, BA, BComm LLB, LLM. Solicitor; b. 25.11.39; m., Astrid Irene Baxter; 3s.   Educ.   Trinity College, Dublin; Queen's University, Belfast; Tulane University, New Orleans.   Member, Northern Ireland Assembly (North Antrim), 1973 - 75; Minister of Information, Northern Ireland Executive, 1974; Chairman (part-time), Industrial Tribunals, Northern Ireland, 1980 - 83; Former Member, Northern Health and Social Services Board; DL, Co Londonderry since 1988; Vice-Lord Lieutenant for Co Londonderry; Member of The Council of The University of Ulster; Member of The Criminal Injuries Appeal Panel (Northern Ireland). Recreations: golf; fishing.   Address: (b.) 3 Ballyhome Road, Coleraine BT52 2LU.   T.-028 207 31552.

Bazley, Dr. Robert Anthony Bryn, BSc, PhD, CGeol, FGS. Consultant Geologist; b. 10.10.36, Barry, South Wales; m., Anne Patricia Patterson; 1s.; 1d. Educ. Wycliffe College, Glos.; University of Wales, Cardiff.   Geologist, British Geological Survey, London, 1962; Senior Geologist, Geological Survey of Northern Ireland, 1966; United Nations Geological Survey of Iran, 1972; Head, Eastern England and London, British Geological Survey, 1977; Head, Geological Survey of Wales, 1981; Director, Geological Survey, Northern Ireland, 1993 - 98. Past Member, Environment Group, Prince of Wales Committee; Past Council Member, Geologists Association of London; Past President, Belfast Geologists Society. Mark Cunningham Award, Dublin; Hon. Professor, University College Wales, Aberystwyth; Hon. Professor, Queen's University, Belfast; Chairman, Northern Ireland Geotechnical Group, 1999; Hon. Research Associate, British Geological Survey; Editor, ES2k (Ireland's geological magazine).   Publications: over 50 publications, mostly maps.   Recreations: boating; rambling; gardening.   Address: (h.) Birch Lodge, 24 Ballymacreely Road, Killinchy, Newtownards, Co Down; T.- 028 97-542018.

Beatty, Prof. Eric Kirkland, OBE, BSc, PhD, CEng, FIAE, FIMechE, FIEI. Advisor to Queen's University Belfast on regional economic development, 2000-02; b. 20.8.40, Londonderry; m., Shirley; 1s.; 1d.   Educ.   Foyle College, Londonderry; Queen's University, Belfast. Graduate Engineer, Sirocco Engineering Works, Belfast, 1963 - 66; Queen's University, Belfast;

Assistant Lecturer, Engineering, 1966 - 68, Manager and Director, Northern Ireland Automation Centre, 1968 - 87, Director, Northern Ireland Technology Centre, 1987-99, Director, Regional Economic Development Office, 1999-2000.   Member: Northern Ireland Training Authority, 1987-90; Manpower Council for Northern Ireland, 1987-90; Technology Board of Northern Ireland, 1988-92; Board of The Industrial Research and Technology Unit, 1992-2000; Steering Committee of Northern Ireland Foresight Initiative, 1998-2002; Council of Irish Academy of Engineering, since 2001. Chairman: IRTU Design Directorate, 1994-2002; Governor: East Antrim Institute of Further and Higher Education, 1998-2002.   Director: Engineering Training Council, 1989-2000; Northern Ireland Chamber of Commerce, 1991-94 & 1999-2002; Manufacturing Technology Partnerships Ltd, 1997-2000; Northern Ireland Growth Challenge, 1988-2001; Business Innovation Links Ltd, since 1998. Awards: MBE for services to industry and education, 1989; OBE for services to economic development in Northern Ireland, 1999; Honorary Professor, Queen's University, 1990; Chartered Mechanical Engineer, 1970; Fellow, Institution of Mechanical Engineers, 1979; Fellow, Institution of Engineers of Ireland, 1999; Fellow, Irish Academy of Engineering, 2000.   Recreations: gardening; swimming.   Address: (h.) 512 Doagh Road, Newtownabbey, Co. Antrim BT36 6UF.   T.-028 9083 2327. e-mail: eric.beatty@care4free.net

Beatty, Malcolm, BSc (For) Hon, MSc, FICF. Chief Executive, Forest Service, since 1998. Educ. Aberdeen University. Joined Forest Service, 1978. Address: (b.) Department of Agriculture and Rural Development, Dundonald House, Belfast BT4 3SB; T.-028 9052 4462.

Beckett, Rev. Robert Campbell, BAgr, MS, PhD, DipTh.   Minister, Crosscollyer Street and Somerton Road, Belfast Congregations of the Evangelical Presbyterian Church of Ireland; Chaplain, St. Mary's University College, Belfast; b. Lisburn, Co Antrim; m., Doreen Anderson; 2s.; 2d.   Educ.   The Wallace High School, Lisburn; Queen's University, Belfast; Ohio State University, USA; Reformed Presbyterian Theological College, Belfast.   Research Assistant, Department of Dairy Science, Ohio State University, 1970 - 74; Animal Geneticist, Department of Agriculture of Northern Ireland, 1974 - 78; Ordained to Ministry of the Evangelical Presbyterian Church in Ireland, 1981. Andrews Travel Scholarship, 1975; Lecturer on Evolution/Creation issues; Chairman, Northern Ireland, Back to Genesis Committee; Youth Camp Leader.   Publications: numerous articles and booklets.   Recreations: walking; swimming; soccer; reading; gardening; DIY. Address: (h.) 1 Green Acres, Newtownabbey, Co. Antrim BT36 6NL.   T.-028 908 38102. e-mail: robertcbeckett@ntlworld.com

Beggan, Anna, LLB.   Solicitor, Arthur Cox, Northern Ireland; b. Co Fermanagh.   Educ.

Queen's University, Belfast. Temporary teaching assistance, Institute of Professional Legal Studies. Recreations: tennis; cycling; sailing. Address: (b.) Arthur Cox Northern Ireland, Capital House, 3 Upper Queen Street, Belfast BT1 6PY. T.- 028 90 230007.

Beggs, Rev. Robert James, Teachers Cert. Retired, Minister Emeritus Free Presbyterian Church, Ballymena; Deputy Moderator of The Free Presbyterian Church of Ulster; b. 5.4.35, Co Tyrone; m., Margaret E Paisley; 1s.; 3d. Educ. Royal School Dungannon; Stranmillis Teaching College, Belfast. Teacher, Dungannon Secondary School, 1958 - 61; Teacher, Ballymoney Secondary School, 1961 - 66; Minister, Ballymena Free Presbyterian Church, 1966-2000. Lecturer, Systematic Theology, Whitefield College of the Bible. Publication: Great is Thy Faithfulness, 1979. Recreations: painting; golf. Address: (h.) 10 Granville Manor, Kells, Ballymena, Co. Antrim BT42 3JE. T.-028 25892189.
e-mail: rj.beggs@btinternet.com

Beggs, Roy, MP, CertEd. Ulster Unionist Member of Parliament (East Antrim) since 1983 (resigned seat, 1985 in protest against Anglo-Irish agreement, re-elected, 1986); b. 20.2.36. Educ. Ballyclare High School; Stranmillis Training College. Teacher/Vice-Principal, 1957 - 83; Councillor, Larne Borough Council since 1973 (Mayor of Larne, 1978 - 83); Member, Northern Ireland Assembly (N Antrim), 1982 - 86. Address: (b.) House of Commons, SW1A 0AA.

Beggs, Roy. BEng (Hons). Member (Antrim East), Ulster Unionist Party, Northern Ireland Assembly, since 1998; b. 3.7.62; m., Sandra Maureen Gillespie; 2 s.; 1 d. Educ. Queen's University Belfast. Vice Chairman, Finance and Personnel Committee; Mem., Committee of the Centre; Mem., Public Accounts Committee; Hon. Secretary, Ulster Young Unionist Council, 1986-87; Mem., Cttee, Raloo Presbyterian Church; Gov., Glynn Primary School; Mem., Ulster Unionist Councillors Association. Recreations: walking; cycling: Officer, 1st Raloo Boys' Brigade. Address: (b.) 32c North Street, Carrickfergus BT38 7AQ. T.-028 9336 2995; Fax: 028 9336 8048. Club: Larne Rugby Football.
e-mail: roy.beggs@btopenworld.com

Bell, Professor David Andrew, BSc, MPhil, DPhil, DSc, CEng, FBCS. Professor of Computer Science, Queen's University Belfast; b. 1946, Belfast; m., Sally; 2s. Educ. Grosvenor High School; Queen's University, Belfast; University of Ulster. Computer Programmer, Hoechst Fibre Industries, 1969 - 72; Teacher, Computing, Rhondda Schools, 1972 - 73; Lecturer/Senior Lecturer/Principal Lecturer, Ulster Polytechnic, 1973 - 84; Reader, University of Ulster, 1984 - 86, Professor, 1986-2002. Publications: over 300 academic research papers; author/editor 9 books including: Evidence Theory, vol 1 and 2 (with J Guan); Distributed Databases,   (with J G

Grimson), 1992. Recreations: walking; jogging; badminton.

Bell, Eileen, BA (Hons). Member (North Down), Alliance Party, Northern Ireland Assembly, since 1998; b. 15.8.43, Dromara, Co Down; m. Educ. Dominican College, Belfast; University of Ulster. Civil servant; Personnel Department, Marks and Spencer; General Secretary, Alliance Party, 1986-90; Peace People/Peace Train, 1990-95; elected to North Down Council, 1993; Member, N.I. Forum, 1996-98; Member, South Eastern Education and Library Board, 1993-99; Member, Local Government Staff Commission, 1997-99; Member, North Down Partnership, 1996-99. Address: (b.) Parliament Buildings, Stormont, Belfast, BT4 3ST; T.-028 90 520 700.

Bell, Prof. Kenneth Lloyd, BSc, MA (Calif), PhD, FInstP, CPhys, FAPS, MRIA. Pro-Vice-Chancellor, Queen's University Belfast, since 2001, Head of School of Maths and Physics, 1998-2001; b. 3.01.41, Portadown; m., Deborah Hilary nee George; 2 s.; 1 d. Educ. Portadown College; Queen's University Belfast. Queen's University Belfast: Assistant Lecturer, 1964-67, Lecturer, 1967-73, Senior Lecturer, 1973-77, Reader, 1977-95, Professor in Theoretical Physics, since 1995. Publications: Supercomputing, Collision Processes and Applications, 1999; Atomic and Molecular Data and their Applications. Recreations: music; reading; walking; watching sport. Address: (h.) 22 Knocklofty Park, Belfast BT4 3NA. T.-02890 653167. e-mail: kl.bell@qub.ac.uk

Bell, Dr. Paul, MD, MRCPsych. Medical Director, South and East Belfast Health and Social Services Trust since 1997; Consultant General Psychiatrist, East Belfast Health and Social Services Trust since 1992; b., 14.4.56, Belfast; m., Teresa; 1s.; 1d. Educ. Methodist College; Queen's University, Belfast. Doctor, general medicine, Lagan Valley and Forster Green Hospitals, 1980; entered Psychiatry, 1982; Qualified Psychiatrist, 1985; Consultant Psychiatrist, Craigavon Area Hospital, 1988; Head, Treatment Services, South and East Belfast Health and Social Services Trust, 1994. Publications: numerous publications in medical journals on psychopharmacology and post traumatic stress disorder in Northern Ireland; Chapter in International Handbook of Stress Disorders (co-author) and in the Encyclopaedia of Stress. Recreations: angling; playing concert flute; indoor football. Address: (b.) South and East Belfast HSST, Knockbracken Healthcare Park, Belfast; T.- 028 90565328.

Bell, William Bradshaw, JP. Member, Northern Ireland Assembly, since 1998 (Chairman, Northern Ireland Public Accounts Committee, since 1999); Member, Lisburn Borough Council, since 1989; b. 9.10.35, Belfast; m., Leona Maxwell; 1 s.; 3 d. Educ. Grosvenor High School. Elected Member, N.I. Constitutional Convention, 1975 - 76; Member, Belfast City Council, 1976 - 85 (Lord Mayor of Belfast, 1979 - 80); Personal Assistant to

Rt. Hon. Sir James Molyneaux, MP, 1976 - 97; Member, N.I. Assembly, 1982 - 86; Lisburn Borough Council: Chairman, Finance and General Purposes Committee, 1993 - 95, Member, Housing Liaison Committee, since 1994, Chairman, Economic Development and Marketing Committee, since 1997; Chairman, South Eastern Building Control Group Committee, since 1993; Member, N.I. Housing Council, since 1994; Member, Board, Northern Ireland Housing Executive, 1997 - 98; UUP Spokesman, Finance and Personnel Department, N.I. Address: (b.) Room 307, Parliament Buildings, Stormont, Belfast BT4 3XX; T.-02890 521344.

Belshaw, Kenneth John Thomas. Non-Executive Director, Grafton Recruitment (Northern Ireland's largest employment agency), Director, since 1983, Co-Founder; b. 14.5.52, Belfast; m., Iris Elizabeth; 1s.; 3d. Educ. Orangefield Boys' School. Production and Media Buyer, BPA Advertising/Publicity Assistant/Sales Representative, Maxol Oil 1968 - 75; Branch Manager, Hestair Plc, Edinburgh, London, 1975 - 79; Managing Director, Marlborough Employment, 1979 - 82. Past Chairman, Irish Federation, Personnel Services, 1986 - 87. Recreations; golf; reading. Address: (b.) Grafton Recruitment, 35 - 37 Queen's Square, Belfast, BT1 3FG; T.- 028-90242824.

Bennett, William Norman, BSc (Econ) Hons, IPFA. Director of Finance, Queen's University Belfast, since 2000; b. 25.3.53, Northern Ireland; m., Mrs Gaye Elizabeth Bennett; 2 s. Educ. Regent House Grammar School, Newtownards; Queen's University Belfast. Entered Health and Personal Social Services in N. Ireland as a Graduate Finance Trainee in 1974 and post qualification; held various middle and senior management posts in the HPSS; latterly Director of Finance at the Royal Hospitals Trust, Belfast. Address: Queen's University Belfast, Belfast BT7 1NN. T.-02890 273018.

Beringer, Dr. Timothy, MD, FRCP, FRCPI. Consultant Physician, Royal Victoria amd Musgrave Park Hospitals since 1985; b. 30.10.53, Belfast; m., Janet Wilson; 1s.; 2d. Educ. Campbell College, Belfast; Queen's University, Belfast. Hon. Senior Lecturer, Queen's University, Belfast; Clinical Director, Care of the Elderly, Green Park Healthcare Trust since 1992. Publications: numerous publications relating to the health care of the elderly. Recreations: golf. Address: (b.) Florence Elliott Unit, Royal Victoria Hospital, Belfast, T.- 02890 633511.

Berry, Paul. Member (Newry and Armagh), Democratic Unionist Party, Northern Ireland Assembly, since 1998; b. 3.6.76. Educ. Tandragee Secondary School; Portadown College of Further Education. Textile industry; youngest Member, Northern Ireland Assembly. Health, Social Services and Public Safety Committee; Standards and Privileges Committee. Address: (b.)

Parliament Buildings, Stormont, Belfast, BT3 4ST; T.- 028 90 521191.

Bharucha, Chitra, MBBS, FRCPath, FRSA. Member of General Medical Council, 1999-2003; Member, Independent Television Commission, 2001-03; Chairman, Advisory Comm. on Animal Feeding Stuffs for Food Standards Agency; b., 6.4.45, Madurai, India; m., Dr. Hoshang Bharucha (see Hoshang Bharucha); 2d. Educ. Ewart School, Madras, India; Christian Medical College, Vellore, India. Past President, Medical Women's Federation, UK; Associate, General Medical Council, since 2003; Vice-Chairman, N I Council for Postgraduate Medical and Dental Education, 1999-2000; WHO expert advisory panel for blood products, 1988-2000; former member: Council, International Society for Blood Transfusion, Council, Royal College of Pathologists; Co-ordinator, Standardisation of Cord Blood Banking in Europe; Northern Ireland Council of BBC, 1996-99; Council, Leprosy Mission (N I), Board of Governors, Methodist College, Belfast, 1990-93; Consultant Haematologist, Belfast City Hospital and Deputy Medical Director, Northern Ireland Blood Transfusion Service, 1981-2000. Nuffield Scholar. Recreations: opera; theatre; hill walking; badminton; experimental cookery. Clubs: Reform, London and Ulster Reform. Address: (h.) 15 Richmond Court, Lisburn, BT27 4QU; T.- 02892-678347.

Bharucha, Hoshang, MBBS, MD, FRCPath. Senior Lecturer, Pathology, Queen's University Belfast since 1974; Consultant Pathologist, Royal Victoria Hospital since 1974; Head, Dept. of Pathology, Queen's University Belfast, since 2001; President, Irish Branch of Association of Clinical Pathologists, 2001; b. 18.11.37, Bombay; m., Dr. Chitra Bharucha (qv); 2d. Educ. Bombay; Royal College of Pathologists; Christian Medical College, Vellore, India.Publications: several papers in professional journals. Recreations: photography; badminton; cycling; Mourne walking. Address: (b.) Institute of Pathology, Royal Victoria Hospital, Belfast; T.- 028 90 89 4618. Fax: 028 90 31 2265. e-mail: h.bharucha@qub.ac.uk

Birnie, Dr. (John) Esmond; BA PhD. Member (South Belfast), Ulster Unionist Party, Northern Ireland Assembly since 1998; UUP Assembly Spokesman on North-South and British-Irish Council and Employment and Learning; Lecturer, Economics, Queen's University, Belfast 1989 - 98 (leave of absence); Senior Lecturer, since 2000; b. 6.1.65. Educ. Ballymena Academy Grammar School; Gonville and Caius College, Cambridge; Queen's University, Belfast. Research Assistant, Northern Ireland Economic Research Centre, 1986 - 89. Publications: Closing the Productivity Gap (with DMWN Hitchens and K Wagner), 1990; East German Productivity (with D M W N Hitchens and K Wagner), 1993; The Competitiveness of Industry in Ireland (with D M W N Hitchens), 1994; Competitiveness of Industry in the Czech Republic

and Hungary (with D M W N Hitchens, J Hamar, K Wagner and A Zemplinerová), 1995; An Economics Lesson for Irish Nationalists and Republicans (with P Roche), 1995; Without Profits or Prophets: A Response to Businessmen and Bishops, 1997; The Firm, Competitiveness and Environmental Regulations (with DMWN Hitchens), 1998; The Northern Ireland Economy (with DMWN Hitchens), 1999; Environmental Regulation and Competitive Advantage (with DMWN Hitchens), 2000; co-author, Can the Celtic Tiger cross the Irish Border?, 2001. Elder, Presbyterian Church. Recreations: jogging; cycling; walking; classical music; military history; arts and architecture; politics; church and community group schemes for unemployment and homelessness. Address: (b.) Northern Ireland Assembly, Parliament Buildings, Belfast, BT4 3XX; T.-028-90291149.
e-mail: esmond.birnie@niassembly.gov.uk

Bisp, Janice, BA (Hons). Home Safety Manager, Royal Society For The Prevention of Accidents; b. 13.9.65, Londonderry; m., Andrew Bisp; 1d. Educ. Limavady Grammar School; University of Hertfordshire. Staff Nurse (RGN): London; Australia; Jersey; Edinburgh; Northern Ireland; Training and Development Manager, NHS Executive, South East England. Recreations: scuba-diving; swimming; walking; reading; DIY. Address: (b.) ROSPA, Nella House, Dargan Crescent, Belfast, BT3 9JP; T.- 028 9050 1160.

Bissett, Alan David, LLB. Partner, Carson McDowell since 2002; b. 1.3.67, Belfast; m., Joanne Walker; 3 d. Educ. Belfast Royal Academy; University of Essex; Guildford School of Law. Admitted as a solicitor in England and Wales and Northern Ireland; Linklaters, London, 1992 - 96. Address: (b.) Carson McDowell, Murray House, Murray Street, Belfast, BT1 6DN; T.- 028 9024 4951; Fax: 028 9024 5768.
e-mail: alan.bissett@carson-mcdowell.com

Black, Dr. Boyd. Subject Leader: Economics and Finance, School of Management and Economics, Queen's University Belfast; b. 3.6.45, Limavady; m., Pat. Educ. Campbell College; Trinity College, Oxford; Columbia University, New York. Secretary, Labour in Northern Ireland (LiNI) – aims to persuade Labour Party to offer membership in N.I. Address: (h.) 19 Church Road, Newtownbreda, Belfast BT8 7AL; T.-02890 273284.

Black, Prof. Norman D., BSc, PhD, FRSM, MIEE. Dean, Faculty of Informatics, University of Ulster, since 2000, Chair, Medical Informatics, since 1999; b. 13.1.54, Belfast; m., Sylvia; 1 s.; 2 d. Educ. Queen's University Belfast. British Telecom: Apprentice Technician, 1971-74, Planning Technician, 1974-76, sponsored student, 1976-80, on special leave, 1980-83, Data Communications Consultant, 1983-85; Lecturer in Electrical and Electronic Engineering, University of Ulster, 1985-90; Assistant Director, Northern

Ireland BioEngineering Centre, 1989-94; University of Ulster: Senior Lecturer, Dept. Electrical and Electronic Engineering, 1990-93, Reader, 1993-96, University Co-ordinator of UoA 26, General Engineering, 1994-99, Director, Northern Ireland BioEngineering Centre, 1994-99, Professor in Digital Communication, 1996-99, Director, Institute of Health Informatics, since 1999, Professor of Medical Informatics, since 1999. President of the European Society for Engineering and Medicine Qualifications (ESEM), since 1999; Fellow of the Royal College of Medicine; Member of the Institute of Electrical and Electronic Engineers (MIEEE), since 1980; Associate Member of the Institute of Electrical and Electronic Engineers, since 1986; Past President of The Ulster Biomedical Engineering Society, 1995-98; Founder Member of the Institute of Telemedicine, 1998. Recreations: DIY; soccer; badminton; tennis; driving. Address: (b.) Faculty of Informatics, University of Ulster, Shore Road, Newtownabbey, Co. Antrim BT37 0QB. T.-028 90 366125.

Black, Professor Robert Denis Collison, MA, BComm, PhD, DSc (Econ), FBA, MRIA, Hon. FTCD. Emeritus Professor of Economics, Queen's University, Belfast; b. 11.6.22, Dublin; m., Frances Mary Weatherup (1953); 1s.; 1d. Educ. Sandford Park School, Dublin; Trinity College, Dublin. Deputy for Professor of Political Economy, Trinity College, Dublin, 1943 - 45; Queen's University, Belfast: Assistant Lecturer, Economics, 1945-46; Lecturer, 1946 - 58; Senior Lecturer, 1958 - 60; Reader, 1961; Professor, 1962 - 85. Pro-Vice-Chancellor, 1971 - 75. Rockefeller Foundation Fellow, USA, 1950 - 51; Visiting Professor, Yale University, USA, 1964 - 65. Research Fellow, Japan Society for Science, 1980; Distinguished Fellow, History of Economics Society, USA, 1987. Publications: Economic Theory and Policy in Context, 1995; Ideas in Economics, 1986; (ed): Papers & Correspondence of William Stanley Jevons, 1972-81; Economic Thought and the Irish Question, 1817 - 1870, 1960. Address: (b.) Department of Economics, Queen's University, Belfast BT7 1NN.

Blackburn, Alan David, LLM, BL. Barrister-at-Law; b. 17.7.52, Greenisland. Educ. Royal Belfast Academical Institution, Queen's University, Belfast. Called to the Bar of Northern Ireland, 1976. Member: Arts Club; Reform Club; Mastermind Club. Recreations: theatre; cinema; music; reading. Address: (b.) Bar Library, Royal Courts of Justice, Chichester Street, Belfast, BT1 3JP; T.- 02890-862035.

Blair, Rev. Dr. Samuel Wesley, BSc (Hons), BD, MSc, PhD, MInstP, CPhys. Methodist Minister, Belfast; Superintendent, Ballynafeigh Methodist Circuit, since 2001; b. 21.4.48, Larne, Co Antrim; m., Mary Elizabeth Jacqueline; 2s.; 1d. Educ. Larne Grammar School; Queen's University, Belfast. Head of Science and Senior Teacher, Larne High School, 1973 - 82; Member, Northern

Ireland CSE Board, 1980 - 82; Methodist Minister: Movilla Abbey, Newtownards, 1984 - 86; Strabane and Newbuildings, 1986 - 94; Lurgan, 1994-2001. Member, Methodist Conference since 1984; District Superintendent, Portadown District, 1999-2001; Secretary: North West District Synod, 1989-94, Portadown District Synod, 1996-99. Member, General Committee, Board of Examiners, Council on Social Responsibility, Budget Committee, MCI; Member, Institute of Physics; Chartered Physicist. Publications: Ministry in a Northern Ireland Village, 1991-92 (Expository Times); The Relationship Between Theology and Physics with special reference to Time, 1994. Recreations: wood working; hill walking; computer studies. Address: (h.)12 Ardenlee Avenue, Belfast BT6 0AA. T.-028 90288303.

Blakiston Houston, Dr. Lucinda Mary Lavinia, DL, BSc (Hons), MSc, PhD, MRSC CChem. Chairman, Council for Nature Conservation and Countryside, since 2002; b. 22.12.56; m., Richard Patrick Blakiston Houston (qv); 4s.; 2d. Educ. St Mary's Convent, Cambridge; Leeds University; Liverpool University; Queen's University, Belfast. Marine Analyst, Welsh Water Authority, 1980 - 82; Marine Chemist, Sultanate of Oman, 1983; Research Assistant, Queen's University, Belfast, 1984 - 87; Managing Director, MacEnCo Ltd, 1987 - 91; Director, McEnco Ltd, 1991 - 94; Member, Laganside Corporation, 1992 - 98; Director, Ulster, North Down and Ards Hospital Trust, 1993 - 95. Director, Opera Northern Ireland, 1993 - 98; Member, Water Chemistry Forum, Royal Society of Chemists, 1993-2000; Member, Northern Ireland Committee, British Council, 1995-98; Member, Museums Steering Group, 1996 - 98; Sheriff of Co Down, 1996; Member, Environmental Health and Safety Committee, Royal Society of Chemists, 1997-2000; Chairman, Northern Ireland Blood Transfusion Service, 1995-2002; Director: Headfort School, Kells, Co Meath, since 2001, Sustrans, since 2001. Recreations: whatever the children enjoy doing, and sometimes theatre; opera; sailing; rare breeds; cycling. Address: (h.) Beltrim Castle, Gortin, Omagh, Co Tyrone, BT79 8PL; T.- 01662-648207. e-mail: lucinda@bhestate.co.uk

Blakiston Houston, Richard Patrick, DL, FRICS; b. 25.7.48, Belfast; m., Lucinda Hubbard (qv); s.; 2d. Educ. Headfort School; Eton College; Royal Agricultural College. Director: Blakiston Houston Estate Co, 1972; Clandeboye Estate Co Ltd, 1982; Dunleath Estates Co Ltd, 1986; Milibern Trust, 1991; Church of Ireland Trustees, 1991; Caledon Regeneration, 1997. Director, Milk Marketing Board since 1997; Director, Blackwood Golf Course Ltd since 1990; Director, Northern Ireland Golf Foundation since 1993; Chairman/Secretary, Ulster Timber Growers Organisation, 1972-96; Director, Caledon Estate. Recreations: tennis; skiing; fishing. Address: (h.) Beltrim Castle, Gortin, Omagh, Co Tyrone, BT79 8PL; T.- 02881 648207.

Blaney (ó Bléine) Roger (Ruairí), MD, DPH, FFCM, FFPHMI. Hon. Senior Lecturer, Queen's University, Belfast; Hon. Consultant in Community Medicine, Royal Victoria Hospital and Eastern Health and Social Services Board; b. 9.5.31, Belfast. m., Brenda Quinn; 2s.; 3d. Educ. St Peter's Public Elementary School; St Patrick's College, Armagh; Queen's University, Belfast. Research Fellow, Guy's Hospital, London, 1961 - 64; Assistant Senior Medical Officer, Northern Ireland Hospitals Authority, 1964 - 68; Queen's University, Belfast: Senior Lecturer, Social and Preventive Medicine, 1968 - 88; Head, Department of Community Medicine and Medical Statistics, 1985 - 88; Consultant, Social and Preventive Medicine, Royal Victoria Hospital and EHSSB, 1968 - 88. President, Acadamh na Lianna, 1979 - 81; Vice-Chairman, Ulster Liberal Party, 1972; Member, Panel for Social Medicine and Epidemiology, EEC, Brussels, 1978 - 87; Chairman, Education and Information Panel, Ulster Cancer Foundation, 1977 - 97; Vice-President, Ulster Cancer Foundation since 1997; Vice-Dean, Faculty of Public Health Medicine, Royal College of Physicians, Ireland, 1984 - 85 and 1997 - 99; Elected member, Coiste Gnó Gaelic League, 1996 - 2002; Trustee, Iontaobhas ULTACH since 1990; President, Belfast Literary Society, 1997 - 98. Carnwath Medal in Public Health, 1961; Noel Hickey Medal in Irish Social Medicine, 1994. Publications: Belfast: 100 years of Public Health, 1988; Presbyterians and the Irish Language, 1996; Notaí on Lia, 1999; various chapters in books and articles in Irish on medical matters in An tUltach and LA. Recreations: genealogy; photography; short wave radio listening. Address: (b) Ulster Cancer Foundation, 40-42 Eglantine Avenue, Belfast, BT9 6DX; T.- 02890 421922.

Blayney, John Robert, BSc (Hons), MSc, DASE. Director, East Antrim Institute of Further and Higher Education, since 1998; b. 15.7.48, Belfast; m., Norma (nee Todd); 1 s.; 1 d. Educ. Belfast Royal Academy; Queen's University Belfast. Assistant Teacher, Coleraine Academical Institution, 1972-75; Head of Department: Ballycastle High School, 1975-81, Lurgan College, 1981-84; Newtownabbey College of Further and Higher Education: Senior Lecturer/Head of Department, 1984-89, Vice-Principal, 1990-94; Deputy Director, East Antrim Institute of Further and Higher Education, 1994-97. Member of Board of Governors, Ballyclare High School, since 1994. Publication: NEBSM Levels in Strategic Management, 2002. Recreations: golf; rugby; reading. Address: (b.) East Antrim Institute of Further and Higher Education, 400 Shore Road, Newtownabbey BT37 9RS. T.-02890 855003. e-mail: john.blayney@eaifhe.ac.uk

Bleakley, David Wylie, CBE, PC, BA, MA (Hons), Dip Econ. Writer, Lecturer, Politician; b. 11.1.25, Belfast; m., Winifred Wason; 3s. Educ. Belfast College of Technology; Ruskin College,

Oxford; Queen's University Belfast. Lecturer and Principal, Belfast College of Further Education; Lecturer, Kivukoni Adult Education College, Dar-es-Salaam; Labour MP, Northern Ireland Government; Privy Councillor/Minister, Community Relations, Northern Ireland Government; Member, Northern Ireland Assembly and Constitutional Convention. General Secretary, Irish Council of Churches; President, Church Missionary Society, London, active in Church of Ireland; Privy Councillor; Advisor, Northern Ireland Peace Talks Conference, 1996 - 98. Regular Broadcaster. Publications: author of many publications including; Brian Faulkner; Sadie Patterson, Peace Maker; Peace in Ulster; Peace in Ireland – Two States, One People, 1996; books on industrial affairs; Centenary Biography: C S Lewis, At Home in Ireland, 1998. Recreations: family and friends; exploring the world of C S Lewis. Address: (h.) 8 Thornhill, Bangor, Co Down, BT19 1RD; T.- 02891-454898.

Blease, Lord, Baron of Cromac in the City of Belfast, William John JP, DLitt, LLD, Hon. FBIM. Member House of Lords; b. 28.5.14; m., Sarah Evelyn Caldwell (dec.); 3s.; 1d. Educ. Belfast College of Technology; NCLC. Apprenticed, Retail Provision Trade, 1929; Branch Manager, Retail Grocery, 1938 - 40; Administrative Clerk, Harland and Wolff Shipyard, 1940 - 45; Belfast Co-operative Society, 1945 - 59; Divisional Councillor, Union of Shop Distributive Workers, 1945 - 59; Irish Congress of Trade Unions: Northern Ireland Official, 1959 - 75; Executive Consultant, 1975 - 76; Executive Member, Northern Ireland Labour Party, 1949 - 59 (Deputy Chairman, 1957 - 58); Created Life Peer, 1978. House of Lords Parliamentary Labour Party (opposition) spokesperson on Northern Ireland Affairs, 1979 - 82. Member Northern Ireland Economic Council, 1964 - 75; Member, Local Government Appeals Tribunals, 1974 - 83. Ford Foundation Travel Award, USA, 1959. Hon. Resident Fellow, New University of Ulster, 1976 - 83; Joint Hon. Resident Fellow, Trinity College, Dublin, 1976 - 79; JP, Belfast since 1976; Hon. DLitt, University of Ulster, 1972; Hon. LLD, Queen's University, Belfast, 1982; New Ireland Peace Trophy, 1971 - 74. Publications: The Trade Union Movement in Northern Ireland, Encyclopedia of Labour Law, Vol. 1, 1983. Recreations: reading; gardening; DIY. Address: (b.) House of Lords, London SWIA OPW.

Bloomfield, Sir Kenneth Percy, KCB, MA (Oxon), LLD (Hons. QUB), DUniv. (Hons. Open U.), D.Litt (Hons. Univ. of Ulster). Chairman, Bangor and Holywood Town Centre Management Ltd, since 2000; Co-Commissioner, Independent Commission for the Location of Victims' Remains, since 1999; Trustee of Musuems and Galleries of Northern Ireland, since 2002; Trustee of the Ulster Historical Foundation, since 1992; Governor of the Royal Belfast Academical Institution, since 1984; Member of the Management Committee of Armagh Observatory and Planetarium, since 1996;

Honorary Fellow of St. Peter's College, Oxford, since 1990; b. 15.4.31, Belfast; m., Mary Elizabeth Ramsey; 1 s.; 1 d. Educ. Royal Belfast Academical Institution; St. Peter's College, Oxford. Held various posts in N. Ireland Civil Service, 1952-91 (including service in New York as Deputy Director of British Industrial Development Office, 1960-63), culminating in post of Head of NI Civil Service and Second Permanent Under Secretary of NI Office, 1984-91. N. Ireland National Governor of the BBC and Chairman of Broadcasting Council for N. Ireland, 1991-99; Chairman of Trustees of BBC Children in Need, 1992-98. First Chairman of NI Higher Education Council, 1993-2001; member of the Senate at Queen's University, 1991-93; Member of Law Reform Advisory Committee, 1991-97; Commissioner of NI Victims Commission and author of the report "We Will Remember Them", 1997-98; Chairman, Review of Criminal Injuries Compensation, 1998-99. Undertook fundamental review of dentists' pay throughout the UK in 1992; headed top-structure review of the UK Dept. of Social Security in 1993. Served at various times on NI Advisory Board of Bank of Ireland, Board of Co-operation North, Board of Green Park Healthcare Trust and other bodies. Member of the Clothier Review of Jersey's system of government, and still engaged as a consultant to States of Jersey; also at various times engaged as a consultant by AHS Emstar, the Stationery Office, Land Securities Trillium and Helm Corporation (for service in Bangladesh). Publications: Stormont in Crisis, 1994; contributor to several anthologies and books of essays; articles in Political Quarterly; Parliamentary Brief; Fortnight and other publications. Recreations: swimming in the sea; travel; opera and theatre; reading history and biography; watching rugby football. Address: 16 Larch Hill, Craigavad, Holywood BT18 0JN. T.-028 90 428340. e-mail: kenbloomfield@tiscali.co.uk

Boggs, Rev. Robert Ernest, BA, MA. Presbyterian Minister; b., 20.12.39, Londonderry; m., Mary Jane McAllen Heron; 1s.; 1d. Educ. Foyle College; Trinity College, Dublin. Licensed in Faughanvale Presbyterian Church, 1965; Ordained, Cregagh Presbyterian Church, 1966; Rasharkin, 1968; Donaghadee Presbyterian Church, 1972; United Church of Canada, Harrington Harbour, 1974; Quyon, Quebec, 1975; Moy and Benburb, 1977; Downpatrick, Ardglass and Strangford, 1993. Moderator, Synod of Armagh and Down, 1993; Convenor, War Memorial Hostel Committee, 1984 - 91. Publications: A Short History of Rasharkin Presbyterian Church, 1970. Recreations: golf; cars (ex stock car driver). Address: (h.) 18 Strangford Road, Downpatrick; T.- 028 44615201.

Boohan, Margaret I., BA, MSc. Lecturer, Medical Education Unit, Queen's University of Belfast, since 1993. Educ. University College, Galway; Queen's University of Belfast. Research Fellow, Northern Ireland Council for Educational

Research, 1988 - 90; Research Associate, Department of General Practice, Queen's University of Belfast. Address: (b.) First Floor, Whitla Medical Building, 97 Lisburn Road, Belfast BT9 7DL; T.-02890 272188.

Boore, Professor Jennifer Ruth Pryse, OBE, RGN, RM, RNT, BSc (Hons), PhD, FRCN. Professor of Nursing since 1984; Co-ordinator of Academic Affairs in Nursing, University of Ulster since 1996; b. 6.12.43, Birmingham. Educ. Westminster Hospital, London; University of Surrey; University of Manchester. Staff Nurse, Westminster Hospital, London, 1964 - 65; Relief District Nurse/Midwife, Cardiganshire County Council, 1967; Sister/Acting Matron, District Hospitals, Tasmania, Australia, 1967 - 68; Relieving Sister-in-Charge, District Nursing Centres, Royal Hobart Hospital, Tasmania, 1968 - 69; Staff Nurse, Westminster Hospital, London, 1969 and 1970; Clinical Teacher, Crumpsall Hospital, Manchester, 1972 - 73; DHSS Research Fellow, Department of Nursing, University of Manchester, 1973 - 76; Sister, Withington Hospital, Manchester, 1976 - 77; Lecturer, Nursing Studies, University of Edinburgh, 1977 - 79; Lecturer, Nursing Studies, University of Hull, 1979 - 84; Head, Department of Nursing, University of Ulster, 1984 - 94. Fellow, Royal College of Nursing, 1993; OBE, 1996; Member of the National Board for Nursing, Midwifery and Health Visiting for Northern Ireland. Publications: 53 publications including 4 books and 9 chapters in books. Recreations: science fiction; ancient history; tapestry; swimming; food and wine. Address: (b.) School of Nursing, University of Ulster, Cromore Road, Coleraine, BT52 1SA; T.-02870-324274.

Boreham, Professor Colin, BA (Hons), MA, PhD. Professor of Sport and Exercise Science, University of Ulster since 1996; b. 26.3.54, Luton; m., Susan Jane; 1s.; 2d. Educ. Bournemouth School for Boys; Birmingham University; University of California, Berkeley. Lecturer in Exercise Physiology, Queen's University, Belfast, 1977 - 89; Director, Physical Education; Queen's University, Belfast, 1989 - 96. Represented Great Britain and Northern Ireland in the Decathlon, Los Angeles Olympic Games, 1984. Recreations: travel; good food and wine. Address: (b.) School of Applied Medical Sciences and Sports Studies, University of Ulster, Jordanstown, Shore Road, Newtownabbey, Co Antrim, BT37 0QB; T.- 028 90366665.

Boreland, Dr. Paul Constantine, BSc, PhD, CIBiol, FIBiol, FIBMS. Principal Microbiologist, Antrim Area Hospital since 1994; b. 20.3.45, Belfast; m., Pamela Virginia McKay; 1s.; 1d. Educ. Masonic Boys' School, Dublin; Queen's University, Belfast; University of Ulster. Scientific Officer, Virology Department, Veterinary Research Labs, 1965 - 71; Lecturer, Biological Sciences, Belfast College of Technology, 1974 - 77; Senior Microbiologist,

Waveney Hospital, Ballymena, 1977 - 86; Principal Microbiologist, Waveney Hospital, 1986 - 94. Publications: numerous papers published on whooping cough; bacteriuria screening and automation in medical microbiology. Recreations: cricket umpiring; golf; sea fishing; chess; reading. Address: (b.) Microbiology Department, Antrim Laboratory, Antrim Area Hospital, 45 Bush Road, Antrim, BT41 2RL T.- 028 94 424000; Ext. 4850.

Borooah, Professor Vani Kant, MA, PhD. Professor, Applied Economics, University of Ulster since 1987; b., 27.12.47, India; m., Vidya Borooah; 1s. Educ. St Edmund's College; University of Bombay; University of Southampton. Lecturer, Economics, University of Deli, 1969 - 73; Doctoral Student, University of Southampton, 1973 - 78; Senior Research Officer, Department of Applied Economics, University of Cambridge, 1977 - 87; Fellow, Queen's College, Cambridge, 1979 - 87. Publications: Political Aspects of the Economy, 1983; The Structure of Consumption Decisions, 1989; Regional Income Inequality and Poverty in the United Kingdom, 1991; Growth, Unemployment, Distribution and Government, 1996; Logit and Probit Ordered and Multinomial Models, 2001. Recreations: cricket; running; opera. Address: (h.) 3 St John's Park, Belfast, BT7 3JF; T.-028-9096 1357.

Botteley, John. Theatre Director, Grand Opera House, Belfast, since 2003; b. 1949, Birmingham. Educ. Westminster College, Oxford. Entertainments Officer, Royal Viking Cruise Line, 1973-76; Stage Manager/Actor/Teacher, Nottingham Playhouse, 1976-79; Artistic Director, Gazebo Theatre-in-Education Company, 1979-86; Performing Arts Co-ordinator, Wolverhampton Council, 1986-89; Chief Executive: Wolverhampton Grand Theatre, 1989-92, Anvil Concert Hall, Basingstoke, 1992-95; Head of Theatres, Arts and Festivals, Bradford Council, 1995-2003. Member of Council, Theatrical Management Association. Address: (b.) The Grand Opera House, Belfast BT2 7HR. T.-028 9024 0411.

Bowen, David, Dip Ed. General Secretary, Irish Football Association since 1983; b. 26.7.55, Belfast; m., Karen. Educ. Kelvin High School; Stranmillis College. Irish Football Association: Executive Officer, 1978 - 83. Member, FIFA and UEFA Discipline Committees. Recreations: tennis; golf; qualified referee; qualified coach. Address: (b.) Irish Football Association, 20 Windsor Avenue, Belfast BT9 6EE; T.- 028 9066 9458.

Bowen, Martin, OBE, CertEd, DipASEd, MA(Ed). Principal, St. Peter's High School, Foylehill, Derry, since 1989; b. 17.8.50, Londonderry. Educ. St. Columb's College; University of Ulster. St. Joseph's Secondary School, 1971 - 82; St. Mary's High School, 1982 - 84; Northern Ireland Council for Educational Development, 1984 - 89. Vice-Chairman, Founder

Director, Creggan Enterprises Ltd. OBE for services to secondary education 1999. Recreations: reading; walking. Address: (b.) Southway, Foylehill, Londonderry BT48 9SE; T.- 028 7127 3920. e-mail: mbowen@stpeters.derry.ni.sch.uk

Bowler, Professor Peter John, MA (Cantab), MSc, PhD, MRIA. Professor, History of Science, Queen's University Belfast, since 1992; b. 8.10.44; m., Sheila Mary Holt; 1s.; 1d. Educ. Alderman Newton's School, Leicester; King's College, Cambridge; University of Sussex; University of Toronto. Assistant Professor, University of Toronto, 1971 - 72; Lecturer, Science University of Malaysia, 1972 - 75; Assistant Professor, University of Winnipeg, 1975 - 79; Lecturer, Queen's University Belfast, 1979 - 87; Reader, Queen's University Belfast, 1987 - 92. Publications: Evolution: The History of an Idea, 1982; Charles Darwin: The Man and his Influence, 1991; The Fontana History of the Environmental Sciences, 1992. Recreations: reading science fiction; walking. Address: (b.) School of Anthropological Studies, Queen's University Belfast, Belfast, BT7 1NN; T.- 02890-273882.

Bowman-McAlister, Colette, LLB (Hons) BL. Barrister-at-Law since 1993; b. 17.8.68, Belfast. Educ. Rathmore Grammar School, Belfast; Queen's University, Belfast. Address: (b.) Bar Library, Royal Courts of Justice, Chichester Street, Belfast, BT1 3JP.

Boyd, Eric William, BMus (Hons), ALCM, Hon. MA. Head of Music Services, North Eastern Education and Library Board since 1994; b. 1.1.55, Glasgow; m., Joan; 2s. Educ. The High School of Glasgow; University of Glasgow. Joined Music Service, North Eastern Education and Library Board, 1977: Head of Music Centres, 1986. Member, various interboard groups and curriculum panels; Chairman, Coleraine International Choral Festival; Member, Board of Governors, Coleraine Academical Institution. Hon. MA, University of Ulster, 1996. Address: (b.) Music Service, North Eastern Education and Library Board, Antrim Board Centre, 17 Lough Road, Antrim, BT41 4DH; T.- 028 94 482231; Fax: 028 94 460224. e-mail: eric.boyd1@btopenworld.com

Boyd, Norman. Member (South Antrim), Northern Ireland Unionist Party, Northern Ireland Assembly, 1998-2003; m.; 1 s.; 1 d. Educ. Belfast High School. Career in banking. Worshipful Master in Orange Lodge; Past Chairman, Ballymena and District Apprentice Boys; Party Whip, Northern Ireland Unionist Party; Boys Brigade Holder of Queens and President's Badges. Address: (b.) Room 303, Parliament Buildings, Stormont, Belfast, BT4 3XX. T.-028 90521733. Fax: 028 90521 754. Constituency Office: 38 Main Street, Ballyclare, Co. Antrim BT39 9AA. T.-028 93349132. Fax: 028 93349128.

Boyd, Trevor Dempster, MBE, BSc, FRMetS, AMInstE. Retired; b. 19.11.31, Belfast; m.,

Heather Lilian Elaine Andrews. Educ. Uppingham; Queen's University of Belfast. Linen Manufacturer, Industrial Manager in Petroleum Industry. Recreations: energy conservation; meteorology; climatology; natural history; lepidoptera. Address: (h.) 12 Woodland Avenue, Helen's Bay, Bangor, Co Down BT19 1TX; T.-028 91852276.

Boyle, Edward Arthur Harry, DL, JP. Farmer; b. 13.7.43, London; m., Alison Margaret Smith; 2s.; 1d. Educ. Fettes College; Harper Adams Agricultural College. Began farming Ardnargle, 1969. Appointed Justice of the Peace, Co Londonderry, 1978; Appointed High Sheriff, Co Londonderry, 1978; Appointed Deputy Lieutenant, Co Londonderry, 1984; Appointed General Commissioner of Income Tax, 1989; Appointed Trustee, Limavady War Memorial Trust, 1990; Appointed to Advisory Committee of Justices of the Peace, Co Londonderry, 1995; Chairman, British Heart Foundation, Limavady Branch since 1996; Vice-Chairman, Northern Ireland Self-Catering Holiday Association, 1997; Chairman, Ulster Gliding Club, 1985 - 93. Recreations: shooting; gliding; power flying; golf. Address: (h.) Ardnargle, Limavady, Co Londonderry, BT49 9DW. e-mail: eahboyle@hotmail.com

Bracefield, Hilary Maxwell, MUniv (Open), MA (Hons), DipMus, Dip Tchg, LTCL. Head of Music, University of Ulster; b. 30.6.38, Dunedin, New Zealand. Educ. Otago Girls' High School, Dunedin; University of Otago, New Zealand. Teacher, Bayfield High School, Dunedin, 1961 - 70; Lecturer, Worcester College of Education, 1974 - 76; Lecturer, Music, Ulster Polytechnic, 1976 - 84; Senior Lecturer, University of Ulster 1984-2003. Council Member, Incorporated Society of Musicians, 1980 - 86 and since 2001; Member: Arts Council of Northern Ireland Advisory Panels, 1983 - 93; Board, Contemporary Music Centre, Dublin, 1985 - 93; Council, Royal Musical Association, 1988-93, 1997-2003; Chairman, Belfast Music Society, 1988 - 90; Chairman, Newtownabbey Borough Arts Advisory Committee, 1993 - 95; Chairman, CCEA, Music Panel, 1996-2000. Blair Trust Travelling Award, 1970. Lecturer/Critic/Broadcaster. Publications: contributor to numerous journals. Recreations: film; theatre; reading. Address: (h.) 103 Monkstown Road, Newtownabbey, Co. Antrim BT37 0LG. T.-028 9086 9044.

Bradford, Conor Lindsay Hamilton, BA (Oxon). BBC Television News Anchorman; b. 30.4.58, London. Educ. Winchester College; Keble College, Oxford. Insurance Broker, Lloyds of London; Fine Art Lecturer, British Institute, Florence; Manual Labourer, Oil rigs, Scotland; Joined BBC Northern Ireland, 1983; Reporter, Good Morning Ulster; Presenter radio news, Newsbreak; Television Anchorman, Spotlight. Sony Award, Best Radio Current Affairs programme; Recreations: golf; architecture.

Address: (b.) BBC Broadcasting House, Ormeau Avenue, Belfast BT2 8HQ; T.- 02890-338000.

Bradley, Andrea Michele, MA, Dip Hist Art, CALS, CPLS. Assistant Solicitor, P J G Bradley since 1992; b. Belfast. Educ. Dominican College, Belfast; University of Edinburgh; Exeter College, University of Oxford; Queen's University, Belfast. Research, Oxford University, 1987; Qualified as a Solicitor, 1992. Publications: The Christopher Hewitt Collection, Ashmolean Museum, 1987. Recreations: reading; music; art; food; travel. Address: (h.) 24 Colenso Court, Colenso Parade, Belfast; T.- 028 90662034.

Bradley, Professor Martin Eugene Joseph, FRCN, MSc, BEd, DipNurs, Dip (HEcon), RGN, RMN, RNT. Director, Royal College of Nursing, N. Ireland; b. 23.6.50, Belfast; m., Nuala; 2 c. Bigger Prize, Educational Studies; University of Ulster, 1985; Visiting Professor, University of Ulster; Vice-Chairman, Northern Ireland Association for Mental Health; Fellow of the Royal College of Nursing, 2000. Address: (b.) Royal College of Nursing, 17 Windsor Avenue, Belfast BT9 6EE. T.-028 90 66 8236.

Bradley, Peadar John (P.J.). Member (South Down), Social Democratic and Labour Party, Northern Ireland Assembly since 1998; b. 28.4.40, Warrenpoint, Co Down; m.; 3 s.; 5 d. Educ. Technical School, Warrenpoint; St Colman's College, Newry. Property surveyor and valuer; appointed FIAVI (Fellow of Irish Auctioneers& Valuers Institute), 1998; part-time farmer; elected to Newry and Mourne Council, 1981 (Chairman of Council); Member, Youth Committee for Northern Ireland, 1978-81; Member, Rent Committee for Northern Ireland, 1987-90. Address: (b.) Parliament Buildings, Stormont, Belfast, BT4 3ST; T.- 02890-520700.
e-mail: pj.bradley@niassembly.gov.uk

Brady, Hilary Anne, MBA, DMS, DIP PE, MILAM, MCIM. Head of Development Services and Deputy Chief Executive, Newtownabbey Borough Council; b. 27.8.49, Larne. Educ. Larne Grammar School; Ulster College of Further Education; University of Ulster. Ballymena Academy, 1970 - 75; Ballymena Borough Council, 1975 - 79; Belfast City Council, 1979 - 81; Lisburn Borough Council, 1981 - 93. Recreations: golf; theatre; hockey. Address: (b.) Newtownabbey Borough Council, Mossley Mill, Newtownabbey BT36 5QA. T.-02890 340000.
e-mail: hbrady@newtownabbey.gov.uk

Brady, Noel, BA, MInstD, AInstSMM. Managing Director, S x 3 Ireland (a leading figure in the IT services sector in Northern Ireland); Chairman, Northern Branch, Sales Institute of Ireland, since 2003; b. 3.12.57, Belfast; m., Barbara; 3 s. Educ. La Salle; University of Ulster. Civil Servant, 1974-91; Business Development Director, ICL Group Ltd, 1998-99. Member of: Northern Ireland Committee of IOD, the NI

Council of CBI, Institute of Sales and Marketing Directors. Recreations: running; keep fit; Irish history. Address: (b.) S x 3, Hillview House, 61 Church Road, Newtownabbey BT36 7SS. T.- 02890 857160.

Brady, Most Rev. Sean, BA, STL, DCL. Archbishop of the Metropolitan See of Armagh and Primate of All Ireland since 1996; b. 16.8.39, Laragh, Co Cavan. Educ. Caulfield National School, Laragh; St Patrick's College, Cavan; St Patrick's College, Maynooth, Co Kildare, Ireland; Pontifical Irish College, Rome. Ordained Priest, 1964; Professor, St Patrick's College, Cavan, 1967 - 80; Vice-Rector, Irish College, Rome, 1980 - 87; Rector, Irish College, Rome, 1987 - 93; Parish Priest, Castletara, Co Cavan, 1993 - 94; Coadjutor, Archbishop of Armagh, 1995 - 96. Chairman, Irish Episcopal Conference since 1996; Chairman, Standing Committee, Irish Episcopal Conference since 1996. Address: Ara Coeli, Armagh, BT61 7QY.
e-mail: admin@aracoeli.com
website: www.armagharchdiocese.org

Brennan, Jean, BA (Hons). Arts Development Officer, Omagh District Council since 1994; b. Dublin. Educ. University of Ulster; Trinity College, Dublin. Previously Artistic Director, The Garage Theatre, Monaghan; worked for Axis Ballymun's Arts and Community Resource Centre. Address: (b.) Omagh District Council, The Grange, Mountjoy Road, Omagh, Co Tyrone, BT79 7BL.

Brennan, Martin John, LLB, CPLS. Solicitor since 1984; b. 27.11.57, London; m., Clare; 2s. Educ. St Patrick's College, Armagh; Queen's University, Belfast. Special interest in immigration Law. Recreations: rowing, Past Chairman, Irish amateur rowing union, Ulster branch. Address: (b.) 117 University Street, Belfast; T.-028 90233477.
e-mail: martinbrennan@dnet.co.uk

Brett, Sir Charles (Edward Bainbridge), Kt, CBE, MA. Consultant, L'Estrange & Brett, Solicitors, Belfast, 1994-98 (Partner, 1954 - 94); Vice-Chairman, Arts Council of Northern Ireland 1994 -98; President, Ulster Architectural Heritage Society since 1979; b. 30.10.28; m., Joyce Patricia Worley; 3s. Educ. Rugby School; New College, Oxford. Journalist, Radiodiffusion Française, Continental Daily Mail, 1949 - 50; Solicitor, 1953. Member: Child Welfare Council of Northern Ireland, 1958 - 61; Northern Ireland Committee, National Trust, 1956 - 83 and 1985 - 93; Board, Arts Council, Northern Ireland, 1970 - 76 and 1994-99; Chairman: Northern Ireland Labour Party, 1962; Ulster Architectural Heritage Society, 1968 - 78; HEARTH Housing Association, 1978 and 1985-2000; Chairman, Northern Ireland Housing Executive, 1979 - 84; Chairman, International Fund for Ireland, 1986 - 89; Board Member, Irish Architectural Archive, Dublin, 1985 - 88. Hon. Member, Royal Society of Ulster

Architects, 1973; Hon. MRIAI, 1988; Hon. FRIBA, 1987. Hon. LLD, Queen's University, Belfast, 1989. Publications: Buildings of Belfast 1700 - 1914, 1967 and 1985; Court Houses and Market Houses of Ulster, 1973; Long Shadows Cast Before, 1978; Housing A Divided Community, 1986; Buildings of County Antrim, 1996; Buildings of County Armagh, 1999; Buildings of North County Down, 2002; Five Big Houses of Cushendun, 1997; Handbook to a Hypothetical City (as Albert Rechts), 1986; lists and surveys for Ulster Architectural Heritage Society, National Trusts of Jersey and Guernsey, Alderney Society. Address: Waterside, 13 Shore Road, Greenisland, Co. Antrim BT38 8UA.

Brewer, Professor John David, BA, MSSc, FRSA. Professor of Sociology, Queen's University of Belfast, since 1991, Head of School of Sociology and Social Policy, 1993-2002, Director of the Centre for the Social Study of Religion, 1999-2002; b. 15.9.51, Ludlow, Shropshire; divorced; 1 s.; 1 d. Educ. Lacon Childe's School, Cleobury Mortimer, Shropshire; Nottingham University; Birmingham University. Lecturer in Sociology: University of Natal, 1977 - 80, University of East Anglia, 1980 - 81, Queen's University of Belfast, 1981 - 91; Visiting Fellow, Yale University, 1989; Visiting Fellow, St. John's College, Oxford, 1992; Visiting Fellow, Corpus Christi College, Cambridge, 2002-03; Martin Weiner Distinguished Lecturer, 2000, Brendeis University, USA. Publications: Mosley's Men: The BUF in the West Midlands, 1984; After Soweto: An Unfinished Journey, 1987; The Police, Public Order and the State (Co-Author), 1988; Can South Africa Survive? (Editor), 1989; The Royal Irish Constabulary: An Oral History, 1990; Inside the RUC: Routine Policing in a Divided Society, 1991; Black and Blue: Policing in South Africa, 1994; Restructuring South Africa (Editor), 1994; The Police, Public Order and the State (2nd Edition) (Co-Author), 1996; Crime in Ireland 1945-95: Here Be Dragons (Co-Author), 1997; Anti-Catholicism in Northern Ireland 1600–1998: The Mote and the Beam, 2000; Ethnography, 2000. Recreations: classical music; theatre; books; fine art; hill-walking; swimming; cricket; squash; travel; his children. Address: (b.) School of Sociology and Social Policy, Queen's University of Belfast, Belfast BT7 1NN; T.-02890 273129.

Briggs, Richard Peter, BSc (Hons), PhD, CBiol, FIBiol, FLS. Principal Scientific Officer and Programme Leader, Aquatic Systems Group, DARD (NI) and Honorary Lecturer, Queen's University Belfast, since 1992; b. 12.6.45, Slough, Bucks; m., Margaret Rose Briggs; 1 s.; 1 d. Educ. Broadlands Secondary School, Keynsham; City of Bath Technical College; Queen's University Belfast. Fisheries Scientist, DANI Fisheries Research Laboratory, Coleraine, 1975 - 92. Research into stock assessment, population dynamics and general biology of marine species. Past Chairman (1992) of NI Branch of Institute of Biology; Member of International Council for the

Exploration of the Sea Working Group for Nephrops. Publications: over 100 in scientific and popular press. Recreation: judo black belt (5th Dan) and former international. Director of Examiners and Senior Coach; President of NI Judo Federation; Executive Committee member of Commonwealth Judo Association; Director of NI Commonwealth Games Council and NI Sports Forum. Address: (b.) AFESD, Department of Agriculture and Rural Development, Newforge Lane, Belfast BT9 5PX. T.-028 7025 5503. e-mail: richard.briggs@dardni.gov.uk

Briggs, Robert Samuel, JP, DMS, I Eng, MIEE, MCMI, MIMF. Managing Director, Ecoat Ltd, Lisburn and Newtownards; m., Evelyn, 2 s. Educ. Lisburn College; University of Ulster. Engineering Apprenticeship, Short Brothers and Harland, Belfast. Vice President, Institute of Metal Finishing; Founder Member and Membership Secretary of IMF Ireland; Member of Association of JP's N. Ireland. Address: (h.) 'Tara' 12 Moira Road, Ballinderry Upper, Lisburn, Co Antrim BT28 2HQ. T.-028 9260 4798. e-mail: samec@btinternet.com

Brittain, Rosemary Jean Elizabeth, Cert Ed, MSc Ed Management. Principal, Dundonald Primary School since 1995; b. 7.2.54, Randalstown, Co Antrim; m., Edward; 1s.; 2d. Educ. Regent House Grammar School, Newtownards; Stranmillis College; University of Ulster at Jordanstown. Assistant Teacher, Glenwood Junior School, 1975 - 76; Assistant Teacher, Millisle Primary School, 1981-88; Vice Principal, Portavogie Primary School, 1988 - 1989; Principal, Portavogie Primary School, 1989 - 95. Recreations: golf; gardening; reading. Address: (b.) Dundonald Primary School, 10 Church Green, Dundonald, BT16 2LP; T.- 02890-482680.

Brodie, William Andrew, MA (Oxon), MA (QUB), PGCE, DipICT. Adviser, North Eastern Education and Library Board, since 1991; b. 17.9.55, Lisburn; m., Vanessa; 1 s.; 2 d. Educ. Bangor Grammar School; Magdalen College, Oxford. Teacher, 1978-90: The Boys' Model School, Belfast, Belfast Royal Academy, Bloomfield Collegiate. Awarded title of "Chevalier dans l'Ordre des Palmes Academiques" by French Government, 2001 for services rendered in promoting French language and culture. Recreations: church involvement; travel; music; wine. Address: (h.) 5 Ballyloughan Park, Ballymena BT43 5HW. T.-028 25643759. e-mail: billbrodieNEELB@hotmail.com

Brookborough, Viscount Alan Henry Brooke, DL. b. 30.6.52. Educ. Harrow; Millfield; Royal Agricultural College, Cirencester; m., Janet Elizabeth Cooke. Commission, 17th/21st Lancers, 1971; Transferred to Ulster Defense Regiment, 1977; Royal Irish Regiment, 1992; Lieutenant-Colonel, 1993; Hon. Colonel, 4th/5th Battalion, The Royal Irish Rangers since 1997. Executive

Director, Green Park Health Care Trust, 1993-2001; Director, Basel International (Jersey); Personal Lord in waiting to Her Majesty the Queen since 1997. Member: Select Committee on European Communities, Sub-Committee D Agriculture and Food, 1989 - 93 and 1994 - 97; Sub-Committee B since 1998; Member, All Party Defence Study Group. Vice President, Somme Association since 1990; President, Army Benevolent Fund, Northern Ireland since 1995. Deputy Lieutenant, Co Fermanagh since 1987; High Sheriff, Co Fermanagh, 1995; Elected to remain in the House of Lords, 1999; Member, Northern Ireland Policing Board, since 2001. Recreations: shooting; fishing; gardening. Address: (h.) Colebrooke, Brookeborough Enniskillen, Co Fermanagh. BT94 4DW; T.-028-89-531402.

Brown, Rev. Andrew Walton Thomas, BSc (Hons), BD. Presbyterian Minister; b. 24.4.64, Portadown; m., Lorraine; 1s.; 1d. Educ. Banbridge Academy; Reading University; Union Theological College, Belfast. Geophysical Analyst. Address: (h.) Churchtown Manse, 193 Drumnagarner Road, Kilea, Co Londonderry, BT51 5TP; T.-028 2954 0599.

Brown, Very Rev. Andrew William Godfrey, BA, BD, PhD, LittD, DD FRHistS. Minister, Ballycastle Presbyterian Church, 1963-2001; Former Moderator, General Assembly, Presbyterian Church in Ireland, 1988 - 89; b. 22.4.36, Belfast; m., Margaret Elizabeth Mary Anderson; 1s.; 2d. Educ. Royal Belfast Academical Institution; Down High School, Downpatrick; Queen's University, Belfast. Ordained, 1960. Former Convener, Overseas Board, Church and Government Committee and Convener, Board of Studies, General Assembly. Publications: numerous historical articles and contributor to several historical books. Recreations: history; walking; ornithology; railways. Address: (h.) 11, Cedar Avenue, Ballycastle, Co. Antrim BT54 6DE. T.- 028 207 62231.

Brown, Dr. John Francis, BA, PGCE, MA, PQH (NI), PhD. Principal, St. Colman's College, Newry, since 2000; b. 23.6.50, Hilltown, Ireland. Educ. St. Colman's College, Violet Hill, Newry; Queen's University, Belfast. Assistant Lecturer, Newry F. E. College, 1974-82; St. Colman's College, Newry: Assistant Teacher, 1982-94, Vice-Principal, 1994-2000. Address: (b.) St. Colman's College, Violet Hill, 46 Armagh Road, Newry, Co. Down BT35 6PP. T.-028 3026 2451. e-mail: fbrown@stcolmans.newry.ni.sch.uk

Brown, Professor Kenneth Douglas, MA, PhD, FRHistS. Queen's University, Belfast: Pro Vice Chancellor (Planning and Resources), since 2002, Professor, Economic History, since 1988, Dean, Faculty of Legal, Social and Educational Sciences, 1997-2002; b. 28.11.43, Nottingham; m., Elizabeth Beesley; 3s.; 4d. Educ. Carlton le Willows Grammar; Reading University; McMaster University; Kent University. Joined Queen's University, Belfast, 1969: Assistant Lecturer, 1969 - 70; Lecturer, 1970 - 77; Reader, 1977 - 88; Dean, Faculty of Economics, 1989 - 92. Royal Historical Society Whitfield Prize, 1977. Publications: author and editor of 8 books, including most recently a comparative economic and social history of Britain and Japan since 1900, 1998. Recreations: model soldiers; gardening; woodwork; Arsenal FC. Address: (b.) Vice Chancellor's Office, Queen's University, Belfast, Belfast, BT7 1NN.

Brown, Professor Norman MacAllan Dear, BSc, PhD, FRSC, CChem, EurChem. Professor, Chemistry, University of Ulster since 1991; b. 27.11.37, Alloa, Scotland; m., Joan Hunter Brown; 2s.; 1d. Educ. Alloa Academy, University of Strathclyde. Research Fellow, University of Glasgow, 1966 - 69; New University of Ulster: Lecturer, 1969 - 76; Senior Lecturer, 1976 - 88; Reader, 1988 - 91. Recreations: DIY; hill walking. Address: (b.) University of Ulster, Cromore Road, Coleraine, BT52 1SA; T.- 02870 324420.

Brown, Dr. Robert Adrian (Bob), BSc, PhD. b. 19.8.50, London; m., Linda R Johnston. Educ. Cranleigh School, Surrey; Queen's University, Belfast. Research Assistant, Department of Zoology, Queen's University, Belfast, 1973 - 76; Research Fellow, Royal Society European Exchange Scheme, Kristineberg, Sweden, 1977 - 78; Research Fellow, University of West Indies, Jamaica, 1978 - 80; Head Warden, National Trust's Strangford Lough Wildlife Scheme, 1981 - 91; Director, RSPB (Northern Ireland), 1991-2003. Member: Strangford Lough Management Committee, 1992-2001; Northern Ireland Bio-Diversity Group; Council for Nature Conservation and the Countryside, Rural Stakeholders' Forum, and other conservation committees; Chairman of the Board of Trustees for the Environmental Information Centre in Northern Ireland. Radio and television contributor. Publications: Strangford Lough: the Wildlife of an Irish Sea Lough, 1990; over 20 papers in biological and conservation journals; articles on wildlife in magazines and newspapers. Recreations: painting/sketching; sailing; hill walking; music; travel (especially South America and Polar Regions); country wines. Address: (h.) 4 Green Row, Castleward, Strangford, Co. Down BT30 7LR. T.-028 44 881636.

Browne, David Hugh. Belfast City Councillor; b. 10.11.58, Belfast; m., Jacqueline; 2d. Educ. Dunlambert Secondary School. Member, Belfast Education and Library Board; Grove Housing Association Chairman; Member, Police Partnership Board; Member, North Belfast Partnership Board. Recreations: fishing; target shooting; computers. Address: (h.) 202a Skegoneill Avenue, Belfast, BT15 3JW; T.- 02890-771757. e-mail: d.browne@ntlworld.com

Browne, Donald John Woodthorpe, MA, JP. b. 1.12.24, London; m., Dinah Browne; 1s.; 1d. Educ. Dulwich College; Hertford College, Oxford. Submarine Officer, RNVR, 1943 - 46; Glaxo Laboratories Ltd, 1950 - 66; Deputy Managing Director, Cerebos Agriculture Ltd, 1966 - 69; Chairman, Hays Oils and Chemicals Ltd, 1970 - 84; Retired, 1984. Lay Observer, Law Society of Northern Ireland, 1987 - 1991; Professional Conduct Committee, Law Society of Northern Ireland, 1994 - 97; Tribunal Member, Social Security Appeals, 1985 - 96; Justice of the Peace since 1975. Member, Board of Visitors, Belfast Prison, 1973 - 79; Executive Member, Northern Ireland Association for Care and Resettlement of Offenders, 1972 - 86 (Chairman, 1975 - 80). Address: (h.) 186 Newcastle Road, Seaforde, Co Down, BT30 8NZ; T.- 028 4481 1732.

Brownlees, William Victor, BA (Hons), CPFA. Clerk and Chief Executive, Armagh City and District Council, since 2001; b. 24.5.65. Educ. Ballymena Academy; Queen's University, Belfast; University of Ulster; Open University. Assistant Auditor, National Audit Office, 1988-90; Senior Accountant, Price Waterhouse, 1990-92; Principal Accountant, Reigate and Banstead Borough Council, 1992-94; Principal Accountant, CSL Managed Services, 1994-95; Head of Accounting Services, CSL Managed Services, 1995-97; Assistant Director of Social Services, East Sussex County Council, 1997-2001; Clerk, Southern Group Environmental Health Committee, since 2001. Recreations: current affairs; reading; music. Address: The Palace Demesne, Armagh BT60 4EL. T.-028 37529603.
e-mail: v.brownlees@armagh.gov.uk

Brownlow, Robert Harold, BSc, MA. Principal, Ballymena Primary School; b. 11.12.54, Ballymena; m., June Elizabeth Moynan; 2s.; 2d. Educ. University of Ulster. Teacher, Tobermore Primary School; Vice-Principal, Hezlett Primary School; Field Officer, Information Technology, North East Education and Library Board. Address: (b.) Ballymena Primary School, 101 Ballymoney Road, Ballymena, BT43 5BX; T.- 028 25656082.
e-mail: hbrownlow@ballymenaprimary.org

Bruce, Rev. David James, BSSc, BD. General Director, Scripture Union, Northern Ireland since 1992; b. 12.11.57, Banbridge, Co Down; m., Zoe Bruce; 2s.; 2d. Educ. Campbell College, Belfast; Queen's University, Belfast; Christ's College, University of Aberdeen. Travelling Secretary, Universities and Colleges Christian Fellowship, 1982 - 85; Assistant Minister, Wellington Street Presbyterian Church, Ballymena, 1985 - 87; Minister, Clontarf and Ormond Quay and Scots Church, Dublin, 1987 - 92. Address: (b.) Scripture Union, 157 Albertbridge Road, Belfast BT5 4PS; T.-028 9045 4806.

Brush, Samuel John, BEM, JP. Civil Servant; b. 2.8.42, Emyvale Co Monaghan, Ireland; m., Olive Turner (nee Williams); 1s. Educ. Royal School, Dungannon. Seriously injured in a Provisional IRA murder attempt, 1981. Served Ulster Special Constabulary, 1960 - 70; Served in Ulster Defence Regiment, 1970 - 90, achieved rank of Colour Sergeant; Served in Royal Irish Regiment, 1990 - 97, retained the rank of Colour Sergeant. Councillor, Dungannon District Council, 1981 - 93; Awarded British Empire Medal, 1981; Appointed JP, 1984; Chairman, Annahoe Credit Union Ltd since 1990; Senior Shop Steward. Recreations: hill walking; gardening. Address: (h.) 74 Main Street, Ballygawley, Dungannon, Co Tyrone, BT70 2HE; T.- 028 85568293.

Bryans, Lynda. Presenter, Live at Six/Features Reporter, Ulster Television since 1996; b. 3.5.62, Belfast; m., Michael Nesbitt (qv); 2s. Educ. Saintfield High, Ballynahinch College of Further Education. BBC Northern Ireland: Newsreader/Announcer, 1986 - 87; Presenter, Inside Ulster, 1987 - 93; BBC 1: Presenter/Reporter, Here and Now, 1994; Presenter, Animal Hospital, 1994; Presenter, Summer Holiday, 1995; Presenter, Holidays Out, 1995; Presenter, Holiday Ireland, Ulster Television, 1997. Recreations: fly fishing; fitness; family. Address: (b.) NCI Management Ltd, 51 Queen Anne Street, London W1M 0HS.

Buchanan, James McClintock Thompson. Travel and Tourism Consultant; Member, Governing Body, North West Institute of Further and Higher Education; b. 6.6.42, Londonderry; m., Jayne; 1s.; 1d. Educ. Londonderry Model; Londonderry Technical College. Lewis Travel, Londonderry, 1958 - 69; Director and General Manager, Lewis Fastravel Ltd, 1969 - 76; Managing Director, Lewis Fastravel Ltd since 1976. Member: Board of Governors, Faughan Valley High School; Education Board of Derry and Strabane Presbytery. Rotary D1160 Comms. Chair; Paul Harris Fellow, Rotary International; Fellow, Institute of Travel and Tourism. Publications: Londonderry Rotary Club, 75 Years of Service. Recreations: gardening; Rotary; computers. Address: (h.) 98a Duke Street, Londonderry; T.- 028 7134 7659.

Buchanan, Professor Ronald Hull, OBE, BA, PhD. Emeritus Professor, Queen's University, Belfast; Chairman, National Trust in Northern Ireland, 1991-2000; Member, Museums and Galleries Commission, 1995-2000; b. 18.12.31, Belfast; m., Gwendolyn (dec); 1s.; 1d.; m. (2), Rhoma. Educ. Campbell College, Belfast; Queen's University, Belfast. Assistant Lecturer, Queen's University, Belfast, 1955 - 58; Assistant Professor, Montana State University, Montana, USA, 1958 - 59; Queen's University, Belfast, Department of Geography; Lecturer, 1959 - 68; Senior Lecturer, 1968 - 78; Reader, 1978 - 81; Visiting Research Fellow, Cornell University, Ithica, New York, USA, 1968 - 69; Professor and Director, Institute of Irish Studies, Queen's University, Belfast, 1982 - 94. Member, Royal

Irish Academy. Publications: The World of Man, 1971; Man and His Habitat, 1976; Province, City and People (Co-Editor), 1987. Recreations: gardening; walking; sailing. Address: (b.) Compass Hill House, 47 Castle Street, Strangford, Co Down, BT30 7NF; T.- 028 4488 1218.

Buchanan, Rev. William Thomas. Superintendent, Newtownabbey Methodist Mission, 1982 - 2000; b. 26.11.34, Enniskillen; m., Joan; 1s.; 1d. Educ. Portora Royal School; Edgehill Theological College. Greencastle Methodist Church, 1959 - 67; Adare Methodist Church, Co Limerick, 1967 - 70; Ballinamallard Methodist Church, Co Fermanagh, 1970 - 76; Glenburn Methodist Church, Belfast, 1976 - 82. President, Methodist Church in Ireland, 1990 - 91; retired, June 2000. Regular contributor to Thought For The Day, BBC Radio Ulster. Recreations: golf; walking. Address: Fuchsia Cottage, 6 Old Forge Avenue, Newtownards, BT23 8GG.

Bunting, Frank, BA. Northern Secretary, Irish National Teachers Organisation since 1991; b. 19.3.50, Belfast; m., Mary; 3s.; 1d. Educ. St Mary's Christian Brothers School, Belfast; Queen's University, Belfast. Teacher, La Salle Secondary School, Belfast, 1973 - 76; Training and Education Officer, Irish Congress of Trade Unions, 1976 - 91. Chair, Northern Ireland Teachers Council since 1997; Member, Invest Northern Ireland Board, 2000. Recreations: music; reading. Address: (b.) INTO, 23 College Gardens, Belfast, BT9 6BS; T.- 02890 381455.

Burke, Rev. Gareth Norman, BA, DipTh. Minister, Stranmillis Evangelical Presbyterian Church, since 2000; b. 10.11.58, Belfast; m., 2s.; 2d. Educ. Methodist College, Belfast; Queen's University Belfast; Free Church of Scotland College, Edinburgh. Somerton Road Evangelical Presbyterian Church, 1984 - 89; Knock Evangelical Presbyterian Church, 1989-2000. Address: (b.) Stranmillis Evangelical Presbyterian Church, 36 Stranmillis Road, Belfast BT9 5AA.

Burke, Professor Philip George, CBE, BSc, PhD, Hon. DSc Exeter and Queen's University, Belfast, FInstP, FAPS, MRIA, FRS. Emeritus Professor of Mathematical Physics, Queen's University, Belfast since 1998, b., 18.10.32, London; m., Valerie Mona Martin; 4d. Educ. Wanstead County High School, London; University College of the South West of England, Exeter; University College, London. Post Doctoral Research Fellow, University College, London, 1956 - 57; Assistant Lecturer, University of London, 1957 - 59; Research Physicist, Lawrence Radiation Laboratory, Berkeley, USA, 1959 - 62; Research Fellow and then Senior Principal Scientific Officer, AERE Harwell, 1962 - 67; Professor of Mathematical Physics, Queen's University, Belfast, 1967 - 98; Head, Theory and Computational Science Division, Daresbury Lab, England, (joint appointment with Queen's University, Belfast), 1977 - 82; Fellow, University

College London, 1986. CBE, 1993, for services to Science. Guthrie Medal and Prize, Institute of Physics, 1994; David Bates Prize, Institute of Physics, 2001. Publications: over 350 research papers and seven books. Recreations: walking; reading; listening to music. Address: (b.) Department of Applied Mathematics and Theoretical Physics, Queen's University, Belfast, BT7 1NN; T.- 02890-335047. e-mail: p.burke@qub.ac.uk

Burns, Alexander, DA(Edin), FRIBA, MRSUA. Retired Architect; m., Flora (dec.); 2d. Educ. Annadale Grammar School; Edinburgh College of Art. Registered with Architect's Registration Board, 1960; Associate of Royal Institute of British Architects, 1960; Architect, Mountford Piggot and Partners, London, 1960 - 62; Architect, G R Smyth Architects, 1962 - 64; Architect, Houston and Beaumont, Belfast, 1964 - 70; Fellow, Royal Institute of British Architects, 1969; Senior Lecturer, Ulster Polytechnic, 1974; Principal Lecturer, Ulster Polytechnic, 1978; Senior Lecturer, University of Ulster, 1984; Course Director, University of Ulster, 1987-2000. Invited to be Fellow RSA, 1992. Charles Lanyon Memorial Prize, Junior, 1955; Senior, 1966. Publications: design guide on shop fronts. Buildings designed and built include churches, ecclesiastical regalia, banks, houses, shops, furniture and industrial buildings; regular contributor to architectural magazines. Recreations: quality music; high quality design and humour. Address: (h.) 66 Old Manse Road, Jordanstown, Newtownabbey, BT37 0RX; T.- 02890 864290. e-mail: alexburns@tiscali.co.uk

Burns, Professor Duncan Thorburn, BSc, MA, PhD, DSc, HonMPSNI, FICI, CChem, Eur Chem, FRSC, MRIA, FRS Edin. Professor Emeritus of Analytical Chemistry, Queen's University, Belfast; b. 31.5.34, Wolverhampton, England; m., Celia Mary. Educ. Whitcliffe Mount School; University of Leeds. Assistant Lecturer, Physical Chemistry, Medway College of Technology, 1958 - 59; Lecturer, Physical Chemistry, Medway College of Technology, 1959 - 63; Senior Lecturer, Analytical Chemistry, Woolwich Polytechnic, 1963 - 66; Senior Lecturer, Analytical Chemistry, Loughborough University, 1966 - 71; Reader in Analytical Chemistry, Loughborough University, 1971 - 75; Professor of Analytical Chemistry, Queen's University, 1975-99. James Taylor Prize, Sheffield Metallurgical and Engineering Society, 1970; Theophilus Redwood Lectureship, Royal Society of Chemistry, 1982; Royal Society of Chemistry, Sponsored Award and Medal, Analytical Reagents and Reactions,1982; Lavoisier Medal, post Euroanalysis VI (Paris) (GAMS), 1987; Boyle-Higgins Gold Medal, Institute of Chemistry of Ireland, 1990; AnalaR Gold Medal and Lectureship, Royal Society of Chemistry/BDH, 1990; Ehren Nadel in Gold, Analytical Institute, Technical University of Vienna, 1990; The 20th SAC Gold Medal, Royal Society of Chemistry, 1993; The Fritz Pregl Medal,

Austrian Society of Analytical Chemistry within the Austrian Chemical Society, 1993; Royal Society of Chemistry Sponsored Award and Medal, Tertiary Chemical Education, 1995; Robert Boyle Gold Pin, Analytical Division, Royal Society of Chemistry, 1996; Sigillium Magnum Universitatis medal, diploma and gold pin, University of Bologna, 1996; Long Service Award, Royal Society of Chemistry, 1998; Sigillum Medal, post Euro analysis, University of Lisbon, 2000. Chairman Commission V/1 International Union of Pure and Applied Chemistry, 1987 - 89; Titular Member, CTC, since 2000; President, Analytical Division, Royal Society of Chemistry, 1988 - 90. Publications: 7 books; over 350 published papers. Recreations: history of chemistry. Address: (b.) Department of Chemistry, Queen's University, Belfast, Belfast, BT9 5AG; T.- 028 90 668567.

Burns, Michael Robin, LLB (Hons), CPLS. Partner, Russells Solicitors, Belfast; m., Anne Humphries. Educ. The Methodist College, Belfast; Queen's University, Belfast. Cleaver Fulton and Rankin, Solicitors: Pupil Solicitor, 1988 - 89; Assistant Solicitor, 1989 - 95; Associate Solicitor, 1995 - 97; Mills Selig: Associate Partner, 1997 - 99; Partner, 2000-02. Part-time Tutor in Conveyancing, Institute of Professional Legal Studies since 1996; Director, Abbeyfield (Lisburn) Society Ltd since 1996; Member, Environmental and Planning Law Association of Northern Ireland, Secretary, 1999-2000; Vice President, Ulster Reform Club, 2002-03. Recreations: church; reading; walking; jazz; eating out. Address: (b.) Russells the Solicitors, 11 Lower Mary Street, Newtownards, County Down BT23 4JJ. T.-028 9181 4444.

Burns, William, MBE, BA. Freelance Writer and Adjudicator; b. 13.6.41, Larne. Educ. Larne Grammar School; Queen's University, Belfast. Assistant Teacher, Linn Primary School, 1963 - 75; Principal, Olderfleet Primary School, 1975 - 99. Member, Guild of Drama Adjudicators, since 1978; freelance BBC schools script writer; Vice President, Association of Ulster Drama Festivals. Recreation: theatre. Address: (h.) 27 Mill Road, Inver, Larne, Co. Antrim BT40 3BX; T.-028 2827 2840.

Burnside, David W. B., BA, CSM (NI). Ulster Unionist Member of Parliament for South Antrim, since 2001; Chairman, New Century Holdings Ltd since 1995; b. 24.8.51, Ballymoney. Educ. Coleraine Academical Institution; Queen's University, Belfast. Press Officer, Vanguard Unionist Party, 1974 - 78; Public Relations Director, Institute of Directors, 1979 - 84; Public Affairs Director, British Airways, 1983 - 93; Chairman, DBA Ltd since 1993. Director, Northern Ireland Tourist Board, 1990 - 93; Director, Unionist Information Office, GB since 1996. Address: The Hill, Secon, Ballymoney, County Antrim, Northern Ireland BT53 6QB.

Bury, Lady Mairi Elizabeth, JP. Farmer and Estate Owner; b. 25.3.21, Mount Stewart, Newtownards; m., Lt Col. Viscount Bury (dec.) 2d. Educ. privately. Patron, British Red Cross Society, Northern Ireland; Former President and Chairman, Ards Women's Unionist Association, Northern Ireland; Liveryman, Worshipful Company of Air Pilots and Air Navigators; Fellow, Royal Philatelic Society, London. Recreations: philately. Address: (h.) Mount Stewart, Newtownards, Co Down, BT22 2AD; T.- 028 42788217.

Butler, Maurice Richard, LLB. Managing partner, Johns Elliot, Solicitors since 1997; b. 18.2.43, Belfast; m., Margaret Cuffe-Smith; 2d. Educ. Bangor Grammar School, Queen's University, Belfast. Admitted as Partner, Johns Elliot, 1970. Solicitors Disciplinary Tribunal, (Member 1986, President, 1999); Deputy County Court Judge, 1990; Member, Northern Ireland Regional Council, Abbeyfield Society and Abbeyfield (NI) Development Society Ltd. Former Lecturer and Member: Board of Examiners, Law Society of Northern Ireland; Institute of Professional Legal Studies. Former Member: North Down Borough Council; South Eastern Education and Libraries Board; Member, Executive Committee, NI Council of Royal Yachting Association. Recreation: sailing. Address: (b.) Johns Elliot, 40 Linenhall Street, Belfast BT2 8BA. T.- 028 9032-6881.

Byrne, Joe. Member (West Tyrone), Social Democratic and Labour Party, Northern Ireland Assembly, 1998-2003; Vice-Chairman, Social Democratic and Labour Party. Educ. Queen's University, Belfast. College Lecturer; elected to Omagh District Council, 1993 (Chairman); Member, Northern Ireland Forum. Address: (b.) 121 Ormeau Road BT7 1SH; T.- 02890-247700.

C

Caledon, 7th Earl of (Nicholas James Alexander). Lord-Lieutenant, Co Armagh since 1989; b. 6.5.55. Educ. Gordonstoun. Recreations: skiing; tennis; swimming; photography; travel. Address: Caledon Castle, Caledon, Co. Tyrone.

Calvin, Ray, BA, MSc, Cert Ed. General Secretary, Ulster Teachers' Union since 1998; b. 25.9.44, Coleraine; m., Margaret; 1s.; 1d. Educ. Bushmills Grammar School; Stranmillis College; Open University; University of Ulster. Police Constable, 1964 - 66; Full time official, Ulster Teachers' Union, 1971 - 97. Publications: various in-house publications for union; contributor to a sailing magazine. Recreations: sailing; reading; travel. Address: (b.) Ulster Teachers' Union, 94 Malone Road, Belfast, BT9 5HP; T.- 028 9066 2216.

Cameron, Ewen Grant. Editor, The Chronicle, Coleraine; b. 24.11.59, Coleraine; m., Rhonda; 3s.; 2d. Educ. Coleraine Academical Institution. Ulster Television Ltd; The Chronicle, Coleraine; Londonderry Sentinel; Coleraine Tribune; Northern Constitution. Broadcaster, BBC Radio Ulster. Publications: Coleraine FC - A History. Address: (b.) The Chronicle, 20-22 Railway Road, Coleraine, Co Derry, BT52 1PD; T.-028 7034 3344.

Campbell, Professor Bruce M. S., BA, PhD, FRHS, MRIA. Professor, Medieval Economic History, Queen's University, Belfast since 1995 b. 11.6.49, Rickmansworth, Herts. Educ. Durrants Secondary School; Rickmansworth Grammar School; University of Liverpool; Darwin College, Cambridge. Queen's University, Belfast: Lecturer, Geography, 1973 - 89; Lecturer and Reader, Economic and Social History, 1992 - 95. Scholar in residence, Centre for East Anglian Studies, University of East Anglia, 1985. Arthur H Cole Prize, Economic History Association, 1984; Proxime accessit Whitfield Prize for British History, 2000; Member of the Scientific Committee of the Datini Institute, Prato, Italy. Publications: numerous articles on Medieval agriculture and economy, including Agrarian Production and its Distribution in the London Region c 1300 (joint author), 1993; English Seigniorial Agriculture, 1250 - 1450, 2000. Recreations: grooming the dog; gardening; opera; travel. Address: (b.) School of Geography, Queen's University, Belfast, Belfast, BT7 1NN; T.- 028 9027 3345. e-mail: b.m.campbell@qub.ac.uk

Campbell, David Alan, BA, ACII. Director, Marsh Ltd; b. 8.11.53, Belfast. Educ. Royal Belfast Academical Institution; University of Ulster. Associated British Foods Plc, 1975 - 76; Joined Marsh UK Ltd, 1976. Past President, Belfast Insurance Institute. Recreations: tennis;

theatre; music; soccer. Address: (b.) Bedford House, Bedford Street, Belfast, BT2 7DX; T.-028 9055 6100.

Campbell, Derek, MA, BEd. Principal of Carrickfergus College, since 2001; b. 27.12.53, Dungannon; m., Sandra Weglarz; 1 s.; 1 d. Educ. Royal School, Dungannon; Dungannon Secondary; Stranmillis College; University of Ulster. Teacher of Physical Education, Ballymena Boys Secondary, 1976-78; Teacher of Physical Education and Geography, Ballee High School, 1978-82; Glengormley High School: Head of Physical Education Department, 1978-90, Vice Principal, 1990-2001. Recreation: outdoor pursuits. Address: (b.) Carrickfergus College, 110 North Road, Carrickfergus, Co. Antrim BT38 7QX. T.-028 93362347. email: info@carrickcollege.carrickfergus.ni.sch.uk

Campbell, Prof. Frederick Charles, MB, ChB, FRCS, MD (Hons). Professor of Surgery at Queen's University Belfast, since 2000; b. 6.11.51; m., Miss Eilish O'Connor; 2 s. Educ. Glasgow University. University of Dundee: Lecturer in Surgery, 1984-88, Senior Lecturer in Surgery, 1988-94, Reader in Surgery, 1994-96, Wellcome Fellow, Dept. of Biochemical Medicine, 1993-95; Professor of Gastroenterological Surgery, University of Newcastle upon Tyne, 1996-99. Publication: Small Bowel Enterocyte Culture and Transplantation, 1994. Recreation: reading. Address: (b.) Department of Surgery, Queen's University of Belfast, Institute of Clinical Science, Grosvenor Road, Belfast, Northern Ireland. T.-028 90635019.

Campbell, Gregory Lloyd. Elected MP, June 2001; Member (East Londonderry), Democratic Unionist Party, Northern Ireland Assembly, since 1998; Leader, Democratic Unionist Group, City Council of Londonderry; b. 15.2.53, Londonderry; m., Elizabeth Frances; 1s.; 3d. Educ. Londonderry Technical College. Civil Servant, 1973 - 82; Member, Northern Ireland Assembly, 1982 - 86; Civil Servant, 1986 - 93; Self employed since 1993. Negotiator, All Party Talks, 1991 - 92 and 1996 - 98; Democratic Unionist Party Security Spokesperson since 1994; Fair Employment Spokesperson, 1981 - 94; Regional Development Minister, NI Assembly, 2000-2001. Publications: Discrimination - The Truth, 1987; Discrimination - Where Now?, 1993; Ulster's Verdict on the Joint Declaration, 1994; Working Towards 2000, 1998. Recreations: reading; soccer; music. Address: (b.) Constituency Office, 25 Bushmills Road, Coleraine, BT52 2BP; T.- 02870 327 327; (b.) 14 Main Street, Limavady BT49 0EU; T.-028777 66060; Fax: 028777 69531. e-mail: colerainehq@dup.org.uk

Campbell, Henrietta, CB, MD, FFPH. Chief Medical Officer, Dept. of Health, Social Services and Public Safety, since 1994; b. 2.11.48, Kilkeel, Co. Down; m., Rev. W. M. Campbell; 1 s.; 2 d. Educ. Kilkeel High School; Queen's University

Belfast. General Practitioner, 1974-83; Senior Medical Officer, DHSS, 1983-94. Awarded CB in Jan. 2000; Hon. Fellow, Royal College GPs; Royal College of Physicians Ireland; Royal College of Physicians and Surgeons, Glasgow. Recreations: gardening; arts and crafts. Address: (b.) Castle Buildings, Upper Newtownards Road, Belfast BT4 3SQ. T.-02890 520563.

Campbell, Jennifer Ann, BPhil, MEd. Principal, D H Christie Memorial Primary School, Coleraine; b. 1.1.53, Ballyrashane, Coleraine; m., William James Campbell; 1s.; 2d.(dec.) Educ. Coleraine High School; Bingley College of Education, Yorkshire. Teacher, Drumard Primary School, Tamlaght O'Crilly, 1974; Principal, Eden (Ballymoney) Primary School, 1983 - 93; Principal, Knockahollet Primary School, Loughgiel, 1993-2002. Part-time student, 1986 - 94. Presently studying for MBA (International School Leadership), Univ. of Hull P-T. Founder Member, North Ulster Small Schools Association, 1983; Member, Working Party for Religious Education, 1991 and RE Review Group, 2002. Publications: What are School Inspectors Looking For in Primary Schools?, 1992; Support for Rural Education in the North Eastern Board: An Investigation into Clustering as a Means of Survival, 1994; 'Lift Off' Human Rights Education sponsored by Amnesty International; a cross border initiative, 2002. Recreations: theatre goer; home computing; reading and travel. Address: (h.) 4 Castlewood Avenue, Coleraine, Co Londonderry BT52 1JR; T.- 028 7035 4889. e-mail: lisnamac@btinternet.com

Campbell, Commander Peter Colin Drummond, LVO, OBE, DL. b. 24.10.27, Ballycastle, Co Antrim; m., Lady Moyra Campbell CVO; 2s. Educ. Cheltenham College. Royal Navy: Commanded H M Ships, Floriston; Shavington; Eastbourne; Equerry to Her Majesty The Queen, 1957 - 60; Director, Belfast Steamship Company and Anglo Irish Transport, 1967 - 75; Northern Ireland Director, Abbey National Building Society, 1983 - 89; Representative in Ireland, The Irish Society, 1974 - 95. Freeman, City of London, 1975; High Sheriff, Co Antrim, 1985; Life Vice-Pres., Royal Naval Assoc. Address: (h.) Hollybrook House, Randalstown, Co Antrim, BT41 2PB; T.- 02894 472224.

Campbell, Peter Gerard, BBS. Solicitor; b. 22.2.61, Derry; m., Clare; 1s.; 3d. Educ. Trinity College, Dublin. Qualified, 1988; Solicitor, Campbell Fitzpatrick. Chairman, Belfast Solicitors Association. Recreations: family; cycling; skiing; golf. Address: (b) 51 Adelaide Street, Belfast. T.-028 9032 7388. e-mail: peter@campbell.fitzpatrick.co.uk

Campbell, Robert David Stewart, BAgr. Chief of Staff to the First Minister of Northern Ireland since 1998; Managing Director, The Somme Association Ltd, 1990 - 98; b. 25.5.65, Belfast; m., Linda Wilson; 2s. Educ. Wallace High School,

Lisburn; Queen's University, Belfast. Part-time Farmer. Member, Ulster Unionist Council, since 1983; Ulster Unionist Councillor, Lisburn Borough Council, 1989 - 93; Member, Northern Ireland Forum (Lagan Valley), 1996 - 98; Member, Ulster Unionist Negotiating Team, All Party Talks, 1996 - 98. Chairman: Agricultural and Fisheries Committee, Strategic Investment Project Board, 2001-02, Maze Prison Consultative Panel, since 2003, Aberdeen Angus Quality Beef Limited, 1998-2002. Recreations: shooting; breeding pedigree Aberdeen Angus cattle. Address: (b.) Parliament Buildings, Stormont, Belfast, BT4 3JN.

Campbell, Rev. Dr. Samuel James, BA, MDiv, DipEd. Minister, Cooke Centenary Presbyterian Church; b. 11.9.38, Belfast; m., Ruth Gill; 3s.; 1d. Educ. Royal Belfast Academical Institution; Queen's University, Belfast; Princeton Theological Seminary, USA. Teacher, Kelvin Secondary School, Belfast; Assistant Minister, Great Victoria Street Presbyterian Church, Belfast; Chaplain, Livingstonia Secondary School, Malawi; Senior Lecturer, Zomba United Theological College, Malawi; Hon. Lecturer, Department of Religious Studies, University of Malawi. Currently Hon. Secretary, Churches' Council for Health and Healing in Ireland since 1991; Convener, Overseas Board, Presbyterian Church in Ireland, 1993-2000; Member, Irish Council of Churches since 1987; Chair, Board of Overseas Affairs, Irish Council of Churches, since 2003; Trustee, Christian Aid, London, 1995-2002. Recreations: hill walking; golf. Address: (h.) 15 Park Road, Belfast, BT7 2FW.

Campbell, Dr. Trefor, CBE. Managing Director, Moy Park Limited, since 1983; b. 18.9.43, Ballymena; m., Maureen; 1 s.; 1 d. Joined Moy Park's former holding company, Moygashel Limited, 1960. Fellow of the Royal Agricultural Societies; Fellow of the Royal Society for the Encouragement of Arts, Manufacturers & Commerce; Honorary Vice President of the Institute of Food Science and Technology; Board Director, InterTradeIreland; Board Member of Centre for Competitiveness; Director of British Poultry Council; Trustee, Northern Ireland Food and Drink Association, Educational Trust Fund; Trustee of the Northern Ireland Assembly and Business Trust; Member of Education and Training Affairs Committee of the CBI; awarded OBE for services to the food industry; awarded the CBE in 2000; Honorary Doctorate from Queen's University Belfast; Chairman, Northern Ireland Food and Drink Association, 1996-98. Recreations: horses; classic cars; motor racing/sports. Address: (b.) Moy Park Limited, 39 Seagoe Industrial Estate, Craigavon BT63 5QE. T.-02838 368004.

Campbell, Rt. Hon. Sir (William) Anthony, Rt. Hon Lord Justice Campbell. Lord Justice of Appeal, Supreme Court of Judicature of Northern Ireland, 1998; b. 30.10.36. Educ. Campbell College, Belfast; Queens' College, Cambridge.

Called to the Bar (Gray's Inn), 1960; Called to the Bar of Northern Ireland, 1960; QC (NI), 1974; Senior Crown Counsel in Northern Ireland, 1984 - 88; Judge of the High Court, 1988 - 98. Chairman, Council of Legal Education in Northern Ireland since 1994; Chairman, Judicial Studies Board, NI, since 1995. Address: (b.) Royal Courts of Justice, I Chichester Street, Belfast, BT1 3JY.

Canning, Professor David James, BA (QUB), PhD (Cantab). Professor, Economics, Queen's University Belfast since 1993; b., 16.3.58, Strabane; m., Hye Sun; 1s.; 1d. Educ. The Academy, Omagh; Queen's University, Belfast; Cambridge University. Fellow, Pembroke College, Cambridge, 1984 - 87; Jean Monnet Fellow, European University Institute, 1987 - 88; Lecturer, LSE, 1988 - 89; Lecturer, Cambridge University, 1989 - 91; Associate Professor, Columbia University, 1991 - 93. Visiting Professor, Harvard University, 1997 - 99. Address: (b.) School of Management and Economics, Queen's University Belfast, Belfast, BT7 1NN.
e-mail: d.canning@qub.ac.uk

Capper, Derek, Cert Ed, BA. Principal, Anahilt Primary School since 1984; b. 14.4.49, Belfast; m., Elizabeth; 1s.; 1d. Educ. Royal Belfast Academical Institute; Stranmillis College; Open University. Assistant Teacher, Downey House, 1970 - 75; Crawfordsburn Primary School: Vice-Principal, 1975 - 78; Principal, 1978 - 84. Reader, Diocese of Down and Dromore (C of I). Scout Movement (NI): Scout Leader, 1970 - 77; Assistant District Commissioner, 1973 - 77; District Commissioner, 1977 - 84; Assistant Chief Commissioner, 1984 - 87; County Commissioner, 1987 - 94; Chairman, National Beaver Scout Advisory Board, 1992 - 95; Member, Committee of Council, UK Scout Movement, 1993 - 96 and 1996-99; Chairman, Programme and Training Sub-Committee UK, 1996 - 99; Youthnet Executive, 2000-03; Member, NI Youth Council, 2003-06; Treasurer, Youthnet, 2003-06. Publications: Challenge and Adventure. Recreations: fishing. Address: (b.) Anahilt Primary School, 248 Ballynaninch Road, Hillsborough BT26 6BP; T.-028 9263 8557.

Caraher, Professor Brian Gregory, BA, MA, PhD. Professor of Literature, School of English, Queen's University, Belfast since 1993; Head, Graduate Teaching and Research; b. 17.2.51, Indianapolis, Indiana, USA; m., Elizabeth Anne (Lizanne) Dowds; 2s. Educ. Brebeuf Preparatory School, Indiana; Wabash College; SUNY at Buffalo. Assistant Professor, Eastern Illinois University, 1980 - 82; Assistant and Associate Professor, Indiana University, 1982 - 93; Fulbright Senior Lecturer, Aarhus University, Denmark, 1992 - 93. Postdoctoral Fellow: Northwestern University, Chicago, USA, 1981; Vanderbilt University, Nashville Tennessee, USA, 1984. Publications include: Wordsworth's 'Slumber' And The Problematics of Reading, 1991; Intimate Conflict: Contradiction in Literary and

Philosophical Discourse, 1992; Trespassing Tragedy, 2004. Recreations: walking; hill and mountain walking; baseball; cinema; reading. Address: (h.) 125 Upper Malone Road, Belfast BT9 6UF. T.-028 90 96 31 76.

Cardwell, Alan A. C., BSc (Hons), CEng, MICE, MCIPS. Chief Executive, Carrickfergus Borough Council, since 1999. Educ. Annadale Grammar School; Queen's University, Belfast. Northern Ireland Civil Service, 1972-99. Address: (b.) Town Hall, Carrickfergus, Co. Antrim BT38 7DL. T.-028 9335 1604.

Carlisle, David Wilson Hugh, BSc (Hons), Master Mariner. Regional Principal Nautical Surveyor, Maritime and Coastguard Agency, Northern Ireland; b. 22.10.52, Belfast; m., Jacqueline; 1s.; 1d. Educ. Royal Belfast Academical Institution; John Moore's University and Nautical College, Liverpool. Fifteen years at sea with BP, Mobil and CP Ships, rising to Chief Officer; Accounts Manager, United States Lines; Marine Consultant and Surveyor, Houston, Texas and Liverpool; Marine Surveyor, Maritime and Coastguard Agency since 1992. Recreations: squash; swimming; sailing. Address: (b.) Maritime and Coastguard Agency, Marine Office, Quay Street, Bangor BT20 5ED. T.-028-91-475310.

Carlisle, Tania Elizabeth, BA (Hons). Learning and Performance Manager, Arts & Business NI, Northern Ireland, since 2001; b. 25.2.74, Belfast; m., Robert Jonathan Carlisle. Educ. Sullivan Upper School; University of Kent at Canterbury; Trinity College, Dublin. Graduate Management Development Programme, 1996 - 97; Administrator, Kabosh Productions Ltd, 1997-99. Northern Ireland Representative, Independent Theatre Council, 1997-99. Recreations: camping; cooking; complimentary medicine. Address: (b.) Arts & Business, 53 Malone Road, Belfast BT9 6RY. T.-028 9066 4736.

Carragher, Anna, BA. Controller, BBC Northern Ireland since 2000; b. 9.7.48, Belfast; m., Alain Le Garsmeur; 2s.; 1d. Educ. St Dominic's High School, Belfast; Queen's University, Belfast. Studio Manager, 1970 - 74; Producer, Today, Radio 4, 1974 - 83; Producer, Breakfast Time, 1983 - 84; Producer, Newsnight, 1984 - 85; Producer, Question Time, 1985 - 89; Producer, Any Questions, Any Answers, 1989 - 92; Editor, Election Call, 1992 - 95; Head of Programmes, BBC Northern Ireland, 1995 - 97, Head of Broadcast, 1997-2000. Sony Award, 1994. Recreations: theatre; hill walking; opera. Address: (b.) BBC Northern Ireland, Ormeau Road, Belfast BT2 8HQ; T.-028 9033 8200.

Carrick, William Mervyn. Member (Upper Bann), Democratic Unionist Party, Northern Ireland Assembly, since 1998; Alderman, Deputy Mayor, Craigavon, 1997 - 98; Mayor, 1998 - 99; b. 13.2.46, Portadown; m., Ruth; 3s.; 1d. Educ.

Portadown Technical College. Elected Local Government Representative, 1990-2001; Director Portadown 2000, 1990-2001; Elected Member, Northern Ireland Forum for Political Dialogue, 1996-98. Address: (h.) 72 Dungannon Road, Portadown, Co Armagh; T.-028 38 336392.

Carson, Ciaran Gerard, BA. Writer and Poet. b. 9.10.48, Belfast; m., Deirdre; 2 s.; 1 d. Educ. St. Mary's Christian Brothers' School; Queen's University Belfast. Literary and Traditional Arts Officer, Arts Council of Northern Ireland, 1975-98; Gregory Award, 1976; Alice Hunt Bartlett Award, 1988; Irish Times/Aer Lingus Award, 1990; T S Eliot Prize for Poetry, 1993. Publications include: First Language, 1993; Opera Et Etcetera, 1996; The Irish For No, 1987; Belfast Confetti, 1989; The Star Factory, 1997; Shamrock Tea, 2001. Recreations: playing traditional music.

Carson, Professor David James, PhD. MBA, FCIM, FAM. Professor of Marketing, University of Ulster, since 1992; b. 11.4.47, Belfast; m., Lynn. Educ. Queen's University of Belfast; University College, Dublin. Editor, European Journal of Marketing; Vice President, Academy of Marketing; Member, Academic Senate, and Board, Chartered Institute of Marketing; Reviewer and Review Board Member, several international journals; External Examiner, numerous universities, UK, Ireland and Australia; Visiting Professor: University of Auckland, 1995; Monash Business School, Melbourne, 1996 and 2000; Queensland University of Technology, Brisbane, 1996; University of Southern Queensland, 1998; has held wide variety of consultancy posts with independent enterprises; long-term Advisor: Disney Corporation, Florida, and Stena Line Ferry Company. Publications: over 100 academic publications. Recreations: sailing; pub conversation. Address: School of Marketing, Entrepreneurship and Strategy, University of Ulster at Jordanstown, Shore Road, Newtonabbey, Co. Antrim BT37 0QB.

Carson (Margaret) Joan. Member (Fermanagh and South Tyrone), UUP, Northern Ireland Assembly, since 1998; Member, South Tyrone and Dungannon Borough Council, 1997-2001; b. . 29.1.35, Enniskillen; m., James; 2 s.; 1 d. Educ. Girls' Collegiate School, Enniskillen; Stranmillis College, Belfast. Teacher: Enniskillen Model Primary School, 1956 - 62, Granville Primary School, Dungannon, 1972 - 79, Dungannon Primary School, 1979 - 82; Principal Teacher, Tamnamore Primary School, 1982 - 88. Recreations: ornithology; painting; reading. Address: 115 Moy Road, Dungannon; T.-018687 84285. e-mail: joancarsonuup@yahoo.co.uk

Carson, Norman D., FCCA. Executive Director of Finance, South and East Belfast Health and Social Services Trust since 1994; b. Belfast; m., Hazel; 1s.; 2d. Auditor/Senior Auditor, Department of Health and Social Security, Health Service Audit, 1969 - 77; Management

Accountant/Assistant Treasurer, Eastern Health and Social Services Board, 1977 - 90; Director of Finance, South and East Belfast Community Unit, 1990 - 94. Past President: Chartered Association of Certified Accountants (Irish Region); Health Service Society; Ulster District Society; Past Chairman. Northern Ireland Branch, Healthcare Financial Management Association (HFMA). Address: (b.) South and East Belfast Trust, Knockbracken Healthcare Park, Saintfield Road, Belfast, BT8 8BH; T.- 028 9056 5668.

Carswell, Rt. Hon. Sir Robert. Kt PC MA. Lord Chief Justice of Northern Ireland since 1997; b. 28.6.34, Belfast; m., Romayne Winifred Ferris OBE JP (see Romayne Winifred Carswell); 2d. Educ. Royal Belfast Academical Institution; Pembroke College, Oxford; University of Chicago Law School. Called to the Bar, Northern Ireland, 1957; Practised at the Bar, 1958 - 84; Counsel to HM Attorney General for NI, 1970 - 71; Queen's Counsel, 1971; Senior Crown Counsel in NI, 1979 - 84; Bencher, Inn of Court, Northern Ireland, 1979; Called to English Bar, Gray's Inn, 1972 (Hon. Bencher, 1993); Judge, High Court of Justice, Northern Ireland, 1984; Judge in charge of Queen's Bench Division, 1988 - 93; Set up and ran the Commercial List, 1992 - 93; Lord Justice of Appeal, 1993 - 97. Knighted 1988; Member, Privy Council, 1993; Pro-Chancellor and Chairman of Council, University of Ulster, 1984 - 94; Governor, RBAI since 1967; Chairman, Board Governors, RBAI, 1986 - 97; Chairman, Law Reform Advisory Committee for Northern Ireland, 1989 - 97; Chairman, Council of Law Reporting for Northern Ireland, 1987 - 97; Chairman, Distinction and Meritorious Service Awards Committee of DHSS, 1995 - 97; Former Member, Law Advisory Committee, British Council; Chancellor, Diocese of Armagh and Diocese of Down and Dromore, 1990 - 97; Hon. Bencher, King's Inns, Dublin, 1997. Member of Scout movement for over 60 years: Chairman, Belfast Scout Council, 1969 - 93; President, Northern Ireland Scout Council since 1993. Recreations: golf (former golf club captain), hillwalking; music; architecture; antiquities; conservation; wildlife. Address: (b.) Royal Courts of Justice, Chichester Street, Belfast, BT1 3JF. T.- 02890 724603.

Carswell, Romayne Winifred, OBE, BA, LLB, JP. Lord Lieutenant, County Borough of Belfast, since 2000; b. Belfast; m., Rt. Hon. Sir Robert Carswell (q.v.); 2d. Educ. Victoria College, Belfast; Queen's University, Belfast. Assistant Principal, Northern Ireland Civil Service, 1959 - 61; Member and Deputy Chairman, Police Complaints Board for Northern Ireland, 1977 - 94; Part-time Member, Industrial Tribunals, 1987 - 97; President, Friends of the Ulster Museum. Trustee, Ulster Historical Foundation; Governor, Victoria College, Belfast, 1979 - 99 (Vice-Chairman 1995 - 99); DL Belfast 1997-2000; C St J 2000; Trustee, Winston Churchill Memorial Trust, 2002. Recreations: hill walking; heritage; conservation; wildlife. Address: (b.) Lord Chief Justice's Office,

Royal Courts of Justice, Chichester Street, Belfast, BT1 3JF; T.- 02890 724603.

Cartin, Edward, BSc (Econ). DPM, MBA, FCA. Chief Executive, QUBIS Ltd since 1985; b. 23.6.49, Co Derry; m., Joan; 2s.; 1d. Educ. St Columb's College; Queen's University, Belfast; University of Ulster. Chartered Accountant, Price Waterhouse, 1970 - 75; Analyst, Northern Ireland Finance Corporation, 1975 - 77; Company Secretary, Keenfoods, 1982 - 85; PA Management Consultants - Manager Londonderry Enterprise Zone, 1982 - 85. Director or Secretary of a number of high technology companies associated with QUBIS Ltd. Past Committee Member: Ulster Society of Chartered Accountants; British Institute of Management; Northern Ireland Small Business Institute; Past Director: YES - Enterprise Scheme (NI) Ltd (now Prince's Trust), Northern Ireland Blood Transfusion Service; Trustee, Drake Music Project. Sir Charles Harvey Award, Irish Management Institute. Former Chairman, University Companies Association (UNICO); Fund Manager, University Challenge Fund. Publications: various papers presented on technology transfer and corporate venturing. Recreations: windsurfing; hill walking. Address: (b.) QUBIS Ltd, Lanyon North, The Queen's University of Belfast, Belfast BT7 1NN. T.-028 9068 2321.

Cartmill, David Hugh, LLB (Hons), LLM, BL, FCIArb. Barrister-at-Law since 1980; b. 27.10.56, Belfast; m., Kristina; 5s. Educ. Belfast Royal Academy; Queen's University, Belfast; University of Ulster, Jordanstown. Attorney at Law, California, 1985. Fellow of Chartered Institute of Arbitrators since 1995. Address: (b.) Bar Library, Royal Courts of Justice, Chichester Street, Belfast, BT1 3JP; T.- 028 9056 2043.

Carver, Dr. Anthony Frederick, BMUS, PhD. Senior Lecturer, Queen's University, Belfast since 1984; b. 16.11.47, Brighton; m., Margaret Janis; 2s.; 1d. Educ. Westlain Grammar School; University of Birmingham. Queen's University, Belfast; Lecturer, Department of Music, 1973 - 84; Director, School of Music, 1990 - 95. Publications: Cori Spezzati (2 vols.), 1988; Irish Church Praise, 1990. Recreations: reading; gardening; model railways; charity shops; going barefoot. Address: (b.) School of Music, Queen's University, Belfast, Belfast, BT7 1NN; T.- 028 9033 5208.

Casey, Simon Christopher, BA, CPLS. Principal, Casey and Casey Solicitors Newry; b. 15.8.57; m., Margaret Casey; 3d. Educ. Abbey Grammar School, Newry; Trinity College, Dublin; Queen's University, Belfast. Served pupillage in NIHE before opening own practice. Recreations: swimming; reading; enjoying family life. Address: (b.) 25-27 Lower Catherine Street, Newry, Co Down; T.- 028 302 66214.

Cassells, David Brian, JP. Retired Headmaster; b. Lurgan; m., Maree Cassells; 2d. Educ. Lurgan College; Stranmillis College. Vice-Principal, Dickson Primary School, Lurgan, 1974 - 79; Principal, Lurgan Model Primary School, 1979 - 83; Headmaster, King's Park Primary School, 1983-2000. Chairman, Northern Ireland Branch, Inland Waterways Association; Vice President, Inland Waterways Association of Ireland; Chairman, Craigavon Museum Services; Chairman, South Ulster Housing Association; Member of Ulster Waterways Group. Address: (h.) 2 Cherryville Park, Lurgan, Co Armagh, BT66 7BA; T.-028 3832 5329.

Cassidy, Arlene Audrey Elizabeth, BSSc, DipSocW, CQSW. Director, Parents and Professionals and Autism (PAPA) since 1997; b. 12.6.53, Belfast; 1s.; 1d. Educ. Carolan Grammar School; Queen's University, Belfast; University of Stirling. Social Worker, Eastern Health and Social Services Board, 1974 - 76 and 1977 - 80; Senior Practitioner, Barnardo's Learning Difficulty Projects, 1980 - 92; Development Officer, PAPA, 1992 - 97. Research undertaken, Assessment of Need Study, (author and co-researcher); Co-ordinator, Northern Ireland, TEACCH Evaluation, Co-editor, Northern Ireland Diagnostic Research: Autism and Keyhole Early Intervention Project for Autism. Address: (b.) PAPA Resource Centre, Donard House, Knockbracken Healthcare Park, Saintfield Road, Belfast, BT8 8BH; T.-028 90 401729.

Cassidy, Very Rev. Herbert, MA. Dean of Armagh since 1989 and Keeper of Public Library; b. 25.7.35, Cork; m., Elizabeth Ann Egerton; 1s.; 2d. Educ. Cork Grammar School; Trinity College, Dublin. Assistant Curate, Holy Trinity, Belfast, 1958 - 60; Assistant Curate, Christ Church, Londonderry, 1960- 62; Incumbent, Aghavilly and Derrynoose, Armagh, 1962 - 65; Bishop's Curate, St Columba, Portadown, 1965 - 67; Incumbent, St Columba, Portadown, 1967 - 84; Dean of Kilmore, 1984 - 89. Recreations: music; travel; reading. Address: (b.) The Library, Abbey Street, Armagh, BT61 7DY; T.- 01861-523142.

Castle Stewart, 8th Earl of, Arthur Patrick Avondale Stuart. BA, FBIM. b. 18.8.28. Educ. Brambletye; Eton; Trinity College, Cambridge. Patron, Holywood Rudolf Steiner School; Vice President and Member, Peggy Guggenheim Museum Advisory Board. Recreations: forestry; choral singing; walking. Address: (h.) Stuart Hall, Stewartstown, Co Tyrone, BT71 5AE.

Caul, Dr. Brian, BA, Dip AppSoc Stud, PhD. Senior Honorary Research Fellow, University of Ulster, since 2000. Educ. Queen's University, Belfast; University of Liverpool; Trinity College, Dublin; m. Sandra; 2d. Social Welfare Officer, Belfast, 1964 - 66; Child Care Officer and Assistant Area Children's Officer, Lancashire, 1967 - 70; Assistant to County Children's Officer, Co Antrim, 1979 - 73; Ulster Polytechnic:

Lecturer, Social Work, 1973 - 74; Senior Lecturer, Social Work, 1974 - 80; Principal Lecturer, Applied Social Studies, 1980 - 84; Head of Student Services, University of Ulster, 1984 - 96; Director of Student Affairs, University of Ulster, 1996-2000. Chairperson and Member, Governing Body, Causeway Institute of Further and Higher Education since 1995; Board of Directors of Association of Northern Ireland Colleges, since 2000; Executive Committee UKCOSA 1989-2000; Member of Advisory Group of RNID (NI), since 2001; Board of Directors, The Blind Centre Northern Ireland, 1988 - 98. Current Research - The Quality of Life of Blind and Partially Sighted People in Northern Ireland. Publications: 8 books including; Towards a Federal Ireland, 1995;Value Added: Personal Development of Students in Higher Education, 1993; A Service For People, 1992; The Right to Learn (RNID 2001); numerous articles and conference papers. Recreations: watercolour painting; creative writing; playing mediocre golf; reading social history and biographies; theatre; squash; travel; playing piano; listening to jazz music; Ulster Orchestra season ticket holder. Address: (h.) 20 Islandtasserty Road, Coleraine, BT52 2PN; T.- 01265-823540; (b.) 01265-324215.
e-mail: b.caul@ulster.ac.uk

Chakravarathy, Prof. Usha, MBBS, FRCS, PhD. Professor, Ophthalmology and Vision Science, Queen's University Belfast, since 1999; Consultant, Royal Victoria Hospital, since 1994; b. 15.3.53, Madras, India; m., James Barbour; 1 s.; 1 d. Educ. Presentation Convent, Church Park, Madras, India; Madras Medical College, India. House Jobs (SHO level), Southampton Eye Unit (SHO), 1976-77, Whipps Cross Hospital (SHO), 1978; Amersham Hospital Bucks (SHO), 1979-80; Southampton Eye Unit (Registrar), 1980-82; Belfast RVH (Senior Registrar), 1982-85; part time Fellow (Career Break), 1986-88; Wellcome Lecturer, Honorary Senior Fellow, RVH, 1988-91; Juvenile Diabetes Foundation Career Dev. Award/Lecturer, 1992-93; Wellcome Senior Lecturer, QUB/Honorary Consultant, RVH, 1993-98. Publications: over 70 papers. Scientific Advisor to Medical Research Council, RNIB, College of Ophthalmologists, and Alliance International. Recreations: tennis; music. Address: (b.) Ophthalmic Directorate, RVH, Belfast. T.-02890 240503 ext. 3954.

Chambers, Dr. George, CBE, BSc, PhD, DSc, CChem, FRSC, FCIM, FRAgS. Chairman, NI Panel Council for Awards Royal Agricultural Societies, since 2001; Trustee, Ulster Historical Foundation, since 1991; b. 1.1.28, Dunmore, Ballynahinch, Co Down; m., Elizabeth Barr; 1s.; 1d. Educ. Shaftesbury House. Belfast; Queen's University, Belfast. Assistant Lecturer, Chemistry, Queen's University, Belfast, 1950 - 54; Research Chemist, Alkali Division ICI Cheshire, 1954 - 58; Chief Chemist, Milk Marketing Board, Northern Ireland, 1958 - 63; Chief Executive, Milk Marketing Board, Northern Ireland, 1963 - 88;

Chairman of four associate companies of Milk Marketing Board, Northern Ireland, 1982 - 88; Chairman, Dairy Produce Packers Ltd, Coleraine, 1989 - 92; Chairman, Sedgwick Northern Ireland Risk Services Ltd, 1991 - 99; Chairman, Ulster Historical Foundation, 1995-2000. Member, British Overseas Trade Advisory Committee, 1975 - 80; Chairman, Export Committee, Northern Ireland Chamber of Commerce, 1975 - 82; President, Society of Dairy Technology, UK and Ireland, 1976 - 77; Member, Northern Ireland Economic Council, 1977 - 87; President, Northern Ireland Chamber of Commerce and Industry, 1979 - 80; Chairman, CBI Northern Ireland, 1983 - 85; Member, Police Authority for Northern Ireland, 1985 - 91; Co-ordinator Northern Ireland Partnership, 1986 - 89; member, Technology Board for Northern Ireland, 1986 - 90; Chairman, Management Group, NI Library and Information Plan, 1990 - 93; Chairman, Food Research Advisory Committee, Queen's University, Belfast, 1993 - 96; Governor, Linen Hall Library, 1986 - 97; Northern Ireland Representative, Central Probation Council, 1991 - 97; Member, Probation Board for Northern Ireland, 1991 - 97; Member, UK Library and Information Commission, 1995 - 98. Belfast Cup for Agricultural Achievement, late 1970s; Gold Medal, UK and Irish Society of Dairy Technology, 1993. Publications: Faces of Chance: Bicentennial History of Northern Ireland Chamber of Commerce and Industry, 1984. Recreations: local history; gardening; walking; tennis; watching cricket and rugby football. Address: (b.) Ulster Historical Foundation, Balmoral Buildings, 12 College Square East, Belfast, BT1 6DD; T.- 02890-332288.

Charles, Dr. Darryl Keith, BEng, PGCE, MSc, PhD. Lecturer, University of Ulster, since 2001; b. 31.7.66, Brisbane, Australia. Educ. Cookstown High School; Queen's University Belfast; Stranmillis College, Belfast; University of Ulster, Coleraine. Teacher, Portadown College, 1989-95; Head of Information Technology, Cox Green School, 1995-96; Lecturer/Senior Lecturer, University of Paisley, 1996-2001. Member of the National Institute for Learning and Teaching (ILT). Publications: various articles in journals and contributions to books. Recreations: 3D computer graphics and game technology; photography; hill walking; soccer. Address: (h.) Millview Cottage, Corkhill Road, Cookstown, Co. Tyrone. T. (b) +44 028 70324582. e-mail: dk.charles@ulst.ac.uk

Charley, Colonel (Robin) William Robert Hunter, OBE, JP, DL. Retired Army; b. 25.4.24, Dunmurry, Co Antrim; m., Catherine Janet Kingan; 3d. Educ. Elm Park School; Cheltenham College; Queen's University, Belfast; Army Staff College. Enlisted, Royal Ulster Rifles (RUR) from Queen's University Officer Training Corps, 1943; Commissioned RUR, 1944; 2 RUR, Palestine, 1945; ADC, 3rd Division, Egypt, 1946; 2 RUR, 1947, UK I RUR, 1948; ADC GOC EAD, 1949 - 50; IRUR, Korea, 1950 - 51; Commonwealth

Division Battle School, Japan, 1951; Adjt. I RUR, Hong Kong, 1952 - 53; Adjt. Depot, RUR, 1953 - 55; War Office, 1955 - 57; Staff College, 1958; Headquarters 4th Division BAOR, 1959 - 60; 6 RUR (TA), 1960 - 61; 1 RUR, 1962 - 63; Headquarters, BAOR, 1963 - 64; C O. Queen's University Officer Training Corps, 1965 - 68; Headquarters Northern Ireland, 1969 - 71; Staff, Northern Ireland Polytechnic, 1971 - 73; Re-employed, Regimental Association Secretary /Regimental Secretary, Royal Irish Rangers, 1974 - 89. JP, Co Down since 1977; High Sheriff, Co Antrim, 1978; Deputy Lieutenant, Co Down since 1986; OBE, 1989; OStJ, 1975; CStJ, 1982; KStJ, 1993. Chairman, Royal Ulster Rifles Association, 1969 - 74 (Vice-President since 1974); Chairman, Royal Ulster Rifles Officers Club since 1990; Trustee, Royal Ulster Rifles Museum since 1965; Hon. Colonel, Army Cadet Force, Antrim and Belfast Battalion, 1989 - 92; Chairman, ACFA (NI), 1979 - 86 (President, 1996-2000); President, 36th Ulster Division, OCA, since 1977; President BKVA (Ireland), since 1986. Director, St John Ambulance Association, 1975 - 85; Librarian, St John Commandery of Ards, since 1986; Hon. Secretary, Forces Help Society, 1964 - 90; Chairman, SSAFA/Forces Help Northern Ireland, 1990 - 96; Member, Northern Ireland War Pensions Committee, 1969 - 79; Board Member: Clifton House, 1983-2001; FARSET Youth Development Board since 1986; Hon. Treasurer, Somme Association since 1990; Chairman, Somme Heritage Centre since 1992; Member, Northern Ireland War Memorial Building Council since 1986; President, Queen's University, Belfast Officer Training Corps Association, 1994 - 97; President, Newtownards Society, since 2003; Vice-President, Not Forgotten Association; Vice-President, Cancer Research Campaign, Northern Ireland. Rectors Church Warden: Helens Bay, 1971 and Christ Church, Carrowdore, 1990; Hon. Treasurer, Christ Church, Carrowdore, 2003; Hon. Sec., RUKBA Newtownards and North Down area. Member: OMRS; OMSA, Medal Society of Ireland; Military History Society of Ireland; North of Ireland Family History Society; Irish Genealogical Society; Army and Navy Club; Ulster Reform Club; Royal British Legion. Recreations: militaria and military history; gardening; genealogy and family history; photography. Address: (h.) Ballyblack Lodge, 16 Ballyblack Road, Newtownards, Co Down, BT22 2AP; T.-028 9181 2379.
e-mail: wrhcharley@aol.com

Cheesman, Rev. Graham Jonathan, Dip Th, BD (Hons), MPhil, ALBC. Principal, Belfast Bible College since 1988; b. 19.2.50, West Drayton, Middlesex; m., Menita França Da Silva; 2s.; 1d. Educ. Cheltenham Grammar School; London Bible College; London University. Pastor, Waltham Abbey Baptist Church, Essex; Missionary Lecturer and Head, Theological Division, Samuel Bill Theological College, Nigeria. Publications: Mission Today, 1989; Hyperchoice, 1997. Recreations: walking; chess.

Address: (b.) Belfast Bible College, Glenburn Road South, Dunmurry, Belfast, BT17 9JP; T.-9030 1551.

Chesney, George Cecil, BA, LLB, LLM. Barrister-at-Law; b. 17.6.53, Ballymena; m., Lorna Constance Brandon. Educ. Portora Royal School, Enniskillen, University of Bristol; Queen's University, Belfast; Open University. Called to the Bar, Northern Ireland, 1983; Called to the Bar, Middle Temple, England, 1988; Called to the Bar, Republic of Ireland, King's Inn, 1997. Recreations: hillwalking; stone masonry. Address: (b.) Bar Library, Royal Courts of Justice, Chichester Street, Belfast. T.- 028 90562174.

Clark, Henry Wallace Stuart, MBE, DL. Retired Linen Manufacturer; Writer; Director, Upperlands Development Group; b. 20.11.26, Northern Ireland; m., June Elisabeth Lester Deane; 2s. Educ. Shrewsbury School. Lieutenant, RNVR, 1945 - 47 (bomb and mine disposal); Cattleman, Merchant Navy, 1947 - 48; District Commandant, Ulster Special Constabulary, 1955 - 70; Major, Ulster Defence Regiment, 1970 - 81. Foyle's Lecturer, USA tour, 1964; Led Church of Ireland St Columba commemorative curragh voyage, Derry to Iona, 1963; Director and Skipper, Lord of the Isles Voyage, Galway to Stornaway in a sixteenth century galley, 1991. DL, 1962; High Sheriff, Co Londonderry, 1969; Vice-Lord Lieutenant, Co Londonderry, 1970-77. Publications: North and East Coasts of Ireland (co-author), 1957; South and West Ireland (co-author), 1972; Sailing Around Ireland, 1976; Linen on the Green, 1982; Lord of the Isles Voyage, 1993; Upperlands History and Visitors Guide, 1998; Sailing Around Russia, 1999; Guns in Ulster, 2002; Rathlin - Its Island Story, 1991; Brave Men and True (Early Days in the Ulster Defence Regiment), 2002. Recreations: sailing to islands. Address: (h.) Gorteade Cottage, Upperlands, Co Londonderry, BT46 5SB; T. -028 796 42737.

Clark, Paul Thompson. Presenter, Live at Six, Ulster Television; b. 4.12.53, Belfast; m., Carol; 2s. Educ. St Mary's Christian Brothers School, Belfast; College of Business Studies. BBC Radio Northern Ireland, 1974 - 80; RTE, Radio, Dublin, 1980 - 83; BBC Radio Northern Ireland/London, 1983 - 85; BBC Television, Northern Ireland, 1985 - 88; Joined Ulster Television, 1989. Features Journalist of the Year, 1994 and 1997; Television Personality of the Year, 1994 and 1995; Various documentaries have won national and international awards; Andrew Cross Award for documentary Living on the Edge, 1998; Christian Broadcasting Council Gold Award (UK) for documentary, A second Calling, 1998; Christian Broadcasting Council Bronze award, "Look, No Hands!", 2002; Andrew Cross Award for documentary "Look, No Hands!", 2003. Recreations: tennis; walking old railways. Address: (b.) Ulster Television, Havelock House, Ormeau Road, Belfast, BT7 1EB; T.- 028 90262000.
e-mail: paulclark@utvplc.com

Clarke, Alan. Chief Executive of the Northern Ireland Tourist Board, since 2001. Career History: over 20 years experience in tourism throughout the United Kingdom commencing in Northern Ireland followed by appointments in Wales and Devon; for the past 11 years: Director of Marketing for Edinburgh and Lothians Tourist Board, then Chief Executive of Aberdeen and Grampian Tourist Board. Chartered Member of the Institute of Marketing and Member of the Institute of Direct Marketing. Recreations: sport; gardening; antiques; watercolours and family. Address: (b.) St. Anne's Court, 59 North Street, Belfast BT1 1NB. T.-028 90231221.

Clarke, Morina Geraldine. Regional Services Manager, Epilepsy Action, since 1997; b. Belfast. Industry, 1966 - 77; Health Service, 1977 - 80; Voluntary Sector, since 1980. Editor, EA local magazine, Searchlight. Address: (b.) Room 110, Bostock House, Royal Hospitals Trust, Belfast BT12 6BA. T.-02890 315914.

Clarke, Dr. Robin Blakely, BSc (Hons), DPhil, Ceng, MIMechE, FIED. Head of School, School of Electrical and Mechanical Engineering, University of Ulster; b. 19.11.55; Belfast; m., Margaret; 2s.; 2d. Educ. Grosvenor High School; Queen's University, Belfast; University of Ulster. Design and Test Engineer, Davidson and Co, Belfast; Lecturer, Ulster Polytechnic, 1981 - 84. Consultant to local industry. Publications: over 30 articles and conference papers published in national and international journals and periodicals. Recreations: family; outdoor activities. Address: (b.) School of Electrical and Mechanical Engineering, University of Ulster, Shore Road, Newtownabbey, BT37 0QB; T.-02890 366271.

Clarke, Thomas Alan, BSc (Hons), MSc. Chief Executive, Northern Ireland Tourist Board, since 2001; b. 10.4.51; m., Mary; 1 d. Educ. Lurgan College; University of Ulster; University of Strathclyde. Principal Officer, Tourism, Gwent County Council, 1979-86; Head of Tourism, Devon Tourism, 1986-90; Director, Marketing and Membership Services, Edinburgh and Lothians Tourist Board/Edinburgh Tourist Board, 1990-97; Chief Executive, Aberdeen and Grampian Tourist Board, 1997-2001. Recreations: rugby; soccer; cricket; gardening; photography; antiques. Address: (b.) St. Anne's Court, 59 North Street, Belfast BT1 1NB. T.-028 9089 5511. e-mail: a.clarke@nitb.com

Cleland, Professor David James, BSc, PhD, CEng, FICE, FstructE. Professor, School of Civil Engineering, Queen's University, Belfast; m., Roberta; 2s.; 1d. Educ. Portadown College; Queen's University, Belfast. Assistant Lecturer, Queen's University, Belfast; Design Engineer, Dr I G Doran and Partners; Lecturer/Senior Lecturer/reader, Queen's University, Belfast. Address: School of Civil Engineering, Queen's University, Belfast, BT7 1NN; T.-02890-335474.

Clements, William James, BA (Hons), MSc. Secretary, North of Ireland Bands' Association since 1992; b. 23.12.44, Belfast; m., Isobel; 1s.; 2d. Educ. Larne Grammar School; University of Ulster at Jordanstown. Brass Band League (NI): Vice-Chairman, 1996 - 97; Chairman, 1998 - 98. Recreations: sport; music. Address: (b.) North of Ireland Bands' Association, 28 Knockfergus Park, Greenisland, Carrickfergus, BT38 8SN; T.- 028 90866179.

Close, Seamus, OBE. Member (Lagan Valley), Alliance Party, Northern Ireland Assembly, since 1998; Member, Lisburn Borough Council, since 1973; Company Director, since 1986; b. 12.8.47, Lisburn; m., Deirdre McCann; 3 s.; 1 d. Educ. St. Malachy's College, Belfast; College of Business Studies. Delegate to Atkins Conference on Northern Ireland, 1980; Chairman, Alliance Party, 1981 - 82; Member, Northern Ireland Assembly, 1982 - 86; Deputy Leader, Alliance Party, 1991-2001; Key Negotiator, Brooke–Mayhew Talks, 1991 - 92; Mayor of Lisburn, 1993 - 94; Member, Forum for Peace and Reconciliation, Dublin, 1994 - 95; Member, Northern Ireland Forum, 1996; Key Negotiator, "Good Friday Agreement", 1996 - 98. Recreations: sports; family; current affairs. Address: (h.) 123 Moira Road, Lisburn BT28 1RJ; T.-028 92 670639.

Clyde, Wilson. Member (South Antrim), Democratic Unionist Party, Northern Ireland Assembly, since 1998; b. 8.4.34, Kilbegs, Antrim; m.; 1 s. Elected to Antrim Borough Council, 1981; Member, Northern Ireland Forum, 1996-98. Address: (b.) Parliament Buildings, Stormont, Belfast, BT3 4ST; T.- 028 90 521111.

Cobain, Fred. Member (North Belfast), Ulster Unionist Party, Northern Ireland Assembly, since 1998. Elected to Belfast City Council, 1985; Lord Mayor, 1990. Address: (b.) Parliament Buildings, Stormont, Belfast BT4 3ST; T.-02890 520700.

Cockroft, Rev. Lena, BLS, BD. Former Moderator, Non Subscribing Presbyterian Church; b. 26.6.53, Belfast; m., Rev. Brian Stuart Cockroft; Educ. Princess Gardens, Finaghy (now Hunter House College); Queen's University, Belfast; Manchester University. Assistant in charge, Dromore Branch Library; Training for the Ministry, 1979 - 81; Ordained, 1982; Minister, Glenarm and Cairncastle Non Subscribing Presbyterian Churches since 1982; Minister, Ballymoney since 1997. Sunday School Convener, 1985 - 89 and 1994 - 97. Publications: Hymns of Faith and Freedom (co-author). Recreations: golf; photography; reading; watching and listening to whodunnits. Address: (h.) 24 Main Street, Greyabbey, Co Down, BT22 2NE; T.-028 4278 8650.

Coey, Alastair Dunlop, BSc, Dip Arch, MUBC. Principal Architect, Alastair Coey Architects since 1993; b. 4.9.50, Belfast; m., Anne; 1s. Educ. Grosvenor High School; Queen's University,

Belfast; University College, Dublin. Architectural Assistant, Robert McKinstry and Melvyn Brown Architects, 1977 - 80; Bank Architect, Ulster Bank Ltd, 1980 - 83; Principal, Alastair Coey Architect, 1983 - 90; Partner, Coey Whitley Architects, 1990 - 93; Principal, Alastair Coey Architects, since 1993. Runner-up, Royal Institute of Chartered Surveyors Conservation Award, 1992; Winner, Royal Society of Ulster Architects Conservation Award, 2000. Publications: Taken for Granted, 1984. Recreations: squash. Address: (b.) Alastair Coey Architects, Belmont Gate Lodge, 96 Sydenham Avenue, Belfast, BT4 2DT; T.- 02890-872400. e-mail: info@alastaircoeyarchitects.com

Coghlin, Hon Mr Justice Patrick, Kt, LLB, DipCrim, QC. High Court Judge since 1997; b. 7.11.45, Manchester; m., Patricia Ann Elizabeth; 1s.; 3d. Educ. Royal Belfast Academical Institution; Queens University of Belfast; Christ's College, Cambridge. Called to the Bar of Northern Ireland, 1970; Called to the Bar of England and Wales, 1975; Junior Crown Counsel, Northern Ireland, 1983 - 85; Senior Crown Counsel, Northern Ireland, 1993 - 97. Vice-President VAT Tribunal, (NI), 1990 - 93; Member, Law Reform Advisory Committee (NI), 1988 - 93; Called to the Bar New South Wales, 1992; Called to the Bar of Ireland, 1993; Chairman, Bar Council (NI), 1991 - 93; Deputy County Court Judge, 1983 - 94; QC, 1985; President, Lands Tribunal NI, 1999; Commercial List Judge, 1999; Deputy Chairman, Parliamentary Boundary Commission for NI, 1999; Vice-Chairman, Mental Health Review Tribunal NI, 1987-97; Council Member of The Association of European Competition Law Judges, 2002. Recreations: rugby; soccer; reading; squash; travel. Address: (b.) Royal Courts of Justice, Chichester Street, Belfast, BT1 3JF; T.- 02890-235111.

Cole, John Senan, BSc (Hons), DAAS, MSc (Proj Man), RIBA, PPRSUA. Chief Executive, NI Health and Social Services Estates Agency (Health Estates), since 2003; b. 9.3.51; m., Shirley; 1 s.; 2 d. Educ. Queen's University Belfast. Publication of a range of articles for professional journals. Chairman of Habinteg Housing Association (Ulster); Member of Council: The Royal Institute of British Architects, The Royal Society of Ulster Architects; Board Member, The Rethinking Construction Centre for Northern Ireland; External Examiner, School of Architecture, Queen's University Belfast. Recreations: mountain walking; music. Address: (b.) Health Estates, Stoney Road, Belfast BT16 1US. T.-028 9052 3823. e-mail: john.cole@dhsspsni.gov.uk

Coleman, Patricia Maureen, BA, DBA, Cert. Prof. Legal Stud. Sole Practitioner, P M Coleman and Co, Solicitor since 1994; m., John Stevenson Coleman; 1s; 2d. Educ. Ballymena Academy, Co Antrim; Queen's University, Belfast. Assistant Solicitor, James Ballentine and Son, 1985 - 91; Assistant Solicitor, Gordon F W McIlrath and Co, 1991 - 94. Top Student, Land Law, 1984.

Recreation: farming. Address: (b.) Dromore House, 174 Dunminning Road, Glarryford, Ballymena, BT44 9ET; T.-02825-685204.

Colhoun, Angela Freda, MA. HM Coroner for Fermanagh and Omagh, since 1990; Deputy District Judge, since 1986; b. Omagh, Co Tyrone. Educ. Wycombe Abbey School; Trinity College, Dublin. Member, Council, Omagh Chamber of Commerce; Omagh Task Force; Trustee, Omagh Lawn Tennis Club. HM Coroner for Fermanagh and Omagh, 1990-2002; High Sheriff, County Tyrone, 1999. Recreations: history; literature; golf. Address: (b.) AF Colhoun and Co., 21 Market Street, Omagh, Co Tyrone BT78 1EE; T.-028 82 242136.

Collier, Brother Patrick Christopher, FSC, TC, BA, HDipEd. Principal, De La Salle High School since 1987; b. 24.5.42, Co Meath, Ireland. Educ. De La Salle College, Waterford, Ireland; De La Salle Training College, Waterford; University College, Dublin; Maynooth University. Teacher, Dublin Primary School, Waterford, 1963 - 73; Teacher, De La Salle College, Waterford, 1973 - 74; Teacher, St Malachy's High School, Portadown, 1975 - 81; Vice-Principal/Principal, Drumcree High School/St Malachy's High School, Portadown, 1981 - 87; Career Break, 4 months renewal in Ministry, All Hallows, Dublin/6 months Human Development Council, New Mexico, USA, 1994 - 95. Assessor, Council for Catholic Maintained Schools, for the appointment of Principals and Vice-Principals, 1990. Recreations: golf; music; skiing. Address: (b.) De La Salle High School, Struell Road, Downpatrick, Co Down, BT30 6JR; T.- 028 4461 2520.

Collins, Ann. Director of Shopmobility Belfast Ltd, since 1995; b. Belfast; 2 s. Educ. Girls Model Secondary School. Honorary Secretary, Northern Ireland Group, Disabled Drivers Association; Vice-Chair: Executive and Management of National Disabled Drivers Association, National Federation of Shopmobility. Recreations: reading; painting; relaxing; surfing the net. Address: (b.) Unit 26, Victoria Centre, Victoria Square, Belfast BT1 4TL; T.-028 90 808092.

Collins, Thomas Brendan, BA, FRSA. Director of Communications, Queen's University, Belfast since 1999; b. 12.8.59, Birmingham; m., Maureen; 1 s.; 1 d. Educ. St Colman's College, Newry, Co Down; University of Ulster at Coleraine; City University, London. Reporter, Carrickfergus Advertiser, 1983 - 84; Editor, Carrickfergus Advertiser, 1984 - 85; Deputy Chief Sub-Editor, News Letter, 1985 - 88; Chief Sub-Editor, News Letter, 1988 - 90; Deputy Editor, The Irish News, 1990 - 93; Editor, The Irish News, 1993 - 99. Chairman, Ulster Orchestra since 2001; Fellow of the Royal Society of Arts, since 2003. Recreations: classical music; opera; reading. Address: (b.) Queen's University, Belfast.

Connolly, James Denis Rentoul, MB, BCh, FFARCSI. Medical Director, Green Park Healthcare Trust since 1997; Consultant Anaesthetist, Musgrave Park Hospital and Belfast City Hospital since 1983; Chairman, British Society of Orthopaedic Anaesthetists; b. 29.12.44, Londonderry; m., Patricia Margaret Lynas; 3s. Educ. Foyle College, Londonderry; Queen's University, Belfast. Consultant Anaesthetist, Lagan Valley Hospital, 1975 - 83; Clinical Director, Theatres and Anaesthetics, Green Park Healthcare Trust, 1992 - 96; Clinical Director, Anaesthetics and Orthopaedics, Green Park Healthcare Trust, 1996 - 97. Member: Association of Anaesthetists, Great Britain and Ireland; American Society of Regional Anaesthesia; European Society of Regional Anaesthesia (National Committee Member, Great Britain and Ireland, 1992 - 95 and 1996 - 98); Secretary, Great Britain and Ireland zone since 1998; Chairman, British Society of Orthopaedic Anaesthetists, 1999-2002. Recreations: walking; swimming; reading. Address: (b.) Musgrave Park Hospital, 5th Floor, McKinney House, Stockman's Lane, Belfast BT9 7BJ; T.-02890-669501, ext. 2985.

Connolly, Paul, BA. News Editor, Belfast Telegraph since 1998; b. 28.8.64, Ballymena. Educ. Queen's University, Belfast. Reporter, Co Down Spectator, 1987 - 88; Reporter/News Editor/Deputy Editor, Sunday News, 1988 - 93; Assistant News Editor, News Letter, 1993 - 96; Security Correspondent, Belfast Telegraph, 1996 - 98; Political Correspondent, Belfast Telegraph, 1998; Freelance Northern Ireland Correspondent, Time Magazine, 1995-98. Shortlisted, Specialist Correspondent of the Year, UK Press Gazette National Awards, 1997. Recreations: skiing; travel; music; gym; dining out/socialising. Address: (b.) Belfast Telegraph, 122 - 144 Royal Avenue, Belfast, BT1 1EB; T.- 02890 264420.

Connolly, Professor Sean Joseph, BA, DPhil, MRIA. Professor, Irish History, Queen's University, Belfast; b. 9.12.51, Dublin; m., Mavis Bracegirdle; 1s.; 1d. Educ. St Paul's College, Raheny; University College, Dublin; University of Ulster. Archivist, Public Record Office of Ireland, 1977 - 80; Lecturer, History, St Patrick's College, Dublin, 1980 - 81; Joined University of Ulster, 1981; Lecturer/Reader/ Professor. Publications: Priests and People in Pre-Famine Ireland, 1982; Religion, Law and Power, The Making of Protestant Ireland, 1660 - 1760, 1992; Oxford Companion to Irish History, (gen. ed.), 1998. Recreations: film and video. Address: (b.) School of Modern History, Queen's University, Belfast, BT7 1NN; T.- 02890 333423.

Connor, Rodney Eric, BSc (Econ), DMS. Chief Executive, Fermanagh District Council, since 2000; b. 25.3.51, Castlederg, N. Ireland; m., Elizabeth; 1 s.; 3 d. Educ. Strabane Grammar School; Queen's University Belfast. Recreation Dev. Officer, 1974-77; Director of Recreation, 1977-92; Director of Environmental Services,

1992-2000. Fermanagh Enterprise; Irish Central Border Area Network. Recreation: golf. Address: (b.) The Town Hall, Enniskillen, Co. Fermanagh, N. Ireland BT74 7BA. T.-028 66 325050.

Conway, Chris, BSc (Hons), MBA. Vice-President, European Supply Chain Operations, Nortel Networks (Europe, Middle East (EMEA), Africa), since 2000; b. 26.11.63, Dungannon, NI; m., Anne; 2 s.; 1 d. Educ. St. Patrick's College, Knock; University of Ulster, Jordanstown. Address: (b.) Doagh Road, Newtownabbey, Co. Antrim BT36 6XA.

Cook, David Somerville, MA. Solicitor, Senior Partner, Messrs Sheldon and Stewart, Solicitors, Belfast; Chairman, Craigavon and Banbridge Community Health and Social Services Trust, 1994-2001; President, Alliance Party, 1992-93; b. 25.1.44; m., Mary Fionnuala Ann Deeny; 4s.; 1d. Educ. Campbell College, Belfast; Pembroke College, Cambridge. Alliance Party of Northern Ireland: Founder Member, 1970; Hon. Treasurer, 1972 - 1975; Central Executive Committee, 1970 - 78 and 1980 - 85; Deputy Leader, 1980 - 84; Chairman, Police Authority for Northern Ireland, 1994-96. Chairman, Northern Ireland Voluntary Trust, 1979-99; Belfast City Councillor, 1973 - 85; Member, Northern Ireland Assembly 1982 - 86; Alliance party Candidate, 1974, 1982, 1986 and 1987; Candidate, European Elections, 1984. Trustee: Ulster Museum, 1974 - 85; The Buttle Trust, 1991-2001; Vice-President, Northern Ireland Council on Alcohol, 1978 - 83; Member: Northern Ireland Council, European Movement, 1980 - 84; Committee, Charity Know How Fund, 1991 - 94; Executive Committee, Association of Community Trusts and Foundations, 1992-98 (Chairman, 1994 - 95); Executive Committee, RBL Housing Association Ltd, 1994-99; Director: Ulster Actors' Company Ltd, 1981 - 85; Crescent Arts Centre, Belfast, 1994 - 96. Governor, Brownlow College, 1994-98. Publications: Blocking the Slippery Slope, 1997. Recreations: pamphleteering; marmalade making; observing politicians; hunting on foot. Address: 70 Donegall Pass, Belfast BT7 1BU.

Cooke, John Peavey, DL. Retired Managing Director; b. 16.5.22, Belfast; m., Nan Josephine Acheson; 2 s.; 1 d. Educ. Bryanston Public Sch. Seaman/Sub-Lieutenant/Lieutenant/Lieutenant Commander RNVR; Director/Managing Director, Family Linen Business, retired, 1987. Former High Sheriff, Co Antrim. Recreations: gardening; Address: (h.) Owensland Cottage, 11 Old Ballybracken Road, Doagh, Ballyclare, Co Antrim, BT39 0SF; T.- 028 933 40441.

Cooke of Islandreagh, Baron of Islandreagh in the County of Antrim, Victor Alexander Cooke, OBE, DL, CEng, FIMechE, MA. Chairman: Henry R Ayton Ltd, Belfast, 1970 - 89; Springvale EPS Ltd 1964-2000; b. 18.10.20; m., Alison Sheila Casement; 2s.; 1d. Educ. Marlborough College, Wiltshire; Trinity College, Cambridge. Engineer

Officer, Royal Navy, 1940 - 46; Joined Henry R Ayton, 1946. Chairman: Belfast Savings Bank, 1963; Harland and Wolff Ltd, 1980 - 81 (Director, 1970 - 87); Director, Northern Ireland Airports, 1970 - 85. Member: Senate, Parliament of Northern Ireland, 1960 - 68; Northern Ireland Economic Council, 1974-78; Commissioner, Belfast Harbour, 1968-79; Commissioner of Irish Lights, 1983-96 (Chairman of Commissioners, 1990 - 92). Deputy Lieutenant, Co Antrim, 1970. Recreations: sailing; shooting.

Cooke, Rev. William Dennis Davison, BA, BD, MTh, PhD. Principal, Edgehill Theological College, Belfast since 1984; b. 3.12.38, West Indies; m., Joan; 2s.; 1d. Educ. Methodist College, Belfast; Queen's University, Belfast; Lexington Theological Seminary, Lexington, Kentucky, USA. Methodist Minister: Portstewart, 1968 - 71; Leeson Park, Dublin, 1971 - 75; Woodvale, Belfast, 1977 - 80; Senior Tutor, Edgehill College, 1980 - 84. Council Member, Glencree Centre for Reconciliation, Dublin, 1972 - 77; Convener, Methodist Faith and Order Committee, 1976 - 84. Publications: Persecuting Zeal – A Portrait of Ian Paisley, 1996. Recreations: gardening; swimming; walking. Address: (b.) Edgehill Theological College, 9 Lennoxvale, Belfast; T.- 02890-665870.

Cooper, Gary, Dip MD, BEd (Hons), MEd. Headmaster, Knockmore Primary and Special Unit School, Lisburn since 1993; m., Sharon Cooper; 1s. Educ. Sullivan Upper School, Holywood; Queen's University, Belfast; University of Ulster. Senior Management, Cavehill Primary School, 1985 - 92. Hon. Secretary, Lisburn Area Principals, 1995 - 96; Member: MENCAP, family advisory committee, Board of Governors, Kings Road Nursery School, Board of Governors, Longstone Special School. Publications: Educational Development in Northern Ireland during the Second World War, 1990; The Political Role of the Monarchy this Century, 1985; various articles including, Cavehill Railway School, 1989; The Special Child, 1994; Mountbatten: Tarnished Hero, 1997; The Church and Education, 2001; Educating the Special Needs Child in South Africa, 2003. Address: (b.) Knockmore School, Hertford Crescent, Lisburn, BT28 1SA; T.- 028 92662600.
e-mail: jcooper@knockmoreps.lisburn.ni

Corken, Tina, BEd (Hons), DASE, MPhil. Head, Dunmurry High School, since 2000; b. Belfast; m., Peter Corken; 1 s.; 1 d. Educ. Finaghy P. S.; Princess Gardens Grammar School; Queen's University Belfast. Dunmurry High School, since 1974: various posts in both curriculum and pastoral care areas. Address: (b.) Dunmurry High School, River Road, Belfast BT17 9DS. T.-028 90622828.
e-mail: tcorken@dunmurry.belfast.ni.sch.uk

Cormack, Professor Robert John, MA, FRSA. Principal, UHI Millennium Institute, since 2001;

Queen's University Belfast: Professor of Sociology, 1994-2001, Pro Vice-Chancellor, 1995-2001; b. 14.12.46, Blantyre; m., Elisabeth; 1s.; 2d. Educ. Montrose Academy; University of Aberdeen. Queen's University, Belfast: Lecturer, 1973 - 87; Senior Lecturer, 1987 - 89; Reader, 1989 - 94; Head of Department, Sociology and Social Policy, 1991 - 93; Dean, Faculty of Economic and Social Sciences, 1993 - 95. Publications: After the Reforms (with R D Osborne and A M Gallagher eds.), 1993; Education and Policy in Northern Ireland, 1987; Discrimination and Public Policy (with R D Osborne), 1991. Recreations: walking in the Highlands. Address: (h.) UHI Millennium Institute, Caledonia House, 63 Academy Street, Inverness IV1 1BB. T.-01463 279212.

Corr, Daniel Anthony. Northern Ireland Manager, Nationwide Building Society since 1988; b. 17.6.44, Whiteabbey; m., Irene; 1s.; 2d. Educ. St Malachy's College. Joined Nationwide Building Society, 1967: worked in branches in, Belfast, Bangor, Lisburn, Portadown. Chairman, Building Societies Association and Council of Mortgage Lenders, 1996 - 97 and 1990 - 92; Board Member: Northern Ireland Co-ownership Housing Association, Business in the Community (NI), Learning and Skills Advisory Board; Council Member: General Consumer Council for Northern Ireland, Common Purpose; Member, Accreditation Panel, Investors in People. Recreations: youth work; church work Irish President; Irish Christian Endeavour, 1993-94. Address: (b.) 53 Royal Avenue, Belfast, BT1 1LX; T.-02890-880252.

Corrigan-Maguire, Mairead, Co-Founder and Hon. Life President, Community of the Peace People; b. 27.1.44; m., Jackie Maguire; 2s.; 3 step c. Educ. Miss Gordon's Commercial College, Belfast. Secretarial career prior to becoming initiator of Peace Movement in Northern Ireland, 1976; Chairman, Peace People Organisation, 1980 - 81. Hon. Dr of Law, Yale University, 1976; Nobel Prize for Peace (jointly with Betty Williams, see Elizabeth Williams); Carl-von-Ossietzky Medaille for Courage, Berlin, 1976. Address: (b.) 224 Lisburn Road, Belfast, BT9 6GE; T.- 02890-663465.

Cory, Michael, BSc (Hons), MPhil. FRICS, C.Dir. Chief Executive, Ordnance Survey of Northern Ireland, since 1999; b. 19.12.58, England; m., Angela; 2 s.; 1 d. Educ. University of Newcastle upon Tyne. Directorate of Overseas Surveys (Liberia, Malawi, North Yemen), 1980 - 86; Ordnance Survey of Great Britain, 1986 - 94; Controller of Mapping, Ordnance Survey Ireland, 1994 - 99. Address: (b.) Colby House, Stranmillis Court, Belfast BT5 9BJ; T.-02890 255702.

Cosgrove, Mary Geraldine. General Secretary, Social Democratic and Labour Party; b. 23.6.52, Belfast; m., Mervyn; 1 s.; 4 d. Address: (b.) 121 Ormeau Road, Belfast BT7 1SH. T.-028 90247700. e-mail: gerry.cosgrove@sdlphq.ie

Coulter, Mabel Diane Margaret, LLB, MPhil. Principal, M. Diane M. Coulter Solicitors; b. 27.1.70, Kilkeel, Co Down;. Educ. Kilkeel High School; Queen's University, Belfast. Part-time Tutor, Land Law and Conveyancing, Queen's University, Belfast since 1994. Butterworth's Law Prize, Best Student; Butterworth's Law Prize, Most Promising Student; ECHR Prize; Guinness Law Prize, Best Student in Licensing Law, 1998. Treasurer, Newry and Banbridge District Solicitors Association; Chairperson of Daisy Hill Breast Cancer Support Group; Member of Northern Ireland Medico-Legal Society; The Employment Lawyers Group and Family Law Association; Vice Chairman of Southern Group Enterprises Limited and Southern Group Business Connections Limited and Practices in three jurisdictions, Northern Ireland, Republic of Ireland, England and Wales rolls of solicitors. Publications: A History of Registration of Deeds in Ireland. Recreations: travel; reading; hockey. Address: (b.)127a Harbour Road, Kilkeel, Co. Down BT34 4AU. T.- 028 417 69772.
e-mail:diane@dianecoultersols.co.uk

Coulter, Rev. Robert. Member (North Antrim), Ulster Unionist Party, Northern Ireland Assembly since 1998. Retired Presbyterian clergyman; Lecturer in Religious Studies; elected to Ballymena Council, 1985; served as Mayor; Member, Northern Ireland Forum, 1996-98. Address: (b.) Parliament Buildings, Stormont, Belfast, BT4 3ST; T.-02890 52146.

Courtney, Angela Maria, OBE. Director, NI Women's Aid since 1995; b. 11.8.43, Gateshead, Co Durham, England; m., Alan Denton Courtney; 2s. 1d. Educ. Convent of Sacred Heart Grammar School, Newcastle-upon-Tyne. Volunteer Member, Belfast Women's Aid, 1977 - 86; Member, Executive Committee, NI Council for Voluntary Action, 1981 - 86; Secretary, N I Women's Aid Federation, 1983 - 91; Regional Development Worker, N I Women's Aid Federation, 1994 - 95. UK Representative, European Observatory on Violence Against Women since 1997. Runs training workshops and seminars, regular conference speaker on domestic violence locally, nationally and internationally. Publications: some poetry. Recreations: gardening; walking; singing. Address: Central Office, 129 University Street, Belfast BT7 1HP. email:angiecourtney@aol.com; niwaf@dnet.co.uk

Courtney, Annie, RGN. Health Promoter for European Pilot Project; Board member, Northern Ireland Tourist Board since 1994; Councillor, Derry City Council 1985- 1987 and former Mayor; m., Sydney; 3 children. Educ. St Margaret's Convent Grammar School, Edinburgh. Student Nurse, City and County Hospital; Staff Nurse, Altnagelvin Area Hospital, 1961; Theatre Sister, St Coiles Hospital, Campberwell, 1961 - 62; Altnagelvin Hospital: Theatre Staff Nurse, 1967 - 74; Theatre Manager, 1974 - 85; Day Care Unit Manager, 1985 - 92; EAPH Co-ordinator, 1992 -

97. Deputy Mayor, Derry, 1992 - 93; Mayor, Derry, 1993 - 94. Member, CNCC; FCB for Northern Ireland, 1995 - 2000; Christian Heritage Promotions since 1996. Recreations: reading; politics. Address: (h.) St Giles Hospital, BT47 2PC.

Courtney, Roger Brian, MBE, BSSc (Hons), CCYW, DMS, MSc. Freelance Management Advisor in the Voluntary and Public Sectors, since 1998; b. 13.4.54, Belfast; m., Christine Courtney; 1s.; 2d. Educ. Royal Belfast Academical Institution; Queen's University, Belfast; University of Ulster; South Bank University, London. Clerk, Ulster Bank Ltd, 1972 - 74; Co-ordinator, Crescent Arts Centre, 1978 - 80; Organising Secretary, Belfast Simon Community, 1981 - 85; Chief Executive, Simon Community, Northern Ireland, 1985 - 98. Chair, War on Want NI, since 1998; Trustee of the Blackburn Trust, since 1987; Founder and Chair of NI Council for the Homeless, 1984-86; Director, NI Quality Centre, 1997-2000; Chair, ACOVO (NI), 1992-95; Chair, Housing Rights Service, 1992-96. Publications: The Northern Ireland Fundraising Handbook; Planning a Fundraising Strategy; Fundraising through Trusts; Making a Difference: The Story of the Simon Community in Northern Ireland; Understanding Homelessness; Managing Voluntary Organisations – New Approaches; Inventing the future: The Strategic Management of Voluntary Organisations; 'Mentoring: a guide for the journey'; The Strategic Management of Voluntary Non profit Organisations. Recreations: singing; song writing; appreciation of opera; athletics, from the safe distance of an armchair; the joy of fatherhood. Address: (h.) 20 Bryansburn Road, Bangor, Co Down, BT20 3SB; T.-028 91 270332. e-mail: roger.courtney@btinternet.com

Cowan, Professor Colin, BSc, PhD, CEng, FIEE, SMIEEE. Nortel/Royal Academy of Engineering Professor of Telecommunications Systems Engineering at Queen's University, Belfast since 1996; b. 6.12.55, Newry, Co Down. Educ. Foyle College; University of Edinburgh. University of Edinburgh: Lecturer, Electrical Engineering, 1980 - 89; Reader, Electrical Engineering, 1989 - 91; Loughborough University: Professor, Signal Processing, 1991 - 96; Head of Department, Electronic and Electrical Engineering, 1994 - 96; Currently Visiting Professor. Address: (b.) Department of Electrical and Electronic Engineering, Queen's University, Belfast, Stranmillis Road, Belfast, BT9 5AH.

Craig, Leslie, OBE. Director, Rural Development Council; Member, Ulster Unionist Council; Director, Food Safety Promotion Board (North/South Implementation Bodies); b. 25.10.60, Londonderry; m., June; 2s. Educ. Strabane Grammar School; Greenmount College, Antrim. Family Farm interests and working in Agri-services industry; Previous Chairman, Northern Ireland Agricultural Producers Association (NIAPA), 1995-99. Holds a Diploma in Rural Development; studying part-time for MSc with Queen's University Belfast @ Rural College Draperstown. Recreations: reading; rural development interest; motor-cycles; family holidays. Address: (h.) Binnelly House, 222 Berryhill Road, Dunamanagh, Strabane, Co. Tyrone BT82 0NB. T.-028 71 398333.

Craig, Rev. Ronald Gavin, BA, DD. Retired Presbyterian Minister; b. 14.4.16, Belfast; m., Isobel Stewart Kelly; 1s., 1d. Educ. Royal Belfast Academical Institution; Queen's University, Belfast; Presbyterian College, Belfast. Minister: Glennan and Middletown, 1944 - 48; Woodvale Park, Belfast, 1948 - 69; 1st Carrickfergus, 1969 - 82; Moderator, General Assembly, 1980; Missionary in Malawi, 1983 - 85. Former member, Government Youth Committee; Sports Council; UNESCO; North Eastern Education Board. Publications: Treasure in Earthen Vessels; For the Healing of the Nation. Irish Rugby International, 1938; Cricket, inter provincial Ulster, 1941 and 1947. Address: (h.) 16 Movilla Gardens, Portstewart, BT55 7BF; T.- 028 70836345.

Craig, Rev. William, MA, BD, DD. Retired Presbyterian Minister and former Moderator of the General Assembly; b. 1.8.18, Comber, Co Down; m., Maud Macrory; 1s.; 1d. Educ. Royal Belfast Academical Institution; Queen's University, Belfast. Minister, Ebrington Presbyterian Church, Londonderry, 1945 - 48; Minister, 1st Portadown Presbyterian Church, 1948 - 84. Moderator, General Assembly of Presbyterian Church in Ireland, 1979 - 80; Chairman, Northern Ireland Keswick Convention, 1977 - 91. Recreations: walking; cycling; reading. Address: (h.) 15 Earlsfort, Old Kilmore Road, Moira, Craigavon, BT67 0LY; T.- 02892-612376.

Craig, William Phillip. Regional Organiser, The Royal British Legion in Northern Ireland since 1994; b. 19.2.49, Montrose, Scotland. Educ. Grove Academy, Dundee. Royal Corps of Signals, 1965 - 89; Pensions Officer, The Royal British Legion, Northern Ireland, 1990 - 93. Recreations: fly-fishing; DIY. Address: (b.) Royal British Legion, 9-13 Waring Street, Belfast, BT1 2EU; T.-02890-321683.
e-mail: bcraig@britishlegion.org.uk

Cramsie, Alexander James. Regional Organiser, Army Benevolent Fund (NI) since 1984; b, 31.5.41, Hexham; m., Bridget Duke; 2s. Educ. Wellington College; Royal Military Academy, Sandhurst. QRIH, 1961 - 84; Commanded QOY, 1980 - 84; Farmer. Recreations: racing; field sports. Address: (b.) Army Benevolent Fund (NI), TA Centre, Artillery Road, Coleraine, BT52 2AE; T.- 028 7034 4407.

Crane, Professor Jack, MB, FRCPath, DMJ, FFPathRCPI. State Pathologist for Northern Ireland since 1990; Professor, Forensic Medicine, Queen's University, Belfast; b. 29.1.54, Belfast. Educ. Methodist College, Belfast; Queen's University, Belfast. House Officer, Royal Victoria Hospital, Belfast; Senior House Officer in Pathology, Royal Victoria Hospital, Belfast; Tutor/Registrar in Pathology, Royal Victoria Hospital and Queen's University, Belfast; Assistant State Pathologist for Northern Ireland, 1985 - 90. Consultant Advisor in Pathology, International Criminal Tribunal for the former Yugoslavia; Examiner in Forensic Medicine, Royal College of Pathologists and University College, Galway; Pathology Convenor, Society of Apothecaries of London; Member of Professional Conduct Committee of General Medical Council. Publications: Self-assessment in Pathology. Recreations: wine; antiques; squash. Address: (b.) Institute of Forensic Medicine, Grosvenor Road, Belfast, BT12 6BS; T.- 028 90 634648. e-mail: j.crane@qub.ac.uk

Crawford, Charles Randall, JP; b. 14.11.33, Coleraine; m., Elizabeth Hayes; 3d. Educ. Coleraine Academical Institution; Proprietor, Randall Crawford Pest Control, Coleraine. Tax Commissioner; Member, Independent Tribunal Service; Member, Coleraine Borough Council, 1973 - 86; Deputy Mayor, 1981 and 1984. Coleraine District President A.E.U., 1960-86. Recreation: world travel. Address: (h.) 34 Buskin Way, Coleraine, BT51 3BE; T.- 028 703 44873.

Crawford, Paul Andrew, BA, LLB, MA. Partner, Crawford Scally and Co Solicitors, Strabane; b. 30.4.48, Strabane, Co Tyrone; m., Helena Laird; 2d. Educ. Christian Brothers Grammar School, Omagh, Co Tyrone; Trinity College, Dublin. Secretary, Strabane Solicitors Association; Solicitor, Strabane District Council. Chairman, Strabane and District Community Work Programme Ltd. Recreations: travel; community organisations; Rotary movement. Address: (b.) Crawford Scally and Co, Solicitors, 45 Bowling Green, Strabane, Co Tyrone, BT82 8BW; T.- 028 7188 3591.

Crawford, Professor Robert James, FREng, PhD, DSc, FIMechE, FIM. Professor of Engineering Materials, Queen's University, Belfast since 1989; b. 6.4.49, Lisburn; m., Isobel Catherine; 2s.; 1d. Educ. Lisburn Technical College; Queen's University, Belfast. Queen's University, Belfast: Assistant Lecturer, Engineering 1972; Lecturer, Mechanical Engineering, 1974; Senior Lecturer, 1982; Reader, 1984; Professor, 1989; Director of School, 1989; Director, Polymer Processing Centre, 1996; Chairman, Board of Governors, North Down and Ards Institute, 1995 - 98; Professor of Mechanical Engineering, Auckland, New Zealand, 1999-2001; Pro Vice Chancellor, Queen's University Belfast, 2001. Member of Board of: Invest Northern Ireland, since 2002, Investment Belfast. Publications: Mechanics of Engineering Materials (2nd edn.), 1996; Plastics Engineering (3rd edn.), 1998. Netlon medal for contribution to polymer processing, 1996. Recreations: reading; gardening. Address: (b.) School of Mechanical and

Manufacturing Engineering, Queen's University, Belfast, BT9 5AH; T.-028 90274700. e-mail: r.crawford@qub.ac.uk

Crawford, Simon Patrick, MA. Solicitor, Peden and Reid Solicitors; b. 29.2.68. Educ. Campbell College, Belfast; Oxford University. Recreations: rugby; reading; travelling. Address: (b.) Peden and Reid Solicitors, 22 Callender Street, Belfast BT1 5BU. T.-02890 325617. e-mail: peden-reid@dnet.co.uk

Creaner, Sarah Margaret Mary, LL.B. Deputy Resident Magistrate since 1980; Proprietor, rare breeds farm since 1994; b. 28.9.41, Downpatrick; m., John Francis Creaner; 2s.; 2d. Educ. Mount St Catherine's School, Armagh; Queen's University, Belfast. Qualified as a Solicitor, 1965; Office of Director of Law Reform, Stormont, 1965 - 68; Practicing Solicitor, 1972 - 94. Recreations: farming; gardening; conservation. Address: (h.) 5 Largy Road, Kilcoo, Newry, Co Down, BT34 5JJ; T.- 028437-78687/70083. e-mail: slievenalargy@aol.com

Creed, Angus Francis Roche, MA (Cantab). Partner, Arthur Cox, Northern Ireland, Solicitors since 1996; b. 10.6.51, Nottingham; m., Rosemary Ann Edith Creed; 3s,; 1d. Educ. Campbell College, Belfast; Pembroke College, Cambridge. In-house Legal Advisor, Bank of Ireland, 1976 - 87; Partner, Norman Wilson and Co Solicitors, 1987 - 96; Norman Wilson merged with Arthur Cox, 1996. Recreations: golf; gardening; reading; music. Address: (b.) Capital House, 3 Upper Queen Street, Belfast BT1 6PU. T.- 02890-230007.

Creighton, Dawn Marie, BL. Barrister-at-Law since 1986; b. 1.12.61, Belfast; m., Patrick M Hirst; 1d. Educ. Victoria College, Belfast; Queen's University, Belfast. Admitted to the Honourable Society of the Inn of Court of Northern Ireland and to the degree of Barrister-at-Law, 1986; Called to the Bar of Ireland, 1996; Temporary Teaching Assistant, Institute of Professional Legal studies since 1994. Recreations: equestrianism; travel; tennis. Address: (b.) Bar Library, Royal Courts of Justice, Chichester Street, Belfast, BT1 3JP; T.- 028 9024 1523.

Creighton, Samuel John, LL.B. Solicitor. b. 17.1.59, Belfast; m., Fiona Jill McFetridge. Educ. Queen's University, Belfast. Admitted as a Solicitor, 1983; Established Creighton and Co, Solicitors, 1987. Recreations: tennis; fishing. Address: (b.) 122 Bloomfield Avenue, Belfast, BT5 5AE; T.- 02890-732461.

Crilly, Rev. Oliver, BA (Hons), MPhil. Parish Priest, Ardmore, Co. Derry, since 1999; b. 5.7.40, Curran, Co.Derry. Educ. St Columb's College, Derry; St Patrick's College. Maynooth; University of Ulster at Coleraine. Teacher, St Patrick's Maghera, Co Derry, 1965 - 69; Director, Veritas

Publications, Dublin, 1969 - 77; Director, Catholic Communications Institute of Ireland, 1977 - 82; Curate, Parish of Camus, Strabane, Co Tyrone, 1982 - 89; Parish Priest, Melmount, Strabane, Co. Tyrone, 1989-99. Chair, Religious Press Association of Ireland, 1970 - 73; Member, National Executive, The National Conference of Priests of Ireland; Member, Irish Commission for Justice and Peace, 1980 - 85; Member, North Review, (independent review of parades and marches), 1996 - 97; Member, Western Education and Library Board, 1987 - 97. Frequent Broadcaster, BBC, RTE, Radio na Gaeltachta, TG4; Presenter first Irish Language Documentary, BBC2 Northern Ireland. Recreations: leisure cycling; drawing cartoons. Address: (h.) Parochial House, 49 Ardmore Road, Derry BT47 3QP. T.- 028 7134 9490. e-mail: ocrilly@aol.com

Crilly, Rev. Patrick Joseph, BA, BD. Parish Priest, Desertmartin, Co Derry since 1997; b., 24.4.44, Co Derry. Educ. St Columb's College, Derry; St Patrick's College, Maynooth; Université de Toulouse, France. Teacher, St Patrick's High School, Maghera, Co Derry, 1969 - 80; Vocations Director, Derry Diocese, 1975 - 84; Hospital Chaplain, Altnagevin Hospital, Derry, 1982 - 87; Administrator, Our Lady of Lourdes Parish, Derry, 1987 - 97. Member, Northern Ireland Leadership Team of Marriage Encounter, 1980 - 82; Member, Western Education and Library Board, 1989 - 97 (Chairman, Youth Committee, 1995 - 97; Chairman, Further Education Committee, 1993 - 97); Chaplain to Foyle Hospice, 1991 - 97. President, Cumann Na Sagart since 1999. Poet and Literary Critic in Irish Language. Regular Broadcaster, BBC Radio and Radio Highland. Publications: Ceantair Shamhalta, 1972; Uaigneas, 1974; Vocation, a Call to Relationship, 1984. Recreations: cycling. Address: (h.) 50 Tobermore Road, Desertmartin, Magherafelt, Co Derry, BT45 5LE; T.- 028-7963 2196.

Crothers, Professor Derrick Samuel Frederick, BA, MA (Oxon), PhD, CPhys, FInstP, EurPhys, CMath, FIMA, CEng, FIEE, MNYAS, MRI, ILTM, MRIA, FAPS. Professor of Theoretical Physics, Queen's University Belfast since 1985; b. 24.6.42, Belfast; m., Eithne A Crothers; 2s.; 1d. Educ. Rainey Endowed School, Magherafelt; Balliol College, Oxford; Queen's University Belfast. Joined Queen's University, Belfast, 1966: Lecturer in Applied Mathematics and Theoretical Physics, 1966 - 76; Reader in Applied Mathematics and Theoretical Physics, 1976 - 85; Lecturer in Physics, University College, London, 1970 - 71; Member, Alliance Party of NI, since 1971; Elected (South Antrim) Ist NI Assembly, 1973-75; Education and Commerce Consultative Committees, 1973; Lisburn Election Agent, 1972-83; Professeur Associe à la Premiere Classe, University of Bordeaux I, 1984; EPSRC PI: Rolling Programme of Research in Theoretical Atomic, Molecular and Optical Physics at QUB, 1988-2000: £4.61 M; UK Chair, UK-Japan Collaboration of Theoretical Atomic Collisions and UK Contact Point in Computational Physics: Theoretical Atomic and Molecular Physics: SERC Monbusho Aide Memoire, 1988 - 98; Head, Theoretical and Computational Physics Research Division, Queen's University Belfast, 1989 - 2001. Elected Member of the Royal Irish Academy, 1991. Long Term Visiting Scientist, Institute for Theoretical Atomic and Molecular Physics, Harvard University, 1993. Elected Fellow of the American Physical Society, 1994 for distinguished research on atomic collision theory. Member, Council of the Institute of Mathematics and its applications, 1996 - 99; Chair, Collision Physics Group, Division of Atomic, Molecular, Optical and Plasma Physics Division, IOP, 1997 - 98; UK Representative, Executive Committee, International Conference for the Physics of Electronic and Atomic Collisions, 1997 - 99; Member of the Institute of Learning and Teaching, 2000; Member, Council of NCUP, 2002-04. Publications: over 300 on collision theory, light and heavy particles, ferromagnetism; Supercomputing, Collision Processes and Applications (ed) 1999; Relativistic Heavy-Particle Collision Theory, 2000; 9 chapters in books including ch. 16 on David R. Bates, Creators of Mathematics: The Irish Connection, 2000. Recreations: rugby union football; North of Ireland FC, 1962-99, Chair, 1980-83, Convenor, 1989-91; Belfast Harlequins RFC, 1999-. Address: (b.) David Bates Building, Department of Applied Mathematics and Theoretical Physics, Queen's University Belfast, Belfast, BT7 1NN; T.- 02890-335048. e-mail: d.crothers@qub.ac.uk

Croxford, Richard Alan, BSc (Hons), PG Acting Dip, MA. Artistic Director of Replay Productions, since 2000; Actor/Director, since 1999; Actor, since 1984; b. 20.10.62, Liverpool. Educ. George Watson's College, Edinburgh; Southampton University. Seventeen years as a professional actor including Blood Brothers, Albery Theatre, London; The Mousetrap - St. Martin's Theatre, London; International Tours with the English Shakespeare Company and Broadway Musical Company; numerous highly successful tours throughout Ireland as a Director. Member: Lisburn Arts Advisory Committee for Lisburn Council, Management Committee, Ulster Association of Youth Drama. Recreations: theatre; cinema; food/drink; swimming; tennis; skiing. Address: (b.) Replay Productions, Old Museum Arts Centre, 7 College Square North, Belfast BT1 6AR. T.-028 90 322 773. e-mail: replay@dircon.co.uk

Crute, Paul, BA, MA (distinction), PGCE (distinction). Headmaster, Royal School Armagh, since 2002; Chair of Visiting Teams for Accreditation of International Schools on behalf of Council of International Schools, since 2001; Chair of Armagh District Scouts, since 2002; b. 18.1.61, Consett, Co. Durham; m., Catherine Elizabeth Ann nee Gibson. Educ. Hartlepool Grammar School (which became Brinkburn Comprehensive School); University of Stirling; University of Liverpool; University of Bath.

French Teacher/Assistant Headmaster (Bruce House), Gordonstoun School, Elgin, Moray, 1985-88; Head of Modern Languages, British International School, Cairo, Egypt, 1988-92; Housemaster, Belvedere House, Aiglon College, Switzerland, 1992-99; Member of SMT, Aiglon College, Switzerland, Accreditation Officer and Deputy Headmaster (Curriculum), 1998-2002. Leader and membership of the pilot project Ruamkan, Thai Hill Tribes Charity. Recreations: squash; skiing; travel; reading. Address: Headmaster's Residence, 5 College Hill, Armagh BT61 9DF. T.-028 37523282.

Cullen, Professor Bernard, BA, BSc (Econ), MA, PhD. Professor of Philosophy since 1992, Dean, Faculty of Humanities since 1998, Queen's University, Belfast; b. 11.1.50, Belfast; m., Jean Murray; 1s.; 1d. Educ. Queen's University, Belfast; Sorbonne, Paris; University of Michigan. Lecturer, Queen's University, Belfast, 1974; Research Fellow, Alexander von Humboldt Foundation, Germany, 1987; Dean, Faculty of Theology, Queen's University, Belfast, 1993 - 97. Fellow of the Royal Society of Arts; Member, International Psychoanalytical Association. President, Irish Philosophical Society, 1989 - 92, Associate Member, British Psychoanalytical Society; Chair, Staff Commission for Education and Library Boards; President, Irish Association for Cultural Economic and Social Affairs, 1995 - 97. Publications: Hegel's Social and Political Thought, 1979; Hegel Today, 1987; Discriminations Old and New, 1992. Recreations: golf; reading newspapers; swimming; cycling; cinema. Address: (b.) Queen's University, Belfast BT7 1NN; T.- 028 9033 5348.

Cullington, John Donald, MA (Cantab), BMus, DMus, FRCO, LRAM, ARCM, Cert Ed. Piano Tutor, University of Ulster at Jordanstown; b., 12.9.37, Spilsby, Lincs; m., Stella Juliet Goodall; 2d. Educ. Sandbach School, Cheshire; Selwyn College, Cambridge. Assistant Master, Bradford Grammar School/Watford Grammar School, 1960 - 62; Sub-Organist, St Mary's Cathedral, Edinburgh/Assistant Director of Music, Edinburgh Academy, 1963 - 65; Director of Music, Samuel Marsden Collegiate School, Wellington, New Zealand, 1965 - 67; Music Lecturer, Huddersfield Polytechnic, 1968 - 71; Senior/Principal Lecturer, Music, Northern Ireland Polytechnic, 1971 - 75; Director of Music, St Paul's Cathedral, Dunedin, New Zealand, 1975 - 78; Principal Lecturer, Music, Ulster Polytechnic, 1979 - 84; Senior Lecturer, Music, University of Ulster, 1984 - 97; Head, Music Department, 1984 - 88. Sawyer Prize, ARCO Organ Performance. Publications: On the Dignity and Effects of Music, 1996; 'That Liberal and virtuous art: three humanist treatises on music', 2001. Numerous live performances and broadcasts in New Zealand and Northern Ireland. Address: (h.) 113 Station Road, Greenisland, Carrickfergus, Co Antrim, BT38 8UW; T.- 028 90 863852.

Cunningham, Brett. Area Operations Manager, West Scotland and Northern Ireland Region Maritime and Coastguard Agency, Northern Ireland, since 2000; b. 24.5.45. Joined Coastguard in 1972 after a career flying helicopters in the RN. Most recent appointment: Clyde Maritime Rescue Co-ordination Centre as Regional Inspector. Address: (b.) Maritime and Coastguard Agency, Bregenz House, Quay Street, Bangor, Co. Down. T.-02891 475301.

Cunningham, John Bernard, MA. Retired Headmaster; b. 9.5.44, Co Donegal; m., Ann Monaghan; 2s.; 2d. Educ. St Michael's Grammar School, Enniskillen; St Joseph's Training College, Belfast; Open University; Durham University. Assistant Teacher, Legamagherry Primary School, Co Tyrone, 1965 - 67; Assistant Teacher, Montiagh Primary School, Co Fermanagh, 1967 - 69; Headmaster, St Davogs Primary School, Co Fermanagh, 1969 - 95. Chairman, Erne Heritage Tour Guides. Publications: Castle Caldwell and its Families; Lough Derg Legendary Pilgrimage; Mysterious Boa Island; John O'Donovan's Letters from Fermanagh, 1834; 25 books written, ghost written or contributed to; numerous articles. Recreations: drama; golf; rough shooting; internet; travel. Address: (h.) Commons, Belleek, Co Fermanagh; T.- 01365-658327.
e-mail: adam4eves@aol.com
web: erneheritagtours.com

Cunningham, Sarah Christina (Sadie). Vice-Chairman, Board of Governors, Newry and Kilkeel Institute of Further and Higher Education, since 1998; Immediate Past President, Northern Ireland Chamber of Trade; b. 24.12.39, Newry, Co Down; m., Charles; 1s.; 3d.. Educ. Sacred Heart Grammar School. Partner with husband in Children's Fashion and Schoolwear (now retired). Employers Member, Industrial Tribunals since 1990; President, Northern Ireland Chamber of Trade, 1993 - 97; Member, Business Leadership Team, Business in the Community, Newry; Hon. Member, Newry Chamber of Commerce. Address: (h.) Aveen, Damolly Village, Newry, Co Down; T.- 028 302 64959.

Curl, Professor James Stevens, PhD, FSA, DiplArch, DipTP, AABC, RIBA, MRIAI, ARIAS, MRTPI, FSA Scot. Emeritus Professor of Architectural History; b. 26.3.37, Belfast; m., Professor Stanislawa Dorota Iwaniec; 2 d. Educ. Campbell College, Belfast; Belfast College of Art; Oxford School of Architecture; University College, London. Architectural Assistant, Belfast, 1958 - 61; Senior Architect, Oxford, 1963 - 69; Private Practice, Oxford, 1969 - 70; Architectural Editor, Survey of London, 1970-73; Consultant Architect, European Architectural Heritage Year, Scottish Civic Trust, 1973-75; Conservation Department, Hertfordshire County Council, 1975 - 78; School of Architecture, Leicester: Senior Lecturer, 1978 - 88, Professor, 1988 - 98, Emeritus Professor and Senior Research Fellow, 1998-2000; The Queen's University of Belfast: Professor of Architectural History and Senior Research Fellow, 2000-02. British Academy Awards; RIBA Research Award; Authors' Foundation Award; Ulster Arts Club Prize; Sir Charles Lanyon Prize; Visiting Fellow, Peterhouse, University of Cambridge, 1992 and 2002; Liveryman, Worshipful Company of Chartered Architects of the City of London. Publications: Death and Architecture, 2002; Piety Proclaimed, 2002; Kensal Green Cemetery, 2001; The Oxford Dictionary of Architecture, 1999, 2000; The Victorian Celebration of Death, 2000; The Honourable The Irish Society and the Plantation of Ulster, 1608-2000, 2000; Victorian Churches, 1995; Egyptomania, 1994; Georgian Architecture, 1993; A Celebration of Death, 1993; Encyclopaedia of Architectural Terms, 1993 and 1997; Classical Architecture, 1992 and 2001; The Art and Architecture of Freemasonry, 1991 and 2002 (Winner of Sir Banister Fletcher Award for Best Book of the Year, 1992); Victorian Architecture, 1990; The Londonderry Plantation 1609 - 1914, 1986; The Life and Work of Henry Roberts 1803 - 76, 1983; The Egyptian Revival, 1982. Recreations: music; food; wine; literature; travel. Address: (h.) 15 Torgrange, Holywood, Co Down, BT18 0NG; T.- 028 90 425141.

Curran, Edmund, BSc, DipEd. Editor, Belfast Telegraph, since 1993; b. 29.9.44, Belfast; m., Pauline; 2 s.; 2 d. Educ. Royal School, Dungannon; Queen's University, Belfast. Belfast Telegraph: Trainee Journalist, 1966, Feature Writer, 1968, Leader Writer, 1969, Assistant Editor, 1973, Deputy Editor, 1974; Editor, Sunday Life, 1988-93. Member of The Press Complaints Commission, since 2002. Recreations: tennis; golf. Address: (b.) 124-144 Royal Avenue, Belfast BT1 1EB; T.-02890 264000.

Curran, Edwin Paul, BSc, PhD, AFIMA. Lecturer, University of Ulster; m., Elizabeth; 3 s. Educ. Queen's University, Belfast. Address: (b.) School of Computing and Mathematics, University of Ulster, Shore Road, Newtownabbey, Co Antrim, BT37 0QB. e-mail: ep.curran@ulster.ac.uk

Cushnahan, Samuel. Director, Families Against Intimidation and Terror; Executive Committee, Widows and Widowers against Violence (voluntary capacity); b. 28.2.45, Belfast; m., Norah; 2s.; 2d. Educ. St Patrick's Comprehensive School, Belfast. Merchant Seaman; Floor Layer/Carpet Fitter; Owner Contracting business; Food and Licensing Trade, owner The Arlington Hotel and Restaurant until destroyed in a fire bomb attack in 1977; Property Development. Participated in the development of television programmes on the effects of violence on groups within Northern Ireland. Elected Vice President of International Federation of Human Rights Groups Against Terrorism "IFHRGT", based in Algeria, Feb. 1999; Founder Member of Northern Ireland Human Rights Alert (NIHRA), May 1996; Founder Member, Northern Ireland Committee Against Terror (NICAT). Recreations: current

affairs; reading; walking; squash. Address: (h.) 3
Glastonbury Avenue, Antrim Road, Belfast BT15
4DL; T.-90-295727.

D

Dallat, Dr. Cahal Alphonsus, JP, BA, Dip Ed Admin, MPhil, DLitt, FRSAI. Author and Historical Consultant; b. 12.11.21, Ballycastle, Co Antrim; m.,1. Mary Gilligan (dec.); m., 2. Moira Mullan (dec.); 3s.; 4d. Educ. St Malachy's College; Queen's University, Belfast; University of Ulster at Coleraine. P Dallat and Sons, Building Contractors, 1943 - 57; Teacher, Technology, Mathematics and History, Star of the Sea Secondary School, Ballycastle, 1957 - 63; Headmaster, Star of the Sea Secondary School, 1963 - 78 (on secondment, Project Officer, Schools Cultural Study Project, University of Ulster, 1974 - 76); Deputy Head, Cross and Passion College, 1978 - 84. Member: Ballycastle Urban Council, 1946 - 57; Co Antrim Welfare Committee, 1948 - 58; Ulster Countryside Committee, 1970-89; Historic Monuments Council (NI), 1983-89; Vice-Chairman, Northern Health and Social Services Board, 1977 - 86; Member, Northern Ireland Health and Social Services Central Services Agency, 1977 - 86; Chairman, Northern Ireland Health and Social Services Training Council, 1983 - 89; Member, Council for the Professions Supplementary to Medicine (London), 1983 - 91; Chairman, Convocation, University of Ulster, 1986 - 90; Council Member, University of Ulster, 1984 - 89; President, Alumni Association, University of Ulster since 1989; Patron, Alumni Association since 1998. Justice of the Peace since 1965; Hon. DLitt, University of Ulster, 1991. Founder Member and Past Chairman, Federation for Ulster Local Studies; Founder member and Past Chairman, Ulster History Trust; Member Ulster Dialect Dictionary Advisory Committee, 1991 - 95. The Cahal Dallat Cultural Diversity Fellowship on Regional History was established by the Northern Ireland Community Relations Council in 1998; Director of the John Hewitt International Summer School, since 1993; President, Multiple Sclerosis Society, since 2001. Northern Ireland Publications include: A Study of the Teaching of Local History in Selected Post-Primary Schools in Northern Ireland, 1978; Caring By Design (HMSO), 1983; Rooms of Time (HMSO), 1988; McCahan's Local Histories, 1988; The Road to the Glens (Friar's Bush Press), 1989; A Tour of the Causeway Coast (Friar's Bush Press), 1990; Antrim Coast and Glens (HMSO), 1990; Altnagelvin's Thirty Glorious Years and Two Hundred Years of Medical Care in the City of Derry, 1991; Ulster Images for Social Studies (with Jack McKinney) (EDCO), 1992; Ballycastle and the Heart of the Glens (Cottage Publications), 1994; Editor of the Glynns, the Journal of the Glens of Antrim Historical Society (from Vol. 16 to Vol. 28). Recreations: folk music; genealogy. Address: (h.) 9 Atlantic Avenue, Ballycastle, Co Antrim, BT54 6AL; T.- 028 207 62467. e-mail: cahaldallat@ireland.com

Dallat, John. Member (East Londonderry), Social Democratic and Labour Party, Northern Ireland Assembly, since 1998; b. Rasharkin, Co Antrim; m.; 2 s.; 1 d. Educ. University of Ulster and Galway University. Teacher of Business Studies, 1968-98; Councillor, Coleraine Borough Council, since 1977; Deputy Mayor, 1995-97; Mayor, 2001-2002; Director and Treasurer, Kilrea, Rasharkin and Dunloy Credit Union. Address: (b.) Parliament Buildings, Stormont, Belfast, BT4 3ST; T.- 028 295 41880.

Dalm, Amanda Victoria (Mandy), FIPA. Managing Director, Navigator Blue Ltd since 1990; b. Bangor, Co Down; m., Pim Dalm; 1d. Educ. Glenlola Collegiate School. Advertising Sales, Century Newspapers, 1973 - 74; Account Executive, The Agency (formerly RMB Advertising Ltd), 1974; Director, 1977; Founding Board Member. RMB Advertising Plc/Deputy Divisional Managing Director, Osprey Communications Plc, 1984 - 90; Bought The Agency from Osprey Plc, 1990, now re-named Navigator Blue Ltd. Lifetime Fellowship, Institute of Practitioners in Advertising, 1997. Recreations: horse riding; spending precious time with family. Address: (b.) Navigator Blue Ltd, The Baths, Ormeau Avenue, Belfast, BT2 8HS; T.- 028 9024 6722.

Daly, His Eminence Cardinal Cahal Brendan, BA (Hons), MA, DD, LPh. Roman Catholic Archbishop Emeritus of Armagh; b. 1.10.17. Educ. St Malachy's Belfast; Queen's University, Belfast; St Patrick's, Maynooth; Institut Catholique, Paris. Ordained, 1941; Lecturer, Scholastic Philosophy, Queen's University, Belfast, 1945 - 62; Reader, 1962 - 67; Consecrated Bishop, 1967; Bishop of Ardagh and Clonmacnois, 1967 - 82; Bishop of Down and Connor, 1982 - 90; Archbishop of Armagh and Primate of All Ireland, 1990 - 96; Cardinal, 1991. Retired, 1996. Honorary Doctorates: Queen's University, Belfast; University of Dublin; National University of Ireland; Notre Dame University, Indiana, USA; St John's University, New York, USA. Publications: Morals, Law and Life, 1962; Natural Law Morality Today, 1965; Violence in Ireland and Christian Conscience, 1973; Theologians and Magisterium, 1977; Peace, the Work of Justice, 1979; The Price of Peace, 1991; Tertullian the Puritan and his Influence, 1993; Moral Philosophy in Britain from Bradley to Wittgenstein, 1996; Steps on my Pilgrim Journey, 1998; chapters in: Prospect for Metaphysics, 1961; Intellect and Hope, 1968; New Essays in Religious Language, 1969; Understanding the Eucharist, 1969. Address: (h.) Ard Mhacha, 23 Rosetta Avenue, Ormeau Road, Belfast, BT7 3HG.

Daly, Most Rev. Edward, BPh, BD, DLitt. Retired Bishop of Derry; b. 5.12.33, Co Donegal. Educ. St Columb's College, Derry; Lateran University, Rome. Curate, Castleder, Co Tyrone, 1957 - 62; Curate, St Eugene's Cathedral, Derry, 1962 - 73; Religious Broadcasting, RTE, Dublin,

1973 - 4; Bishop of Derry, 1974 - 93. Publications: The Clergy of the Diocese of Derry, an Index, 1997; Mister, Are You A Priest, 2000. Recreations: reading. Address: (h.) Gurteen, 9 Steelstown Road, Derry, BT48 8EU.

Darby, Professor John, OBE, BA, DPhil. Professor of Comparative Ethnic Studies, University of Notre Dame, Indiana; Professor in Ethnic Studies, University of Ulster, 1985-98; Senior Research Fellow, INCORE, since 1998; b. 18.11.40, Belfast; m., Marie Darby; 2s. Educ. St Patrick's College, Armagh; Queen's University, Belfast. Teacher, St Malachy's College, Belfast, 1963 - 71; Research Publications Officer, Northern Ireland Community Relations Commission, 1971 - 74; Lecturer, Social Administration, New University of Ulster 1974 - 85; Director, Centre for the Study of Conflict, 1985 - 91; Director, Initiative in Conflict, Resolution and Ethnicity (INCORE), 1993 - 97. President, Ethnic Studies Network; Hon. Professor, University Sunderland; Jennings Research Fellow, US Institute of Peace, Washington DC, 1998. Publications: 11 books including; Scorpions in a Bottle, 1997; The Management of Peace Processes, 2000; The Effects of Violence on Peace Processes, 2001; Guns and Government, 2002. Recreations: golf; orchid cultivation. Address: (h.) 61 Strand Road, Portstewart, BT55 7LU; T.- 01265-833098.

Dardis, Anthony James (Tony), MA, Mlitt, MA(Ed). Principal, East Tyrone College of Further and Higher Education since 1994; b. 8.1.48, Magherafelt, Co Londonderry; m., Tillie; 3s.; 1d. Educ. St Patrick's College, Armagh; Rainey Endowed, Magherafelt; Trinity College, Dublin; University of Ulster. Omagh Technical College: Lecturer, English, 1971 - 73; Head of Academic and General Studies, 1973 - 86; Vice-Principal, Omagh College of Further Education, 1986 - 94; Course Tutor/Counsellor, Open University, 1972-2000. Member, Western Education and Library Board, 1993 - 94; Member, Western Health and Social Services Council, 1991 - 94. Recreations: reading. Address: (b.) East Tyrone College of Further and Higher Education, Circular Road, Dungannon, Co Tyrone, BT71 6BQ; T.- 028 87 722323.

Davidson, Norman. Chief Executive, Lisburn City Council since 1996; 2s.; 1d. Eastern Health and Social Services Board; Belfast City Council; Community Relations Commission; Deputy Chief Executive, Lisburn Council, 1989. Recreations: sport. Address: (b.) Lisburn Council, Island Civic Centre, The Island, Lisburn BT27 4RL. T.-028 9250 9250.

Davies, Professor Raymond Jeremy Hugh, MA, PhD. Professor, Biochemistry, Queen's University, Belfast since 1991; b. 14.8.42, Wolverhampton; m., Janet Elizabeth Craig; 2s.; 1d. Educ. St Mary's School, Nairobi, Kenya; Jesus College, Cambridge. Research Fellow, California Institute of Technology, USA, 1966 - 68; MRC

Junior Research Fellow, University of Kent, Canterbury, 1968 - 70; Lecturer/Reader/Professor, Queen's University, Belfast since 1970; Head of Biochemistry Division, 1988 - 95. Chairman, Irish Area Section, Biochemical Society, 1995 - 98. Publications: over 100 published papers in scientific journals, Royal Irish Academy Medal for Biochemistry, 1993. Recreations: tennis; travel. Address: (h.) 21 Viewfort Park, Belfast, BT17 9JY; T.- 028 90 614554. e-mail: j.davies@qub.ac.uk

Davis, Brian Wilson, BSc (Econ), FCA. Managing Director, Nambarrie Tea Company Ltd since 1992; m., Rosemary 1s.; 1d. Educ. Wallace High School; New University of Ulster. Chartered Accountant, Deloitte and Co, 1972 - 77; Chief Accountant, Thomas McMullan and Co Ltd, 1977 - 79; Financial Controller, Dale Farm Dairies Ltd, 1979 - 87; Factory Manager, Dale Farm Ice Cream Ltd, 1988 - 90; General Manager, Dale Farm Ice Cream Ltd, 1990 - 92. Recreation: Ulster U 21 Hockey Coach. Address: (b.) Nambarrie Tea Company Ltd, 21 Victoria Street, Belfast, BT1 3GD; T.- 02890-326618.

Davis, Ivan. Member (Lagan Valley), Ulster Unionist Party, Northern Ireland Assembly, 1998-2003; NI Assembly Deputy Whip, UUP, 1998-2003; Chief Whip, UUP, 2002-03; b. 16.4.37, Lisburn; m.; 3 s.; 1 d. Educ. Lisburn Public School. Member, Northern Ireland Assembly, 1982-86; Member, Northern Ireland Forum, 1996-98; Member of Lisburn City Council, since 1973. Address: (b.) Room 278, Parliament Buildings, Stormont, Belfast, BT4 3XX; T.- 02890-521029/521749. e-mail: ivan.davis@niassembly.gov.uk

Davis, Dr. John, PhD, MSc, BAgr. Director, Agricultural and Food Economics, School of Agriculture and Food Science, Queen's University, Belfast and Department of Agriculture and Rural Development (DARD), since 1992; Hon. Secretary, Agricultural Economics Society (UK); Managing Editor, Euro Choices; b. 28.6.51, Belfast; m., Dorothy Elaine Davis; 1s.; 1d. Educ. Wallace High School, Lisburn; Queen's University, Belfast; University of Newcastle-upon-Tyne. Queen's University, Belfast: Lecturer, Business Economics, 1977 - 81; Lecturer, Agricultural Economics/ Senior Agricultural Economist, DANI, 1982 - 87; Senior Lecturer/Principal Agricultural Economist, DANI, 1987 - 92. Publications: An Economic Analysis of Early Retirement and Setting Up Young Farmers' Schemes in Northern Ireland, 2002; Economics of Marketable Surplus Supply: A Theoretical and Empirical Analysis for China; China's Grain Supply and Demand: The Challenge of Feeding a Billion (with L Wang), 1999; Rural Change in Ireland (ed.), 1999. Recreations: running; cycling; gardening. Address: (b.) School of Agriculture and Food Science, Queen's University, Belfast, Newforge Lane, Belfast, BT9 5PX; T.- 028 9025 5204. e-mail: john.davis@qub.ac.uk

De Brun, Bairbre. Member (West Belfast), Sinn Fein, Northern Ireland Assembly, since 1998; b. Dublin. Educ. University College, Dublin; Queen's University, Belfast. Teacher. Address: (b.) Parliament Buildings, Stormont, Belfast BT4 3ST; T.-02890 520700.

Deery, Aidan, BCL. Senior Partner, Deery McGuiness and Co Solicitors since 1997; Mullingar, Co Westmeath, Ireland; m. Kathleen Bernadette McLister; 1s.; 1d. Educ. Christian Brothers School, Monaghan; University College, Dublin. Solicitors Apprentice, McKinty and Wright Solicitors; Solicitor, L'Estrange and Brett; Sole Practitioner, AF Deery and Co, 1982 - 97. Recreations: played representative squash and tennis for Ulster and Ireland; county football; music. Address: (b.) 179 - 181 Victoria Street, Belfast; T.- 02890-233268.

Dempsey, John Patrick, MBA, BSc (Hons) Elect. Engr. Chief Executive, Ballymoney Borough Council, since 1998; b. 18.3.51, Ballymena; m., Liz; 3 s.; 4 d. Educ. St. Columb's College, Derry; Queen's University Belfast; University of Ulster. Engineer: Short Bros, Belfast: Jun - Sept 1972, BBC Belfast, 1972-76, Roads Service, Coleraine, 1976-87, Roads Service, Belfast, 1988-97; Ballymoney Borough Council, since 1998. Director of ACORN (Local Enterprise Agency); Ballymoney Regeneration Co and Ballymoney Borough Local Strategy Partnership; Secretary, SOLACE, NI Branch. Recreations: gardening; motorcycling. Address: (b.) Riada House, 14 Charles Street, Ballymoney, Co Antrim BT53 6DZ. T.-028 2766 0237.
e-mail: john.dempsey@ballymoney.gov.uk

De Silva, Professor Amilra Prasanna, BSc, PhD. Professor, School of Chemistry, Queen's University, Belfast since 1997; b. 29.4.52, Colombo, Sri Lanka. Educ. St Thomas' College, Mount Lavinia, Sri Lanka; University of Colombo, Sri Lanka; Queen's University, Belfast. Lecturer, Department of Chemistry, University of Colombo, Sri Lanka, 1980 - 86; Queen's University, Belfast: Lecturer, School of Chemistry, 1986 - 91; Reader, 1991 - 97. Publications: chapters and papers published in numerous books, most recently: Dalton Perspectives, 2003; Handbook of Photochemistry and Photobiology, 2003. Recreation: percussion. Address: (b.) School of Chemistry, Queen's University, Belfast, Belfast, BT9 5AG; T.- 02890-274422.
e-mail: a.desilva@qub.ac.uk

Devlin, Dr. Rosemary, BSSc (Hons), PhD, PGCE. Member, Viewer Consultative Committee, Independent Television Commission, 1993-97; b. 25.11.56, Belfast; 1s.; 2d. Educ. St Genevieve's High School; Queen's University, Belfast. Couple Counselling Certificate. Recreations: family; reading; aerobics; Glens of Antrim. Address: (h.) 103 Brooke Drive, Belfast, BT11 9NJ; T.- 02890-592199.

Diamond, Thomas, BSc, MD, FRCS, FRCSI. Consultant in General and Hepatobiliary Surgery, Mater Hospital, since 1992; Honorary Senior Lecturer in Surgery, Queen's University of Belfast, since 1996; Regional Adviser in Surgery for Northern Ireland, since 1999; b. 10.2.56; m., Emma Diamond; 1 s.; 3 d. Educ. The Queen's University of Belfast. General Surgical Training in N. Ireland; Specialist Hepatobiliary Surgical Training in Paris. Editorial Board Member, British Journal of Surgery. Publications: books: 2; original papers: 78; abstracts published: 45. Address: (b.) Mater Hospital, Crumlin Road, Belfast BT14 6AB.

Dickson, Alexander Norman, MSc, BA, Cert Ed, ACP, DipRSA. Headmaster, Clounagh Junior High School since 1996; b. 11.11.40, Portadown; m., Hazel Best; 1d. Educ. Portadown Technical College; Stranmillis Training College. Appointed Clounagh Junior High School, 1963: Assistant Teacher, General Subjects, 1963 - 68; Assistant Teacher, Special needs, 1968 - 73; Head, Geography, 1973 - 84; Vice-Principal, 1984 - 92; Senior Vice-Principal, 1992 - 95. Recreations: walking; stamp and coin collecting; gardening. Address: (h.) 7 Richmond Chase, Mullavilly, Tandragee, Craigavon, Co Armagh, BT62 2NP; T.-(b.) 028 3833 2717.

Dickson, Professor Brice, BA, BCL, MPhil, Barrister-at-Law. Chief Commissioner, Northern Ireland Human Rights Commission since 1999; b. 5.12.53, Belfast; m., Patricia Mallon; 1 step d. Educ. Regent House, Newtownards; Wadham College, Oxford. Leverhulme European Studentship, University of Paris, 1976 - 77; Law Lecturer, Leicester University, 1977 - 79; Law Lecturer, Queen's University, Belfast, 1979 - 91; Professor of Law, University of Ulster, 1991 - 99. Salzburg Fellow, 1985; Churchill Fellow, 1994. Publications: The Legal System of Northern Ireland, 2001; Civil Liberties in Northern Ireland: The CAJ Handbook, 2003; Introduction to French Law, 1994; Human Rights and the European Convention, 1997; The House of Lords: Its Parliamentary and Judicial Roles (with P Carmichael), 1999. Recreations: reading novels; playing and watching sport; philately. Address: (h.) 33 Maryville Park, Belfast BT9 6LP.

Dickson, David Ronald, MEd, BEd (Hons), Adv Cert Ed. Principal, The Armstrong Primary School, Armagh, since 2001; b. 9.6.66, Banbridge; m., Lynda Margaret Parr; 1 d. Educ. Banbridge Academy; Stranmillis College; Queen's University, Belfast. Teacher, Edenderry Primary School, Banbridge, 1988 - 92; Vice-Principal, Windsor Hill Primary School, Newry, 1993 - 96; Principal, Iveagh Primary School, Rathfriland, 1996-2001. Recreations: cricket (Millpark CC); reading; interest in agriculture and the countryside. Address: (b.) Armstrong Primary School, College Hill, Armagh BT61 9DF. T.-028 37523003.

Dickson, Dr. Glenn Raymond, PhD, MSc, MIBiol, CBiol, FIBMS, FRMS. Senior Lecturer,

Anatomy, Queen's University Belfast since 2001, Head of Tissue Engineering Team, Trauma Research Group; b. 13.9.49, Belfast; m., Heather Dickson; 2s. Educ. Orangefield Boys' High School; Queen's University, Belfast. Medical Laboratory Scientific Officer, Department of Forensic Medicine, Queen's University, Belfast and Ministry of Home Affairs, 1968; Anatomy Department, Queen's University, Belfast: Electron Microscope Technician, 1971; Electron Microscopist, 1975; Research Officer, 1978; Senior Research Officer, 1983; Visiting Scientist and Lecturer, Laboratory for Musculoskeletal Research, Rappaport Family Institute for Research in the Medical Sciences, Israel Institute of Technology, Haifa, 1988; Lecturer, Anatomy, Queen's University Belfast, since 1992. Secretary, Ulster Biomedical Engineering Society since 1996; Hon. Treasurer, Northern Ireland Branch, Institute of Biology. Member and Fellowship, 11 Scientific Societies; President, NI Biomedical Engineering Society, 1999. External Examiner: University of London; University of Bath; National University of Ireland; Royal College of Surgeons, Ireland. Publications: Methods of Calcified Tissue Preparation, 1984; Over 100 Scientific papers. Recreations: country and forest walking; swimming; DIY; theatre; music. Address: (b.) Anatomy, School of Medicine and Health Sciences, Queen's University, Belfast, Medical Biology Centre, 97 Lisburn Road, Belfast, BT9 7BL; T.- 02890 272143; 669501 Ext. 2858. e-mail: G.Dickson@qub.ac.uk

Dinnen, Very Rev. John Frederick, MA, BD, MTh. Dean of Down/Rector of Hillsborough; b. 16.12.42, Belfast; m., Jane Margaret; 3 s. Educ. Foyle College, Derry; Trinity College, Dublin; Queen's University, Belfast. Assistant Curate: All Saints, Belfast; St Thomas, Dublin; St Brigid, Glengormley; Dean of Residence, Queen's University, Belfast. Address: (h.) 17 Dromore Road, Hillsborough, Co Down, BT26 6HS.

Dinsmore, Adeline. Headmistress, Ashfield Girls' High School, since 2001. Address: (b.) Ashfield Girls' High School, Holywood Road, Belfast BT4 2LY. T.-028 90 471744.

Dinsmore, Francis James, JP. Chairman, Francis Dinsmore Ltd; b. 12.2.27, Kells. Co Antrim; m., Phyllis F Allen; 3s.; 2d. Educ. Coleraine Academical Institution; Queen's University, Belfast. Managing Director, Francis Dinsmore Ltd, 1947 - 97. Recreations: sailing. Address: (h.) Templemoy House, Kells, Co Antrim, BT42 3JL; T.-02825-892829.

Dixon, The Very Rev. Dr. Samuel John, BA, DD. Convenor of Overseas Board of the Presbyterian Church in Ireland, since 2000; Moderator, P.C.I., 1998 - 99; Minister, 1st Antrim Presbyterian Church since 1980; b. 30.3.43, Co Monaghan; m., Claire Bentley; 2d. Educ. Clones High School; Magee University College; Trinity College, Dublin; New College, Edinburgh; Assembly College, Belfast (now known as Union Theological College). Assistant Minister, Carnmoney, 1966 - 70; Minister, First Rathfriland, 1970 - 80; Moderator, Presbyterian Church in Ireland, 1998-99; Chairman of Irish Council of OMF International, 1984-2000. Recreations: squash. Address: (h.) 11 Greystone Road, Antrim, BT41 1HD; T.- 028 94463289. e-mail: claire@dixon2002.plus.com

Dodds, Nigel Alexander, OBE, MA, BL. Member of Parliament for North Belfast, since 2001; Member (North Belfast), Democratic Unionist Party, Northern Ireland Assembly since 1998; Councillor, Belfast City Council since 1985; Secretary, Ulster Democratic Unionist Party since 1993; b. 20.8.58, Londonderry; m., Diana Jean Harris; 2s.; 1d. Educ. Portora Royal School, Enniskillen; St John's College, Cambridge; Institute of Professional Legal Studies, Queen's University, Belfast. Barrister-at-Law. Lord Mayor of Belfast, 1988 - 89 and 1991 - 92; Former Vice-President, Association of Local Authorities of Northern Ireland; Member, Senate, Queen's University, Belfast, 1989 - 93; Member, Northern Ireland Forum for North Belfast, 1996 - 98; Minister for Social Development, 1999-2000 and since 2001. McMahon Studentship for Law, Cambridge University, 1980 - 84. Scholarship, St John's College, Cambridge, 1979. Recreations: reading; travel. Address: (b.) Belfast City Hall, Belfast, BT1 5GS; T.- 02890-320202.

Doherty, Arthur, BEd, ATC. Member (East Londonderry), SDLP, Northern Ireland Assembly, since 1998; Member, Limavady Borough Council, since 1977; b. 19.1.32, Donegal; m., Mary Farrell; 1 s.; 2 d. Educ. St. Columb's College, Derry; St. Mary's College of Education, Belfast; University of Ulster at Jordanstown. Teacher, St. Columba's Primary School, Derry, 1953 - 57; Principal: Duncrun Primary School, Magilligan, 1957 - 67, Roemill Primary School, Limavady, 1967 - 69; Teacher, Art and Design, St. Mary's High School, Limavady, 1969 - 89. Member, Western Education and Library Board, 1993 - 98; Former Member and Vice-Chair of Governing Body, Limavady College of Further Education; Chair, Forum for Local Government and the Arts, 1995 - 99; Member, Council for Nature Conservation and the Countryside, 1995-2001; Mayor, Limavady Borough Council, 1993 - 94. Recreations: wife and family; reading; crosswords; galleries and museums; walking (slowly); swimming. Address: (h.) Gartan, 30 Tircreven Road, Magilligan, Limavady BT49 0LN; T.-028 7775 0287.

Doherty, Henry, JP. Legal Executive; b. 19.1.43, Derry; m., Phyllis; 2s.; 2d. Educ. Long Tower; Derry Municipal Technical College. Cleaver Fulton Rankin Solicitors since 1970. Former Member, Board of Visitors, Crumlin Road Prison; Justice of the Peace; Former Vice President, Irish Amateur Boxing Association; Chairman, General Commission, Inland Revenue Belfast Division; Member (HEROBC) Joint Advisory Committee,

University of Ulster and Queen's University Belfast; Executive Director, Golden Gloves Sporting Club, Ireland; Member, Central Council, IABA; Treasurer, Social Democratic Labour Party. Recreations: music; football; boxing; theatre. Address: (h.) 43 Harberton Park, Belfast, BT9 6TX; T.- 02890-662904; Fax: 02890 201885.

Doherty, Pat. Member (West Tyrone), Sinn Fein, Northern Ireland Assembly, since 1998; Member of Parliament, since 2001; b. 18.7.45, Glasgow; m.; 2 s.; 3 d. National Organiser, Sinn Fein, 1985-88, Vice-President, since 1988; Member, Sinn Fein talks team, 1997-98; founder Member, local Credit Union. Address: (b.) Parliament Buildings, Stormont, Belfast, BT4 3ST; T.- 02890-520700.

Doherty, Dr. Paul, BSc, PhD, LTCL, FRGS. Lecturer, School of History and International Affairs, University of Ulster since 1992; b. 7.9.48, Belfast; m., Valerie Ann Doherty; 2d. Educ. Sullivan Upper School; Queen's University, Belfast. Queen's University, Belfast: Research Assistant, 1971 - 73; Postgraduate Student, 1973 - 75; Lecturer, School of Environmental Studies, Ulster Polytechnic, 1975 - 84; Lecturer, Department of Environmental Studies, University of Ulster, 1984 - 92. Publications: Geographical Perspectives on the Belfast Region, 1990; Ethnic Residential Segregation in Belfast (with M A Poole), 1995; Ethnic Residential Segregation in Northern Ireland (with MA Poole), 1996. Recreations: playing the organ; motor caravanning. Address: (b.) School of History and International Affairs, University of Ulster at Jordanstown, Shore Road, Newtownabbey, Co Antrim, BT37 0QB; T.- 02890-366460.

Dolan, Aidan, BSc (Hons), MEd (Ed Mg), CertEd. Headteacher, Integrated College, Dungannon, since 1995; Trainer/Asssessor for PQH (NI), since 1999; Assessor, Threshold Pay for Teachers, since 2001; b. 7.8.54, Enniskillen, Co. Fermanagh. Educ. St. Michael's College, Enniskillen; Queen's University Belfast. Computer Programmer, 1977-78; Senior Lecturer, Dungannon FE College, 1979-95. Address: (b.) 21 Gortmerron Link Road, Dungannon, Co. Tyrone BT71 6LS. T.-028 87 724401.
e-mail: adolan@intcollege.dungannon.ni.sch.uk

Dolan, Peter Anthony, BA (Hons), Dip Arch, RIBA. Chartered Architect, partner of private practice; b. 30.11.66; m., Niamh; 2s; 1d. Educ. Christian Brothers Grammar School, Omagh; Manchester Polytechnic. Recreations: all sports particularly football and golf. Address: (b.) ADP Architects, 1 Holmview Terrace, Omagh BT79 0AH. T.-02882 244411.

Dolk, Prof. Helen Margaret, BA (Hons), PhD. Professor of Epidemiology and Health Services Research, University of Ulster, since 2000; b. 28.6.60, Netherlands. Epidemiologist Research Fellow at Catholic University of Louvain, Brussels, 1984-91; Lecturer/Senior Lecturer in Environmental Epidemiology, London School of Hygiene and Tropical Medicine, 1991-2000. Main interests: environmental health; perinatal health; disease registers and surveillance; inequalities in health. Address: (b.) Room IFO8, Faculty of Life and Health Sciences, University of Ulster, Newtownabbey, Co. Antrim BT37 0QB.

Donaldson, Adrian, MSc, MBA, FCMI. Chief Executive, Castlereagh Borough Council, since 1997; b. 26.2.55, Belfast, Northern Ireland; m., Pamela; 1 s.; 1 d. Educ. Friend's Grammar School, Lisburn; University of Ulster; Cranfield University. Past Chairman and President of Belfast Round Table; Fellow of The Chartered Institute of Management; Member of The Local Government Staff Commission; Member of The Northern Ireland Joint Council for Local Government Services. Recreations: golf; hiking; sub aqua. Address: Castlereagh Borough Council, Civic and Administrative Offices, Bradford Court, Upper Galwally, Castlereagh BT8 6RB. T.-028 90 494506. e-mail: chiefexec@castlereagh.gov.uk

Donaldson, Jeffrey Mark, MP. Member of Parliament (Lagan Valley) since 1997; b. 7.12.62, Kilkeel, Co Down; m., Eleanor; 2d. Educ. Kilkeel High School; Castlereagh College, Belfast. Agent, Rt. Hon. Enoch Powell, MP, 1983 - 84; Personal Assistant, Rt. Hon. James Molyneaux MP, 1984 - 85; Member, Northern Ireland Assembly, 1985 - 86; Partner, Financial Services and Estate Agency Business, 1986; Honorary Secretary, Ulster Unionist Council, 1988-2000, Vice President, 2000; Negotiator for Ulster Unionist Party, Northern Ireland Talks, 1991 - 98; Member, Northern Ireland Forum, 1996 - 98. Recreations: church activities; historical sites; walking; reading. Address: (b.) House of Commons, London, SW1A 0AA; T.- 028 9266 8001.
e-mail: jeffreydonaldsonmp@laganvalley.net

Donaldson, Thomas Watters Perry, JP, FInstD. Chairman/Director, North Down Group; b. 27.2.45, Belfast. Educ. Regent House, Newtownards. Management/Sales, James McVeigh and Sons Ltd, 1963 - 71; Formed Perry Donaldson and Co Ltd (Chairman and Managing Director), 1971; Formed Subsidiary Company, Perry Pac Ltd (Chairman and Managing Director), 1981; Former member, BBC Agricultural Advisory Committee; past-president, Belfast Battalion Boys' Brigade; Lay Magistrate; Chairman, Board of Governors, Dundonald Primary School; Elder/member of committee, Dundonald Presbyterian Church; Member, Boys' Brigade UK Executive; Vice President, Symington Memorial Silver band. Address: (h.) 262 Belfast Road, Dundonald. T.-028 9182 2264.
e-mail: perrydonaldson@northdowngroup.com

Donnan, Prof. Hastings, DPhil, MRIA, AcSS. School of Anthropological Studies, Queen's University Belfast; b. 12.3.53, Northern Ireland; m., Katharine Marshall; 3 d. Educ. Bangor Grammar School; Queen's University Belfast;

University of Sussex. Member of the Royal Irish Academy and a Founding Academician in the Academy of Learned Societies for the Social Sciences; carried out field research in the Himalayan foothills of northern Pakistan and along the Irish border. Publications include: Marriage among Muslims, 1988; Borders: Frontiers of Identity, Nation and State, 1999; Islam, Globalization and Postmodernity, 1994; Irish Urban Cultures, 1993; Culture and Policy in Northern Ireland, 1997; Border Identities: Nation and State at International Frontiers, 1998; Interpreting Islam, 2002. Completed a European Union funded project on 'Border Cities and Towns: Causes of Social Exclusion in Peripheral Europe', 1997-2001; directed a project on migrant athletes funded by the Sports Council for Northern Ireland, 2000-2002. Address: (b.) School of Anthropological Studies, Queen's University, Belfast BT7 1NN. T.-00 44 028 9027 3878. e-mail: h.donnan@qub.ac.uk

Donnelly, Brenda, LLB. Official Solicitor to the Supreme Court, since 1998; b. 6.11.62, London. Educ. Mercy Primary School, Belfast; Belfast Royal Academy; Queen's University of Belfast. Pupil Solicitor, Elliott Duffy Garrett, Solicitors, Belfast, 1986 - 87; Legal Adviser, Northern Ireland Court Service (Lord Chancellor's Department), 1987 - 95; Solicitor to HM Coroner for Greater Belfast and Deputies, 1992 - 95; Principal Legal Assistant to Lord Chief Justice, 1995 - 98. Recreations: theatre; cooking. Address: (b.) Royal Court of Justice, Belfast BT1 3JF.

Donnelly, Patrick Gerard, DipQS, MRICS, MBIFM. Director of Physical Resources, University of Ulster since 1993; b. 16.3.56, Ballycastle, Co Antrim; m., Joan; 1s.; 4d. Educ. Cross and Passion College, Ballycastle; University of Ulster at Jordanstown. Quantity Surveyor: Dalzell and Campbell, 1975 - 77; John Laing Construction, 1979-79; Ferris Craig and Moore, 1980 - 84; Project Manager/Quantity Surveyor, Building Design Partnership, 1984 - 88; Assistant Estates and Building Officer, Queen's University, Belfast, 1988 - 93. Address: (b.) University of Ulster, Cromore Road, Coleraine, BT52 1SA; T.-028 7032 4133.

Donnelly, Tom, MBE, JP, DL. Early Retirement, 2000; b. 25.5.39, Belfast; m., Rosemary; 2 s.; 1 d. Educ. St. Malachy's College, Belfast. Area Business Manager, Proton Cars (UK) Ltd, 1998-2000; Operations Director, Motor Vehicle Imports (NI) Ltd (an Inchcape Company), 1977-98; Development Officer, ICI Fibres Ltd, 1965-77; appointed Commissioner, Northern Ireland Human Rights Commission, 1999; Member, Advisory Committee on appointment of General Commissioners of Income Tax, since 1996; awarded MBE and appointed Deputy Lieutenant, County Borough of Belfast, 1987; appointed Justice of the Peace, 1985; Treasurer and Chairman, Northern Ireland Festival for Youth Society 1973 - 86; Member, Duke of Edinburgh

Award Scheme 25th Anniversary Appeal Fund Committee; Patron, Belfast Charitable Trust for Integrated Education; Belfast City SDLP Councillor; Treasurer, Belfast City Council, Road Safety Committee; Treasurer, Belfast Royal Academy Parents' Union; Board Member: Ulster Folk and Transport Museum; Dutch Help Northern Ireland Foundation; Member: Corrymeela Centre for Reconciliation; Irish Management Institute. Recreations: gardening; reading; walking.

Doran, Professor Isaac Gregg, OBE, BSc, (Hons), MSc, PhD, FICE, FISE, FIEI, FGS. Hon. Senior Research Fellow, Geotechnics, School of the Built Environment, Queen's University, Belfast; b. 18.1.23, Belfast; m., Ainslie Elizabeth Graham; 1s.; 2d. Educ. Methodist College, Belfast; Queen's University, Belfast. Queen's University, Belfast: Research Assistant; Lecturer, School of Engineering; Senior Scientific Officer, Materials Testing Station; Private Practice as Consulting Engineer; Senior Partner Dr IG Doran and Partners. Millar Prize, Institution of Civil Engineers. Recreation: contemplation. Address: (h.) 47 Derryvolgie Avenue, Belfast, BT9 6FN; T.-028 9066 0521. e-mail: g.doran@qub.ac.uk

Doran, Noel. Editor, Irish News. Address: (b.) 113-117 Donegall Street, Belfast BT1 2GE.

Dorman, John Michael Addison, MA (Oxon). Partner, Mackenzie and Dorman, Solicitors since 1972; b. 11.2.43, Belfast; m., Penelope Georgina Hudson; 2s. Educ. Campbell College, Belfast; Oxford University. Oxford University Rugby Blue; Ulster Rugby Cap. Recreations: hill walking; skiing; sailing. Address: (h.) 29 Knockdene Park North, Belfast, BT5 7AA; T.-02890-650392.

Dornan, Brian, BSS, MPhil, CQSW. Director of Social Services, Southern Health and Social Services Board, since 2001; b. 3.3.51, Belfast; m., Laraine Greer; 3d. Educ. Royal Belfast Academical Institution; Trinity College, Dublin; York University. Probation Officer, Northern Ireland Probation and After Care Service, 1975 - 76; Eastern Health and Social Services Board: Social Worker, 1976 - 77; Senior Social Worker, 1977 - 81; Assistant Principal Social Worker, 1981 - 84; Principal Social Worker, 1984 - 88; Assistant Director of Social Services, 1988 - 90; Director, Community Services, Down Lisburn Health and Social Services Trust, 1990-2001. Publications: Personal Social Services in Northern Ireland: Perspectives on Integration, 1993. Address: (b.) SHSSB, Tower Hill, Armagh BT61 9DR. T.-028 3741 4610.

Dougal, Andrew Patrick, OBE, BA, DBA, MCIPD, FIPR. Chief Executive, Northern Ireland Chest Heart and Stroke Association since 1983; b. 27.8.50, Belfast; m., Fiona Marion O'Donovan; 1 s. Educ. St Malachy's College, Belfast; Queen's University, Belfast; Ulster Polytechnic. Registrar, St Louise's Comprehensive College, Belfast, 1975

- 83. Former Chairman: Institute of Personnel and Development (NI); Association of Chief Officers of Voluntary Organisations; Council of the European Movement (NI); Treasurer, World Heart Federation, 1995 - 98. OBE, 1996. Former Fellow, Salzburg seminar, 1986; Paul Dudley White Fellowship, American Heart Association, 1997. Recreations: music (choral, orchestral and opera); swimming; horse riding; rugby.   Address: (b.) Northern Ireland Chest Heart and Stroke Association, Chamber of Commerce House, 22 Gt. Victoria Street, Belfast BT2 7LY.   T.- 02890-320184. e-mail: adougal@nichsa.com

Douglas, Boyd.   Member (East Londonderry), United Unionist Assembly Party, Northern Ireland Assembly, 1998-2003; b. 13.7.50, Limavady; m.; 2 s; 2 d. Educ. Burnfoot Primary School; Dungiven Secondary School; Strabane Agriculture College. Farmer. Elected to Limavady Council, 1997. Address: (b.) Parliament Buildings, Stormont, Belfast, BT4 3XX; T.- 028 90 521141. e-mail: boyd.douglas@tibus.com

Douglas, James Frederick, BM, BCh, MA, BCL (Oxon), FRCP (UK). Consultant Nephrologist, Belfast City and Royal Victoria Hospitals since 1975; b. 22.9.38, Portadown, Co Armagh; m., Giselle Sookan Lim; 3s. Educ. Portora Royal School, Enniskillen; Oxford University; Queen's University, Belfast.   Called to the Bar (Middle Temple Hons), 1961; Posts in Legal Publishing and Professional Teaching, 1961 - 64; Qualified in Medicine, 1964 - 69; Junior House Officer, Royal Victoria Hospital, 1969 - 70; Junior Posts in Clinical Pharmacology, Medicine, casualty, Opthalmology and Renal Medicine, 1971 - 73; Registrar/Senior Registrar in Nephrology, 1973 - 75.   FRCP (UK), 1986; Senior Nephrologist/ Clinical Director, Department of Nephrology, 1988 - 96. Member: UKTSSA, 1995-2002; ULTRA since 1995; Renal Association; British Transplantation Society, Council Member and Archivist, since 2002; International Society of Nephrology; American Society of Nephrology; Irish Transplantation Society; European Dialysis and Transplantation Association, (EDTA); Ulster Medico-Legal Society; Corrigan Club.   Medical Adviser, N. Ireland Kidney Research Fund; Chairman, Northern Ireland Transplant Games Association.   Publications: numerous articles on renal failure, acute and chronic; transplantation; the law and renal medicine; renal toxicology; contributions to textbooks on similar matters. Recreations: golf; cricket; chess; astronomy; hill walking; books.   Address: (b.) Belfast City Hospital, Lisburn Road, Belfast BT9. e-mail: jamesfdouglas38@hotmail.com

Douglas, Dr. John, DD. Minister, Lisburn Free Church since 1976; Clerk of Presbytery since 1970; Principal Whitefield College of the Bible since 1979; b. 18.6.33, Newtownards, Co Down; m., Eunice; 2s.; 4d. Educ. Theological Hall of the Free Presbyterian Church of Ulster. Joint Assistant Minister, Mount Merrion Free Presbyterian Church, Belfast, 1954 - 56; Minister, Portavogie/Ballyhalbert, 1956 - 67; Lecturer and Registrar, Theological Hall, 1965; Minister, Moneyslane, Co Down, 1967 - 76. Has preached in conferences and as an evangelist throughout the UK, Spain, Germany, Africa, Australia, Canada, USA. Conducts bible tours to Israel. Publications: book on Charismatic movement. Address: (h.) 40 Lombard Avenue, Lisburn; T.- 028 92 588 375.

Dowdall, Prof. J. M., CB, BSc (Econ). Comptroller and Auditor General, Audit Office, Northern Ireland since 1994; Professor, Faculty of Business and Management, University of Ulster, since 2002; b. 6.9.44; m., Aylerie Houston; 3s.; 1d. Educ.   King Edward's School, Surrey; Queen's University, Belfast.   Member of CIPFA, since 2001.   Economics Lecturer, Royal University of Malta, 1966 - 69; Political Economics Lecturer, University of Aberdeen, 1969 - 72; Economic Adviser, Department of Commerce, Northern Ireland, 1972 - 78; Principal, Department of Commerce, 1979 - 82; Assistant Secretary, Department of Finance and Personnel, Northern Ireland, 1982 - 85; Deputy Chief Executive, Industrial Development Board, Northern Ireland, 1986 - 89; Under Secretary, Department of Finance and Personnel, Northern Ireland, 1989 - 94. Address: (b.) Northern Ireland Audit Office, 106 University Street, Belfast, BT7 1EU; T.- 028 9025 1059.

Drake, Michael McMullan, MBE. Agriculture Editor, Belfast Telegraph; b. Downpatrick; m., Vanessa; 2s.; 1d.   Mourne Observer, 1959 - 63; Mirror Group, 1963 - 65; Down Recorder, 1965 - 73; Joined Belfast Telegraph, 1973. Publications: written widely on agricultural issues, conservation, art and antiques, including art and antiques column in the Belfast Telegraph; recent book: Breaking New Ground - 50 years of NI Agriculture. Recreations: collecting art and antiques. Address: (b.) Belfast Telegraph, 124-144 Royal Avenue, Belfast, BT1 1EB.

Dudley, Miriam, MA (Cantab), MA (Sheffield). Director, SLS Legal Publications (NI).   Educ. Belfast Royal Academy; University of Cambridge; University of Sheffield.   Fellow, Institute of Continuing Professional Development.   Address: (b.) SLS Legal Publications (NI), School of Law, Queen's University, Belfast, Belfast, BT7 1NN; T.- 028 9033 5224.

Duffin, Beth. Formerly Regional Manager, Royal National Lifeboat Institution, 1983 - 98; b. 28.5.38, Larne, Co Antrim; 2s.   Industrial Appeals Organiser, Dr Barnardos, 1978 - 83.   Past Chairman, Larne Drama Festival; Vice President, Association of Ulster Drama Festivals. Recreations: amateur theatre; gardening; family. Address: (h.) 10 Argyll Avenue, Larne BT40 2JX. T.- 028 2826 0330.   e-mail: bethduffin@aol.com

Duffy, Gavan, LLB (Hons).   Barrister-at-Law; b. 22.12.67, Belfast; m., Gemma Dougal; 3 s.; 1 d.

Educ. St Patrick's College, Armagh; Queen's University, Belfast. Called to the Bar, Northern Ireland, 1991; Member, Prison Board of Visitors, 1998-2001. Recreations: films; theatre; squash; swimming. Address: (b.) Bar Library, Royal Courts of Justice, Chichester Street, Belfast BT1 3JP; T.- 028 90562222.

Duly, Rev. James Alexander, BSC (Econ), BD. Supply Preacher, Reformed Presbyterian Church; b. 12.3.59, Belfast; m., Anna Elizabeth Millar; 2s. Educ. Grosvenor High School, Belfast; University of Wales, Aberystwyth; Union Theological College, Belfast. Minister, Presbyterian Church in Ireland, 1986 - 91; Joined Reformed Presbyterian Church of Ireland, 1993. Hon. Secretary, Magherafelt Arts Advisory Committee. Published Poet. Magill Bursary for Preaching, 1985; President, Students' Council, Union Theological College, 1984. Recreations: reading; cinema reviews; collecting books, catechisms and Irish stamps; reading; writing poetry; listening to music; psalmody; current affairs; amateur philosopher. Address: (h.) 9 Balmoral Avenue, Whitehead, Co. Antrim BT38 9QA.

Dumigan, John Joseph, MSc, PPBEng, FBEng, MRICS. Group Chief Building Control Officer, South Eastern Group of Councils since 1994; b. 11.1.48, Newtownards; m., Marleen; 3s.; 1d. Educ. Newtownards College of Further Education; University of Ulster. Draughtsman, Department of the Environment, 1965 - 75; Building Control Officer, South Eastern Group of Councils, 1975 - 79; Fire Specialist, South Eastern Group of Councils, 1979 - 84; Deputy Chief Building Control Officer, South Eastern Group of Councils, 1984 - 94. Recreations: golf. Address: (b.) c/o Down District Council, 24 Strangford Road, Downpatrick, Co Down, BT30 6SR; T.- 02844-610827.

Dunbar, John James, MBE, UD, DL, Cert Ed, Cert RSc. Retired Secondary Headteacher; b. 14.4.36, Newtowstewart; m., Mary Kathleen Young; 3s. Educ. Omagh Academy; Stranmillis College, Belfast. Teacher, Rural Science, Kesh Intermediate School, 1957 - 61; Teacher Rural Science, General Subjects, Omagh High School, 61 - 63; Vice-Principal, Castlederg High School, 1963 - 80; Principal, Castlederg High School, 1980 - 92. Military Service: 6 U.D.R., 1970 - 90: Commissioned as 2nd Lt, 1970; 1st Lt, 1972; Captain, 1973; Major, 1974; Retired as Major Bn 2ic, 6 U.D.R., 1990. Member, Governing Body, Omagh College of Further Education; Chair of Newtownstewart Townscape Heritage Initiative. MBE, 1981; Deputy Lieutenant, Co Tyrone since 1985. Recreations: salmon and trout fishing; gardening; hobby farming. Address: (h.) 76 Dublin Street, Newtownstewart, Co Tyrone; T.- 028 8166 1330.

Duncan, Rev. Eric. Superintendent, Lisbellaw Tempo and Maguires Bridge Circuit, since 2000; b. 20.9.38, Carlisle; m., Dorothy Frances Duncan.

Educ. Belfast Royal Academy; Chatam College of Technology; Queen's University, Belfast. Work Study Engineer, 1958 - 75. Fellow, Work Study Society. Recreations: golf; walking. Address: (h.) The Methodist Manse, Main Street, Mullybritt, Lisbellaw, Co Fermanagh BT94 5ER. T.-028 6638 7211.

Duncan, William John, DMS, MBA. European Director of Youth for Christ International; b. 23.4.52, Belfast; m., Maisie; 2d. Educ. Friends School, Lisburn; University of Ulster. Recreations: church; conversation; travel; entertaining; photography; sport. Address: (b.) 54 Main Street, Ballynahinch, Co. Down BT24 8DN. T.-028 9756 0021.

Duncan, William Kenneth, LLB. Solicitor; Deputy District Judge since 1993; b. 22.10.56, Omagh; m., Hilary Anne Duncan; 2d. Educ. Omagh Academy; Queen Mary College, University of London; Queen's University, Belfast. Admitted as a Solicitor, 1979; Partner, McConnell and Fyffe, 1984, Senior Partner, 2000. Recreations: reading; rugby union football. Address: (b.) The Old Rectory, 21 Church Street, Omagh. T.-028 82 242 099.

Dundee, Frederick Alexander, JP, BSc, MPSNI. Pharmaceutical Chemist; b. 24.1.30, Belfast; m. 3s.; 1d. Educ. Royal Belfast Academical Institution; Queen's University, Belfast. Qualified as a pharmacist, 1953; succeeded to family business, 1960. Address: (h.) 42 Ballynure Road, Ballyearl, Newtownabbey, Co. Antrim BT36 5SJ.

Dunlop, Jayne Alexandra, BLib, MSc (Econ), FRGS. Careers Information Officer, University of Ulster at Coleraine since 1995; Alliance Councillor, Ballymena Borough Council, 1997-2001; Chair, Alliance Party N. Ireland, since 2002; b. 26.6.62, Ballymena. Educ. Ballymena Academy; University College of Wales, Aberystwyth. Special Cataloguer, Dr Williams' Library, London, 1984 - 87; Assistant Librarian, Royal Geographical Society, 1987 - 90; Librarian, Royal Geographical Society, 1991 - 94; Assistant Librarian, Northern Ireland Housing Executive, 1994-95. Recreations: tennis; reading. Address: (h.) 64 Glenhugh Park, Ahoghill, Ballymena, Co Antrim, BT42 1LR; T.- 028 2587 1220.

Dunlop, Very Rev. John, CBE. Minister, Rosemary Presbyterian Church, Belfast since 1978; b., 19.9.39, Newry, Co Down; m., Rosemary Willis. Educ. Newry Grammar School; Royal Belfast Academical Institution; Queen's University, Belfast; New College, University of Edinburgh; Assembly's College, Belfast. United Church of Jamaica, Grand Cayman, 1968 - 78. Member, Senate, Queen's University, Belfast, 1987 - 99; Eisenhower Fellow, 1989; Moderator of the General Assembly of the Presbyterian Church in Ireland, 1992; Co-convenor, Presbyterian Church's Church and Government Committee, 1996-2003. Hon. DD, Presbyterian Theological

Faculty of Ireland and Trinity College, Dublin; Hon LLD, University of Ulster and Queen's University Belfast. Publications: A Precarious Belonging. Address: (h.) 17 Innisfayle Park, Belfast, BT15 5HS; T.- 028 9077 8164; Fax: 028 9077 8164.
e-mail: jdunlop@presbyterianireland.org

Dunlop, William John Thistle, JP. Retired Farmer; b. 5.1.31, Portadown; m., Alicia Trueman; 2d. Educ. Portadown College. Recreations: reading; walking; church work; lay reader. Address: (h.) Fox Park, 52 Drumanphy Road, Portadown, Craigavon BT62 1SN; T.- 028 38 851244.

Dunluce, The Viscount, Randal Alexander St John McDonnell, BA. Private Client Fund Manager, Sarasin Investment Management Ltd, London since 1997; b. 2.7.67. Educ. Gresham's School, Norfolk; Worcester College, Oxford. NCL Investments Ltd, London, 1992 - 97. Recreations: vintage cars; reading; walking and shooting. Address: (h.) Glenarm Castle, Glenarm, Co Antrim, BT44 0BD; T.- 028 28 841203.

Dunn, Alistair, BSc (Econ), FRICS, ACIArb. Managing Director, Lisney; b. 5.9.47, Belfast; separated; 3d. Educ. Royal Belfast Academical Institution; Queen's University, Belfast. Northern Ireland Valuation Office, 1971 - 79; Property Services Agency, 1979 - 81; Lisney Commercial Property Consultants: 1981; Partner/Director, 1986 - 94; Managing Director since 1994. Chairman RICS in NI, 2001/2; Chairman SDP (NI), 1988 - 90; Chairman, Campaign for Equal Citizenship, 1991 - 94. Recreations: mountaineering; golf; tennis; reading; music; juggling. Address: (b.) Lisney, 5 Linenhall Street, Belfast, BT2 8AA; T.- 02890 501525.

Dunn, Norman, MA, DMS, MILAM, MInstWM, MInstM. Town Clerk and Chief Executive, Newtownabbey Borough Council since 1996; b. 20.6.42, Belfast; m., Maureen; 2s.; 2d. Educ. Ballyclare High School; University of Ulster. Local Government Officer, Newtownabbey Borough Council since 1959: Roles in Administration and Finance; Recreation, 1971; Director, Leisure and Technical Services. Recreations: golf; gardening; food and wine; reading. Address: (h.) 11 Doagh Road, Newtownabbey, Co Antrim, BT37 9PA; T.- 02890-862960.

Durkan, Mark. Member (Foyle), Social Democratic and Labour Party, Northern Ireland Assembly, since 1998; b. 26.6.60, Derry; m. Educ. St Columb's College, Derry; Queen's University, Belfast; Magee College, Derry. Assistant to John Hume, MP, 1984-98; Chairperson, SDLP, 1990-95; Derry City Council, 1993-2000; Minister of Finance and Personnel, Northern Ireland Assembly, 1999-2001, Deputy First Minister, 2001-02. Member, Northern Ireland Forum, 1996; SDLP Negotiator, Castle Buildings talks, 1996-98;

Member, N.I. Housing Council, 1993-95; Member, Western Health and Social Services Council, 1993-2000. Address: (b.) Parliament Buildings, Stormont, Belfast, BT4 3ST; T.- 02890 521319.

E

Eadie, Roland Rennie Alistair, FRICS, DL. Consultant Chartered Surveyor; b. 21.8.44, Enniskillen; m., Lois Cecily Sullivan. Educ. Portora Royal School, Enniskillen. Qualified as Chartered Surveyor, 1968; Fellow, Royal Institution of Chartered Surveyors, 1978; Senior Partner, Eadie McFarland and Co, Enniskilen, 1971 - 96. Deputy Lieutenant, Co Fermanagh since 1978; High Sheriff, Co Fermanagh, 1984. Governor, Portora Royal School, 1997-2001. Chairman, Enniskillen Yacht Club Charitable Trust, 1986-2003; Member: Historic Buildings Council for Northern Ireland, 1987 - 90; Ulster Countryside Commission for Northern Ireland, 1980 - 86; Lord Chancellor's Advisory Committee (Fermanagh), 1985 - 97; Northern Ireland Milk Quota Tribunal, 1982 - 84; Black Inquiry into Inland Fisheries in Northern Ireland, 1978 - 80; Board Member, Countryside Alliance (NI), 1998-2003; Joint-Chairman, Hunting Association of NI, 1998-2001. Recreations: hunting and field sports; conservation of historic buildings and the natural heritage; racing and the breeding of National Hunt bloodstock; collecting early Irish glass. Address: (h.) Aghavea Glebe, Brookborough, Co Fermanagh, BT94 4LP; T.- 028-89-531310.

Eakins, Dr. William Arthur, CBE, TD, DL, MB, BcH, FRCPI, FFOM (London), FFOMRCPI. Dean, Faculty of Occupational Medicine, Royal College of Physicians Ireland; b. 1.8.32, Belfast; m., Helen Smith; 2s.; 2d. Educ. Campbell College, Belfast; Queen's University, Belfast. General Medical Practitioner and Police Surgeon, Belfast, 1958 - 75. Regional Medical Officer, Northern Ireland Post Office and British Telecom; Queen's Hon. Physician, 1983 - 85. Board Member, BT and Post Office Boards, 1975 - 90. Commanding Officer TA General Hospital, 1981 - 84; Hon. Colonel, Northern Ireland Field Ambulance, 1987 - 98; Deputy Lieutenant, Belfast since 1992; Lieutenant of Commandery of Ards of Order of St John, 1992-99; OStJ since 1992; Knight of the Order of St John. Member, Northern Ireland Mountain Leadership Board, 1978 - 84; Chair, Eastern Division, BMA, 1986; Chairman, War Pensions Appeals Board, 1991 - 97; President, Standing Medical Boards, Ministry of Defense, 1993 - 97. Campbell Young Prize, General Practice, 1981. Publications: various papers on alcohol and driving; mountain medicine. Recreations: military history; watching rugby; hill walking; shooting. Address: (b.) Commandery of Ards, Erne, Knockbracken Healthcare Park, Saintfield Road, Belfast; T.- 02890-799393. e-mail: aeakins36A@hotmail.com

Eames, The Lady Ann Christine, LLB (Hons), MPhil. A Northern Ireland Commissioner for Human Rights; b. 21.1.43, Dublin; m., Most Rev. Lord Robert Eames (see Lord Robert Eames); 2s.

Educ. Ashleigh House, Belfast; Queen's University, Belfast. President Derry and Raphoe Mothers' Union, 1976 - 80; Vice-President Down and Dromore Mothers' Union, 1980 - 86; President, Armagh Mothers' Union, 1987 - 94; President, Girls' Friendly Society, Armagh, 1987 - 97; All Ireland Vice-President, Mothers' Union since 1987; World President, Mothers' Union, 1995-2000. Member, Advisory Board for Cross-community Trust for Youth in Northern Ireland; Past President, Old Ashleighans Association. Recreations: sailing; family. Address: (h.) See House, Cathedral Close, Armagh, BT61 7EF; T.- 01861-522851.

Eames, Most Rev. Lord Robert Henry Alexander, LLB (Hons), LLD, PhD, DD, DLitt. Archbishop of Armagh and Primate of all Ireland, Metropolitan since 1986; b. 27.4.37, Belfast; m., Anne Christine Daly (see The Lady Eames); 2s. Educ. Methodist College. Belfast; Belfast Royal Academy; Queen's University, Belfast; Trinity College, Dublin. Research Scholar and Tutor, Law Faculty, Queen's University, Belfast, 1960 - 63; Curate Bangor, 1963 - 66; Rector, Gilnahirk, Co Down, 1966 - 74; Rector, Dundela, Co Down, 1974 - 75; Bishop of Derry and Raphoe, 1975 - 80; Bishop of Down and Dromore, 1980 - 86. Select Preacher: Oxford University, 1987; Cambridge University, 1990; University of Edinburgh, 1993. Chairman, Archbishop of Canterbury's Commission on Women Bishops, 1988; Chairman, Inter-Anglican Theological and Doctrinal Commission since 1991; Chairman, Anglican Communion Finance Committee since 1996; Elected Hon. Bencher Lincoln's Inn, 1999. Publications: The Quiet Revolution, 1970; Through Suffering, 1973; Chains to be Broken, 1992 and 1993. Created Life Peer, Lord Eames of Armagh, 1995. Recreations: sailing; rugby; reading. Address: (h.) See House, Cathedral Close, Armagh, BT61 7EE; T.- 01861-522851.

Eaton, James Thompson, CBE, TD. Lord-Lieutenant, County Borough of Londonderry, 1986-2002; b. 11.8.27; m., Lucy Edith Smeeton; 1 s.; 1 d. Educ. Campbell College, Belfast; Royal Technical College, Glasgow. Managing Director, Eaton and Co Ltd, 1965 - 80. Member, Londonderry Development Commission, 1969-73 (Chairman, Education Committee, 1969-73); Chairman, Londonderry Port and Harbour Commissioners, 1989 - 95 (Member, 1977-95; Vice Chairman, 1985). Served North Irish Horse (TA), 1950-67 (Major, 1961). Hon. Col, 1st (NI) Bn, ACF, 1992-98. High Sherriff, Co. Londonderry, 1982. Recreations: military history; gardening. Address: Cherryvale Park, Limavady, Co. Londonderry BT49 9AH.

Ekin, Thomas Alexander, BSc, FCA. Managing Director, Linfield Properties since 1990, Hollinvest Ltd; Belfast City Councillor since 1997; b. 26.2.41, Ballymena; m., Ann; 4d. Educ. Campbell College, Belfast; Queen's University, Belfast. Chartered Accountant, Belfast and

London, 1962 - 70; Economist, Anglo-American Corporation, South Africa, 1970 - 77; Senior Executive, Northern Ireland Development Agency, 1977 - 79; Managing Director, Springtown Engineering Ltd, 1980; Financial Director, Linfield Group Ltd, 1981; Chairman/Chief Executive, Linfield Group Ltd, 1986 - 90. Chairman, Management Charter Initiative, 1987 - 90; Non Executive Director, Training and Employment Agency, 1987 - 91; Chairman, Alliance Party of Northern Ireland, 2000-02. Recreations: golf; mountain climbing; making progress. Address: (h.) 4 Malone Hill Park, Belfast, BT9 6RD; T.- 028 90 669449. e-mail: tom@weaverscourt.com

Elder, Catherine Hazlett, JP. Retired Director of Nursing; b. 25.11.30, Belfast. Educ. Miss Dunn's Private Business School; University of Manchester. Student Nurse, Belfast City Hospital, 1948 - 52; Student Midwife, Hope Hospital, Salford, 1954 - 56; Student Health Visitor, Salford Health Authority, 1958 - 59; District Midwife and approved District Teacher, Salford, 1956 - 59; Assistant Matron, Stretford Memorial Hospital, Stretford, 1970 - 71; Deputy Principal Nursing Officer, Hope Hospital, Salford, 1971 - 80; Director of Nursing, Salford Health Authority Community, 1980 - 84; Director of Nursing, Causeway Unit of Management, 1984 - 90; Retired, 1990. Recreations: reading; music (classical and sacred); antiques. Address: (h.) Villa Bella, 11 Old Coach Road, Portstewart, Co Londonderry, BT55 7BX; T.- 01265-834970.

Elliott, Frank Alan, CB, BA, DUniv. Chairman, Chief Executives' Forum, 1997-2001; b. 28.3.37, Belfast; m., Olive Lucy; 1 s.; 2 d. Educ. Royal Belfast Academical Institution; Trinity College, Dublin. Entered Northern Ireland Civil Service, 1959; Senior Civil Servant, since 1972; Permanent Secretary, Department of Health and Social Services, 1987 - 97. Chairman, Public Examination Panel, Draft Regional Strategic Framework for Northern Ireland (reported January 2000). Chairman, Mediation NI and Regional Chairman, Leonard Cheshire. Publication: Curing and Caring. Recreations: motoring; the arts. Address: (h.) 180 Crawfordsburn Road, Bangor, Co. Down BT19 1HY; T.-028 9185 3709.

Ellis-Farquhar, Rev. Gabrielle, A. J., BA DipTh, MTh. Presbyterian Minister, Ballycarry, Co Antrim since 1994; Member of World Alliance of Reformed Churches European Area Committee; b. Dublin; m. Maurice Farquhar BA, LTCL. Educ. Bertrand and Rutland; Diocesan Girls' School; Trinity College, Dublin; New College, University of Edinburgh. Personnel Department, Bank of Ireland, 1975 - 81; Administrator, Dublin Central Mission, 1981 - 84; Manager, Barret Cheshire Homes, Dublin, 1984 - 86; Studying for the Ministry, 1987; Assistant Minister, Hillsborough Presbyterian Church, 1991. Recreations: classical music; playing organ and piano; gardening.

Address: (h.) 34b, Manse Road, Ballycarry, Co Antrim, BT38 9HW; T.- 028 93 372380.

Elsdon, Rev. Dr. Ronald, BA, BD, PhD, PhD. Rector, St. Bartholomew's Belfast, since 2002; Church of Ireland Chaplain, Stranmillis University College, since 2002; Curate, Ballymena and Ballyclug, 1999-2002; Former Co-ordinator Crosslinks (formerly Bible Churchmen's Missionary Society), 1989 - 97; b. 31.7.44, Newcastle-upon-Tyne; m., Janice Margaret Beddow; 2s. Educ. Tiverton Grammar School, Devon; Cambridge University. Post Doctoral Fellow, University of Manchester, 1969 - 71; Lecturer, Geology; University College, Dublin, 1971 - 89. Church of Ireland Lay Reader, 1971 - 99; Member, Church of Ireland General Synod, 1977 - 99, 2003-. Publications: five books. Recreations: photography; railways; birdwatching; books; music. Address: (h.) St. Bartholomew's Rectory, 16 Mount Pleasant, Stranmillis, Belfast BT9 5DS. e-mail: stbartholomew@connor.anglican.org

Emerson, Peter John. Director, The De Borda Institute since 1996; b. 8.7.43, Oxford. Educ. Franciscan College, Buckingham; Royal Naval College, Dartmouth; Queen's University, Belfast. Naval Officer, H M Submarines, 1961 - 70; Volunteer Teacher, Nairobi, 1970 - 73; Travel writer, cycling across Central Africa, 1974; Youth Community Worker, Belfast, 1975 - 78; Travel writer, cycling across North Africa, 1979; Joint Founder, CND (NI), 1980; Joint Founder, Northern Ireland Green Party, 1981; Farm Manager, Farset City Farm, 1983; Student, Slavonic Studies, 1984 - 88; Russian-English Translator, Moscow, 1988 - 90; Travel writer, cycling Moscow to Tirana, 1990 - 91; Farmer, Farset City Farm, 1991 - 92; War Correspondent, Bosnia, 1993; Author, 1994. Fluent in Russian, speaks some French, Serbo-Croat, Swahili and Gaelic. Publications: Inflation? Try a Bicycle, 1978; Northern Ireland, That Sons May Bury Their Fathers, 1979; Consensus Voting Systems, 1991; What an Extraordinary Title for a Travel Book, 1991; A Bosnian Perspective, 1993; The Politics of Consensus, 1994; Beyond the Tyranny of the Majority, 1998; Preferendum Social Survey, 1998; From Belfast to the Balkans, 2000; Defining Democracy, 2002. Recreations: climbing mountains; classical music; gardening. Address: (h.) The De Borda Institute, 36 Ballysillan Road, Belfast, BT14 7QQ; T.- 02890-711795. e-mail: pemerson@deborda.org

Emery, James Andrew. Councillor, Ulster Unionist Party, Strabane District Council since 1989; b. 4.4.44, Castlederg. Educ. Castlederg High School; Edwards Primary School. Member, Kirk Session since 1975; Member, Orange Order; Member, Royal Black Institution; School Governor since 1987; Chairman, Castlederg Charity Band Parade Committee, 1983-2003; Lay Preacher; Chairman, Londonderry Post Office Advisory Committee, 1993, 1994 and 1998; Member, Somme Advisory Council (NI) since

1989; Chairman, Strabane District Council Cultural and Arts Committee, 1998-99, 2001-02; Chairman, Strabane District Council, 2003-04; Member, Strabane District Policing Partnership, since 2002. Boys Brigade Officer since 1963. Boys' Brigade Long Service Gold Brooch, 1997. Publications: The Passing Years of a Country Lodge, 1990; Historical Recollections, 1995; 1st Castlederg Boys' Brigade, 1947 - 97, 1997; Castlederg Royal Black Centenary Booklet, 1991. Recreations: photography; gardening; local history; genealogy. Address: (h.) Edward's View, 8 Lurganbuoy Road, Churchtown, Castlederg, Co Tyrone, BT81 7HS; T.- 028 8167 1014. Fax: 028 8167 1014.

Empey, Sir Reg N. M., KB, OBE, BSc. Member (East Belfast), Ulster Unionist Party, Northern Ireland Assembly, since 1998; Minister for Enterprise, Trade and Investment in Northern Ireland Executive, 1999-2002; Belfast City Councillor, since 1985; Member, European Committee of the Regions, Brussels, 1994-2002; b. 26.10.47, Belfast; m., Stella Ethna Donnan; 1s.; 1d. Educ. Royal School, Armagh; Queen's University, Belfast. Ulster Young Unionist Council: Publicity Officer, 1967- 68; Vice-Chairman, 1968 - 72; Chairman, Vanguard Unionist Party, 1974 - 75; Member, East Belfast, Northern Ireland Constitutional Convention, 1975 - 76. Member: Belfast Harbour Commission, 1985 - 89; Eastern Health and Social Services Board, 1985 - 86; Ulster Unionist Council since 1987 (Hon. Secretary, 1990 - 96; Vice-President, since 1996); Lord Mayor of Belfast, 1989 - 90 and 1993 - 94 (Deputy Lord Mayor, 1988 - 89); Board: Laganside Corporation, 1992-98; Police Authority for Northern Ireland, 1992-2001; KB, 1999. Recreations: walking; gardening. Address: (b.) Knockvale House, 205 Sandown Road, Belfast, BT5 6GX.

English, Prof. Richard, MA, PhD. Professor of Politics, Queen's University Belfast, since 1999; b. 16.12.63, Belfast; m., Maxine Cresswell; 2 d. Educ. Queen Elizabeth's Hospital, Bristol; Keble College, Oxford. Publications: Ernie O' Malley: IRA Intellectual, 1998; Armed Struggle: the history of the IRA, 2003. Recreations: opera; jazz; The Arsenal. Address: (b.) School of Politics, Queen's University Belfast BT7 1PA. T.-02890 273328. e-mail: r.english@qub.ac.uk

Ennis, Professor Madeleine, BSc, PhD. Professor of Immunopharmacology, Department of Clinical Biochemistry, Queen's University Belfast; b. 26.2.53, London. Educ. University College London. Post Doctoral Research Fellow: University College London, 1977 - 80; Royal Postgraduate Medical School, London, 1980 - 82; Philipps University of Marburg, Germany, 1982 - 89; Lecturer, Department of Clinical Biochemistry, Queen's University Belfast, 1989 - 96; Senior Lecturer, Department of Clinical Biochemistry, Queen's University Belfast, 1996-99; Professor, Department of Clinical Biochemistry, Queen's

University Belfast, since 1999. Recreation: travel. Address: (b.) Department of Clinical Biochemistry, Institute of Clinical Science, Queen's University Belfast, Grosvenor Road, Belfast BT12 6BJ; T.-028 90 263107. e-mail: m.ennis@qub.ac.uk

Enniskillen, 7th Earl of, Andrew John Galbraith Cole; b. 28.4.42. Educ. Eton. Managing Director, Kenya Airways, 1979 - 81; Executive Vice-Chairman, AAR Health Services since 1991. Address: (b.) House of Lords, London, SW1A 0PW.

Erne, 6th Earl of, Henry George Victor John Crichton, JP. Lord-Lieutenant, Co Fermanagh since 1986; b. 9.7.37. Educ. Eton. Lieutenant, North Irish Horse, 1959 - 66. Member: Royal Ulster Agricultural Society; Royal Forestry Society. Justice of the Peace, Co Fermanagh. Address: (h.) Crom Castle, Newtownbutler, Co Fermanagh, BT92 8AP.

Erskine, Rev. William Paul Henry, MA, BD. Minister, Windsor Presbyterian Church, Belfast since 1994; b. 24.8.46, Bangor; m., Christine Margaret Boal; 1d. Educ. Bangor Grammar School; Royal Belfast Academical Institution; Trinity College; Dublin; University of Edinburgh; Union Theological College, Belfast. Ordained, Assistant Minister, Belmont Presbyterian Church, 1974; Minister, 1st and 2nd Ramelton and Kilmacrenan Presbyterian Churches, 1976 - 85; Minister, 2nd Comber Presbyterian Church, 1985 - 94. Elected Scholar, Trinity College, Dublin, 1967. Recreations; reading; meeting people; walking in the Donegal hills. Address: (h.) 63 Balmoral Avenue, Belfast, BT9 6NY; T.- 028 90666785.

Ervine, David Walter. Member (East Belfast), Progressive Unionist Party, Northern Ireland Assembly, since 1998; Belfast City Councillor; b. 21.7.53, Belfast; m., Jeanette; 2s. Educ. Orangefield Boys' Secondary School. Address: (h.) 182 Shankhill Road, Belfast, BT13 2BL; T.- 02890-326233.

Erwin, Dr. Barbara Erwin, BSc, PhD, MBA, CBiol, MIBiol, ALCM. Director (Staff and Student Services), Stranmillis University College, since 1998; b. 6.9.44, Belfast; m., Dr. David George Erwin, OBE; 1 s.; 1 d. Educ. Sale County Grammar School for Girls; Queen's University Belfast; University of Ulster, Jordanstown. Assistant Teacher of Biology, 1967-69; Lecturer in Science, 1969-76; Senior Lecturer in Biology, 1976-84; Head of Science, 1984-89; Senior Tutor, Practical Studies, 1989-98. Parades Commissioner, 1998-2000; Women's National Commissioner, since 2003; QAA Institutional Auditor. Recreations: gardening; dressmaking. Address: (h.) Quoile Quay House, 25 Quoile Road, Downpatrick BT30 6SF. e-mail: b.erwin@stran.ac.uk

Evans, Professor John David Gemmill, BA, MA, PhD, MRIA, MILT. Professor of Logic and Metaphysics, Queen's University of Belfast, since 1978; Chair, Philosophy Panel, Research Assessment Exercise 2001, since 1998; Chair, Committee on General Policy, International Federation of Philosophical Societies, since 1998; b. 27.8.42, London; m., Rosemary. Educ. St. Edward's School, Oxford; Queen's College, Cambridge. Fellow, Sidney Sussex College, Cambridge, 1964 - 78; Visiting Professor, Duke University, North Carolina, USA, 1972 - 73; Chair, Royal Irish Academy National Committee for Philosophy, 1984 - 88; Member, Philosophy Panel, Research Assessment Exercise, 1995 - 96; Member, Board of NI Arts Council, 1991-93; Governor, Strand Primary School, since 2002. Publications: Aristotle's Concept of Dialectic; Moral Philosophy and Contemporary Problems; Aristotle; Teaching Philosophy on the Eve of the Twenty-First Century. Recreations: mountaineering; astronomy; poker. Address: (b.) School of Philosophical Studies, Queen's University of Belfast, Belfast BT7 1NN.

Ewart, Professor Robert Wallace, OBE, MSc, CEng, FBCS. Pro Vice-Chancellor and Provost, University of Ulster at Belfast, 1998-2002; Dir., Springvale Project, Univ., of Ulster, 1994-2002; b. 4.11.38, Ballymena; m. 2d. Educ. Ballymena Academy; Queen's University, Belfast. Data Processing Manager, Queen's University, Belfast, 1961 - 73; Head of Management Services, Oxford University, 1973 - 76; Head of School, Computer Science, Ulster Polytechnic, 1976 - 84; Appointed Professor, 1982; Head, Computer Science, University of Ulster, 1984 - 85; Dean, Faculty of Informatics, University of Ulster, 1985 - 88; Dean, Faculty of Business and Management, University of Ulster, 1988 - 94; Visiting Professor, University of Loughborough, 1984 - 87; Member, Library and Information Commission, 1998-2000; Board Member, Northern Ireland Growth Challenge, 1997-2001; Chairman, Ufi N. Ireland Advisory Panel, since 2000; Member: Ortus Board, since 1994, Sentinus Board, since 2000. Recreations: sport (largely spectator rather than participant); rugby; tennis; squash. Address: (b.) University of Ulster at Belfast, York Street, Belfast, BT15 1ED; T.- 028 90 267330.
e-mail: rw.ewart@ulster.ac.uk

Ewart, Sir (William) Michael. b. 10.6.53. Educ. Radley. 7th Bt of Glenmachen, Co Down and of Glenbank, Co Antrim. Address: (h.) Hill House, Hillsborough, Co Down, BT26 6AE.

Eyre, Charles George, BA. Retired Methodist Minister; Former Chairman, Irish Council of Churches; b. 2.6.25, Belfast; m., Betty Muriel Shier, 1s.; 2d. Educ. Coleraine Academical Institution; Queen's University, Belfast; Edgehill Theological College. Methodist Minister, 1947 - 92. Secretary, Methodist Church in Ireland, 1977 - 90; President, Methodist Church in Ireland, 1982 - 83; Chairman, Irish Council of Churches, 1988 - 90. Recreation: music. Address: (h.) 364 Upper Ballynahinch Road, Lisburn, BT27 6XL; T.- 028 9263 9044.

F

Faithfull, Philip Charles Raymond, BEd (Hons). Clerk and Chief Executive of Strabane District Council, since 2001; b. 15.6.54, Strabane; m., Hazel Rebecca Faithfull. Educ. Strabane Grammar School; University of Ulster. P E Teacher, Boys' Model Secondary School, Belfast, 1978 - 80; Assistant Manager, Lisnagelvin Leisure Centre, Londonderry, 1980 - 81; Joined Omagh District Council, 1981, Chief Contract Services Officer, 1981-2001. Member, Institute of Quality Assurance; Fellow, Institute of Leisure and Amenity Management, 1997; Member, Institute of Sport and Recreation Management. ILAM Leisure Manager of the Year Award, 1991; Special Merit, Local Government Officer of the Year Awards, 1992. Recreations: golf; collecting MG sports cars; model cars; antiques and militaria. Address: (b.) Strabane District Council, 47 Derry Road, Strabane, Co. Tyrone BT82 8DY. T.-02871 382204.

Farahmand, Prof. Kambiz, BSc MSc, PhD, FIMA. Professor in Mathematics, University of Ulster; b. 1954, Tehran, Iran; m., Ann Lois; 3s.; 1d. Educ. Jam High School, Tehran; University of London; Chelsea and Kings Colleges. Lecturer, University of Natal; Senior Lecturer, University of Capetown; Visiting Lecturer, University of Bristol; Lecturer, University of Ulster. Publications: Topics in Random Polynomials, 1998. Address: (b.) Department of Mathematics; University of Ulster at Jordanstown, Shore Road, Co Antrim, Newtownabbey, BT37 0QB. e-mail: k.farahmand@ulst.ac.uk

Farren, Sean Nial, BA, MA, DPhil, HDipEd. Member (North Antrim), SDLP, Northern Ireland Assembly, since 1998; Senior Lecturer, University of Ulster, since 1970; b. 6.9.39, Dublin; m., Patricia Clarke; 1 s.; 3 d. Educ. Colaiste Mhuire, Dublin; National University of Ireland (UCD); Essex University; University of Ulster. Teacher: Catholic Training College, Bo, Sierra Leone, West Africa, 1961 - 64, Institut Stavia, Estavayer-Le-Lac, Switzerland, 1964 - 65, St. Vincent's Secondary School, Dublin, 1965 - 67, Holy Trinity Secondary School, Kenema, Sierra Leone, 1967 - 69; Lecturer/Senior Lecturer, School of Education, University of Ulster, since 1970 (currently on leave of absence). Chair, SDLP Executive, 1980 - 84. Address: 30 Station Road, Portstewart BT55 7DA; T.-01265 833042. e-mail: sn.farren@btinternet.com

Farry, Dr. Stephen Anthony, BSSc, PhD. Councillor, North Down Borough Council since 1993/Alliance Party General Secretary; Deputy Mayor, 2002-03; b. 22.4.71, Newtownards, Co Down. Educ. Our Lady and St Patrick's College; Queen's University, Belfast; Doctorate in International Relations. Director, North Down Development Organisation since 1996; Research Consultant to Alliance Talks delegation, 1996 - 98; North Down Borough Council since 1993; Chairman, Finance Sub-committee; Queen's Parade Working Group since 1998; Deputy Mayor, 2002-03; Party Organiser, Alliance Party, 1997-2000; Alliance Party Policy Officer and General Secretary, since 2000; Parliamentary Candidate, Fermanagh and South Tyrone, 1997; Northern Ireland Assembly Candidate, Fermanagh and South Tyrone, 1998; Candidate, NI Assembly, North Down, 2003; Political Party Trainer, National Democratic Institute for International Affairs; Advisor, Alliance Party Assembly Member, since 1999. Contributor to several newspapers and magazines. Recreations: snooker; cricket; international affairs. Address: (h.) 26 Morston Park, Bangor, Co Down, BT20 3ER; T.-01247-451161. e-mail: stephen.farry@northdown.gov.uk

Favis-Mortlock, David Thomas, PhD, BA (Hons). Lecturer, School of Geography, Queen's University Belfast, since 2000; b. 27.8.53, Romford. Educ. Barstable Grammar/Technical, Basildon, Essex; SE Essex College of Technology; University of Lancaster; University of Brighton. Computer Programmer, Redman Heenan (Engineers) Ltd, 1976-78; Musician, Self-employed, 1978-85; Project Leader, Rural Warwickshire Agency, 1982-85; Computing Supervisor, Countryside Research Unit, Brighton Polytechnic, 1985-87; Trainer, then Director of Training, Brighton Computer Training Centre, 1987-89; Occasional Lecturer, University of Brighton, 1989-93; Owner/Senior Consultant, Jupiter Computer Consultants, 1988-94; Visiting Assistant Professor, USDA-ARS National Soil Erosion Research Laboratory, 1996; Research Scientist 1A, Environmental Change Institute, University of Oxford, 1993-2000. Elected Council Member for the British Society of Soil Science, 2001-2003; Committee member for South-East England Soils Discussion Group, 1991-97; Member of: International Society for Soil Science, International Association of Hydrological Sciences, American Geophysical Union, World Association for Soil and Water Conservation, European Society for Soil Conservation, Soil and Water Conservation Society, British Geomorphological Research Group, British Society for Soil Science, South-East England Soils Group. Publications: over 30 scientific papers on soil erosion by water. Recreations: playing music; reading; vipassana meditation; travel. Address: (b.) Queen's University Belfast, School of Geography, Belfast BT7 1NN. T.-02890 335283.

Fawcett, Dr. Liz, BA, MSc, PhD. Lecturer in Media Studies, University of Ulster since 1995; b. 3.2.61, Surrey. Educ. Manchester University; Queen's University, Belfast. News Trainee, BBC, 1983 - 84; Regional Journalist, TV News, BBC South and West, 1985 - 87; BBC Northern Ireland: Reporter, TV News, 1987 - 88; Business Correspondent, 1988 - 90; Social Affairs

Correspondent, 1990 - 93; Regional Education Correspondent, 1994. Northern Ireland representative, Transport 2000. Recreations: campaigning on transport issues; art; cinema; music. Address: (b.) School of Communication, Faculty of Arts, Design and Humanities, University of Ulster, York Street, Belfast, BT15 1ED; T.- 028 9026 7371.

Fearon, Michael, BA (Hons). Chief Executive, Cinematic World Screen Festival for Young People, since 2001; b. 31.7.69, Newry. Educ. St. Colman's College; Thames Valley University. Address: 3rd Floor, Fountain House, 17-21 Donegall Place, Belfast BT1 5AB.

Fee, Professor Howard, MD, PhD, FFARCSI. Professor of Anaesthetics, Queen's University, Belfast since 1995; Consultant Anaesthetist, Royal Victoria Hospital and Musgrave Park Hospital, Belfast; b. Belfast; m., Eileen Hutchinson; 1s. Educ. Royal Belfast Academical Institution; Queen's University, Belfast. Member, War on Want team, India, 1970; Qualified in medicine, 1972; Senior Lecturer, Anaesthetics, Queen's University, Belfast, 1982 - 95. Assistant Editor, Anaesthesia since 1991. Speciality Adviser, Northern Ireland Council for Postgraduate Medical Education, 1987 - 96; Board member, Faculty of Anaesthetists, RCSI, 1986 - 96; Vice-Dean, Faculty of Anaesthetists, RCSI, 1997 - 98; Examiner, Royal College of Anaesthetists, London since 1989; Member, External Advisory Panel, Committee on Safety of Medicines since 1995. Publications: Anaesthetic Physiology and Pharmacology (joint ed.), 1996. Recreations: pianoforte; organ; private pilot. Address: (b.) Department of Anaesthetics, Queen's University, Belfast BT7 1NN; T.- 02890-335785.

Fee, John. Member, (Newry and Armagh), Social Democratic and Labour Party, Northern Ireland Assembly, 1998-2003; b. Newry, Co Down; m. Elected to Newry and Mourne Council, 1988; Member, SDLP talks team, Castle Buildings Talks, 1996-98; Member, European Committee of the Regions, 1995. Address: (b.) Parliament Buildings, Stormont, Belfast, BT4 3ST; T.- 02890-520700.

Fell, Sir David, KCB. Chairman, Northern Bank Ltd since 1998; b. 20.1.43; m., Sandra Jesse Moore; 1s.; 1d. Educ. Royal Belfast Academical Institution; Queen's University, Belfast. Sales Manager, Rank Hovis McDougall Ltd, 1965 - 66; Teacher, 1966 - 67; University Research Associate, 1967 - 69; Northern Ireland Civil Service: Ministry of Agriculture, 1969 - 72; Department of Commerce, 1972 - 82 (Under Secretary, 1981); Under Secretary, Department of Economic Development, 1982; Deputy Chief Executive, Industrial Development Board for Northern Ireland, 1982 - 84; Permanent Secretary, Department of Economic Development, 1984 - 91; Head of Northern Ireland Civil Service and Second Permanent Under Secretary of State, Northern

Ireland Office, 1991 - 97. Chairman, Opera Northern Ireland, 1998 - 99; Chairman, Boxmore International Plc 1998-2000; Chairman, the Prince's Trust, Volunteers since 1998; Director, National Australia Group Europe Ltd since 1998; Chairman, National Irish Bank since 1999; Director, Fred Olsen Energy ASA 1999-2003; Director, Dunloe Ewart Plc 1998-2002; Director, Chesapeake Corporation, since 2000; Chairman, Harland and Wolff Group plc, 2001-02; Chairman, Titanic Properties Ltd, since 2001; Chairman, Titanic Quarter Ltd, since 2001; President, The Extern Organisation since 1998; Chairman, Prince's Trust Council, Northern Ireland since 1999; Fellow of the Institute of Bankers, 1998; D.Univ (University of Ulster), 2003. Recreations: music; golf; rugby union. Address: (b.) Northern Bank Ltd, Head Office, PO Box 183, Donegal Square West, Belfast, BT1 6JS; T.- 02890-245277.

Ferguson, Gail C., MInstD. Chief Executive and Company Secretary, Filor Housing Association Ltd since 1990; b. 1.5.64, Banbridge; divorced, 2s.; 1d. Educ. Banbridge High School; Banbridge College. Filor Housing Association Ltd: Personal Assistant, 1986 - 87 Housing Officer, 1987 - 88; Finance Manager, 1988 - 90. Part-time panel member, Industrial and Fair Employment Tribunals (NI). Member: Chartered Institute of Housing, Institute of Directors, Chartered Institute of Personnel and Development. Recreations: reading; psychology. Address: (h.) 34 Clareglen, Belfast BT14 8LU. T.-02890 729829. (b) 282-290 Crumlin Road, Belfast BT14 7EE. T.-02890 351131.

Ferris, Jack Wilson, BSC, M Ed, FIMA, JP. Headmaster, Down High School since 1989; b. 26.5.46, Kircubbin, Co Down; m., Deirdre; 2s.; 1d. Educ. Regent House, Newtownards; Queen's University, Belfast. Insurance Industry, 1968 - 70; Mathematics Teacher: Ballymena Academy, 1970 - 72; Campbell College, 1972 - 77; Head of Mathematics/Housemaster, Campbell College, 1977 - 88 (Teacher, University of Chicago, 1982 - 83). Lay Magistrate, Juvenile and Family Courts. Recreations: golf; squash; philately; gardening. Address: (b.) Down High School, Mount Crescent, Downpatrick, BT30 6EU; T.- 02844-612103.

Finlay, Mark James, BSc, MRICS, MAPM. Managing Director: SDG Ireland Ltd, SDG (Scotland) Limited, Scarloch Limited, SDG (Properties) Limited, Ulster and London Land Limited. Directorships: Belfast Harbour Commissioners, Rosyth Europarc Ltd., Shepborough Developments (Liverpool) Ltd, Scarborough Development Company Limited: Aberdeen Buildings (Belfast) Ltd. Former Directorships: Mallusk Group of Companies, GWM Developments Ltd, GWM Investments Ltd, Rathmore Ltd, Ulster Automobile Club Ltd; b. 14.9.66, Lisburn, Co. Antrim; m. Karen; 1 d. Educ. Methodist College, Belfast; University of Ulster. Other: Member of the Institute of Directors Economic Policy Committee; former Chairman,

Newtownards Round Table; Committee, Knock Presbyterian Church; former Chairman, RICS General Practice Division in Northern Ireland; Member: Ulster Reform Club, Malone Golf Club. Recreations: Church; golf; motor sport. Address: (b.) Floral Buildings, 2-14 East Bridge Street, Belfast BT1 3NQ.
e-mail: mark.finlay@sdgroup-plc.com

Finnis, Professor Michael William, BA (Cantab), PhD, CPhys, FInstP. Professor of Atomistic Theory of Materials, Queen's University, Belfast since 1995; b. 14.9.49, Margate, Kent. Educ. Jesus College, Cambridge University. Scientist, Theoretical Physics Division, AERE Harwell, 1974 - 88; Alexander von Humbolt Fellow/Scientist, Fritz-Haber-Institut, Berlin, 1988 - 90; Leader, Theory Group, Max-Planck-Institut für Metallforschung, Institut für Werkstoffwissenschaften, Stuttgart, 1990 - 95. Publications: over 80 papers on the theory of materials. Recreations: viola da gamba and recorder playing; jogging. Address: (b.) Atomistic Simulation Group, School of Mathematics and Physics, Queen's University, Belfast, Belfast BT7 1NN; T.- 02890-335330.

Fitzgibbon, Ali, BA, PGD. Administrator, Replay Productions since 1997; b. 4.8.72, Cork, Ireland; m., Glenn Patterson. Educ. University College, Cork. PR/Marketing Officer, Graffiti Theatre Company/ Everyman Palace Theatre; Freelance marketing including work for Lavitt's Quay Gallery; Collins Press and Cork Aids Alliance; Administration: Community Arts Forum, Belfast, 1994; Belfast Community Circus, 1994; Freelance work included, Ballysillan Community Festival, 1995; Tour Manager, Loved Ones, Old Museum Arts Centre, 1996; Lyric Theatre, 1996. Recreations: reading; interior decorating; cooking. Address: (b.) Replay Productions Ltd, Old Museum Arts Centre, 7 College Square North, Belfast, BT1 6AR; T.-028 90322773.
e-mail: replay@dircon.co.uk

FitzPatrick, Robert John, BA, Dip Ed. Dip Curric St, MA. Regional Training Unit Associate; Headmaster, Ballyclare High School, 1990-2000; b. 1937, Belfast; m., Muriel Craig; 1s.; 1d. Educ. Methodist College, Belfast; Queen's University, Belfast; University of Ulster. Joined Ballyclare High School, 1960: Assistant History Teacher, 1960 - 66; Head , History Department, 1966 - 80; Vice-Principal, 1980- 84; Inspector of Schools, Department of Education (NI), 1984 - 90. Recreations: golf; hill walking; painting; reading. Address: (h.) Ossory, Demesne Road, Holywood; (b.) Regional Training Unit, Black's Road, Balmoral, Belfast. T.-028 90 618121.

Fitzsimmons, Dr. Alan, BSc, PhD, FRAS. Reader in Astrophysics, Queen's University, Belfast since 1997; b. 31.1.64, London. Educ. The Turnpike School, Newbury; Sussex University; Leicester University. Queen's University, Belfast: Post Doctoral Fellow, 1988 - 93; Lecturer, 1993 - 97.

Publications: over 90 scientific papers and reports. Recreations: waiting in airport departure lounges. Address: (b.) Astrophysics and Planetary Science Division; Queen's University, Belfast, Belfast, BT7 1NN; T.- 02890-273124.

FitzSimons, Thomas Marsden, BA (Hons). Retired Teacher; Councillor, North Down Borough Council since 1993; Mayor of North Down, 1998 - 99; b. 31.8.25, Belfast; m., Beth FitzSimons; 1s.; 1d. Educ. Royal Belfast Academical Institution; Queen's University, Belfast. Language Teacher: Ballymena Academy, 1948 - 49; Royal Belfast Academical Institution, 1949 - 62; Head of Languages/Senior Teacher, Glenlola Collegiate, 1962 - 89. Lay reader, Church of Ireland. Publications: two text books; Mon Bac; Mon Brevet. Recreations: tennis (Ulster veteran); operatics; music; drama. Address: (h.) 12 Charles Mount, Bangor, BT20 4NY; T.- 028 91 468167.

Flanagan, James. Deputy Editor, Belfast Telegraph since 1996; b. 25.6.60, Belfast; m., Colette Marie; 1s.; 1d. Educ. Annadale Grammar School; Thomson Regional Newspapers Training Centre, Cardiff. Trainee Reporter, East Antrim Times, 1979 - 80; Chief Reporter/Office Manager, East Antrim Times, 1980 - 83; Belfast Telegraph: Senior Reporter, 1983 - 87; Energy Correspondent, 1987 - 88; Assistant News Editor, 1988 - 91; News Editor, Sunday Life, 1991 - 93; Deputy Editor, Sunday Life, 1993 - 96. Recreations: football; rugby. Address: (b.) Belfast Telegraph, 124 Royal Avenue, Belfast; T.- 01232-264402.

Flanagan, Sir Ronnie, OBE, MA. HM Inspector of Constabulary, since 2002; b. 25.3.49. Educ. Belfast High School; University of Ulster. Joined PSNI as Constable, 1970; Chief Constable, Police Service of Northern Ireland, 1996-2002. Address: (b.) c/o Home Office, 50 Queen Anne's Gate, SW1H 9AT.

Flannagan, Thomas William, BSc (Hons), Cert Ed, DASE. Headteacher, Portadown College; b. 2.11.46, Portadown; m., Sylvia; 1s.; 1d. Educ. Queen's University, Belfast. Science Teacher, Royal School, Armagh; Head, Biology, Belfast Royal Academy; Science Inspector, Education and Training Inspectorate (NI). Recreations: gardening; racquet sports; cricket. Address: (h.) 3 Sandhill Court, Calvertsown Road, Portadown, BT63 5XP; T.- 028 38343671.

Fleck, Kate. Manager, Diabetes UK, since 2000. Address: (b.) Diabetes UK, John Gibson House, 257 Lisburn Road, Belfast BT9 7EN. T.-028 9066 6646. Fax: 028 9066 6333.
e-mail: n.ireland@diabetes.org.uk

Fleck, Professor Robert, BSc, PhD, CEng, FIMechE, MSAE. Professor of Mechanical Engineering; School of Mechanical and Manufacturing Engineering, Queen's University, Belfast; b. 22.10.51, Ballymena; m., Linda; 3s.; 1d. Educ. Ballymena Technical College; Queen's

University, Belfast. Manager, New Products, Mercury Marine, Wisconsin, USA, 1976 - 82; Joined Queen's University, 1982. Consultant to automotive companies around the world. Publications: named author on over 30 internationally published technical papers. Address: (b.) Queen's University, Belfast, Ashby Building, Stranmillis Road, Belfast, BT9 5AH; T.- 02890-274116.

Ford, David. Member (South Antrim), Alliance Party, Northern Ireland Assembly, since 1998; m.; 3 d.; 1 s. Senior Social Worker, NHSSB, 1980-90; General Secretary, Alliance Party, 1990-98; elected to Antrim Borough Council, 1993-2001; Alliance Chief Whip, 1998-2001, Party Leader, 2001. Address: (b.) Parliament Buildings, Stormont, Belfast, BT4 3XX; T.- 028 9052 1314. e-mail: david.ford@allianceparty.org

Forde, Patrick Mathew Desmond. JP DL. Vice Lord Lieutenant, Co. Down; b. 12.12.40, Belfast; m., Lady Anthea Lowry-Corry; 3s.; 1d.   Educ. Eton; Greenmount Agricultural College. Farmer, Nursereyman, Forester, Plant Collector; Councillor, Down District Council, 1977 - 85. Address: (h.) Seaforde, Downpatrick, Co Down, BT30 8PG; T.- 02844-811225.

Foreman, Sir Philip Frank, CBE, FREng, FIMechE, DL, Hon. DSc, Hon. DTech, Hon. DUniv, Hon. FRAeS. Chairman, Progressive Building Society, 1990-2000; b. Suffolk; m., Margaret Cooke; 1s. Educ. Soham Grammar School, Cambs; Loughborough University. Royal Naval Scientific Service, 1943 - 58; Short Bros Plc, 1958 - 88 (Managing Director, 1967 - 88; Chairman, 1983 - 88); Director, Progressive Building Society, 1987-2000 (Chairman, 1990-2000); Director, Simon Engineering Plc, 1987 - 92 (Chairman, 1991 - 92); Director, Ricardo Group Plc 1988 - 98 (Chairman, 1992 - 97). Board member, British Standards Institution, 1986 - 98 (Chairman, 1988 - 91; President, 1994 - 98); Member, Northern Ireland Economic Council, 1972 - 88; Trustee, Scotch-Irish Trust of Ulster since 1987; Member, Senate, Queen's University, Belfast, 1993-2002. Papers presented to Royal Aeronautical Society and Institution of Mechanical Engineers. Recreations: gardening. Address: (h.) 26 Ballymenoch Road, Holywood; T.-028 90 425673.

Forsythe, John W, LLB. Partner, Diamond Heron Solicitors since 1988; b. 27.6.61, Belfast; m., Lynn; 1s.; 1d. Educ. Methodist College, Belfast; Queen's University, Belfast. Admitted as Solicitor, 1985. Recreations: tennis; bridge; golf. Address: (b.) Diamond Heron Solicitors, Diamond House, 7-19 Royal Avenue, Belfast, BT1 1FB; T.- 02890-243726.

Foster, Elizabeth Ann, BA. Principal, Kilskeery Independent Christian School, 1979 - 91 and since 1992; b. 27.10.46, Co Antrim; m., Rev Ivan Foster (qv); 3s.; 3d. Educ. Ballymena Academy; Queen's

University, Belfast. Youth Employment Officer, 1967 - 68; Teacher, Fivemiletown High School, 1974 - 79. Reid-Harwood Scholarship in Modern Languages, 1964; Blayney Exhibition in Modern Languages, 1965. Publications: The Story of Joseph; Behold My Servant; 3 booklets on Mark's Gospel; children's tracts. Recreations: walking; reading. Address: (b.) Kilskeery Independent Christian School, Old Junction Road, Kilskeery, Co Tyrone, BT78 3RN; T.- 028 8956 1564.

Foster, Rev. Ivan. Minister, Kilskeery Free Presbyterian Church since 1978; b. 8.11.43, Co Fermanagh; m., Elizabeth Ann (q.v); 3s.; 3d. Educ. Ashfield Technical College; Free Presbyterian Theological Hall. News Film Editor, Ulster Television, 1962 - 64; Student Minister, 1965 - 68; Ordained, Lisbellaw Free Presbyterian Church, 1968. Councillor, Omagh District Council, 1982 - 86; Member, Northern Ireland Assembly for Fermanagh and Co Tyrone, 1982 - 86; Convener, Free Presbyterian Church Board of Education; Administrator, Kilskeery Independent Christian School. Publications: Patrick, Apostle of Ireland; The Williamite Wars and The Ulster Protestant; The Department of Education's Plan to Strangle our Protestant Heritage; Shadow of the Antichrist – Exposition of the book of Revelation; The Burning Bush, (monthly newsheet, ed.). Radio preacher on four weekly gospel broadcasts from Monaghan, Dublin and Donegal. Recreation: walking. Address: (h.) 51 Old Junction Road, Kilskeery, Co Tyrone, BT78 3RN. T.-028 8956 1564. e-mail: theburningbush@ivanfoster.org

Foster, Samuel, CBE, FIRSO (Hon), CQSW. Member (Fermanagh and South Tyrone), UUP, Northern Ireland Assembly, since 1998; Minister of Environment, NI Assembly, 1999-2002; Member, Fermanagh District Council, 1981-2001 (Chairman, 1995 - 97); b. 7.12.31, Lisnaskea, Co. Fermanagh; m., Dorothy C. Brown; 2 s.; 1 d. Educ. Enniskillen Technical College; Rupert Stanley College, Belfast; Ulster Polytechnic, Jordanstown, Belfast. Printer, Compositor, Proof Reader, 1946 - 66; Senior Education Welfare Officer, 1966 - 79; Social Worker (Special Child Care), Wirral Social Services, 1979 - 81; Social Worker, WHSSB, 1981 - 96. Company Commander, UDR (4th Bn.), rank of Major, 1970 - 79. Publication: Recall – A Little Bit of Orangeism in Fermanagh...And All That. Recreations: sport; campanology; debate. Address: 35 Derrychara Road, Enniskillen BT74 6JF; T.-028 66 323594.

Fraser, Alasdair MacLeod, Kt, CB, QC. Director of Public Prosecutions since 1989; b. 29.9.46, Glasgow; m., Margaret Mary Fraser, 2s.; 1d. Educ. Sullivan Upper School; Trinity College, Dublin; Queen's University, Belfast. Called to the Bar, Northern Ireland, 1970, Bencher 1999; Department of the Director of Public Prosecutions: Court Prosecutor, 1973; Assistant Director, 1974; Senior Assistant Director, 1982; Deputy Director, 1988. Address: (b.) 93 Chichester Street, Belfast BT1 3JR. T.-028 90542444.

Fraser, Professor Thomas Grant, MA, PhD, FR Hist S. Professor of History, University of Ulster since 1991; b. 1.7.44, Kilwinning, Scotland; m., Grace Frances Armstrong; 1s.; 1d. Educ. Irvine Royal Academy, Irvine, Scotland; University of Glasgow; London School of Economics. University of Ulster: Lecturer, History, 1969 - 85; Senior Lecturer, 1985 - 91; Head, Department of History, 1988 - 94; Head, School of History, Philosophy and Politics, 1994 - 98. Fullbright Scholar in Residence, Indiana University, South Bend, USA, 1983 - 84. Chairman, Northern Ireland Museums Council since 1998; Trustee, National Museums and Galleries of Northern Ireland since 1998. Publications: Joint editor, Studies in Contemporary History series, MacMillan Press; Partition in Ireland, India and Palestine, 1984; The USA and the Middle East since World War 2, 1989; The Arab-Israeli Conflict, 1995; Ireland in Conflict, 1922 - 98, 1999; The Middle East, 1914 - 79 (ed.), 1980; Conflict and Amity in East Asia (with P Lowe), 1992; Men, Women and War (with K Jeffrey), 1993; Europe and Ethnicity, 1996 (with S Dunn), 1996. Recreations: listening to music; travel. Address: (h.) 7 Circular Road, Castlerock, Co Londonderry, BT51 4XA; T.- (b.) 01265-44141.

Frawley, Tom. Assembly Ombudsman and Commissioner for Complaints for Northern Ireland, since 2000. Address: Progressive House, 33 Wellington Place, Belfast BT1 6HN. T.-028 9023 3821.

Freedman, Anthony Howard. Insurance Broker; b. 9.12.34, London; m., Olive Sara; 2s. Educ. St Marylebone Grammar School, London. Royal Artillery; Merchant Navy; British European Airways; Hotel and Catering Management. Secretary, Bangor Chamber of Commerce Ltd; Past Chairman, Board of Directors, Ulster Society for the Prevention of Cruelty to Animals; Chairman, Bangor Branch, USPCA; Vice Chairman, Animal Welfare Federation Northern Ireland; Chairman, Better Bangor Campaign; Chairman, Bangor Road Safety Committee; Vice-President, North Down Scouts Association; Toyota North Down Cycling Club; Northern Ireland Chamber of Trade; Association of Jewish Ex Servicemen (AJEX); NDBC Equality and Good Relations Consultative Panel. Recreations: eating out; cooking; enjoying my family. Address: (h.) 15 James Mount, Bangor, Co Down. BT20 4NR; T.-028 9146 7932.

Freeman, Prof. Ruth Edwina, PhD, MSc, MMedSc, BDS, DDPH, RCS(Eng). Professor, Dental Public Health, Queen's University, Belfast since 2000; b. 10.8.54, Glasgow. Educ. Laurel Bank School, Glasgow; Belfast Royal Academy; Queen's University, Belfast; University of London. Research Student, Queen's University, Belfast, 1979 - 83; Lecturer, Dental Public Health, University College, London, 1985 - 89; Lecturer, Paediatric and Preventative Dentistry, 1990 - 94; Senior Lecturer, Dental Public Health, Queen's

University, Belfast, 1994-2000. Member, British Confederation of Psychotherapists, 1997. Publications: Centres and Peripheries of Psychoanalysis (with R Ekins), 1994; The Selected Anna Freud (with R Ekins), 1998; The Psychology of Dental Patient Care: the Common Sense Approach, 2000. Recreations: reading; walking; theatre; art. Address: (b.) School of Clinical Dentistry, Queen's University, Belfast, Belfast, BT12 6BP; T.-028-9024-0503 ext. 3827.

Fulton, Elizabeth Jean, OBE, MBA, BA, FCIH, MRICS, DMS. Chief Executive, B.I.H Housing Association since 1995; b. 27.2.54, Belfast. Educ. Carolan Grammar School, Belfast; Queen's University, Belfast; University of Ulster. Graduate Trainee Manager/Housing Officer/Senior Housing Officer, Northern Ireland Housing Executive, 1975 - 82; B.I.H Housing Association: Housing Manager, 1982 - 85; Director of Housing, 1985 - 95. Recreation: classical music. Address: (b.) Russell Court, Claremont Street, Belfast, BT9 6JX; T.-02890-320485.
e-mail: j.fulton@bih.org.uk

Fulton, Richard, LLB. Partner, Mills Selig, Solicitors since 1994; b. 4.11.53, Belfast; m., Barbara Fulton; 2d. Educ. Dalriada Grammar School; Queen's University, Belfast. Admitted as a Solicitor in England, 1980; Partner, Blaser Mills, 1982 - 90; Joined Mills Selig, 1991. Recreations: snow skiing; windsurfing; hill walking; music. Address: (b.) Mills Selig, 21 Arthur Street, Belfast, BT1 4GA; T.- 02890 243878.

G

Gallagher, Tommy. Member (Fermanagh and South Tyrone), Social Democratic and Labour Party, Northern Ireland Assembly, since 1998; b. 17.8.42, Ballyshannon, Co Donegall; m.; 2 s.; 1 d. Educ. Queen's University, Belfast; St Joseph's College of Education. Secondary school teacher; elected to Fermanagh Council, 1989; Member, Western Education and Library Board; Member, SDLP talks team, Castle Buildings talks, 1996-98; founder Member, Fermanagh Business Initiative; former President, Belleck Chamber of Commerce; Inter-County Gaelic footballer and hurler. Address: (h.) 39 Darling Street, Enniskillen BT74 7DP.

Gamble, Professor Harold Samuel, BSc, PhD, CPhys. Professor of Microelectronic Engineering, Queen's University, Belfast; b. 21.5.45, Dromore, Co Down; m., Isobel; 1s.; 1d. Educ. Banbridge Academy; Queen's University, Belfast. Temporary Engineering Lecturer,   Queen's University, Belfast, 1969-70; Research Engineer, Standard Telecommunications Laboratory, Essex, 1970 - 72; Research Associate, Queen's University, Belfast, 1972 - 73; Joined Academic Staff, 1973. Recreations: DIY.   Address: (b.) Electrical Engineering Department, Queen's University, Belfast, Ashby Building, Stranmillis Road, Belfast; T.- 01232-274063.

Gardiner, Keith R., MD, MCh, FRCS (Gen). Consultant Colorectal Surgeon, Royal Victoria Hospital, Belfast, since 1995; Honorary Senior Lecturer in Surgery, The Queen's University of Belfast, since 2000; b. 13.3.60, Belfast; m., Ruth; 2 d. Educ. Belfast Royal Academy; Queen's University of Belfast. House Officer, Royal Victoria Hospital, 1983 - 84; Anatomy Demonstrator, Queen's University of Belfast, 1984 - 85; Senior House Officer, Belfast Surgical Rotation, 1985 - 87; NI Registrar Rotation, 1987 - 89; DHSS Research Fellow, 1989 - 91; Research Fellow, Johns Hopkins Medical Institutions, Baltimore, 1991 - 92; Senior Registrar, NI Surgical Training Scheme, 1992 - 95; Senior Lecturer in Surgery, Queen's University of Belfast, 1995 - 99. Chairman, NI Regional Basic Surgical Training Committee, 1997-2002; Programme Director for General Surgery Training (NI), since 2000. Address: (b.) Department of Surgery, Royal Victoria Hospital, Grosvenor Road, Belfast BT12 6BA; T.-028 90633205.

Gibson, Christopher Duffield, OBE, DUniv, BAgr. Chairman, Civic Forum, 2000; Pro-Chancellor, Queen's University Belfast, 1999; Independent News and Media (NI) Ltd, Board Member, 2000; b. 1.4.40, Belfast; m., Jennifer Jane; 2d. Educ. Campbell College, Belfast; Queen's University, Belfast. Technical Executive, Richardsons Fertilisers, Belfast, 1965; ICI, Ireland,

Dublin: Sales Manager, 1973, General Manager, Agriculture, 1978; Managing Director, 1982; Commercial Director, Irish Fertiliser Industries, Dublin, 1989; Golden Vale UK, Belfast: Managing Director, 1992, UK Director, 1996. Chairman, Centre for Cross Border Studies; Trustee, Irish School of Economics.   Address: (h.) 18 Ballymorran Road, Killinchy, Newtownards, Co Down, BT23 6UE; T.- 028 9754 2527. e-mail: chrisdgibson@compuserve.com

Gibson, Professor Christopher Edward, BSc, PhD, DSc, CBiol, FIBiol. Professor in Aquatic Science, Queen's University, Belfast since 1993;Senior Principal Scientific Officer since 1992; b. 23.3.44, Ashford, Kent; m., Jennifer Margaret Uden; 1s.; 2d. Educ. Wanstead County High School; University College of North Wales, Bangor. Joined Department of Agriculture, Northern Ireland, 1968.   Fellow, Institute of Biology, 1997; President British Phycological Society, 1999. Publications: 92 scientific papers on freshwater and marine ecology. Lay reader, Church of Ireland. Recreations: gardening; travelling. Address: (b) AESD, Newforge Lane, Belfast, BT9 5PX; T.- 01232-255509.

Gibson, Professor Norman James, CBE, BSc (Econ), PhD, MRIA. Emeritus Professor of Economics; b. 13.12.31, Co Fermanagh; m., Faith Gibson; 2s.; 1d. Educ. Portora Royal School; Queen's University, Belfast. Queen's University, Belfast: Assistant Lecturer, Economics, 1956 - 59; Lecturer, 1959 - 62; University of Manchester: Lecturer, 1962 - 66; Senior Lecturer, 1966 - 67; Visiting Associate Professor of Economics, University of Wisconsin, USA, 1967; New University of Ulster: Professor of Economics, 1968 - 84; Dean, School of Social Sciences, 1968 - 71; Pro Vice-Chancellor, 1975 - 78 and 1982 - 84; University of Ulster: Professor of Economics, 1984 - 96; Pro-Vice-Chancellor: (Academic Planning), 1984 - 88; (Planning) 1988 - 92; (Planning and Research), 1992 - 93; Deputy to Vice Chancellor, 1992 - 93. Commonwealth Fund Fellowship, 1958 - 59, University of Chicago; CBE, 1991; Member, Royal Irish Academy, 1975. Publications: Economic Activity in Ireland: A Study of Two Open Economies (with J E Spencer, joint ed.), 1977; The Financial System in Northern Ireland, 1982; Northern Ireland and Westminster: Fiscal Decentralisation, 1996.   Recreations: reading; studying Irish conflict; walking. Address: (h.) 39 Glenbroome Park, Newtownabbey, Co Antrim, BT37 0RL; T.- 028 9086 0066. e-mail: normgib@tiscali.co.uk

Gilbert, Raymond, MA, BEd, DASE, FPEA. Assistant Senior Education Officer, SEELB; b. 27.8.57, Belfast; m., Joanna Marian Gilbert; 2d. Educ. Carrickfergus Grammar School; Stranmillis College; Queen's University, Belfast. Teacher, Ardnaveigh High School, Antrim, 1980 - 86; Lecturer, Stranmillis College, 1986 - 91; Assistant Advisor, P E, North Eastern Education and Library Board, 1991 - 92. Fellow, Physical Education

Association of the United Kingdom since 1995. Recreations: golf; reading. Address: (b.) South Eastern Education and Library Board, Grahamsbridge Road, Dundonald, Belfast, BT16 0HS; T.- 01232-90566288.
e-mail: ray.gilbert@seelb.org.uk

Gildernew, Michelle. Member (Fermanagh and South Tyrone), Sinn Fein, Northern Ireland Assembly, since 1998; Sinn Fein Member of Parliament (Fermanagh and South Tyrone), since 2001. Educ. University of Ulster, Coleraine. Address: (b.) Parliament Buildings, Stormont, Belfast, BT4 3ST; T.- 02890-520700.

Gillan, Dr. Mark Andrew, BEng (Hons); PhD, CEng, MAIAA, MRAES. Aeronautical Engineering Lecturer, Queen'sUniversity, Belfast, 1995 -98; Lecturer, Queen's University, Belfast since 1995; b. 25.1.68, Bangor, Co Down; m., Dominique L P Gillan. Educ. Bangor Grammar School; Queen's University, Belfast. Research Fellow, Queen's University, Belfast, 1993 - 94; Research Scientist, Short Bros Plc, 1994 - 95; Advisor of Studies, Queen's University, Belfast since 1997; Director, Northern Information Technology and Engineering Consultancy Ltd.. Publications: 30 technical papers. Recreations: golf. Address: (h.) 40 Bitterne Drive, Goldsworth Park, Woking, Surrey, GU21 33U; T.- 01483-729967.

Gillen, Hon. Sir John, Hon, Mr Justice, KT, BA (Oxon). Judge at the High Court of Justice Northern Ireland since 1999; b. 18.11.47, Belfast; m., Claire McCartney; 2d. Educ. Methodist College, Belfast; The Queen's College, Oxford. Called to Bar, Northern Ireland, 1970; Barrister, 1970 - 83; Queen's Counsel since 1983. KT, 1999. Recreations: sport; music; reading. Address: (b.) Bar Library, Royal Courts of Justice, Belfast, BT1 5RG; T.- 01232-241523.

Gillespie, Dr. Alan Raymond, CBE, BA Hons (Cantab), MA, PhD, DUniv. Chairman, Ulster Bank Group, since 2001; Chairman, University Challenge Fund (NI), since 2000; Patron, the Queen's University of Belfast Foundation, since 2003; b. 31.7.50, Belfast; m., Ruth Milne; 1 s.; 1 d. Educ. Grosvenor High School, Belfast; Clare College, Cambridge University. Citicorp: London, 1976 - 80, Geneva, 1981 - 83, London, 1984 - 86; Goldman Sachs and Co.: New York, 1986 - 87, London, 1987 - 99; Member, Northern Ireland Industrial Development Board, 1995-96, Deputy Chairman, 1996-98, Chairman, 1998-2002; Chief Executive, Commonwealth Development Corporation plc, 1999-2002; President, European Development Finance Institutions, 2001-02. Member, Board, Elan Corporation plc; Member, Board, Co-operation Ireland; Member, Advisory Board, Judge Institute of Management Studies, University of Cambridge. Recreations: golf; tennis. Address: Ulster Bank Limited, 11-16 Donegall Square East, Belfast BT1 5UB. T.-02890 276000.

Gillespie, Prof. John H., BA, PhD, DipTh, FIL. Head of School of Languages and Literature, University of Ulster, since 1999, Director of Research, Faculty of Arts, since 1988, Professor of French Literature, since 2003; b. 2.3.48, Belfast; m., Rosalind; 2 d. Educ. Royal Belfast Academical Institution; Queen's University Belfast. New University of Ulster, 1974-84; University of Ulster, since 1984, Head, Research Graduate School, Faculty of Art, Design and Humanities, 1996-99. Chair, Modern Language Association of Northern Ireland; Chair, University Council of Modern Languages for Northern Ireland; Committee, UK Society for Sartre Studies; Member of ECONI. Recreations: reading; music (playing and listening); running. Address: (b.) School of Languages and Literature, University of Ulster at Coleraine, Cromore Road, Coleraine, Co. Londonderry BT52 1SA. T.-028 70 324578.
e-mail: j.gillespie@ulster.ac.uk

Gillespie, Kenneth Mathew, DMS. Executive Commissioner, The Scout Association, Northern Ireland Scout Council since 1992; b. 29.8.51, Carrickfergus; m., Joan; 3s.; 1d. Educ. Carrickfergus Technical College; University of Ulster. Accountancy, Carrickfergus Borough Council, 1969 - 72; Branch Manager, Blacks of Greenock/Waycastle Ltd, South of England, 1972 - 77; Installment Credit, NIIB/UDT, 1977 - 86; Northern Ireland Field Officer, Northern Ireland Scout Council, 1986 - 92. Recreations: scouting; badminton; caravan. Address: (b.) The Scout Association, Northern Ireland Scout Council, 109 Old Milltown Road, Belfast, BT8 7SP; T.- 028 90492829. e-mail: k.gillespie@scoutsni.com

Gillespie, William Fulton, OBE, TD, BA JP, DL. Chairman, John Sinton Ltd since 1990; Chairman, Fire Authority for Northern Ireland, since 2003; b. 18.9.31, Belfast; m., Winifred Mary Sinton; 2s. John Sinton Ltd: Manager, 1957; Director, 1960; Managing Director, 1972. Vice Chairman, TAVR Association of Northern Ireland; Former Colonel, Territorial Army (North Irish Horse/Royal Signals); President, South East Branch, Institute of Management; Fellow, Chartered Institute of Building; Fellow, Association of International Accountants; Fellow, Institute of Directors. Chairman, Southern Education Board, 1986 - 87; Chairman, Southern Health and Social Services Board, 1994-2003; Chairman, CITB (NI), 1993-2002. Former President, Construction Employers Federation; Former Chairman, N I Region, Junior Chamber of Commerce; Appointed Justice of the Peace, 1992; Appointed Deputy Lieutenant Co Armagh, 1984; High Sheriff, Co Armagh, 1989; OBE, 1989; Chairman, Agricultural Wages Board since 1999; Chairman, General Commissioners for Tax, Bann Central Division. Publications: History of the Territorial Army. Recreations: railways; gardening. Address: (h.) Ballymore Lodge, Tandagee, Craigavon, Co Armagh; BT62 2JY; T.- 028 38840362.

Gilliland, Dr. Albert Brian, BA, PhD, DLit, Dip RD, ACoP, FCollP, MCMI. Principal, Cairnshill Primary School, Belfast since 1987; b. Enniskillen, Co Fermanagh; m., Elizabeth Livingstone; 5d. Educ. Portora Royal School, Enniskillen; Stranmillis College, Belfast. Teacher, Strand Primary School, Belfast, 1967 - 76; Vice-Principal, Kilmaine Primary School, Bangor, 1976 - 87. Secretary of Northern Ireland Schools' Football Association; Past Chairman of Schools' FA and Schools' International Board. Recreations: sport; reading; travel. Address: (b.) Cairnshill Primary School, Belfast, BT8 6RT; T.-028 9070 5122; Fax: 028 9040 3015.

Gilliland, David Jervois Thetford, BA; LLB. Senior Partner, Caldwell and Robinson, Solicitors since 1970; b. 14.7.32, Donegal, Ireland; m., 1. Patricia Wilson (m. diss.); m., 2. Jennifer Johnston; 2s.; 3d. Educ. Wrekin College; Dublin University; Trinity College, Dublin. Solicitor, 1957, took over Todd and Mark Solicitors, 1957; took over Caldwell and Robinson Solicitors, 1970. Member, Independent Television Authority with special responsibility for Northern Ireland, 1965 - 70; Chairman, Northern Ireland Heritage Gardens Committee since 1992. Member: International Dendrology Society; Royal Horticultural Society; Royal Photographic Society; National Trust; Friend, Chelsea Physic Garden. Member, Clyde Cruising Club. Recreations: dendrology; photography; cruising. Address: (b.) 11 Castle Street, Londonderry; T.- 02871 261334. e-mail: candr@iol.ie

Gilliland, John William David, HND, FRAgS. President, Ulster Farmers' Union; NI Commissioner, Agricultural and Environment Biotechnology Commission; Managing Partner, Brook Hall Estate, Farming; Chairman and Director, Rural Generation Ltd; Chairman, Rural Support; Member of N. Ireland Authority For Energy Regulation; Member of N. Ireland Economic Development Forum; Director of Action Renewables; b. 16.5.65, Londonderry; m., Catherine Christine Knox; 3 s.; 1 d. Educ. Coleraine Academical Institution; East of Scotland College of Agriculture. Founded Brook Hall Estate Farm Business, 1989; Founder Member of Ulster Arable Society, 1994; Chairman, N. Ireland's Farm Quality Assured Cereals Scheme, 1995-2000; Director, Home Grown Cereal Authority, 1994-2003; Member of Local Branch RNLI, 1995-2000; Member of British Biogen; Member, Department of Agriculture For N. Ireland's Research and Development Strategy Committee, 1996-98; UK Alternate Member to DG Ag.of EU Commission's Advisory Committee on Energy Crops; Fellow of The Royal Agricultural Societies of the UK; Chairman, UFU Seeds and Cereals Committee, 1996-2000; Winner, All Ireland Tillage Farmer of the Year, 1992; All Ireland Farm Sprayer Operator of the Year, 1993; All Ireland Environmental Award, 2000; Pioneer and UK's first developer of On Farm Willow Biomass, combined heat and power units, to

manufacture renewable energy. Recreations: family; sailing; travelling to study world systems of agriculture. Address: (b.) The Red Lodge, Brook Hall Estate, 67 Culmore Road, Londonderry BT48 8JE. T.-02871 354635/07850 389666.

Gilpin, David Howard, BA DipTh. Presbyterian Minister, Moira, since 2001; Redrock and Druminnis, 1989-2001; b. 5.9.59; Ballymoney, Co Antrim; m., Catherine Anne; 1s.; 1d. Educ. Belfast Royal Academy; Larne Grammar School, Queen's University, Belfast. Lay Evangelist, Methodist Church, Lurgan Circuit, 1981 - 82; Lay Assistant, Sinclair Seaman's Presbyterian Church, Belfast, 1982 - 83; Assistant Minister, Ballyholme Presbyterian Church, Bangor, 1985 - 89; Ordained, 1987. Recreations: golf; swimming; watching rugby. Address: (h.) 6, Station Road, Moira BT67 0NE. T.-028 92611252.

Gilpin, Geraldine Patricia, LLB. Northern Ireland Regional Co-ordinator, Abbeyfield Society since 1996; Director, Abbeyfield NI Development Society; b. 3.12.57, Belfast; m., John Gilpin; 2s. Educ. Carolan Grammar School; Queen's University, Belfast. Director, Extra Care for Elderly People, until 1987; career break to raise family. Recreations: clarinet teacher, City of Belfast School of Music since 1978. Address: (b.) Abbeyfield Regional Office, 3 Grand Parade, Belfast, BT5 5HG; T.- 028 90402045.

Girvan, Hon. Mr Justice (Sir Frederick Paul), BA (Cantab). High Court Judge since 1995; b. 20.10.48, Larne, Co Antrim; m., Karen Elizabeth Joyce; 2s.; 1d. Educ. Larne Grammar School; Belfast Royal Academy; Clare College, Cambridge; Queen's University, Belfast. Called to the Bar of Northern Ireland, 1971; Called to the Inner Bar of Northern Ireland, 1982; Junior Crown Counsel (Chancery), 1976 - 82; High Court Judge since 1995; Chancery Judge since 1997. Knighted, 1995. Chairman, Law Reform Advisory Committee for Northern Ireland since 1997; Chancellor, Archdiocese of Armagh. Recreations: painting; walking; badminton; golf; reading. Address: (b.) Royal Courts of Justice, Chichester Street, Belfast BT1 3JP; T.- 02890-235111.

Girvan, Lady Karen Elizabeth, LLB, Barrister-at-Law. NI Chairman, Action Medical Research, since 2002; Trustee, Grand Opera House, Belfast, since 2000; b. 16.12.52, Omagh; m., Sir F. P. Girvan; 2 s.; 1 d. Educ. Coleraine High School; Queen's University Belfast. Practised at NI Bar, 1975-77; Founder of Sparks NI, 1986 (Sporting Partners of Action Medical Research Committee). Former Governor, Methodist College, Belfast. Recreation: walking. Address: (h.) 5 Ballygrainey Road, Craigavad, Co. Down BT18 0HE. T.-028 90 423673. e-mail: karengirvan@utvinternet.com

Glasgow, Dr. John Frederick Turnbull, BSc, MD, FRCPCH, FRCP(L) FRCP(I), FFAEM, MFPaed, RCP(I), DCH. Independent Consultant Paediatrician; b. 27.1.38, Co Down; m., Dr. Judith

Gray; 3s. Educ. Royal Belfast Academical Institution; Queen's University, Belfast. Qualified in Medicine, 1963; House Officer, Royal Victoria Hospital, Belfast, 1963 - 64; House Physician, Hospital for Sick Children, Great Ormond Street, London, 1969, specialising in Paediatrics since 1966; Resident/Clinical Fellow, Hospital for Sick Children, Toronto, Canada, 1969 - 71; Consultant Paediatrician, since 1971; Senior Lecturer, Queen's University, Belfast, 1971, Acting Head of Department, 1984 - 85, Reader in Child Health, 1987-2003. Publications: Management of Injuries in Children (with H K Graham), 1997; numerous papers in academic and medical journals. Recreations: golf; bird watching; gardening; military history. Address: (h.) 12 Old Coach Road, Upper Malone, Belfast, BT9 5PR; T.- 028 90-290296.

Glendinning, Ronald Ivan. National Chairman of Fundraising, Royal British Legion; b. 11.9.49, Limavady; m., Margaret Jane Scott; 2s.; 1d. Educ. Limavady High School. Purchasing Officer in Education; National Council, Royal British Legion; Director, Poppy Factory; Former Chairman, Royal British Legion, Northern Ireland. Address: (h.) 36 Drumceatt Park, Limavady, BT49 9HE; T.-028777-64434; (b.)TRBL, 48 Pall Mall, London SW1Y 5JY.

Glendinning, Will, BSc, Cert Ed, JP. Chief Executive, Community Relations Council since 1997; m., Maura Maginn; 1d. Educ. Campbell College; Queen's University, Belfast; University of York. Teacher, Belfast High, 1975 - 82; Member, Belfast City Council, 1977 - 87; Member, Northern Ireland Assembly, 1982 - 86; Education Officer, Northern Ireland Council on Alcohol, 1986 - 87; Northern Ireland Regional Co-ordinator, Help the Aged, 1987 - 90; Development Officer, Community Relations Council, 1990 - 97. Chair, Northern Ireland Association of Citizen's Advice Bureaux, 1991 - 95. Recreations: sheep farming. Address: (b.) Community Relations Council, 6 Murray Street, Belfast, BT1 6DN; T.-028 9022 7500.

Glenny, Rev. James Brownlee (Lee), BSc, PGCE, DASE, MA. PhD. Minister, Holywood Methodist Church, since 2001; b. 2.1.45, Omagh, Co Tyrone; m., Mave; 1d. Educ. Omagh Academy; Queen's University, Belfast; New University of Ulster. Mathematics Teacher, Methodist College, Belfast, 1971 - 83; Training for Methodist Ministry, 1983 - 85; Minister, South Derry Mission, 1985 - 89; Minister, Seymour Hill, Dunmurry and Upper Falls Methodist Churches, 1989 - 94; Minister, Donaghadee Methodist Church, 1994-2001. Member, Ministry of Healing Committee; Member, Churches' Council for Health and Healing in Ireland; District Education Secretary; Sec. of the Northern Executive of Board of Education; Former District Secretary, World Development and Relief. Recreations: bowling; being taken for a walk by the dog. Address: (h.) 22

My Lady's Mile, Holywood, Co. Down BT18 9EW. T.-028 9042 2061.

Good, Rev. George Harold, OBE, STM. Methodist Minister; President, Methodist Church in Ireland, 2001-2002; b. 27.4.37; Londonderry; m., Clodagh Coad; 2s.; 3d. Educ. Methodist College, Belfast; Edgehill Theological College; CTS, Indianapollis, USA. Served Congregations in Northern Ireland and the Republic; Director, Corrymela Community, 1973 - 78; Northern Ireland Supplementary Benefits Commissioner, 1974 - 80; Chairman, Northern Ireland Association for the Care and Resettlement of Offenders (NIACRO), 1991-2000. Member, UK Social Security Advisory Committee, 1980 - 98; Chair, Review of Northern Ireland Council of Social Services, 1982 - 83; Chair, Personal Social Services Advisory Committee, 1984 - 92; Governor, Methodist College, Belfast; Governor, Greenwood Assesment Centre; Governor, Edgehill Theological College; Member: New Deal task force on unemployment, 1997 - 99; Northern Ireland Human Rights Commission since 1999. Recreations: painting; photography; sea angling; travel. Address: (h.) 4 Brown's Park, Marino, Co. Down BT18 0AB.

Good, Richard James, BA. Adviser to the Speaker, Northern Ireland Assembly, since 2002; b. 23.8.72, Belfast. Educ. Methodist College, Belfast; Queen's University Belfast. Assistant to Leader of Alliance Party, 1994 - 96; Press Officer, Alliance Party, 1996 - 98; General Secretary, Alliance Party, 1998-2000; General Manager, Marketing and Communications, Irish League of Credit Unions, 2000-2001; Councillor, North Down Borough Council, 1997-2001; Media and Public Relations Officer, Independent Television Commission, 2001-02. Address: (h.) 18 Meadow Grove, Crawfordsburn, Co. Down BT19 1JL.

Gordon, Rev. James, MA BD. Minister, 1st Presbyterian Church, Donaghadee since 1994; b. 1.3.49, Belfast; m., Sarah Alexandra Mary Angela Carson; 1s.; 1d. Educ. Belfast Royal Academy; Magee University College, Londonderry; Trinity College, Dublin; Queen's University, Belfast; Assembly's College, Belfast. Ordained, 1974; Minister Glenwherry, Co Antrim 1976 -94; Clerk of the Presbytery, Ballymena, 1983 - 94. General Assembly Boards and Committee memberships: General Board, 1983 - 95, 2000-; Business Board, 1983 - 93; Doctrine Committee, 1985 - 94; Recognised Ministries, 1985 - 94; Forces Committee, 1987 - 95; Peace and Peacemaking, 1990 - 95, 2000-; Chaplains' Committee, since 2000. Member: Christian Education Committee, Boys' Brigade (NI), 1979 - 82; PCI Inter Church Relations Board, 1981 - 90, 2001-03; Irish Church Relations Committee, 1981 - 90; PCI Representative, Irish Council of Churches, 1983 - 90; Officiating Chaplain (OCF), 1985 - 94; Member: Commission on the Union of Congregations since 1995; Convenor, Manses Committee, 1997-2002; Member, Church and

Government Committee, since 2002; United Appeal Board, 1995 - 99; Judicial Commission, since 2003; Chairman, Board of Governors: Moorfields C P School, 1978 - 94; Ballyvester CP School, 1994-2000; Member, Board of Governors: Ballymena Academy, 1989 - 94, Ballyvester CP School, since 2000. Recreations: reading; walking; travel; gardening. Address: (h.) The Manse, 5 Meeting House Point, Edgewater, Donaghadee, BT21 OJN; T.-02891-883990.

Gordon, John Gerard, LLB. Managing Partner, Napier and Sons Solicitors since 1985; b. 27.11.57, Belfast; m., Patricia Crossin; 3d. Educ. St Malachy's College; Queen's University, Belfast; Institute of Professional Legal Studies. Qualified as a solicitor, 1982, Part-time Lecturer, Insolvency, Queen's University, Belfast. Council Member, Law Society of Northern Ireland since 1987; Treasurer, Law Society of Northern Ireland since 1996; Member, Lord Chancellor Advisory Committee on Insolvency, holder, Insolvency Practitioners License. Publications: chapter, Grier and Floyd Personal Insolvency; numerous articles on insolvency. Recreations: basketball. Address: (b.) Napier and Sons, 1-9 Castle Arcade, Belfast; T.- 02890-244602.

Gorman, Sir John. Member (North Down), Ulster Unionist Party, Northern Ireland Assembly, since 1998. Educ. Rockport; Portora Royal School, Enniskillen; Haileybury/Imperial Service College; Glasgow University; Harvard Business School. District Inspector of RUC, 1946-60; British Overseas Airways, British Airways, 1960-79; Deputy Chairman and Chief Executive, Northern Ireland Housing Executive, 1979-86; Director, Institute of Directors, 1988-96; Chairman, Northern Ireland Forum for Political Dialogue, 1996-1998. Knighted, 1998. Address: (b.) Parliament Buildings, Stormont, Belfast, BT4 3XX; T.-028 90520306.

Gorman, Professor Jonathan Lamb, MA, PhD (Cantab). Professor of Moral Philosophy, Queen's University, Belfast since 1995; b. 14.1.46, Middlesex; m., Kyra Hodges; 1s.; 2d. Educ. Merchant Taylor's School; University of Edinburgh; Peterhouse, Cambridge. Research Fellow, Philosophy, University of Birmingham, 1973 - 75; Lecturer, Social Philosophy, Queen's University, Belfast, 1976 - 85; John Milton Scott Visiting Professor, Queen's University, Ontario, 1981; Visiting Fellow and Senior Fulbright Scholar, Princeton University, USA, 1982; Queen's University, Belfast: Senior Lecturer, Philosophy, 1985 - 90; Reader in Philosophy, 1990 - 95; Head, Department of Philosophy, 1993 - 97; Head of School of Philosophical Studies since 1998. Publications: The Expression of Historical Knowledge, 1982; Understanding History, 1992; Rights and Reason, 2003; over 100 other papers and publications. Recreations: rare. Address: (b.) School of Philosophical Studies, Queen's University, Belfast, Belfast BT7 1NN; T.- 02890-273624.

Gormley, Kathleen, BA (Hons), MA, PQH. Principal, St. Cecilia's College, since 2002; b. 7.6.61, Belfast; m., Neil Gormley; 1 s. Educ. Our Lady's Grammar School, Newry; University of Ulster. Teacher of History and Politics, St. Cecilia's College, 1985-93; Field Officer for History with the Western Education & Library Board, 1993-95. President of North West Archaeological and History Society, 1991-95; Director, Hon. Secretary, Chairperson of the Education Committee of the Federation for Ulster Local Studies, 1992-96; Member of the Historic Monuments Council for Northern Ireland, 1993-97; Trustee of the Foyle Trust for Integrated Education, 1992-97; Member of Bishop Eames Cross Community Group, 1987-95; Director and Chair of St. Columb's Park House, 1999-2001; Member of Foyle Common Purpose, since 2003. Currently studying for an MBA in International Educational Leadership. Publications: The Wilsons and MacMahons - two families in Co. Monaghan, 1845-1920, 1994; Seige City, 1990; Island Divided, 1996; The Norman Impact and the Medieval World, 1997; The Middle Ages, 1997; Rivalry and Conflict, 1995; Rivalry and Conflict in Derry, Ireland and Europe, 1996; History Forum and DoE. Recreations: fitness and historical research on World War 1. Address: (b.) St. Cecilia's College, Bligh's Lane, Derry BT48 9PJ. T.-028 71 281800.
e-mail: office@stceciliascollege.com

Gormley, Dr. Mark John James, MB, DCH, FRCP, FRCP(I), MD. Consultant Physician since 1985 and Clinical Director since 1990, Mater Hospital Trust; b. 16.6.52, Belfast; m., Lorell Morris; 1d. Educ. St Malachy's College, Belfast; Queen's University, Belfast. General Medicine, Belfast Hospitals; Resident Physician in Diabetes, Hôpital Bichat, Paris, 1981 - 82. Publications: numerous papers published concerning physiology of non-insulin dependent diabetics. Recreations: swimming; music; opera; literature; cooking. Address: (b.) Mater Hospital, Crumlin Road, Belfast, BT14 6AB; T.- 02890-741211, Ext 2330.

Gowdy, David Clive, CB, BA, MSc. Permanent Secretary, Department of Health, Social Services and Public Safety, since 1999; b. 27.11.46, Belfast; m., Linda Doreen Traub (see Linda Gowdy); 2d. Educ. Royal Belfast Academical Institution; Queen's University, Belfast. Assistant Principal, Ministry of Finance, 1970; Deputy Principal, Department of the Civil Service, 1973; Principal, Northern Ireland Office, 1976; Assistant Secretary, Department of Commerce, 1980; Executive Director, Industrial Development Board, 1983; Under Secretary, Department of Economic Development, 1987; Under Secretary, Department of Health and Social Services, 1990; Director of Personnel, Department of Finance and Personnel, 1994; Permanent Secretary, Department of Health and Social Services, 1997. Awarded CB in June 2001. Recreations: reading; music; tennis; golf. Address: (b.) Department of Health, Social

Services and Public Safety, Castle Buildings, Stormont, Belfast, BT4 3SJ; T.- 02890-520559.

Graham, Professor Brian James, BA, PhD. Professor of Cultural Heritages and Director, Academy for Irish Cultural Heritages, University of Ulster, Magee Campus, since 2001; b. 19.6.47, Belfast; m., Valerie Graham; 2s. Educ. Annadale Grammar School; Queen's University, Belfast. Lecturer/Senior Lecturer, Ulster Polytechnic, 1972 - 79; Principal Lecturer, Ulster Polytechnic, 1979 - 84; Senior Lecturer, University of Ulster, 1984 - 93; Reader in Geography, University of Ulster, 1993 - 96; Professor of Human Geography, University of Ulster, 1996-2001. Publications: An Historical Geography of Ireland (co-ed.), 1993; Geography and Air Transport, 1995; In Search of Ireland: A Cultural Geography (ed.), 1997; Modern Europe, Place, Culture and Identity (ed.), 1998; Modern Historical Geographies (ed.), 1999; A Geography of Heritage (joint author), 2000. Recreations: walking; reading; classical music. Address: (b.) Academy for Irish Cultural Heritages, University of Ulster, Magee Campus, Northland Road, Londonderry BT48 7JL. T.- 02871 325462.

Graham, Cecil W L, LVO, OBE, BSC (Econ). b. 11.6.33, Belfast; m., June; 1s.; 1d. Educ. Belfast College of Technology; Queen's University, Belfast. Apprentice, Printing Industry; Awarded King George VI Leadership/Training Bursary; worked in British Guiana, for St Johns Ambulance, 1957 - 58; Training and Extension Secretary, Boys' Brigade in Northern Ireland, 1958 - 70; Publicity Officer, Ulster Savings Committee, 1970; Deputy Training Manager, Distributive Industry Training Board, 1970 - 74; Northern Ireland Civil Service, 1974 - 94; Chief Executive, Action Mental Health, 1994-2002. Previously President and Executive Chairman, European ACCEPT network. Assisted formation of Princes Trust in Northern Ireland, 1976 (former Chairman, Local Committee and National Vice-Chair, 1989 - 95); Vice-Chair, Princes Trust Volunteers, 1990 - 98; Chairman, Churches Youth Service Council, 1986 - 93. National Training Award, 1994; Former Member, Institute of Personnel Management; Member, Eastern Health and Social Services Council; Governor, Castlereagh College of Further Education; Directorships: UK Social Firms Ltd; Acceptable Enterprises (Larne) Ltd; Hillsborough New Horizons; Scrabo Catering; LVO, 1996; OBE, 1995. Recreations: sport; DIY; church activities. Address: (h.) 97 Orby Drive, Belfast, BT5 6AG; T.- 02890-289702. e-mail: cecilgrahamni@fsmail.net

Graham, David Alexander, OBE, BA. Chief Executive, Fane Valley Co-operative Society Ltd since 1993; Vice Chairman, Northern Ireland Dairy Association; b. 16.8.47, Co Fermanagh; m., Joanna; 1d. Educ. Portora Royal School; University of Ulster at Jordanstown. Fane Valley Co-op Society: Trainee Manager, 1968 - 69; Assistant Dairy Manager, 1968 - 71; Dairy Manager, 1971 - 88; General Manager, 1988 - 93. Recreations: outdoor bowls. Address: (b.) Fane Valley Co-op Society, Alexander Road, Armagh; T.- 028 37 522344. e-mail: davidgraham@fanevalley.co.uk

Graham, Edwin, BSc. Director, Lurgan Council for Voluntary Action since 1994; b. 12.6.57, Enniskillen; m., Mahvash Aminian; 1s.; 1d. Educ. Enniskillen High School; Portora Royal School; University of Ulster. Co-ordinator, Enniskillen Together, 1987 - 91; Community Relations Training Officer, Northern Ireland Council For Voluntary Action, 1991 - 94. Chairperson of the Joint Government and Voluntary Sector Forum; Secretary, Baha'i Council for Northern Ireland; Chairman, Craigavon and Banbridge Local Health and Social Care Group. Recreations: sailing; gardening; poultry rearing. Address: (b.) Mount Zion House, Edward Street, Lurgan BT66 6DB. T.- 028 3832 2066. e-mail: edwin@gawleysgate.co.uk

Graham, Stanley Samuel Bumper. Assistant Secretary, Northern Ireland Public Service Alliance since 1989; b. 14.2.58, Belfast. Educ. Wallace High School, Lisburn. Civil Servant, 1974 - 82; Executive Officer, Northern Ireland Public Service Alliance, 1982 - 89. Member/Secretary, Irish Congress of Trade Unions, Northern Ireland Youth Committee, 1982 - 90; Member/Chairperson, South East Belfast Local Manpower Committee, 1983 - 90; Member, Manpower Council Youth Training Programme Standing Committee, 1983 - 90; Member, Board of Belfast Harbour Commissioners, 1994-2001; Lisburn Peace and Reconciliation Partnership Board, since 1999. Recreations: golf; hockey; reading; music; football. Address: (h.) 8 Greenbank, Harmony Hill, Lisburn, Co Antrim, BT27 4JF; T.- 01846-673996.

Graham, Professor William (Bill), BSc, PhD, FInstP, FAPS. Professor of Physics, Queen's University, Belfast since 1995; Director, International Research Centre for Experimental Physics, since 2000; b. 11.6.49, Belfast; m., Professor B Hannigan; 2s. Educ. Annadale Grammar School; Queen's University, Belfast. Staff Scientist, Lawrence Berkley Laboratory, California USA, 1974 - 78; Lecturer, Physics, University of Ulster, 1979 - 88; International Fellow, SRI International, California, USA, 1988; Queen's University, Belfast: Lecturer, Physics, 1989 - 90; Reader, 1990 - 95. Researcher in technological plasmas and atomic collisions. Recreations: running; hiking; food and drink; hanging out with Ben and Ross. Address: (b.) Department of Pure and Applied Physics, Queen's University, Belfast, Belfast, BT7 1NN; T.- 028-90-273564. e-mail: B.Graham@qub.ac.uk

Gray, David William, BSc (Econ) (Hons), LGSM, FCA. Partner, McClure Watters, Chartered Accountants since 1997; b. 28.7.54, Bangor, Co Down; m., Jill; 3s.; 2d. Educ. Bangor

Grammar School; Queen's University, Belfast. Price Waterhouse: Trainee Accountant, Belfast, 1976 - 80; Audit Manager, 1980 - 85; Project Manager, New York, 1985 - 86; Senior Manager, Belfast, 1986 - 87; Director, Corporate Lending, Investment Bank of Ireland, 1987 - 88; Partner, Coopers and Lybrand, Belfast, 1988 - 94; Managing Director, Pace Corporate Services Ltd, 1994 - 97. Past Chairman, Ulster Society of Chartered Accountants; Joint Secretary, Institute of Chartered Accountants in Ireland; Director, Ulster, North Down and Ards Hospital Trust; Chairman, Board of Governors, Bangor Grammar School. Recreations: reading; clay pigeon shooting; rowing, university blue, represented Ireland, 1977 - 81, British and World Masters Champion, 1996 and 1997. Address: (b.) 14 James Street South, Belfast. T.-028 9023 4343.

Gray, Richard John, LLB. Solicitor of the Supreme Court of Northern Ireland, Partner, L'Estrange and Brett, Solicitors, Belfast since 1996; b. 21.2.66, Belfast; m., Kerry Philippine Cushnan; 2s.; 1d. Educ. Methodist College, Belfast; Queen's University, Belfast; Institute of Professional Legal Studies, Belfast. Called to the Bar of Northern Ireland, 1989; Cameron Markby Hewitt, City of London (now Cameron McKenna), 1989 - 92; Requalified as solicitor in England and Wales and Northern Ireland, 1992; Joined L'Estrange and Brett, 1992. Lord Chief Justice Prize, First in Year, 3rd and 4th years at University. Publications: a number of professional articles and seminars. Recreations: keeping fit; keeping up with my young family; reading. Address: (b.) L'Estrange and Brett, Arnott House, Bridge Street, Belfast BT1 1LS; T.- 02890 230426

Gray, Rev. William Harold, BA, BD. Retired Minister, Presbyterian Church in Ireland; b. 1.7.26, Belfast; m., Jean Kelly; 2s.; 1d. Educ. Methodist College, Belfast; Queen's University, Belfast; Stranmillis Training College; Union Theological College, Belfast; New College, University of Edinburgh. Teacher, Belfast Boys' Model School, 1948 - 52; Minister: Newmills Presbyterian Church, 1956 - 69, with Carland Presbyterian Church, 1960 - 69; Woodvale Presbyterian Church, 1969 - 76; Harmony Hill Presbyterian Church, 1976 - 91. Former member, South East Education and Library Board (Chairman, 1985 - 87); Former Trustee and Governor, Wallace High School, Lisburn (Chairman of Board of Governors, 1992 - 97). Recreations: travel; walking; gardening. Address: (h.) 6 Fairway Crescent, Belfast, BT9 5NN; T.- 028-9062 7712.

Greene, Hugh Francis, BSc (Hons), DAAS, RIBA. Principal, Hugh Greene Chartered Architect; b. 31.3.56, Kilkeel, Co Down; m., Rosemary Neely; 1s.; 1d. Educ. Queen's University, Belfast. Kennedy FitzGerald Architects, Belfast, 1983 - 85; Scott MacLynn Architects, 1985 - 88; BDP, Belfast, 1988; Private practice, 1994. Recreations: hill-walking;

photography. Address: (b) 16 Rosepark, Belfast, BT5 7RG; T.-028 9041 0202.

Greenfield, Tanya Dawn, BA (Hons), DipAA. Development Manager, Arts Council of Northern Ireland, since 2002; b. 27.3.63, Wimbledon; m., Ronald McGill; 2 s (1 deceased). Educ. Tolworth Girls School; John Beddoes School; Rippowam High School; New University of Ulster; University College Dublin. Belfast Folk Festival, 1986 – 87; Old Museum Building and Theatre Ireland, 1987 - 88; CIRCA Publications, 1988 - 89; Arts Theatre, 1989 - 90; Hanna Greenfield, 1990 - 94; Tyrone Guthrie Centre, 1990 - 94; many other freelance positions; Arts Council of Northern Ireland: Lottery Officer, 1994 - 95, Lottery Officer (Head of Unit), 1995 - 97; Lottery Director, 1997-2002. Recreations: travelling; reading; theatre; archaeology. Address: (h.) 33 Manse Road, Cloughey, Newtownards, Co. Down BT22 1HS. T.-028 427 72670.

Greer, Professor Desmond, QC (Hon.), LLD, BCL. Professor of Common Law, Queen's University, Belfast since 1973; b. 31.8.40, Limerick; m., Diana Stevenson; 1s.; 1d. Educ. Bishop Foy School, Waterford; Methodist College, Belfast; Queen's University, Belfast; Wadham College, Oxford. Tutor, Legal Method, University of Pennsylvania Law School, 1964 - 66; Queen's University, Belfast: Lecturer, Law, 1966 - 73; Professor since 1973; Dean, Faculty of Law, 1973 - 76; President, Irish Association of Law Teachers, 1980 - 81; Dean, Faculty of Law, 1983 - 86; Visiting Professor: University of Western Ontario, 1976 - 77; Cornell Law School, USA, 1990 - 91. Member: Standing Advisory Commission on Human Rights, 1982 - 86; Law Reform Advisory Committee for Northern Ireland, 1989 - 97; Chairman, Hamlyn Trustees, 1993 - 98; President, Irish Legal History Society, 1997-2000. Publications: various books, articles and reports especially on compensation for crime victims and Irish legal history. Recreations: hill walking; bridge. Address: (b.) School of Law, Queen's University, Belfast, Belfast, BT7 1NN; T.- 028 9024 5133.

Greer, Rev. Dr. Robert James (Robin), BSc, MPhil, CChem, MRSC, BD, PhD, DTh, FETS. Minister, Tandragee Presbyterian Church; b. Ballymena; m., Alison Elizabeth Culbert, BSc RGN (Nursing Sister: Belfast City Hospital). Educ. Ballymena Academy; University of Ulster; King's College, University of Aberdeen; Union Theological College, Belfast; European Theological Seminary, Birmingham. Gallaher, Research Chemist; Ordained, Presbyterian Church in Ireland, 1991. Member, Ulster Cancer Foundations ASH Committee, 1993-98; Convenor, Alcohol and Drug Education Committee of P.C.I., 1993 - 97; Volunteer: Benevolent Fund, Royal Society of Chemistry. Publications: Thesis: Studies in the Synthesis of Quininoline Alkaloids, 1987; Revival Fact or Fiction? 2001; Evolution Fact or Fiction? 2002; several papers in scientific and Biblical journals and magazines. Address: (h.) The Manse, Tandragee, Co Armagh, BT62 2EU; T.-028 38 840 303.

Greer, Rev. Thomas William Alexander, LLB BD. Minister, Molesworth Presbyterian Church, Cookstown, since 2001; b. 13.10.63, Ballymena, Co Antrim; m., Heather Malcomson; 1 d. Educ. Ballymena Academy; Queen's University, Belfast; Union Theological College; Belfast. Ordained 1990; Assistant Minister, Greenwell Street Presbyterian Church, Newtownards, 1990 - 93; Minister, Cavanleck and Aughentaine Presbyterian Churches, 1993 - 98; Minister, Macrory Memorial, Newington and Sinclair Seamen's Presbyterian Churches, Belfast 1998-2001. Deputy Imperial Grand Chaplain, Royal Black Institution; Deputy Grand Chaplain of Ireland, Loyal Orange Institution; Assistant Sovereign Grand Master, Royal Black Institution. Recreations: travel; listening to music; reading; golf; gardening. Address: (h.) 119A Coolreaghs Road, Cookstown, Co. Tyrone BT80 8QN. T.-028 8676 6998.

Gregg, Rev. Richard David, BSc, BD. Minister, Burnside Presbyterian Church; b. 12.12.70, Ballymena; m., Deirdre Elizabeth. Educ. Cambridge House Boys' Grammar; Queen's University, Belfast. Computer Software Engineer, Kainos Software, Belfast; Assistant Minister, 1st Antrim Presbyterian Church. Recreations: golf; reading; caravanning. Address: (h.) Mill Road, Portstewart, BT55 7SW; T.- 02870-836984.

Grew, James, CBE, JP, DL, FInstD. Treasurer, National Art Collections Fund, Northern Ireland, 1999-2001; Chairman, Giants Causeway-Bushmills Railway, 1999; Chairman, Lloyds TSB Foundation Board for Northern Ireland 1991-99; b. 25.10.29, Portadown; m., Pauline Peta Cunningham; 2s.; 2d. Educ. Downside. Founder Chairman and Managing Director, Abbicoil Springs Ltd, Portadown, 1957 - 96. President, Portadown Rotary Club, 1969 - 70; Member: Security Advisory Committee, J Police Division, 1971 - 73; Northern Ireland Community Relations Commission, 1971 - 74; Northern Ireland Economic Council, 1970 - 74; Craigavon Development Commission, 1971 - 73; Crawford Commission on Broadcasting Coverage, 1973 - 74; Justice of the Peace since 1974; Member: BBC General Advisory Council, London, 1976 - 81; BBC Northern Ireland Advisory Council, 1976 - 81; Chairman: Lisburn and District Group Training Scheme, 1977 - 78; Lisburn and District Youth Opportunity Workshop, 1980 - 81; Director, Management Development Services, Northern Ireland, Ltd, 1975 - 90; Member: Standing Advisory Commission on Human Rights, 1980 - 82; Post Office Users National Council, London, 1976 - 81; Chairman, Post Office Users Council, Northern Ireland, 1976 - 81; President, Brownlow Citizens Advice Bureau, 1976 - 80; Appointed Deputy Lieutenant, Co Armagh, 1981; Member: Northern Ireland Advisory Committee, Independent Broadcasting Authority, 1981 - 83;

Member, Advisory Committee, Automation Centre, Queen's University, Belfast, 1984 - 87; Director, Northern Ireland Transport Holding Company, 1983 - 86; First Chairman, Probation Board for Northern Ireland, 1982 - 87; Director, Northern Ireland Railways, 1982 - 91; Deputy Chairman, TSB Foundation Board For Northern Ireland, 1987 - 91; First Chairman, Independent Commission for Police Complaints, Northern Ireland, 1988 - 97; CBE, 1989; Member, Abbey National Advisory Board, 1990 - 93; Director, International Association for Civilian Oversight of Law Enforcement (IACOLE), USA, since 1989 (Vice-President, 1991 - 93; President, 1994 - 95); Director, Bannside Development Agency Ltd, 1990-99 (Chairman, 1992 - 96); Director: Portadown Integrated Primary School Ltd, 1990 - 93; NIR Leasing Ltd, 1990 - 91; Novatech Ltd, 1990 - 94; Novatech Seed Fund Board, 1991 - 94; Director and Secretary, Northern Ireland Council for Integrated Education, 1991 - 93; Associate Member, International Association of Chiefs of Police, 1991 - 96; Member, Advisory Committee on the Ulster Defence Regiment, 1990 - 92; Trustee: Ulster Defence Regiment Benevolent Fund, 1990-2002; Royal Irish Regiment Museum, Ballymena, 1993-2003; Member: Territorial Auxiliary and Volunteer Reserve Association for Northern Ireland, 1988-2002; Army Cadet Force Association, 1987; Lord Chancellor's Committee for Appointments. Member: Armagh Club; Knight of Malta, 1998. Recreations: sailing; gardening. Address: (h.) Peacefield, Ballinacorr, Portadown, BT63 5RJ; T.- 02838 350065.

Gribben, William. Principal, Bocombra Primary School, Portadown since 1990; b., 23.2.47, Ballymena; m., Edna Gribben; Educ. Ballymena Academy; Stranmillis College, Belfast. Teacher, Grove Primary School, 1968 - 70; Teacher/Vice Principal, Edenderry Primary School, Portadown, 1970 - 90. Introduced mini-rugby to Northern Ireland with Ronnie Lamont, 1972, Recreations: rugby coach, Portadown RFC. Address: (b.) Bocombra Primary School, 1 Old Lurgan Road, Portadown, BT63 5SG; T.- 028 3833 6749. e-mail: wgribben@bocombra.portadown.ni.sch.uk

Guckian, Francis Gerard, CBE, JP, DL. Director, Londonderry Chamber of Commerce since 1996; b. Claudy, Co Londonderry; m., Eillen Josephine; 2s.; 2d. Educ. St Columb's College. Proprietor and Managing Director, Clothing Manufacturers; Proprietor, Retail Clothing Firm. Chairman, Shirt Manufacturers Federation (NI); President, Londonderry Chamber of Commerce; Member, Londonderry Harbour Commission; Chairman, Londonderry Economic Standing Committee; Chairman, Western Health and Social Services Board; Chief Commissioner Planning Appeals Committee (NI); Member BBC Nothern Ireland Advisory Council; Member, Review Committee on Higher Education; Member, Parades Commission (NI). Past President, St Columb's Union; Past Member, Board of Governors, St Columb's College. High Sheriff,

Londonderry. Recreations: golf – past president/past captain City of Derry Golf Club, and past captain, Greencastle Golf Club; theatre.

Guelke, Professor Adrian Blanchard, BA, BA (Hons), MA, PhD. Professor of Comparative Politics, Queen's University, Belfast since 1997; b., 15.6.47, Pretoria, South Africa; m., Brigid Erin Bates; 1s.; 1d. Educ. Diocesan College, Cape Town, South Africa; University of Cape Town; London School of Economics. Temporary Lecturer, Comparative African Government and Law, University of Cape Town, 1969; Lecturer in Politics, Queen's University, Belfast, 1975 - 92 (Reader, 1992); Jan Smuts Professor of International Relations; University of Witwatersrand, Johannesburg, 1993 - 95; Lecturer in Politics, Queen's University, Belfast, 1996 - 97. Publications: Northern Ireland: The International Perspective, 1988; Age of Terrorism and the International Political System, 1995; South Africa in Transition, 1999; co-editor, A farewell to arms?: from 'long war' to long peace in Northern Ireland. Recreations: wine tasting; opera. Address: (b.) School of Politics, Queen's University, Belfast, Belfast, BT7 1PA; T.- 028-90273658.

Guest, Michael. Chief Executive, Royal Ulster Agricultural Society. Address: (b.) The King's Hall, Balmoral, Belfast BT9 6GW. T.-02890 665225.

Gunn-King, Brian James, MSc, DT&CP, FRTPI, FRSH, FLand Inst, FFB, FRSA, FIVU, MCMI, MIHBC, MUDG. Planning and Conservation Consultant; Hon. Treasurer, Vegetarian Society of Ulster since 1998; b. 28.7.33, Coventry; m., Margaret C Gunn-King; 2d. Educ. Henry VIII Grammar School (now Coventry School); College of Art and Design, Trent University; University of Ulster at Coleraine. Ordnance Surveyor, MAFF, West Midlands; Geodetic Computer, War Office; TV Network Planner, Rediffusion, East Midlands, Nottingham; Technical Planning Assistant, Notts County; Planning Assistant, Lincoln City; Planning Assistant, Review of City Plan, Leicester City; Chief Assistant Planner, Central Area Plan, Royal Tunbridge Wells, Kent; Deputy Town Planner, Reigate/Redhill, Surrey; Assistant Chief Planner, Antrim and Ballymena New Towns Commission, Department of the Environment (NI); Principal Planner (upper grade), Ballymena Planning Division, Department of the Environment (NI), 1973 - 93; Consultant for "Planning Aid" Belfast, since 2001; Judge for NIA Council, 1997 - 2002; Judge for Best-Kept Competition, 1996-2003 and for NI Amenity Council. Former Gen. Secretary/Executive/Vice-President, International Vegetarian Union, 1969 - 87, Fellow of IVU 2000; Hon. Treasurer Vegans International since 1994; Committee Member/Joint Vice-President/President/Hon. Treasurer, Vegetarian Society of Ulster 1968 - 2003; Chairman, Ulster Society for the Preservation of the Countryside, 1991 - 2000; Committee Member, RTPI (NI); Founder Member,

IHBC (NI), 1997. J N Mankar Animal Trophy of India. Publications: over 30 planning reports published. Recreations: landscapes; listed buildings; photography; specialised botanic international philately; veganic horticulture; historic research; world tree planter. Address: (h.) Braidujle, 120 Knockan Road, Ballycloghan, near Broughshane, Ballymena, BT43 7LE; T.- 02825 861202.

H

Hadden, Professor David Robert, MD, FRCP (Edinburgh), FRCP (London). Hon. Consultant Physician, Royal Victoria Hospital, Belfast; Hon. Professor of Endocrinology, Queen's University, Belfast; b. 24.5.36, Portadown, Co Armagh; m., Dr Diana Sheelagh Mary Martin; 1s.; 2d. Educ. Campbell College, Belfast; Queen's University, Belfast. House Physician/Research Fellow, Royal Victoria Hospital, Belfast, 1959 - 62; Fulbright Travelling Fellowship, Johns Hopkins Hospital, Baltimore, USA, 1962 - 64; MRC Infantile Malnutrition Research Unit, Kampala, Uganda, 1965 - 66; Department of Experimental Medicine, University of Cambridge, 1966 -67. Member: Ulster Medical Society (President, 1995 - 96); Irish Endocrine Society (President, 1987 - 89); Association of Physicians, GB and Ireland; Royal Society of Medicine; British, European and American Societies for Endocrinology and Diabetes. Lectures: Annual Oration, Royal Victoria Hospital, 1996; Jorgen Pedersen Lecture, Diabetes Pregnancy Study Group, 1997; Arnold Bloom Lecture, British Diabetic Association, 1997; Scott-Heron Lecture, Royal Victoria Hospital, 2000. Publications: Diabetes and Pregnancy, an International Approach to Diagnosis and Management, 1996; numerous research articles and chapters in British, European and international journals of endocrinology and diabetes. Chairman, Board of Governors, Victoria College, Belfast, 1995-2002. Recreations: restoration and care of old houses and gardens. Address: (b.) Regional Endocrinology and Diabetes Centre, Royal Victoria Hospital, BT12 6BA; T.- 02890-894798.

Hagan, John Patrick (Sean), LLB DipLaws, FCIArb, Legal Associate RTPI. Solicitor; b. 3.9.43, Portadown; m., Philomena; 4s.; 1d. Educ. Christian Brothers, Greenpark, Armagh; Queen's University, Belfast. Solicitor in private practice and planning advisor. Past President, Portadown Chamber of Commerce; Past President, Portadown Rotary Club; Hon. Secretary, Ulster Architectural Heritage Society. Recreations: walking; architectural heritage; reading. Address: (w.) Montrose House, 17-21 Church Street, Portadown, Craigavon; T.- 02838 333333. e-mail: sean@jphagan.com

Hall, John. Businessman; b. 14.9.41; Runcorn, Cheshire; m., Charlotte; 4d. Educ. Clones High School. Farmer; master butcher; property. Past President, Master Butchers' Association. Recreations: rambling. Address: (h.) 8 Lowroad, Islandmagee, Larne, BT40 3RD; T.-02893 353264. e-mail: ford.farm@nieland.com

Hall, Robert Edmund, ScB, BA (Hons) (Oxon), MA (Oxon), MSIEPM. Lecturer in History and Philosophy of Science, Queen's University Belfast

1972-2000; continuing as scholar and consultant (science in Islamic world); b. 13.8.39; Wichita, Kansas, USA. Educ. Brown University; Oxford University; Harvard University; The Warburg Institute, Stanford University; Hebrew University, Jerusalem. Temporary appointments: Conoco; Stanford University; Harvard University, IBM; The Van Leer Foundation, Jerusalem. Publications: professional articles on the history of medieval Islamic science, its background in Greek science, its place in the middle ages, and its influence on western science in the middle ages, renaissance and early modern period; Science in the contemporary Islamic world. Recreations: travel; photography; art and architecture; classical music. Address: (h.) 28 Balmoral Court, Belfast BT9 7GR. T.-028-90660496. e-mail: r.e.hall@ukonline.co.uk

Hall, Major William Joseph, JP. Lord-Lieutenant, Co Down, since 1996; b. 1.8.34; m.; Jennifer Mary Corbett; 1 s.; 1 d. Educ. Ampleforth College, York. SSC, Irish Guards, 1952-56; W.C. Pitfield & Hugh McKay, investment management co., then Shell Oil, Canada, 1956-62; dir. of own wine wholesale business, also sheep farmer and commercial narcissus bulb grower, 1962-90, retired. Mem., Lord Chancellor's Adv. Committee on JPs, since 1975 (Chairman, Ards Div., since 1996). County Down: JP 1973; DL 1975-93; High Sherriff, 1983; Vice Lord Lieutenant, 1993-96. NI ACF, 1967-79 (Hon. Major, 1980; President, NI ACFA, 1999-2002); Pres., RFCA NI, since 2000; Chairman, Ulster Br., Irish Guards Assoc., since 1979. Hon. Col. 1st Bn (NI), ACF, since 2003. CStJ 1997. Address: The Mill House, Narrow Water, Warrenpoint, Co. Down BT34 3LW. T.-028 4175 4904.

Hall-Callaghan, Avril Elizabeth, BSc, MSc. Assistant General Secretary, Ulster Teachers' Union since 1997; b. 14.4.54, Lurgan, Co Armagh; m., Don; 1d. Educ. Lurgan College; University of Ulster. Mathematics Teacher, Coleraine Girls' School, 1976 - 81; Field Officer, Ulster Teachers' Union, 1981 - 97. Member: Irish MENSA, Industrial Court, Northern Committee of ICTU (Irish Congress of Trade Unions). Recreations: horse riding; swimming. Address: (b.) Ulster Teachers' Union, 94 Malone Road, Belfast, BT9 5HP; T.- 02890-662216.

Halliday, Professor Henry Lewis, MD, FRCPE, FRCP, FRCPCH. Consultant Paediatrician, Royal Maternity Hospital and Royal Hospital for Sick Children, since 1979; Hon. Professor of Child Health, Queen's University, Belfast since 1992; b. 29.11.45, Belfast; m., Marjorie Edna; 1s.; 2d. Educ. Belfast Royal Academy; Queen's University, Belfast. Neonatal Research Fellow, Case Western Reserve University and Rainbow Children's Hospital, Cleveland, Ohio, USA, 1976 - 77; Neonatal Research Fellow, Cardiovascular Research Institute, University of California and Children's Hospital, San Francisco, USA, 1977 - 78. Graduated MD, Queen's University, Belfast,

1980. Past President: Irish Perinatal Society; Irish and American Paediatric Society; European Society for Paediatric Research; Chief Editor of Biology of the Neonate; Chair of NI Forum for Health Care Research; Chair of Child Health and Welfare Research Groups. Publications: 2 books and 86 book chapters; 244 peer reviewed publications in medical journals. Recreations: golf; gardening; listening to music. Address: (b.) Regional Neonatal Unit, Royal Maternity Hospital, Belfast, BT12 6BB; T.- 02890-894687. e-mail: h.halliday@qub.ac.uk

Hamilton, Heather A., BSc (Econ), ACA. Deputy Director of Finance, Queen's University Belfast, since 1995; b. 24.7.60, Belfast; m., Gary; 2 s.; 1 d. Educ. Belfast Royal Academy; Regent House; Queen's University. Touche Ross and Co., London, 1982-86; Hong Kong of Shanghai Bank, London, 1986-88; James Capel and Co, Stockbrokers, London, 1988-90; Queen's University Belfast, since 1990. Address: Queen's University Belfast BT7 1NN. T.-90 273731.

Hamilton, Rory Hamish, BA, LLB. Retired Solicitor; b. 13.9.46, Coleraine; m., Maureen Frances Brolly; 2s. Educ. Portora Royal School; Coleraine Academical Institution; Trinity College, Dublin. Joined Wray and Baxter (now known as Macaulay Wray) on graduation. Hon. Member, College Historical Society, Trinity College, Dublin; Former President and Secretary, Antrim and Derry Branch, Trinity College, Dublin Association. Recreations: golf; rugby; walking; reading. Address: (h.) 6 Randal Park, Portrush, BT56 8JJ; T.-028 7082 4819.

Hammond, Philip Alexander, MA, BMus, DMus. Arts Development Director, Arts Council of Northern Ireland, since 2002; b. 5.5.51, Belfast. Educ. Campbell College, Belfast; Queen's University Belfast. Director of Music, Cabin Hill Preparatory School, Belfast; Tutor in Music, Queen's University Belfast; Director of Music, Arts Council of Northern Ireland; Director of Performing Arts, Arts Council of Northern Ireland, 1995-2002. Hon Sec (Representative), Royal Society of Musicians of Great Britain; Board Member of Arts Care; Composer, Writer, Broadcaster and Performer. Recreations: swimming; antiques; travel. Address: (b.) The Arts Council of Northern Ireland, 77 Malone Road, Belfast BT9 6AQ. T.-02890 385200.

Hanna, Brian P., CBE, FCIEH, DMS, DSc (Econ). President of Chartered Institute of Environmental Health, 2002-2005; Member of the UK Sustainable Development Commission; b. 15.12.41, Belfast; m., Sylvia; 1d. Educ. Royal Belfast Academical Institution; Belfast College of Technology; Ulster College, Northern Ireland Polytechnic. Belfast Corporation: Clerical Assistant, City Treasurer's Department, 1959, Clerical Officer, Health Department, 1960 - 61; Pupil Public Health Inspector, 1961 - 65; Public Health Inspector, 1965 - 73; Senior Training Advisor, The Food and Drink Industry Training Board, 1974 - 75; Principal Public Health Inspector, Eastern Group Public Health Committee, Castlereagh Borough Council, 1975 - 77; Belfast City Council: Deputy Director, Environmental Health Services, 1978; Director, Environmental Health Services, 1984; Director of Health and Environmental Services, 1992; Chief Executive, 1994-2002. Member of the Senate of Queen's University Belfast; Governor of the Royal Belfast Academical Institution. Past President, Irish Hockey Union. Recreations: hockey. Address: (h.) 27 Clonevin Park, Lisburn, Co. Antrim BT28 3BJ. e-mail: bphanna@btopenworld.com

Hanna, Carmel. Member (South Belfast), Social Democratic and Labour Party, Northern Ireland Assembly, since 1998; Minister for Employment and Learning; b. Warrenpoint; m.; 1 s.; 3 d. Educ. Our Lady's Grammar School, Newry, Co Down. Registered nurse; and midwife; elected to Belfast City Council, 1997. Chair, All-Party Group on International Development. Address: (b.) Parliament Buildings, Stormont, Belfast, BT4 3XX. T.- 028 90 520369. (b.) Constituency Office, 17 Elmwood Mews, Belfast BT9 6BD. T.-028 90 683535. e-mail: carmel.hanna@niassembly.gov.uk

Hanna, Marjorie, BA (Hons). Principal, Carhill Integrated Primary School; b. 30.10.51, Ballymoney. Educ. Victoria College, Belfast; New University of Ulster, Coleraine. Teacher, Moorfield Primary School, Ballymena; Teacher, Lincoln School, Dominican Republic; Panaga School, Brunei, Borneo. Recreations: theatre; gardening. Address: (b.) Carhill Integrated Primary School, 78 Carhill Road, Garvagh, Coleraine, BT51 5PQ; T.-028 2955 8635.

Hanna, Dr. Samuel A, PhD, MSc, BAgr, AdvDipEd, PGDipAgric Comm, MCIM. Director (Corporate Planning), North East Institute of Further and Higher Education; b. 1958, Ballymena; m., Margaret B Corrigan; 1s.; 2d. Educ. Ballymena Academy; Queen's University, Belfast. Address: (b.) North East Institute of Further and Higher Education, Fountain Street, Antrim BT41 4AL. T.-028 94463916.

Hannigan, Prof. Bernadette Mary, BA (Mod.), PhD, FIBMS. Dean, Faculty of Life and Health Sciences, University of Ulster, since 1999, Professor of Biomedical Sciences, since 1997; b. 26.3.59, Kilsallaghan, Co Dublin; m., Prof. Bill Graham; 2 s. Educ. Trinity College, Dublin; National University of Ireland. Recreations: motherhood; marathon running; garden taming. Address: University of Ulster, Faculty of Life and Health Science, Cromore Road, Coleraine BT52 1SA. T.-028 70324491.

Hannon, Right Rev. Brian Desmond Anthony, BA, MA, Div. Test. Church of Ireland, Bishop of Clogher, 1986-2001; b. Lurgan; m., Maeve Geraldine Audley Butler; 3s. Educ. St Columba's

College, Rathfarnham, Co Dublin, Ireland; Trinity College, Dublin. Curate, All Saints, Clooney, Co Londonderry, 1961 - 64; Rector, Desermartin, 1964 - 69; Rector, Christ Church, Londonderry, 1969 - 82; Rural Dean of Londonderry Rural Deanery, 1977 - 82; Rector, Enniskillen Cathedral, 1982 - 86; 1982, Canon; Dean of Clogher, 1985. Member, World Council of Churches Central Committee, 1983 - 93; Chairman, Western Education and Library Board, 1985 - 87 and 1989 - 91; President, Church Mission Society Ireland, 1990 - 96; President, Irish Council of Churches, 1992 - 94; Co-Chairman, Irish Inter-Church Meeting, 1992 - 94. Publications: Christ Church, Londonderry, Milestones, Ministers and Memories. Recreations: walking; travel; sport; photography; music. Address: Drumconnis Top, 202 Mullaghmeen Road, Ballinamallard, Co. Fermanagh BT94 2DZ. T.-028 6638 8557. e-mail: bdah@btinternet.com

Harbison, Joan Irene, CBE, BA, MSc. Chief Commissioner, Equality Commission for Northern Ireland, since 1999; b. 21.1.38, Belfast; m., Jeremy Harbison; 1 d. Educ. Victoria College, Belfast; Queen's University of Belfast. Teacher, Orangefield Girls' School; Lisburn Technical College; Senior Lecturer, Stranmillis College of Education, 1975 - 97. Chairman, NIACAB, 1995; Member: Eastern Health and Social Social Services Board, 1984-88 (Deputy Chair, 1988-90), SACHR, 1990-93 (Deputy Chair, 1993-96), Human Fertilisation and Embryology Authority, 1990-96, General Dental Council, 1989-99; Chair, Commission for Racial Equality for Northern Ireland, 1997-99. Publications: three books on the effects of the troubles on children in Northern Ireland. Recreations: food; travel; reading; embroidery. Address: Equality Commission for Northern Ireland, Equality House, 7-9 Shaftesbury Square, Belfast BT2 7DP; T.-028 90 500688.

Haren, Dr. Patrick, BSc, PhD, MBA, FIEE, FENG. Group Chief Executive, Viridian Group Plc; b. 4.8.50; m., Anne; 2s. Educ. Queen's University, Belfast; University College, Dublin. Research Fellow, CERN, Geneva, 1976 - 77; Various Senior Managerial and Engineering positions with Electricity Supply Board, Ireland, 1978 - 88; Director, New Business Investment, Electrical Supply Board, 1989 - 92. Board Member, Invest NI. Recreations: skiing; hill walking; languages. Address: (b.) Viridian Group Plc, 120 Malone Road, Belfast, BT9 5HT.

Hargan, Karen Frances. BA (Hons). HR Executive, Desmond and Sons Ltd., since 1995; b. 20.6.66; Londonderry; 1 s.; 2 d. Educ. Thornhill College; University Ulster. HR Manager, Desmond and Sons Ltd., 1993 - 95. Member, Police Authority for Northern Ireland; Governor, Lumen Christi College, Derry.

Hargie, Prof. Owen David William, BA, DipEd, PhD, AFBPsS, CPsychol. Professor of Communication, University of Ulster, since 1991;

Adjunct Professor, Norwegian University of Science and Technology, since 1999; b. 19.1.50, Ballycastle; m., Patricia. Educ. Ballycastle High School; Queen's University Belfast. Lecturer: Cregogh Technical College, 1973-75, Ulster Polytechnic, 1975-77, Senior Lecturer, 1977-84, University of Ulster, 1984-91. Associate Fellow and Chartered Member of British Psychological Society; Executive Council Member of European Communication Association. Publications: author of 18 books and over 100 book chapters and journal articles. Keynote speaker at numerous International Conferences. Recreations: jogging; music; animal rights. Address: School of Communication, University of Ulster, Jordanstown, Newtownabbey BT37 0QB. T.-028 9036 6230. e-mail: odw.hargie@ulster.ac.uk

Harkness, George Douglas Brown, MA, FCA. Non Executive Director, Northern Bank, National Irish Bank, since 1996; Non Executive Director, Dale Farm, since 1998; Honorary Treasurer, University of Ulster, since 2000; b. 5.8.38, Belfast; m., Elisabeth; 2 s.; 3 d. Educ. Campbell College; Cambridge University. Craig Gardner, Belfast, 1960-72; Asworth Rowan Craig Gardner, Partner, Price Waterhouse NI, 1972-98. Former Non Executive Director, Ulster, Northern Down and Ards HSS Trust; Chairman, Abbeyfield Belfast Society Ltd; Vice Chairman, Habinteg Housing Association; Director, Ulster Orchestra Society; Past Captain, Royal Belfast Golf Club; Past President, Rotary Club of Belfast East. Recreations: golf; bridge. Address: (h.) 18 Castlehill Road, Belfast BT4 3GL. T.-028 90653695. e-mail: george@harkness2.freeserve.co.uk

Harland, Robert Wallace (Robin), MB, BCh, BAO, FRCGP, FISM, DUniv. Retired doctor; Chairman, British Association of Sport and Medicine (Northern Ireland), 1993-2000; Member, Senate, Queen's University Belfast, 1992-2001; b. 7.3.26, Belfast; m., Mary Kennedy (dec.); 5s. Educ. Methodist College; Queen's University, Belfast. Partner in General Practice, Sherburn (Durham), 1950 - 70; Medical Officer RAMC, 6th Royal Tank Regiment, 1953 - 55; Senior Medical Officer, University Health Service; Queen's University, Belfast, 1970 - 91. Medical Officer, Northern Ireland Commonwealth Games Council, 1976 - 90; Hon. Secretary, British Student Health Association, 1975 - 80; President, British Student Health Association, 1989 - 90; President, Ulster Medical Society, 2000 - 2001. Butterworth Gold Medal, Royal College of General Practitioners, 1978. Recreations: walking; gourmet cooking. Address: (h.) 6 Castlehill Road, Belfast, BT4 3GL; T.-028 9065 3682.

Harper, Professor David Benjamin, BSc, PhD, CChem, FRSC. Professor Emeritus, Queen's University Belfast, since 2003; b. 13.8.42. Educ. Park High School, Birkenhead; University of Bristol; Wye College, University of London. SRC Post Doctoral Fellowship, University of London,

1967 - 68; NRC Post Doctoral Fellowship, Prairie Regional Laboratory, Saskatoon, Canada, 1968 - 70; Wellcome Research Fellowship, University of Newcastle-upon-Tyne and University of Kent at Canterbury, 1970 - 72; Queen's University Belfast: Special Lecturer/Lecturer, Department of Food and Agricultural Chemistry, 1973 - 82; Senior Lecturer, 1982 - 88; Reader, 1988 - 92, Professor of Microbial Biochemistry, Department of Food Science, 1992-2002. Publications: over 100 refereed research publications. Recreations: gardening; beekeeping; planting trees. Address: (b.) School of Agriculture and Food Science, Queen's University Belfast, Newforge Lane, Belfast, BT9 5PX; T.- 02890 255343. e-mail: david.harper@dardni.gov.uk

Harper, William, DL, BSc (Hons), MSc. Retired Headmaster; b. 25.6.42, Belfast; m., Pamela; 2s.; 2d. Educ. Sullivan Upper School; Queen's University, Belfast; University of Ulster. Head, Junior Science, Portora Royal School, 1965 - 67; Omagh Academy: Head, Geography (senior teacher). 1967 - 81; Second Master, 1981 - 85; Headmaster, Omagh High School, 1985-2001. Captain Dungannon Rugby Club, 1967; Captain, Omagh Rugby Club Commodore, Lough Erne Yacht Club, 1993; President, Omagh Rugby Club, 1995 - 97; Chairman, Omagh Academicals Rugby Football Club, since 2003. Rotarian. Recreations: sailing; gardening. Address: (h.) The Old Manse, Ballynahatty, Omagh, Co Tyrone; BT78 1QN; T.- 02882 243035.

Harrison, Albert. Managing Director, Belfast International Airport. Address: (b.) Aldergrove, Crumlin, Co Antrim, BT29 4AB; T.-028 9448 4848.

Harrison, Stephen Joseph, BSc, DASE. Principal, Gilnahirk Primary School, since 2002; b. 20.10.60, Belfast; 2s.; 1d. Educ. Wallace High School; New University of Ulster at Coleraine. Teacher, Crumlin Primary School, Co Antrim, 1985 - 90; Vice-Principal: Edenderry Primary School, Portadown, 1991 - 97, Hart Memorial Primary School, 1997-2001. Recreations: orienteering (British instructor). Address: (b.) Gilnahirk Primary School, 148 Gilnahirk Road, Belfast BT5 7QQ. T.-02890 401697.

Harrison, Terry, LLB. Partner, Harrison and Barbour Solicitors, since 1997; b. 10.4.56; m., Catherine Lavery; 2s.; 2d. Educ. Belfast Royal Academy; Queen's University, Belfast. Assistant Solicitor, C & H Jefferson, 1979 - 87; Partner, Geo L Maclaine, 1987 - 94; Head, Legal Department, Northern Bank Ltd, 1994 - 97. Recreations: rugby; cricket; reading. Address: (b.) Scottish Provident Building, 7 Donegall Square West, Belfast; T.- 02890-322322.

Hart, His Honour Judge Anthony, QC. Recorder of Belfast, since 1997; Presiding Judge of the County Court in NI, since 2002; b. 30.4.46, Belfast; m., Mary Morehan; 2s.; 2d. Educ. Portora

Royal School, Enniskillen; Trinity College, Dublin; Queen's University, Belfast. Called to the Bar, Northern Ireland, 1969; Called to the Bar, England and Wales, 1975; QC, 1983; Junior Crown Prosecutor, Co Londonderry, 1973 - 75 and Co Down, 1975 - 79; Part-time Chairman, Industrial Tribunals, 1980 - 83; Deputy County Court Judge, 1983 - 85; County Court Judge, 1985. Member: Council for Legal Education for Northern Ireland, 1977 - 83; Review Committee of Legal Education (NI), 1984 - 85; Standing Advisory Commission on Human Rights, 1984 - 85; Criminal Justice Consultative Group (NI), 1993-99 (now Criminal Justice Issues Group); Judicial Studies Board (NI), 1993 - 97; Chairman: County Court Rules Committee since 1997; Council of HM County Court Judges in Northern Ireland, 1995 - 98; Member, Civil Justice Reform Group, 1998-99. Chancellor, Diocese of Clogher (Church of Ireland) since 1990; President, Irish Legal History Society, 1991 - 94. Publications: Criminal Procedure in Northern Ireland (Consultant Ed.), 1989; Brehons, Serjeants and Attorneys (Contributor), 1990; Explorations in Law and History (Contributor) 1995; A History of the King's Serjeant at Law in Ireland: Honour rather rather than advantage, 2000. Recreations: reading. Address: (b.) Northern Ireland Court Service, 9-15 Bedford Street, Belfast, BT2 7LT; T.- 028 90328594.

Haslett, Victor Campbell, CBE, ACII, FBIBA, FIMgt. Chairman, Multiple Sclerosis Society NI; Deputy Chairman, Willis Harris Marrian Limited; Chairman, Property News.com Ltd; b. 7.9.39, Belfast; m., Sheila; 3 d. Educ. Campbell College. Inspector, Royal Insurance Co., Belfast, 1958-71; Agency Superintendent, Royal Insurance Co., Liverpool, 1972; Harris, Marrian and Co., Belfast: Manager, 1973, Chairman and Chief Executive, 1983-97; Deputy Chief Executive and Chairman of four Group Companies, Willis Corroon Ltd, London, 1990-97; Chairman, Willis Harris Marrian, Belfast, 1997-2001. Board Member: International Fund for Ireland, Ulster Community Investment Trust, Emerging Business Trust, Enterprise Equity (NI) Ltd, Enterprise Equity (Ire) Ltd, Investment North America; President, NI Chamber of Commerce; Trustee, Multiple Sclerosis Society. Clubs: Royal Belfast Golf Club, Royal North of Ireland Yacht Club, Ulster Reform Club. Address: (b.) Multiple Sclerosis Society, 34 Annadale Avenue, Belfast BT7 3JJ.

Haslett, Rev. William Larmour, MA. Minister, Ballyblack Presbyterian Church, Newtownards since 1986; b. 30.10.40, Belfast; m., Doris Isobel O'Neill; 2 s. (1 dec.); 1d. Educ. Royal Belfast Academical Institution; Magee University College, Londonderry; Trinity College, Dublin; The Presbyterian College, Belfast. Assistant Minister, Newtownbreda Presbyterian Church, Belfast, 1966 - 69; Minister, Downshire Road, Presbyterian Church, Newry, 1969 - 73; Minister, Newark Parish Church, Port Glasgow, Renfrewshire/Chaplain: Port Glasgow High

School; Broadstone Jubilee Hospital, Port Glasgow; Inverclyde Royal Hospital, Greenock, 1973 - 86; Moderator, Presbytery of Greenock, 1984 - 85; Chaplain, Ards Hospital, Newtownards since 1987. Convener, General Assembly's Committee on Stewardship and Lay Evangelism, 1969 - 73; Convener, General Assembly's Committee on Broadcasting, Television and AVA, 1991 - 97; Moderator, Presbytery of Ards, 1996 - 97. Involved with Northern Ireland Association for Mental Health; Newry Community Service Council; The Samaritans, 1969 - 73. Fellowship in Continuing Education, Virginia Theological Seminary, Alexandria, USA, 1968. Publications: Newark Parish Church, Port Glasgow, Chronicles of two hundred years, 1774 - 1974, 1975. Recreations: puppetry, member: the British puppet and model theatre guild; Union Internationale de la Marionnette. Address: (h.) 17 Ballyblack Road, Newtownards, BT22 2AP; T.- 028 91 813141.

Hassard, Ronnie, MA, BEd, DASE, AdvCertEd. Principal, Wellington College Belfast, since 2000; b. 31.10.52, Enniskillen, Co Fermanagh; m., Audrey (nee Marshall); 2 s.; 1 d. Educ. Portora Royal School; Queen's University Belfast; Stranmillis College; University of Ulster. English Teacher, Model Boys' School, Belfast, 1975-77; Head of English and Senior Teacher, Ballyclare High School, 1977-93; Vice Principal, Grosvenor Grammar School, 1993-2000. Recreations: local history; gardening; reading; music. Address: (b.) Wellington College Belfast BT7 3HE. T.-02890 642539. e-mail: info@wellington.belfast.ni.sch.uk

Hastings, Dr William George, CBE, JP, FIOD, FIM, FHCIMA. Chairman, Hastings Hotels Group Ltd.; b. 17.10.28, Belfast; m., Joy Hamilton; 1s.; 3d. Educ. Royal Belfast Academical Institution. Past Chairman: Institute of Directors, (NI); Chamber of Commerce and Industry (NI); President, Chartered Institute of Marketing,(NI); Chairman, St Patrick's Visitor Centre; Chairman (NI), Trustee (UK), Help the Aged; Landmark Ltd (Merrion Hotel, Dublin); Lloyds Underwriter; Patron of Crimestoppers (NI). Paul Harris Fellow, Rotary; President: NI Polio Fellowship, Ulster Youth Orchestra, Northern Ireland Chest Heart and Stroke Association; Past President, Prince's Trust (NI); Board member, Down Cathedral. Recreation: golf. Address: (b.) Midland Buildings, Whitla Street, Belfast, BT15 1NH; T.- 01232-745251.

Haughey, Denis. Member (Mid Ulster), Social Democratic and Labour Party, Northern Ireland Assembly, 1998-2003; Junior Minister, 2000-03. Educ. Queen's University, Belfast. Founder Member, SDLP; elected to Northern Ireland Assembly, 1982; elected to Cookstown Council, 1989; Member, talks team, Castle Buildings talks, 1996-98; Member, European Union Committee of the Regions. Address: (b.) 54A William Street, Cookstown BT80 8NB. T.-02886 763349.

Haughey, Edward, OBE, JP, FRCSI. Founder Chairman/Managing Director, Norbrook Laboratories Ltd since 1980; m., Mary Gordon Young; 2s.; 1d. Educ. Christian Brothers School, Dundalk, Co Louth, Ireland. Board Member, Warrenpoint Harbour Authority, 1986 - 89, Director, Bank of Ireland Management, Northern Ireland, 1987-99; Director, Bombardiers Shorts Plc. Member, Forum for Peace and Reconciliation since 1996; Trustee: Dublin City University since 1995, Royal College of Veterinary Surgeons; Member, Senate of Ireland 1994-2002; Former Government spokesman in the Senate on Northern Ireland. Permanent Vice-President, Anglo-Chilean Society, 1995; Honorary Consul for Chile. Hon. LLD NUI, 1997, Hon. DBA, International Management Centres, 1992; Hon. Fellow of RCSI 1998; Trustee of the Royal College of Veterinary Surgeons, since 2001. Clubs: Reform Club, Belfast; University and Kildare Street Club, Dublin; Farmers' Club, London. Publications: Bibliographical Details - Out On Their Own by Ivor Kenny. Recreations: history of architecture; shooting; fishing. Address: (b.) Station Works, Camlough Road, Newry, Co Down, BT35 6JP; T.- 028 3036 9824.

Hawkins, Dr. Stanley Arthur, BSc (Hons), MB, BCh, BAO, FRCP. Reader in Neurology, Queen's University of Belfast, since 1997; Consultant Neurologist, Royal Hospitals Trust, since 1981; Consultant Neurologist, Belfast City Hospital, since 1986; 2.3.48, Downpatrick, Co. Down; m., Fiona; 3 s. Educ. Belfast Royal Academy; Queen's University of Belfast. Senior House Officer/Tutor, Royal Victoria Hospital, Belfast, and Mater Hospital, Belfast, 1973 - 74; Northern Ireland Neurology Service: Registrar in Neurology, 1974 - 76, Senior Registrar in Neurology, 1976 - 79; Resident Registrar, National Hospital, London, 1979 - 81; Senior Lecturer/Consultant Neurologist, Belfast, 1981 - 97; Visiting Professor, University of California, Los Angeles, 1984. Publications: 170 papers and abstracts in academic journals. Recreation: gardening. Address: (h.) 177 Malone Road, Belfast BT9 6TB; T.-02890 682274.

Hawthorne, Dr. Colin, PhD, FInstE, FCIBSE, MInstR. Consulting Engineer, Managing Director, Delta RAC Design Ltd since 1998; b. 20.3.61, Belfast; m., Kim; 1s.; 1d. Educ. Hopefield School; University of Ulster at Coleraine. Technical Director, Bel-Air Refrigeration Ltd, 1988 - 96; Technical Manager, BL Group, 1996 - 98. Chartered Engineer, 1997. Address: 1 Red Fort Drive, Carrickfergus, Co Antrim; T.- 028 9335 9090. e-mail: ch@delta-design.fsnet.co.uk

Hay, Prof. Roderick James, MA, DM, FRCP, FRCPath, FMedSci. Dean of the Faculty of Medicine and Health Sciences, Head of the School of Medicine, Professor of Dermatology, Queen's University Belfast, since 2002; b. 13.4.47, Cobham; m., Delyth (nee Price); 2 d. Educ. Wellington College; Oxford University; Guys Hospital Medical School. House and Registrar appointments, Guys Hospital, 1971-75; Senior Registrar, Wellcome Research Fellow, Institute of Dermatology, London Sch. of Hygiene and Tropical Medicine, Centre for Disease Control, Atlanta, USA, 1975-79; Senior Lecturer, then Reader in Clinical Mycology, London Sch. of Hygiene and Tropical Medicine, 1979-89; Mary Dunhill Professor of Cutaneous Medicine, UMDS/KCL, 1989-2002; Dean of the Institute of Dermatology, Guys, Kings and St. Thomas' Med. Sch., 1995-2000; Dean for External Affairs, UMDS/KCL, 1995-2002.   Visiting Professor, London Sch. of Hygiene and Tropical Medicine, since 1996. Chairman, International Foundation of Dermatology, since 2002; President, British Association of Dermatology, 2001-02; President, European Confed of Medical Mycology, 1999-2002; Member, International Committee of Dermatology; Non Executive Director, EHSSB, since 2002.   Publications: over 400 scientific publications; 5 books. Recreations: gardening; music.   Address: (h.) High Knowle, 46 Craigdarragh Road, Helens Bay, Co. Down B19 1UB. T.-0289 185 3930. e-mail: r.hay@qub.ac.uk

Hay, William. Member (Foyle), Democratic Unionist Party, Northern Ireland Assembly, since 1998; b. 16.4.50, Donegall; m.; 3 s.; 2 d. Educ. Faughan Valley High School, Londonderry. Haulage contractor; elected to Derry City Council, 1981; Mayor, 1993; Member, Western Education and Library Board, since 1998; Member, Northern Ireland Housing Council, since 1998; Member, Londonderry Port and Harbour Commission, since 1998. Address: (b.) Parliament Buildings, Stormont, Belfast, BT4 3ST; T.- 01232-520700.

Hayes, William David, BEd, DASE. Principal, Carr Primary School; b. 20.10.47, Belfast; m., Joyce Hayes; 1s.   Educ.   Orangefield Boys' Secondary School; Stranmillis College. Engineer; Sales Rep; Student; Teacher.   Recreations: swimming; soccer; Sunday School superintendent. Address: (b.) Carr Primary School, 336 Comber Road, Lisburn, Co Antrim, BT27 6YE; T.- 02892-638615.

Haylett, Thomas Anthony, MA, BA (Hons). Police Superintendent; District Commander, Larne, since 2002; Chief Inspector, Musgrave Street, since 2001; b. 6.6.60, Scarborough; m., Jean; 3 s. Educ. Scarborough Sixth Form College; University of Ulster, Jordanstown. Police Officer, 22 years; service in RUC/PSNI; Police service centred around response policing/ uniform/community/training.   Recreations: reading; fitness. Address: (b.) 2 Hope Street, Larne BT40 2UR. T.-028 2827 1050. e-mail: thomas.haylett@psni.pnn.police.uk

Heaney, Dr. Liam, MB, BCL, MRCP, MD. Consultant Physician, Belfast City Hospital, since 1999; Senior Lecturer in Respiratory Medicine, Queen's University Belfast, since 1999; b. 2.2.65, Omagh, Co. Tyrone; m., Susan; 1 s.; 2 d. Educ. St. Colmans College, Newry; Queen's University

Belfast. Post-Graduate Training, NI and London; Consultant Physician appointment, Craigavon Hospital, 1999.   Member of British Thoracic Society; British Society of Allergy and Clinical Immunology; Ulster Thoracic Society. Recreation: football.   Address: (b.) Level 8, Belfast City Hospital, Lisburn Road, Belfast.   T.-028 90263821. ext. 3158.

Hedley, Margaret Anne, BSc, Adv Dip Ed. Head of School, East Down Institute; b. 19.7.43, Belfast; m., Kenneth Hedley; 1s.; 1d. Educ. Belfast High School; Queen's University, Belfast. Lecturer, Newtownabbey Technical College; Teacher, Antrim High School; Assistant Principal, Newcastle College.   Recreations: golf; skiing. Address: (h.) 30 Ardluin Heights, Newcastle, Co Down, BT33 0RA; T.- 013967-24234.

Hegarty, Most Rev. Seamus, BA, HDE, DD. Bishop of Derry since 1994; b. 26.1.40, Kilcar, Co Donegal, Ireland. Educ.   St Eunan's College, Letterkenny, Ireland; St Patrick's College, Maynooth, Co Kildare, Ireland; University College, Dublin.   Dean of Studies, Holy Cross College, 1967 - 71; Headmaster, Holy Cross College, 1971 - 81; Bishop of Raphoe, 1982 - 94. Recreations: angling; bridge.   Address: (h.) Bishop's House, St Eugene's Cathedral, Derry, BT48 9AP; T.- 028-71262302; Fax: 028-71371960.

Henderson, Deric. Ireland Editor, The Press Association, since 1998; b. Omagh; m., Clare; 2 s. Tyrone Constitution, 1969-73; Belfast Telegraph, 1973-80; Press Association, since 1980. Recreations: golf (Royal Portrush) and (Dunmurry); Irish Art. Address: Queen's Building, 10 Royal Avenue, Belfast BT1 1DB. T.-028 90 245008. e-mail: derich@pa.press.net

Henderson, Michael John, ABICS.   Alderman, Castlereagh Borough Council; b. 6.7.56, Belfast; m., Arenee; 1s.; 2d. Educ HMF Junior Soldiers. Her Majesties Forces, 1972 - 80; Stores Manager, C W S, 1980 - 82; Stores Manager, Haydock Ltd, 1982 - 87; Regional Sales Manager, Diversey-Lever since 1987. Member, Eastern Health and Social Services Council; Mayor, Castlereagh Borough Council, 2003-04; appointed to Castlereagh District Policing Partnership, 2003. Cyprus UN Medal; GSN (NI) medal; TAVR (LS) medal.   Recreations: Lions Club TAVR. Address: (h.) 6 Killnyure Crescent, Carryduff, Belfast, BT8 8EF; T.- 02890 815883.

Henderson, Oscar William James, OBE, DL, FBIM. Chairman, Universities Press (Belfast) Ltd; Director of other Northern Ireland Companies; b. 17.8.24, Belfast; m., Rachel Primrose Forrest; 3d. Educ.   Brackenber House, Belfast; Bradfield College, Berkshire, England. Irish Guards, 1942 - 47; Belfast Newsletter: Trainee, 1947; Junior Manager, 1949; Managing Director, 1959; Chairman/Managing Director, Century Newspapers, 1963 - 89; Founder Director (longest serving director), Ulster Television Plc, 1958 - 94; Director, Ewart Plc, 1986 - 95 (Chairman, 1988 - 90); Director, Capital Gearing Trust Plc since 1962; Director, Ulster Sheltered Employment Ltd, 1962 - 92 (Chairman, 1979 - 92); Director, Northern Salmon Ltd since 1988 (Chairman, 1988 - 90). Member, Northern Ireland Chamber of Commerce since 1960 (President, 1988); Member, British Institute of Management since 1968 (Fellow, 1977); Member, Northern Ireland Parliament, 1953 - 58. Recreations: gardening; fishing; DIY; reading. Address: (h.) 47 Moss Road, Holywood, Co Down, BT18 9RU; T.- Holywood 763145.

Henderson, Samuel Kendrick, B Ed, MSc. Principal, Dunclug Primary School, Ballymena; b. 23.11.46, Tobermore, Co Londonderry; m., Anne; 2s. Educ., Rainey Endowed Grammar; Stranmillis College; Queen's University, Belfast; University of Ulster at Jordanstown. Assistant Teacher: Portstewart Primary School; Randalstown Central Primary School; Vice-Principal, Ballee Primary School; Principal, Whitehouse Primary School. Recreations: sport; theatre; travelling. Address: (b.) Dunclug Primary School, Doury Road, Ballymena. T.-02825-652327. khenderson@dunclugps.ballymena.ni.sch.uk

Hendron, Dr. Joe. Member (West Belfast), Social Democratic and Labour Party, Northern Ireland Assembly, 1998-2003. Educ. Queen's University, Belfast. Doctor; former Belfast City Councillor; Member, New Ireland Forum, 1983; MP, West Belfast, 1992-97; Member, Northern Ireland Forum, 1996; Member, SDLP talks team, Castle Buildings, 1996-98. Address: (b.) Parliament Buildings, Stormont, Belfast, BT4 3ST.

Henry, William George. General Manager, National Air Traffic Services Belfast; b. 2.12.50, Belfast; m., Denise Henry; 3s. Educ. Grosvenor High School, College of Air Traffic Control, Bournemouth. Air Traffic Control: Belfast; Ulster Radar, Bishopscourt; Scottish Air Traffic Control Centre; Henley Management College; FAA Academy, Oklahoma. Recreations: rugby. Address: (b.) Belfast International Airport, BT29 4AA; T.- 02894-484258.

Henstock, Professor Ralph, MA (Cantab), PhD (London). Emeritus Professor, Pure Mathematics, University of Ulster at Coleraine; b., 2.6.23, Nottinghamshire; m., Marjorie Jardine (deceased); 1s. Educ. The Henry Mellish County Secondary School, Notts; St John's College, Cambridge; Birbeck College, London. Experimental Officer (statistics), Ministry of Supply, 1943 - 46; Assistant, Department of Pure Maths, Bedford College, London, 1947 - 48; Lecturer, Birbeck College, London, 1948 - 51; Queen's University, Belfast: Lecturer, 1951 - 56; Senior Lecturer/Reader, 1960 - 64; Lecturer, Bristol University, 1956 - 60; Reader, Lancaster University, 1964 - 70; Professor of Mathematics, New University of Ulster, 1970 - 88, (retired

1988); Leverhulme Emeritus Research Fellowship, 1988 - 90. Publications: Theory of Integration, 1963; Linear Analysis, 1968; Lectures on the Theory of Integration, 1988; The General Theory of Integration, 1991; 45 papers in prestigious journals. Recreations: New Testament Christianity; poetry, science fiction. Address: (h.) 11 Regent Park, Portstewart, Co Londonderry, BT55 7NP; T.- 02870 832397.

Hepburn, Professor Claude, BSc, MSc, DSc, ANCRT, FRSC, FIM, CEng, FRSA. Emeritus Professor of Polymer Engineering, University of Ulster since 1991; b. 31.3 35, Edinburgh; m., Evelyn Janet Loretta Pearce; 3s.; 2d. Educ. Boroughmuir High School, Edinburgh; Heriot-Watt University, Edinburgh. Product and Materials Engineer, North British Rubber Company, 1958 - 61; Development Process Engineer, Midland Silicones, 1961 - 63; Chief Technical Engineer, Rubber and Plastics Research Association, 1963 - 65; Research Manager, J H Fenner, Power Transmission Engineers, 1965 - 69; Senior Lecturer, Loughborough University, 1969 - 91. Publications: Elastomers: Criteria for Engineering Design (with R J W Reynolds), 1979; Rubber Technology and Manufacture (with C M BLow), 1992; Polyurethane Elastomers, 1992. Hancock Gold Medal, Institute of Materials, 1993. Recreations: mountaineering; golf; shooting. Address: (h.) 39 Upper Station Road, Greenisland, Carrickfergus, BT38 8RA; T.-02890-861726. e-mail: claudehepburn@bigfoot.com

Hermon, Lady Sylvia, MP. Ulster Unionist Member of Parliament (North Down), since 2001; b. 18.8.55; m., Sir John Hermon; 2 s. Educ. Dungannon High School for Girls; Aberystwyth University, Wales. Lecturer, European, international and constitutional law, Queen's University, 1978-88. Chair, North Down Support Group Marie Curie Cancer Care, since 1998; Member, Friends of Bangor Community Hospital, since 2000. Constituency chair, North Down constituency party, since 2001; UUP Spokesperson for: Home Affairs, since 2001, Youth and Women's Issues, since 2001, Culture, Media and Sport, since 2002; Vice-chair, All Party: Police Group, since 2002, Dignity at Work Group, since 2003; author and committee member addressing Patten Report Criminal Justice Review, 2000; Ulster Unionist Executive, 1999; Constituency chair, North Down Unionist Constituency Association, since 2001. Publication: A Guide to EEC Law in Northern Ireland, 1986. Recreations: fitness training; swimming; ornithology; letter writing; proof reading. Address: (b.) House of Commons, London SW1A 0AA. T.-020 7219 8491. e-mail: jamisons@parliament.uk

Hewitt, Frank. Chief Executive, Northern Ireland Chamber of Commerce. Address: (b.) 22 Great Victoria Street, Belfast BT2 7BJ. T.-02890 244113.

Hewitt, Paul Deane, BA, DipEd, MA, FRSA, FCIM. Headmaster, The Royal School, Dungannon since 1984; b. 1.5.47, Belfast; m., Christine Mary Burns; 1s.; 2d. Educ. Royal Belfast Academical Institution; Queen's University, Belfast; L'Université de Montpellier; University of London. Assistant Master, Belfast Royal 1970 - 84; Form Master, Belfast Royal Academy, 1973 - 84. Chairman: Northern Ireland Boarding Schools Partnership, since 2002, Post Primary Principals' Association (SELB); Member: Admiralty Interview Board since 1988, Youth Council for Northern Ireland, since 2000, Secondary Heads Association since 1984; Fellow, Royal Society for the Arts since 1992; Fellow, Institute of Management since 1986. Member: Portstewart Golf Club; Dungannon Football Club; Dungannon Golf Club. Contributor to magazines and newspapers on educational, rugby, boarding and religious subjects. Recreations: golf; rugby; cricket; music. Address: (b.) Headmasters Residence, The Royal School, Dungannon, BT71 6AS; T.- 028-8772-2710.

Hewitt, Victor Alan, LLB, LLM. Senior Partner, L'Estrange & Brett Solicitors, Belfast since 1994; b, 8.3.41, Belfast; m., Ruth Hewitt; 1s.; 2d. Educ. Royal Belfast Academical Institution; Queen's University, Belfast; University of Michigan. Admitted as a Solicitor, 1967; Partner in L'Estrange & Brett, Solicitors since 1969. Council Member, Law Society of Northern Ireland since 1991, President, 2001-2002; Council Member, Society for Computers and Law, 1981 - 87; Member, Law Reform Advisory Committee for Northern Ireland, 1997-2001. Recreations: golf; music; reading. Address: (b.) L'Estrange & Brett, Solicitors, Arnott House, 12-16 Bridge Street, Belfast, BT1 1LS.

Higgins, The Hon Mr Justice (Sir Malachy Joseph) , LLB, BL. Judge of the Supreme Court in Northern Ireland; b. 30.10.44, Bangor, Co Down; m. Dr Dorothy Ann Grech; 3d. Educ. St Mac Nissi's College, Garron Tower; Queen's University, Belfast; Middle Temple. Called to the Bar of Northern Ireland, 1969; Called to the Irish Bar, 1978; Queen's Counsel, 1985; County Court Judge, 1988 - 93; Recorder of Londonderry, 1990 - 93; County Court Judge for Armagh, 1993; Judge, High Court of Justice, 1993; Bencher, Inn of Court, Northern Ireland, 1993, Treasurer, 2001; Judge, Family Division, 1996-2001; Member, Board of Governors, Sullivan Upper School, Co Down. Recreations: gardening; golf; sailing; walking. Address: (b.) Royal Courts of Justice, Belfast.

Hilditch, David William. Member, (East Antrim), Democratic Unionist Party, Northern Ireland Assembly, since 1998; former Mayor of Carrickfergus; b. 27.3.63, Larne; m., Wilma; 2s. Educ. Carrickfergus Grammar School. Royal Mail; 4th term as local councillor, Carrickfergus Borough Council. Recreations: soccer enthusiast and former player; golf. Address: (b.)

Constituency Office, 22A High Street, Carrickfergus, BT38 7AA; T.- 02893-329980.

Hilditch, Stephen Robert, MBE, BSc, DASE. Headmaster, Belfast High School since 1987; b. 6.6.46, Whitehead, Co Antrim; m., Anne; 2s. Educ. Larne Grammar School; Queen's University, Belfast. Assistant Teacher, Physics, Grosvenor High School, 1968 - 72; Head, Physics Department, Grosvenor High School, 1972 - 82; Vice-Principal Wallace High School, Lisburn, 1983 - 87. Recreations: rugby (refereeing): Ulster Society Rugby Football Referees, 1972; Ulster Inter-Provincial Panel, 1978; Irish international panel, 1984 - 1995, has officiated in 16 countries and 17 major international matches including three world cups; Schools Committee, Ulster Branch IRFU; Coach to Irish Referees; Appointed Sports Council of Northern Ireland, 1993, Vice-Chairman, 1994-2000; International Rugby Board Referee Assessor, 2001; Vice-President, IRFU (Ulster Branch), 2001, President, 2003/4. Address: (h.) 3 Edgcumbe Drive, Belfast, BT4 2EN; T.- 02890-653028.

Hill, Prof. Brian Joseph, BSc, DPhil. Professor Emeritus, Textiles Technology, University of Ulster; b. 11.2.38, Belfast; m., Margaret Maud Gamble; 2 d. Educ. Methodist College, Belfast; Queen's University, Belfast. Linen Research Association: Research Student, 1956 - 61; Research Officer, 1961 - 67; Lambeg Industrial Research Association: Assistant Head, Testing Department, 1967 - 77; Head of Flammability Research, 1969 - 77; Ulster Polytechnic: Lecturer, 1977 - 78; Senior Lecturer, 1978 - 84; University of Ulster: Lecturer, 1984 - 90; Senior Lecturer, 1990 - 96; Reader, 1996-2000. Publications: over 70 papers published in international journals. Recreations: sport (mainly rugby and cricket). Address: (h.) 4, Broughton Gardens, Belfast BT6 0BB.

Hill, Dr. Brian William, PhD (Mech Eng), MSc (Edu Man), BSc (Hons). Principal Lecturer, COE Manufacturing and Motor Vehicle Engineering, North East Institute of Further and Higher Education; b. 7.12.55, Antrim; m., Jane, 1s.; 1d. Educ. Ballymena Academy; Queen's University, Belfast. Production Manager, Sperrin Metal Products; Lecturer, Newtownabbey Technical College; Senior Lecturer, Antrim Technical College; Head of Manufacturing and Motor Vehicle Engineering, North East Institute. Publications: author of AutoCAD Training Manuals. Recreations: session clerk in Presbyterian church. Address: (b.) North East Institute of Further and Higher Education, Ballymena Campus, Trostran Avenue, Ballymena, Co Antrim, BT43 7BN; T.- 028 2566 4254. e-mail: bhill@nci.ac.uk

Hill, Dr. Frances Margaret, BA, MBA, PhD, ILTM, GradCIPD. Senior Lecturer, School of Management and Economics, Queen's University, Belfast; m., Brian Hill; 2d. Educ. Methodist

College, Belfast; Queen's University, Belfast. Personnel Manager, 1974 - 80; Research Officer, Equal Opportunities Commission, 1981 - 82; School of Management and Economics, Queen's University, Belfast since 1982. Publications: numerous academic papers concerning organisational change. Recreations: cycling; listening to music; reading. T.- 028 90 335011.

Hill Geoff, BA. Features and Travel Editor, News Letter, Belfast; b. 21.5.56, Omagh. Educ. The Academy, Omagh; Queen's University, Belfast. News Reporter, Tyrone Constitution, Omagh; News Reporter, News Letter, Belfast; Sub-Editor, The Irish News; Deputy Chief Sub-Editor, Newsletter; News Reporter, The Sun, London and Glasgow. Northern Ireland Features Journalist of the Year; Four UK Travel Writer of the Year Awards; European Travel Writer of the Year Award; Irish Travel Writer of the Year Award. Publications: Ulster Joke Book; Smith (novel). Recreations: volleyball, Irish caps record holder with 122 appearances for Northern Ireland; flying. Address: (h.) 36 Brookvale Avenue, Belfast BT14 6BW; T.- 028 90 286000. (b.) News Letter, 46-56 Boucher Crescent, Belfast, BT12 6QY; T.- 028 90 680013. e-mail: g.hill@newsletter.co.uk

Hill, John McCready. Energy Manager; b. 6.5.49; m., Daphne Hill; 1d. Educ. Ballymena Technical College. Estates Officer: Lagan Valley Hospital, Lisburn; Musgrave Park Hospital, Greenpark Healthcare Trust since 1991. Associate Member, Institute of Energy. Recreations: golf, Galgorm Castle Golf Club. Address: (b.) Estates Services Department, Musgrave Park Hospital, Stockman's Lane, Belfast; T.- 02890-669501, Ext. 2729.

Hill, Martin, BA. News Editor, Sunday Life since 1997; b. 4.10.62. Educ. St Malachy's College, Belfast; Queen's University, Belfast. Reporter, News Letter, 1988 - 91; Reporter, Belfast Telegraph, 1992 - 96; Reporter, Sunday Life, 1996 - 97. Recreations: venery. Address: (b.) Sunday Life, 124-144 Royal Avenue, Belfast, BT1 1EB; T.- 02890-264311.

Hill, Myrtle, BA, PhD. Director, Centre for Women's Studies, Queen's University of Belfast, since 1994, Senior Lecturer, since 1998; b. 25.1.50, Belfast; 2 d. Educ. Larkfield Secondary School; Queen's University of Belfast. Lecturer, Continuing Education, Queen's University of Belfast, 1992 - 98. Board Member, Irish Journal of Feminist Studies; Chair, Ulster Local History Trust; Committee Member, Women's History Association of Ireland. Publications include: Aspects of Irish Studies (co-editor), 1990; Evangelical Protestantism in Ulster, 1740–1900 (co-author), 1992; Image and Experience: Photographs of Irishwomen c. 1880–1920 (co-author), 1993; 1798: Rebellion in Down (co-editor), 1998; Sources and Resources in Local History (co-editor), 1998; Women of Ireland, Image and Experience c. 1880-1920 (2nd edn), co-

author, 1999; The Time of the End: Millenarian Beliefs in Ulster, 2001; Women in Ireland: A Century of Change, 2003. Recreations: reading; walking; keep fit. Address: (b.) 1-3 College Park East, Belfast BT7 1NN; T.-02890 335318.

Hill, Prof. W. John, MA, PhD, FRSA. Professor of Media Studies, University of Ulster, since 1998; b. 15.2.54. Educ. The Academy, Annan; University of Glasgow; University of York. Lecturer in Media Studies, University of Ulster, 1978-88, Senior Lecturer in Media Studies, 1988-98. Senior Research Fellow, AHRB Centre for British Film and Television Studies, 2001-2002; Founding Chair, Foyle Film Festival, 1987; Chair, Northern Ireland Film Council, 1994-97; Governor, British Film Institute, 1994-97; Member of the Communications, Cultural and Media Studies panel for the HEFCE Research Assessment Exercise, 1996; Chair, Working Group on the Film Industry in Europe, European Institute for the Media, since 1998; Director, UK Film Council, since 1999. Publications include: Sex, Class and Realism: British Cinema, 1956-63, 1986; co-author, Cinema and Ireland, 1987; co-editor, The Oxford Guide to Film Studies, 1998, and British Cinema in the 1980s, 1999. Address: (b.) School of Media and Performing Arts, University of Ulster, Coleraine BT52 1SA. T.-028 7032 4262. e-mail: wj.hill@ulst.ac.uk

Hillan (nee Daly), Sheelagh Elizabeth, MBE, DL, BSc, BTh, MPSNI. Director, J J Daly & Co (Randalstown) Ltd; Owner, Laverty's Bar, Ranaldstown, b., 30.11.48, Belfast; m., James Hillan, LLB, FCA; 4 children; Educ. Cross and Passion College, Ballycastle; Queen's University, Belfast. Member: Ulster Chemist Association Executive, (Past President); Pharmaceutical Contractors Committee, Northern Ireland, (Past Chairman); President of Pharm. Soc. of NI; Lay Member of NI Mental Health Rev. Tribunal; Non Executive Director, Homefirst Community Trust; Director, Northern Pharmacies; Vice Chairman of the Board of Antrim New Horizons (Action Mental Health); Trustee, Ulster Chemists Association; Member of the Council for the Regulation of Healthcare Professionals (CRHP). Recreations: skiing; golf; bridge. Address: (b.) Maine House, 2 Neillsbrook Road, Randalstown BT41 3AE. T.- 02894 472245.

Hillan, Dr. Sophia Mary, BA, MA, PhD. Associate Director, Institute of Irish Studies, Queen's University, Belfast since 1993; Acting Director, 1997 - 98; b. 14.5.50, Belfast; m., Eunan King (separated); 1s.; 1d. Educ. St Dominic's High School, Belfast; Queen's University, Belfast. English Teacher: St Dominic's High School, Belfast, 1974 - 75 and 1984 - 86; Greendale Community School, Dublin, 1975 - 80; Part-time Tutor, Carysfort College, Co Dublin, 1979 - 83; Research Fellow, Institute of Irish Studies, Queen's University, Belfast, 1986 - 88; Senior Lecturer, Stranmillis College, 1988 - 90; Institute of Irish Studies:Part-time Lecturer, 1990 - 93.

Publications: The Silken Twine: A Study of the works of Michael McLaverty, 1992; In Quiet Places, The Uncollected Letters, Stories and Critical Prose of Michael McLaverty (ed.), 1989; Hope and History: Eyewitness Accounts of Life in Twentieth-Century Ulster (co-editor), 1996; The Edge of Dark: A Sense of Place in the Writings of Michael McLaverty and Sam Hanna Bell, 2000. Address: (b.) Institute of Irish Studies, Queen's University, Belfast, 8 Fitzwilliam Street, Belfast, BT9 6AW; T.- 01232-273386.

Hinds, Dr. Eileen Kathleen, BA, BEd, MA, DPhil. Retired Principal; b. 27.4.41, Lisbellaw, Co Fermanagh; m., Richard Hinds; 1s.; 1d. Educ. Collegiate School, Enniskillen; Queen's University, Belfast. Omagh Academy; English Teacher, 1962; Head of English, 1965; Vice-Principal, 1978 - 95; Principal, Drumragh Integrated College, Omagh, 1995-2001. Appointed, Curriculum Committee, CEA, 1997. Recreations: amateur drama; theatre; painting. Address: (h.) 4 Gortmore Drive, Omagh, Co Tyrone, BT78 5EA; T.-02882 243635.

Hogg, Clarence Thomas, MBE, UD, JP, DL. Former Area Manager, Banking Division, Lombard & Ulster; b. 6.4.38, Belfast; m., Anne Phyllis Waring Arnold Robb; 1s.; 1d. Educ. Downey House; Brackenbecker House School; The Marine Radio College. Penninsular and Oriental Steam Navigation Co, 1956 - 58; Carplant (UDT), 1959 - 69; Joined Lombard and Ulster, 1969. President, Belfast Junior Chamber of Commerce, 1974/1975; Member, Northern Ireland Chamber of Commerce and Industry, 1972-1988; Chairman, Board of Governors: Belfast College of Business Studies, 1981-85, Bloomfield Collegiate School, 1993-99; Member, Belfast Education and Library Board, 1981-85; Member of the Police Authority for Northern Ireland, 1986-94; Chairman, Northern Ireland Regional Committee for Lay Visiting, 1993-94; Member of the Probation Board for Northern Ireland, 1994-2000; Chairman, Milibern Trust; Director, Blind Centre for Northern Ireland; Director/Treasurer, Clanmil Housing Ltd; Director, Northern Ireland War Memorial Building; Member, Advisory Committee of General Commissioners of Income Tax; Lieutenant Colonel, Ulster Defence Regiment, 1972-1990; Trustee, Ulster Defence Regiment Benevolent Fund; Vice Chairman, Reserve Forces and Cadets Association, Northern Ireland; Member: Ulster Reform Club; Army and Navy Club. Recreations: antiques; walking. Address: (h.) 27 Massey Avenue, Belfast BT4 2JT.

Hooks, Bryan John. Editor, Banbridge Chronicle since 1989; b. 10.7.58; widower; 1s.; 1d. Educ. Markethill Junior High School; Armagh College of Further Education. Reporter: Ulster Gazette, Armagh, 1975 - 78; Lurgan Mail, 1978 - 82; Deputy Editor: Castlereagh Courier, 1982 - 84; Lurgan Mail, 1984 - 88. Recreations: tennis; swimming; reading; travelling. Address: (b.) Banbridge Chronicle Press Ltd, 14 Bridge Street,

Banbridge, Co Down, BT32 3JS; T.- 018206-62322.

Hool, Jonathan Harris Edwin, LLB. Managing Partner, Harrisons Solicitors; b. 22.2.57, Belfast; m., Gillian Patricia MacDermott; 2s.; 1d. Educ. Royal Belfast Academical Institution; Queen's University, Belfast. Solicitor, TG Menary, Lurgan, 1980 - 85 (incorporating McCracken McFadden, 1982); Principal, Galway McIlwaine and Seeds incorporating George H Leitch, 1985 - 94. Member, Institute of Directors; Founder member, Northern Ireland Young Solicitors Group; Member, Professional Firms Group (Prince of Wales Trust). Recreations: cricket – MCC Area Representative, Ireland; Belfast Harlequins CC, Leprechauns CC; rugby – member, Instonians RFC; golf – Royal Belfast Golf Club, Malone Golf Club. Address: (b.) Victoria House, 54-58 Chichester Street, Belfast, BT1 4HN; T.- 02890-323843. Fax: 02890 330187. e-mail: Jonathan.Hool@harrisonll.com

Hopkins, Anthony Strother, CBE, BSc (Econ), FCA, CIMgmt. Chairman, Laganside Corporation since 1997; b. 17.7.40, Bangor; m., Dorothy, Moira Hopkins JP; 1s.; 2d. Educ. Campbell College; Queen's University, Belfast. Chief Executive, Northern Ireland Development Agency, 1979 - 82; Industrial Development Board; Deputy Chief Executive, 1982 - 88; Chief Executive, 1988 - 92; Senior Partner, Deloitte and Touche, 1992-2001. Chairman, Northern Ireland Higher Education Council, since 2002; Chairman, Milk Marketing Board since 1995; Member, Northern Ireland Tourist Board, 1992 - 98; Deputy Chairman, Probation Board for Northern Ireland, 1997 - 98; Member, Ulster Business School, Advisory Board, 1995-99; Chairman, Northern Ireland Region, Institute of Management, 1992 - 97; Member, Advisory Board, Crescent Capital (NI), since 1996; Director, QUBIS Ltd, since 2002; Member, Belfast Festival at Queen's Board, since 2002; Visiting Professor, University of Ulster, since 1993. Member, various charity appeal committees including Relate, The Prince's Trust, Mencap, Bryson House. Recreations: tennis; golf. Address: (b.) Laganside Corporation, Clarendon Buildings, Belfast.

Hopkins, Dorothy Moira, BA (Hons), JP. Lay Panel Member, Youth Court; b. 24.7.41, Armagh; M., Anthony S Hopkins CBE (qv); 1s.; 2d. Educ. Armagh Girls' School; Queen's University, Belfast. News Division, BBC, London; British Universities Sports Federation. President, Ulster Womens' Squash Rackets Association, 1981; Vice-President, Irish Womens' Squash Rackets Association, 1983; Irish Delegate, International Squash Rackets Federation, 1984 - 86; Relate Counsellor; 1993-2001. Member, Board, Trustees of Relate in Northern Ireland, 1999-2001. Recreations: golf; tennis.

Horner, Thomas Mark, BA (Cantab). Queens Counsel since 1996; b. 3.7.56, Belfast; m., Karin vander Ree; 2s.; 1d. Educ. Campbell College; St Catharine's College, Cambridge. Called to the Bar of Northern Ireland, 1979; Called to the Irish Bar, 1996; Called to Senior Bar, 1996. Publications: Guidelines for the Assessment of General Damages on Personal Injury Cases in Northern Ireland. Recreations: rugby; golf; reading. Address: (h.) 15 Castlehill Road, Belfast. T.- 02890-655352.

Houston, Deane, MIMgt, MIDM. Chief Executive, Blind Centre for Northern Ireland since 1978; b. 13.6.51; m., Helen; 1s.; 1d. Educ. Methodist College, Belfast. Winston Churchill Travelling Scholarship, 1987. Address: (b.) 70 North Road, Belfast BT5 5NJ.

Houston, Professor, Samuel Kenneth, BSc, PhD, CMath, FIMA, ILTM. Professor of Mathematical Studies, University of Ulster since 1996; b. 13.1.43, Belfast; m., Patricia Ann McVittie; 1s.; 2d. Educ. Royal Belfast Academical Institution; Queen's University, Belfast. Lecturer, Applied Mathematics, Sheffield University, 1967 - 73; Resident Post Doctoral Associate, Goddard Space Flight Center, USA, 1969 - 70; Principal Lecturer in Mathematics, Ulster Polytechnic, 1974 - 84; Head, Department of Mathematics, University of Ulster, 1984 - 94; Senior Lecturer, University of Ulster, 1994 - 96. Publications: Developments in Curriculum and Assessment in Mathematics (ed.), 1993; Developing Rating Scales for Undergraduate Mathematics Projects (with C R Haines and A Kitchen), 1994; Innovations in Mathematics Teaching (ed.), 1994; Enhancing Student Learning through Peer Tutoring in Higher Education (with S Griffiths and A Lazenbatt), 1995; Mathematical Modelling (with J S Berry), 1995; Supercalculators through the Curriculum (with M Fitzpatrick, joint eds.), 1997; Teaching and Learning Mathematical Modelling (with W Blum, I Huntley and N T Neill, joint eds.), 1997; Creators of Mathematics - The Irish Connection (ed.), 2000; co-editor, Modelling and Mathematics Education - ICTMA 9: Applications in Science and Technology, 2001; co-editor, Mathematical Modelling in Education and Culture, 2003; co-editor, Mathematical Modelling: A Way of Life, 2003. Recreations: photography; golf; NSM in Church of Ireland. Address: (b.) School of Computing and Mathematics, University of Ulster at Jordanstown, Shore Road, Newtownabbey, BT37 0QB; T.-028 9036 6953.
e-mail: SK.Houston@ulster.ac.uk
web: http://www.infj.ulst.ac.uk/staff/sk.houston

Hudson, Dr. Paul David, BA, PhD. Senior Lecturer, Operational Research; Queen's University, Belfast; b. 1.10.40, Kent; m., Pauline Rodinson; 3s. Educ. The Skinners' School, Tunbridge Wells, Kent; Fitzwilliam House, Cambridge; Manchester University. Research Associate, Department of Astronomy, Columbia University, New York, USA, 1966 - 67; Research Associate, Department of Space Science, Rice University, Houston Texas, USA, 1967 - 69;

Research Fellow, Department of Physics, Imperial College, London, 1969 - 70; Lecturer in Applied Maths/Senior Lecturer, Queen's University, Belfast since 1970. Member of Senate, Queen's University, Belfast, 1986 - 90 and since 1991; Member, National Executive, Association of University Teachers, 1983 - 99 (President, 1990 - 91). Recreations: DIY. Address: (h.) 11 Ravenshill Park, Belfast, BT6 0DE; T.-02890-641508. e-mail: p.hudson@qub.ac.uk

Hughes, Breedagh, BA (Hons), RGN, RM. Secretary, Northern Ireland Board, Royal College of Midwives; b. 12.8.58, Dublin, Ireland; m., Peter Hughes; 2s. Educ. St Dominic's High School, Belfast; Queen's University Belfast. General Nurse training, Belfast City Hospital, 1982 - 85; Staff Nurse, Belfast City Hospital, 1986 - 87; Midwifery Training, Jubilee Maternity Hospital, Belfast. 1987 - 88; Midwife, Royal Maternity Hospital, Belfast, 1988 - 96; Midwifery Sister, Neonatal Intensive Care Unit, Royal Maternity Hospital, Belfast, 1996 - 97. Recreations: hill-walking; ethics in health care. Address: (b.) Royal College of Midwives, 58 Howard Street, Belfast, BT1 6PJ; T.- 028 9024 1531.
e-mail: bhughes@rcmnib.org.uk

Hughes, Col. James, CBE, KStJ, TD, MA, MEd, DL. Retired Deputy Principal, Stranmillis College of Education; b. 25.1.17, Campbeltown, Scotland; m., Emily Walker; 4d. Educ. Regent House Grammar School, Newtownards; Stranmillis College; Trinity College, Dublin; Queen's University, Belfast. War Service, Royal Artillery, 1939 - 46; Teacher/Vice Principal, 1946 - 48; Senior Lecturer, Higher Education, 1948 - 56; Principal Lecturer, Higher Education, 1956 - 70; Deputy Principal, Stranmillis College, 1970 - 82; Retired, 1982. MBE, 1945; OBE, 1961; CBE, 1975; French Legion d'Honeur, 1983; Knight of the Order of St John, 1990. National Chairman, Royal British Legion, 1972 - 75; National Vice-President, Royal British Legion since 1980; Patron, RBL Poppy Factory; President, Clanmil Housing Association; President, Kilcreggan Homes; Hon. President, Belfast Battalion Boys Brigade. Recreations: reading; voluntary charitable work. Address: (h.) Kintyre, 28 Beechgrove Drive, Castlereagh, Belfast, BT6 0NW; T.- 02890-793956.

Hughes, John Gerard, BSc, PhD, FBCS. Pro-Vice-Chancellor (Research and Development), University of Ulster, since 2000; b. 28.8.53, Belfast; m., Maura; 2 s. Educ. Christian Brothers' Grammar School, Belfast; The Queen's University of Belfast. Lecturer in Computer Science, The Queen's University of Belfast, 1981-84; Research Scientist, International Atomic Energy Agency, Vienna, 1984-85; University of Ulster: Reader in Information Systems, 1988-91, Head of Department of Information Systems, 1989-93, Dean of the Faculty of Informatics, 1993-2000. Fellow of the British Computer Society; BCS IT Professional of the Year, 1997; Member of: the

Conference of Professors of Computer Science, the Institute of Electrical and Electronic Engineers, USA, the Association for Computing Machinery, USA; Director: Synergy Centres Ltd, UUTECH Ltd, UUSRP Ltd, NISP (Holdings) Ltd, HERO Ltd, eyespyfx Ltd, EFMB Ltd, Greenshoots Ltd. Recreations: politics; history; travel; soccer; film. Address: (b.) University of Ulster, Cromore Road, Coleraine BT52 1SA. T.-028 7032 4343. e-mail: jg.hughes@ulster.ac.uk

Hull, Professor, M Elizabeth C, BSc, PhD, CEng, FBCS.   Professor of Computing Science, University of Ulster; Director of Quality, Faculty of Informatics; b. 19.5.53, Belfast.   Educ. Strathearn School; Queen's University, Belfast. Programmer, Ulster Polytechnic. 1975 - 77; Analyst/Programmer, Northern Ireland Civil Service, 1977 - 78; Research Assistant, Queen's University, Belfast, 1978 - 80; Lecturer/Senior Lecturer, University of Ulster, 1981 - 86; Director, Northern Ireland Regional Transputer Support Centre, 1988 - 91; Head, Department of Computing Science, University of Ulster, 1986 - 96.   Currently Computing College Member, ESPRC Information Technology; Professional Examination Board, British Computer Society; Member, Accreditation and Exemptions Committee, British Computer Society; Editorial Boards: Springer-Verlag, Internal Journal of Project Management.   Publications: over 70 academic papers. Recreations: golf. Address: (b.) School of Computing and Mathematics, University of Ulster, Newtownabbey, Co Antrim, BT37 0QB; T.- 028 9036 8846. e-mail: mec.hull@ulster.ac.uk

Hume, John, MP, MEP, MA. SDLP Member of Parliament (Foyle), Social Democratic and Labour Party, since 1983; Member (Northern Ireland) European Parliament since 1979; Leader, Social Democratic and Labour Party 1979-2001; Member (Foyle), Social Democratic and Labour Party, Northern Ireland Assembly 1998-2000; b. 18.1.37; m., Patricia; 2s.; 3d. Educ. St Columb's College, Derry; St Patrick's College, Maynooth, Co Kildare, Ireland. Member of Parliament (Foyle) Northern Ireland Parliament 1969 - 73; SDLP Member, (Londonderry), Northern Ireland Assembly, 1973 - 75; Member, Northern Ireland Constitutional Convention, 1973 - 76; Member, Northern Ireland Assembly, 1982 - 86. Address: (b.) 5 Bayview Terrace, Derry, BT48 7EE; T.- 01504-265340.

Hunter, Dr. Desmond Morrison, MA, PhD, ARAM, FRCO, LRAM, Special Dip.   Senior Lecturer, Music, University of Ulster since 1992; b. 13.4.46, Londonderry; m., Joan Patricia Good; 2d.   Educ.   Down High School, Downpatrick; Methodist College, Belfast; Royal Academy of Music, London; Antwerp Conservatoire; University College, Cork. Tutor, City of Belfast School of Music, 1969 - 72; Ulster Polytechnic: Lecturer, Music, 1972 - 80; Senior Lecturer, 1980 - 84; Lecturer, Music, University of Ulster, 1984 -

92; International Organ Recitalist since 1968, numerous solo performances including major festivals in Belgium, France, Germany, Holland, Ireland, Italy, Switzerland, UK and USA; Broadcasts (radio and television), BBC, BRT, ITV, RTE; CD Recordings on organ and harpsichord (including the first complete recording of the organ sonatas of Stanford, 1994).   First prizewinner, National Organ Competition, England, 1970; Premier Laureat, Concours National Biennal D'Orgue, Belgium, 1969; 2nd Prizewinner, International Organ Festival, St Albans, 1975. Associate, Royal Academy of Music, 1973; awarded a National Teaching Fellowship, 2000. Publications: numerous articles in books and journals in UK, USA and Ireland; contributor to The New Grove Dictionary of Music and Musicians. Recreations: golf; swimming; walking. Address: (h.) 3 Bayswater, Clooney Road, Derry BT47 6JL.

Hussey, Derek Robert, CertEd. Member (West Tyrone), UUP, Northern Ireland Assembly, since 1998; Strabane District Councillor, since 1989; Deputy Chairman, Assembly Standards and Privileges Committee; b. 12.9.48, Padstow, Cornwall; m., Karen; 2 s.; 1 d. Educ. Omagh Academy; Stranmillis College. Teacher of Business Studies, Glencairn Girls Secondary School, Belfast, 1971 - 72; Head of Business Studies, Castlederg High School, 1972 - 98; Proprietor, The Castle Inn, Castlederg, since 1993; UUP Member, West Tyrone, Northern Ireland Forum, 1996 - 98. Recreations: football; jogging; loyal orders; country and western music; singing; travel. Address: (b.) 48 Main Street, Castlederg, Co. Tyrone; T.-028 81679299/8167 1501.

Huston, Adrian Robert Arthur, JP BSc.   Tax Consultant, Partner, Huston and Co since 1992; b. 11.7.63, Coleraine; m., Felicity Huston (qv); 2s. Educ.   Coleraine   Academical   Institution; Southampton University.   Ernst and Whinney, Chartered Accountants, 1985 - 86; Inspector of Taxes, Inland Revenue, 1986 - 92.   Member: Police Authority for Northern Ireland, 1997-2001; Lord Chancellor's Legal Aid Advisory Committee since 1997; House Committee, Royal British Legion Housing Association 1994-99; Industrial Tribunals panel, since 1996; Vice-Chairman, Federation of Small Businesses, 1996-98; Officer, Territorial Army, Military Police, 1986 - 92; Agricultural Wages Board for Northern Ireland, 2000-03.   Part-time farmer.   Recreations: Indian cookery; cinema. Address: (b.) Huston & Co Tax Consultants   and   Accountants,   481   Upper Newtownards Road, Belfast, BT4 3LL; T.- 028-9080-6080. e-mail: adrian@huston.co.uk

Huston, Felicity Victoria, BA.   Partner/Tax Consultant, Huston and Co since 1994; b. 28.5.63, Antrim; m., Adrian Huston (q.v); 2s.   Educ. Strathearn School; Campbell College; Nottingham University.   Local Government Officer, Coventry City Council, 1985 - 87; Project Control Officer, Open University, 1987 - 88; H M Inspector of

Taxes, 1988 - 94. Member, General Consumer Council of Northern Ireland, 1996-2000 (Deputy Chairman 1999-2000); Energy Convenor, GCCNI; Member, Personal Investment Authority Consumer Panel, 1997 - 99; Member, Post Office Users Council, 1996 - 99, Member: Social Security Tribunals, 1994 - 99; Industrial Tribunals Panel, 1999-2000; Hon. Treasurer, Belfast Charitable Society; Member, Northern Ireland Charities Advisory Committee, 1998-2000; Chairman, NI Consumer Committee for Electricity, 2000-03; Commissioner, House of Lords Appointments Commission, since 2000; Director: Moyle Holdings Ltd; Moyle Interconnector (Financing) PLC; Moyle Interconnector Ltd; Cassandra Consulting NI Ltd. Recreation: vegetarian cookery. Address: (b.) Huston and Co, 481 Upper Newtownards Road, Belfast, BT4 3LL; T.- 028-9080-6080. e-mail: felicity@huston.co.uk

Hutchieson, Doris, BA (Hons), PGCE, FRSA. Headmistress, Coleraine High School; m., Ron Hutchieson. Educ. Glenlola Collegiate School, Bangor; Queen's University, Belfast. Assistant Lecturer, North Down Further Education College; Senior Teacher, Glenlola Collegiate School, Bangor. President, Secondary Heads Association (NI), 1997; Member, Court, University of Ulster; Member, UCAS Northern Ireland Standing Group; Chairman, NE Post-Primary Heads Association; Member, Rotary International; High Sheriff, County of Londonderry, 1999. Recreations: gardening; travel. Address: (b.) Coleraine High School, Lodge Road, Coleraine, Co Londonderry, BT52 1LZ; T.- 028 703 43178.

Hutchinson, Billy. Member (North Belfast), Progressive Unionist Party, Northern Ireland Assembly, 1998-2003. Elected to Belfast City Council, 1997. Address: (b.) Parliament Buildings, Stormont, Belfast, BT4 3ST.

Hutchinson, Prof. Robert Watson, BSc, MA. Dean, Faculty of Business and Management, University of Ulster, since 2001, Professor of Business Finance, since 1996; b. 18.01.50, Belfast; m., Linda; 1 s.; 2 d. Educ. Belfast High School; University of Ulster; University of Warwick. Lecturer in Economics (part-time), Coventry Polytechnic; Lecturer in Economics, University of Ulster, Senior Lecturer in Financial Economics, Head of School of Business, Retail and Financial Services. Executive Committee, Irish Economics Association; Visiting Research Fellow, Central Bank of Ireland; Adviser on Financial Services activities. Address: (b.) Faculty of Business and Management, University of Ulster, Coleraine, Co. Londonderry. T.-028 90 366350. e-mail: r.hutchinson@ulster.ac.uk

Hutchinson, Roger. Businessman; Member (East Antrim), Northern Ireland Unionist Party, Northern Ireland Assembly, 1998-99, Independent Unionist, 1999-2003; b. East Antrim; m., Educ. Larne Technical College. Minister, Elim Church for fifteen years. Press Officer, Business and

Professional People for the Union. Address: (b.) Parliament Buildings, Stormont, Belfast, BT4 3ST; T.- 02890-520700.

Hutchinson, Very Rev. Samuel, BA, BD, MTh, DD. b. 14.9.37, Belfast; m., Margaret Kerr. Educ. Royal Belfast Academical Institution; Queen's University, Belfast; Assembly's College, Belfast. Assistant Minister, Oldpark, Belfast, 1962 - 66; Minister, Gilford Presbyterian Church, 1966 - 85; Minister. Gilford Presbyterian Church with Clare, 1967 - 85; Deputy Clerk, General Assembly, 1985 - 90; Clerk of the General Assembly, Presbyterian Church in Ireland, 1990-2003. Moderator, General Assembly, 1997. Recreations: reading; walking; travel. Address: (h.) 32 Aberdelghy Park, Lambeg, Lisburn, BT27 4QF; T.- 02892-665586. e-mail: samuelhutchinson@yahoo.co.uk

Hyland, Davy, BSc (Econ), PGCE. Chairman, Newry and Mourne District Council, since 1993; School Teacher, since 1979; b. 25.2.55, Newry, Co. Down; m., Bronagh (nee Lamph); 1 s.; 1 d. Educ. St. Colman's College, Newry; Aberystwyth; Manchester University. Teacher, Rathmore Grammar School, 1982-92; elected to Newry and Mourne District Council in 1993-97 and 2001. Member of various local community groups including Armagh Road; Mourneview Park; Derrybeg; Carnaget; Drumalane; Carlingford Park. Recreations: does not drive - cycles everywhere. Address: (h.) 15 Sean O'Neill Park, Newry, Co. Down. T.-028 302 66633.

I

Irvine, Henry, QPM, PgDip, A and LS, MA, FCIS. District Commander, Strandtown Police Station, since 2001; b. 15.5.54, Bangor; 1 s.; 2 d. Address: (h.) Strandtown PSNI Station, 1-5 Dundela Avenue, Belfast BT4 3BQ. T.-028 9065 0222 ext 25068.

Irvine, John Walter, LLB, LLM. Partner/Head, Corporate Department, L'Estrange Brett Solicitors, Belfast since 1987; b. 18.9.57, Enniskillen; m., Andrea; 1 s. Educ. Portora Royal School; Queen's University, Belfast; Queen's University, Kingston, Ontario, Canada. Lecturer, Law, University of Central Lancashire, 1983 - 84; Tutor, Law, University of Exeter, 1984 - 85; Joined L'Estrange and Brett, 1985: Apprentice, 1985 - 86; Admitted as Solicitor, 1986. Teaching Fellow, Queen's University, Kingston, Ontario, 1982 - 83; Visiting Research Fellow, Centre for Industrial Relations, Kingston, Ontario, 19832 - 83. Publications: Numerous articles and contributions to national and international law journals. Recreations: football; fishing; squash. Address: (b.) L'Estrange and Brett, Solicitors, Arnott House, 12-16 Bridge Street, Belfast, BT1 1LS. T.-02890-230426. email:john.irvine@lestrangeandbrett.com

Irwin, Rev. David Crawford, MA, BD, DMin. b. 10.7.37; m., Flora Mary (Maureen) MacManaway; 3d. Educ. Campbell College, Belfast; Trinity College, Dublin; Edinburgh University; Union Theological College. Belfast; Princeton Theological Seminary, USA. Assistant Minister, Woodvale Park Presbyterian Church, Belfast, 1962 - 66; Minister, Groomsport Presbyterian Church, Co Down, 1966 - 91; Minister, McCracken Memorial Presbyterian Church, 1991-2003. Publications: Tides and Times in the Port: a Narrative History of the Co Down Village of Groomsport, 1991. Recreations: sport; photography; travel. Address: (h.) 11 Strangford Avenue, Belfast, BT9 6PG; T.- 028 9066 5739.

Irwin, Professor George William, FREng, MRIA, BSc (Hons), PhD, DSc, CEng, FIEE, FInstMC, Sen MIEEE. Chair of Control Engineering, Queen's University Belfast since 1989; Director, Virtual Engineering Centre, Queen's University Belfast; b. 19.9.50, Bangor, Co Down; m., Margaret Yvonne; 1s. Educ. Sullivan Upper School, Holywood; Queen's University, Belfast. Lecturer, Department of Engineering Mathematics, Loughborough University of Technology, 1976 - 80; Queen's University, Belfast: Lecturer, Department of Electrical Engineering, 1980 - 87; Reader, 1987 - 89. Chair, IEE Control Division, London, 1997 - 98; Chair, IEE (NI Centre), 1997 - 98; Chair, UK Automatic Control Council, since 2001. Awards: Honeywell Prize, Institute MC, 1994; IEE Kelvin Premium,

1985; IEE Heaverside Premium, 1987; IEE Mather Premium, 1991; IEE Hartreee Premium, 1996; Best Paper, Czech Academy of Science, 1997; Inst. M.C; Honeywell International Medal, 2002. Non-executive director, Anexb Ltd. Publications: over 300 publications and five edited books; Editor-in-Chief, Control Engineering Practice IFAC Journal 1998-2002; Chair, UK Automatic Control Council, 1998-2002. Recreations: swimming; reading; Portballintrae; walking. Address: (b.) Electrical and Electronic Engineering, University Belfast, Belfast, BT9 5AH; T.- 028 9033 5439. e-mail: g.irwin@ee.qub.ac.uk

Irwin, Gordon, OBE, ACMA, FILT, FCIT, JP. Chief Executive, Belfast Harbour Commissioners. Address: (b.) Harbour Office, Corporation Square, Belfast, BT1 3AL; T.- 028 9055 4422.

Irwin, William Kenneth, MA (Ed Mgt), BEd, BA, PGDipGC, AdvDip EM. Headmaster, Carrickfergus Grammar School since 1990; b. 11.6.50, Belfast; m., Margaret Alison Starret; 3s. Educ. Methodist College, Belfast; Queen's University of Belfast. Teacher, Carrickfergus Grammar School, 1973 - 79; Head, Mathematics, Whitehead High School, 1979 - 81; Senior Teacher, Laurelhill High School, 1981 - 88; Vice-Principal, Newtownbreda High School, 1988 - 90. Recreations: reading; walking. Address: (h.) 3 Lonsdale Court, Jordanstown, BT37 0FA; T.- 028 90 863001.

Iwaniec, Professor, Stanislawa Dorota. Professor of Social Work, Queen's University Belfast, Director of the Institute of Child Care Research; b. 20.4.40, Krasiczyn, Poland; m., James Stevens Curl (qv); 2s. Educ. Kraków Lyceum, Sienkiewicza; Jagiellonian University, Kraków; University of Leicester. Teacher, Biology Kraków, 1963 - 64; Social Worker, Leicestershire Social Services, 1972 - 77; Researcher/Clinician, Department of Child Health, Leicester Royal Infirmary, 1977 - 82; Supervisor/Director, Student Unit, Leicester, 1982 - 92. Publications: The Emotionally Abused and Neglected Child - Identification, Assessment and Intervention, 1995; Making Research Work: Policy, Practice in Child Care (joint ed. with J Pinkerton), 1998; Child Welfare - Policy and Practice: Current Issues in Child Care Research (joint ed. with M Hill), 2000; Children who Fail to Thrive: A Practice Guide, 2004; numerous international papers on failure to thrive in children, parenting, attachment, emotional abuse and neglect, and behaviour management of children and adolescents. Recreations: music; opera; mushroom picking; walking. Address: (b.) Department of Social Work; Queen's University, Belfast, 7 Lennoxvale, Belfast, BT9 5BY; T.- 02890 335401.

Iyer, Dr. Venkat, BSc (Hons), LLM, PhD. Barrister-at-Law; Senior Lecturer in Law, University of Ulster at Jordanstown, since 1995; Editor, The Commonwealth Lawyer, since 1999; b. 26.6.57, India; m., Shanti Sarma. Educ. University of Bombay; Queen's University, Belfast. Advocate, Bombay High Court, 1981-90; Research Officer, Queen's University, Belfast, 1990-95; Nuffield Fellow, Wolfson College, Cambridge, 1990. Publications: several books, including Database on States of Emergency, 1995; Media Monitors in Asia, 1997; Democracy, Human Rights and the Rule of Law, 2000; Constitutional Perspectives, 2001. Recreations: reading; travelling; writing. Address: (b.) School of Law, University of Ulster at Jordanstown, Shore Road, Newtownabbey BT37 0QB; T.-02890 368876. e-mail: v.iyer@ulst.ac.uk

J

Jackson, Prof. Alvin, MA, DPhil, FRHistS. Professor of Modern Irish History, Queen's University, Belfast since 1999; 13.3.61; m., Joyce Kelso; 2 s.; 1 d. Educ. Grosvenor High School; Corpus Christi College, Oxford; Nuffield College, Oxford. Junior Fellow, Institute of Irish Studies, Queen's University, Belfast, 1985 - 86; Post Doctoral Fellow of the British Academy, 1986 - 88; Lecturer, Modern History, University College, Dublin, 1988 - 91; Lecturer, Modern History, Queen's University, Belfast, 1991 - 95, Reader, 1995-99; Salzburg Fellow, 1990; Burns Visiting Professor, Boston College, USA, 1996 - 97; British Academy Research Reader, 2000-2002. Publications: The Ulster Party, 1989; Sir Edward Carson, 1993; Colonel Edward Saunderson, 1995; Ireland, 1798 - 1998; Home Rule: An Irish History, 2003. Address: (b.) School of Modern History, Queen's University, Belfast BT7 1NN; T.- 01232-245133.

Jackson, Professor John Dugald, BA, LLM, Barrister-at-Law, Bar of Northern Ireland, England and Wales; Professor of Public Law, Queen's University, Belfast since 1995; Director of Institute of Criminology and Criminal Justice, Queen's University, Belfast; b. 13.6.55, Belfast; m., Katharine Jackson; 1s.; 1d. Educ. Coleraine Academical Institution; University of Durham. Taught, University of Wales; Queen's University, Belfast; City University, London; University of Sheffield until 1995. Visiting Scholar, Swiss Institute of Comparative Law, 1985; Deputy Director, Institute for the Study of the Legal Profession, Sheffield, 1994; Visiting Professor, Hastings College of the Law, University of California, 2000. Publications: numerous articles on criminal procedure and criminal justice; Books include Called To Court, A Public View of Criminal Justice (with C Harvey and R Kilpatrick), 1991; co-author: Judge Without Jury, 1995, The Judicial Role in Criminal Proceedings, 2000. Recreations: cycling; tennis; swimming. Address: (b.) School of Law, Queen's University, Belfast, Belfast, BT7 1NN; T.-02890-335019. e-mail: j.jackson@qub.ac.uk

Jamieson, John Trevor. Superintendent Minister, Larne Circuit Methodist Church in Ireland since 1997; b. 13.12.50, Carrickfergus; m., Helen Miriam Nesbitt; 2s.; 1d. Educ. Carrickfergus Secondary Intermediate School (now Carrickfergus College); Queen's University, Belfast. Worked in industry until 1983; entered Methodist Ministry, 1984; Londonderry, Strabane, Inishowen, Limavady Mission Circuit, 1986 - 89; Lurgan Circuit, 1989 - 94; Superintendent, Charlemont and Cranagill Circuit, 1994 - 97; Synod Secretary of the North East District, since 2002. Member of the North Eastern Education and Library Board, 2001; Governor: Larne and Inver Primary School, Carnlough Controlled Integrated Primary School, Rostulla Special School, Jordanstown; Former Governor of several primary schools, Co Armagh; Former Governor, Lurgan Junior High School. Recreations: golf; gardening; computers. Address: (h.) 110 Glenarm Road, Larne, BT40 1DZ; T.- 028 28 272586.

Jamison, David, LLB. Partner, Carson and McDowell Solicitors since 1994; b. 23.11.64, Stoke-on-Trent; m., Sara E Jamison. Educ. Carrickfergus Grammar School; University of Manchester. Admitted as Solicitor in England, 1989; Solicitor, Prudential Corporation plc, Holborn, 1989 - 93; Admitted as a Solicitor, Northern Ireland, 1994. Address: (b.) Murray House, Murray Street, Belfast, BT1 5HS; T.-02890-244951.

Jamison, Nicola H.G., LLB, MBA, DIC. Chief Executive, Federation of The Retail Licensed Trade Northern Ireland, since 2000; b. 24.12.67, Bangor; m., Dr. David Carruthers; 1 s. Educ. Glenlola Collegiate, Bangor; Queen's University Belfast; Imperial College London. Lloyds Bank, 1990-93; Senior Legal Adviser, The Building Societies Association and Council of Mortgage Lenders (London), 1993-2000. Address: (b.) 91 University Street, Belfast BT1 1HP. T.-90 32 7578.

Jarritt, Professor Peter H., BSc, PhD, FIPEM. Chief Executive, Northern Ireland Regional Medical Physics Agency, since 2003; Scientific Director of the Northern Ireland PET Institute, since 2002; Consultant Clinical Scientist, Royal Victoria Hospital Belfast, since 2000; Hon. Professor, Queen's University Belfast, since 2001; b. 31.7.51, Ipswich; m., Moire; 2 s. Educ. Reading University; King's College London. Member: European Association of Nuclear Medicine, British Nuclear Medicine Society; Fellow of Institute of Physics and Engineering in Medicine. Address: (b.) Northern Ireland Regional Medical Physics Agency, Royal Victoria Hospital, Belfast BT12 6BA. T.-028 9031 1844.

Jay, Richard, MA, MPhil. Assistant Director, Institute of Lifelong Learning, Queen's University Belfast, since 2003, Academic Director, Armagh Campus, since 1999; b. 16.12.46, Bury, Lancs; m., Fionnuala Jay-O'Boyle; 1 s.; 1 d. (previous marriage). Educ. Bury Grammar School; Brasenose and Nuffield Colleges, Oxford. Lecturer in Government, University of Essex, 1971-73; Lecturer and Senior Lecturer in Politics, Queen's University Belfast, since 1974. Member, NI Civic Forum; Governor, North East Institute of FHE. Publications: author, Joseph Chamberlain: A Political Study, 1981; other works on history and politics. Recreations: dogs; opera. Address: (b.) Armagh Outreach Campus, 39 Abbey Street, Armagh BT61 7EB. e-mail: r.jay@qub.ac.uk

Jedrzejewski, Jan Pawel, MA, DPhil. Senior Lecturer in English and Comparative Literature,

University of Ulster, since 2001; b. 2.7.63, Poland. Educ. Stanislaw Wyspianski Grammar School, Lodz, Poland; University of Lodz, Poland; Worcester College, University of Oxford. University of Lodz: Junior Teaching Assistant, 1984-85, Teaching Assistant, 1985-87, Senior Teaching Assistant, 1988-89; Tutor in English Literature, Wadham College, St. Edmund Hall, Oxford, 1991-92; Tutor in Polish, St. Clare's, Oxford, 1991-92; Lecturer in English and Comparative Literature, University of Ulster, 1993-2001. Publications: Thomas Hardy and The Church, 1996; Editor: Thomas Hardy, Outside The Gates of The World, 1996, Joseph Sheridan Le Fanu, The Cock and Anchor, 2000; co-gen. editor, The Complete Critical Guide to English Literature, since 2000. Recreations: reading; current affairs; travel; film; chess. Address: (b.) School of Languages and Literature, University of Ulster, Coleraine, Co. Londonderry BT52 1SA. T.-028-70324553.

Jeffcutt, Professor Paul, BSc, MEd, PhD, FRSA. Chair of Management Knowledge and Director of the Centre for Creative Industry, Queen's University of Belfast, since 1997; b. 5.2.52, Cheltenham. Educ. Saintbridge School, Gloucester; University of London; University of Manchester. Sales, Marlon Marketing, 1974 - 75; Production Control, British Leyland, 1976 - 77; Management Training, EF Institute, 1978 - 79; Training Consultant, Fielden House, 1981 - 85; Lecturer in Educational Studies, University of Southampton, 1985 - 89; Lecturer in Organisational Behaviour, University of Stirling, 1989 - 94; University of Hull: Senior Lecturer in Management, 1994 - 97; Director, Institute for Organisational Analysis, 1995 - 97. Member, Governing Council, British Academy of Management, since 1996; Chair, UK Creative Industry Research Network, since 1997; Member, Governing Council, UK Academy for the Social Sciences, since 2000. Publications include: Understanding Management: Culture, Critique and Change, 1995; Theatre and Performance in Organisation, 1996; Management Education and Critical Practice, 1997; From the Industrial to the Post-Industrial Subculture, 1999; Management and the Creative Industries, 2000; Creativity and Convergence in the Knowledge Economy, 2001; The Foundations of Management Knowledge, 2003. Recreations: writing and reading poetry; hillwalking; cycle touring; travel photography. Address: (b.) School of Management and Economics, Queen's University of Belfast, Belfast BT7 1NN; T.-02890 273112.

Jeffrey, William Henry. Chairman Emeritus, Federation of Small Businesses, Northern Ireland; Alliance Party Councillor, Belfast City Council, 1974 - 78; b. 15.2.34, Belfast; divorced; 1s.; 1d. Educ. Masonic Boys' School, Dublin. Self employed for 35 years, current business, Arrow Mobile Promotions. Joint Chair, Consultative Forum, EU special support programme for peace and reconciliation in Northern Ireland and the six border counties of Ireland; Member (and Past Chair), Publicity Association of Northern Ireland; Member, Employers Panel, Industrial Relations Tribunal (NI); Member, Management Committee, Lisburn Victim Support; Governor, Castlereagh Further Education College, Belfast; T&EA NI Management Council; Member, Queen's University Forum for Lifelong Learning; Member, University of Ulster Advisory Board of The Faculty of Business and Management; Business Sector Representative on the Civic Forum. Regular contributor on business affairs, press, radio and television. Recreations: reading; photography; writing; speaking; star gazing; public affairs. Address: (h.) 110 Gregg Street, Lisburn, BT27 5AW; T.- 028 9263 4949.

Johnston, Donald Ernest, BSc, PhD, CChem, FRSC, FIFST. Senior Lecturer, Food Science Department, Queen's University of Belfast; Principal Scientific Officer, Food Chemistry Branch, Department of Agriculture and Rural Development for Northern Ireland; b. 20.12.46, Belfast; m., Eleanor Margaret Coyle; 2 s.; 1 d. Educ. Regent House Grammar School; Queen's University of Belfast. Appointed Lecturer in Food Chemistry, Queen's University of Belfast, 1972. Committee Member, Royal Society of Chemistry Food Group. Publications: Joint Editor, three books. Recreations: cycling; hill-walking; quizzes. Address: Agriculture and Food Science Centre, Newforge Lane, Belfast BT9 5PX; T.-028 9025 5331. e-mail: donald.johnston@dardni.gov.uk

Johnston, Professor George Dennis, DSc, MD, PhD, FRCP, FRCPI. Whitla Professor, 2000; Professor of Clinical Pharmacology, since 1996; b. 9.9.46, Belfast; m., Barbara Johnston; 1s.; 2d. Educ. Grosvenor High School; Queen's University, Belfast. Consultant Physician/Lecturer in General Medicine/Clinical Pharmacology, 1977 - 79; Merck Sharp and Dohme International Fellow in Clinical Pharmacology, 1979 - 80; Senior Lecturer, 1980 - 89; Reader, 1989 - 96; Head of Department. Chairman, Drugs and Therapeutics Committees, DHSS (NI); Director of Drugs and Poisons Unit, Eastern Health and Social Services Board; Member, Executive Committee, British Hypertension Society. Publications: over 200 papers, reviews and books in Cardiovascular Pharmacology. Recreations: choral and orchestral music; drama. Address: (b.) Department of Therapeutics and Pharmacology, Whitla Medical Building, 97 Lisburn Road, Belfast, BT9 7BL; T.-02890-335772. e-mail: g.d.johnston@qub.ac.uk

Johnston, Joseph Mervyn, BSc (Hons), M Ed. Principal, Lurgan Junior High School since 1996; b. 11.7.59, Lurgan; m., Shirley Helena; 1s.; 2d. Educ. The Royal School, Armagh; Queen's University, Belfast. Lecturer, Ballymena Technical College, 1981 - 86; Teacher, Lurgan Boys' Junior High School, 1986 - 89; Principal, Newtownhamilton High School, 1989 - 96. Address: (b.) Lurgan Junior High School,

Toberhewny Lane, Gilford Road, Lurgan, BT66 8SU; T.- 02838 323243.

Johnston, Neil. Arts, Folk Music and Features Writer, Belfast Telegraph; b. 1.11.43, Ballymena; m., Myrtle Speirs; 1s.; 1d.   Educ.   Omagh Academy.   Journalist: Tyrone Constitution, Omagh, 1964 - 68; Belfast News Letter, 1968 - 70; Belfast Telegraph since 1970. Recreations: golf; playing guitar; Irish traditional music, blues, jazz; songwriting; reading. Address: (h.) 9 Nottinghill, Malone Road, Belfast; T.- 028 90 666393.

Johnston, Peter Henry, MEng, ACGI. Head of Broadcasting, BBC Northern Ireland since 1994; b. 20.1.66, Ballymena, Co Antrim; m., Jill; 1 s.; 1 d. Educ. Ballymena Academy; Imperial College, London University.   Business Consultant, Shell International, 1988 - 90; Senior Associate, Coopers and Lybrand Management Consultants, 1990 - 94. Address: (b.) BBC Northern Ireland, Broadcasting House, Ormeau Avenue, Belfast BT2 8HQ; T.- 02890 338979.

Johnston,   William   James, FCA. Former Chairman, Northern Ireland House Building Council; b. 3.4.19; m., Joan Elizabeth Nancye Young; 2d. Educ.   Portora Royal School, Enniskillen. Professional Accountancy, 1937 - 44; Antrim County Council, 1944 - 68 (Deputy Secretary, 1951 - 68); Belfast City Council: Deputy Town Clerk, 1968 - 73; Town Clerk, 1973 - 79; Secretary, Association of Local Authorities of Northern Ireland, 1979 - 82; Director, Northern Ireland Advisory Board, Abbey National Building Society, 1982 - 89; Chairman, National House Building Council, 1989 - 95. Member: Northern Ireland Advisory Council, BBC, 1965 - 69; Council ICAI, 1967 - 71; Northern Ireland Tourist Board, 1980 - 85; Local Government Staff Committee, 1974 - 85; Public Service Training Council (formerly Public Service Training Committee), 1974 - 83; (Chairman, 1974 - 83); Arts Council of Northern Ireland, 1974 - 81; Chairman, Extra Care for Elderly People Ltd since March 1999.   Northern Ireland Representative, Duke of Edinburgh's Commonwealth Study Conference, Canada, 1962. Recreations: golf; live theatre. Address: 19a Windsor Avenue, Belfast, BT9 6EE; T.- 028 90 669373; 4 Riverside Close, Cushendall, BT44 0NR; T.- 028 217 72013. e-mail: bill@cushendall.freeserve.co.uk

Jones, Rev. Stewart Robert, BD, Dip Soc Stud, MTh, MA DPhil. Minister, Kilcooley Presbyterian Church since 1990; b. 8.9.57, Newry; m., Patricia; 3d.   Educ.   Newry High School; Queen's University,   Belfast;   University   of   Ulster. Ordained, McQuiston Memorial Church, 1983; Minister, 2nd Castlederg, 1984 - 90. Publications: Israel in the Carter Years, 1993. Recreations: church history; Irish history; Middle East history. Address: (h.) 9 Lord Warden's Meadow, Bangor, BT19 1YS; T.- 02891-460250.

Jordan, Deborah Mary, MA (Cantab). Barrister-at-Law; b. 21.2.69, Belfast; m., Jonathan Park. Educ. Strathearn School Belfast; Sidney Sussex College, Cambridge. Called to the Bar, England and Wales, 1992; Pupillage, 5 Essex Court, Temple, London, 1992 - 93; Tenant of 5 Essex Court, Temple, London, 1993 - 94; Called to the Bar, Northern Ireland, 1994. Recreations: sailing; golf; tennis.   Address: (b.) Bar Library, Royal Courts of Justice, Chichester Street, Belfast, BT1 3JP; T.- 02890 241523.

K

Kane, Gardiner. Member (North Antrim), Democratic Unionist Party, Northern Ireland Assembly, 1998-2003; b. 25.11.47, Ballymoney; m.; 2 s.; 3 d. Farmer; elected to Moyle Council, 1985 (Chairman, 1990 and 1996); President, Association of Local Authorities N.I., 1994-96; Member, Fire Authority for N.I., since 1993; Member, Local Government Staff Commission, since 1993; Member, N.I. Housing Council, since 1989; Member of the Assembly's Agriculture and Rural Development Committee, since 1998. Address: (b.) Parliament Buildings, Stormont, Belfast, BT4 3ST; T.- 02890 521108.

Kay, Professor Edward Albert (Ted), BSc, PhD. Principal Engineer, Halcrow Group, since 1992; Visiting Professor, Civil Engineering, Queen's University, Belfast; b., 14.5.43, Wolverhampton; m., Hilary Knott; 2s.; 1d. Educ. Methodist College, Belfast; Queen's University, Belfast. Site Engineer, Babtie, Shaw and Morton, 1969 - 70; Design Engineer, R Travers; Morgan and Partners, 1970 - 75; Materials Specialist, Halcrow International Partnership, Dubai, 1976 - 82; Project Engineer, Sir William Halcrow and Partners, Cardiff, 1982 - 84; Chairman, Materials and Building Maintenance Department, Travers Morgan, 1984 - 92. Publications: Assessment and Renovation of Concrete Structures, 1992. President, Concrete Society, 2000-01. Recreations: entries in biographical works of reference; walking; travel. Address: (b.) Halcrow Group Ltd, Vineyard House, 44 Brook Green, London, W6 7BY; T.- 0207-602 7282. e-mail: kayea@halcrow.com

Keegan, Geraldine Mary Marcelea, OBE, MEd, Dip Ed, FRSA. Headmistress, St Mary's College, Londonderry; b. Aghadowey. Educ. Thornhill College, Londonderry; St Mary's Teacher Training College, Belfast; Manchester University; University of Ulster. Teacher, Music, Maths and English, St Mary's Secondary School, Londonderry; Senior Lecturer, St Mary's Teacher Training College, Belfast; Deputy Director, Centre for Education Management. Pro-Chancellor, University of Ulster since 1997. Recreations: classical music; travel.

Keenan, Cormac, LLB. Principal, Keenan Solicitors since 1997; b. 28.1.69, Belfast. Educ. St Malachy's College; Queen's University, Belfast. Donnelly and Wall Solicitors: Apprentice, 1991 - 93; Assistant Solicitor, 1993 - 96. Address: (b.) 54 Knockbreda Road, Belfast; T.- 02890-493349.

Keith, William James, MSc, BEd. Headmaster, Belfast Boys' Model School, since 1990; b. 23.3.48, Belfast; m., Denise; 3 s. Educ. Royal Belfast Academical Institution; Queen's University of Belfast; Stranmillis College; University of Ulster. Posts at Belfast Boys' Model School, since 1971. Recreation: rugby. Address: (h.) 183 Lower Braniel Road, Belfast BT5 7NP; T.-01232 594826.

Kells, Ronald David, OBE, DL, BSc (Econ), FCIS, FIB. Former Group Chief Executive, Ulster Bank Ltd, 1994 - 98; b. 14.5.38. Educ. Bushmills Grammar School; Sullivan Upper School; Queen's University, Belfast. Joined Ulster Bank, 1964; retired, 1998. Addres: (b.)10 Upper Knockbreda Road, Belfast, BT6 9QA; T.- 028 90796518.

Kelly, Rt. Hon. Sir Basil, KT, PC, PC (NI), BA, LLB, Barrister-at-Law, QC. Retired Lord Justice of Appeal; b. 10.5.20, Co Monoghan, Ireland; m., Pamela Colthurst; 1d. Educ. Methodist College, Belfast; Trinity College, Dublin. Called to the Bar of Northern Ireland, 1945; Called to the English Bar (Middle Temple), 1970. Bencher 2001; Queen's Counsel, 1957. Member of Parliament, Northern Ireland Parliament (Mid-Down constituency), 1964 - 72; Attorney General for Northern Ireland, 1968 - 72; Judge, High Court of Justice in Northern Ireland, 1973 - 84; Lord Justice of Appeal, Supreme Court of Judicature (NI), 1984 - 95. Chairman, Council of Legal Education, 1989 - 93; Chairman, Judicial Studies Board, 1993 - 95; Member, Law Advisory Committee, British Council, 1982 - 92; United Kingdom representative, international association of Judges, 1980 - 95. Recreations: music; golf. Address: (b.) Royal Courts of Justice, Chichester Street, Belfast, BT1 3JF; T.- 01247-852635.

Kelly, David James, BSc (Hons), MRICS, MBEng. Chief District Building Control Officer, Moyle DC, since 1988; b. 20.3.52, Ballymoney; m., Heather; 2 d. Educ. Dalriada School, Ballymoney; University of Ulster. Jordanstown. Career History: W. & J. Taggart, Building and Civil Engineering Contractors; W. H. Stephens, Chartered Surveyors; Moyle District Council Building Control Dept., since 1977. Recreations: cycling; keep fit; walking. Address: (b.) Moyle District Council, Sheskburn House, 7 Mary Street, Ballycastle, Co. Antrim BT54 6QH. T.-028 207 62225. e-mail: davidkelly@moyle.council.org

Kelly, Elaine, LLB (Hons). Barrister-at-Law since 1992; b. 13.9.67, Belfast. Educ. St Dominic's High School, Belfast; Queen's University, Belfast. Recreations: hockey. Address: (b.) Bar Library, Chichester Street, Belfast; T.- 02890-241523.

Kelly, Gerald Edward, BA (Hons), MSc. Chief Executive, North and West Housing Ltd since 1980. Educ. University of Ulster; Heriot-Watt University, Edinburgh. Development Officer, Fold Housing Association, 1977 - 79. Address: (b.) North and West Housing Ltd, 18 Magazine Street Londonderry, BT48 6HH; T.- 02871 263819. e-mail: g.kelly@nwh-group.com

Kelly, Gerry. Member (North Belfast), Sinn Fein, Northern Ireland Assembly, since 1998. Educ. St

Peter's Secondary School, Belfast. Member, Sinn Fein talks team, Castle Buildings, 1996-97. Address: (b.) Parliament Buildings, Stormont, Belfast BT4 3ST; T.-01232 520700.

Kelly, John. Member (Mid Ulster), Sinn Fein, Northern Ireland Assembly, since 1998. Seaman; elected to Magherafelt District Council, 1997. Address: (b.) Parliament Buildings, Stormont, Belfast, BT4 3ST; T.- 028 90521633.

Kelly, Margaret Jeanette, MBE, JP, BA (Hons), PGCE. Director, Speedwell Trust since 1991; b. 29.3.53, Dungannon; m., Pearse; 1d. Educ. Dungannon High School for Girls; Manchester University; Didsbury College of Education. Teacher: Extra-Mural Board, Stockholm University (British Centre), 1975 - 76; John Bunyan Upper School, Bedford, 1976 - 78; Dungannon High School for Girls, 1978 - 86; Royal School, Dungannon, 1986 - 88; Benburb Youth and Resource Centre, 1989 - 91. Co-founder, Windmill Integrated Primary School; author of teaching materials. Recreations: family; walking; reading; theatre; tennis. Address: (b.) The Speedwell Trust, Parkanaur Forest Park, 57a Parkanaur Road, Castlecaulfield, Dungannon, Co Tyrone, BT70 3AA; T.- 028 8776 7392.

Kelly, Rosemary. Chair, Arts Council of Northern Ireland. Address: (b.) 77 Malone Road, Belfast BT9. T.-02890 385200.

Kelly, Sarah Ann, BA, DASE, MSc. Head Teacher, Thornhill College, Derry; b. 20.4.49, Tyrone; m., Des Kelly; 2s.; 1d. Educ. Loreto Convent, Omagh; Queen's University, Belfast. Teacher, Bearnageeha, Belfast; Vice-Principal, St Mary's College, Derry; Principal, St Joseph's Secondary School, Derry. Recreations: reading; walking. Address: (b.) Thornhill College, Culmore Road, Derry BT48 8JF. T.-02871 355800.

Kelly, Tom, BSc (Hons), MInstD, PRCA, MICC. Managing Director, Drury Communications (NI) Ltd since 1994; b. 17.8.63; m., Patricia Jackson. Educ. Abbey Grammar School, Newry; University of Ulster at Jordanstown. Parliamentary Assistant to Seamus Mallon MP, 1986 - 88; Executive Director, Social Democratic and Labour Party, 1988 - 90; Mentor Business Consultancy, 1990 - 94. Director, Drury Communications Ltd, Republic of Ireland since 1998; Director, Newry Credit Union Ltd since 1987; Chairman, Newry Town Centre Partnership since 1998. Former Vice-Chairman, Social and Democratic Labour Party, 1988 - 90; Associate, National Democratic Institute for International Affairs, Washington DC. Recreations: golf; gaelic football; politics. Address: (b.) DCL Public Relations (N) Ltd, 2 Donegall Square East, Belfast BT1 5HB. T.-02890 339949. e-mail: tom@dclmedia.com

Kennedy, Dr. Dennis, BA, PhD. Political Commentator; Lecturer, Institute of European Studies, Queen's University of Belfast, 1993-2001; President, Irish Association for Cultural, Economic and Social Relations, 1999-2000; b. 3.8.36, Lisburn; m., Katherine Hickey; 2 s.; 1 d. Educ. Wallace High School; Queen's University of Belfast; Trinity College, Dublin. Journalist, Belfast Telegraph, 1959 - 66; News Editor, LWF Broadcasting Service, Addis Ababa, Ethiopia, 1966 - 68; Deputy Editor, Irish Times, 1968 - 85; European Commission Representative, Northern Ireland, 1985 - 91. Publications: The Widening Gulf – Northern Attitudes to the Independent Irish State, 1919-1949, 1988; Living With The European Union – The Northern Ireland Experience, 1999. Address: (h.) 3 Mornington, Belfast BT7 3JS; T.-028 90641729. e-mail: dennis.kennedy1@ntlworld.com

Kennedy, Gary George, B Ed, DASE. Principal Waringstown Primary School since 1991; b. 26.9.54, Bessbrook, Co Armagh; m., Margaret Gray; 1s.; 3d. Educ. Newry High School; Stranmillis College; Queen's University, Belfast. Teacher, Sir Robert Hart Memorial Primary School, Portadown, 1977 - 83; Principal, Annaghmore Primary School, Portadown, 1983 - 91. Fellow, Royal College of Preceptors since 1991. Past Chairman, Northern Ireland Schools' Football Association; Vice Chairman, Schools' Association Football International Board (SAFIB). Publications: An Examination of the Nature and Fortunes of Craigmore National School, 1872 - 1952, 1983. Recreations: being with my family; watching Linfield FC; hill walking. Address: (b.) Waringstown Primary School, 1 Banbridge Road, Waringstown, Craigavon, County Armagh, BT66 7QH; T.-028 38881367. gkennedy@waringstown.waringstown.ni.sch.uk

Kennedy, Hazel Kathleen Elizabeth, LLB (Hons). Solicitor since 1984; b. 27.6.60. Educ. Coleraine High School; Queens University, Belfast. Address: (b.) 111 Dunboe Road, Macosquin, Coleraine; BT51 4JS; T.- 028 703 56346.

Kennedy, Rev. Hugh P, KM, BA, STB, MTh, DD. Parish Priest, Sacred Heart Parish, Belfast since 1997. Educ. St Malachy's College, Belfast; Queen's University, Belfast; Pontifical Gregorian University, Rome; Institut Catholique de Paris; St Patrick's College, Maynooth, Co Kildare, Ireland. Ordained Priest, Irish College, Rome, 1981; Curate:Castlewelan, 1981 - 82; Glenravel, 1982 - 85; Post graduate studies, Paris, 1985 - 88; Curate, St Paul's, Falls Road, Belfast, 1988 - 90; Doctoral Studies, Maynooth, 1990 - 94; Curate, St Bernadette's Parish, Belfast, 1994 - 97. Member, Irish Commission for Liturgy since 1988; Chairman, Ulster Historic Churches Trust; Chief Chaplain, Irish Association, Sovereign Order of Malta. Publications: articles in theological periodicals in Ireland and Germany. Recreations: opera; choral music; architectural studies; boating. Address: (b.) Sacred Heart Presbytery, 1a Glenview Street, Belfast, BT14 7DP; T.- 02890 351851.

Kennedy, John, JP. Former Secretary of the Association of Justices of the Peace (NI); b, 22.4.49; m., Karin Greig; 2s.; 1d. Educ. Hopefield School, Newtownabbey. Trustee and Honorary Treasurer, First Newtownabbey Linfield Supporters Club. Recreations: watching soccer, rugby; playing golf. Address: (h.) Princes Crescent, Newtownabbey BT37 0BA.

Kennedy, Professor Liam, DPhil. Professor, Economic and Social History, Queen's University, Belfast since 1998; b. 10.8.46, Co Tipperary, Ireland; div., 1d. Educ. Cistercian College, Roscrea; University College, Cork; University of York. Lecturer, Queen's University, Belfast, 1981 - 93; Reader in Economic and Social History, Queen's University, Belfast, 1993 - 98. Publications: The Modern Industrialisation of Ireland, 1989; Colonialism, Religion and Nationalism, 1996. Secretary, Peace Train; Founder Member, Northern Ireland Human Rights Alert. Recreations: reading; talking; theatre. Address: (h.) 39 Rugby Road, Belfast, BT7; T.-028-90-322067.

Kennedy, Michael Gerald, BA, DASE, BPhil, MSc. School Principal, St Colman's High School, Strabane since 1994; b. 2.12.45, Lifford, Co Donegal; m., Anne Nelis; 1s.; 2d. Educ. St Columb's College, Derry; De La Salle College of Education, Manchester. Assistant Teacher, St Patrick's Secondary School, Dungannon, 1967 - 68; Head of PE, St Colman's Secondary School, Strabane, 1968 - 72; Chifubu Secondary School, Zambia, 1972 - 74; Head of Maths, St Colman's High School, 1974 - 88; Organiser, Strabane Teachers' Centre, Western Education and Library Board, 1988 - 90; Assistant Education Officer, Advisory Support Services, Western Education and Library Board, 1990 - 94. Founder Member, Strabane United '68 FC, 1968-72; Founder Member, Zenith Basketball Club, 1968-72; Soccer Coach to Zambia Schoolboy International Team, 1973 - 74; Soccer Coach, Tyrone Youth Team, 1975 - 76. Treasurer, Strabane History Society, 1989-2003; Director: Strabane Training Services, Strabane Enterprise Agency; Chairman, NI Secondary Committee NAHT. Publications: By the Banks of the Mourne, A History of Strabane, 1996; Strabane Through The Millennium, An Illustrated Chronology 1179-2000, 2001; Half Hanged McNaughten (with D Canning), 1992; co-editor, "Fair River Valley" by Jim Bradley et al., 2000. Recreations: golf; travel; reading; local history. Address: (b.) St Colman's High School, 35 Melmount Road, Strabane BT82 9EF. T.-028 71 382562.

Kennedy, Thomas Daniel (Danny). Member (Newry and Armagh), Ulster Unionist Party, Northern Ireland Assembly since 1998; Chairman, Education Committee, Northern Ireland Assembly; Ulster Unionist District Councillor, Newry and Mourne District Council since 1985; b. 6.7.59, Newry, Co Down; m., Karen Susan; 2s.; 1d. Educ. Newry High School. Employed by British Telecom, Northern Ireland, 1978 - 98. Chairman, Newry and Mourne District Council, 1994 - 95; Member, Ulster Unionist Party since 1974: Contested Newry and Armagh seat, General Election, 1997. Member, Northern Ireland Tourist Board, 1996 - 98; Sabbath School Superintendent; Clerk of Session, Bessbrook Presbyterian Church. Recreations: family; church activities; reading; sport (purely spectating). Address: (b) Advice Centre, 107 Main Street, Markethill, Co. Antrim BT60 1PH. T.-028 3755 2831; Fax: 028 3755 2832.
e-mail: cllrdanny.kennedy@btinternet.com

Kennedy, Tony, BSc, MSc. Chief Executive, Co-operation Ireland since 1992; b. 19.4.48, Lisburn; m., Ann Godfrey; 1s.; 2d. Educ. Royal Belfast Academical Institution; Loughborough University; University of Ulster. Northern Ireland Housing Executive: Belfast Region Information Officer, 1972 - 74; Area Manager, North Belfast, 1974 - 79; Regional Controller, North West, 1979 - 83; Chief Housing Officer, Wakefield Metropolitan District Council, 1983 - 92. Deputy Director, John Hewitt International Summer School; Deputy Chair, Ulidia Housing Association. Recreations: cycling; reading; gardening. Address: (b.) 7 Botanic Avenue, Belfast, BT7 1JG; T.-01232-321462.
e-mail: tkennedy@cooperationireland.org

Kennedy, Rev. William Alistair, MA. Minister, Trinity Presbyterian Church, Bangor since 1993; b. 20.7.43, Downpatrick, Co Down; m., Anna May Currie; 2d. Educ. Belfast High School; Queen's University, Belfast; Assembly's College, Belfast. Assistant Minister, Wellington Presbyterian Church, Ballymena, 1969 - 73; Minister, Rasharkin Presbyterian Church, 1973 - 1980; Minister, St Andrews Presbyterian Church, Belfast, 1980 - 93. Co convener, Coleraine Assembly Committee, 1988 - 92; Co-convener, Presbyterian Church of Ireland's, Strategy for Mission Committee, 1991 - 98; Convener, PCI Board of Communications, since 2002; Member, Central Religious Advisory Committee, 1993 - 97; Member, UK Board, Latin Link with strong interest in South America.. Regular contributor, BBC Northern Ireland, Thought For The Day. Recreations: Irish studies; history; environment, walking. Address: (h.) Trinity Manse, 211 Gransha Road, Bangor, Co Down, BT19 7PU; T.-028 9127 4860.

Kernan, Patrick, BA, Dip Ed. Vice-Principal, Our Lady and St Patrick's College, Knock since 1985; b. 11.4.44, Co Armagh; m., Sheelagh Kernan; 4s.; 1d. Educ. St Patrick's College, Armagh; Queen's University, Belfast. Teacher, St Thomas' Intermediate School, Belfast, 1966 - 68; Appointed, St Patrick's College, Knock, 1968: Vice-Principal, 1977 - 85. Member, various Irish language organisations including Lecale Gaelic Society. Recreations: films; music; languages; French impressionism. Address: (h.) 15 Knockchree Road, Downpatrick, Co Down, BT30 6RP; T.- 01396-613709.

Kernohan, Professor George, BSc, PhD. Professor, Health Research, University of Ulster; b. 24.12.58, Carrickfergus; m., Anne Munn; 3s.; 2d. Educ. Belfast High; Ulster Polytechnic; Queen's University, Belfast. 20 years wide ranging experience in health research. Fellow, Royal Academy of Medicine, Ireland; Teacher, evidence-based practice; Chartered Physicist; Former Chairman, UNITE Solutions Ltd. Internet Services Provider. Address: (b.) School of Health Sciences; University of Ulster, Newtownabbey, BT37 0QB. T.-02890-366532.
e-mail: wg.kernohan@ulster.ac.uk
http://www.ulster.ac.uk/staff/wg.kernohan.html

Kernohan, Stephen. Editor, East Antrim Gazette Series since 1997; b. 11.3.61, Londonderry; m., Janette; 2d. Educ. Ballymena Academy. Trainee Journalist, Ballymena Guardian, 1978 - 80; Senior Journalist, Ballymena Observer, 1980 - 84; Deputy Editor, Ballymena Times, 1984 - 97. Recreations: armchair sport; gardening. Address: (b.) Carrickfergus Advertiser, 31a High Street, Carrickfergus, BT38 7AN; T.- 01960-363651.

Kerr, Christopher, BA, MSc, MIMgt, MIFireE. Fire Brigade Area Commander for Belfast, since 2003; b. 10.12.64, Belfast; m., Kathryn; 2 s. Educ. Sullivan Upper School, Holywood; University of Ulster at Jordanstown. Northern Ireland Fire Brigade: Operational Fire Officer, Belfast, 1985-93; District Commander, Co. Tyrone, 1993-96; returned to Belfast in 1996 and moved to headquarters in 1999 as Operations Officer for the Brigade. Lectured Internationally on Disaster Management and Planning as part of the European Exchange of Experts Programme, 2001; Area Commander for Greater Belfast, since 2003; Past President of Institution of Fire Engineers (Northern Ireland); Graduate of The Federal Executive Institute, Charlottesville, Virginia, USA, 2002. Recreations: fishing; hill walking; reading; classical music. Address: (b.) Fire Brigade Eastern Command, Bankmore Street, Belfast BT7 1AQ. T.-028 90 310360.

Kerr, Rev. David James, BA, MMin Theol. President, Churches Together in Britain and Ireland, since 2002; Superintendent, Belfast Central Mission, 1987-2003; b. 28.5.37, Belfast; m., Eileen Samson; 4s.; 1d. Educ. Sullivan Upper Grammar School; Edgehill Theological College; Queen's University, Belfast; University of Sheffield. Minister: Rathcoole, Newtown Abbey, 1964 - 69; Limerick Methodist Church, 1969 - 75; Ballyholme Bangor Methodist Church, 1975 - 81; Knockbreda Belfast Methodist Church, 1981 - 87; President, Methodist Church in Ireland, 1998 - 99. Member, BBC Northern Ireland Religious Affairs advisory Panel; Chairman, Inter Churches Affairs Board, Irish Council of Churches; Trustee, Methodist Church in Ireland since 1989; Chairman, Belfast District of Methodist Church, 1992 - 98. Publications; contributor to Esteem; essays in honour of Eric Gallagher; contributor to Belfast: Faith in the City; contributor to Sources:

Letters from Irish People on Sustenance for the Soul. Recreations: hill walking; music; reading. Address: (h.) 8 Wynard Park, Belfast BT5 6NS. T.-02890 229883.

Kerr, Dr. Edwin, CBE, BSc, PhD, FIMA, FBCS. Chairman, Vocational and Academic Board, Institute of Health Care Developments, 1996-2000; b. 1.7.26; m., Gertrude Elizabeth Turbitt; 1s.; 2d. Educ. Royal Belfast Academical Institution; Queen's University, Belfast. Assistant Lecturer, Mathematics, Queen's University, Belfast, 1948 - 52; Lecturer, Mathematics, Birmingham College of Technology (now University of Aston in Birmingham), 1952 - 55; Lecturer, Mathematics, Manchester College of Science and Technology (now UMIST), 1956 - 58; Head, Department of Mathematics, Royal College of Advanced Technology, Salford (now University of Salford), 1958 - 66; Principal, Paisley College of Technology, 1966 - 72; Chief Officer CNAA, 1972 - 86; Chairman and Chief Executive, Examination Board for Financial Planning, 1987 - 89; Chief Executive, College for Financial Planning, 1988 - 96. Member: Advisory Committee on Supply and Training of Teachers, 1973 - 78; Advisory Committee on the Supply and Education of Teachers, 1980 - 85; Board for Local Authority Higher Education, 1982 - 85; Board for Public Sector Higher Education, 1985 - 86; Member and Vice-Chairman, Continuing Education Standing Committee, 1985 - 88. President: Society for Research into Higher Education, 1974 - 77; The Mathematical Association, 1976 - 77. Hon. FCP, 1984; Hon. Fellow: Coventry Lancaster, Newcastle-upon-Tyne, Portsmouth and Sheffield Polytechnics, 1986; Huddersfield Polytechnic and Paisley College of Technology, 1987; Goldsmiths' College, University of London, 1991; DUniv: Open University, 1977; Paisley, 1993; Hon DSc, Ulster, 1986; Hon. DEd CNAA, 1989. Publications: An Introduction to Numerical Methods (with R Butler), 1962; numerous mathematical and educational papers. Recreations: gardening. Address: (h.) 59 Craigdarragh Road, Helen's Bay, Co Down, BT19 1UB; T.- 028 9185 2748.

Khosraviani, Kourosh, MD, FRCS Ed (Gen Surg), FRCSI. Senior Lecturer, Queen's University Belfast, Consultant Colorectal Surgeon, since 2001; b. 21.11.65, Tehran, Iran. Educ. Methodist College, Belfast; Queen's University of Belfast. Completion of Higher Professional Training in Northern Ireland; spent one year at St. Marks Hospital, London; International Centre for Management of Colorectal Disorders. Address: (b.) Department of Surgery, Institute of Clinical Science, Royal Group of Hospitals, Grosvenor Road, Belfast BT12 6BJ. T.-90240503.

Kilbane, Dr. Paula, CBE, MB, Msc, FRCP, FFPH. Chief Executive, Eastern Health and Social Services Board since 1995; b. 1950, Belfast; m., James Kilbane, 1s.; 1d. Educ. St Louis School,

Kilkeel; Sion Hill School, Dublin; Trinity College Dublin; Queen's University, Belfast. Junior Doctor, Royal Victoria Hospital, 1973 - 76; Post graduate Training, London, 1976 - 80; Consultant in Public Health, NETRHA/LSTHM, 1980 - 86; Consultant, Eastern Health and Social Services Board, Belfast, 1986 - 90; Director, Public Health; Southern Health and Social Services Board, 1990 - 93; Chief Executive, Southern Health and Social Services Board, 1993 - 95. Member: Institute of Directors; Society of Social Medicine; Democratic Dialogue. Publications: various medical papers; Information on Aids/HIV. Recreations: France; food; fitness. Address: (b) Eastern Health and Social Services Board, 12-22 Linenhall Street, Belfast, BT2 8BS; T.- 028 90 321313 Ext. 2526.

Kilclooney, Rt. Hon. The Lord Kilclooney of Armagh (John David Taylor). Deputy Leader, Ulster Unionist Party; MP for Strangford, Westminster, 1983-2001; Member (Strangford), Ulster Unionist Party, Northern Ireland Assembly since 1998; House of Lords, since 2001; b. 24.12.37, Armagh City; m., Mary Frances Todd; 1s.; 5d. Educ. The Royal School, Armagh; Queen's University, Belfast. MP for Northern Ireland, Stormont, 1965 - 73 (Cabinet Minister, Home Affairs, Northern Ireland, 1970 - 72); Member, Northern Ireland Assembly; Member, Northern Ireland Constitutional Convention; Member, Northern Ireland Assembly; Member, European Parliament, 1979 - 89; Member, Assembly of the Council of Europe since 1997; Member, Northern Ireland Forum, 1996-97; Member, NI Assembly, since 1998. Privy Counsellor since 1970. Publications: Northern Ireland – The Economic Facts (co-author). Recreations: horticulture; travel; antiques. Address: (h.) Mullinure; Armagh City; BT61 9EZ; T.- 01861-522409.

Kilmurray, Avila, MA. Director, Community Foundation for Northern Ireland, since 1994; b. 21.7.52, Dublin; m., Brian Gormally; 1 s.; 2 d. Educ. Roslyn Park School, Sandymount, Dublin; University College Dublin; Australian National University. Community Worker, Derry, 1974 - 77; adult education, Derry, 1977 - 80; Community Development, Northern Ireland Council for Voluntary Action, 1980 - 85; Co-ordinator, Rural Action Project, 1985 - 90; Women's Officer, ATGWU, 1990 - 94. Trustee, Community Development Foundation; Recreations: reading; writing; history. Address: (b.) Citylink Business Park, Albert Street, Belfast BT12 4HB. T.-028-90245927.

Kinahan, Dr. Kathleen, MBE, MB, BS, JP. Retired Doctor; b. 18.12.14, Crumlin; m., Charles (dec.); 3s. Educ. Downe House, Newbury; London School of Medicine. Children's Ward, Singapore, 1946; Children's Ward, Malacca, Malaya, 1947. Church of Ireland Adoption Committee; Member, Lay Panel, Juvenile Courts; Chairman, Association of Prison Visitors;

Chairman, NIACRO. Recreations; gardening; arts and crafts. Address: (h.) 53 Broadacres, Templepatrick, Ballyclare, Co Antrim, BT39 0AY; T.- 028 9443 2379.

Kincade, Dr. James, CBE, MA, BLitt, PhD, Hon LLD. Former Principal, Methodist College, Belfast; b. 4.1.25, Londonderry; m., Elizabeth Fay Piggot; 1s.; 1d. Educ. Foyle College, Londonderry; Magee University College; Trinity College, Dublin; Oriel College, Oxford; University of Edinburgh. Royal Air Force, 1943 - 47; Master, Merchiston Castle School, Edinburgh, 1952 - 61; Visiting Professor of Philosophy, University of Indiana, USA, 1959; Headmaster, Royal School, Dungannon, 1961 - 74; Principal, Methodist College, Belfast, 1974 - 88; Retired, 1988. National Governor, BBC Northern Ireland, 1985 - 91; Member, Senate, Queen's University, Belfast, 1978 - 98; Director Design Council, NI, 1990 - 93 (Design Council UK, 1993 - 95). Recreations: gardening; golf. Address: (h.) Greenfields, 10a Harry's Road, Hillsborough, Co Down, BT26 6HJ; T.- 02892-683865.

King, Professor David John, MD, FRCPsych, FRCP(I), DPM. Professor of Clinical Psychopharmacology, Queen's University of Belfast, since 1995 (Assistant Head, School of Medicine (Research), since 1998); Consultant Psychiatrist, Holywell Hospital, Antrim, since 1972; Executive Medical Director, Homefirst Community Health and Social Services Trust, 1996-99; b. 25.11.40, Liverpool; m., Anne; 2 s. Educ. Larne Grammar School; Queen's University of Belfast. Senior House Officer/Registrar in Psychiatry, Belfast and University of Sheffield, 1965 - 69; Andy Darlington Memorial Fellow, Mental Health Research Fund, 1969 - 72; Assistant Professor of Psychiatry, Dalhousie University, Nova Scotia, 1973 - 75; Queen's University of Belfast: Senior Lecturer, Department of Therapeutics and Pharmacology, 1975 - 86, Reader in Neuropharmacology, 1986 - 95. President, Ulster Neuropsychiatric Society, 1996 - 98; Member of Council of British Association for Psychopharmacology, 1992-96; Chair of DHSSPS R & D Office Neuroscience Recognised Research Group, since 2001; Royal Irish Academy Award of Merit and Silver Medal in Pharmacology and Toxicology, 2001. Publications: Seminars in Clinical Psychopharmacology (Editor); over 90 scientific publications. Recreations: swimming; sailing; music; gardening. Address: (b.) Department of Therapeutics and Pharmacology, Whitla Medical Building, 97 Lisburn Road, Belfast BT9 7BL; T.-028 9033 5771. e-mail: d.king@qub.ac.uk

King, Steven Alistair William, BA (Hons). Political Adviser, The Rt. Hon. David Trimble, MP, since 1999; Adviser to Sir John Gorman since 1998; Member, Senate, Queen's University of Belfast; Special Adviser, Right Hon. John D Taylor, MP, 1994-99; b. 10.11.72, Chester. Educ. The Leas School; The Grange School; Oxford

University; Queen's University, Belfast; University of Ulster. Journalist since 1994, Contributor; The Irish Times; The Belfast Telegraph. Ulster Unionist Talks Support Team, 1996 - 98; Secretary, The Irish Association, 1995-2002; Member Committee: NIGRA. Recreations: theatre; Irish/British history; smoking. Address: (h.) 429 Holywood Road, Belfast BT4 2LN. T.-02890 765500.

Kingston, Professor Arthur Edward, BSc, PhD, FRAS, FInstP MRIA, MIAA. Professor of Theoretical Physics, Queen's University, Belfast since 1983; Professor Emeritus, since 2000; b. 18.2.36, Armagh; m., Rachel Helen, McCann; 1s.; 1d. Educ. Armagh Royal School; Queen's University, Belfast. Lecturer, University of Liverpool, 1961 - 63; Research Fellow, University of Colorado, USA, 1963 - 64; Queen's University, Belfast: Lecturer, 1964 - 68; Senior Lecturer, 1968 - 71; Reader, 1971 - 83; Professor, Theoretical Physics since 1983; Dean, Faculty of Science, 1989 - 93; Director, School of Mathematics and Physics, 1990 - 93; Provost of Science and Agriculture; Queen's University, Belfast, 1993 - 98, Emeritus Professor, since 2000. Publications: over 260 scientific papers. Member, Royal Irish Academy; Member, International Academy of Astronautics. NASA Public Service Award for work on Spacelab 2 Satellite. Recreations: reading; walking; theatre. Address: (b.) School of Mathematics and Physics, Bates Building, Queen's University, Belfast, BT7 1NN; T.- 02890-273175.

Kirk, Alan Norman Samuel, BA (Hons). Partner, Joseph Lockhart and Son, Solicitor; b. 30.9.48, Belfast; m., Rosie; 2d. Educ. Portora Royal School; Trinity College, Dublin. Past captain, Malone Golf Club; Governor, Hunterhouse College. Recreations: golf; travel; family. Address: (b.) 24 Bachelors Walk, Lisburn, BT28 1XJ; T.- 028-9266-3225.

Kirkpatrick, Prof. Laurence Samuel, BA, BD, MTh, PhD. Professor of Ecclesiastical History, Union Theological College and Queen's University Belfast, since 1996; Assistant Dean, Institute of Theology, Queen's University Belfast, since 2001; b. 10.9.56, Belfast; m., Pamela; 2 s.; 1 d. Educ. Methodist College, Belfast; The Queen's University Belfast; Glasgow University. Minister of Muckamore, Presbyterian Church, 1984-96; Presbyterian Chaplain in Muckamore Abbey Hospital, since 1985. Council Member, Presbyterian Historical Society. Recreations: squash; golf; gardening. Address: (b.) Union Theological College, 108 Botanic Avenue, Belfast BT7 1JT. T.-028 90205080.

Kirk-Smith, Michael David, BSc (Hons) Bio Phys, PNSc, PhD (Psych), MBA, ACCA Dip, CPsychol, AFBPS. Reader in Behavioural and Health Sciences, University of Ulster, since 1992; Director of Responsa Ltd, since 2001; Research Scientist; b. 26.4.51, Belfast. Educ. Methodist College, Belfast; Portora Royal School,

Enniskillen; King's College, London; University of Birmingham. Currently Reader in the Institute of Postgraduate Medicine and Health, University of Ulster; previously Senior Lecturer, University of Sheffield, 1989-92; Manager of the Behavioural Sciences Program, Unilever Research, Birkenhead, 1986-89; Corporate Strategist, Cambridge Life Sciences, Cambridge Science Park, 1982-86; Biotechnology Consultant, PA Centre for Advanced Study, Cambridge, 1981; Research Fellow in Molecular Sciences and Psychology, University of Warwick, 1978-81. British Psychological Society; papers in learned journals; referee to learned journals and ESRC. Recreations: running; sailing; music. Address: (b.) University of Ulster, Newtownabbey BT37 0QB. T.-02890 280669. e-mail: mks@ulst.ac.uk

Knox, Professor Colin Gerard, BA, MSc, PhD. Professor, Public Policy, University of Ulster since 1995; b. 2.7.53, Lurgan, Co Armagh; m., Veronica Knox; 1s. 1d. Educ. St Patrick's College, Armagh; University of Ulster; University of Loughborough; Queen's University, Belfast. Administrative Trainee, Cardiff City Council, 1972 - 74; Senior Local Government Officer, Cardiff City Council/Dungannon District Council, 1974 - 84; Lecturer, Public Policy, University of Ulster, 1984 - 91; Senior Lecturer/Reader, 1991 - 95. Recreations: running; swimming; reading. Address: (b.) School of Policy Studies, University of Ulster, Jordanstown BT37 0QB. T.-028 90 366378.

Knox, David Alan, BA (Hons), MA, DipAS Ed, Grad CertEd. Headmaster, Ballyclare High School (Grammar), since 2000; b. 11.12.52, Belfast; m., Patricia Kennedy; 2 d. Educ. Bangor Grammar; University of Ulster. Assistant Teacher, Cambridge House Boys' Grammar School, 1975; Head of English Department, 1978; Acting Vice Principal, 1993; Senior Teacher, 1995; Vice Principal, Victoria College, Belfast, 1997. Recreations: theatre; musical concerts; reading; travel. Address: (b.) 31 Rashee Road, Ballyclare, Co. Antrim BT39 9HJ. T.-028 9332 2244.

Kula, Dr. Erhun BSc, MSc, PhD. Writer and Economist; Senior Lecturer, University of Ulster since 1987; Advisor to the Economic and Social Research Council in the creation of multimillion pound research centres in the UK; b. 1945, Istanbul; m., Karen Kula; 1s.; 1d. Educ. Sultanahmet Lycee of Commerce, Istanbul; Marmara University; University of Wales; University of Leicester. Lecturer: University College of Swansea, 1980 - 82; New University of Ulster, 1982 - 87; Visiting Professor, University of New Mexico, 1992; Visiting Professor, Environmental Economics, University of Bosphorous, 1995; Tutor and Examiner, Centre for Financial and Management Studies, University of London since 1995; External examiner, University of Hong Kong. Publications: 8 books and over 50 scientific papers mostly in international journals. Recreations: cycling; reading.

Kumar, M. Satish, PhD (JNU), MPhil Geog (JNU), MA, BA Econ (NEHU). Lecturer, Human Geography, Queen's University Belfast, since 2000; b. 26.9.59, Shillong, Meghalaya, India; 1 s. Educ. St. Edmund's School, Shillong, India. Commonwealth Fellow, Department of Geography, University of Cambridge, 1997-98, Visiting Fellow, Fitzwilliam College, 1998-99, Affiliated Lecturer, Dept. of Geography and Dept. of Land Economy, 1998-99; Assistant Professor, Jawaharlal Nehru University, 1991-2000, Associate Professor, Human Geography, 2000-03. SGI Merit Award for Peace, Culture and Education from Japan for contributions to community and youth development, 1992; Distinguished Leadership Award, American Biographical Institute, 1996; India-European Union Global Peace and Friendship Award, 2003; Boovigyan (Earth Scientist) Indian National Leadership Award, 2002. Recent publications: contributions to books and journals in the UK and India including The Indian Journal of Labour Economics; Local Environment. Recreations: photography; trekking; films; music. Address: School of Geography, Queen's University Belfast, Belfast BT7 1NN. T.-028 9027 3479.

Kyle, Maree, Dip HS, ACIH. Chief Executive, Larne and District Housing Association Ltd since 1993; b. 28.1.48, Belfast; m., James Kyle; 1s.; 2d. Educ. Larne High School; University of Ulster. Recreations: golf; reading; gardening. Address: (b.) 93 Main Street, Larne, BT40 1HJ; T.- 028 2827 6431.

L

Lacey, Lewis John, BA (Hons), Dip Ed, DASE, MEd. Headmaster, Strabane Grammar School since 1996; b. 14.9.49, Belfast; m., Irene; 1s.; 2d. Educ. Wellington College, Belfast; University of Ulster; Queen's University, Belfast. Head of History, Antrim Grammar School, 1980- 89; Vice-Principal, Foyle and Londonderry College, 1989 - 95; Senior Vice-Principal, Foyle and Londonderry College, 1995 - 96. Recreations: fly fishing; hill walking; cooking; anything historical. Address: (b.) 4 Liskey Road, Strabane, BT82 8NW; T.- 02871 382319.

Laird, The Lord Laird of Artigarvan. Chairman, John Laird Group of Communication Companies; Member, House of Lords, since 1999; b. 23.4.44, Belfast; m., Caroline Ethel; 1s.; 1d. Educ. Royal Belfast Academical Institution. Bank Official, 1963 - 67; Bank Inspector, 1967 - 68; Computer Programmer, 1968 - 73; Northern Ireland MP, (St Annes), 1970 - 73; Member, Northern Ireland Assembly, 1973 - 75; Member, Northern Ireland Convention, 1975 - 76; Founded, John Laird Public Relations, 1976. Chairman, Northern Ireland Branch, Institute of Public Relations, 1989 - 92; Fellow, Institute of Public Relations since 1992; Visiting Professor, Public Relations, 1993; Currently: Governor, Royal Belfast Academical Institution; Council Member, Ulster Society; President, European Movement. Chairman of Ulster Scots Agency. Filmed and Published Videos: Trolleybus Days in Belfast; Swan Song of Steam in Ulster; Twilight of Steam in Ulster; Waterloo Sunset; Rails in the Isle of Wight. Recreations: interest in history of Northern Ireland, Europe and railways; cricket; rugby; politics Address: (b.) John Laird Group, 104 Holywood Road, Belfast, BT4 1NU; T.- 028 90471282; (h.) 43 Earlswood Road, Belfast, BT4 3EA.

Lambkin, Brian Kevin, MA (Cantab), Dip Ed. MA, DPhil. Director, Centre for Migration Studies at the Ulster American Folk Park; b. 18.4.53, North Shields; m., Dr. M K Muhr; 2s.; 1d. Educ. The John Fisher School, Purley; Queens' College, Cambridge. Rathmore Grammar School, 1977 - 81; Lagan College, 1981 - 97: Principal, 1993 - 97. Publications: Interpreting Northern Ireland After The Conflict, 1996. Recreations: Northumbrian small pipes. Address: (b.) Centre for Migration Studies at the Ulster American Folk Park, Omagh, BT78 5QY; T.- 028 82 256315.

Langhammer, Mark Francis, BA DipSocSc, Cert Ed, MIMgt. Regional Manager Ufi (learndirect); Director, Dunanney Centre; b. 10.3.60, Belfast; m., Margaret; 1d.; 1s. Educ. Edinburgh University; Queen's University Belfast. Member: Irish Labour Party, GMBATU; Labour Councillor, Newtownabbey Borough Council, since 1993; Chair: Newtownabbey Economic Development Unit, since 1995, Northern Ireland Association of Citizens Advice Bureaux, 1994 - 98, Playboard, Northern Ireland, 1998-99; Member, North East Education and Library Board, since 2000. Address: (h.) 477 Shore Road, Coastguard Row, Whiteabbey, Co Antrim BT37 0SP; T.- 028 9086 3609.
e-mail: mlanghammer@newtownabbey.gov.uk

Lappin, Professor Terence Robert James, MSc, PhD, FRCPath, FRSC. Professor, Haematology, Queen's University, Belfast; b. 20.6.44, Belfast; m., Frances Gillian Arnott; 2s.; 1d. Educ. Friends' School, Lisburn; Queen's University, Belfast. Biochemist, Royal Victoria Hospital, Belfast, 1966 - 83; Top Grade Scientist, 1983 - 97: Queen's University, Belfast: Hon. Lecturer, 1988, Hon. Reader, 1991, Chair of Haematology, 1997, Deputy Director, Cancer Research Centre, 1999; Scientific Secretary, British Society for Haematology, 2003; Wellcome Research Travel Grant, Visiting Scientist, University of Chicago, 1982. Member: Association, Clinical Biochemists; Royal Society of Chemistry; British Society for Haematology; International Society for Experimental Hematology; Ulster Society of Pathologists; American Society of Hematology; European Haematology Association; Irish Haematology Association; American Society for the Advancement of Science; Editorial Board, Experimental Haematology, 1994 - 96. Publications: Volume 717, Annals of the New York Academy of Sciences (with I N Rich, joint eds.); 90 scientific papers. Recreations: sporting activities especially hockey; reading; music; travel. Address: (b.) Department of Haematology, Queen's University of Belfast, Tower Block, Belfast City Hospital, Lisburn Road, Belfast BT9 7AB; T.- 02890-263718.
e-mail: t.lappin@qub.ac.uk

Larkin, Dr. Michael James, BSc, PhD. Senior Lecturer in Bacteriology; Queen's University, Belfast since 1995; b. 26.3.55, Coventry; m., Sheila Patrick; 2d. Educ. Ullathorne Grammar School, Coventry; University of Cardiff. Lecturer, Queen's University, Belfast; Chairman, Questor Centre, Queen's University, Belfast since 1980. Publications: over 60 scientific papers articles and reviews; Immunological and Molecular Aspects of Bacterial Patnogenesis (co-author), 1995. Address: (b.) The Questor Centre, Queen's University of Belfast, Belfast BT9 5AG; T.- 02890-335577.

Laverty, John. NCTJ. Sports Editor, Belfast Telegraph since 1996; b. 12.11.62, Co Antrim. Educ. St Louis Grammar School, Ballymena; Belfast College of Business Studies. News Reporter, Ballymena Times, 1983 - 86; Belfast Telegraph: News Reporter, 1986 - 87; Cricket/Junior Football Correspondent, 1987 - 88; Football Correspondent, 1988 - 91; Chief Football Writer, 1991 - 96. Chairman, Northern Ireland Football Writers' Aassociation. Highly Commended, Northern Ireland Sports Journalist of the Year, 1993 and 1996. Recreations: fast cars;

table quiz; legal fiction. Address: (b.) Belfast Telegraph, 122 Royal Avenue, Belfast, BT1 1EB; T.- 02890-264466.

Lavery, Dr. Irvine, MBE, BA (Hons), MSc, DPhil, Master Mariner, FCIT, FNI, MIHT. Transport Development Manager, Translink; b. 4.11.42, Belfast; m., Sandra; 1s.; 1d. Educ. Annadale Grammar School; Queen's University, Belfast; Cranfield University; University of Ulster. Officer, Captain, Merchant Navy; Lecturer; Ulster Polytechnic; University of Ulster; Senior Lecturer, Transport Studies, University of Ulster. Past Chairman, Northern Ireland Section, Institute of Transport; Transport Consultant; Frequent Speaker, International Transport Conferences. Active in the voluntary sector, including Age Concern; Disability Action. Frequent media contributor on transport issues. Awarded an MBE for services to transport in June 2003 Birthday Honours Awards. Publications: over 80 research and consultancy reports and papers. Recreations: church activities; travel; theatre; rambling. Address: (b.) Translink, Central Station, Belfast, BT1 3PB; T.- 028 9089 9475.

Leonard, Prof. Brian Edmund, BSc (Hons), PhD, DSc, MRIA. Emeritus Professor of Pharmacology, Nat. Univ. Ireland, Galway (NUIG), since 1999; Visiting Professor: Dept., Therapeutics, Queen's University Belfast, since 2000, University of Maastricht, Netherlands, since 2002; b. 30.5.36, Winchester, Hants; m., Helga Muelpfordt; 2 d. Educ. University of Birmingham. Lecturer in Pharmacology, School of Pharmacy, Nottingham University, 1962-68; Technical Officer (Research), ICI Ltd, Macclesfield, 1968-71; Head: Neurochemistry Group, Organon International, Holland, 1971-74; Prof. of Pharmacology, NUIG, 1974-99. President Elect: Int. Coll. Psychopharmacology. Publications: Fundamentals of Psychopharmacology, 1992, 1997; Fundamentals of Psychoneuroimmunology, 2000; approx. 400 publications in Neuropharmacology and Psychopharmacology. Recreations: Entomology; music (classical); gardening. Address: (h.) Currabhaitia, Tullykyne, Moycullen, Co. Galway. T.-+353-91-555292.

Leonard, Paul F., BSc, MSc, FCA. Chief Executive, Clarendon Fund Managers Ltd, since 2001; Former Chairman, Ulster Society of Chartered Accountants; b. Belfast; m., Gillian; 2 s.; 2 d. Educ. Queen's University Belfast; University of Ulster. Chartered Accountant, KPMG Belfast, 1982-88; Senior Executive, Enterprise Equity (NI), Ltd, 1988-89; Director, Corporate Banking and Head of Financial Services, Bank of Ireland, 1990-2001. Address: (b.) 12 Cromac Place, Belfast BT7 2JB. T.-028 9032 6465.

Leong, Fee Ching, BSc (Hons), DSM, AMIPD. Equality Consultant/Trainer and Director, OMI Consultancy, since 1998; Board Member: FOLD Housing Association & FOLD Housing Trust; Member, Employers' Panel, Fair Employment

Tribunal (Northern Ireland), since 1999; Commissioner, Churches Together in Britain and Ireland's Churches' Commission for Racial Justice, since 1994; b. 25.6.55, Ipoh, Perak, Malaysia; 2 d. Educ. Convent of the Holy Infant Jesus, Ipoh, Perak, Malaysia; National Junior College, Singapore; Queen's University of Belfast; Open University. Research Officer, School of Chemistry, Queen's University of Belfast; Care Assistant, Faith House Residential Home, Belfast; Lecturer, Castlereagh College of Further and Higher Education, Belfast; Chinese Welfare Association (N.I.): numerous posts including Welfare Rights Adviser, Advocate, Interpreter, Project Manager, Training Executive; Ethnic Minority Columnist, BBC Radio Ulster; Co-ordinator, Multicultural Resource Centre (N.I.). Commissioner, Commission for Racial Equality for Northern Ireland, 1997 - 99; Member of Senate, Queen's University of Belfast, 1999-2002; Member, Active Community Initiative Monitoring Committee; Honorary Secretary, Belfast Central Community and Police Liaison Committee; Member, Eastern Health and Social Services Board's Registration and Inspection Advisory Committee; Presbyterian Church in Ireland's Inter-Church Relations Board (and Member, Race Relations Committee). Publications include: Caring for Children from Ethnic Minorities in Northern Ireland (Editor), 1996; A Literature Review of Ethnic Minority Health and Social Care Needs, 1996; Anti-Racism Training in Northern Ireland (Co-Author), 1996; Understanding Racism (Co-Author), 1999; A Unique Way of Sharing, 2001; ESOL: Interpreting the Way Forward, 2002; Caring for Difference, 2003. Recreations: culinary interests; embroidery; rock-painting; sketching; hill-walking; swimming; dancing; drumming; listening to music (especially reggae); socialising. Address: 37 Saintfield Road, Ballygowan, Co. Down BT23 6HB; T.-028 9052 1677.

Leslie, James Seymour, MA. Member (North Antrim), UUP, Northern Ireland Assembly, 1998-2003; Junior Minister, 2002; b. 1.3.58, Singida, Tanzania. Educ. Dalriada School, Ballymoney; Eton College, Windsor; Queens' College, Cambridge. Standard Chartered Bank, 1980 - 84; Guinness Mahon and Co. Ltd., 1985 - 87; Guinness Flight Global Asset Management Ltd., 1987 - 97. Recreations: sailing; hill-walking; bridge. Address: (b.) Parliament Buildings, Stormont, Belfast BT4 3ST.

Leslie, Prof. Julian, MA, DPhil, CPsychol, FPsSI. Professor of Psychology, University of Ulster, since 1986; b. 19.9.49, London, m., Rosanne Cecil; 2 s. Educ. Dulwich College, London; Merton College, Oxford University. Lecturer in Psychology, New University of Ulster, Coleraine, 1974-84; Senior Lecturer in Psychology, University of Ulster, 1984-85, Head of Department of Psychology, 1985-94. Honorary Director of Institute of Counselling and Personal Development; Irish delegate to scientific committee of European Federation of Psychology

Association; Chair of undergraduate accreditation committee of Psychological Society of Ireland. Publications: numerous scientific papers and five books on behaviour analysis. Recreations: keeping goats and growing trees (separately). Address: (b.) School of Psychology, University of Ulster at Jordanstown, Newtownabbey BT37 0QB. T.- 02890 366943.

Lewis, Richard Gregory, JP, BSc (Econ.), CPFA. Chief Executive, Moyle District Council; b. 7.4.53, Burnley, Lancashire; m., Marian; 2s.; 1d. Educ. University of Hull. Inland Revenue; District Audit Service, Audit Commission for local authorities, England and Wales; Department of Environment (NI) Local Government Auditor. Recreations: sailing; golf; family activities. Address: (b.) Moyle District Council, 7 Mary Street, Ballycastle, Co Antrim, BT54 6QH; T.- 028 2076 2225.

Lewis, Dr. Sheena E.M., BSc, PhD, PGCHET. Reader in Obstetrics and Gynaecology, since 2000; b. 2.5.56, Lisburn; m., R. Paul Lewis; 2 s.; 1 d. Educ. Ashleigh House School; Queen's University Belfast. Lecturer in Obstetrics and Gynaecology, Queen's University Belfast, 1995-2000. Invited Speaker at International Conferences on male infertility; Member: British Fertility Society, British Andrology Society. Publications: over 60 academic research papers; reviewer for numerous journals and charities. Recreations: cookery; gardening; travel. Address: (b.) School of Medicine, Obstetrics and Gynaecology, Queen's University Belfast. T.-028 90 894633.

Lewsley, Patricia. Member (Lagan Valley), SDLP, Northern Ireland Assembly, since 1998; b. 3.3.57; 3 s.; 2 d. Educ. St. Dominic's High School; University of Ulster at Jordanstown. Director, City West Action; Chairperson, Men's Advisory Project. Address: (h.) 34 Alina Gardens, Areema, Dunmurry BT17 0QJ; T.-028 9087 4206.

Liddy, Dr. Brian, BSc (Hons), PhD, PGCE, AdvDipEdM. Education Officer (Planning and Development), Southern Education and Library Board, Armagh, since 1988; b. 20.5.46, Holywood, Co. Down; m., Briege; 4 d. Educ. St. Mary's Grammar School, Belfast; Queen's University of Belfast; Open University. Research Fellow in Electron Optical Chronography, Queen's University of Belfast, 1971-72; Science Teacher, St. Malachy's College, Belfast, 1972-78; Assistant Education Officer, Southern Education and Library Board, 1978-88. Recreation: golf. Address: (b.) 3 Charlemont Place, The Mall, Armagh BT61 9AX. T.-028 3751 2228. e-mail: brian.liddy@selb.org

Lilley, Robert Hugh. OBE. Editorial Director, Belfast Telegraph Newspapers, 1993-98; retired; b. 4.12.38, Belfast; m., Georgina; 2d. Educ. Larne Grammar School. Joined Belfast Telegraph, 1957: Political Correspondent, 1962 - 64 and 1967 - 69; Political Correspondent, Thomson Regional Newspapers, 1965 - 67; Belfast Telegraph: Assistant Editor, 1970 - 71; Deputy Editor, 1971 -

74; Editor, 1974 - 92. Golden Pen of Freedom Award, Federation International des Editeurs et Publications, 1977; Hon. MA, Open University, 1978. Recreation: golf. Address: (h.) 8 Church Avenue, Jordanstown, Newtownabbey, Co. Antrim BT37 0PJ.
e-mail: RandG_Lilley@UKGateway.net

Lindsay, Martin. Editor and General Manager, Sunday Life, Belfast; b. 26.12.45, Belfast; m., Yvonne; 1 s.; 2 d. Junior Reporter, Morton Publications; Trainee Reporter, East Antrim Times; News Reporter, Chief Reporter, Belfast Telegraph; News Reporter, Scottish Daily Express; Deputy News Editor, Belfast Telegraph, Assistant to the Editor, then Deputy Editor. Newspaper Focus UK Regional Editor of the Year, 1996. Recreations: angling; golf. Address: (b.) Sunday Life, 124 Royal Avenue, Belfast, BT1 1EB; T.- 02890-264309.
e-mail: martin.lindsay@belfasttelegraph.co.uk

Linton, Dr. David, BSc (Hons), PhD, CEng, MIEE, SMIEEE. Senior Lecturer in Electrical Engineering, Queen's University Belfast, since 1999; Professional Electrical Engineer, since 1983; b. 7.2.61, Ballymena, Co. Antrim; m., Phyllis. Educ. Ballymena Academy; Queen's University Belfast. Lucas Stability: Applications Manager, 1983-87, New Products Development Manager, 1987-89; Lecturer in Electrical Engineering, Queen's University Belfast, 1989-99. Member: Institute of Electrical Engineers (UK), Institute of Electrical and Electronic Engineers (USA); Church Elder. Recreations: church work; singing; music. Address: (b.) Queen's University Belfast, School of Electrical and Electronic Engineering, Ashby Building, Stranmillis Road, Belfast. T.-028 9027 4265. e-mail: d.linton@ee.qub.ac.uk

Livingstone, Professor David Noel, OBE, BA, Dip Ed, PhD, FBA, MRIA, FRSA, CGeog, MAE, AcSS. Professor of Geography and Intellectual History, Queen's University, Belfast; b. 15.3.53, Banbridge; m., Frances Allyson Haugh; 1s.; 1d. Educ. Banbridge Academy; Queen's University, Belfast. Queen's University, Belfast: successively Curator of Maps, Lecturer then Reader; British Association for the Advancement of Science, The Charles Lyell Lecturer, 1994; Visiting Professor, Geography and History of Science, Calvin College, Grand Rapids, Michigan, USA, 1989 - 90; Visiting Professor of History, Notre Dame University, Indiana, USA, 1995; Visiting Noted Scholar, University of British Columbia, 1999. Elected Fellow, British Academy, 1995; Elected Member, Royal Irish Academy, 1998; Elected Member, Academia Europaea, 2002; Elected Academician, Academy of Learned Societies for the Social Sciences, 2002; British Academy Research Reader, 1999 - 2001. Admiral Sir George Back Award, Royal Geographical Society, 1997; Centenary Medal, Royal Scottish Geographical Society, 1998; Hettner Lectures, University of Heidelberg, 2001; Murrin Lectures, University of British Columbia, 2002; Templeton

Lecture Award, 1999. Publications: Nathaniel Southgate Shaler, 1987; Darwin's Forgotten Defenders, 1987; The Preadamite Theory, 1992; The Geographical Tradition, 1992; Human Geography, 1996; Ulster-American Religion, 1999; Geography and Enlightenment, 1999; Science, Space and Hermeneutics, 2002; Putting Science in its Place, 2003. Recreations: music; photography. Address: (b.) School of Geosciences, Queen's University, Belfast, Belfast, BT7 1NN; T.-01232-335145.

Livingstone, Prof. Margaret Barbara Elizabeth, BEd, MSc, MSc, DPhil, RNutr. Professor of Human Nutrition, University of Ulster, since 2001; b. 29.1.50, Armagh; m., Harold John Stewart. Educ. Armagh Girls High School; University of London; University of Ulster. Teacher of Home Economics, Inner London Education Authority, 1972-73; Senior Lecturer: School of Home Economics, Ulster Polytechnic, 1973-84, Home Economics, University of Ulster, 1984-90, Nutrition, 1990-99, Reader in Nutrition, 1999-2001. Member: Nutritional Sciences Committee, Royal Irish Academy; Chairperson, Nutrition Society (Irish section); Member, Board of Governors of the British Nutrition Foundation. Recreation: hill walking. Address: (b.) School of Biomedical Sciences, University of Ulster, Coleraine, Co. Londonderry BT52 1SA. T.-028 7032 4471. e-mail: mbe.livingstone@ulster.ac.uk

Lockett, John A, BA, MEd, CTC. Headmaster, Grosvenor Grammar School; b. 5.4.48, Belfast; m., Vera; 2s.; 1d. Educ. Royal Belfast Academical Institution; Queen's University, Belfast. Head of Biology, Lurgan Boys' Junior School; Head of Careers, Banbridge Academy; Vice-Principal, Grosvenor Grammar School. Council for Education in World Citizenship: President (NI); Vice President (UK); Chairman, Heritage Railway Association. Recreations: walking; railway enthusiast; travel; music. Address: (b.) Grosvenor Grammar School, Cameronian Drive, Belfast, BT5 6AX; T.-02890-702777.

Lockington, Very Rev. Dr. John William, BA, BD, MTh, PhD, DD. Minister, Clogherney Presbyterian Church, Larne since 2003; b. 28.4.44, Belfast; m., Elizabeth Norma Knox; 1s.; 2d. Educ. Belfast High School; Queen's University, Belfast; Presbyterian College, Belfast. Assistant Minister, Ballysillan Presbyterian Church, 1969 - 71; Minister: Ballyroney and Drumlee Presbyterian Churches, 1971 - 81; Mall Presbyterian Church, Armagh, 1981 - 89; Gardenmore, Larne, 1989-2003; Moderator, General Assembly of the Presbyterian Churchin Ireland, 1999 - 2000. Publications: Ballyroney, Its Church And People; History of the Mall Presbyterian Church, 1837 - 1987; Robert Blair of Bangor. Recreations: philately; watching soccer; reading. Address: (h.) 65 Rock Road, Beragh, Sixmilecross, Omagh BT79 0QN. T.-028 8075 7022.

Logue, Dr. Kenneth John, MA, PhD. b. 15.2.48, Glasgow; 1d. Senior Programme Officer, Atlantic Philanthropies. Educ. Kirkaldy High School, Fife, Scotland; Edinburgh University. District Secretary, Workers Educational Association, South East Scotland, 1976 - 83; Director, Northern Ireland Council on Alcohol, 1984 - 88; Proprietor, Kenneth Logue Associates, Community Development Advisors, 1988 - 93; Partner, Murtagh and Logue Partnership, Management and Development Consultants, 1993 - 96; Proprietor, Ken Logue Consulting, 1996 - 98. Formerly Chairperson, War on Want, Northern Ireland; Director: Crescent Arts Centre, Belfast; Glencairn Enterprises Ltd; New Agenda; Chairperson, WEA, Bangor; Formerly Treasurer, WEA, Northern Ireland; Former Vice-Chairperson, Northern Ireland Council for Voluntary Action. Publications: Popular Disturbances in Scotland, 1780 - 1815, 1979; Community Development in Northern Ireland: Perspectives of the Future (with N Fitzduff), 1991; Anti-sectarianism in the Community and Voluntary Sector, 1993; Anti-sectarianism: A Framework for Action (with W Glendinning), 1994; District Councils and Rural Development, 1995; Accommodating Change: Active Community Relations (with D Smyth), 1996. Recreations: recreational basketball; football with Ballyholme BFC. Address: (h.) 25 Dorman's Court, Donaghader, Co Down BT21 0JL. T.-028 9188 4269.

Lomas, Garth, MA, FCA. Partner, Moore Stephens, Chartered Accountants since 1988; b. 8.11.51, Lurgan, Co Armagh; m., Barbara Mason; 2d. Educ. Lurgan College; Trinity College, Dublin. Training as Accountant, Deloitte Haskins and Sells, 1975 - 79; Senior Auditor, Deloitte Haskins and Sells, Middle East, 1980 - 81; Established own practice, Northern Ireland, 1982 - 87. Recreations: young family. Address: (b.) 7 Donegall Square West, Belfast, BT1 6JH; T.-02890-329481.

Long, Professor Adrian Ernest, BSc, PhD, DSc. Professor, Civil Engineering, Queen's University Belfast, since 1976; b. 15.4.41, Dungannon; m., Elaine Margaret Long; 1s.; 1d. Educ. Royal School, Dungannon; Queen's University, Belfast. Bridge Design Engineer, Toronto, Canada, 1967 - 68; Assistant Professor, Department of Civil Engineering, Queen's University, Kingston, Canada, 1968 - 71; Lecturer, Civil Engineering, Queen's University, Belfast, 1971 - 75; Visiting Professor, Royal Military College, Kingston, Canada, 1975 - 76; Queen's University, Belfast: Head, Department of Civil Engineering, 1977 - 89; Director, School of the Built Environment, Queen's University, Belfast, 1989 - 98; Dean, Faculty of Engineering, 1988 - 91; 1998-2002; Elected Vice President, Institution of Civil Engineers, London, 1999, President, 2002-03. UK representative, EU Cost Urban Civil Engineering Technical Committee since 1992. Esso Energy Gold Medal, Royal Society of London, 1994; Coopers Hill Medal, 1988; Telford Premium 1988,

1998 and 2002; Baker Medal, 1998, Institution of Civil Engineers, London; State of the Art Civil Engineering Award, American Society of Civil Engineers, USA, 1973; Fellow, Royal Academy of Engineering (UK), 1989; Fellow, American Concrete Institute, 1996; Fellow, Irish Academy of Engineering, 1998. Recreations: church; travel; walking; gardening; occasional golf. Address: (b.) School of Civil Engineering, David Keir Building, Queen's University Belfast, BT7 1NN; T.- 028 90 274005.

Longley, Michael. Writer and Poet. b. 1939, Belfast. Educ. Trinity College, Dublin. Teacher, then worked for the Arts Council of Northern Ireland, 1970-91. Publications: No Continuing City, 1969; Exploded View, 1973; The Echo Gate, 1979; Gorse Fires, 1991 (Whitbread Prize for Poetry); The Weather in Japan, 2000.

Loughlin, Bernard. Director, SmART INNS and Farrera Fabulosa SL; b. 3.2.50, Belfast; m., Mary Kathleen Rogan; 1s.; 1d. Educ. St Malachy's College, Belfast; Queen's University Belfast. Extensive travels in Europe as, variously, shepherd, grape harvester, teacher of English, trawlerman, then Founding Director of The Tyrone Guthrie Centre of Annaghmakerrig for 18 years. Founding Secretary of Res Artis - International Association of Residential Arts Centres; member of other regional, national and international boards and bodies. Publication: The Guinness Book of Ireland (ed.). Radio and television programmes and documentaries. Recreations: bird-watching; gardening; reading and travel. Address: El Refugi Irlandes, Can Felip, Farrera de Pallars, Lleida, Catalunya, Spain.
e-mail: smartinns@worldonline.es

Loughlin, Dr. James, BA, PhD, FRHistS. Reader in History, University of Ulster, since 1999; b. Portadown, Co. Armagh; m., Jacinta Haddock; 2 d. Educ. Northern Ireland Polytechnic; Trinity College, Dublin. Teacher, 1982-84; Research Fellow, Institute of Irish Studies, Queen's University Belfast, 1985-88; Lecturer in History, Magee College, University of Ulster, 1988-97, Senior Lecturer in History, 1997-99. Publications: Gladstone, Home Rule and The Ulster Question, 1882-93, 1986; Ulster Unionism and British National Identity, since 1885, 1995; The Ulster Question, since 1945, 1998. Address: (b.) School of History and International Affairs, Magee College, University of Ulster, Londonderry. T.- 02871 375346. e-mail: jp.loughlin@ulster.ac.uk

Loughrey, Stephen Victor Patrick, BA, PGCE, MA. BBC Director, Nations and Regions, since 2000; b. 29.12.55; m., Patricia; 1s.; 2d. Educ. Loreto, Milford; University of Ulster; Queen's University, Belfast. Research Studentship, Trent University, Ontario, Canada, 1977 -78; Teacher, St Colms High School, Draperstown, 1978 - 84; BBC Northern Ireland: Producer, Education, 1984 - 88; Head of Educational Broadcasting, 1988 - 91; Head of Programmes, 1991 - 94; Controller, BBC

Northern Ireland, 1994-2000. Publications: joint editor. Ulster Local Studies, 1988 - 91; People of Ireland (ed.), 1988. Recreations: walking; talking. Address: (b.) BBC Broadcasting House, Portland Place, London W1A 1AA. T.-0208 743 8000.

Lowry, Major (Barry) Charles William McCaughey, MBE, TD, MIB. Hon. Chairman, The Not Forgotten Association (N I Branch); b. 24.6.39, Belfast; m., Rosemary; 1s.; 1d. Educ. Belfast Royal Academy; Campbell College, Belfast. Belfast Banking Co Ltd/Northern Bank Ltd, 1957 - 90 (Assistant Manager); Member, Institute of Bankers of Ireland; Member of The Order of The British Empire; NY Hons 1998. Territorial Army: Queen's University, Belfast Officer Training Corps, 1957 - 62; Commissioned, 152 (U) Regiment, Royal Corps of Transport, 1969 - 84, Rank of Major and position on retiring in 1984, Regimental Paymaster RAPC (V). Territorial Decoration, 1984. Director (Training) of St John Ambulance N I; Officer of The Order of St. John of Jerusalem and Chapter Member of The Commandery of Ards; Past President of Belfast Benevolent Society of St. Andrew; Executive Committee Member, SSAFA Forces Help N I; Member, Belfast Charitable Society. Recreations: stamp and coin collecting; native American ethnology; golf. Address: (h.) 44 Ormiston Crescent, Belfast, T.- 02890-652462.

Lowry, Dr. Roger Clark, OBE, BSc, FRCP, FRCPI. Consultant Physician, Belfast City Hospital, 1970-98; b. 20.9.33, Belfast; m., Dorothy Joan; 4s.; 1d. Educ. Campbell College; Queen's University, Belfast. Associate Professor, University of Tennessee, 1976 - 77. OBE, June 2001. Recreations: golf; gardening; tennis. Address: (h.) 49 Belfast Road, Newtownards, Co Down BT23 4TR; T.- 028 9181 3284.

Lucas, Philip Alistair, BSSc (Hons), MSc. Director of Development and Leisure Services, Antrim Borough Council since 1990; b. 3.6.55, Belfast; m., Daphne Lucas, 1s.; 2d. Educ. Royal School, Armagh; Queen's University, Belfast; Loughborough University. Assistant Manager, Connah's Quay Sports Centre, North Wales, 1977 - 78; Assistant Manager, Coventry Sport and Recreation Centre, 1978 - 82; Manager, Maysfield Leisure Centre, Belfast, 1982 - 85; Deputy Chief Leisure Services Officer, Ards Borough Council, 1985 - 90. Member, Board of Governors, Templepatrick Primary School. Recreation: golf. Address: (b.) Antrim Borough Council, The Steeple, Antrim; T.- 028 9446 3113.

Lutton, Joan Ellen, B Ed (Hons), Cert Ed. Principal, The Thompson Primary School since 1990; b. 14.4.50, Belfast; m., Clifford T Lutton; 2s.; 1d. Educ. Belfast High School; Queen's University, Belfast/Stranmillis College. Assistant Teacher: Mossley Primary School, 1971 - 75; Ballyduff Primary School, 1979 - 86; Vice-Principal Mallusk Primary School, 1986 - 90. Address: (b.) Thompson Primary School, 42

Mossley Road, Ballyrobert, Ballyclare, Co Antrim, BT39 9RX; T.- 028 93-352361; (h.) 028 93-340184.

Lyle, David, MCIM. Chief Executive, McCann-Erickson, Belfast; b. 2.6.50, Donaghadee; m., Helen; 1s.; 3d. Educ. Regent House Grammar School; Queen's University, Belfast. Trainee, Advertising and sales, Oneida Silversmiths, Bangor, 1972 - 75; Account Executive, Armstrong Long, Advertising, 1975; Promoted to Board; Training for the Ministry, Reformed Theological College, Belfast, 1984 - 86; Creative Director, Armstrong Long Advertising, 1986; Managing Director, McCann-Erickson, Belfast, 1986-87. Member, Design and Art Directors Association and Creative Circle; Chartered Institute of Marketing; McCann-Erickson Global SISU, Award, 1988; McCann-Erickson UK Agency of the Year Award, 1989; International H W McCann Leadership Award, 1990; Creative Award Credits include: Gold Hollywood Ollies; Mobius Golds; Chicago, Epica Gold; London International Winners; Golden Awards of Montreaux; New York Festivals Silvers; Two Pani Grand Prix and Millennium Award; Roses Grand Prix; Roses and Kinsale Golds; IPA Area Effectiveness Awards and AME World Medals. Recreations: health club; cinema; travel. Address: (b.) McCann-Erickson Belfast, 31 Bruce Street, Belfast, BT2 7JD; T.- 02890-331044. e-mail: david_lyle@europe.mccann.com

Lynas, Rev. Robert Victor Alexander, OBE, BA, BD, DD. b. 17.1.20, Belfast; m., Margaret E Rainey; 3s.; 1d. Educ. Methodist College. Belfast; Queen's University, Belfast; Union Theological College, Belfast. Minister: Trinity Presbyterian Church, Ahoghill, 1943 - 47; Gardenmore Presbyterian Church, Larne, 1947 - 87; Clerk, Presbytery of Carrickfergus, 1974-1999. Moderator, Synod of Ballymena and Coleraine, 1965; Moderator, General Assembly, Presbyterian Church in Ireland, 1972; General Assembly Committees: Convener, State of Religion, 1953 - 63; Central Ministry Fund, 1962 - 73; Ministry and Pensions Board, 1961 - 76; Church and Government Committee, 1973 - 81. Member, Board of Governors, Larne Grammar School since 1949 (Chairman 1966-2000). Recreations: gardening; walking. Address: (h.) 19 Wheatfield Heights, Ballygally, Larne, BT40 2RT; T.- 02828-583643.

Lynden-Bell, Professor Ruth Marion, MA (Cantab), PhD (Cantab), ScD (Cantab), FRIC, FInstP. Professor of Condensed Matter Simulation, Queen's University of Belfast since 1995; b. 7.12.37, Welwyn Garden City; m., Professor Donald Lynden-Bell (qv); 1s.; 1d. Educ. King Edward VI High School, Birmingham; Newnham College, Cambridge. AAUW Fellow, California Institute of Technology, 1961 - 62; Fellow and College Lecturer, New Hall Cambridge, 1962 - 65; Lecturer, Chemistry, University of Sussex, 1965 - 72; Fellow, College Lecturer, New Hall Cambridge, 1972 - 95; College Lecturer, St John's College, 1975 - 95; Newton Trust Lecturer, University of Cambridge, 1993 - 95. Publications: Nuclear Magnetic Resonance Spectroscopy (with R K Harris); numerous academic papers in scientific journals. Recreations: walking. Address: (b.) Atomistic Simulation Group, School of Mathematics and Physics, Queen's University, Belfast, Belfast BT7 1NN; T.- 02890 335329.

Mc/Mac

McAdam, Dr. James H., BSc, MAgr, PhD, ARAgS, MIBiol, CBiol. Principal Scientific Officer, Department of Agriculture and Rural Development, since 1987; Reader, Queen's University, Belfast since 1997; b. 15.1.52, Donaghadee, Co Down. Educ. Coleraine Academical Institution; Queen's University, Belfast. Pasture Agronomist, Falkland Islands, 1976 - 79; Senior Scientific Officer, Department of Agriculture for Northern Ireland, 1980 - 87; Lecturer, Queen's University, Belfast, 1982 - 97. Publications; Wild Flowers of the Falkland Islands; The Upland Goose; over 100 scientific papers; Editor, The Falkland Islands Journal. Recreations: sailing; local and natural history. Address: (b.) Agriculture and Food Science Centre, Newforge Lane, Belfast, BT9 5PX; T.-028 90255275. e-mail: jim.mcadam@dardni.gov.uk

McAdams, Seamus, BA (Hons), DipM, MCIM. Chief Executive, Tyrone Economic Development Initiative since 1994; b. 24.11.65, Derry; m., Sharon; 2s. Educ. St Columb's College, Derry; University of Ulster at Jordanstown. Assistant Quality Control Manager, Adria Ltd, 1988 - 89; Marketing Consultant, Matrix Business Services, 1989 - 90; Chief Executive, North West Marketing, 1990 - 92; Marketing Manager, McCormack Homes, 1992 - 94. Recreations: cycling; soccer; music. Address: (h.) 64 Derry Road, Omagh. T.-028 8224 8444.

McAleer, James J., MD, FRCP, FRCR. Senior Lecturer and Consultant in Clinical Oncology, since 1992; b. 1.10.57, Omagh; m., Geraldine; 3 d. Educ. Omagh Christian Brothers Grammar School; Trinity College, Dublin. Special interest: clinical trials and new drug development (main interests: breast, testicular cancer and malignant melanoma). Trustee, Friends of Montgomery House. Recreations: cycling; golf; woodcarving. Address: (b.) Belfast City Hospital, Lisburn Road, Belfast BT9; T.-01232 329241, Ext. 3079.

McAleese, Janice Lynda Ingrid, BA (Hons) Textile Design. Chief Executive, Northern Ireland Events Company, since 2003, Company Secretary, since 2001; b. 19.5.64, Enniskillen. Educ. Omagh Academy; University of Ulster. Previous experience includes managing export markets in Japan, USA and The Middle East; youth work, fundraising company administration and event management. Recreations: motor sports; arts and crafts. Address: (b.) Northern Ireland Events Company, Redwood House, 66 Newforge Lane, Belfast BT9 5NW. T.-028 9066 6661. e-mail: info@nievents.co.uk

McAllister, Dr. Hector Gerard, PhD, MSc, BSc, CEng, MIEE. Associate Head of School, Computing and Mathematics, Faculty of Engineering, University of Ulster; b. 23.12.48, Larne; m., Patricia Margaret Fitzsimons; 1s.; 2d. Educ. Larne Technical College; Queen's University, Belfast; University of Ulster. Publications: 60 publications in journals, books and conferences. Recreations: reading; walking. Address: (b.) Faculty of Engineering, University of Ulster at Jordanstown, Shore Road, Newtownabbey, BT37 0QB; T.- 028 90368156. e-mail: hg.mcallister@ulster.ac.uk

McArdle, Dr. Fergus, EdD, MA MEd, BSc, BA, PGCE. Headmaster, St Patrick's Grammar, Downpatrick since 1985; b. 22.3.49, Dundalk. Educ. Maynooth; University of Wales, Swansea; University of Washington D.C., USA; Queen's University, Belfast; Open University. Teacher, St Patrick's Grammar, Downpatrick, 1972 - 81; Head of Department, St John's College, Washington D.C., 1981 - 85. Recreations: hill walking; reading. Hon. EdD, University of Ulster, 1998. Address: (b.) St Patrick's Grammar School, Saul Street, Downpatrick, BT30 6NJ; T.- 028 4461 9722.

McAuley, Chrissie, Member (Sinn Féin) for Upper Falls, Belfast City Council, since 1998 (Chair, Development Committee, since 2001); b. 1.11.55, Belfast; m., Richard; 1 s.; 2 d. Educ. St Louise's Comprehensive College. PA to Manager, RK Binney Finance Ltd., 1973 - 75; Northern Reporter, Republican News, 1979 - 89; Press Officer, 1989 - 94; Sinn Féin: National Head, Education Department, 1994 - 96, Publications Editor, International Department, 1990 - 97; Community Economic Development Work, 1995 - 98. Anchor of Sinn Fein's Human Rights/Equality Advisory Teams. Publications: The RUC: Nationalist Women's Experience, 1996; Women in a War Zone, 1995. Recreations: writing; oil painting; horse-riding; walking. Address: (b.) City Hall, Belfast; T.-01232 808404.

McAuley, Linda Jane. Radio Presenter, Consumer Affairs and Freelance Journalist; b. 27.9.54; m., Paul Wilson; 3s. Educ. Glenola Collegiate School; The Mount, York. Address: (h.) 85 Groomsport Road, Bangor, Co Down, BT20 5NG; (b.) T.-028 9033 8315.

McBain, James Benjamin, BA, Dip Ed, DASE. Principal, Omagh Academy; b. 18.8.44, Portadown; m., Pauline Anne Cooper; 2s.; 1d. Educ. Portadown College; Queen's University, Belfast. Assistant Teacher, Geography, Portadown College, 1966 - 70; Head, Geography, Royal School, Armagh, 1970 - 74; Belfast Royal Academy: Head, Geography/Teacher, I/C General Studies/ Chair, Curriculum Committee, 1974 - 84. Revisor, A-Level Geography, 1984-93; Secretary, Secondary Heads Association (NI), 1993 - 98; President, Secondary Heads Association (NI), 1999 - 2000. Recreations gardening; walking; swimming; church activities. Address: (b.) Omagh Academy, 21 - 23 Dublin Road, Omagh, BT78 1HF; T.- 02882-242688. e-mail: info@omaghacademy.omagh.ni.sch.uk

McBrearty, Paul. Director of Corporate Affairs, Lisburn Health Centre. Address: (b.) Level 5, Lisburn Health Centre, Linenhall Street, Lisburn, Co. Antrim BT28 1LU. T.-028 92 665181.

McBride, Anne, BA (Hons). Principal, The Wallace High School, Lisburn, since 2000. Address: 12a Clonevin Park, Lisburn, Co. Antrim BT28 3AD. T.-02892 672311.

McCalden, Brian, BA (Hons). Editor, Penton Publications (NI Medicine Today); b. 20.12.55, Belfast; m., Gladys; 1s.; 1d. Educ. Annadale Grammar School, Belfast; University of Ulster. Public Relations Officer, Northern Ireland Training Authority/Industrial Training Boards, 1985 - 88; Public Relations Consultant, Derek Murray Communication, Belfast, 1988 - 89; Editor, Ulster Magazines, Belfast, 1989 - 90; Joined Greer Publications, Editor, 1990. Founding Chairman, Ulster Van Writers' Association since 1997. Recreations: current affairs; reading. Address: (b.) Penton Publications, 38 Heron Road, Sydenham, Belfast BT3 9LE.
e-mail: brian.mccalden@pentonpublications.co.uk

McCann, Barbara Anne. Presenter/Reporter, GMTV News/Reuters Television since 1996. Educ. Dominican College, Fortwilliam; St Genevieve's, Andersontown; University of Ulster at Jordanstown; College of Business Studies. Reporter, Downtown Radio, 1978; Chief Reporter, East Antrim Times, 1978 - 79; Senior Reporter, Downtown Radio, 1979 - 87; Freelance, UTV/BBC/TV AM, 1987 - 88; Northern Ireland Correspondent/Foreign Correspondent, TV AM, 1988 - 92; Freelance Correspondent, GMTV/SKY/Reuters Television, 1992 - 96; Producer/Director documentaries shot in Brazil, Uganda, The Philippines, Bangladesh, India; Producer/Director, Corporates; Patron, Friends of Jessica, Charity, Northern Ireland. Recreations: golf; collecting fine art; horse riding; painting; theatre; opera. Address: (b.) GMTV, Fanum House, 108 Great Victoria Street, Belfast, BT2 7BL; T.- 0374-274754/01232-234098.

McCann, John. Managing Director, Ulster Television. Address: (b.) Ulster Television, Havelock House, Ormeau Road, Belfast BT7 1EB. T.-028 9032 8122.

McCann, Robert William Crowe, LLB, DBA. Partner, Mills Selig Solicitors; b. 7.1.53, Belfast; m., Dr. Gillian Martin; 1s.; 1d. Educ. Grosvenor High School; Queen's University, Belfast. Recreations: golf; music. Address: Mills Selig, Solicitors, 21 Arthur Street, Belfast BT1 4GA. T.-028 9024 3878.

McCanny, Prof. John Vincent, CBE, BSc, PhD, DSc, FRS, FREng, MRIA, FIEEE, FIEE, FInstP, FRSA, CEng, CPhys. Professor of Microelectronics Engineering, Queen's University, Belfast since 1988; Member, NI Information Age Initiative, 1999-2002; b. 25.6.52, Ballymoney; m., Maureen B Mellon, 1s.; 1d. Educ. Dalriada Grammar School, Ballymoney. Educ. University of Manchester; New University of Ulster. Lecturer/Post Doctoral Research Fellow in Physics, New University of Ulster, Coleraine, 1977 - 79; Scientific Civil Service: Higher Scientific Officer, 1979 - 82; Senior Scientific Officer, 1982 - 83; Principal Scientific Officer, 1983. Department of Electrical and Electronic Engineering, Queen's University, Belfast: Lecturer, (IT Research), 1984 - 87; Reader, 1987 - 88. Chair, IEEE Technical Committee on Design and Implementation of Signal Processing Systems, 1999 - 2001; Member of IEEE Signal Processing Technical Directions Committee, 1999-2001; Member, Royal Academy of Engineering, Engineering Standing Committee, since 2001; Member of Office of Science and Technology Foresight Panel on Information Technology Communications and Multi-Media, 2001-02; Royal Society Sectional Committee 4 (Engineering and Technology), 2004-07; Steering Committee, DTI Electronics Innovation and Growth Team, since 2003; Royal Society Fellowships Committee (Chemistry and Engineering), 2003-06. Royal Academy of Engineering Silver Medal, 1996; IEEE 3rd Millennium Medal, 2000; Millennium Product Award, 2000; Northern Ireland Information Technology Award, 1987; Department of Trade and Industry SMART Awards for Enterprise, 1988, 1990 and 1995; Research chosen as UK Exemplar by SERC/DTI, 1993, 1994, 1995 and 1999. Publications: 5 edited books; 250 peer reviewed scientific papers; 20 patents. Co-Founder 1988 APT Ltd, 1994 Amphion Semiconductor Ltd (Chief Technology Officer). Recreations; swimming; golf; swimming; Manchester United FC; photography; music. Address: (b.) School of Electronics Engineering, Queen's University, Belfast, Ashby Building, Stranmillis Road, Belfast, BT9 5AH; T.- 02890-335438.

McCarney, Dr. Willie, OBE, JP, MA, BA, DPhil, Dip Computer Studies and Applications, Teacher's Cert. Lecturer (retired); b. 31.8.38, Bangor, North Wales; widower. Educ. Christian Brothers Grammar School, Omagh; St Joseph's Teacher Training College; Open University; Queen's University, Belfast; University of Ulster at Jordanstown. Lay Magistrate, Belfast Youth Court and Belfast Family Proceedings Court; Justice of the Peace for the City of Belfast; President, International Association of Youth and Family Judges and Magistrates; Editor, Lay Panel Magazine (Magazine of the Northern Ireland Youth and Family Courts Association); Editor-in-Chief, The Chronicle (Magazine of the International Association of Youth and Family Judges and Magistrates). Board of Directors, Glenmona Children's Home. Recreation: ornithology. Address: (h.) St Martin, 175 Andersontown Road, Belfast, BT11 9EA;T.- 028 9061 5164. e-mail: w.mccarney@btconnect.com

McCartan, Prof. Eamonn G. Chief Executive, Sports Council of Northern Ireland since 1994; Professor, University of Ulster, Faculty of Business and Management (School of Leisure and Tourism). Former teacher, Business Studies: Queen's University, Belfast; Open University; Assistant Director, Physical Education, Queen's University, Belfast. Chair: Community Relations Council, Northern Ireland; Trustee, Youth Sports Trust, UK; Council Member, Northern Ireland Chest Heart and Stroke Association; Board Member, Co-operation Ireland. Address: (b.) Sports Council of Northern Ireland, House of Sport, Upper Malone Road, Belfast, BT9 5LA; T.- 028 90 381222.

McCarthy, Kieran, JP. Member (Strangford), Alliance Party, Northern Ireland Assembly; Retailer, Kircubbin; b. 9.9.42, Kircubbin; m., Kathleen; 2 s.; 2 d. Elected to Ards Borough Council, 1985, Alderman, 1997; Talks Delegate, Strangford Alliance Party. Recreations: cycling; gardening; reading. Address: (h.) Loughedge, 3 Main Street, Kirkcubbin, Co. Down; T.-028 427 38221.

McCartney, Dr. Mark, BSc, MSc, PhD, PGCE, MInstP, CPhys. Lecturer in Mathematics, University of Ulster, since 1999; b. 17.4.67, Lisburn; m., Karen Patricia; 1 s. Educ. Lisnagarvey High School; Friends' School, Lisburn; Queen's University Belfast. Lecturer in Mathematics, University of Abertay Dundee, 1994-98; Research Officer, University of Ulster, 1998-99. Publications: numerous papers in learned journals; co-editor, Physicists of Ireland, 2003. Recreations: reading; amateur astronomy. Address: (b.) School of Computing and Mathematics, University of Ulster, Jordanstown, Co. Antrim. T.-028 90366590. e-mail: mark.mccartney@physics.org

Macartney, Nigel S., MA (Cantab), DipLib, CertEd, FRSA. Director of Information Services, University of Ulster, since 1999; b. 7.7.47, Manchester; m., Yolande; 1 s. Educ. Sale County Grammar School for Boys; Corpus Christi College, Cambridge. Various posts, Leeds City Libraries, 1968-72; Librarian, Hertfordshire College of Agriculture and Horticulture, 1972-77; Hatfield Polytechnic/University of Hertfordshire: Senior Tutor Librarian, 1978-79; Deputy Librarian, 1979-82, Librarian, 1982-95; Director of Research and Innovation Centre, British Library, 1995-99. Library and Information Services Council, since 2000; NE Education and Library Board, since 2001; British Library Think Tank, 2000-2001. Recreations: sport; travel; local history. Address: (b.) Department of Information Services, University of Ulster, Cromore Road, Coleraine, Co. Londonderry BT52 1SA. T.-028 7032 4245.

McCartney, Robert Law, QC, MP, LLB (Hons). Member of Parliament (North Down), 1995-2001; Member (North Down), UK Unionist Party,

Northern Ireland Assembly since 1998; Barrister-at-Law; b. 24.4.36; m., Maureen Ann Bingham; 1s.; 3d. Educ. Grosvenor Grammar School, Belfast; Queen's University, Belfast. Called to the Bar , Northern Ireland, 1968; Member, Northern Ireland Assembly, 1983 - 87; Leader, Unionist Party Talks/ Forum Delegate since 1996. President, Campaign for Equal Citizenship, 1986 - 88. Publications: Liberty and Authority in Ireland, 1985; McCartney Report on Consent, 1997; McCartney Report on the Framework Document, 1997. Recreations: reading (biography and military history); walking. Address: (b.) 10 Hamilton Road, Bangor, BT20 4LE; T.- 02891-272994.

McCaughan, Rt Rev. Monsignor Colm, BA. Chancellor, Diocese of Down and Conner since 1993; b. 12.11.27, Glenshesk. Educ. St Malachy's College, Belfast; Queen's University, Belfast; Maynooth College. Diocesan Adviser in Religious Education, 1957 - 69; Secretary, Diocesan Education Committee, 1969 - 85; Director, Council for Catholic Maintained Schools, 1985 - 93. Recreations: reading. Address: (h.) 6 Waterloo Park North, Belfast, BT15 5HW; T.- 028 90778111.

McCaughan, Professor Daniel Vincent, OBE, BSc, PhD, DSc, FREng, FIEE, FRAeS, FInstP, FIEI, CEng, FInstD, FIAE. Partner, McCaughan Associates, since 2001; Adviser, Trireme Partners, New York, USA, since 2002; President and COO, Cambridge Display Technology (CDT) Ltd, Cambridge, 2000-2001; b. 1942, Ballycastle; m., Anne Kinsella; 1s. Educ. Queen's University, Belfast. Member, Technical Staff, Bell Laboratories, USA, 1968 - 74; Senior Principal Scientific Officer, Scientific Civil Service, 1974 - 81; Manager, Solid State Devices Research Laboratories, GEC, 1981 - 85; Technical Director, Marconi Electronic Devices Group, 1987 - 88; Technical Director, GEC Electronics Devices Group, 1987 - 88; Director, Northern Ireland Telecoms Engineering Centre, STC then Northern Telecom/Nortel, 1988 - 93; Chief Scientist BNR/Nortel Technology, 1994 - 96; Chief Scientist, Nortel Satellite Networks 1996-2000. Chairman: Technology Board for Northern Ireland, 1986 - 92; IRTU/DED, 1993; Professorial Fellow, Queen's University Belfast since 1988; Visiting Professor, UMIST, Manchester, since 2002; Member: Foresight panels, DTI, UK and DED, NI. Publications: over 100 books/papers/patents etc. Recreations: fungi; mountains; glass; photography. Address: (b.) McCaughan Associates, 20 Circular Road East, Holywood BT18 0HA. T.-02890 428366. Fax: 02890 428367.

McCaughey, Dr. William John, BA, MA, MVB, PhD, MRCVS, FRAgS. Veterinary Surgeon; b. 27.11.37, Broughshane, Co Antrim; m., Diana Mary Craig; 1s.; 1d. Educ. Ballymena Academy; Trinity College, Dublin; Ohio State University, USA; Open University. Fulbright Scholar, Ohio State University, USA, 1960 - 61; Lecturer,

Preventive Veterinary Medicine, Trinity College, Dublin, 1961 - 65; Senior Veterinary Research Officer, VRL, Department of Agriculture of Northern Ireland, 1965 - 72; Lecturer, Animal Health, Queen's University, Belfast, 1971 - 72; Research Scientist, Agriculture Canada, 1972 - 73; Senior Veterinary Research Officer, VSD, Department of Agriculture of Northern Ireland, 1973 - 92; Senior Lecturer, Veterinary Science, Queen's University, Belfast, 1976 - 97; Dean, Royal College Veterinary Surgeons, 1986 - 90; Deputy Chief Veterinary Research Officer, Veterinary Sciences Division, Department of Agriculture for Northern Ireland, 1992 - 97. Member, Veterinary Products Committee, DEFRA, 1998-2005; Member, Veterinary Residues Committee, DEFRA, 2001-2004. Publications: 117 in refereed journals; 105 in non-refereed journals. Recreation: licensed radio amateur. Address: (b.) 19 Caherty Road, Broughshane, Antrim BT42 4QA.

McClarty, David. Member (East Londonderry), UUP, Northern Ireland Assembly, since 1998; b. 23.2.51, Coleraine; m., Norma; 2 s. Educ. Coleraine Academical Institution; Magee College, Londonderry. Insurance Underwriter, 1973 - 84; Insurance Consultant, 1984 - 98. Mayor of Coleraine, 1993 - 95; Freeman, City of London. Recreations: sport; reading; music; amateur dramatics. Address: 22 Slievebanna, Coleraine, Co. Londonderry BT51 3JG; T.-07771 605617. e-mail: david.mcclarty@niassembly.gov.uk

McCleary, Anne. Chief Executive, The Compensation Agency. Address: (b) Royston House, 34 Upper Queen Street, Belfast, BT1 6FD; T.- 028 9024 9944.

McClelland, Donovan. Member (South Antrim), Social Democratic and Labour Party, Northern Ireland Assembly, 1998-2003; Former Deputy Speaker of NI Assembly; b. Toome, Co Antrim; m.; 2 s.; 1 d. Educ. Ballymena Academy; Queen's University, Belfast. University Lecturer; elected to Antrim Borough Council, 1989; Deputy Mayor, 1998; Member, SDLP talks team, 1991; Member, Northern Ireland Forum, 1996; Member, SDLP talks team, Castle Buildings talks, 1996-98; Chairman of Committee on Standards and Privileges, NI Assembly. Address: (b.) Parliament Buildings, Stormont, Belfast, BT4 3ST; T.- 01232-520700.

McClelland, Norman, BSc, GHTI, PGCE. Principal, Lisnagarvey High School, Lisburn, since 1982; b. 22.4.43, Lisburn; m., Dorothy; 1 s.; 1 d. Educ. Lisburn College of Technology; Belfast College of Technology; Queen's University Belfast; Warwick University. Lisnagarvey High School: Teacher, 1967-70, Head of Science Dept., 1970-76, Deputy Principal, 1976-82; Seconded to Warwick University, 1989-90. Graduate of Head Teacher into Industry. Recreation: golf. Address: (b.) Warren Gardens, Lisburn BT28 1HN. T.-028

92 662636.
e-mail: nmcclelland@lisnagarvey.lisburn.ni.sch.uk

McClelland, Prof. Roy, MD, PhD, FRCPsych. Professor of Mental Health, Queen's University Belfast, since 1985; Consultant Psychiatrist, since 1976; b. 13.3.43, Londonderry; m., Hazel; 1 s.; 1 d. Educ. Foyle College, Londonderry; Queen's University; University of London. Senior Lecturer, from 1976. Trustee, NI Centre for Trauma and Transition; Member, Corrymeela Community. Address: (b.) Department of Mental Health, Queen's University Belfast, Belfast. T.-02890 335 790.

McClelland, William Morris, MB, BCh, BAO, FRCPath. Chief Executive/Medical Director, Northern Ireland Blood Transfusion Service; b. 22.6.45; m., Margaret Christine; 1s.; 2d. Educ. Portadown College; Queen's University, Belfast. House Officer, Belfast City Hospital, 1971 - 72; Senior House Officer/Registrar, Belfast City Hospital, 1972 - 75; Senior Registrar, Haematology, Royal Victoria Hospital, Belfast, 1975 - 78; Deputy Director, Northern Ireland Blood Transfusion Service, 1978 - 80. Address: Northern Ireland Blood Transfusion Service, Belfast City Hospital, Lisburn Road, Belfast, BT9 7TS; T.- 028 90 321414.
e-mail: chiefexec@nibts.n-i.nhs.uk

McClinton, Samuel Ivor, BSc, Dip Ed, BA (Hons), MSc, MBCS, ILTM. Senior Lecturer, School of Computing and Maths, University of Ulster since 1984; b. 14.5.47, Belfast; widowed; 1s.; 1d.; remarried in 1998. Educ. Boys' Model School, Belfast; Queen's University, Belfast; Open University. Head, Maths, Dunmurry High School, 1969 - 75; Lecturer, Department of Computing Science, Ulster Polytechnic, 1976 - 78; Senior Lecturer, Ulster Polytechnic, 1978 - 84; Lecturer, University of Ulster, 1984 - 91; Course Director, BSc Honours Computing Science (part-time), 1996-2002; Faculty Board since 1988. Distinguished Teaching Award, University of Ulster, 1991. Recreations: crosswords; DIY. Address: (b.) School of Computing and Maths, University of Ulster, Shore Road, Newtownabbey, BT37 0QB; T.- 01232-366673.

McCloy, Alison Elizabeth, BA, MSc, MInst Public Relations. Communications Manager, British Red Cross since 1998; b. 13.9.50, Corbridge, England; m., Maurice McCloy; 3d. Educ. Sullivan Upper School; Newbury Girls' Grammar School; Queen's University, Belfast; University of Ulster. Trainee Bank Manager, National Westminster Bank Plc, Reading, 1972 - 73; Teacher, Geography, Shaw House School, Newbury, 1973 - 78; Junior Researcher, Institute of Irish Studies, Queen's University, Belfast, 1985 - 86; Education Officer, Ulster Wildlife Trust, 1986 - 88; Public Affairs Officer, Royal Society for the Protection of Birds, 1988 - 98;. School Governor. Publications: Strangford Lough Bibliography, 1986. Recreations: walking; bridge; golf; travel;

painting. Address: (h.) 51 Ballycoan Road, Belfast BT8 8LL; T.- 02890-645584; (b.) British Red Cross, 87 University Street, Belfast, BT7 1HP; T.- 02890-246400.

McCluggage, David Campbell. JP. Retired; Landowner; b. 5.7.28; m., Margaret Jane McCluggage; 2s.; 3d. Educ. Portora Royal School, Enniskillen; Wreckin College, Wellington, Shropshire; Northampton Technical College. Chairman, Shoe Manufacturer and Distributor; Forestry. Justice of the Peace since 1988.

McClure, Rev. Colin David, BSc, BD, MSSc. Minister, First Larne Presbyterian Church; Member, Southern Education and Library Board; b. 28.1.62, Belfast; m., Jane Margaret Henderson; 1s.; 1d. Educ. Royal Belfast Academical Institution; Queen's University, Belfast; Union Theological College; United Theological College of the West Indies. Assistant/Student, Webster Memorial United Church, Kingston, Jamaica; Ordained, Fisherwick Presbyterian Church, Belfast. Representative, Irish Council of Churches; Member, General Assembly Committees including: Irish Church Relations; World Church Relations; World Development; Union Commission - Convener, Personnel and Planning Committee; Boys' Brigade Training Officer; PCI representative to the United Reformed Church's Ecumenical Committee; Board of Governors at Larne and Inver PS and Olderfleet PS; Governor, Banbridge Academy and Larne Grammar School. Recreations: music; keyboards; male voice choir; swimming; camping and caravanning. Address: (h.) The Manse, 154 The Roddens, Larne BT40 1PN. T.-028 28272441. e-mail: cmcclure@presbyterianireland.org

McClure, Prof. Neil, MD, FRCOG. Professor of Obstetrics and Gynaecology, Queen's University, Belfast since 2000; b. 9.7.59, Newtownards; m., Jennifer, Jane Bunting; 1s; 3d. Educ. Regent House School; Queen's University, Belfast. Fellow, Reproductive Medicine, Brown University, Providence, Rhode Island, USA, 1990; Sub-speciality Senior Registrar, Reproductive Medicine, Monash University, Australia, 1991 - 92. Publications: papers in The Lancet, Human Reproduction, Fertility and Sterility. Recreations: pipe organs; motorbikes; horses. Address: (b.) School of Medicine, Obstetrics and Gynaecology, Institute of Clinical Science, Grosvenor Road, Belfast. T.-028 90 894600. e-mail: n.mcclure@qub.ac.uk

McCluskey, David Rolande, MD (Hons), FRCP, FRCPI. Consultant Physician, Royal Victoria Hospital, since 1984; Head of Department of Medicine, Queen's University of Belfast, (Assistant Head, School of Medicine, since 1998); b. 6.1.52, Portadown; m., Barbara Jane Clyde; 2 s. Educ. Portadown College; Queen's University of Belfast. Recreation: golf. Address: Department of Medicine, Institute of Clinical Science, Grosvenor Road, Belfast BT12 6BA; T.-028 90 632707. e-mail: d.mccluskey@qub.ac.uk

McCollum, Anne, CBE, DL, HonDR Lit. b. 9.5.34, Belfast; m., Lord Justice McCollum (see Rt. Hon. Lord Justice McCollum); 6s.; 2d. Educ. St Dominic's College, Belfast. Member, Lloyds TSB Foundation, since 2001; Member, Board of Trustees, Shorts Bombardier Charitable Foundation since 1994; Chairman, Mater Hospital Trust, since 1999. Recreations: golf; walking; theatre; reading.

McCollum, Rt Hon. Lord Justice Liam. KB. Lord Justice of Appeal since 1997; b. 13.1.33, Rathmullan, Co Donegal, Ireland; m., Anne Fitzpatrick (see Anne McCollum); 6s.; 2d. Educ. Waterside Boys' School; St Columb's College; University College, Dublin. Called to the Bar, Northern Ireland, 1955; Called to the Irish Bar, 1963; Queen's Counsel, 1971; High Court Judge, 1987. Knight Batchelor, 1988; Privy Councillor, 1997. Address: (b.) Royal Courts of Justice, Chichester Street, Belfast BT1; T.- 01232-235111.

McConkey, Professor Roy, BA, PhD, FPsSI. Professor of Learning Disability, School of Nursing, University of Ulster; b. 19.6.48. Belfast; m., Patricia; 1s.; 1d. Educ. Belfast High School; Queen's University, Belfast. Hester Adrian Research Centre, University of Manchester, 1970 - 77; Senior Research Officer, St Michael's House, Dublin, 1977 - 88; Director of Training and Research, Brothers of Charity, Scotland, 1988 - 97. Consultant: UNESCO; Save the Children (UK), Cheshire Foundation International; British Council. Address: (b.) School of Nursing, University of Ulster, Shore Road, Newtownabbey, BT37 0QB; T.- 02890-368889 e-mail: r.mcconkey@ulster.ac.uk

McCormack, Prof. Brendan, DPhil (Oxon), BSc (Hons), PGCEA, RGN, RMN. Professor of Nursing, University of Ulster, since 2000; Director of Nursing Research and Development, Royal Hospitals Trust, Belfast, since 2000; b. 11.8.62, Mullingar, Ireland; m., Mary; 1 s.; 1 d. Educ. Vocational School, Moate, Co. Westmeath; University of Oxford. Head of Practice Development, Oxfordshire Community Health Trust, 1993-96; Director of Gerontological Nursing, Royal College of Nursing, London, 1996-2000. Member, Institute of Learning and Teaching. Publication: Negotiating Partnerships with Older People, a person-centred approach, 2001. Address: (b.) 3rd Floor, Bostock House, Royal Victoria Hospital, Grosvenor Road, Belfast BT12 6PA. T.-028 9063 5332.

McCormack, Feargal, BSc (Econ), FCA, FIMC, MIMgt. Managing Partner, FPM Chartered Accountants; b. 13.5.60, Newry; m., Anne; 2 s. Educ. Abbey Christian Brothers Grammar School, Newry; Queen's University Belfast. General Practice Manager, KPMG, Belfast, 1987; Principal Officer, Industrial Development Board, 1987 - 90;

Founded FPM Chartered Accountants, 1991. Board Member of InterTradeIreland, the Cross Border Trade and Business Development Body; Immediate Past Chairman, Ulster Society of Chartered Accountants; Secretary of Newry Chamber of Commerce and Trade; Chairman of Greenshoots Newry Limited; Secretary of Vela Microboards Northern Ireland Limited; Chairman, Sacred Heart Trust Armagh; Board Member, EquityNetwork. Recreations: sport; current affairs. Address: (b.) FPM Chartered Accountants, Dromalane Mill, The Quays, Newry, Co. Down BT35 8QF.

MacCormack, Rev. James T, BA, BD, MTh. Retired Methodist Minister; b. 11.3.26, Dublin; m., Joan C Shier; 1s.; 2d. Educ. Wesley College, Dublin; Dublin University; Edgehill Theological College; Queen's University, Belfast. Methodist Minister: Dublin Central Mission, 1947 - 49; Zambia, 1952 - 63; Co Fermanagh, 1963 - 66; Zambia, 1966 - 71; Belfast, 1971 - 77; Co Antrim, 1977 - 84; Theological College, 1984 - 91; Co Down, 1991 - 94. Publications: Should We Drink?; Various English Texts translated into Tonga of Zambia; Revision of Tonga Bible, 1967 - 71; Thoughts from a warmed heart, 2002: Commentary on John Wesley's Notes on the New Testament. Recreations: rugby (1938 - 45 and 1949 - 51); squash (1945 - 48 and 1970 - 74); walking; photography; mountain walking. Address: (h.) 14 Malone View Road, Belfast, BT9 5PH; T.- 028 90611931.

McCosker, John Joseph, BSc, FASI, ACIB. Surveyor and Architectural Consultant; Member, Fire Authority for Northern Ireland; b. 30.4.47, Strabane; m., Eileen O'Kane; 4s.; 1d. Educ. St Colman's High School; Open University. Joined Architects firm, Given Wallace and Partners, 1969; Fellow, Architects and Surveyors Institute, 1998. Started own Architectural and Surveying Consultancy Practice, 1977. Recreations: golf; swimming; bridge. Address: (b.) McCosker and Associates, 46 Derry Road, Strabane, Co. Tyrone BT82 8LD. T.-028 71882138.

McCourt, Robert, BSc, CEng, FIEE. Group Director of Engineering, Ulster Television since 1988; b. 16.1.53, Belfast; m., Hilary; 3d. Educ. Methodist College, Belfast; Queen's University, Belfast. Product Development Engineer, Strathearn Audio, 1976 - 77; Vision Control Engineer leading to Broadcast Systems Manager, BBC, 1977 - 88. Recreations: running. Address: (b.) Ulster Television, Havelock House, Ormeau Road, Belfast, BT7 1EB.
e-mail: rmccourt@utvplc.com

McCracken, Dr. Alistair Ross, BSc, PhD, MIBiol, CBiol. Principal Scientific Officer, Department of Agriculture and Rural Development, Northern Ireland; Senior Lecturer, Department of Applied Science, Queen's University, Belfast; 10.4.51, Belfast. Educ. Ballyclare High School; University of Strathclyde;

Queen's University, Belfast. Postdoctoral Appointment, Queen's University, Belfast, 1976 - 79; Joined Department of Agriculture of Northern Ireland, Higher Scientific Officer, 1979. President, Society Irish Plant Pathologists. Editor, Annals of Applied Biology. Publications: scientific papers published on topics including, rust control in short rotation coppice willow, apple canker epidemiology, fungi. Interested in methods to encourage development of student skills; frequent speaker on disease control especially in the garden. Recreations: music, especially Mahler; reading; youth work. Address: (b.) Applied Plant Science Division, Department of Agriculture and Rural Development, Northern Ireland, Newforge Lane, Belfast BT9 5PX; T.-028 902 55244.
e-mail: alistair.mccracken@dardni.gov.uk

McCracken, Dr. Kathleen Luanne, BA (Hons), MA, PhD. Lecturer, English and American Studies, University of Ulster at Jordanstown since 1992; b. 26.10.60, Canada; partner, Dr. Arthur Aughey; 1d. Educ. Grey Highlands Secondary School, Ontario, Canada; York University, Toronto; University of Toronto. Course Director, York University, Toronto, 1985 - 89; Course Director, University of Toronto, 1985 - 89; Part-time Tutor, Trinity College, Dublin, 1990 - 91. Canadian Social Sciences and Humanities Research Council Postdoctoral Research Fellowship, 1989 - 91. Publications: 4 volumes of poetry: Reflections, 1976; Into Celebration, 1980; The Constancy of Objects, 1988; Blue Light, Bay and College, 1991; A Geography of Souls, 2002. Recreations: swimming; photography. Address: (b.) Faculty of Humanities, University of Ulster at Jordanstown, Shore Road, Newtownabbey, Co Antrim, BT37 0QB; T.- 01232-366192.
e-mail: kl.mccracken@ulster.ac.uk

McCrea Rev. Dr. (Robert Thomas) William. Member (Mid Ulster), DUP, Northern Ireland Assembly, since 1998; Member, Magherafelt District Council, since 1973, Chairman, since 2002; Minister, Calvary Free Presbyterian Church, Magherafelt, since 1969; b. Stewartstown; m., Anne; 2 s.; 3 d. Educ. Cookstown Grammar School; Theological Hall, Free Presbyterian Church of Ulster. Civil Servant, 1966; Free Presbyterian Minister of the Gospel, since 1967; Member, Mid Ulster, Northern Ireland Assembly, 1982 - 86; MP Mid Ulster, 1983-97; MP for South Antrim, 2000-01. Hon. DD, Marietta Bible College; Gospel recording artist (silver, gold and platinum discs). Publication: In His Pathway – The Story of Rev. William McCrea. Recreations: music; horse-riding. Address: (b.) 11 Ballyronan Road, Magherafelt, Co. Londonderry BT45 6BP.

McCready, Desmond Turner, BA, PGCE, MEd, PGCert EdMgt. Lecturer, Sociology/Religious Studies, Armagh College of Further and Higher Education, since 1985; b. 13.2.54, Lisburn, County Antrim; m., Diane; 1 s.; 1 d. Educ. Dromore Secondary School, County Down; Lisburn Technical College, County Antrim; Queen's

University Belfast; Edgehill College, Ormskirk, Lancs; University of Ulster, Jordanstown. Professional educator, Further Education, since 1980; Head of School, Armagh College of FE, 1998-2003; Part-time Prison teacher, HMP Maze, 1980-81, 1985-86, 1986-87. Publications: Return to Study: A Guide for Mature Students, 1989; wrote Foreword of 'Peaceful Wartime' (autobiographical account of Britain and Ireland during the Second World War), 1999. Recreations: enjoy travel (have visited some 20 countries); cinema; theology; current affairs; modern history; music; keep fit; cooking; complementary therapies. Address: (h.) 32 Parkland Avenue, Lisburn, Co. Antrim BT28 3JP. T.-02892 588421. e-mail: d.mccready1@ntlworld.com

McCreery, David Garfield, B Ed. Headmaster, Killinchy Primary School since 1983; b. 13.8.48, Newtownards; m., Margaret; 2d. Educ. Regent House Grammar School; Stranmillis College, Belfast. Brownlee Primary School, Lisburn, 1971 - 73; Principal, Ardmilan Primary School, Killinchy, 1973. Address: (h.) 57 Comber Road, Killinchy, Newtownards, Co Down, BT23 6PD; T.- 02897 541679.

McCullough, Rev. Professor John Cecil, BA, BD, PhD. Principal, Union Theological College 1998-2003; Prof. of New Testament, since 1988; b. 13.2.42, Ahoghill; m., Dorothy Irene McCullough; 1s.; 1d. Educ. Ballymena Academy; Queen's University, Belfast. Assistant Minister, Trinity Presbyterian Church, Bangor, 1965 - 68; Minister, Muckamore Presbyterian Church, 1968 - 75; Professor of New Testament and Academic Dean, Beirut, Lebanon, 1975 - 83; Professor and Sub-Dean, Dunedin, New Zealand, 1984 - 88. Editor, Irish Biblical Studies. Recreations: walking. Address: (b.) Union Theological College, 108 Botanic Avenue, Belfast, BT7 1JT. e-mail: jc-mccullough@union.ac.uk

McCully, Madelaine K. Studio Owner; Writer and Storyteller; b. 17.6.44, Derry; m., Thomas McCully; 2d. Educ. Thornhill College, Derry; Belfast College of Art; West of England College of Art; Bristol University. Began teaching art, 1967; Various exhibitions in Derry and Belfast paintings and prints; various commissions undertaken; Bookbinding and Restoration Department, University of California Berkeley, 1976 - 77; Exhibited Book bindings in Handbinding Today, San Francisco Museum of Modern Art, 1978; Left teaching to open own studio in Derry, specialising in book binding. Publications: Leather Book Restoration Manual; Designed Book of Gospels for City of Bregenz, Austria. Recreations: oral history; reading; co-ordinator for Worldwide Marriage Encounter. Address: (b.) 9 Kingsfort Crescent, Derry, BT48 7TB; T.- 028 71350612

McCutcheon, Dr. William Alan, MA, FSA, MRIA. Consultant and Author. Educ. Royal Belfast Academical Institution; Queen's University Belfast. Director: Survey of Industrial

Archaeology, Ministry of Finance, Northern Ireland; Keeper, Technology and Local History, Ulster Museum; Director, Ulster Museum. Hon Senior Fellow, School of Geosciences, Queen's University Belfast, 1999. Publications: The Canals of the North of Ireland, 1965; Railway History in Pictures, Ireland, Vol. 1, 1969, Vol. 2, 1970; Travel and Transport in Ireland (contributor), 1973; Folk and Farm (contributor), 1976; Wheel and Spindle - Aspects of Irish Industrial History, 1977; The Industrial Archaeology of Northern Ireland, 1980; Some People and Places in Irish Science and Technology (contributor), 1985; An Economic and Social History of Ulster, 1820-1939 (contributor), 1985; numerous articles and papers in professional journals. Address: (h.) Ardmilne, 25 Moira Drive, Bangor, Co Down, BT20 4RW; (028) 9146 5519.

McDade, Rev. Edward Ivan, BSc (Econ), Dip Th, MInstPS. Methodist Minister, Cullybackey (Co Antrim), since 2001; b. 1951, Belfast; m., Heather. Educ. Grosvenor Grammar School; University of Ulster at Jordanstown; Belfast College of Further and Higher Education; Queen's University, Belfast. Clerical Officer, Central Records Office, 1970 - 73; Northern Ireland Electricity: Management Trainee, 1973 - 75; Supplies Officer, 1975 - 80; Purchasing Supplies Officer, Central Services Agency, 1980 - 84; Training for the Ministry, 1984 - 87; Methodist Minister: Newtownabbey Methodist Mission, 1987 - 91; Portrush and Portstewart Methodist Churches, 1991 - 96; Methodist Minister, Irvinestown and Pettigo, 1996-2001. Aer Lingus Young Manager of the Year Award, 1976. Recreations: playing at playing golf; reading; walking; travelling. Address: (h.) 30 Shelling Hill Road, Cullybackey, Co. Antrim BT42 1NF. T.-028 2588 0271.

MacDermott, Rt. Hon. Sir John Clarke. Lord Justice of Appeal, Supreme Court of Judicature, Northern Ireland, 1987 - 98; b. 1927. Educ. Campbell College, Belfast; Trinity Hall, Cambridge; Queen's University, Belfast. High Court Judge (NI), 1973 - 87. Address: (b.) 6 Tarawood, Holywood, Co Down BT18 0HS.

McDonald, James Oliver, LVO, MBE, KCSG, KCHS, JP, MSc, FSCA, DL. Independent Assessor for Military Complaints Procedures; b. 21.9.37, Belfast; m., Deirdre; 1s.; 1d. Educ. St Mary's Christian Brothers Grammar School; University of Ulster at Coleraine. Chief Accountant, Jas P Corry and Co Ltd, 1964 -74; General Manager, Hull Group, 1974 - 80; Senior Accountant, Northern Ireland Housing Executive, 1980 - 87; Chief Finance Officer, Down District Council, 1987 - 90; Chief Officer, Labour Relations Agency, 1990 - 96. Member, Post Office Users Council, 1987 - 95; Member, Advisory Committee on Telecoms, 1987 - 95; Member, Police Authority for Northern Ireland, 1994-2001; Chairman, Prince's Trust Action; Board Member, Prince's Youth Business Trust, 1983-2001; Vice

Chairman, Prince's Trust Council (NI), since 1999; Chairman: Youthnet, 1996-2000, Royal Ulster Constabulary GC Foundation, 2001; Board Member: Voluntary Services, 2002, Reach Volunteering, 2003. Recreations: local history; military history; eating out. Address: (h.) 50 Malone Park, Belfast, BT9 6NN; T.- 01232-667350.

McDonald, Joe, BSc, (Econ), MSc. Assistant Secretary and Press Officer, Ulster Farmers' Union since 1995; b. 20.1.72, Lurgan, Co Armagh. Educ. St Michael's Senior High School, Lurgan; Queen's University, Belfast. Field Staff Member/Hatchery Manager, Moy Park Ltd, 1994 - 95. Recreations: all sports participating and watching; playing and listening to music. Address: (b.) Ulster Farmer's Union, 475 Antrim Road, Belfast, BT15 3DA; T.- 02890-370222.

McDonald, John Gary. Business and Finance Editor of Irish News, since 2000; b. 25.4.62, Banbridge; m., Jayne; 1 s.; 1 d. Educ. Banbridge Academy. Trainee Reporter/Senior Reporter, Banbridge Chronicle, 1979-86; Ulster Star (Lisburn): Senior Reporter, 1986-87, Deputy Editor, 1987-89; Editor, Mid-Ulster Mail (Cookstown, Co. Tyrone), 1989-95; Editor, Ulster Business Magazine, 1995-98; Ireland Sub-Editor of Press Association, 1998-2000. Northern Ireland Business Journalist of The Year, 2000. Recreations: play bag pipes competitively; sports enthusiast (freelance reporter on men's hockey for a number of newspapers and BBC Northern Ireland). Address: (b.) 113-117 Donegall Street, Belfast BT1 2GE. T.-028 9033 7469.

McDonald, Martin. Chief Executive, Rural Development Council of Northern Ireland since 1999. m., Anne; 1s.; 2d. Educ. St Colman's College, Newry; Queen's University Belfast. Joined Down County Council, 1973-74; Department of Environment, Planning Service, 1974-90; Rural Area Co-ordinator, Department of Agriculture, 1990-98. Chair of numerous local networks. Address: (b.) Rural Development Council for Northern Ireland, 17 Loy Street, Cookstown, BT80 8PZ; T.- 016487-66980. e-mail: mmcdonald@rdc.org.uk

McDonnell, Dr. Alasdair, MB, BCh, DCH, DRCOG. Member (South Belfast), Social Democratic and Labour Party, Northern Ireland Assembly, since 1998; Belfast City Councillor since 1977; Deputy Mayor of Belfast, 1995 - 96; b. 1.9.49, Cushendall; m., Olivia Nugent; 1d.; 1 s. Educ. Garron Tower; University College, Dublin. Family Doctor, in an inner city Belfast practice. SDLP Candidate (S Belfast) in every parliamentary election since 1979. Recreations: skiing; farming; promoting tourism and trade and regenerating the economy of Belfast through information technology and biomedical technologies. Address: (h.) 22 Derryvolgie Avenue, Belfast, BT9 6FN; T.- 028-90-662170; (b.) Ormeau Health Centre, 139 Ormeau Road,

Belfast; T.- 028-90-326030; (b.) Political Offices, 150 Ormeau Road, Belfast; T.- 028-90-242474; (b.) 384 Parliament Buildings, Stormont. T.-028 90520329.

McDonough, Dr. Niall Anthony, BA (Mod), PhD. Marine Biologist; Manager, Centre for Marine Resources and Mariculture (C-Mar), Queen's University Belfast, since 2002; b. 2.11.71, Drogheda, Republic of Ireland; m., Oonagh. Educ. St. Mary's Diocesan School, Drogheda, Ireland; Trinity College Dublin; Queen's University Belfast. Career History: Research Fellow, C-Mar, Queen's University Belfast; Resource Development Officer, Cross - Border Aquaculture Initiative; Development Officer, Environmental Change Institute, National University of Ireland, Galway. Recreations: golf; reading; travelling. Address: (b.) Queen's University, Marine Laboratory, 12 The Strand, Portaferry, Co. Down BT22 1PF. T.-028 42729648. e-mail: niall.mcdonough@qub.ac.uk

McDonough, Roisin. Chief Executive, Arts Council of Northern Ireland. Address: (b.) MacNeice House, 77 Malone Road, Belfast BT9 6AQ. T.-02890 385200.

McDowell, Sir Eric Wallace, CBE, DSc (Econ), FCA. Chairman, Capita Management Consultants Ltd, 1991 - 98; b. 7.6.25, Belfast; m., Helen Lilian Montgomery; 1s.; 2d. Educ. Royal Belfast Academical Institution. Qualified as CA, 1948; Partner, Wilson, Hennessey and Crawford, 1952 - 73; Partner, Deloitte, Haskins and Sells, 1973 - 80; Senior Partner, Belfast 1980 - 85; Director: Northern Ireland Transport Holding Company, 1971 - 74; Spence Bryson Ltd, 1986 - 89; TSB Bank Northern Ireland Plc, 1986 - 92; First Trust Bank Ltd, 1992 - 96; Shepherd Ltd since 1992. Member: Advisory Committee, Northern Ireland Investment Fund for Charities, 1975 - 98 (Chairman, 1980 - 98); Northern Ireland Economic Council, 1977 - 83; Industrial Development Board for Northern Ireland, 1982 - 91 (Chairman, 1986 - 91); Broadcasting Council for Northern Ireland, 1983 - 86. Member: Executive Committee Relate (NI), 1981-2001; (Chairman, 1992 - 96); Board of Trustees, National Relate, 1992-2000; Presbyterian Church in Ireland Trustee since 1983; Member: Executive Committee, Abbeyfield Belfast Society since 1986 (Treasurer, 1986-99); Member: Board of Governors, Royal Belfast Academical Institution since 1959 (Chairman 1977 - 86); Council, Institute of CAs in Ireland, 1968 - 77 (President 1974 - 75); Senate, Queen's University, Belfast, 1993 2001. Hon. DSc (Econ), Queen's University, Belfast, 1989. Recreations: current affairs; music and drama; foreign travel. Address: (h.) Beechcroft, 19 Beechlands, Belfast, BT9 5HU.

McDowell, Sid, CBE. Chairman, Northern Ireland Housing Executive, since 1995. Educ. Methodist College, Belfast; Ruskin College, Oxford. Compositor. Former senior trade union official at Northern Ireland Public Service Alliance, 1965-94; Chairman, Educational Guidance Service for Adults, 1990-98; Deputy Chairman, Co-operation North. Chairman, Local Government Staff Commission for Northern Ireland, since 1996; Civil Service Commission, since 1999; Vice-President, NI Association for Spina Bifida and Hydrocephalus; President, Lisnagarvey Operatic Society. Address. (b.) NI Housing Executive, Housing Centre, 2 Adelaide Street, Belfast BT2 8PB; T.- 028 9024 0588.

McElduff, Barry. Member (West Tyrone), Sinn Fein, Northern Ireland Assembly, since 1998. Educ. Queen's University, Belfast. Address: (b.) Parliament Buildings, Stormont, Belfast BT4 3ST.

McElhinney, William, Cert Ed, B Ed, B Phil, MSc, PGCCE. Principal, Ashlea Primary and Nursery School, Londonderry since 1991; b. 12.6.54, Co Donegal, Ireland. Educ. Foyle College, Londonderry; University of Bristol; University of Ulster. Assistant Teacher: Model Primary School, Londonderry, 1977 - 80; Lisnagelvin Primary School, Londonderry, 1980 - 86; Principal, Sandville Primary School, Co Tyrone, 1986 - 91. Recreations; music; gardening; youth work; church activities.   Address: (b.) Ashlea Primary School, 163 Stevenson Park, Tullyally, Londonderry, BT47 3QT; T.- 028 7134 7950.

McElnay, Professor James Charles, BSc, PhD, FPSNI MRPharms, FCCP. Dean, Faculty of Science and Agriculture, Queen's University Belfast, since 2002; b. Ballymoney, Co Antrim; m., Diana Marie McElnay; 2s.; 1d.   Educ. Dalriada School, Ballymoney; Queen's University Belfast. Lecturer, Pharmacology, 1979 - 80, Queen's University Belfast; Research Fellow, Clinical Pharmacy, University of Iowa, USA, 1980 - 81; Visiting Lecturer, Clinical Pharmacy, University of Zimbabwe, 1982; Queen's University, Belfast: Lecturer, Biopharmacy, 1981 - 90; Senior Lecturer, Pharmacy Practice, 1990 - 91; Visiting Professor, Clinical Pharmacy, University of Houston, Texas, USA, 1991 - 92; Queen's University Belfast: Reader, Pharmacy Practice, 1992 - 94; Head, School of Pharmacy, 1994-2002; Professor of Pharmacy since 1996. Co-Director, Antrim Area Hospital Academic Practice Unit since 1995. Chairman, UK Heads of School of Pharmacy, 1998-2000; President, Pharmaceutical Society of Northern Ireland, 1999-2001. Recreations: salmon fishing; theatre; cinema. Address: (b.) School of Pharmacy; Queen's University Belfast, BT9 7BL; T.- 02890-335800.

McElwee, Dorothy, BSSc (Hons), MIPD, ADFE. Head, Department of Business and Management Studies, North West Institute of Further and Higher Education since 1996; b. 13.8.58, Londonderry; m., Paul Ashley McElwee; 3s.; 1d. Educ. Foyle and Londonderry College; Queen's University, Belfast. Part-time Lecturer, Further Education, 1980 - 84; Personnel Manager, Contract Shirts,

1984 - 88; Training and Enterprise Manager, L E A, 1989 - 91; North West Institute of Further and Higher Education: Senior Lecturer, 1991 - 94; Principal Lecturer, 1994 - 96. Bank of Ireland, Best Overall Student Award for Postgraduate Diploma in Personnel Management. Recreations: gym; walking; golf; swimming. Address: (h.) 93 Westlake, Enagh Lough, Londonderry; T.- 02871-342724.

McEvoy, Prof. Kieran Patrick, LLB (Hons), MSc,   PhD.   Professor of Law, Institute of Criminology and Criminal Justice, Queen's University Belfast, since 2000; b. 22.4.67, Newry; m., Lesley Emerson. Educ. Abbey Christian Brothers Grammar School, Newry; Queen's University Belfast; University of Edinburgh. Information Officer, NIACRO, 1990 - 95; Assistant Director, Institute of Criminology and Criminal Justice, Queen's Univ. Belfast, 1995-2000.   Chairperson, Committee on the Administration of Justice (CAJ) 1997-99. Publications: Crime, Criminology and Locale in Northern Ireland, 2000; Paramilitary Imprisonment in Northern Ireland, 2001; Criminology and Conflict Resolution, 2002. Recreations: reading; five-a-side football; cinema. Address: (b.) School of Law, 27 University Square, Queen's University Belfast, Belfast BT7 1NN; T.- 02890-273873.

McEwen, Professor Alexander, BA (Hons), PhD, Cert Ed, FRSA. Professor of Education, Queen's University, Belfast since 1997; b. 6.3.45, Belfast; m., Helen McEwen; 2s.; 1d. Educ. Grosvenor High School, Belfast; Queen's University; Stranmillis College, Belfast; Middlesex University. Teacher, London and Essex, 1966 - 74; Queen's University, Belfast: Lecturer, 1974; Senior Lecturer, 1987; Dean, Faculty of Education, 1994; Reader, 1995. Recreations: fixing things; mountaineering; singing. Address: (b.) School of Education, Queen's University, Belfast, 69-71 University Street, Belfast, BT7 1HL; T.- 02890-335940.

Macfadyen, Professor Amyan, MA DSc. Emeritus Professor of Biology, University of Ulster; b. 11.12.20, Kent; m., Ursula Margaret Hampton (dec.); 3s.; 1d. Educ. Dauntseys; Oxford University.   Royal Electrical and Mechanical Engineers, 1939 - 46; Research Officer, Bureau of Animal Population, 1948 - 57; Department of Zoology, Swansea University: Lecturer/Senior Lecturer/Reader,   1957-65;   Professor, Jordbundsbiologisk Institutet, University of Aarhus, Denmark, 1965 - 66; Professor of Biology, New University of Ulster, 1966 - 86, retired, 1986. Past President: British Ecological Society; International   Association   for   Ecology. Publications: Animal Ecology, 1957 (2nd edn, 1963); IBP Handbook on Terrestial Productivity, 1970; Advances in Ecological Research (ed.) 1969-86; Approximately 90 scientific papers. Recreations: gardening; walking; travel; reading; natural history. Address: (h.) 23 Mountsandel

Road, Coleraine, BT52 1JE; T.- 028703-42112.
e-mail: amyan@gn.apc.org

McFarland, Alan. Member (North Down), Ulster
Unionist Party, Northern Ireland Assembly, since
1998; b. 9.8.49, Londonderry; m.; 1 s.; 2 d. Educ.
Campbell College, Belfast; Royal Military
Academy, Sandhurst. Former Major, Royal Tank
Regiment; Parliamentary Assistant, Westminster;
Director, Somme Heritage Centre, Newtownards;
Member, Northern Ireland Forum, 1996; Former
Deputy Chair, Regional Development Committee,
NI Assembly; Member, NI Policing Board.
Address: (b.) Parliament Buildings, Stormont,
Belfast BT4 3XX; T.-028 9052 1528.
e-mail: alanmla@hotmail.com

McFarland, Brian Charles, Dip ID (Hons).
Communications Co-ordinator for Slavic Gospel
Association (UK) Ltd since 1999; b. 1.3.49,
Dungannon, Co Tyrone; m., Phyllis Boyd; 2s.
Educ. Dungannon Royal School; Belfast College
of Art. Craigavon Development Commission,
1970 - 73; Department of the Environment,
Graphic Design Unit, 1973 - 89; Regional
Representative Ireland for Slavic Gospel
Association (UK) Ltd, 1989 - 99. Recreations:
golf; reading; family. Address: (b.) 36 Moss Park,
Richhill, Co Armagh, BT61 9PT; T.-028 3887
0025. e-mail: brian.mcfarland@sga.org.uk

McFarland, Sir John Talbot, 3rd Baronet of
Aberfoyle, Londonderry, TD. Chairman: Malvey
Ltd, 2000-01; J.T. McFarland Holdings Ltd, 1984-
2001; McFarland Farms since 1980; b. 3.10.27,
Londonderry; m., Mary Scott Watson; 2s.; 2d.
Educ. Marlborough College; Trinity College,
Oxford. Captain RA (TA), retired 1967;
Chairman: R C Malseed and Company, 1957 - 90;
Lanes (Derry) Ltd, 1977 - 84; Lanes (Fuels) Oils
Ltd; Lanes Patent Fuels Ltd; Holmes Coal Ltd;
Alexander Thompson and Company Ltd; Nichol
Ballintyne Ltd; J W Corbett Ltd; Wattersons Ltd.
Chairman, Londonderry Lough Swilly Railway
Company, 1978 - 81; Director: Londonderry
Gaslight Company, 1958 - 89; Donegal Holdings
Ltd, 1963 - 85; G Kinnaird and Son Ltd, 1981 - 95;
Windy Hills Ltd, 1994 - 95; Wallcoatings, Dublin
Ltd. Councillor, Londonderry County Borough
Council, 1955 - 69; Member: NW HMC, 1960 -
73; Londonderry Port and Harbour
Commissioners, 1965 - 73; Joint Chairman,
Londonderry and Foyle College, 1971 - 76. High
Sheriff, Co Londonderry, 1958; City of County of
Londonderry, 1965 - 67; DL, Londonderry, 1962.
resigned 1982. Recreations: shooting; golf.
Address: (h.) Dunmore House, Carrigans, Co
Donegal; T.- 07491 40120. Fax: 07491 40336.

McFerran, Francis Donal, LLB, MPhil. Solicitor
of Supreme Court, (NI); b. 28.5.41, Ballymena, Co
Antrim; m., Anne Higgins; 2s.; 2d. Educ. St
Patrick's College, Armagh; Wallace High School,
Lisburn; Queen's University, Belfast. Admitted as
Solicitor, 1972; Deputy Resident Magistrate, 1980
- 85; Deputy County Court Judge since 1991.

Master of Philosophy, Medical Ethics and Law,
1994. Legal Member, Mental Health Tribunal,
1997; Professional Conduct Committee, General
Medical Council, 1997. Life Sentence Review
Commissioner, since 2001; Secretary of Solicitors
Disciplinary Tribunal. Recreation: sailing.
Address: (b.) PO Box 138, Holywood BT18 9HG.
T.-02890 425522.

McFerran, John Christopher Herdman, JP. b.
16.4.37, Carrickfergus; m., Elizabeth Murray
Mudie; 1s.; 1d. Educ. Mourne Grange; St
Edwards School, Oxford. Lieutenant, North Irish
Horse (TA) 1956- 63; Proprietor and Managing
Director, Carpex (NI) Ltd Belfast, 1972 - 90.
Director, Herdmans Ltd Sion Mills since 1980.
Governor, Rockport Prep School, Craigavad since
1974. Chairman, Helen's Bay Residents
Association; Vice Chairman, SSAFA Forces Help,
N. Ireland; Commodore, Royal North of Ireland
Yacht Club, 1989 - 90; Vice Chairman, Association
of Justice of Peace, N. Ireland. Recreations:
sailing; golf. Address: (h.) 56 Church Road,
Helen's Bay, Co Down, BT19 1TP; T.- 028 9185
2265. email:christopher.mcferran@btinternet.com

McGarry, Colm, MSc, DMS, FCIPD. Chief
Executive and Town Clerk, Larne Borough
Council, since 1998; m., Nuala; 2 s.; 2 d. Address:
(b.) Smiley Buildings, Victoria Road, Larne, Co.
Antrim BT40 1RU. T.-028 2827 2313.

McGavock, Professor Hugh, MD, BSc, FRCGP.
Prescribing Science Section, School of Nursing,
University of Ulster; b. 13.4.39, Larne; m., Dr.
Elizabeth McGavock; 3s. Educ. Belfast Royal
Academy; Queen's University, Belfast. RMO,
Royal Victoria Hospital, Belfast, 1964 - 65;
Medical Officer, Research, Royal Army Medical
Corps, Farnborough, 1965 - 70; General
Practitioner, 1971 - 80; Government Medical
Officer since 1980, former Principal Medical
Officer; Member, Committee on Safety of
Medicines, London; Postgraduate Course
Organizer, Northern Ireland Council for
Postgraduate Medical and Dental Education.
Chair, National and International Research Bodies.
Publications: 65 scientific research articles;
Author, 'How Drugs Work', 2002; Editor, Practice
Formulary; Handbook of Drug Use Research;
chapters in textbooks; numerous guest lectures.
Recreations: music; tennis; hill walking.
Address:(h.) 55 Culcrum Road, Cloughmills, Co
Antrim, BT44 9NJ; T.- 02827 638258.

McGeown, Prof. Mary Graham, CBE, MB,
BCL, MD, PhD, FRCP (Ed, L, I), DSc (Hon.)
DMSc (Hon.). Professorial Fellow, Queen's
University, Belfast since 1988; b. 19.7.23, Lurgan;
m., Joseph Maxwell Freeland (dec.) ; 3s. Educ.
Lurgan College; Queen's University, Belfast.
House Physician/Surgeon, Royal Victoria
Hospital, Belfast, 1947 - 48; House Officer, Royal
Belfast Hospital for Sick Children, 1948; Assistant
Lecturer, Pathology, Queen's University, Belfast,
1949 - 50; Assistant Lecturer, Biochemistry,

Queen's University, Belfast, 1950 - 53; Research Fellow, MRC, 1953-56, Royal Victoria Hospital, 1956-58; Senior Hospital Medical Officer, Renal medicine, 1958 - 62; Consultant Nephrologist, Belfast City and Royal Victoria Hospitals, Belfast, 1962 - 88; Physician in administrative charge, Renal unit, Belfast City Hospital, 1968 - 88. Chairman, UK Transplant Management Committee, 1983 - 90; President, Ulster Medical Society, 1984 - 85; Medical Advisor, Northern Ireland Kidney Research Fund, 1972 - 88 (Patron since 1988); Hon. member, Renal Association of GB (President, 1986 - 87); Hon. Member, British Transplantation Society since 1987; Archivist 1987-90; Chairman, Supervisory Committee on Organ Transplantation, 1985 - 89; Hon. member, European Renal Association; Chairman, Corrigan Club, 1987. Publications: Clinical Management of Electrolyte Disorders, 1983; Clinical Management of Renal Transplantations, 1993; numerous articles and book chapters on kidney diseases, kidney transplantation, calcium metabolism and kidney stones. Recreations: gardening; antiques; cooking. Address: (h.) 14 Osborne Gardens, Belfast, BT9 6LE; T.- 028 90-802934.

McGilly, Patrick Joseph, Cert Ed. Retired Headmaster; b. 21.3.39, Enniskillen; m., Angela Duffy; 1s.; 4d. Educ. St Columb's College, Derry; St Joseph's College of Education, Belfast. Former Vice-Principal, St Comhghall's Secondary School, Lisnaskea; Former Principal, St Mary's Primary School, Newtownbutler, Co Fermanagh; Former Headmaster, St Ronan's Primary School, Lisnaskea, Co Fermanagh. Address: (h.) 'Drumsastry', Newtownbutler, Enniskillen, Co Fermanagh, BT92 8ED; T.- 028 677 38661.

McGimpsey, Michael Henry, BA. Businessman; Member (South Belfast), Ulster Unionist Party, Northern Ireland Assembly, since 1998; Minister for Culture, Arts and Leisure, since 1999; UUP Assembly spokesman on Security/Home Affairs; b. 1.7.48, Donaghadee, Co. Down; m.; 1s.; 1d. Educ. Regent House Grammar School; Trinity College Dublin. Elected Councillor, Belfast City Council (Laganbank Ward), 1993; Member, Queen's University Senate. Publications: many articles in various newspapers and periodicals. Recreations: reading; walking; gardening. Address: (b.) UUP Advice Office, 127-145 Sandy Row, Belfast BT12 5ET. T.-028 90 245801; Fax: 028 90 245801.

McGinnis, William, OBE, DL, MSc, FRSA, FCIM. Chairman, The McAvoy Group Ltd, The Learning and Skills Advisory Board; b. 24.1.49; m., Elizabeth; 2 d. Board Member: Invest Northern Ireland; Board Member, Sector Skills Development Agency; Member of National Employment Panel. Address: (b.) 76 Ballynakilly Road, Dungannon BT71 6HD. T.-028 8774 0372; (b) Department for Employment and Learning, Adelaide House, 39-49 Adelaide Street, Belfast. T.- 028 9025 7802.

McGivern, Colm, BA (Hons), MSSc. Assistant Director (Education), Workers Educational Association; b. 9.8.72, Newry Co Down. Educ. St Colman's College, Newry; Queen's University, Belfast. Students' Union, Queen's University, Belfast: Vice-President (Education), 1994 - 95; President, 1995 - 96. Member, Senate, Queen's University, Belfast since 1996. Recreations: middle-distance running; theatre; cinema. Address: (b.) 1 Fitzwilliam Street, Belfast, BT9 6AW; T.- 02890 329718.

McGivern, Gerard, BA (Hons), MCIM, MIED. Director of District Development, Newry and Mourne District Council, since 2000; b. 22.3.58, Newry; m., Roisin; 2 s. Educ. Abbey Grammar CBS, Newry; Trinity College Dublin. Development Supervisor, Mournecraft Ltd, Newry, 1981-85; Manager, Lecale Youth Trainee Workshops, Downpatrick, 1985-90; Manager, Banbridge Enterprise Centre, Banbridge, 1990-92; Banbridge District Council: Development Manager, 1992-99, Director of Development, 1999-2000. Member: Institution of Economic Development, Chartered Institute of Marketing; Director, East Border Region Ltd. Address: (b.) Newry and Mourne District Council, Greenbank Industrial Estate, Newry BT34 2QU. T.-028 3031 3233. e-mail: districtdevelopment@newryand mourne.gov.uk

McGlone, Patrick Joseph (Patsy), BA (Hons). Councillor, Cookstown District Council since 1993; b. 8.7.59, Magherafelt, Co Derry; m., Geraldine O'Neill. Educ. St Trea's, Ballymaguigan, Magherafelt; Rainey Endowed School, Magherafelt; University of Ulster. Member, Executive SDLP, 1984 - 86; General Secretary, SDLP, 1986 - 91; media consultant; Member, Northern Ireland Forum for Constituency of Mid-Ulster, since 1996; SDLP Delegate, multi-party peace talks, concluding in Good Friday Agreement 1998. Chairman, SDLP Association of Councillors, since 1999; Member: SDLP Ruling General Council, Northern Ireland Housing Council, Housing Benefit Review Panel; Board Member, Foras na Gaeilge (cross-border Irish language promotional and funding agency set up as integral part of Good Friday Agreement); Member, EU Community Support Framework Monitoring Committee for Northern Ireland. Contributor and political commentator to magazines; Writer specialising in Irish Language/Gaelic culture, writing in English and Irish. Recreations: reading; cycling; fishing; wildfowling. Address: (h.) 'Sliabh an Doire', Spring Road, Ballylifford, Ballinderry Bridge, Cookstown, Co Tyrone BT80 0BD. T.-02879 418778.

McGoldrick, Sister Julie, MRelSc, BEd (Hons). Principal, Sacred Heart Grammar School, Newry; b. Johnstone, Scotland. Recreations: golf; cycling; music; Celtic FC. Address: (b.) Sacred Heart Grammar School, 10 Ashgrove Avenue, Newry BT34 1PR.

McGrady, Edward Kevin (Eddie), MP, FCA. Member of Parliament (South Down), since 1987; Member (South Down), Social Democratic and Labour Party, Northern Ireland Assembly, since 1998; b. 3.6.35, Downpatrick, Co Down; m., Patricia Swail; 2s.; 1d. Educ. St Patrick's Grammar School, Downpatrick. Chartered Accountant. First Chairman, SDLP; Councillor, Downpatrick Urban District Council until 1973; Councillor, Down District Council, 1973 - 89; Member Northern Ireland Assembly, 1973; Minister for Co-ordination and Planning. Chairman, ONC on several occasions; Member of the NI Affairs Committee in Westminster; Member of the NI Policing Board. Recreations: walking; gardening; choral music. Address: (b.) 30-32 Saul Street, Downpatrick, Co Down, BT30 6NQ; T.- 01398-612882.

McGrady, Rev. Feargal Patrick, KCHS, KGCO, Ch.LJ, BEd, BD. Curate in the Parish of Drumbo and Carryduff since 1998; b. 12.6. 60, Downpatrick, Co Down. Educ. St Patrick's High School, Downpatrick; St Joseph's College of Education; St Patrick's College, Maynooth, Co Kildare, Ireland. Ordained into the Priesthood, 1985; Chaplain, Royal Victoria Hospital, Belfast, 1985 - 86; Curate: Castlewellan, Co Down, 1986 - 89; Portaferry, Co Down, 1989 - 92; Curate in the Parish of Ballymena, Co Antrim, 1992 - 98. Knight of the Holy Sepulchre of Jerusalem (an order under the protection of the Holy See), 1993; Knight, Commander, 1996. Publications: Deich mBliana ag Fás – Ten years a growing: The Crusading Spirit in Medieval Ireland and the Establishment of the Order of the Holy Sepulchre in Ireland 1986, 1999; Ecclesiastical Knight of Grace of the Sacred and Military Constantinian Order of St. George (Royal House of Bourbon - Two Sicilies), 2001; Chaplain of St. Lazarus of Jerusalem, 2001. Address: (h.) 79 Ivanhoe Avenue, Carryduff, Belfast BT8 8BW.

McGrath, Brian. Chief Executive, Londonderry Port & Harbour Commissioners. Address: (b.) Harbour Office, Port Road, Lisahally, Londonderry BT47 6FL. T.-028-71-860555.

McGrath, Sinead, LLB. Solicitor since 1996; b. 27.2.72, Belfast. Educ. Dominican College, Fortwilliam, Belfast; Queen's University, Belfast. Recreations: netball; swimming. Address: (b.) L'Estrange and Brett Solicitors, Arnott House, 12-16 Bridge Street, Belfast, BT1 1LS; T.- 02890-230426.

McGrath, Thomas, OBE, FCII, FInst, AM(Dip). Regional Director, Marsh (UK) Ltd; b. 18.11.44, Belfast; m., Marjorie; 2d. Educ. Belfast High School. Various positions, Sun Alliance, 1962 - 72; W J Palmer Group, 1972 - 74; Joined Marsh UK Ltd, 1974: Director, 1978; Chief Executive, 1987; Managing Director, Marsh & Mclennan Inc, 1992. Visiting Lecturer to universities and professional bodies. Past President, Belfast Insurance Institute; Past Chairman, College of

Business Styudies; Past Board Member, Braidside Integrated Primary School; Past Chairman, Rathgael Training School; Past Examiner, Chartered Insurance Institute. Member, Probation Board for Northern Ireland; Chairman, Northern Ireland Tourist Board; Director, The Ireland Funds; Member, Board of Governors, Belfast High School; Chairman, Education Committee of the Institute of Directors; Vice Chairman, NIBEP; Board Member, Tourism Ireland Ltd; Member of the Board of Trustees of Arthritis Research. Recreations: walking; reading (biography and military history); charitable work; traditional jazz; public service. Address: (b.) Marsh UK Ltd, Bedford House, Bedford Street, Belfast, BT2 7DX; T.- 02890 556100.

McGreal, Professor William Stanley, Professor, School of the Built Environment, University of Ulster since 1998; b. 11.11.50, Whitehead, Co Antrim; m., Irene; 1s.; 1d. Educ. Larne Grammar School; Queen's University, Belfast. Graduate Demonstrator, Department of Geography, Queen's University, Belfast, 1976 - 79; Lecturer, School of Surveying, Ulster Polytechnic, 1979 - 84; School of the Built Environment, University of Ulster: Lecturer/Senior Lecturer/Reader 1984 - 98. Publications: Urban Regeneration: Property Development and Investment; European Cities, Planning Systems and Property Markets; Cities in the Pacific Rim; European Valuation Practice. Recreations: travel; walking. Address: (b.) School of the Built Environment; University of Ulster, Shore Road, Newtownabbey, Co Antrim BT37 OQB; T.- 02890-366566. e-mail: ws.mcgreal@ulster.ac.uk

McGreevy, Marian, BEd (Hons), DipEd. Principal Teacher, St. Colmcille's High School, since 1994; b. 17.6.54, Enniskillen. Educ. Mount Lourdes, Enniskillen; Sedgley Park, Manchester; Warwick University. Posts at: Bishop Ullathorne, Coventry, 1975 - 78, Ash Green, Warwickshire, 1979 - 83, Exhall School, Warwickshire, 1983-86; Advisory Teacher, Warwickshire LEA, 1986 - 87; TVEI Assistant Adviser, Warwickshire, 1987 - 89; Adviser, Shropshire, 1989 - 94. Recreations: theatre; hill-walking; reading. Address: (b.) Crossgar, Co. Down BT30 9EY; T.-028 44 830311.

McGrillen, John, MSc, MBA. Clerk and Chief Executive, Down District Council, since 1999; b. 13.3.62, Co. Down. Educ. St. Patrick's Grammar School, Downpatrick. Short Bros. PLC, 1984 - 87; Industrial Development Board: Dusseldorf, 1989 - 93, Belfast, 1993 - 97; Chief Executive, Northern Ireland Public Sector Enterprises Ltd., 1997 99. Recreations: travel; soccer; gaelic football. Address: (b.) Down District Council, 24 Strangford Road, Downpatrick BT30 6SR.

McGuckian, John Brendan, BSc (Econ). Chairman, Ulster Television Plc since 1991; b. 13.11.39, Co Antrim; m., Carmel McGowan; 2s.; 2d. Educ. St MacNissi's College, Co. Antrim; Queen's University, Belfast. Chairman,

Cloughmills Manufacturing since 1967; Director: Munster and Lenster Bank since 1972; Allied Irish Bank Plc since 1976; Harbor Group Ltd since 1978; Aer Lingus Plc, 1979 - 84; Unidare Plc since 1987; Irish Continental Group Plc since 1988. Member: Derry Development Committee, 1968 - 71; Laganside Corporation, 1988 - 92; Chairman: International Fund for Ireland, 1990- 93; Tedcastle Ltd, 1996-2001; Northern Ireland Development Board, 1991 - 97; Pro Chancellor, Queen's University, Belfast, 1990-2000. Address: (b.) Ulster Television Plc, Havelock House, Ormeau Road, Belfast, BT7 1EB; T.- 028 9032 8122.

McGuckin, Michael Joseph, BSc, MICE, FIHT. Chief Executive, Cookstown District Council since 1991; b. 23.10.46, Cookstown; m., Marguerite; 5s.; 2d. Educ. Rainey Endowed School, Magherafelt; Queen's University, Belfast. Engineer, Tyrone County Council, 1969 - 73; Senior Engineer, Roads Service, Department of Environment, 1973 - 87; Principal Engineer, Roads Service, Department of the Environment, 1987 - 91. Recreations: sport; gardening. Address: (b.) Council Offices, Burn Road, Cookstown, BT80 8DT; T.- 028867-62205.

McGuigan, Martin, OBE, BA, MSc. Vice President of European Ceramic Operation A.V. X., since 1978; Board Member of A.V.X., Cz; b. 5.3.56; m., Anne; 2 s.; 1 d. Educ. Dalriada School; University of Ulster. ESB, Dublin, 1979-80; A.V.X, since 1980: numerous positions in production, manufacturing, marketing and general management. Recreations: tennis; exercise; skiing. Address: (h.) 53 Knock Road, Ballymoney, Co. Antrim BT53 6LX.

McGuinness, Daniel Joseph, BSSc (Hons). Partner, Deery McGuiness and Company, Solicitors; b. 19.7.54, Belfast. Educ. St Mary's Christian Brothers Grammar School, Belfast; Queen's University, Belfast. Admitted as Solicitor, 1984. Member of Alliance Party of NI, since 1972. Councillor, Belfast City Council, 1977 - 81; Board Member: Northern Ireland Housing Executive, 1982 - 89; Probation Board for Northern Ireland, 1985 - 89; Belfast Education and Library Board, 1989 - 93; Member, Consumer Council for Northern Ireland, 1990 - 96; Non-Executive Director, Eastern Health and Social Services Board, 1991-99, Chairman, 2000. Recreations: politics; driving; reading; music. Address: (h.) 58 Mooreland Park, Belfast, BT11 9AZ; T.- 028 90 614520.

McGuinness, Joseph (Very Rev.), BSc, BD, MTh, PGCE. President, St. Michael's College, Enniskillen, since 2000; b. 4.10.59, Lisnaskea, Co. Fermanagh. Educ. St. Michael's College, Enniskillen; Queen's University Belfast; St. Patrick's College, Maynooth; Institut Catholique, Paris; St. Mary's University College, Belfast. Head of Music, St. Michael's College, 1995-2000. Member, Irish Commission for Liturgy, 1990-2002. Publications: Lough Derg, St. Patrick's

Purgatory, 2000; various articles and reviews. Recreations: music; theatre; art; reading; travel. Address: (b.) St. Michael's College, Chanterhill Road, Enniskillen, Co. Fermanagh BT74 6DE. T.- 028 6632 2935.

McGuinness, Martin, MP. Member of Parliament (Mid-Ulster), Sinn Fein, since 1997; Member (Mid-Ulster), Sinn Fein, Northern Ireland Assembly since 1998; b. 23.5.50. Educ. Christian Brothers Technical College. Address: (b.) Sinn Féin, 55 Falls Road, Belfast, BT12 4PD

McGuinness, Samuel John, BSc, DASE, DPhil, MBA. Headmaster, Limavady Grammar School since 1997; b. 10.1.49, Londonderry; m., Jennifer; 1s.; 1d. Educ. Foyle College, Londonderry; Queen's University, Belfast; University of Ulster, Coleraine. Limavady Grammar School: Assistant Master, 1971; Department Head, 1976; Vice-Principal, 1984; Headmaster. Cookstown High School, 1990. Recreations: golf; rugby; outdoor pursuits; music. Address: (b.) Limavady Grammar School, Ballyquin Road, Limavady, BT49 9ET; T.- 028 777 60950.

McHale, Professor Noel, BSc, PhD, MRPharmS. Dunville Professor of Physiology, Department of Physiology, Queen's University, Belfast since 2000; b. 24.12.43, Armagh; m., Carmel Jean Rafferty; 1s.; 2d. Educ. St Columb's College, Derry; Queen's University, Belfast. Lecturer, Pharmacology, University College, Dublin, 1975 - 77; Lecturer, Physiology, Queen's University, Belfast, 1977 - 87; Visiting Professor in Physiology, University of Mississippi School of Medicine, USA, 1987; Visiting Professor in Physiology, University of Nevada, Reno, USA, 1988; Queen's University, Belfast: Senior Lecturer in Physiology, 1988 - 89; Reader in Physiology, 1989 - 1992; Prof. of Physiology, 1992-2000. President, Biomedical Sciences, Royal Academy of Medicine in Ireland, 1992 - 94; Conway Review Lecturer and Silver Medalist, 1991. Publications: over 150 articles on the lymphatic system. Recreations: tennis; music. Address: (b.) Department of Physiology, Queen's University, Belfast, 97 Lisburn Road, Belfast, BT9 7BL; T.- 02890 335794. e-mail: n.mchale@qub.ac.uk

McHenry, Maurice J, MSc, MInstBiol, Adv Dip Ed. Headmaster, Our Lady of Lourdes, Ballymoney since 1992; b. 23.8.44, Ballycastle; m., Marie; 1s.; 4d. Educ. Ballycastle High; De La Salle College, Manchester. Science Teacher: St Olcan's, Randalstown, 1967 - 72; St Joseph's High School, Coleraine, 1972 - 89; Field Officer (Secondary Science), North East Education and Library Board, 1989 - 92. Publications: John Clarke (with N McHenry). Recreations: farming; television. Address: (h.) 134 Whitepark Rd, Ballintoy, Ballycastle, Co Antrim, BT54 6ND; T.- 012657-62093.

McHugh, Gerry. Member (Fermanagh and South Tyrone), Sinn Fein, Northern Ireland Assembly,

1998-2003; Councillor, Fermanagh Council; Sinn Fein spokesman on agriculture and rural affairs. Address: (b.) Parliament Buildings, Stormont, Belfast, BT4 3ST.

McHugh, Prof. Marie Louise, BA, MSc, PhD. Professor of Organisational Behaviour, University of Ulster, since 2001, Head of School of Business Organisation and Management, since 2001; b. 6.2.61, Enniskillen. Educ. Convent Grammar School, Enniskillen; Queen's University Belfast; University of Ulster. Research Assistant, Northern Ireland Council for Educational Research, 1985-87; Research Officer, University of Ulster, 1987-89, Lecturer in Organisation Studies, 1989-98, Senior Lecturer in Organisational Behaviour, 1998-99, Reader in Organisational Behaviour, 1999-2001. Publications: Managing Change: Rejuvenating Business, 2001; widely published in area of organisational change, employee stress and well-being. Address: (b.) School of Organisation and Management, University of Ulster, Shore Road, Newtownabbey, Co. Antrim BT37 0QB. T.- 028 90 368844. e-mail: ml.mchugh@ulster.ac.uk

McIlhenny, Dr. Alan James, BSc, PhD, AFIMA. Education Consultant, Association of Christian Schools International; b. 22.11.44, Belfast; m., Margaret Twinem; 1s.; 1d. Educ. Annadale Grammar School, Belfast; Queen's University, Belfast; University of Surrey. Maths Teacher, Royal Belfast Academical Institution, 1969 - 74; Head, Maths, Seychelles College, Seychelles, 1974 - 80; Lecturer, Tribhuvan University, Nepal, 1982 - 85; Principal and Founder, Kathmandu International Study Centre, Kathmandu, Nepal, 1985 - 92. Nominated, University of Louisville Grawemeyer International Award in Education, 1992. Publications: various papers and articles in academic journals conferences and magazines. Recreations: walking, camping; photography; music. Address: (b.) 11 Thornhill Park, Lisburn BT28 3EG. T.-02892 604395. e-mail: alan_mcilhenny@acsi.org

McIlrath, George Adams, OBE, FRICS, JP. Freeman of the City of London. Chairman, McIlrath Ltd; b. 7.5.16, Kilrea; m. Vera E Gilmour; 1s.; 1d. Entered family firm, 1932; succeeded father, 1939; extended business by establishing sale of livestock by auction, pigs, 1949; cattle, 1954. Member, Coleraine Rural Council, 1943 - 74 (Former Vice-Chairman and Chairman); Councillor, Londonderry County Council; Mayor of Coleraine, 1980 - 83; High Sheriff, Co Londonderry, 1984; Council Member, New University of Ulster. OBE, 1963. Justice of the Peace since 1946; Former Member, Irish Society Advisory Committee; President, NI Livestock Salesman Association. Address: (h.) The Lorne, Kilrea, Coleraine; T.- 02870-821248.

McIlroy, Duncan Moore, Eur Ing, FIMarEST, CEng. Fishing Vessel Surveyor, Maritime and Coastguard Agency; b. 10.10.40, Belfast; m., June; 2s. Educ. Royal Belfast Academical Institution;

University of Ulster. Engineer Officer/Chief Engineer, Merchant Navy; Manager, Harland and Wolff Shipbuilders; Surveyor, Department of Transport (now Maritime and Coastguard Agency). Recreations: walking; DIY. Address: (b.) Maritime and Coastguard Agency, Marine Office, Bregenz House, Quay Street, Bangor BT20 5ED.

McIlroy-Rose, Andrea K S, LLB. Partner, L'Estrange and Brett; b. 22.4.65, Belfast; m., Nicholas J Rose. Educ. Victoria College, Belfast; University of Reading. Solicitor, Rowe and Maw, City of London, 1988 - 96. Address: (b.) L'Estrange and Brett, Arnott House, 12-16 Bridge Street, Belfast BT1 1LS; T.- 028 90230426.

McIlveen-Wright, Dr. David Roderick, MSc, DPhil, CEng, CPhys, MInstP, MInstE, MCIWM. Business Manager, NICERT, University of Ulster, Coleraine since 1991; b. 22.4.49, Belfast; m. Chantal Cordier. Educ. Wallace High School, Lisburn; University of Ulster at Coleraine; Brock University, Canada. Experimental Officer, GEC Ltd, Hirst Research Centre, London, 1972 - 75; Teaching Assistant, Research Student, Physics, Brock University, Canada, 1975 - 78; Surface Physics Research, PCS Group, Cavendish Laboratory, University of Cambridge, 1978 - 80; Surface Physics Research, Max Planck Gesellschaft, Berlin, Germany, 1981 - 83; Lecturer, Maths and Physics, Overseas departments of American Colleges (Chicago, Texas, and Maryland) in Berlin, 1983 - 91. Publications: over 30 papers published in scientific journals. Vice-Chairman, Institute of Energy (NI branch). Recreations: running; genealogy; dogwalking; environmental issues. Address: (h.) 29 Adelaide Avenue, Coleraine, Co Londonderry, BT52 1LT; T.- 028703-58758. e-mail: david@mcilveen-wright.com

McIvor, Frances Jill, CBE, LLB, D Univ, QSM. New Zealand Honorary Consul in Northern Ireland since 1996; b. 10.8.30, Belfast; m., Rt. Hon. William Basil McIvor (qv); 2s.; 1d. Educ. Methodist College; Lurgan College; Queen's University, Belfast. Assistant Librarian, Queen's University, Belfast, 1954 - 55; Tutor, Legal Research, Queen's University, Belfast, 1965 - 74; Editorial Staff, Northern Ireland Legal Quarterly, 1966 - 76; Librarian, Department of Public Publications, 1977 - 79; Called to the Bar of Northern Ireland, 1980; Deputy Chairman, Radio Authority, 1990 - 94; Northern Ireland Parliamentary Commissioner for Administration and Commissioner for Complaints (Ombudsman), 1991 - 96. Northern Ireland Member, Independent Broadcasting Authority, 1980 - 86; Chairman, Lagan Valley Regional Park Committee, 1984 - 1988 (member since 1975); Ulster Countryside Committee, 1984 - 89; Member, Fair Employment Agency (later Commission), 1984 - 91; Lay Panel, Juvenile Court, 1976 - 77; Lay member, General Dental Council, 1979 - 91; Member, Belfast Voluntary Welfare Society, Bryson House

Committee, 1981 - 90; Board Member, Co-operation North, 1987 - 90; Advisory Panel on Community Radio, 1985 - 86; Chairman, Educational Guidance Service for Adults, 1988 - 90; Northern Ireland Advisory Committee, British Council, 1986 - 98; Chairman, Ulster New Zealand Trust since 1987; Board of Visitors, Queen's University, Belfast since 1988; Fellow Royal Society of Arts, 1988-2000;   Research Ethics Committee, Queen's University, Belfast, 1996-99. Publications: Manual of Law Librarianship, (Irish consultant and contributor), 1976; Elegantia Juris, selected Writings of F H Newark (ed.), 1973; Chart of the English Reports, 1982.   Recreations: gardening; New Zealand. Address: (h.) Larkhill, 98 Spa Road, Ballynahinch, Co Down, BT24 8PP; T.- 028 9756 3534.

McIvor, Rt. Hon. William Basil, PC, OBE, LLB. Retired Resident Magistrate; b. 17.6.28, Pettigo, Co Fermanagh; m., Frances Jill Anderson (see Frances Jill McIvor); 2s.; 1d. Educ. Methodist College, Belfast; Queen's University, Belfast. Called to the Bar of Northern Ireland, 1950; Ulster Unionist MP (Larkfield), Northern Ireland Parliament, 1969; Minister of Community Relations NI, 1970 - 72; Ulster Unionist Member (S Belfast), Northern Ireland Assembly, 1973 - 74; Minister of Education NI, 1974. Fold Housing Association: Founder Member, 1976; Chairman, 1988 - 98; Chairman, All Children Together, 1990 - 94; Governor, Campbell College, 1975 - 91 (Chairman, Board of Governors, 1983 - 85); Chairman, Board of Governors, Lagan College, Belfast,   1981-2003,   President,   2003. Publications: Hope Deferred, Experiences of an Irish Unionist, 1998. Recreations: music (piano); golf; gardening.   Address: (h.) 98 Spa Road, Ballynahinch, Co Down, BT24 8PP; T.- 01238-563534.

Mackay, Rev. Donald Stewart, BSc, BD. Minister, Boveedy and 2nd Kilrea Presbyterian Churches since 1996; b. 19.7.48;, Belfast; m., Elizabeth Margaret Mackay; 3d. Educ. Belfast High School; Queen's University, Belfast. Graduate Analyst, 1973-75, Laboratory Manager, 1975-79, Ruddock and Sherratt Public Analysts; Chemist, Ulster Curer's Association, 1979 - 83; Quality Controller, Dromona Quality Foods, 1984 - 91; studying for Ministry, 1991 - 94; Assistant Minister, Dungannon Presbyterian Church, 1994 - 96.   Address: (h.) 40 Blackrock Road, Kilrea, Coleraine, BT51 5XH; T.-028 295 40258. e-mail: stewart.mackaypci@virgin.net

McKee, Rev. Ian Thomas, B Ed, BD. Secretary, Christian Education and Sunday School Organiser since 1996; b. 17.3.53, Bangor; m., Annette Marie; 2s.; 1d.   Educ.   Grosvenor Grammar School, Belfast; Edgehill College of Further Education; Union Theological College.   Primary School Teacher,   1975 - 76; Minister, St Andrew's Presbyterian Church, Bangor, 1983 - 90; Minister, St Stephen's Comely Bank, Church of Scotland, Edinburgh, 1990 - 96.   Recreations: squash.

Address: (b.) Church House, Belfast, BT1 6DW; T.- 028 90322284.

McKee, Seamus. Broadcaster/Journalist, BBC since 1981; b. Belfast; m., Brenda; 2. Educ. St Malachy's College; Queen's Univ., Belfast (BA). Teacher, Belfast, 1969-81.   Recreations: travel; reading; theatre; music.   Address: (b.) BBC Northern Ireland, Broadcasting House, Ormeau Avenue, Belfast, BT2 8HQ; T.- 01232-338000.

McKee, Thomas James, BA. Regional Official, NASUWT, since 1978; b. 6.1.44, Armagh; m., Esther McKee; 1s.; 1d. Educ. Armagh Royal School; Queen's University, Belfast.   Teacher, Killicomaine Junior High School, Portadown, 1965 - 78. Recreations: reading; serendipity; camping. Address: (b.) NASUWT, Ben Madigon House, Edgewater Road, Belfast, BT3 9JQ; T.- 02890-784480.
e-mail: rc-nireland@mail.nasuwt.org

McKelvey, Dr. James Moorhead, DL, MB, BCh, BAO. General Medical Practitioner since 1959; b. 2.4.33, Belfast; m., Dr. Moira Ruth Hopkins; 1s. Educ.   Campbell College, Belfast; Queen's University, Belfast. Qualified in Medicine, 1958. Recreations: played international rugby and cricket for Ireland in the 1950's.   Address: (h.) 39 Ballynahinch Road, Saintfield, Co Down.

McKelvey, Very Rev. Robert Samuel James Houston, QVRM, TD, BA (Hons), MA (Ed), DMin. Dean of Belfast, since 2001; b. 3.9.42, Antrim; m., Eileen Roberta; 1 s. Educ. RBAI; QUB; TCD; Garrett-Evangelical Theological Seminary, Evanston, Illinois. Curate-Assistant, St. Colman's, Dunmurry, 1967-70; Incumbent, St. Hilda's, Kilmakee, 1970-82; Secretary, General, Synod Board of Education (Northern Ireland), 1982-2001. Recreation: sailing. Address (b.) Belfast Cathedral, Donegall Street, Belfast BT1 9HB. T.-028 9032 8332; Fax: 028 9023 8855.
e-mail: dean@belfastcathedral.org

McKenna, Professor Patrick Gerald (Gerry), DL, BSc, PhD, DSc, LLD, MRIA, CBiol, FIBiol, FIBMS, FRSA. Vice-Chancellor and President, University of Ulster; b. 10.12.53, Co Tyrone; m., Philomena McArdle; 2s. Educ.   St Patrick's Academy, Dungannon; University of Ulster; Queen's University Belfast. University of Ulster: Lecturer, Human Biology and Genetics, 1979 - 84, Senior Lecturer, Biology, 1984 - 88, Professor and Head of Department, Biological and Biomedical Sciences, 1988-94, Dean, Faculty of Science, 1994 - 97, Pro-Vice-Chancellor (Research), 1997-99; Visiting   Professor: University   Kebangsaan Malaysia, 1993, University of Malaya, 1994, University of California at Berkeley, 1995. Chair: Higher Education Funding Councils Research Assessment Exercise, 2001; Other Studies and Professions Allied to Medicine; Vice-Chair, Ulster Cancer Foundation; Chair, UU-Online.com Ltd; Chair, University of Ulster Science Research Parks Ltd, UUTECH Ltd; Board Member, The Scotch-

Irish Trust of Ulster, 2002; Member: Joint Medical Advisory Committee, Northern Ireland Civil Service Appointments and Procedures Review Group (completed 2003), Board of North-South Roundtable Steering Group, Northern Ireland Committee, The British Council, Science, Engineering and Environment Advisory Committee, The British Council, Council and Member, Policy and Finance Committee, Ulster Cancer Foundation, University of Ulster Foundation Board, US-Ireland Research and Development Taskforce; Founding Board member of UK Health Education Partnership; Past Member of Business in The Community Northern Ireland; Chair, Northern Ireland Foresight: Life and Health Technologies Panel, 1996-99; Member: Higher Education Funding Council for England/Department of Health, Nursing and PAMS Research Task Force; Member, Steering Group, E-Nursing Education Consortium; Member, Institute of Biomedical Science: Council, Educational and Professional Standards Committee; External Assessor for Biomedical Sciences: University of Malaya, Hong Kong University Polytechnic; Member, Editoria Boards: British Journal of Biomedical Science, Radiography; Past Chair: Institute of Biology Northern Ireland Branch, UK Heads of Biomedical Sciences; Past Member: Institute of Biology Fellowship Committee, DHSS Clinical Research Awards Advisory Committee, DENI Postgraduate Awards Committee, Medical Physics Agency Board, Council for Professions Supplementary to Medicine MLT Board, Research Committee, Northern Ireland Leukaemia Research Fund etc; Chair of Universities Ireland; Chair of UUSRP Ltd; Chair of UUTECH Ltd; Co-Chair, Working Group on Innovation, North-South Roundtable Group; Non-Executive Director: Northern Ireland Science Park Foundation, e-UK Universities Worldwide, ILEX (Londonderry Urban Regeneration Company). Publications: over 200 scientific papers. Research Grants: over £8m from various sources. Awards: Freedom of the Borough of Coleraine, 2001, Honorary Doctor of Science, National University of Ireland, 2001; Doctor of Laws, Queen's University Belfast, 2002. Club: Reform. Recreations: horse racing; reading. Address: (b.) Vice-Chancellor's Office, University of Ulster, Coleraine BT52 1SA; T.-028 70 324329.

McKeown, Rev. Donal, BA, STB, STL, MBA. Ordained Auxiliary Bishop of Down and Connor, since 2001; b. 12.4.50, Belfast. Educ. St. Mac Nissi's College; Queen's University of Belfast; Pontifical Gregorian University, Rome. Teacher: St. Patrick's College, Knock, Belfast, 1978 - 83, St. Mac Nissi's College, Carnlough, 1983 - 87, St. Malachy's College, Belfast, 1987 - 95 (and Dean, St. Joseph's Seminary, Belfast); President, St. Malachy's College, 1995-2001. Recreation: jogging. Address: 73 Somerton Road, Belfast BT15 4DE. T.-028 9077 6185. e-mail: dmck@downandconnor.org
website: www.downandconnor.org

McKibbin, Brian. Managing Director, The PR Agency since 1997; b. 13.3.61; m., Maeve; 1d. Educ. Royal Belfast Academical Institution. Joined Northern Bank, 1979: Public Relations Officer, 1988; Director, Public Relations, AV Browne Group, 1994; Director, Public Relations, The Manley Group, 1996. Chairman, Publicity Association of Northern Ireland, 1996; Chairman, Institute of Public Relations (Northern Ireland), 1996 and 1997. Recreations: rugby; golf; most other sports. Address: (b.) 721A Lisburn Road, Belfast BT9 7GU; T.- 028 90 222422.

McKie, Professor Peter Halliday, CBE, DSc (Hon.), FRIC, FIQA, FIOD, FIAECompanion IM. Chairman, QUBIS; Senior Partner, PHM Associates; b. 20.3.35, Bristol; m., Jennifer Anne; 3s.; 1d. Educ. Bangor Grammar School; Queen's University, Belfast. Technical Assistant, Courtalds, 1956 - 59; Du Pont, Northern Ireland. USA, Scandanavia, Switzerland, UK, West Virginia, 1959 - 96. Director, Ulster Bank since 1997. Recreations: motoring; motorcycling. Address: (h.) 3 The Rookery, Killinchy, Co Down, BT23 6SY. e-mail: peter.mckie@ntlworld.com

McKinley, Brian, Cert Ed, BA (Hons), RSA Dip IT. Principal, St Joseph's (Meigh) Primary School since 1990; b. 2.7.49, Newry; m., Pamela; 1s.; 1d. Educ. Abbey Grammar School, Newry; St Joseph's/St Mary's Teacher Training College, Belfast. Teacher: St Colman's Abbey Primary School, 1971 - 75; Potiskum Teachers College, Nigeria, 1976 - 78; Cloughoge Primary School, Newry, 1978 - 90. Publications: Understanding Decimalisation, 1971. Recreations: swimming; IT; cycling. Address: (b.) St Joseph's Primary School, 1 Seafin Road, Killeavy, Newry, BT35 8LA; T.- 028 30848331. e-mail: stjonewry@aol.com

McKnight, Agnes, MD, FRCP(Ed), FRCGP, DRCOG. Director of Postgraduate General Practice Education, since 1994; Senior Lecturer in General Practice, Queen's University of Belfast, 1981-2000; b. 26.8.44, Belfast; m., Dr. S.I. Dempsey; 1 s.; 1 d. Educ. Princess Gardens School; Queen's University of Belfast. Chairman, Disability Living Allowance Advisory Board, Northern Ireland; Chairman, National Summative Assessment (General Practice) Board UK; Member, Medicines Commission, UK. Recreations: opera; classical music; travelling. Address: (h.) 4 Bristow Park, Belfast BT9 6TH; T.- 02890 665168.

McKnight, Thomas Rufus, BA (Hons), MDiv, JD. Minister, Queen's Parade Methodist Church, Bangor, since 2000; Superintendent Minister, Ballinamallard Methodist Circuit since 1997; b. 2.6.54, Dallas, Texas USA; m., Elizabeth Maureen Bell; 2d. Educ. David W Carter High School, Dallas; Southern Methodist University, Dallas; University of Texas, Austin; Ashbury Theological Seminary, Kentucky. Licensed to the practice of Law by the State Bar of Texas; Division Order, Legal and Governmental Departments, Sun Oil

Company; Attorney, Pennzoil Company; Attorney and Partner, McKnight and McKnight of Dallas since 1980; Ordained Methodist Minister, 1980, Comber Methodist Church, 1981; Brookeborough, 1984; Highland Park, 1986; Dromore, 1987; Larne, 1991. Chairman, North East District, 1995 - 97. Member: International Society of Theta Phi; Board of Advocates; Kappa MU Epsilon Mathematics Honorary Society; PHI ETA SIGMA Honarary Society; National Forensic League; International Thespian Society; National Honour Society. Recreations: music (cello, guitar, choir). Address: (h.) 9A Chippendale Avenue, Bangor, Co. Down. T.-028 9146 0098.

Maclaran, Michael Walter Savage, BA (Hons), FIFP, MICS, DI Managing Director, Heyn Group Ltd; b. 14.7.48, Belfast. Educ. Marlborough College, Wiltshire, England; Trinity College, Dublin. Joined Heyn Group and associated companies in shipping, transport and engineering services, 1970. Hon. Danish Consul, Belfast, 1975; Hon. Swedish Consul, Belfast, 1976; Hon. Icelandic Consul, Belfast, 1999. Commissioner of Irish Lights (Chairman, 1999-2001); Past President, Northern Ireland Chamber of Commerce and Industry, 1985. Address: (b.) G Heyn and Sons Ltd, 1 Corry Place, Belfast Harbour Estate, Belfast, BT3 9AH; T.- 02890-350000.

McLaughlin, Prof. Eithne, BA, MPhil, PhD. Professor of Social Policy, Queen's University Belfast, since 1995; b. 29.12.59, Omagh, Co. Tyrone; m., Patrick Clarke; 2 s. Educ. St. Dominics High School, Belfast; Loreto Grammar, Omagh; Queen's Belfast; Trinity Hall, University of Cambridge. Member, Commission on Social Justice, 1994-96; Vice Chair and Member, Standing Advisory Commission on Human Rights, 1994-96; Non Executive Director, EHSSB, 1994-2001; Member: Post Primary Review Body, 2001, Human Organs Inquiry, 2001, MAGNI, since 2001. Fellow, Royal College of Arts; FRSA; Fellow, Academy of The Learned Societies of The Social Sciences (AcSS). Address: (h.) 2 Kew Gardens, Belfast BT8 6GN. T.-02890 964073.

McLaughlin, Gerry, MIPD. Director of Human Resources and Operational Services, Sperrin Lakeland Health and Social Care Trust since 1996; b. 29.9.50, Co Tyrone; m., Mary; 2s.; 1d. Educ. St Patrick's Secondary School, Omagh; Belfast College of Technology. Omagh Unit of Management: Clerical Officer, 1969; Higher Clerical Officer, 1972; General Administrative Assistant, 1974; Unit Personnel Officer, 1977; Assistant District Administrative Officer, Fermanagh Unit of Management, 1986; Western Health and Social Services Board: Deputy Area Personnel Officer, 1988; Acting Area Personnel Officer, 1989; Omagh/Fermanagh DMU: Administrative Services Manager, 1990; Business Services Manager, 1991; Director of Human Resources and Operational Services, 1995. Recreation: golf. Address: (b.) Strathdene House,

Tyrone and Fermanagh Hospital, Omagh, Co Tyrone, BT79 ONS; T.- 028 82835248.

McLaughlin, Prof. James Andrew, BSc, PhD, CPhys, MInstP MIEEE. Reader, School of Electrical and Mechanical Engineering, University of Ulster; b. 16.10.60, Coleraine; m., Gemma McLaughlin; 1s. Educ. Dominican College, Portstewart; University of Ulster at Coleraine. Process Management Trainee, Michelin Tyre Co; University of Ulster: Involved in setting up materials and thin film research and the Northern Ireland Bio Engineering Centre; current work has been the focus of Northern Ireland Centre for Advanced Materials and the Biomedical and Environment Sensor Technology Centre (BEST). Secretary, Irish Branch, Institute of Physics; Committee Member various national scientific bodies. Publications: over 100 papers and 6 patents. Recreations: golf; swimming; international travel; spending time with the family. Address: (b.) 25B09, University of Ulster, Shore Road, Newtownabbey, BT37 0QB; T.- 02890-368933.

McLaughlin, Mitchel. Chairperson, Sinn Fein; Member (Foyle), Sinn Fein, Northern Ireland Assembly since 1998; Councillor, Derry City Councillor, 1985 - 99; b. 29.10,45, Derry; m., Mary Lou; 3s. Educ. Christian Bothers, Brow O' the Hill, Derry; North West Centre for Further Education. Engineering Apprenticeship, 1961 - 66; Refrigeration/Air conditioning Engineer, 1966 - 81. Recreations: reading; walking. Address: (b.) Sinn Fein, 44 Parnell Square, Dublin; T.-01 8726100; 01 8726932.

McLaughlin, Peter T, FCCA. Director of Finance and Information, Western Health and Social Services Board, since 2001; b. 27.1.55, Londonderry; m., Catherine McCallion; 2s.; 1d. Educ. Christian Brothers, Brow O' the Hill, Derry; University of Ulster at Jordanstown, Assistant Group Finance Officer, Omagh and Fermanagh Health and Social Services Unit, 1986 - 88; Assistant Treasurer, Western Health and Social Services Board, 1988 - 91; Unit Finance Officer, Foyle Community Unit, 1991 - 1996; Director of Finance, Foyle HSS Trust, 1996-2001. Recreation: photography. Address: (b.) Western Health and Social Services Board, 15 Gransha Park, Clooney Road, Londonderry BT47 6FN. T.- 028 71 860086.

McLean, Robert John, JP. Retired Company Director; b. 30.8.29, Donaghmore, Co Tyrone; m., Joan Margaret Buchanan; 1s.; 2d. Educ. Royal School, Dungannon. Company Director, 1969 - 87. Member and Past Chairman, Dungannon Development Association; Member and Founder Chairman, Dungannon Enterprise Centre; Board member, Irish World; Member and Past President, Donaghmore Historical Society; Past Treasurer, Carland Presbyterian Church; Dungannon Branch Treasurer, Ulster Society for the Prevention of Cruelty to Animals; Chairman, Torrent Valley

Initiative; Justice of the Peace, 1987. President, The Honourable Society Dungannon Senior Golfers; Past President, Dungannon Branch. Rotary International; Secretary, Dungannon Regeneration Partnership. Publications: The Backford Chronicle, 1994; The Old Meeting House at Carland, 1996; Recreations: golf; reading; local history. Address: (h.) 1 Killymeal Road, Dungannon, Co Tyrone; T.- 028 8772 2965.

McLean, Victoria, LLB, LLM. Litigation Partner, Harrisons Solicitors, since 2001; b. 24.9.70, Belfast; m., John; 1 s.; 1 d. Educ. Kilkeel High School; Queen's University Belfast. Recreations: travel; reading; golf; theatre. Address: (b.) Victoria House, 54-58 Chichester Street, Belfast BT1 4HN. T.-02890 323843. e-mail: v.mclean@harrison11.com

McLoughlin, Dr. James Christopher, MD, FRCP,FRCPI. Cons. Physician/Gastroenterologist, Mater Hospital since 1984; Medical Dir., Mater Hospital Trust, 1995-2003; b. 19.12.47, Belfast; m., Rosemary; 1s.; 2d. Educ. St Mary's Grammar Sch., Belfast; Queen's Univ., Belfast. Junior House Officer, Mater Hospital; Registrar/Tutor, Belfast City Hospital; Research Fellow, Royal Victoria Hospital, Belfast; Senior Registrar posts in Belfast Hospitals in General Medicine and Gastroenterology; Consultant Physician, Whiteabbey Hospital, 1979 - 84. Publications: numerous papers published. Recreations: caravanning; fishing. Address: (b.) Mater Hospital Trust, Crumlin Road, Belfast, BT14 6AB; T.-01232-741211 ext. 2512.

McMahon, Gerard, BA, AdvDip, CertEd, PGCTE, PQH. Principal, Corpus Christi College, since 2001; b. 5.7.54, Belfast; m., Katrina; 2 d. Educ. St. Thomas's Secondary School; St. Joseph's TC; Open University; University of Ulster. Various posts of responsibility: St. Thomas's Secondary School, 1976-88; Corpus Christi College: Head of Faculty, 1988-96, Vice Principal, 1996-2001. West Belfast Partnership Board - various committees; Greater Shankill and West Belfast Employment Service Board. Recreations: gardening; two labrador dogs. Address: (b.) Corpus Christi College, Belfast BT12 6FF. email: gmcmahon@corpuschristicollege.ni.sch.uk

McMaster, (Thomas) Brian (Mulholland), MSc, PhD. Senior Lecturer, Pure Mathematics, Queen's University Belfast, since 1994; b. 12.1.46, Bangor, NI; m., Moyra Harrison Cather; 2 d. Educ. RBAI; Queen's University Belfast. Queen's University Belfast: Assistant Lecturer, 1970, Lecturer, 1973, Associate Fellow, Institute of Mathematics and Its Applications, 1980. Recreation: music. Address: Pure Mathematics Department, Queen's University Belfast, Belfast BT7 1NN; T.-02890 273666. e-mail: t.b.m.mcmaster@qub.ac.uk

McMenamin, Eugene. Member (West Tyrone), Social Democratic and Labour Party, Northern Ireland Assembly, since 1998; m.; 4 s. Educ. North

West Institute of Further and Higher Education, Derry. Self-employed electrical contractor; elected to Strabane District Council, 1977; Member, Strabane/Lifford Cross Border Commission; Member, Ulster Tourism Board; Member, Advisory Committee on ravellers; Member, Culture and Arts Committee (Cross Border). Recreations: amateur drama; music; football; collecting stamps and coins; travel; art. Address: (b.) Parliament Buildings, Stormont, Belfast, BT4 3ST.

McMorran, Andrew, MEd, BSc (Hons), DipEd, DASE. Principal, Ashfield Boys' High School, since 1999; b. 12.6.51, Belfast; m., Elizabeth; 1 s.; 3 d. Educ. Belfast Boys Model School; Queen's University Belfast. Teacher, Boys Model, 1975-94; Vice Principal, Ashfield Boys High School, 1994-99. Northern Ireland Schools U-18 National Coach (soccer). Recreation: golf. Address: (b.) Holywood Road, Belfast BT4 2LY. T.-02890 656812. e-mail: office@ashfieldboys.uk

McMorris, Ian, BSc, DPhil, MMII, FCIM. Managing Director, Ulster Weavers Home Fashions Ltd., since 1995; Non Executive Director: Ulster Weavers Apparel Ltd., since 1995, Lagan College Ltd., since 2000; b. 13.11.48, Rusape, S. Rhodesia; m., Lin; 2 s.; 1 d. Educ. Foyle College, Londonderry; New University of Ulster. Cantrell and Cochrane, Belfast, 1976 - 79; Irish Trade Board, Dublin and Duesseldorf, 1979 - 84; Senior Consultant, IMS Condon International, Dublin, 1984 - 87; Director of Strategy Services, PA Consulting Group, Belfast and Dublin, 1987 - 92; Group Marketing Director, Ulster Weavers, 1992 - 95. Chair, Castlereagh Partnership, 1996 - 98; NI Chairman, CBI, 2002, 2003; Council Member, CBI; Former Council Member, Chamber of Commerce; Former Board Member, Growth Challenge (Former Chair, Textile Group); Governor and Chair of Finance, Lagan College; Vice Chairman, CBI NI, 2001, Chairman, since 2002. Recreations: film; theatre; travel; squash; fitness. Address: (b.) Maldon Street, Donegall Road, Belfast BT12 6NZ; T.-02890 329494.

McMullan, Rt. Rev. Gordon, BSc (Econ), PhD, Dip. Rel Stu. ThD, MPhil, DMin. Bishop of Down and Dromore. 1986-97; b. 1934; m., Kathleen Davidson; 2 s. Educ. Queen's University, Belfast; Ridley Hall, Cambridge; Geneva Theological College; University of the South, USA. Publications include: Opposing Violence/Building Bridges, 1996. Address: 26 Wellington Park, Bangor, Co. Down BT20 4PJ.

McMullan, John, BSc, MA, PhD, DSc, CPhys, CEng, FInstP, FInst Energy. Professor of Physics; Director of Energy Research Centre, University of Ulster; b. 5.9.39, Bangor, Co Down; m., Joan; 1s.; 2d. Educ. Bangor Grammar School; Queen's University, Belfast; State University of New York, USA; University of St Andrews. Research Physicist, Cornell Aeronautical Laboratory, Cornell University, Buffalo, New York, 1961 - 64;

Lecturer, Physics, University of St Andrews, 1964 - 67; Joined University of Ulster, 1967: Lecturer; Reader; Professor of Physics. Editor-in-Chief, International Journal of Energy Research since 1975. Publications: over 250 books and papers. Recreations: music; theatre; furniture restoration. Address: (b.) Energy Research Centre, University of Ulster, Cromore Road, Coleraine, Co Londonderry, BT52 ING; T.- 01265-324469.

McMullen, Rev. Charles John Carson, MA, MLitt, BD. Minister, West Presbyterian Church, Bangor since 1999; b. 22.3.60, Omagh; m., Barbara, 2s.; 1d. Educ. Omagh Academy; Trinity College, Dublin; St Antony's College, Oxford; Queen's University, Belfast. Assistant Minister, Harmony Hill, 1986 - 91; Minister, Legacurry Presbyterian Church. 1991 - 99. Convener, National and International Problems' Committee, 1993 - 97; Convener, Magee Fund Scheme Committee, 1993-2000; Chairman, Lisburn Council of Churches, 1996 - 98. Recreations: reading biographies; gardening; walking; theatre and cinema. Address: (h.) 37 Kensington Park, Bangor, BT20 3RF; T.- 02891-454338.

McMullin, Mary Frances, MD, FRCP, FRCPath. Reader in Haematology, Queen's University Belfast; Consultant Haematologist, Belfast City Hospital; b. 4.10.56, Belfast; m., Sean Curran; 2s.; 1d. Educ. Dominican College, Belfast; Queen's University, Belfast. General Training in Haematology, 1980 - 87; Senior Registrar and Research Fellow, Postgraduate Medical School, Hammersmith Hospital, London, 1987 - 91. Address: (b.) Department of Haematology, Queen's University, C Floor, Belfast City Hospital, Lisburn Road, Belfast BT9 7AB. T.-028 90 329241 ext. 2193. e-mail: m.mcmullin@qub.ac.uk

McMurray, Alan Douglas, BA (Hons). Development Officer for Hockey, Ulster Branch, Irish Hockey Union since 1993; b. 14.10.69, Banbridge; m., Naomi Ruth Wayne-Barrett; 1 s.; 1 d. Educ. Friends School, Lisburn; University of Ulster, Belfast. Ulster Branch, Irish Hockey Association. Manager, Irish Under 16 hockey team since 1995. Address: (b.) Hockey Office, House of Sport, Upper Malone Road, Belfast, BT9 5LA; T.- 028 9038 3826. e-mail: alan@ulsterhockey.com

McMurray, Professor Cecil Hugh, CBE, FRSC, FIFST BSc, BAgr, PhD. Consultant on Scientific Affairs in Agri-Food; Director, NICO, since 1992; b. 19.2.42. Educ. Royal Belfast Academical Institution; Queen's University Belfast; University of Bristol. Chief Scientific Officer, Department of Agriculture for Northern Ireland 1988-2002; retired 2002. Address: (h.) 25 Sheridan Drive, Helens Bay, Co. Down BT19 1LB.

McMurray, Thomas Alvin, JP. Retired Newsagent; b. 11.9.21; m., Mary Neill; 2d.. Educ. Lurgan College. Lay Panel Member; Past

President and Captain Lurgan Rugby and Cricket Club; Founder President, Lurgan Lions Club. Address: (h.) 'Ramalta', 12 Rosewood Park, Upper Toberhewny Lane, Lurgan, Co Armagh; T- 028 38322672.

McNally, Geralyn, LLB, LLM, BL. Barrister-at-Law; b. 2.3.70, Dungannon; m., Joseph Barry Mulqueen BL; 1s. Educ. St Patrick Girls' Academy, Dungannon; Queen's University, Belfast; University College, Dublin. Called to the Bar of Northern Ireland, 1994; Member of Irish Bar, since 1998; Part-time Lecturer in Law, 1994 - 2000. Member, Independent Commission for Police Complaints, 1997-2000; Member, Law Reform Advisory Committee for NI, since 2000; Vice Chair, Amnesty International Lawyers' Group NI. e-mail: mulqueen.mcnally@virgin.net

McNamee, Pat. Member (Newry and Armagh), Sinn Fein, Northern Ireland Assembly, since 1998. Councillor, Armagh City and District, since 2001. Address: (b.) Room 330, Parliament Buildings, Stormont, Belfast BT4 3ST; T.- 028 90 521430.

McNaney, Peter, LLB. Chief Executive of Belfast City Council, since 2002. Graduated in law from the University of Manchester, 1980; joined Belfast City Council in 1986; appointed Director of Legal Services in 1995. Address: (b.) Chief Executive's Office, City Hall, Belfast BT1 5GS. T.-028 9027 0202. e-mail: mcnaneyp@belfastcity.gov.uk

McReynolds, Anne, BA (Hons). Director, Old Museum Arts Centre; b. 12.9.65, Ballymena, Co Antrim; m., Terry Loane; 1s. Educ. St MacNissi's College, Garron Tower; Queen's University, Belfast; University of Ulster at Jordanstown. Administrator/Box Office, Belfast Festival at Queen's; Development Officer, Belfast Community Circus. Address: (b.) 7 College Square North, Belfast BT1 6AR. T.-028 90235053.

McRitchie, Ian, BA (Hons), PGCE, MEd. Head of School, Adult and Community Education, Lisburn Institute of Further and Higher Education since 1997; b. 17.2.54, Donaghadee; m., Mary; 2s.; 1d. Educ. Bangor Grammar School; Queen's University, Belfast; University of Ulster. Senior Lecturer, Department of Academic Studies, 1987 - 97. Recreations: hillwalking; gardening; wine making; reading. Address: (b.) School of Adult and Community Education, Lisburn Institute of Further and Higher Education, Castle Street, Lisburn, Co Antrim, BT27 4SU; T.-028 92677225. e-mail: imcritchie@liscol.ac.uk

McRoberts, Robin, MEd, MBA, PGDip, G&C, Dip, RSA, DipAD, ATD. Chief Executive, Action Cancer NI, since 2003; b. Belfast; m.; 3 c. Educ. in Belfast and in Edinburgh. Career History: secondary school teacher, then full-time youth work; various management positions over a 12-year period in one of the Education and Library Boards in NI; counsellor, part-time lecturer and

external examiner; currently teaches the Certificate in Counselling at Queen's University; currently Director of Services and Deputy Chief Executive of Relate NI. Currently completing an MBA degree in health and social care management. Recreations: sport and travel. Address: (b.) Action Cancer, 1 Marlborough Park, Belfast BT9 6XS. T.-028 9080 3344.
e-mail: rmcroberts@actioncancer.org

McSorley, Daniel, BSc, CEng, MICE. Chief Executive, Omagh District Council, since 2001; b. 24.1.54, Co. Tyrone. Address: (b.) The Grange, Mountjoy Road, Omagh, Co. Tyrone BT79 7BL. T.-02882 245321.
e-mail: daniel.mcsorley@omagh.gov.uk

McVeigh, Eddie. Head of Representation, European Commission in NI, since 2002; b. 14.8.53, Kilkeel; m., Hilary; 1 d.; 1 s. Educ. St. Colman's College, Newry; QUB. Local government officer, Wales, 1978-88; Press and PR, European Parliament (Brussels, Strasbourg, and Luxembourg), 1988-96; Senior Press Officer, European Parliament, London, 1996-2002. Recreations: local history; hill walking. Address: (b.) Windsor House, Belfast BT2 7EG. T.-028 9024 0708.

McVey, Joanna, OBE. Chairperson, Rural Development Council of Northern Ireland since 1998; Managing Director, The Impartial Reporter. Chairperson, The Fermanagh Trust; Vice Chairperson, Devenish Partnership Forum. Address: (b.) Rural Development Council for Northern Ireland, 17 Loy Street, Cookstown, BT80 8PZ; T.- 028867-66980.

McWilliams, Anthea M. R., BA (Hons), MA, Independent Dancer; b. 17.11.58, Lisburn; 2 children.; 1gc. Educ. Wallace High School, Lisburn; Middlesex University; University of Ulster. Established Hoi Polloi Community Dance Company, Artistic Director and Choreographer since 1991; Initiated launched and organised Dance NI (a company working to develop dance in Northern Ireland), 1997. Recreations: photography; travel. Address: 34 Station Road, Sydenham, Belfast, BT4 1RF; T.- 02890-653541; Fax: 02890-286025.
e-mail: artactlisburn@aol.com

McWilliams, Professor Monica. Member (South Belfast), Northern Ireland Women's Coalition, Northern Ireland Assembly, 1998-2003; b. 28.4.54, Kilrea, Co Derry; m.; 2 s. Educ. Queen's University, Belfast; University of Michigan. University Lecturer; Professor of Women's Studies, University of Ulster, since 1998; Member, multi-party negotiations and Northern Ireland Forum, 1996-98; J.F. Kennedy Profile in Courage Award, 1998; Avril Harriman Democratic Institute Award, 1998; New York 100 Heroines Award, 1998. Address: (b.) Parliament Buildings, Stormont, Belfast, BT4 3XX; T.- 02890 521463.
e-mail: monica.mcwilliams@niassembly.gov.uk

M

Magee, Brendan. Chief Executive, Driver and Vehicle Licensing Agency (NI) since 1993, Department of the Environment. Career Civil Servant previously holding posts in the Home Office, Price Commission and Employment Department Group. Address: (b.) County Hall, Castlerock Road, Coleraine, BT51 3HS; T.- 028 7034 1249.

Magee, Samuel J., MBE, JP, BA. Chief Executive, Antrim Borough Council since 1973; b. 25.2.44, Hillsborough, Co Down; m., Olive; 1s.; 2d. Educ. Lisburn Technical College; University of Ulster at Jordanstown, Lisburn District Council, 1960; Antrim Rural District Council: Deputy Chief Executive, 1971; Chief Executive, 1972. Recreations: golf. Address: (b.) Antrim Borough Council, The Steeple, Antrim, BT41 1BJ; T.- 028 9446 3113.

Mageean, Professor Vincent, OBE. Lay Observer for Northern Ireland. Address: (b.) Brookmount Buildings, 42 Fountain Street, Belfast BT1 5EE. T.-02890 245028; Fax: 02890 251944.

Magill, William James, MA (Cantab), MA, Cert Ed. Principal, Foyle and Londonderry College since 1994; b. 12.8.50, Belfast. Educ. Royal Belfast Academical Institution; Christ's College, Cambridge; University of Ulster. Assistant Teacher, Sandy Upper School, Bedfordshire, England, 1976 - 80; Deputy Head, New Hall School, Chelmsford, 1980 - 94. President, Northern Ireland Fencing Union. Recreations: fencing; skiing; swimming; theatre. Address: (b.) Foyle and Londonderry College, Duncreggan, Londonderry, BT48 0AW; T.- 028 71 269321.

Maginness, Alban Alphonsus, BA (Hons), BL. Member (North Belfast), Social Democratic and Labour Party, Northern Ireland Assembly, since 1998; Lord Mayor of Belfast, 1997 - 98; b. 9.7.50, Belfast; m., Carmel McWilliams; 3s.; 5d. Educ. St Malachy's College, Belfast; University of ULster; Queen's University, Belfast. Called to the Bar of Northern Ireland, 1976; Called to the Bar of Ireland, 1984; Councillor, Belfast City Council, since 1985; Chairman, SDLP, 1985 - 91; Elected (North Belfast) Northern Ireland Forum/Talks, 1996. Member of the Committee of the Regions (EU); Council Member, Action Cancer; Chair of Assembly's Regional Development Committee. Recreations: music; reading; drama. Address: (h.) 96 Somerton Road, Belfast, BT15 4DE; b.) City Hall, Belfast, BT1 5GS; T.- 01232-770558.

Maginnis of Drumglass, of Carnteel in the County of Tyrone, Lord (Kenneth Wiggins). Member of Parliament (Fermanagh and South Tyrone), 1983-2001; b. 21.1.38; m., Joy Stewart; 2s.; 2d. Educ. Royal School, Dungannon;

Stranmillis Teacher Training College. Teacher: Cookstown Secondary School, 1959 - 69; Drumglass Primary School, 1960 - 66; Principal, Pomeroy Primary School, 1966 - 82; Councillor, Dungannon District Council, 1981 - 93 and since 2001; Member, Northern Ireland Assembly, 1982 - 86; Member, NI Forum, -98. Served, Ulster Special Constabulary, 1958 - 65; Ulster Defence Regiment, 1970- 81, achieved rank of Major, commissioned 1972. Member: House of Commons Select Committee on Defence, 1984 - 85; Deputy Chairman, Assembly's Finance and Personnel Committee, 1982 - 86; Chairman, Assembly's Security and Home Affairs Committee, 1982 - 86; Chairman F and P, Southern Health and Social Services Board, 1989 - 91; Member, Southern Health and Social Services Council, 1991 - 93; Member various Dungannon District Council Committees, (Council Chairman, 1992), Chairman, Dev. Committee; Chairman, District Police Partnership, since 2002 (DPP); Chairman, F & ST Local Strategy Partnership (LSP), since 2001; House of Commons Select Committee on Armed Forces Bill, 1990; House of Commons Select Committee on Northern Ireland, 1995 - 97. Vice-President, Ulster Unionist Council; Member, Executive, Ulster Unionist Party; Spokesman, Defence and Home Affairs, Ulster Unionist Party - House of Lords; Chairman, Moygashel Regeneration project. Publications: McGimpsey and McGimpsey v Ireland, 1990; Witness for the Prosecution, 1993; various articles in national newspapers. Recreations: Rugby. Address: (h.) 1 Park Lane, Ballynorthland, Demesne, Dungannon, Co Tyrone; T.- 077-6776-3763.

Magowan, Robert John, BA, DASE, MSc. Headmaster, Clondermot High School, Londonderry since 1994; b. 7.10.44, Londonderry; m., Margaret Crooks; 1d. Educ. Foyle College, Londonderry; Trinity College, Dublin. Assistant Teacher, Foyle College, 1967; Foyle and Londonderry College: Senior Teacher, 1976; Vice-Principal, 1979. Session Clerk, Waterside Presbyterian Church. Recreations: cricket (former Irish schools selector); Leader, Londonderry Crusaders. Address: (h.) 41 Limavady Road, Londonderry, BT47 1LP; T.- 01504-344091.

Maguire, J., CBE. President, Industrial Tribunals and Fair Employment Tribunal. Address: (b.) Long Bridge House, 20-24 Waring Street, Belfast BT1 2EB. T.- 028 9034 7415.

Maguire, Dr. Terence Anthony, BSc, PhD, MCPP, FPSNI, FPSI, MRPharms (Hon). Principal Pharmaceutical Officer, Dept. Health, Social Services and Public Safety, since 2003; b. 13.6.58, Strabane; m., Catherine; 2s.; 2d. Educ. St Columb's College, Derry; Queen's University, Belfast. Manager, Belfast Pharmacy, 1984 - 86; Pharmacy Proprietor since 1986; Queen's University, Belfast: Research Fellow, 1989; Senior Lecturer, 1994; Director, Northern Ireland Centre for Postgraduate Pharmaceutical Education and Training, 1997-2002. President, Pharmaceutical

Society of Northern Ireland, 1998 - 1999; Vice-Chairman, Pharmacy HealthLink, since 1989; Member, Committee for Safety of Medicine, 2002-2005; awarded Honorary Membership, Royal Pharmaceutical Society of GB, 2001. College of Pharmacy Practice Award, 1989; Glaxo Pharmaceutical Care Award, 1994. Publications: 31 research papers on Pharmacy Practice; book: 'Mind Your Own Business', 2003. Recreations: cycling; running. Address: (b.) 3 Beechmount Avenue, Belfast BT12 7NA; T.-02890 320590; (h) 505, Falls Road, Belfast BT12 6DE; T.-02890 327140.

Mahon, Derek. Writer and Poet. b. 1941, Belfast. Educ. Belfast Institute; Trinity College, Dublin. Journalist/screen writer, London and New York; Taught, Barnard and NYU. Former Writer in Residence, Trinity College, Dublin; Member, Aosdána. Irish Times/Aer Lingus Poetry Prize; C K Scott Moncrieff Translation Prize; Guggenheim Fellowship. Publications: Selected Poems, 1990; Hudson Letter, 1995; Raunes Phaedra, 1996; Collected Journalism, 1996.

Mahood, W Laurence, LL.B.   Head of Commercial Property Department, Elliott Duffy Garrett Solicitors; b. 7.9.53, Belfast; m., Lynda Mahood; 2s. Educ. Royal Belfast Academical Institution; Queen's University, Belfast. Admitted as a solicitor, 1978; Joined Elliott Duffy Garrett, 1978; Partner since 1982. Publications: chapter, Northern Ireland Law in Butterworth's Property in Europe, Law and Practice. Recreations: walking the dog. Address: (b.) Elliott Duffy Garrett, Royston House, 34 Upper Queen Street, Belfast BT1 6FD.

Mallon, Hugh James, MA (EdMgmt), BA, PQH (NI). Headteacher, St. Joseph's Boys' High School, Newry, since 2002; b. 24.1.56, Newry; m., Anne; 1 s.; 3 d. Educ. St. Joseph's Boys' HS, Newry; De La Salle College/Manchester University. Primary Teacher, St. Patrick's Boys' PS, Newry, 1977-79; Teacher/Head of Religion, St. Paul's HS, Bessbrook, 1979-2000; Vice Principal, St. Joseph's Boys' HS, Newry, 2000-02. Recreations: gardening; walking. Address: (b.) 20 Armagh Road, Newry, Co. Down BT35 6DH. T.-028 302 62595.
e-mail: info@stjosephhigh.newry.ni.sch.uk

Mallon, Marie. Director, Human Resources, The Royal Hospitals since 1996; b. 24.11.56, Belfast; 3d. Educ. St Rose's Secondary School; Belfast Institute of Further and Higher Education. Joined Royal Hospitals Trust, 1974, working in a variety of posts including Finance and on secondment to the Joint Councils of Northern Ireland, 1978 - 84; Head Personnel Department, South Belfast Community, 1984; Assistant Group Administrator, South Belfast Community, 1986 - 89; Eastern Health and Social Services Trust: Senior Personnel Manager, 1989; Senior Industrial Relations Manager, 1990 - 93; Deputy Director of Personnel, Royal Hospital, 1993 - 94; Deputy Director,

Human Resources, Central Services Agency, Provider Support Unit, 1994 - 96. Member, Chartered Institute of Personnel Development; Member of Industrial Tribunal. Recreations: reading; activities involving the family. Address: (b.) The Royal Hospitals, Grosvenor Road, Belfast, BT12 6BA; T.- 02890-240503, Ext. 2203.

Mallon, Patrick Eugene, BEd.   Principal, Our Lady's Primary School, Tullysaran since 1997; b. 11.10.58, Portadown; m., Sarah; 1 d.; 1 s. Educ. St Patrick's Grammar, Armagh; St Joseph's College of Education. Teacher St Mary's, Cabragh, 1981 - 89; Principal, Tullymore Primary School, Benburb, 1989 - 97. Recreations: gaelic sports; theatre; travel. Address: (h.) 60 Gorestown Road, Dungannon, Co Tyrone; T.- 028 87784874.

Mallon, Seamus. MP. Member of Parliament, Newry and Armagh since 1986; Member (Newry and Armagh), Social Democratic and Labour Party, Northern Ireland Assembly, since 1998; Deputy First Minister, Northern Ireland Assembly, 1998-2001; b. 17.8.36, Markethill; m., Gertrude Cush; 1d. Educ. Abbey Grammar School, Newry; St Joseph's College of Education, Belfast. Member: Armagh District Council, 1973 - 89; Northern Ireland Assembly, 1973 - 74 and 1982; Northern Ireland Convention, 1974 - 75; Seanad Eireann, 1982; British-Irish Inter Parliamentary Body, 1986. Recreations: golf; angling. Address: (b.) 2 Bridge Street, Newry, BT35 8AE.

Mallory, Professor, J. P., PhD, RIA. Professor in Archaeology, Queen's University, Belfast; b. 25.10.45, San Bernardino, California; marr. diss.; 2s.; 1d. Educ. Occidental College; University of California. US Army (Military Police), 1969 - 72; Graduate Student, University of California, 1972 - 75; Lecturer, University of California, (Los Angeles), 1975 - 77; Visiting Lecturer, Queen's University, Belfast, 1977 - 78; Senior Research Fellow, Institute of Irish Studies, 1978 - 79; Joined Staff, Queen's University, Belfast, 1979. Publications: The Tarim Mummies, 2000; Encyclopedia of Indo-European Culture, 1997; The Archaeology of Ulster, 1991; Aspects of Tain, 1992; In Search of the Indo-Europeans, 1989. Address: (b.) Department of Archaeology, Queen's University, Belfast, Belfast BT7 1NN; T.- 02890-273188.

Manley, Lester Charles. Chief Executive, Dimex Ltd; b. 25.5.61, Belfast; m., Vivienne Manley; 3d. Educ. Methodist College, Belfast; University of Ulster. Recreations: boating; watersport. Address: (b.) Dimex Ltd, Knockbracken Health Park, Saintfield Road, Belfast BT8 8BH.   T.-028 90579000. e-mail: lester@dimex.tv

Mann, Prof. John, BSc (Chem), PhD (Chem), DSc (London). McClay Chair of Biological Chemistry, Queen's University Belfast, since 1999; b. 30.9.45, Dartford, England; m., Rosemary; 1 s.; 3 d. Educ. Dartford Grammar School; University College London. Post Doctoral

Research Fellow: Syntex, Palo Alto, then Harvard; Tutorial Fellow, Jesus College, Oxford; Lecturer, Reader and Professor, Reading University, 1974-99. Publications: Secondary Metabolism, 1978 and 1987; Murder, Magic and Medicine, 1992 and 2000; The Elusive Magic Bullet, 1999. Address: (h.) 6 Ardmore Terrace, Holywood BT18 9BH. T.-02890 335525. e-mail: j.mann@qub.ac.uk

Marchant, Professor Roger, BSc, PhD, DSc, CBiol, FIBiol. Professor of Microbial Biotechnology, University of Ulster since 1986 and Head, School of Applied Biological and Chemical Sciences, 1994-2000; b. 6.7.43, London; 2s.; 1d. Educ. Shene Grammar School; University College London. Quain Student in Biology, University College London, 1967 - 68; New University Of Ulster: Assistant Lecturer, 1968 - 69; Lecturer, 1969 - 76; Senior Lecturer, 1976 - 82; Reader, 1982; University of Ulster: Head, Department of Biology, 1984 - 88. Publications: more than 140 articles in scientific journals and books. Recreation: horticulture. Address: (b.) School of Biological and Environmental Sciences, University of Ulster, Coleraine, BT52 1SA; T.-02870-324450. e-mail: r.marchant@ulst.ac.uk

Mark, John Martin. Board Member, Livestock and Meat Commission since 1997; b. 28.1.58, Limavady; m., Helen Middlemas; 2s. Educ. Portora Royal School; East Of Scotland College of Agriculture. Full time farmer since 1979; Founder Director, Lean and Easy Lamb, 1994. Ulster Farmers Union: Member, 1979 - 2002 (executive member, 1988 - 2002); Member, Central Cattle and Sheep Committee, 1986 - 2002 (Chairman, 1995 - 98); Group Chairman, 1993 - 94; County Chairman, 1997 - 99. Recreations: rugby; golf; tennis; family. Address: (h.) Carrowmena House, 71 Carrowclare Road, Limavady; T.-028 777 62496. e-mail: leanandeasyltd@btinternet.com

Mark, Dr. Rob, PhD, BSc (Hons), MSc, MA, M Ed, DipTRP, Cert Ed. Assistant Director, Lifelong Learning and Senior Lecturer, Adult and Continuing Education, Queen's University Belfast; b. 15.8.53. Educ. Dublin; Queen's University Belfast; University of Ulster; Glasgow University; Hull University. Worked in Universities, Further Education and Community Education; Represents Institute of Lifelong Learning, Queen's University Belfast on a range of professional bodies and organisations in Adult Education locally, nationally and internationally. Research interests are: adult literacy; comparative adult education; European adult education; guidance and counselling in adult education; access to education for disadvantaged adults. Recreations: swimming; outdoor pursuits; travel. Address: (b.) Institute of Lifelong Learning, Queen's University Belfast; T.-028-90335163. e-mail: r.d.mark@qub.ac.uk

Marks, Professor Robert James, BSc, MSc, DIC, PhD, FIBiol, CBiol. Deputy Chief Scientific Officer, Department of Agriculture and Rural Development for Northern Ireland; Professor of

Applied Plant Science, Queen's University, Belfast since 1994; Head, School of Agriculture and Food Science, Queen's University, Belfast since 1999; b. 9.12.45, Belfast; m., Sonia; 1d. Educ. Belfast Royal Academy; Queen's University, Belfast; Imperial College of Science and Technology, London. Lecturer, Applied Entomology, Imperial College of Science/Team Leader, UK Overseas Development Administration Cotton Pest Management Project, Malawi, 1970 - 76; Senior Scientific Officer, Department of Agriculture for Northern Ireland/Lecturer, Agricultural Zoology, Queen's University, Belfast, 1976 - 79; Principal Scientific Officer, DANI, 1979 - 81; Professor of Agricultural Zoology, Queen's University, Belfast/Senior Principal Scientific Officer and Head of Agricultural Zoology Division, DANI, 1981 - 94. Fellow, Institute of Biology; Honorary Academician, Romanian Academy of Agricultural and Forestering Sciences. Publications: senior editor of a definitive book on global distribution, biology and control of potato cyst nematodes; over 40 scientific papers, chapters and articles on entomology, plant nematology and heliculture. Recreations: gardening. Address: (b.) Department of Applied Plant Science, Agriculture and Food Science Centre, Newforge Lane, Belfast, BT9 5PX; T.- 02890-255281.

Marshall, Prof. Alan James, PhD, BSc, SMIEEE. Professor of Telecommunications Networks, Department of Electrical Engineering, Queen's University Belfast since 1993; b. 20.3.59, Belfast; m., Anne; 2 d. Educ. Dunlambert School, Lisburn; University of Aberdeen. Engineer, Standard Telephones and Cables Ltd, 1977 - 80; Design Engineer, Ferranti Avionics, Edinburgh, 1985 - 86; Higher Scientific Officer, Admiralty Research Establishment, Portsmouth, 1987 - 90; Senior Systems Engineer, Northern Telecom, 1990 - 93. Director, Advanced Telecommunications Laboratory. Recreations: hillwalking; swimming; travelling. Address: (b.) Department of Electrical Engineering, Ashby Building, Queen's University Belfast, Stranmillis Road, Belfast, BT9 5AH; T.-02890-274248.

Marshall, Margaret, BA, JP. b. 20.8.33, Co Tyrone; m., Stanley Marshall (dec.) 2s.; 1d. Educ. Alexandra College, Dublin; Trinity College, Dublin. Former Teacher of Classics including three years in Lima, Peru. Social Work Consultant, Family Fund/Independent Living Fund; Alliance Party Councillor, Castlereagh Borough Council, 1993 - 97; Alliance Party spokesperson on Equality and Community Relations; Citizens' Advice Bureau Adviser; Member, Belfast Naturalists' Field Club (former President), Botanical Secretary. Recreations: botany; walking; conservation; travel. Address: (h.) 2 Cairnshill Avenue, Belfast, BT8 6NR; T.- 02890-701537.

Martin, Eamon Columba, BSc, BD, MPhil. President, St. Columb's College, since 2000; b. 30.10.61, Derry. Educ. St. Columb's College; St.

Patrick's College, Maynooth; University of Cambridge. Ordained Priest, 1987; Catholic Curate, St. Eugene's Cathedral, 1987-89; Postgraduate Studies, Queen's University Belfast, 1989-90; Teacher, St. Columb's College, 1990-2000; Postgraduate Studies, University of Cambridge, 1998-99. Consultative Group on Catholic Education. Recreations: music; gardening. Address: (b.) St. Columb's College, Buncrana Road, Derry BT48 8NH.   T.-028 71285000.

Martin, Eric. Managing Director/Owner, Profast Group Ltd; b. 29.5.49, Dromore County Down; m., Marie; 2s.; 1d. Educ. Newtownards College of Further Education; Belfast College of Technology. Production Engineer, Tenneco-Walker (UK) Ltd; Sales Engineer, Demag Ltd; Research and development Engineer, Goodyear Tyre and Rubber Co; Sales Engineer, Pump Services (NI) Ltd; Pipeflow Westwood Ltd: Sales Representative; Sales Manager; General Manager. Recreations: rallying; golf. Address: (b.) 26-30 Rydalmere Street, Belfast; T.-028 90243215.

Martin, Eugene Gerard, BSc, MA, PGCE. Principal, Ulidia Integrated College, since 1997; Director, Northern Ireland Council for Integrated Education, since 2002; b. 6.11.55, Belfast; m., Elizabeth Moyra Spence; 2 s.; 2 d. Educ. St. Patrick's College, Belfast; University of Ulster - Coleraine. Head of Maths, Dundonald Girls High School, Belfast, 1979-87; Head of Maths, Senior Teacher and Pastoral Coordinator, Lagan College, Belfast, 1987-97. Chief Examiner, OCR 'Information Studies', 1992-2002. Recreations: sailing; reading. Address: (b.) 112 Victoria Road, Carrickfergus, Co. Antrim BT38 7JL. T.-028 9335 8500. e-mail: ulidia.college@excite.com

Martin, His Honour Judge, QC (**John Alfred Holmes).** Chief Social Security Commissioner and Chief Child Support Commissioner for Northern Ireland; President of the Pensions Appeal Tribunals, Northern Ireland. Address: (b.) Office of the Social Security Commissioners and Child Support Commissioners, Headline Building, 10-14 Victoria Street, Belfast BT1 3GG.   T.- 02890 728731.

Martin, Joseph, BA, BD.   Chief Executive, Western Education and Library Board, since 1995; b. 13.3.39, Carrickmore; m., Marie McCulgan; 3 s.; 1 d. Educ. St. Patrick's College, Armagh; St. Patrick's College, Maynooth. Teacher, 1963-74; Education Officer, 1974-89; Senior Education Officer, 1989-94. Membership of Society of Education Officers. Address: (b.) Western Education and Library Board, 1 Hospital Road, Omagh BT79 0AW. T.-028 82 411205.

Martin, T. H. B., BA, BSC, A Dip Ed. Principal, Ballyholme Primary School since 1996; b. Ballyclare, County Antrim; 1s.; 2d. Educ. Ballyclare High School; Stranmillis College; Queen's University, Belfast; Open University.

Assistant Teacher, Whitehouse Primary School, 1966 - 69; Vice-Principal, Mossley Primary School, 1969 - 77; Principal, Ballyduff Primary School, 1977 - 96, (seconded to Education and Library Board, Management Development, 1991-95). Director/Assessor, NEAC. Address: (b.) Ballyholme Primary School, 6 Glenburn Park, Bangor, BT20 5RG; T.-028 9127 0392. e-mail: hmartin@ballyholmeps.bangor.ni.sch.uk

Maskey, Alex. Member (West Belfast), Sinn Fein, Northern Ireland Assembly, since 1998. Elected to Belfast City Council, 1983.   Address: (b.) Parliament Buildings, Stormont, Belfast BT4 3XX; T.- 01232-520700.

Mason, Gary James, BA DipTh, DD, DPhil. Minister of Religion since 1987; b. 9.2.58, Belfast; m., Louise; 2s. Educ.   Boys' Model School; Queen's University, Belfast; University of Ulster. Northern Ireland Civil Service, 1974 - 77; Administrator, Health Service, 1977 - 84. British Enkalon Cup, Business Organisation; Minnis Mills Award in Pastoral and Communication Studies. Recreations: squash; gym; swimming; reading. Address: (h.) 34 Cyprus Avenue, Belfast, BT5 5NT; T.-028 90654 305.

Mathews, William, MB, BCH, BAO, FRCS. Retired Surgeon; Councillor, Coleraine Borough Council since 1973; Deputy Mayor, 1993 - 94 and 1997; b. 7.9.17, Cloughmills; m., Florence Hazel Jean; 1s. 1d. Educ. Ballymena Academy; Queen's University of Edinburgh; Royal College of Surgeons, Edinburgh. RAMC, 1941 - 45; Fellow, Royal College of Surgeons, 1949; Consultant Ear Nose and Throat Surgeon, Coleraine and Ballymoney, 1951 - 81. Officers (Brothers), Order of St John. Recreations: bridge; bowls; gardening. Address: (h.) 15 Charnwood Park, Coleraine, BT52 1JZ; T.- 01232-42517.

Maxwell, Andrew John Samuel, BA(Mod), Barrister-at-Law, CPLS. b. 19.12.59, Belfast; m., Aine Hughes; 3d. Educ. Belfast Royal Academy; Trinity College, Dublin. Called to the Bar of Northern Ireland, 1984; Tutor, Institute of Professional Legal Studies since 1987. President, Royal Belfast Academy Old Boys' Association, 1998 - 99. Clubs: Royal Ulster Yacht Club. Address: (b.) Bar Library, 91, Chichester Street, Belfast, BT1 3JQ; T.- 028-90662584. e-mail: counsel@dnet.co.uk

Maxwell, Rev. James Desmond, BA, MDiv, ThM, Presbyterian Minister since 1979/Lecturer Belfast Bible College since 1987; b. 25.8.52, Ballymena, Co Antrim; m., Heather McDowell; 2d. Educ.   University of Ulster; Westminster Seminary;   Philadelphia,   USA;   Princeton Theological Seminary, USA.   Minister, Sunny Corner pastoral Charge, Presbyterian Church in Canada, 1979 - 82; Assistant Minister, Richview Presbyterian Church, Belfast, 1982 - 83; Minister, Berry Street Congregation, Belfast, 1983 - 87. Publications: Life and Limb, 1990. Recreations:

walking; music. Address: (h.) 24 Thistlemount Park, Lisburn, BT28 2UN; T.- 028 92 67 03 10. e-mail: d.maxwell@bigfoot.com

Maxwell, Michael Edmond, BA. Barrister-at-Law; b. 28.9.49, Belfast; m., Nuala Mary McMordie; 1s.; 1d. Educ. Cabin Hill; Glenalmond, Perthshire, Scotland; Trinity College, Dublin. Called to the Bar of Northern Ireland, 1973; Called to the Irish Bar, 1996. Recreations: fishing; game shooting; target rifle shooting. Address: (b.) Bar Library, Royal Courts of Justice, Chichester Street, Belfast, BT1 3JP; T.- 02890 241523.

May, Dr. Forde, BSc, MSc, CDipAF, PhD. Managing Director, Forde May Consulting Ltd and JobMarket NI.com; m., Valerie; 1d. Educ. Portadown College; Queen's University, Belfast; University of Ulster. Research Scientist, Esso; Technical Officer, ICI; Manufacturing Manager, Lucas Stability; Head, Northern Ireland Practice and Worldwide Partner, PA Consulting Group. Recreations: golf; tennis; boating. Address: (b.) Forde May Consulting Ltd, Balmoral House, 77 Upper Lisburn Road, Belfast BT10 0GY. T.-028 9062 88 77. e-mail: forde@jobmarketni.com

Mayne, Dr. C. S. Acting Director, Agriculture Research Institute of Northern Ireland. Address: (b.) Large Park, Hillsborough, Co Down; T.-02892 682484.

Meehan, Prof. Elizabeth Marian, BA, DPhil, FRSA, MNYAS, AcALSS, MRIA. Professor of Politics, Queen's University Belfast since 1991, Director, Institute of Governance, since 2001; b. 23.3.47, Edinburgh. Educ. Peebles Burgh and County High School; Sussex University; Nuffield College, Oxford. Diplomatic Service, 1965 - 73; Studying, 1973 - 79; Lecturer, Politics, Bath University, 1979 - 90; Hallsworth Fellow, Manchester University, 1989 - 90; Dean Faculty of Economics and Social Sciences, Queen's University Belfast, 1995 - 97. Vice-President: Political Studies Association of the UK, Royal Irish Academy; Member, Irish Research Council for the Humanities and Social Sciences; Director, Democratic Dialogue. Publications: Women's Rights at Work, 1985; Citizenship and the European Community, 1993. Recreation: opera. Address: (b.) Institute of Governance, Public Policy and Social Research, Queen's University Belfast, Belfast BT7 1NN; T.- 02890-273288.

Middleton, Dr. Richard, BA, PhD. Reader, American History, Queen's University Belfast; b. 1.4.41, Scunthorpe, Educ. Sir William Borlase's Grammar School; University of Exeter. Exchange Student, College of William and Mary, Virginia, USA, 1966 - 67; Lecturer, Modern History, Queen's University Belfast, 1967 - 72; Fellow, Institute of Early American History and Culture, Williamsburg, Virginia, USA, 1972 - 74; Queen's University Belfast: Lecturer, American History, 1974 - 85; Senior Lecturer/Reader since 1985.

Publications: The Bells of Victory: 1757 - 1762, 1985, reprint 2002; Colonial America, A History: 1600 - 1776, 1992 (1st edn.), 1996 (2nd edn.), (3rd edn.), 2002; Amherst and the Conquest of Canada, 2003. Recreations: tennis; classical music; antiques. Address: (b.) School of Modern History, Queen's University Belfast, Belfast, BT7 1NN; T.- 02890-245133.

Millar, Robert Thomas David, Cert Ed, BA, Dip ASEd. Principal, Carnalridge Primary School, Portrush since 1980; b. 18.7.52, Coleraine; m., Violet Elizabeth Kelly; 1s. Educ. Coleraine Academical Institution; Stranmillis College; Open University; University of Ulster at Coleraine. Teacher: Ballyoran Primary School, Dundonald, 1973 - 79; Killowen Primary School, Coleraine, 1979 - 80. Recreations: Leader, Powerhouse Youth Club, Portstewart Baptist Church. Address: (b.) 135 Atlantic Road, Portrush, BT56 8PB; T.- 02870-822686.

Millar, Ross George, BA, MSc. Director, Leisure Services, Craigavon Borough Council, since 2002; Assistant Director, Environment and Heritage Service, DOE (NI), since 2000, Principal Scientific Officer, since 1997; b. 16.5.52, Portadown; m., Hazel (nee McVittie); 1 s.; 1 d. Educ. Dungannon Royal School; Queen's University Belfast; University of Ulster (Jordanstown). Planning Officer, Department of the Environment (N.I.), 1974-91, Senior Scientific Officer, Environment and Heritage Services, Principal Scientific Officer, (Protected Landscapes), Assistant Director (Head of Countryside & Coast). Member: Irish Planning Institute, Mountaineering Council of Ireland. Recreations: hill walking; cycling. Address: (b.) Craigavon Borough Council, Civic Centre, Lakeview Road, Craigavon BT64 1AL. T.-028 3831 2551. e-mail: ross.millar@craigavon.gov.uk

Miller, Right Rev. Harold Creeth, MA, BA(Theol), DPS. Bishop of Down and Dromore since 1997; b. 23.2.50, Belfast; m., Elizabeth Adelaide; 2s.; 2d. Educ. Belfast High School; Trinity College, Dublin; Nottingham University. Curate, St Nicholas' Carrickfergus, 1976 - 79; Chaplain and Director of Extension Studies, St John's College, Nottingham, 1979 - 84; Chaplain, Queen's University, Belfast, 1984 - 89; Rector, Carrigrohane Union of Parishes, Cork, Ireland, 1989 - 97. Publications: Anglican Worship Today, 1980; Finding a Personal Rule of Life, 1984; New Ways in Worship, 1986; Making an Occasion of It, 1994; Outreach in the Local Church, 2000. Recreations: music; caravanning. Address: (h.) The See House, 32 Knockdene Park South, Belfast, BT5 7AB; T.- 02890-471973.

Millington, Dr. Gordon Stopford, OBE, BSc, FIEI, FICE, FIStructE, FIHT, CEng. Consulting Engineer; b. 29.6.35, Belfast; m., Margaret Jean; 2s.; 1d. Educ. Campbell College; Queen's University, Belfast. Assistant Engineer, Sir William Halcrow, 1957 - 59; Kirk McClure Morton: Engineer, 1960 - 66; Partner, 1966 - 87;

Senior Partner, 1988 - 97. Member, Standing Committee on Structural Safety; Vice-President, Institution of Civil Engineering, 1995 - 97; President, Institution of Engineers in Ireland, 1997 - 98; Past Chairman: Northern Ireland Associations, Institution of Structural Engineers; Institution of Highways and Transportation; Institution Civil Engineers; Institution Engineers of Ireland; Founder Member, Irish Academy of Engineering. Director: Amelwood Ltd, Stranwood Estates Ltd, NI 2000; Past Chairman, Rotary Club of Belfast; Grosvenor Grammar School; President, The Irish Academy of Engineering; Chairman, Ormeau Baths Gallery of Contemporary Art; Past Chairman, NI 2000, Friends of the Ulster Orchestra. Publications: Engineering, the Key; many engineering papers. Recreation: sailing. Address: (h.) 1 Malone View Road, Belfast BT9 5PH. T.- 028 9061 1303.

Mills, C G Michael, OBE, BSc (Econ), DBA, MSc. Group Chief Executive Officer, Ulster Carpet Mills Ltd since 1993; b. 31.8.47, Sydney, Australia; m., Jacqueline; 3d. Educ. Royal School, Dungannon; Queen's University of Belfast; Ulster Business School. Esso UK Plc, 1970 - 88; Group CEO, Ulster Carpet Mills Ltd, since 1988; UK Quality Award for Business Excellence, 1996; IRTU Innovation Award, 2000; Chairman, Business in the Community, Northern Ireland, 1999-2002; Non Executive Director, Emerging Business Trust since 1997. Governor, Victoria College since 1991; Chairman, Carpet Foundation, since 2000; President, European Carpet Association, since 2001; President, Northern Ireland Chamber of Commerce and Industry, 2003/04. Recreations: golf; reading. Address: (b.) Ulster Carpet Mills Ltd, Portadown, BT62 1EE; T.-028 3833 4433. e-mail: mike.mills@ulstercarpets.com

Mills, Maurice William, JP, FCA. Retired; b. 2.7.33, Belfast; m., Ida W M Corry; 1s.; 2d. Educ. Sullivan Upper School, Holywood, Co Down. Qualified as chartered accountant, 1956; Professional accountancy, 1950 - 59 Antrim County Council, 1959 - 61; Belfast Harbour Commissioners, 1961 - 93. Elder, Presbyterian Church in Ireland. Recreations: travel; reading; music; art; watching Rugby Union. Address: (h.) 2 Stormont Park, Belfast, BT4 3GX; T.- 028-90-483256.

Mills, William Stratton, LLB. Consultant, Mills, Selig Solicitors, Belfast, since 2000, Former Senior Partner; Non-Executive Chairman, Hampden Group Plc, 1992 - 99; b. 1.7.32, Belfast; m., Merriel Elinor, Ria Mills; 3s. Educ. Campbell College, Belfast; Queen's University, Belfast. Vice-Chairman, Federation of University Conservative and Unionist Associations, 1952 - 53 and 54, - 55; Admitted a Solicitor, 1958; Member of Parliament (Ulster Unionist), Belfast North, 1959 - 72; Member of Parliament (Alliance) Belfast North, 1973 - 74; PPS to Parliamentary Secretary, Ministry of Transport, 1961 - 64;

Member: Estimates Committee, 1964 - 70; Executive Committee; 1922 Committee, 1967 - 70 and 1973; Hon. Secretary, Conservative Broadcasting Committee, 1963 - 70 (Chairman, 1970 - 73); Member: Mr Speaker's Conference on Electoral Law, 1967; One Nation Group, 1972 - 73. Vice-Chairman, Voluntary Service, Belfast, 1975 - 85; Chairman, Voluntary Service, Belfast Youth Workshop Ltd, 1978 - 89; Founding Chairman, Ulster Orchestra Society Ltd, 1980 - 90; Board Member, Northern Ireland Opera Trust, 1976 - 85 (Hon. Treasurer); Board Member, Castleward Opera since 1987; Retired 1998; Director, Opera RARA since 1997; Council Member, Winston Churchill Memorial Trust, 1990 - 95; Member, Public Records Office NI (PRONI) Advisory Board, since 1996. Arnold Goodman Award for outstanding achievement in the encouragement of business sponsorship for Arts, 1990. Recreations: golf. Address: (h.) 21 Arthur Street, Belfast, BT1 4GA.

Mirakhur, Professor Rajinder K, MBBS, MD, PhD, FRCA, FFARCSI. Professor of Anaesthetics, Queen's University, Belfast since 1996; Consultant Anaesthetist; b. 14.10.45, Srinagar, Kashmir, India; m., Meenakshi; 1s.; 1d. Educ. Medical College, Kashmir; J and K University, India. Residency, 1967 - 70; Lecturer/Assistant Professor, Post Graduate Institute, Chandigarh, India, 1970 - 74; Research Fellow, Royal Victoria Hospital, Belfast, 1975 - 76; Training posts within Northern Ireland until 1980; Consultant Anaesthetist, Royal Victoria Hospital, Belfast, 1980 - 90; Senior Lecturer, Anaesthetics, Queen's University, Belfast, 1990 - 96. Member, Council of the Royal College of Anaesthetics; Past Council Member, Association of Anaesthetics. Publications: Anaesthetics for Eye, Ear, Nose and Throat Surgery, 1985; Multiple Questions in Pharmacology, 1993; over 200 publications in peer-reviewed and international journals. Recreations: computers; reading; travel. Address: (b.) Department of Anaesthetics, Queen's University, Belfast, Whitla Medical Building, 97 Lisburn Road, Belfast BT9 7BL;T.- 01232-335785.

Mitchell, Senator George. Chancellor, Queen's University Belfast. Address: (b.) Queen's University Belfast BT7 1NN.

Mitchell, James Bernard, BA (Hons), DipHSM. Chief Executive, United Hospitals HSS Trust, since 1996; b. 12.5.56, Belfast; m., Rebecca; 1 d. Educ. Grosvenor High School; Queen's University Belfast. General Management Trainee, HPSS, 1978-80; varied managerial positions in SHSSB and EHSSB, 1980-90; Unit General Manager, Loughside Unit of Management, NHSSB, 1990-94; Unit General Manager, United Hospitals Group, NHSSB, 1994-96. Former Chairman, Institute of Health Management, NI. Address: (b.) Bush House, Bush Road, Antrim BT41 2QB. T.- 028 94 424673.

Mitchell, Lesley Rebecca Jane, BA (Hons), MSc, FCCA. Director of Finance, Foyle Health and Social Services Trust, since 2001; b. 23.5.63, Belfast; m., Gardiner Stewart Mitchell; 1d. Educ. University of Ulster at Jordanstown. Qualified Accountant, 1988; Western Health and Social Services Board: Financial Accountant, 1988; Assistant Director of Finance, 1991; Deputy Director of Finance, 2000. Recreations: reading; swimming. Address: (b.) Foyle Health and Social Services Trust, Riverview House, Londonderry; T.- 028 71 266111. e-mail: lmitchell@foylehq.n-i.nhs.uk

Moffet, Trevor Lonsdale. Consultant (Rehabilitation aids and equipment for the Disabled) since 1979; b. 1939, Banbridge; m., Margaret Crawford; 3d. Educ. Royal Belfast Academical Institution; Belfast College of Technology; Borough Polytechnic, London. G N Haden and Sons, Contractors, 1956; Oscar Faber and Partners, Consultants, 1963; Building Design Partnership, 1969; Northern Ireland Housing Executive, 1975; DisableCare, 1982; Access Lifts and Hygiene Services, 1998. Member, Chartered Institution of Building Services Engineers. Design Council Award, 1991; Radio4/Radio Times Award, 1991; Ulster Television/Design Council Innovations Awards, 1991; Gallaher Business Challenge Award, 1990; Archimedes Award, 1991. Publications: contributor: The Ulster Architect, CBISE Journal, Specify, Prospective; teaching papers. Recreations: fishing; photography; inventing products and systems. Address: (b.) 106 Portaferry Road, Newtownards, BT22 2AH; T.-02891-813321.

Moir, Arthur Hastings, LLB. Clerk and Chief Executive Officer to the Northern Ireland Assembly, since 2001; b. 18.10.48, Belfast; m., Catherine. Educ. Belfast Royal Academy; Queen's University of Belfast. Assistant Solicitor, 1974-78; Partner in solicitors' practice, 1978-88; Solicitor in Land Registry, 1988-93; Registrar of Titles and Land Purchase Trustee, 1993-2001; Chief Executive of Land Registers of Northern Ireland, 1996-2001. Publication: The Land Registration Manual, 1994. Address: (b.) Parliament Buildings, Stormont, Belfast BT4 3XX. T.-028 9052 1199.

Moiseiwitsch, Professor Benjamin Lawrence, BSc, PhD, MRIA. Professor Emeritus, Applied Mathematics, Queen's University, Belfast since 1993; b. 1927, London; m., Sheelagh McKeon; 2s.; 2d. Educ. Royal Liberty School, Romford, Essex; University College London. Appointed Queen's University, Belfast: Lecturer/Reader, Applied Mathematics, 1952 - 68; Professor, Applied Mathematics, 1968 - 93; Dean, Faculty of Science, 1972 - 75; Head, Department of Applied Mathematics and Theoretical Physics, 1977 - 89. Member, Royal Irish Academy, 1969. Publications: Variational Principles, 1966; Integral Equations, 1977; numerous articles on theoretical atomic physics. Recreations: music. Address: (h.) 21 Knocktern Gardens, Belfast, BT4 3LZ; T.-

02890-658332. e-mail: b.moiseiwitsch@btinternet.com

Molloy, Francis Joseph, Dip Humanities. Member (Mid Ulster), Sinn Fein, Northern Ireland Assembly since 1998 (Chair, Finance and Personnel Committee); b. 16.12.50, Derrymagowan, Dungannon; m., Ann; 2.; 2 d. Educ. St Patrick's, Dungannon; University of Ulster, Jordanstown. Elected to Dungannon District Council, 1985; elected to N.I. Forum, 1996. Recreations: watercolour painting. Address: (h.) Derrymagowan, Dungannon, Co Tyrone BT71 6SX; T.-018687 48689.

Molyneaux, Lord James Henry of Killead; b. 27.8.20. Educ. Aldergrove. Recreations: music; gardening. Address: House of Lords, London, SW1A 0PW; T.- 020 7219 6707.

Monds, Professor Fabian Charles, CBE, BSc, PhD, CEng, MIEE, MBCS, CCMI. Emeritus Professor of Information Systems, University of Ulster, 2000; National Governor, BBC Northern Ireland, since 1999; Chairman, Invest Northern Ireland, since 2002; Chairman, NI Centre for Trauma and Transformation, since 2001; b. 1.11.40, Omagh; m., Eileen Graham; 2d. Educ. Christian Brothers Grammar School, Omagh; Queen's University, Belfast. Visiting Professor, Purdue University, Indiana, 1965 - 66; Lecturer/Senior Lecturer/Reader, Queen's University, Belfast, 1967 - 87; University of Ulster: Professor of Information Systems, 1987, Dean of Informatics, 1989 - 92, Pro-Vice Chancellor (Planning), 1992-2000, Provost, Magee College, 1995-2000. Publications: An Introduction to Mini and Microcomputers, 1981; The Business of Electronic Product Development, 1984 plus 80 other articles and papers. Recreations: light aircraft. Address: (b.) BBC NI Broadcasting House, Belfast.

Montague, John. Writer and Poet. b. 1929, Brooklyn, New York. Taught in France, Canada, US (UCC). American Ireland Literary Fund Literary Award, 1995. Publications: Rough Field, 1972; Great Cloak, 1978; Dead Kingdom, 1984; Collected Poems, 1993; Time in Armagh, 1993.

Montgomery, Rev. David John, BA (Hons), MDiv. Associate Minister, Knock Presbyterian Church since 1998; b. 18.12.63, Belfast; m., Gwen Dorothy Robinson. Educ. Belfast Royal Academy; University of Stirling; Regent College, Vancouver, B C, Canada. Youth Development Officer, Presbyterian Church in Ireland, 1987 - 90; Youth Reconciliation Officer, Presbyterian Church in Ireland, 1990 - 92; Assistant Minister, Stormont Presbyterian Church, 1995 - 98. Publications: Sing a New Song, 2000. Recreations: music; writing; Manchester City F C. Address: (h.) 5 Kensington Manor, Belfast BT5 6PE; T.- 02890-402619; (b.) 53 Kings Road Belfast, BT5 6JH; T.- 02890-794582.

Montgomery, Patrick David, MA (Cantab). Chairman, Phoenix Natural Gas since 1996; b. 30.12.34, Belfast; m., Geraldine McGladery; 2s.; 1d. Educ. Glenalmond College; Clare College, Cambridge. Managing Director, James Clow and Co Ltd, Belfast, 1970 - 86; President, UKASTA, London, 1985 - 86; Managing Director, John Thompson and Sons Ltd, Belfast, 1986 - 94. Chairman, Large Users Action Group on Northern Ireland Electricity Prices, 1992 - 94; Independent Member, Northern Ireland Economic Council 1993-2003. Recreation: golf. Address: (b.) Phoenix Natural Gas, 197 Airport Road, Belfast BT3 9ED. T.-028 9055 5561.

Montgomery, William Howard Clive. Sotheby's Representative in Ireland; Trustee of the Museums and Galleries of Northern Ireland; Director, International Property and Fine Art Consultancy Ltd; Chairman, Opera Northern Ireland, 1993 - 1998; b. 18.1.40, Oxford; m., 1. Jennifer Dunn (dec.); m., 2. The Hon. Daphne Bridgemen; 1s.; 3d. Educ. Eton College; Royal Agricultural College, Cirencester. Partner, Osborne King and Megran, 1964 - 70; Director, International Land Investments, 1970 - 82; Director, Sotheby's, 1984 - 92; Chairman, Sotheby's International Realty, 1987 - 92; Director, Ermitage Management UK Ltd, 1994 - 97; Director, Abercairney Estates since 1991; Director of Bradford Rural Estates, since 2000; Trustee of the Church of Ireland; Governor, Linen Hall Library; Trustee, Ulster Historical Foundation; Senior Trustee of the Gibson Trust; Chairman: Weston Park Foundation, Weston Park Enterprises Ltd; Governor of several schools. Liveryman of the Goldsmiths' Company, London. Recreations: country sports; opera; architecture; wine. Address: (b.) The Estate Office, Grey Abbey, Newtownards, Co Down, BT22 2QA; T.- 028 4278 8666.

Mooney, Oliver A G, BA (Hons), PGC Ed, MSc. Principal, St. Paul's High School, Bessbrook; b. 27.11.53, Co Armagh; m., Anne; 2s.; 3d. Educ. St Colman's College, Newry; Queen's University, Belfast; University of Ulster at Jordanstown. Joined Abbey Grammar School, Newry; Geography Teacher; Head of Geography; Geography Advisor, Southern Education and Library Board; Principal, St. Joseph's Boys' High School, Newry, 1996-2002. Publications: The Greenest Corner, a video and text resource (co-ed.). Recreations: walking; reading; fishing. Address: (b.) St. Paul's High School, 108 Camlough Road, Newry BT35 7EE. T.-028 30830309.

Moore, James, BA (Hons), MTh. Area Representative, Soldier's and Airmen's Scripture Readers Association since 1981; b. 13.12.39, Belfast; m., Margaret G Moore; 1s.; 1d. Educ. Royal Belfast Academical Institution; Trinity; Liverpool University. Royal Navy, 1957 - 66; Commerce and Industry, 1967 - 81. Recreations: sport; reading. Address: (b.) Apt 74, Rodgers Quay, Carrickfergus, Co. Antrim BT38 8BE. T.- 028 9336-2228.

Moore, Richard John, BSc, FCIM, MRSC. Managing Director, Millward Brown Ulster, since 1981; b. 2.7.48, Belfast; m., Deirdre Calwell; 1s.; 3d. Educ. Royal Belfast Academical Institution; Queen's University, Belfast. Research Chemist/Marketing Executive, Gallaher Ltd. 1971 - 78; Marketing Executive, Northern Ireland Development Agency, 1978 - 81. Chairman, Northern Ireland Branch, Chartered Institute of Marketing, 1994 - 95. Recreations: sailing; bridge; Newcastle United. Address: (b.) Millward Brown Ulster, 115 University Street, Belfast, BT7 1HP; T.- 02890 231060.

Moore, Very Rev. Thomas Robert, DipTh, MA. Dean of Clogher and Diocesan Secretary; b. Co Fermanagh; m., E Hazel Bailey; 1s.; 2d. Educ. Portora Royal School, Enniskillen; Trinity College, Dublin. Ordained Christchurch Cathedral, Dublin, 1968; Curate Assistant: Drumcondra North Strand, with St. Barnabas, Dublin; St Columba, Portadown, Co Armagh; Rector: Kilskeery and Trillick, Co Tyrone, 1973 - 85; Trory and Killaders, Co Fermanagh, 1985 - 94; Rural Dean, Kilskeery Diocese of Clogher; Diocesan Secretary, Diocese of Clogher; Examining Canon, Diocese of Clogher; Prebend of Donacavey, Clogher Cathedral; Prebend of Donaghmore, St Patrick's Cathedral, Dublin; Rector of Clogher and Errigal-Portclare; Dean of St Macartan's Cathedral and Chapter, Diocese of Clogher. Recreations: DIY; interest in the countryside; travel. Address: (h.) The Deanery, 10 Augher Road, Clogher, Co Tyrone, BT76 0AD.

Moore, Sir William (Roger Clotworthy), 3rd Bt, TD, DL.. Deputy Lieutenant, Co Antrim; b. 17.5.27, Belfast; m., Lady Moore; 1s.; 1d. Educ. Marlborough College. RMC Sandhurst Lieutenant, Royal Inniskilling Fusiliers, 1945 - 50; Major, North Irish Horse, 1951 - 63. Grand Juror, Co Antrim, 1952 - 68; Prison Visitor, 1968 - 74; Chairman, Castledillon open prison, 1971 - 72; Member, Parole Board, Scotland, 1978 - 80; High Sheriff, Co Antrim, 1964; Self Employed, 1963-85. Recreations: shooting; golf; river boating. Address: (h.) Moore Lodge, Ballymoney, Co Antrim; T.- 028295-41043.

Morison, Professor John, LLB, PhD. Professor of Jurisprudence, Head of School of Law, Queen's University Belfast. Educ. University College Cardiff, University of Wales. Member, European Group of Public Law; Board Member, European Centre for Public Law, Athens; Member, DSD Taskforce on Resourcing the Voluntary and Community sector; Member of the Council of the Pharmaceutical Society of Northern Ireland; Governor, Malone College, the integrated college of south and west Belfast; Member Board, Democratic Dialogue; Honorary Senior Research Fellow, The Constitution Unit, University of London; Management Board of Institute of

Governance, Public Policy and Social Research, Queen's University Belfast. Address: (b.) School of Law, Queen's University Belfast, Belfast BT7 1NN; T.- 01232-90273475; Fax: 01232-90273376. e-mail: j.morison@qub.ac.uk

Morrell, Leslie James, OBE, JP, BAgr. Hon. Secretary, Oaklee Housing Association since 1992; b. 26.12.31, Enniskillen; m., Anne Wallace ; 2s.; 1d. Educ. Portora Royal School; Queen's University, Belfast. Member: Coleraine Rural District Council, 1962 - 73; Londonderry County Council, 1969 - 73; Coleraine Borough Council, 1973 - 77; Unionist Member (Londonderry) Northern Ireland Assembly 1973 - 75; Minister of Agriculture Northern Ireland Exec., 1973 - 74; Deputy Leader, Unionist Party and Unionist Party of Northern Ireland. Member, BBC General Advisory Committee, 1986 - 91; Chair, Northern Ireland Federation of Housing Associations, 1978 - 80; Founder Chair, James Butcher Housing Association, 1975, Hon. Secretary, until 1992; Chair, Northern Ireland Water Council, 1982 - 93. Executive Governor, Coleraine Academical Institution, 1969-2002. Recreations: reading; travel. Address: (h.) Dunboe House, Castlerock, 133 Quilly Road, Coleraine BT51 4UB; T.- 028 7084 8352. e-mail: lemorrel@lineone.net

Morrice, Jane. Former Deputy Speaker, Northern Ireland Assembly; Member (North Down), Northern Ireland Women's Coalition, Northern Ireland Assembly, 1998-2003. Educ. University of Ulster. Journalist; former Head of European Commission Office in Northern Ireland; founder Member, Women's Coalition; Member, Women's Coalition team, Castle Buildings talks, 1996-98. Address: (b.) Parliament Buildings, Stormont, Belfast, BT4 3XX; T.- 028 90 521297.

Morris, Dr. David, BMus, MMus, PhD. Lecturer in Music, University of Ulster at Jordanstown since 1985; b. 23.7.48, London; m., Rachel Morris (div.); 1s.; 2d.; 2nd m., Anne Montgomery. Educ. Alleyns School, Dulwich; University College, Wales, Durham University. Lecturer in Music, Ulster Polytechnic, 1981 - 84; Lecturer in Music, Queen's University, Belfast, 1982 - 84. International Lutoslawski Prize for Composition, 1991. Recreations: ornithology; lepidoptera. Address: (b.) Music Division, University of Ulster at Jordanstown, BT37 0QB; T.- 028 2884 1284.

Morrissey, John Thomas, LLB. Barrister-at-Law; b. 14.8.63, Belfast; m., Kathryn O'Reilly; 1d; 2 s. Educ. St Patrick's College, Knock; Queen's University, Belfast. Member of the Inn of Court, Northern Ireland since 1987; Tutor in Criminal Law; Queen's University, Belfast 1988-97. Address: (b.) The Bar Library, 91-93 Chichester Street, Belfast BT1 3JQ. T.-028 90 241523.

Morrow, Maurice. Member (Fermanagh and South Tyrone) Democratic Unionist Party, Northern Ireland Assembly, since 1998; Party Chairman, Chief Whip (DUP); Minister for Social Development, July 2000-October 2001. Estate agent; Member, Dungannon and South Tyrone Borough Council, since 1973; Member, Northern Ireland Forum, 1996-98. Address: (b.) Parliament Buildings. Stormont, Belfast, BT4 3ST; T.- 02890-520700. e-mail: maurice@morrow48.fsnet.co.uk

Mortimer, William Jamison, MA, LLB. Barrister-at-Law; b. 12.7.45, Belfast. Educ. Royal Belfast Academical Institution; Trinity College, Dublin. Member of the Inn of Court of Northern Ireland and of the Middle Temple, Barrister-at-Law in practice at the Bar of Northern Ireland. Recreations: cricket; tennis. Address: (b.) Bar Library, 91 Chichester Street, Belfast, BT1 3JQ; T.- 028 90 562082.

Morton, James Neill, BA, BSSc, DASE, MA (Ed), MA, PQH. Headmaster, Portora Royal School, Enniskillen, since 2002; b. 19.3.49, Belfast; m., Linda; 2 s. Educ. Annadale Grammar School, Belfast; The Queen's University Belfast. Assistant Teacher, Annadale GS, Belfast, 1972-77; Campbell College: English Teacher, Head of Dept., Housemaster, Senior Teacher, Head of Sixth Form, Head of Drama, 1977-2002. Founded Annadale Striders Athletic Club, 1973; Coach, NI Athletics Team, Commonwealth Games, 1978. Playwright (4 Professional Productions); Broadcaster, Heritage, BBC Radio Ulster, 2000. Address: (b.) Enniskillen, Co. Fermanagh BT74 7HA. T.-028 6632 2658. e-mail: nmorton@portora.enniskillen.ni.sch.uk

Morton, Very Rev. William Wright, ALAM, BTh, MA. PhD. Rector of Templemore and Dean of Derry since 1997; b. 23.7.56, Co Armagh; m., Rosemary Emily Alexandra Todd; 3s. Educ. Newry Grammar School; Trinity College, Dublin; Queen's University, Belfast. Journalist/Deputy Editor/News Editor, Ulster Gazette, Armagh, 1983 - 85; Ordained Deacon, Christ Church, Limavady, 1988; Curate, Christ Church, Limavady; Ordained Priest, St Columb's Cathedral, Londonderry, 1989; Rector, Conwal Union (Letterkenny) with Gartan, Diocese of Raphoe, 1991. Corkey Biblical Greek Prize, 1986; Downes Public Speaking Prize, 1988; Gold Medal, Public Speaking, London Academy of Music. Recreations: music; reading. Address: (h.) The Deanery, 30 Bishop Street, Londonderry, BT48 6PP; T.- 028 7126 2746.

Moseley, Terence James, BA, FRAS. President and PRO, Magazine Editor, Irish Astronomical Association.; b. 27.2.46, East London, South Africa; m., Moira Noade; 2s.; 1d. Educ. Royal School, Armagh; Portadown College; Queen's University, Belfast. Interregnum Director, Armagh Planetarium, 1968; Teacher, 1971 - 74; Civil Service since 1974. President, Irish Astronomical Association, 1987 - 89, 1995 - 97 and 1999-2002; Recipient, Aidan P Fitzgerald Medal, 1992. Publications: Reaching for the Stars, 1975; regular contributor and book reviewer for various astronomical books, journals and magazines; Chairman, Irish Federation of Astronomical

Societies; Honoured by International Astronomical Union, September 2002, by naming Asteroid 1994 YC2 as "16693 Moseley" in recognition of contribution to astronomy. Recreations: music; reading; observing the heavens. Address: (b.) 6 Collinbridge Drive, Newtownabbey, Co Antrim, BT36 7SX; T.- 028 9058 7658. e-mail: terrymosel@aol.com

Mountgarret, 17th Viscount, Richard Henry Piers Butler; b. 8.11.36. Educ. Eton; Royal Military Academy, Sandhurst. Commissioned Irish Guards (retired rank Captain), 1957 - 64.

Muldoon. Paul. Writer and Poet. b. 1951, Co Armagh. Educ. Queen's University, Belfast. Talks Producer, BBC; Lecturer, Princeton. Gregory Award, 1972; T S Eliot Prize for Poetry. Publications: New Weather; Mules; Why Brownlee Left; Quoof; Meeting the British; Madoc: A Mystery; Annals of Chile.

Muldowney, Patrick, BSc, MSc, DPhil, ALCM, FIMA. Lecturer in Statistics, Magee College, University of Ulster, since 1985; b. 18.3.46, Kilkenny, Ireland; 2 s.; 1 d. Educ. De La Salle College, Waterford; National University of Ireland, Galway. Junior Fellow, University College Galway, 1967-68; University of Michigan: Fulbright Scholar, Teaching Fellow, 1968-70; Research Assistant in Mathematics, New University of Ulster, 1970-74; Lecturer in Statistics, North West Institute of Further and Higher Education, Derry, 1974-85. Member, Irish Mathematical Society, American Mathematics Society. Publications: General Theory of Integration, 1987; New Integrals, 1990; Danta Phiarais Feiriteir (poems of Pierce Ferriter), 1999; co-author (with Brendan Clifford), Bolg An Tsolair (Gaelic magazine of The United Irishmen, 1795), 1999; Danta Eoghain Ruaidh Ui Shuilleabhain (poems of Owen Rua O'Sullivan), 2002. Address: (b.) Magee College, University of Ulster, Northland Road, Derry BT48 7JL. T.-028 71375321. e-mail: p.muldowney@ulster.ac.uk

Mulholland, Prof. Clive W., BSc (Hons), PhD, FIBMS. Director of Lifelong Learning, University of Ulster, since 2000, Professor of Technology Enhanced Learning; b. Belfast. Educ. University of Ulster. Lecturer, Paramedical Sciences, University of Wales, Swansea, 1993-95; Senior Research Fellow, Queen's University Belfast, 1995-97; Director, Virtual School of Biomedical Sciences, University of Ulster, 1997-99, Head of School of Biomedical Sciences, 1999-2000; Visiting Prof., University of Rochester, New York, 2002. Address: (b.) University of Ulster, Shore Road, Newtownabbey, Co. Antrim BT37 0QB. T.- 02890 366059.

Mulholland, Esther, BA (Hons). Development Manager, Moyle District Council, since 1993; b. 3.11.56, Ballycastle; m., Paul; 2 s.; 1 d. Educ. Ballycastle High School; University of Ulster. Community Relations Officer; Bookmaker, own

business; Marketing, Riverside Theatre. Recreation: sailing. Address: (b.) Moyle District Council, Sheskburn House, 7 Mary Street, Ballycastle, Co. Antrim BT54 6QH. T.-028 207 62225.

Mullan, Raymond James, OBE, MSc, BSc Econs (Hons), T Cert. Director, Newry and Kilkeel Institute of Further and Higher Education since 1991; b. Co Antrim; m., Patricia Mullan; 2s.; 2d. Educ. Ballymoney College of Further Education; Queen's University, Belfast; University of Ulster; Manchester University. Lecturer, Business Studies, Downpatrick College of Further Education, 1962 - 76; Head, Department of Business and Management Studies, Newry and Kilkeel College of Higher and Further Education, 1976 - 81. Chairman, Association of College Principals, 1986 - 87; Member: Northern Ireland Colleges Forum, 1996 - 98, Southern Education and Library Board since 1997, NI New Deal Task Force, DETI Economic Development Forum; Chairman, Association of NI Colleges, 1998-2000; OBE awarded in 2001 New Year Honours for services to education. Recreations: sailing; walking; travelling. Address: (b.) Patrick Street, Newry, Co Down BT35 8DN; T.-01693 61071.

Mulligan, Patricia, SRN, ATCL Teachers Certificate Gold Medal (NEA). Part-time Lecturer, Creative Development, Drama, Upper Bann Institute, 1992-2000; b. 11.3.47, Portadown; m., Frank Mulligan; 1s.; 1d. Educ. St Michael's School, Lurgan; Portadown Technical College; Trinity College, London; New Era Academy, London. SRN, Musgrave Park Hospital, 1965 - 68; Staff Nurse, Banbridge Hospital, 1968 - 70; Theatre Sister, Craigavon Area Hospital, 1970 - 75; Drama Teacher, St Michael's Lurgan, 1985 - 88. Regional Representative, Society of Teachers of Speech and Drama (NI); Adjudicator, Amateur Drama Council of Ireland since 1985; Organising Secretary, Banbridge Speech and Drama Festival since 1975; Past Chairman, Banbridge Arts Committee, 1994 - 97; Producer, Stage Struck Drama Group. Recreations: archery (qualified instructor); theatre visits; reading. Address: (b.) 7 Tullyear Avenue, Banbridge, Co Down; T.- 018206 23748.

Mulryne, Thomas Wilfred, MA, EdD. Principal, Methodist College since 1988, Belfast; b. 24.2.44; m., Doreen Patricia Quigley; 3s.; 1d. Educ. Methodist College, Belfast; St Catharine's College, Cambridge. Assistant Teacher, Methodist College, 1965 - 73; Part-time Tutor, Queen's University, Belfast, 1968 - 78; Senior Resident Master, Head of Classics, Methodist College, 1973 - 78; Headmaster, Royal School, Armagh, 1978 - 88. Lay reader, Church of Ireland, diocese of Connor; Chairman Belfast County Scout Council; Member, GBA Executive; Chairman, Curriculum and Assessment Committee (CCEA). Recreations: theatre; music; golf; reading; family. Address: (b.) Methodist College, 1 Malone Road, Belfast, BT9 6BY; T.- 02890-205202.

Murphy, Conor. Member (Newry and Armagh), Sinn Fein, Northern Ireland Assembly, since 1998. Councillor, Newry and Mourne Council, 1989-97. Address: (b.) Parliament Buildings, Stormont, Belfast, BT4 3ST; T.- 01232-520700.

Murphy, Mick. Member, (South Down), Sinn Fein, Northern Ireland Assembly, since 1998. Address: (b.) Parliament Buildings, Stormont, Belfast, BT4 3ST; T.- 01232-520700.

Murphy, Paddy, BA, IRFIVB. Senior Information Officer, NI Department of the Environment, since 2000; Management Consultant/Journalist; b. 7.6.51, Belfast; m., Marie; 1s.; 1d. Educ. St Malachy's College; St Patrick's Novitiate; Queen's University, Belfast. Deputy President/Sports Officer, Student Union, 1973 - 76; Research Project Officer, Sports Council, (NI), 1976; Northern Ireland Civil Service, 1977; Assistant Manager, Maysfield Leisure Centre, Belfast, 1977 - 78; Publicity Officer, Sports Council (NI), 1978 - 87; Assistant Public Relations Officer, Eastern Health and Social Services Board, 1987 - 93; NI Information Service, 1998; Publicity Director, NI Millennium Company, 1999-2000; Secretary, Ethnic Equality Council, 1995 - 98; Vice-Chairman. Public Affairs and Communications Association (NI), 1997 - 98; President, NI Volleyball Association, since 1980; Member, British Volleyball Federation Board, since 1978; Researcher/Writer/Presenter, BBC Radio and Television (NI), 1993 - 97; Consultant, RNID, EHSSB, RCS, Ethnic Equality Council since 1994. Member: NUJ, since 1978, Sports Journalists' Association of Great Britain, since 1978; Secretary, Ethnic Equality Council, 1995-98. International Volleyball referee, 1981-2001; represented Northern Ireland and UK in Volleyball since 1980. Publications: IOC Official Atlanta Guide; poetry published in Poetry Now. Recreations: volleyball; judo; reading; music; pets; cooking. Address: (h.) Nukiwaza, 21 Broughton Park, Ravenhill, Belfast BT6 0BD. T.-02890-963447. e-mail:padymurphy@aol.com /paddy.murphy@doeni.gov.uk.

Murphy, Rt. Hon. Paul (Peter), MA, PC, MP. Secretary of State for Northern Ireland, since 2002; b. 25.11.48. Educ. St. Francis RC Primary School, Abersychan; West Monmouth School, Pontypool; Oriel College, Oxford (Hon. Fellow, 2000). Management Trainee, CWS, 1970-71; Lecturer in History and Government, Ebbw Vale College of Further Education, 1971-87. Member, Torfaen Borough Council, 1973-87 (Chairman, Finance Committee, 1976-86); Secretary, Torfaen Constituency Labour Party, 1974-87. Opposition front bench spokesman for Wales, 1988-94; on NI, 1994; on foreign affairs, 1994-95; on defence, 1995-97; Minister of State, NI Office, 1997-99; Secretary of State for Wales, 1999-2002. Recreation: music. Address: (b.) House of Commons, London SW1A 0AA. T.-020 7219 3463, (office) 01495 750078.

Murray, Denis James, OBE, BA, HDipEd. Ireland Correspondent, BBC since 1988; b. 7.5.51; m., Joyce Linehan; 2 s.; 2 d. Educ. St Malachy's College, Belfast; Trinity College, Dublin; Queen's University, Belfast. Graduate Trainee, then Reporter, Belfast Telegraph, 1975 - 77; Belfast Reporter, RTE, 1977 - 82; BBC: Dublin Correspondent, 1982 - 84; NI Political Correspondent, 1984 - 88. Publications: BBC Guide to 1997 General Election (Contributor), 1997. Recreations: music; reading; sport; family. Address: (b.) c/o BBC, Ormeau Avenue, Belfast, BT2 8HQ; T.- 02890-338000.

Murray, John James, BDS, NUI. Dental Surgeon since 1955; b. Castleblayney, Co Monaghan, Ireland; m., Nancy; 1s.; 1d. Educ. St Edna's Galway; De la Salle, Waterford; University College, Dublin. Dental Surgeon, Loughton Essex; County Dental Officer, Co Monaghan. Past Chairman, Local dentistry Advisory Committee; Central Dental Advisory Committee; Chairman and Hon. Member, Armagh Arts Club; Chairman, Armagh City and District Arts Committee since 1975; Member, Co Armagh Golf Club (Captain, 1974, President, 1991 and 1992). Orthodontic Prize, Dublin Dental Hospital. Recreations: golf; arts; horse racing; painting in oils. Address: (b.) 6 Victoria Street, Armagh; T- 02837-522135.

Murray, Rev. Peter David, BA, BD. Methodist Minister, Glengormley Methodist Church, Newtownabbey since 1998; b. 12.9.52, Malawi; m., Elizabeth; 3s.; 1d. Educ. Methodist College, Belfast; Queen's University. Geography Teacher, Grosvenor High School, 1975 - 83 (Head of department, 1979 - 83); Methodist Minister, Sligo and Drumshanbo Circuit, Ireland, 1987 - 91; Methodist Minister, Carnalea Methodist Church, Bangor, 1991 - 98;. Publications: Northern Ireland (with G Dalton), 1987. Recreations: painting. Address: (h.) 34 Dalewood, Newtownabbey, Co Antrim, BT36 8WR.

N

Naismith, Scott, MA (Hons), PGCE, SQH. Headmaster, Regent House Grammar School, since 2003; b. 29.8.62, Hamilton; m., Wendy; 2 d. Educ. Dalziel High School; Edinburgh University; Moray House College of Education. Taught in Egypt, 1985-87, then at Castlebrae High School, Edinburgh, 1987-1989; George Heriot's School, Edinburgh: History and Modern Studies Teacher, then Head of Department, then Assistant Headteacher, then Depute Headteacher, 1989-2003. Recreations: photography; guitar and mandolin. Address: (b.) Regent House Grammar School, Circular Road, Newtownards, Co. Down BT23 4QA. T.-02891 813234.

Napier, Sir Oliver. Co founder, Alliance Party of Northern Ireland and Leader, 1973 - 84; b. 11.7.35, Belfast; m., Lady Briege Barnes; 3s.; 5d. Educ. St Malachy's College, Belfast; Queen's University, Belfast. Admitted as a Solicitor, 1959; Senior Partner, Napier and Sons; Part-time Lecturer, Queen's University, Belfast; Co-founder Alliance Party of Northern Ireland, 1970; Elected (East Belfast), Northern Ireland Assembly, 1973; Member, Minister of Law Reform Power Sharing Executive, 1974; Elected (East Belfast), Constitutional Convention, 1975 - 76; Councillor, Belfast City Council, 1977 - 89; Elected (East Belfast), Northern Ireland Assembly, 1982 - 86. Elected (North Down), Northern Ireland Forum for Political Dialogue, 1996 - 98; Part of Alliance Party negotiating team, all Party Talks, 1996 - 98. Knighted, 1985; Chair, Standing Advisory Commission on Human Rights, 1988 - 92. Recreations: gardening; travel. Address: (h.) 83 Victoria Road, Holywood, Co Down; T.- Holywood 425986.

Naughton, Martin, Hon. Dr of Laws, UCD and Trinity, Dublin, Queen's, Belfast, University of Ulster, Notre Dame, USA. Chairman, Glen Dimplex, since 1973; b. 2.5.39, Dublin; m., Carmel; 2 s.; 1 d. Educ. De La Salle, Dundalk; Southampton College of Technology. Member, Irish Council of State; Chairman, Cross Border Trade and Business Development Board; ex Board Member, Industrial Development Board (NI); Trustee, Notre Dame. Address: (b.) Glen Dimplex, Ardee Road, Dunleer, Co Louth, Ireland; T.-041-6851700.

Neeson, Sean. Member (East Antrim), Alliance Party, Northern Ireland Assembly, since 1998. Elected to Carrickfergus Borough Council, 1977; Mayor, 1993; Member, Northern Ireland Assembly, 1982-86; Member, Northern Ireland Forum, 1996-98; Member, Alliance talks team, Castle Buildings talks, 1996-98; Vice-Chairperson of Assembly Committee on Enterprise, Trade and Investment. Address: (b.) Parliament Buildings, Stormont, Belfast, BT4 3ST.

Neill, Rose. Television Newscaster/Presenter, BBC Northern Ireland since 1986 and Television Personality; b. Newtownards, Co Down; m., Ivan Wilson; 2s. Educ. The Mount School, York, England; The City and East London College. Full time daily Newscaster/Light Entertainment Presenter/Sports Presenter, Ulster Television, 1978 - 86; BBC, since 1986. Made 3 Medical Documentaries; presenter of shows including: Children in Need, Making a Difference, Lifeline, medical programmes; Presenter live afternoon chat show, BBC Radio Ulster. Hon. Patron, Ulster Cancer Foundation; Committee Member, Northern Ireland Mother and Baby Appeal; Member: Royal Ulster Yacht Club; Strangford Lough Yacht Club. Recreations: sailing; hunting; snow and water skiing; travelling; reading; entertaining. Address: (b.) BBC Newsroom, BBC Northern Ireland, Ormeau Avenue, Belfast, BT2 8HQ; T.- 028 90 338000.

Nelis, Mary. Member (Foyle), Sinn Fein, Northern Ireland Assembly, since 1998. Councillor. Address: (b.) Parliament Buildings, Stormont, Belfast, BT4 3ST; T.- 028 90 520322.

Nelson, Rev. John Wallace, BA, BD, PhD. Clerk of Synod, Non-Subscribing Presbyterian Church of Ireland, 1988-2001; b. 1.10.55, Belfast. Educ. Larne Grammar School, 1967 - 74; Queen's University, Belfast, 1974 - 80; Victoria University of Manchester, 1980 - 83. Minister, Old Presbyterian Church, Ballycarry since 1983; Minister Raloo Non-Subscribing Presbyterian Church since 1983; Clerk of Presbytery of Antrim since 1986. Publications: Congregational Memoirs The Old Presbyterian Church of Larne and Kilwaughter (co-author), 1975; various articles mostly on historical topics. Recreations: study of history with special interest in Irish Presbyterianism. Address: (h.) Drumcorran, 102 Carrickfergus Road, Carnduff, Larne, Co Antrim, BT40 3JX; T.- 02828-272600.

Nelson, Kenneth John. Chief Executive of Larne Enterprise Development Co. Ltd (LEDCOM), since 1992; m., Pauline; 4 d.; 1 s. Address: (b.) LEDCOM Industrial Estate, Bank Road, Larne, Co. Antrim BT40 3AW. T.-028 28270742.

Nesbitt, Dermot W.G., BSc Econ (Hons). Member (South Down), Ulster Unionist Party, Northern Ireland Assembly, since 1998; academic staff, Queen's University, Belfast, 1976-98 (leave of absence); b. 14.8.47, Belfast; m., Oriel; 1 s.; 1 d. Educ. Down High School, Downpatrick; Queen's University, Belfast. Member, SACIIR; Chair: SEELB, Stranmillis College, Belfast. Address: (b.) Parliament Buildings, Stormont, Belfast, BT4 3ST.

Nesbitt, Michael, MA (Cantab), DBA. Presenter Ulster Television News and Current Affairs since 1992; b. 11.5.57, Belfast; m., Lynda Bryans (q.v.); 2s. Educ. Campbell College, Belfast; Jesus College Cambridge; Queen's University, Belfast.

Sports Correspondent, BBC Northern Ireland, 1980 - 86; Presenter, Good Morning Ulster, BBC Radio Ulster, 1986 - 89; Managing Director, Anderson-Kenny Public Relations Ltd, 1989 - 92. Recreations: reading; walking. Address: (b.) c/o Nicola Ibison, NCI Management Ltd, 51 Queen Anne Street, London W1M 0HS.

Nevin, Professor Norman Cummings, OBE, BSc, MD, FFPM, FRCPath, FRCPEd, FRCP. Retired, 2000; b. 10.6.35, Belfast; m., Jean; 1s.; 1d. Educ. Grosvenor High School; Queen's University, Belfast. House Officer, Royal Victoria Hospital, Belfast, 1960 - 61; John Dunville Fellow in Pathology, Queen's University, Belfast, 1961 - 64; Registrar, Medicine, Royal Victoria Hospital, Belfast, 1964 - 65; Medical Research Council Clinical Fellow, London and Oxford, 1965 - 67; Queen's University, Belfast: Lecturer, Human Genetics, 1967 - 68; Consultant/Senior Lecturer, 1968 - 75; Professor of Genetics, 1975-2000; Head, Northern Ireland Regional Genetics Service, Belfast City Hospital, 1975-2000. Gene Therapy Advisory Committee, UK: Member since 1993; Chairman since 1995. Publications: Illustrated Guide to Malformations of the Central Nervous System (with J A C Weatherall), 1983; over 300 peer reviewed publications on congenital abnormalities and genetic disease. Recreations: walking; painting; lecturing on ethical issues in genetics. Address: (h.) 17 Ogles Grove, Hillsborough, BT26 6RS; T.- 01846-689126.

Newell, Cecil Andrew, BD. Retired Methodist Minister; b. 28.10.25, Belfast; m., Sylvia Wilson; 1s.; 1d. Educ. Belfast College of Technology; Edgehill Theological College; London University (external student). Methodist Minister in Ireland, 1945 - 54; Methodist Minister in Zimbabwe, 1954 - 71; Methodist Minister in Ireland, 1971 - 99. President, Methodist Church in Ireland, 1983 - 84. Recreations: golf. Address: (h.) 22 Lord Warden's Parade, Bangor, BT19 1YU; T.-028 91463848.

Newell, Rev. Kenneth Norman Ernest, BA, BD, MTh. Minister, Fitzroy Presbyterian Church, Belfast since 1976; b. 14.5.43, Belfast; m., Valerie Ritchie; 1s.; 1d. Educ. Belfast High School; Queen's University, Belfast; Presbyterian College, Belfast; Ridley Hall, Cambridge; Hendrik Kraemer Institute, Leyden, Holland. Ordained, Hamilton Road Presbyterian Church, Bangor, 1968; Lecturer, New Testament Studies, Theological Academy of the Christian Evangelical Church of Timor, Indonesia, 1971 - 75. Convener, Continental Mission of the Presbyterian Church in Ireland, 1978 - 86; Chaplain to Rt. Hon. Alban Maginness, Lord Mayor of Belfast, 1997 - 98. Co Founder: Fitzroy-Clonard Inter Church Fellowship, 1981; Evangelical-Roman Catholic Theological Conferences, held annually since 1986. Justice Award, Belvedere College, Dublin, 1994. Pax Christi International Peace Award, 1999; involved in preaching at Memorial Service in First Congregational Church, Old Greenwich, USA following September 11th 2001 attacks.

Presented a paper, "Reconciliation in a Socio-political Dimension", to Serbian Bosnian and Croat Church leaders in Belgrade, 1996. Recreations: swimming; watching soccer (Crusaders FC); movies; music. Address: (h.) 64 Maryville Park, Belfast, BT9 6LQ; T.- 02890-874323. e-mail: ken.newell@ntlworld.com

Nicholson, James Frederick, MEP. Member (Northern Ireland) European Parliament since 1994; b. 29.1.45. Educ. Aghavilly Primary School. Councillor, Armagh District Council since 1975; Mayor of Armagh, 1995; Official Unionist Member (Newry and Armagh) Northern Ireland Assembly, 1982 - 86; Official Unionist Member of Parliament, (Newry and Armagh), 1983 - 85.

Nicholson, Rt. Hon. Sir (James) Michael (Anthony), Kt, PC, Rt. Hon. Lord Justice Nicholson. Lord Justice of Appeal, Supreme Court of Judicature, Northern Ireland since 1995; b. 4.2.33. Educ. Downside; Trinity College, Cambridge. Called to the Bar of Northern Ireland, 1956; Called to the English Bar (Gray's Inn), 1963; Hon. Bencher, 1995); Called to the Bar of Ireland, 1975.; High Court Judge, NI, 1986 - 95. President, ICU, 1978; President, NWICU, 1980-87. Address: (b.) Royal Courts of Justice, Chichester Street, Belfast, BT1 1YJ.

Nixon, Ken. Chairman, Northern Ireland Sports Forum, since 2001. Address: (b.) House of Sport, Upper Malone Road, Belfast BT9 5LA. T.-02890 381222.

Norton, Professor, Brian, BSc (Hons), MSc, PhD, DSc, FInstE, CEng. Professor of Built Environmental Engineering, since 1989; Dean of Engineering and Built Environment 1996-2001, University of Ulster; b. 11.12.55, Great Yarmouth; m., Bahara Sorooshian; 2s.; 1d. Educ. University of Nottingham; Cranfield University. Lecturer and Director, Solar Energy Technology Centre, Cranfield, 1987 - 89; University of Ulster: Director, Centre for Performance Research on the Built Environment, 1993 - 94; Head, Department of Building and Engineering, 1992 - 94; ICSU Visiting Professor of Science for Sustainable Development, Nigeria, 1995-99; Head, School of the Built Environment, University of Ulster, 1994 - 96. Member, Construction Industry Training Board, since 1992; Chair, Northern Ireland Business Education Partnership, since 2002; Chair, World Renewable Energy Network, since 1998; Gold Medal of the Amir of Bahrain for outstanding research achievement in the field of solar thermal applications, 1994; Napier Shaw Medal, Chartered Institute of Building Services Engineers, 1996; Institute of Energy's Past Chairman's Medal, 1995; Roscoe Prize, Institute of Energy, 1999. Publications: Solar Energy Thermal Technology, 1992; Passive Solar Schools (co-author), 1993; over 230 academic papers. Recreation: cycling. Address: (b.) University of Ulster, Faculty of Engineering, Shore Road, Newtownabbey BT37 0QB; T.- 02890-366285.

O

O'Brien, Martin Gerald, LLB, CPLS, LLM, Barrister-at-Law; Bar of Ireland; b. 26.2.65, Lurgan. Educ. St John's School, Moy; St Patrick's Academy, Dungannon; Queen's University, Belfast. Member Inn of Court, Northern Ireland practising at the Bar, Northern Ireland since 1989; Member, Bar of Ireland; Part-time Lecturer, Institute of Professional Legal Studies, Queen's University, Belfast. Part-time Chairman, Industrial Tribunals. Recreations: gardening; travel. Address: (b.) Bar Library, Royal Court of Justice, Chichester Street, Belfast, BT1 3JP; T.-02890-241523; (h.) 120 Benburb Road, Tobermasson, Moy, Co Tyrone, BT71 7PZ; T.- 02837-548357.

O'Brien, Martin Oliver, BA, MSSc. Senior Producer religious affairs since 1996/Journalist BBC Northern Ireland; Editor, Sunday Sequence; b. 19.7.54, Enniskillen, Co Fermanagh; m., Kate Toland; 2s.; 2d. Educ. St Joseph's Secondary School, Enniskillen; Fermanagh College of Further Education; Queen's University, Belfast. Reporter, Transport and Tourism Correspondent, Drama Critic, Belfast Telegraph, 1977 - 82; Editor, The Irish News, 1982 - 84; Producer, radio current affairs, BBC Radio Ulster, Good Morning Ulster, 1985 - 89; Senior Producer, Sunday Newsbreak, budget and election programmes, 1989 - 92; Editor, News Intake/responsible for radio and television strategic news planning, 1992 - 95. Member, Senate, Queen's University, Belfast since 1982; Member: various university committees; Board of Governors, Glenveagh School, Belfast since 1998; Board Member/Trustee, Northern Ireland Music Therapy Trust since 1999. Sony Award, Best radio current affairs programme in the UK, Sunday Newsbreak, 1991; Montgomery medal, Irish Association, 1993. Publications: Margaret Thatcher's Irish Legacy, in A Century of Northern Life, 1995. Recreations: country walks; book collecting; having a pint in stimulating company. Address: (b.) BBC Broadcasting House, Ormeau Avenue, Belfast, BT2 8HQ; T.- 02890-338000.

O'Brien, Dr. Matthew Gerard Robert, BA, MA, PhD, FRHist Soc. Senior Lecturer, History, University of Ulster, Magee College since 1994; b. 29.10.56, Fermoy, Co Cork, Ireland; divorced; 1s.; 1d. Educ. Christian Brothers College, Cork; University College, Cork; Peterhouse, Cambridge. Fellow, Institute Irish Studies, Queen's University, Belfast, 1983; History Lecturer, University of Ulster, Magee, 1983 - 94. Publications: author and editor of numerous books and papers on Irish History, 1200 - 1966. Recreations: hill walking; campaign medals. Address: (b.) Magee College, University of Ulster, Londonderry, BT48 7JL.

O'Connell, Joseph Ignatius, MEd, BA, HDip Ed, FRSA, JP. Retired Principal, St Mary's Teacher Training College, Belfast; b. 16.12.30, Crossgar,

Co Down; m., Bogan Mary Catherine; 2d. Educ. Christian Brothers' Grammar School, Belfast; University College, Dublin; Queen's University, Belfast. Teacher: St Mary's College, Port of Spain Trinidad, 1952 - 56; Synge Street Grammar School, Dublin, 1956 - 57; St Mary's Secondary School, Ballycastle, 1957 - 60; St Patrick's Secondary School, Belfast, 1960 - 63; Deputy Principal, St Augustine's Secondary School, Belfast, 1963 - 70; St Joseph's College of Education, Belfast, 1970 - 80; St Mary's College, Belfast: Deputy Principal, 1980-87; Principal, 1987 - 92; Retired, 1992. Recreations: golf; reading; swimming. Address: (h.) 41 Strathmore Park North, Antrim Road, Belfast, BT15 5HQ.

O'Connor, Danny. Member, (East Antrim), Social Democratic and Labour Party, Northern Ireland Assembly, 1998-2003. Educ. St MacNissis College, Garron Tower. Security officer; elected to Larne Borough Council, 1997. Address: (b.) Parliament Buildings, Stormont, Belfast, BT4 3ST.

O'Connor, Emmet, MA (NUI), PhD (Cantab). Lecturer in Politics, University of Ulster, Magee College, since 1985, Senior Lecturer, since 1992; b. 27.12.54, Dublin; m., Colette; 1 s.; 1 d. Educ. De La Salle College, Waterford; University College Galway; St. John's College, Cambridge. Research Fellow, Churchill College, Cambridge, 1983-84; Lecturer, University of Ulster, 1985-2001. Publications: Editor, Saothar, 1983-84, 1986-2003; A Labour History of Ireland, 1824-1960, 1992; Syndicalism in Ireland, 1917-23, 1988. Recreations: chess; squash; hurling. Address: (b.) Magee College, University of Ulster, Londonderry BT48 7JL. T.-02871 375211.

O'Connor, Dr. Francis A., MD, FRCP. FRCPI, FACG. Consultant Physician and Gastroenterologist, Altnagelvin Hospital Trust since 1977; Director of Medical Education, Altnagelvin H & SS Trust; Honorary Senior Lecturer, Queen's University Belfast; b. Belfast; m., Elizabeth Breda; 2s.; 1d. Educ. St Mary's Christian Brothers Grammar School, Belfast; Queen's University, Belfast. Tutor/Registrar in Medicine, Queen's University, Belfast/ Royal Victoria Hospital, Belfast City Hospital Mater Informorum, 1970 - 73; Royal Victoria Hospital Research Fellow, 1973 - 74; Fellow in Gastroenterology, University of Washington, Seattle, USA, 1974 - 75; Senior Tutor/Registrar in Gastroenterology, Royal Victoria Hospital, Belfast, 1975 - 77. Publications: numerous papers in medical and academic journals. Address: (b.) Altnagelvin Area Hospital Trust, Londonderry; T. 01504-345171, Ext. 3354.

O'Connor, Rory, CBE, BComm. Barrister-at-Law, Kings Inns, Dublin; b. Holywood, Co Down; m., Elizabeth Dew; 1s.; 2d. Educ. Christian Brothers School, Belfast; Blackrock College, Dublin; University College, Dublin; Kings Inns, Dublin. Called to the Bar of Ireland, 1949; Resident Magistrate, Kenya, 1956; Magistrate,

Hong Kong, 1962; High Court Judge, Hong Kong, 1977 - 90; High Court Judge, Brunei, 1983 - 90. Member, Judicial Service Commission, Hong Kong, 1987 - 90; Chairman, Board of Review, Long Term Prison Sentences, Hong Kong, 1988 - 90; Member, Gibralter Court of Appeal, 1991 - 97. CBE, 1991. Recreations: travel; reading. Address: (h.) 12 Windermere Crescent, Bangor, Co Down; T.- 02891-271707.

Odling-Smee, Anne Marie, CBE, JP, BA, FRSA. b. 22.12.34, Cheshire; m., William Odling-Smee (see William Odling-Smee); 3s.; 3d. Educ. Kings College, Newcastle; University of Durham. Lecturer, Social Work, Queen's University, Belfast, 1976 - 1991. Member, Belfast Education and Library Board, 1989-2001 (Chair, from 1997); Governor, Integrated Education Fund 1992-2000 (Chair, from 1995); Board Member, Extern Organisation. CBE, 1999. Address: (h.) The Boathouse, 24, Rossglass Road South, Killough, Co. Down BT30 7RA. e-mail: wodlingsmee@aol.com

Odling-Smee, William, FRCS. Senior Lecturer in Surgery, Queen's University, Belfast, 1973-2000; Consultant Surgeon, Belfast City Hospital, 1997-2000; b. 21.4.35; m. Anne M Odling-Smee (qv); 3s.; 3d. Educ. Durham School; University of Durham. St Raphaels Hospital, India, 1961 - 64; Surgical Training, Newcastle-upon-Tyne, 1964 - 68; CMCU, Nigeria, 1969 - 70; Senior Registrar, Royal Victoria Hospital, Belfast, 1970 - 73; Consultant Surgeon, Royal Victoria Hospital, 1973 - 1997. Address: (h.) The Boathouse, 24, Rossglass Road South, Killough, Co. Down BT30 7RA. T.-028 4484 1868; Fax: 028 4484 1143. e-mail: wodlingsmee@aol.com

O'Dowd, Dr. Mary, BA, PhD. Senior Lecturer, Queen's University, Belfast; b. 11.9.52. Educ. Muckross Park College, Dublin; University College, Dublin. Lecturer, School of Modern History, Queen's University, Belfast since 1979. Member, Irish Manuscripts Commission; President of the International Federation for Research in Women's History, since 2000. Publications: Power, Politics and Land, Sligo 1568 - 1688, 1995; Editor of various collections of essays on women and Irish history, including (jtly) Field Day Anthology of Irish Writing Vols 4 and 5, 2002. Address: (b.) School of Modern History, Queen's University, Belfast, Belfast, BT7 1NN; T.- 02890-245133.

O'Fee, Charles Stewart, BA, Grad Cert Ed, DASE. Principal, Lisnasharragh Primary School since 1986; b. 15.5.50, Bangor; m., Jeanette Baxter; 2d. Educ. Sullivan Upper School; Queen's University, Belfast; Stranmillis College. Teacher, Rathmore Primary School, 1973 - 77; Killyleagh Primary School; Vice-Principal, 1977 - 81; Principal, 1981 - 86. Recreations: horticulture; stone wall building; walking holidays; soccer. Address: (b.) Lisnasarragh Primary School, Tudor

Drive, Belfast, BT6 9LS; T.- 01232-401211. e-mail: cofee@lisps.belfast.ni.sch.uk

O'Hagan, Bernard. Chair, City Marketing Committee, Derry City Council; Elected to Derry City Council, 2001; age 41; m. Chair of North West Region Cross Border Group; Member: City of Derry Airport Committee, Policy and Resources Committee, Derry Investment Initiative, Derry Visitor and Convention Bureau, Derry Theatre Trust, NI Local Government Association. Recreations: golf; fishing; walking; reading. Address: (b.) Derry City Council, 98 Strand Road, Derry BT48 7NN. T.-028 7136 5151.

O'Hagan, Dr. Dara, BA (Hons), MSSc, PhD, MLA. Member (Upper Bann), Sinn Fein, Northern Ireland Assembly, 1998-2003; b. 29.8.64, Lurgan, Co Armagh; m., Thomas Mulholland. Educ. St Michael's Grammar School, Lurgan; University of Ulster; Queen's University, Belfast. Recreations: reading; writing. Address: (b.) Parliament Buildings, Stormont, Belfast, BT4 3XX; T.- 028 90521671.

O'Hara, Bill (William P), JP. Hotel Consultant; b. 26.2.29, Bangor; m., Anne O'Hara (nee Finn), MBE; 2s.; 2d. Educ. Castleknock College, Dublin. Trainee, Grand Central Hotel, Belfast; previously Managing Director: O'Hara's Royal Hotel, Bangor; The Irish Whiskey Co.; Abercorn Restaurant; Globe Tavern, Belfast; Lusty Beg Island; Brown Trout Inn and Country Club. Bangor Independent Councillor, 1964 - 74; National Governor, BBC Northern Ireland, 1974 - 79. Recreations: golf; walking; politics. Address: (h.) Summer Cottage, 12 Raglan Road, Bangor, BT20 3TL.

O'Kane, James Patrick Jude, BA (Hons) Acc, CPFA. Registrar, Queen's University Belfast, since 1999; b. 1.3.58; m., Breege; 1 s.; 2 d. Educ. NI Polytechnic; Liverpool Polytechnic. National Finance Trainee, NI Staffs Council for The Health and Social Services, 1979-82; Senior Finance Officer, NI Housing Executive, 1982-84; Deputy Director of Finance, University of Ulster, 1984-92; Director of Finance, North Eastern Education and Library Board, 1992-94; Director of Finance, Queen's University Belfast, 1994-99. Director of the following companies: G. Scope Ltd; QUBIS Ltd; NI Challenge Fund Ltd; NI Science Park Holdings Ltd; Director on Board of Royal Group of Hospitals Trust; Governor of BIFHE and currently Chairman. Recreations: sport; family. Address: (b.) Queen's University Belfast, University Road, Belfast BT7 1NN. T.-028 90 27 2500. e-mail: j.okane@qub.ac.uk

O'Kane, Sally, FPSNI, MPSNI. Director, Pharmaceutical Services, Western Health and Social Services Board/Altnagelvin Hospitals Trust since 1992; b. 7.11.38; m., Bernard; 2s.; 1d. Educ. Dominican College, Belfast; College of Pharmacy, Belfast. Pharmacist, Royal Victoria Hospital, Belfast, 1961 - 63; Pharmacist, Altnagelvin

Hospital, Londonderry, 1969 - 73; District Pharmaceutical Officer, 1973 - 78; Principal Pharmacist, Altngelvin, 1978 - 90; Assistant Unit General Manager, Altnhelvin, 1990- 92. Fellow, Pharmaceutical Society of Northern Ireland, 1998; Evans silver Medal for significant contribution to the practice of pharmacy locally, 1998. Recreations: reading; golf; swimming; skiing. Address: (b.) Department of Pharmacy, Altnagelvin Hospital, Londonderry; T.- 01504- 345171, Ext. 3905.

O'Kane, Winifred (Una), OBE, MEd, DASE, Dip HEd, MIMgt. Headmistress, St Mary's Grammar School, Magherafelt since 1995; b. 22.8.49, Magherafelt. m., Michael O'Kane; 2s. Educ. St Mary's Grammar, Magherafelt; University of Ulster at Jordanstown; Queen's University, Belfast. Teacher, St Colms High School, Draperstown, 1970 - 86; Field Officer, Northern Ireland Council for Educational Development, 1986 - 89; Senior Professional Officer, Northern Ireland Curriculum Council, 1989 - 93; Assistant Director, Northern Ireland Council for the Curriculum, Examinations, Assessment, 1993 - 95. Member, Board of Health Promotion Agency, Northern Ireland. Recreations: reading; walking; theatre. Address: (b.) St Mary's Grammar School, Castledawson Road, Magherafelt, BT45 6AX; T.- 028 796-32320.

O'Loan, Declan, BSc, PGCE, MBA. Head of Maths, St Louis Grammar School since 1987; SDLP Councillor, Ballymena Borough Council since 1993; b. 5.8.51, Ballymena, Co Antrim; m., Nuala (see Nuala O'Loan); 5s. Educ. St MacNissi's College, Co Antrim; Imperial College, University of London; University of Cambridge; University of Ulster. Maths Teacher: Ramsden School, London, 1974 - 76; Rainey Endowed School, Magherafelt, 1976 -80; Overseas Development Administration, Kenya, 1980 - 83; Methodist College, Belfast, 1983 - 87; Member General Council, SDLP, 1996-98 and since 2001; Secretary and Treasurer, Association of SDLP Councillors, 1997-98 and Secretary, since 2001; Member, Ballymena District Partnership, 1996-2001 (Chair, 1998-99); Member, Ballymena CAB Management Committee, 1993 - 97 and since 1998, Treasurer, since 1999; Director and Treasurer, Ballymena Community Forum, since 2000; Member: Community Relations Council Community Advisory Group, 2000-2001, Community Relations Council, since 2001; Member and interim Chair, Ballymena Strategy Partnership, since 2001. Address: (h.) 48 Old Park Avenue, Ballymena, Co Antrim, BT42 1AX; T.- 028 2564 9636.

O'Loan, Nuala Patricia, LLB (Hons). Police Ombudsman for Northern Ireland; b. 20.12.51, Bishops Stortford, England; m., Declan O'Loan q.v.; 5s. Educ. Convent of Holy Child, Harrogate; King's College, University of London; College of Law, London. Solicitor of the Supreme Court of England and Wales since 1976; Law

Lecturer, Ulster Polytechnic, 1976 - 80; Law Lecturer, University of Ulster, 1984 - 92; Jean Monnet Chair in European Law, University of Ulster, 1992-99. Member, Energy and Transport Group, General Consumer Council for Northern Ireland, 1991 - 96 (Convenor, 1994 - 96); Lay Visitor to RUC Stations, 1991 - 97; Member, UK Domestic Coal Consumers Council, 1992 - 95; Member, Ministerial Working Group on the Green Economy, 1993 - 95; Member, Northern Health and Social Service Board, 1993 - 97 (Convenor for Complaints, 1996 - 97); Expert Member, European Commission Consumers Consultative Council, 1994 - 95; Member, Police Authority for Northern Ireland, 1997-2000; Senior Lecturer in Law, University of Ulster, 1994-2000; Chairman, Northern Ireland Consumer Council for Electricity, 1997-2000; Volunteer Member, Accord Counselling and Marriage Care, since 1986. Over 45 publications on consumer law, policing and other issues. Recreations: reading; music. Address: (b.) New Cathedral Buildings, St. Anne's Square, 11 Church Street, Belfast BT1 1PG.

O Murañle, Dr. Eamonn Nollaig, BA, MA, PhD. Reader in Irish and Celtic Studies, Queen's University, Belfast (staff member since 1993); b. 22.12.48, Knock, Co Mayo; m., Mary Teresa Keenan; 1s.; 1d. Educ. Knock National School; St Nathy's College, Ballaghaderreen; St Patrick's College, Maynooth. Placenames Officer, Ordnance Survey of Ireland, Dublin, 1972 - 93; Director and General Editor, Northern Ireland Place-Name Project; Editor, Ainm: Bulletin of the Ulster Place-Name Society. Author of numerous articles, in Irish and English. Books include: Mayo Places: Their Names and Origins, 1985; Béacán/Bekan: Portrait of an East Mayo Parish (co-author), 1986; Logainmneacha na hEireann: Contae Luimnigh (co-author), 1990; The Celebrated Antiquary: Dubhaltach Mac Fhirbhisigh c 1600-71, 1996, reprint, 2002; Cathal Og Mac Maghnusa and the Annals of Ulster, 1998; Irisleabhar Mha Muad 2000: Cead Bliain Slan, 2000. Recreations: reading; writing; listening to music; current affairs. Address: (b.) School of Languages, Literatures and Arts, Queen's University, Belfast, Belfast BT7 1NN; T.- 02890-273694.

O'Neill, The Right Hon. The Lord, TD, DL. Landowner and Company Director; b. 1.9.33; m., Georgina Montague-Douglas-Scott; 3s. Educ. Ludgrove School, Berks; Eton College; Royal Agricultural College, Cirencester. Short Service Commission, 11th Hussars PA O, 1952 - 53; Joined North Irish Horse T A, 1954: Major, Commanding D, North Irish Horse Squadron, Royal Yeomanry Regiment, 1967 - 69; Commanding, North Irish Horse Cadres, 1969 - 71; R A R O, 1971; Hon. Colonel, D, 1986 - 91; Hon. Colonel, 69th (North Irish Horse) Signals Squadron (V), 1988 - 93; Farmer; Company Director: Shane Developments Ltd; Shanes Castle Estates Co; Chairman, Ulster Countryside Committee, 1971 - 75; Chairman, Northern Ireland Tourist Board, 1975 - 80; Trustee,

Ulster Folk and Transport Museum, 1969 - 90, (Vice-Chairman, 1987 - 90); President, Northern Ireland Association of Youth Clubs (Youth Action); Chairman, Finance Committee, Royal Agricultural Society, 1974 - 83; President, Royal Ulster Agricultural Society, 1984 - 1986; Member, National Trust Committee for Northern Ireland, 1980 - 91 (Chairman, 1981 - 91); Member, Council for Nature Conservation and The Countryside, 1989 - 92; Commissioner, Museums and Galleries Commission, 1987 - 94; Chairman, Northern Ireland Museums Advisory Committee, 1989 - 93; Chairman, Northern Ireland Museums Council, 1993 - 98; President, The Railway Preservation Society of Ireland since 1964; Lord-Lieutenant, Co Antrim, 1994. Recreations: shooting; walking; swimming; motor cars old and new; railways; boats; gardening.

O'Neill, Eamonn. Member (South Down), Social Democratic and Labour Party, Northern Ireland Assembly, 1998-2003. Teacher; elected to Down Council, 1977. Address: (b.) SDLP Constituency Office, 60 Main Street, Castlewellan, Co Down BT31 9DJ. T.-028 43778833. Fax: 028 43778044. e-mail: e.oneill@sdlp.ie

O'Neill, Dr. Gerard Michael, BSc, PhD, MBA, MInstPhys, ACA. Director (Corporate Services), Labour Relations Agency, since 2001; Non Executive Board Member, NI Regional Medical Physics Agency, since 2001; b. 22.1.51, Belfast; m., Imelda; 2 d. Educ. St. Malachy's College; Queen's University; University of Ulster. Industry for 11 years (mainly in product development quality and technical support); Manager in Information Technology, Public Sector, 1987-93; Internal Audit, 1993-2001; became a Senior Manager in 2001. Address: (b.) Labour Relations Agency, 2-8 Gordon Street, Belfast BT1 2LG. T.-028 90 337428. e-mail: gerry.o'neill@lra.org.uk

O'Neill, Maurice. Group Editor, Northern Newspaper Group since 1991; b. 11.10.38, Ballymena; m., Jean; 1d. Educ. Ballymena Academy. Joined Ballymena Observer, 1955; Founding Editor, Ballymena Guardian, 1971. Publications: Ballymena – An Historical Companion. Recreations: stamp collecting. Address: (b.) Ballymena Guardian, 83-85 Wellington Street, Ballymena; T.-02825 641228.

O'Neill, Peter, MSSc, BSc. Director, National Union of Students - Union of Students in Ireland, since 1987; b. 24.7.59, London; m., Tess O'Neill. Educ. St Patrick's Academy, Dungannon; Queen's University, Belfast. President, Queen's University, Belfast Student Union, 1983 - 84; Education Officer, Union of Students In Ireland, 1984 - 85; Member of Court, University of Ulster. Publications: Student Community Relations Guide, 1997; Promoting and Managing Diversity in Colleges of Further and Higher Education in Northern Ireland, 1998. Recreations: current affairs; reading; travel; local history. Address: (b.) 29 Bedford Street, Belfast, BT2 7EJ.

O'Neill, Seamus, MEd. MSc, BEd. Headmaster, Drumcree College since 1994; b. 23.12.45, Lurgan; m., Mairie; 3s,; 2d. Educ. St Colman's College; Queen's University, Belfast. Assistant Teacher, St Malachy's Boys' School, 1969; Vice-Principal St Malachy's Boys'High School, 1978; Vice-Principal, Drumcree College, 1985. Chairperson, Ministerial Northern Ireland Working Party on careers education, 1988-89. Recreations: hill walking; photography. Address: (h.) 22 Derrymore Road, Gawley's Gate, Lurgan, BT67 0BW; T.- 028 92 651 526.

O'Neill, Prof. Shane T., MA, PhD. Professor of Political Theory, Queen's University Belfast, since 2002, Head of the School of Politics and International Studies, since 2001; b. 31.3.65, Dublin; m., Grace McCarthy; 2 s. Educ. Belvedere College, Dublin; University College, Dublin; Glasgow University. Lecturer in Political Theory, Department of Government, University of Manchester, 1993-94; Lecturer in Politics, Department of Politics, Queen's University Belfast, 1994-98, Reader in Politics, School of Politics, 1998-2002. Publications: Impartiality in Context, 1997; Reconstituting Social Criticism (Editor), 1999. Recreations: music; sport. Address: (b.) School of Politics and International Studies, 21 University Square, Queen's University Belfast BT7 1PA; T.-028 9027 3276.

Orde, Hugh Stephen Roden, OBE, BA Hons (Public Admin and Mgt). Chief Constable, Police Service of Northern Ireland, since 2002; b. 27.8.58; m., Kathleen Helen; 1 s. Educ. University of Kent at Canterbury. Joined Metropolitan Police, 1977; Sergeant, Brixton, 1982; Police Staff Coll., 1983; Inspector, Greenwich, 1984-90 (Bramshill Schol., 1984-87); Staff Officer to Dep. Assistant Commander, SW London, as Chief Inspector, 1990; Chief Inspector, Hounslow, 1991-93; Superintendent, Territorial Support Group, 1993-95; Detective Chief Superintendent, Major Crimes, SW Area, 1995-98; Commander, Crime, South London, 1998; Dep. Assistant Commander, 1999-2002. Recreations: marathon running; wine; gardening. Address: (b.) Police Service of Northern Ireland, Knock Road, Belfast BT5 6LE.

O'Reilly, Prof. Margaret Dolores, BEd (Hons), MA PhD. Professor of International Business Strategy and Head of School of International Business, University of Ulster; b. 3.12.60, Belfast; m., John Parr; 1 d. Educ. Dominican College, Belfast; Queen's University, Belfast; University of Ulster; University of Surrey. Teacher, St Bride's School, Belfast, 1983 - 87; Investment Consultant, Trustee Savings Bank, 1987 - 89; Fulltime study, 1989 - 90; Staff member, University of Ulster since 1990. Jean Monnet Research Fellow, European University Institute, Florence Italy, 1996 - 97. Vere Foster Gold Medal (distinguished teaching award) Irish National Teachers Association, 1983; Chairman, Air Transport Users Council of the Chambers of Commerce of Ireland, 1998-2001; Represents Ireland at the Federation of Air

Transport Users Representatives in Brussels; Member: Academy of International Business; Institute of Management; Strategic Planning Society; Transport Studies Organisation; Non Executive Director of the Ufi Charitable Trust and Ufi Ltd; member of the Board of the Information age Initiative; Director of the Derry Investment Initiative. Recreations: international travel; cooking; opera. Address: (b.) University of Ulster at Magee, Faculty of Business and Management, Carrickmore House, Rock Road, Londonderry, BT48 7JL; T.- 028 7137 5288.

Orr, Professor Jean Agnes, BA, MSc, RGN, RHV. Head, School of Nursing and Midwifery, Queen's University Belfast since 1991, Professor of Nursing Studies, since 1991; b. 10.9.43. Educ. Princess Gardens; Ulster Polytechnic; Manchester University. Lecturer, Social and Health Sciences, Ulster Polytechnic, 1979 - 81; Lecturer, Nursing, Manchester University, 1981 - 89; Senior Lecturer, Nursing, University of Manchester, 1989 - 91. Patron of WAVE Trauma Centre in Northern Ireland; Trustee of Marie Curie Cancer Care; Trustee of the Child Development Programme in Bristol; Adjunct Professor, University of Massachusetts at Amherst; Executive Committee member of the Council of Deans and Heads of UK University Faculties for Nursing, Midwifery and Health Visiting; representing Northern Ireland; Member of Queen's University, Belfast Senate and Women's Forum. Recreations: good food; good wine; theatre and travelling. Address: (b.) School of Nursing and Midwifery, Queen's University Belfast, Medical Biology Centre, 97 Lisburn Road, Belfast BT9 7BL. T.-028 9027 2079.

Osborn, Helen, BLib, MLib, MCILIP. Head of Libraries and Information, Western Education and Library Board, since 2000; b. 8.6.59, Bromsgrove, England; m., Geoff Thomas. Educ. University College of Wales, Aberystwyth. Chief Librarian, Newport, South Wales, 1993-2000. Recreations: walking; cycling. Address: (b.) Library Headquarters, 1 Spillars Place, Omagh, Co. Tyrone BT78 1HL. T.-028 8225 3644.

Osborne, Professor Robert David, BA, PhD. Professor of Applied Policy Studies, University of Ulster since 1995; b. 30.12.50, Derry; m., Frances Merle; 2d. Educ. Ysgol Dewi Sant, Wales; Queen's University, Belfast. Research Assistant, Queen's University, Belfast, 1973 - 74; Research Student, Queen's University, Belfast, 1974 - 76; Research Officer, Fair Employment Agency, 1976 - 78; Lecturer, Social Policy, Ulster Polytechnic, 1978 - 85; University of Ulster: Senior Lecturer, Social Policy, 1985 - 92; Reader, Public Policy, 1992 - 95. Member, Standing Advisory Commission on Human Rights, 1998. Publications: 5 books including: Higher Education in Ireland: North and South, 1996; After the Reforms: Education Policy in Northern Ireland, 1993. Recreations: walking; steam railways; keeping poultry; gardening. Address: (b.) School of Public Policy, Economics and Law, University

of Ulster, Shore Road, Newtownabbey, Jordanstown, Co Antrim, BT37 0QB; T.- 02890-366322.

Othick, John. Director, Centre of Canadian Studies, Queen's University, Belfast, 1989-2000; b. 5.1.41, Merseyside. Educ, Wallasey Grammar School, Merseyside; Queen's University, Belfast. Lecturer, Economic History, Queen's University, Belfast, 1967 - 95; Course Tutor, Open University, 1970 - 94. President, British Association for Canadian Studies, 1994 - 96; Chair, Belfast Branch, United Nations Association, 1996-2000. Recreations: walking; swimming. e-mail: johnothick@aol.com

Outram, Victor George, MA. DASE. Headmaster, Enniskillen High School since 1987; b. 18.12.46, Articlave, Co Londonderry; m., Kate; 2s.; 1d. Educ. Coleraine Academical Institution; Trinity College, Dublin. Recreations: sport; refereeing rugby football. Address: (b.) Enniskillen High School, Derrychara, Enniskillen, Co Fermanagh, BT94 6JL; T.- 02866 322923.

Owen-Jones, Sheila M., PhD, MSc, BA (Hons), FRSA, PGCE. Principal Chief Executive, North East Institute of Further and Higher Education; b. Newry; 1s.; 1d. Educ. University of Wales. Assistant Director, Further and Higher Education, Clwyd Local Education Authority; Senior Education Officer, Post 16, Glamorgan Local Education Authority; Senior Education Officer for Further and Higher Education, Gwent Local Education Authority. Publications: research articles for Welsh History Review; Oral History etc. Member, Institute of Directors; Member of Board of Association of Colleges (AOC); Member of the Governing Body, Institute of Technology, Sligo; Chair of Lobbying Committee of Association of NI Colleges; Member of the Senate of Queen's University. Recreations: hill walking; swimming; painting; films. Address: (h.) Trostan Avenue, Ballymena, Co Antrim, BT43 7BN; T.- 028 2563 6222.

Owens, Dr. Francis Joseph, BSc, PhD, CEng, MIEE, Senior Lecturer, University of Ulster at Jordanstown since 1990; b. 17.11.53, Ballygawley, Co Tyrone; m., Mary Campbell; 3s.; 1d. Educ. Glencull Primary School; St Ciaran's High School, Ballygawley, Co Tyrone; Christian Brothers Grammar School, Omagh, Co Tyrone; Queen's University, Belfast. Lecturer, Department of Electronics, Dundalk Regional Technical College, 1979 - 80; Lecturer, School of Electrical and Electronic Engineering, Ulster Polytechnic, 1980 - 84; Lecturer, Department of Electrical and Electronic Engineering, University of Ulster, 1984 - 90. Publications: 50 research papers; 1 text book - Signal Processing of Speech, 1993. Recreations: reading; gardening; DIY. Address: (b.) School of Electrical and Mechanical Engineering, University of Ulster at Jordanstown, Newtownabbey, Co. Antrim BT37 0QB; T.- 028 90366513.

P

Paisley, Ian, Jnr. Member (North Antrim), Democratic Unionist Party, Northern Ireland Assembly since 1998; b. 12.12.66; m.; 2 d. ; 1 s. Educ. Shaftesbury House College; Methodist College, Belfast; Queen's University, Belfast. Political researcher and author, since 1989; Member, Northern Ireland Forum, 1996-98. Recreations: food; rugby; reading; motor-racing; collector of cartoons and political caricatures from 19th-century. Address: (b.) Parliament Buildings, Stormont, Belfast, BT4 3ST; T.- 02890-520700.

Paisley, Rev. Ian Richard Kyle, MP, DD. Member of Parliament, Antrim North; Member, European Parliament, Northern Ireland; Member (North Antrim), Democratic Unionist Party, Northern Ireland Assembly since 1998; Minister, Martyrs Memorial Church, Belfast; b. 6.4.26, Armagh; m., Eileen Emily Cassells; 2s.; 3d. Educ. Ballymena Technical College; South Wales Bible College; Reformed Presbyterian Theological Hall. Ordained, Minister, Ravenhill Evangelical Mission Church (now Martyrs Memorial Church), 1946; Elected MP, Bannside, Stormont Parliament, 1970; Elected, Antrim North, Westminster Parliament, 1970; Elected MEP, 1979. Publications: Christian Foundations; The '59 Revival; Exposition on Romans; America's Debt to Ulster. Recreations: collecting rare books; reading. Address: (h.) The Parsonage, 17 Cyprus Avenue, Belfast; T.- 02890-651574. e-mail: ian.r.k.paisley@btinternet.com

Palmer, George Albert, BA (Hons), Dip Ed. Former Senior Partner, Peden and Reid Solicitors; b. 7.1.37, Lurgan; m., Valerie Ellenor Eva Palmer; 2s. Educ. Lurgan College; Queen's University, Belfast. Schoolmaster: Dunlambert Boys School; Friends School, Lisburn. Former President, Northern Ireland Association of Schoolmasters (now NASUWT); Former Chairman, Belfast Solicitors' Association; former President, Law Society of Northern Ireland. Recreations: golf; gardening; travelling. Address: (b.) 22 Callender Street, Belfast BT1; T.-02890 325617.

Parker, Rev. Thomas Alexander Noble, BA. Retired Presbyterian Minister; b. 16.1.16, Letterkenny, Co Donegal, Ireland; m., Anne McCormack; 2s.; 1d. Educ. Magee University College; Trinity College, Dublin; Princeton Theological Seminary, New Jersey, USA; Assembly's College, Belfast. Ordained, Minister of Maze Presbyterian Church, 1940; Chaplain RAF LongKesh, 1942 - 48; Organiser, Religious Education for Day Schools, Presbyterian Church in Ireland, 1947 - 73; Chaplain, Lissue Children's Hospital, 1950 - 89; Chaplain, H M Prison Maze, 1970 - 82; Retired from Ministry, 1981. Recreations: gardening; bowls. Address: (h.) 8 Springburn Park, Lisburn, Co Antrim, BT27 5QZ; T.-028 92664082.

Parr, Gerard Patrick, BSc (Hons), PhD, FBCS, MIEE, CEng, MIEEE (USA). Senior Lecturer in Telecommunications, University of Ulster at Coleraine; since 1996; Director, Causeway Data Communications Ltd since 1997; b. 28.12.61, Hilltown, Co Down; m., Heather Joy; 2d. Educ. St Mark's High School, Warrenpoint; Newry College of Further and Education; University of Ulster at Coleraine; University of Southern California, Los Angeles, USA. Graduate Researcher, University of Ulster, 1984 - 85; Visiting Scientist, University of Southern California, 1985 - 86; PhD Researcher, University of Ulster, 1986 - 89; Lecturer, University of Ulster, Magee College, 1988 - 96. Technical Consultant for Telecommunications Sector to the Industrial Development Board of Northern Ireland since 1990. Member, technical editorial board, IEEE Network Journal (USA); Chairman, Internetworking session, International Symposium on Internetworking '92, Bern, Switzerland; Member, International Technical Programme Committee of USA, AGM SIGCOMM '94; Invited to sit on International Technical Programme Committee, International Symposium on Internetworking '94, France; Reviewer, EPSRC Communications/ Distributed Systems funding committee (UK) until 1999; Member, ECOM EEIG SIG, for Cross Border Information Technology and Telecommunications; Member, BT Information, Communications and Entertainment Consortium, 1994; External Examiner for Telecommunications Engineering, Zagazig University, Egypt, 1995; Member, BT Corporate Advisory Committee for Education and Training in the UK since 1995; External Academic Referee for numerous journals. Publications: over 70 publications ranging from journals and conferences, academic research papers, book chapters and editorials in China the UK, the USA and Ireland; Advisor, Northern Ireland Growth Challenge; Consultant, DED Telecommunication Review for Future Strategy. Recreations: good red wine to wash down spicy food; DIY; gardening; walking and enjoying our coastline; racquet sports (former captain intervarsity badminton team); travel. Address: (b.) Causeway Data Communications Ltd, South Buildings, University of Ulster at Coleraine, BT52 1SA; T.- 01265-324131.

Patterson, Dr. Gertrude, MA, MLitt, PhD. Head of English, Stranmillis University College, Belfast, 1991-2003; b. 26.9.38, Ballymena; m., Peter Frost. Educ. Ballymena Academy; Trinity College, Dublin. Head of English, Cambridge House School, 1960 - 65; Postgraduate research, Trinity College Dublin, 1965 - 67; Stranmillis College, Belfast: English Lecturer, 1967; Principal Lecturer, 1974; Dean of Women Students, 1982. Member: Board of Governors, Ballymena Academy, Education and Establishment committees; Poetry Society of Great Britain; Arts Council for Northern Ireland (former member combined arts committee, literary awards panel); National Association for the Teaching of English.

Visiting Lecturer, University of Trölhattan/Uddevalla, Vänsersburg, Sweden. Publications: books; T.S. Eliot, Poems in the Making, 1971; Things Made and Things Said: Teachers, Pupils and the Craft of Writing, 1999; numerous articles and chapters on the works of T.S Eliot and W. B. Yeats including, The Longer Poems of T.S. Eliot, The Yeats Eliot Journal, 1978; The Challenge of the Verse Play, Yeats Eliot Journal, 1981; Consultant Editor, T.S Eliot Review, 1972; Consultant Editor, Yeats Eliot Journal, 1973; many lectures published. Regular speaker at international conferences. Recreations: reading; theatre; cooking; painting; travel. Address: (b.) Department of English, Stranmillis University College, Belfast, T.-028-90 384337. e-mail: g.patterson@stran-ni.ac.uk

Patterson, Rev. Margaret Ruth, OBE, BA, MSW, BD, Hon PhD. Director, Restoration Ministries since 1991; b. 25.10.44, Belfast. Educ. Glenola Collegiate School, Bangor; Queen's University, Belfast; University of Toronto; Edinburgh University; Union Theological College, Belfast. Assistant to Presbyterian Chaplain, Queen's University, Belfast, 1968 - 71; Ordained (first woman in Ireland) 1976; Assistant Minister, Gardenmore Presbyterian Church, Larne, 1976 - 77; Minister, Kilmakee Presbyterian Church, Dunmurry, 1977 - 91. Will Y Darling Memorial Prize, University of Edinburgh; 2000 University of Edinburgh/Royal Bank of Scotland Alumna of the Year Award; awarded an honorary doctorate in 2001 from the Presbyterian Theological Faculty of Ireland. Recreations: walking; reading; swimming. Address: (b.) Restoration Ministries, 4 Thornhill Road, Dunmurry, Belfast, BT17 9EJ; T.-028 9062 1867.

Patterson, William James, BA, MBA, FCIPD. Chief Executive, Labour Relations Agency since 1996; b. 1952, Belfast; m., Geraldine Patterson; 2d. Educ. Annadale Grammar School, Belfast; Queen's University, Belfast; University of Ulster. Industrial Relations Officer, Magnesium Electron Ltd, Manchester, 1978 - 80; Personnel Officer and Manager, Northern Ireland Housing Executive, 1980 - 90; Director, Personnel and Administration, Loughside Unit, Northern Health and Social Security Board, 1990 - 93; Head of Human Resources, Belfast City Council, 1993 - 96. Address: (b.) Labour Relations Agency, 2-8 Gordon Street, Belfast, BT1 2LG; T.-028 90 321442. e-mail: wpatterson@lra.org.uk

Patton, Marcus Murray, OBE, BSc, Dip Arch, RIBA, MSAI, ARUA. Director, Hearth Housing Association and Hearth Revolving Fund since 1978; b. 23.8.48, Enniskillen; m., Joanna Mules, 3s. Educ. Campbell College; Queen's University, Belfast. Architect, Robert Hurd and Partners, Edinburgh; Senior Planner, Glasgow District Council; Freelance Artist and Musician; Partner, West Port Books, Edinburgh. Conductor, Palm Court Orpheans. Publications: Central Belfast; Buildings of Bangor; The Opera Hat of Sir

Hamilton Harty; The Diamond as Big as a Square (co-author); Ireland (illustrator); Scotland (Illustrator); Bugs, Bites and Bowels (Illustrator). Recreations: drawing things; playing music that is too difficult. Address: (h.) Ingledene, Sans Souci Park, Belfast, BT9 5BZ; T.-9066 7352.

Patton, Rev. William Donald, BSSc, BD, PhD. Minister, Randalstown Presbyterian Old Congregation, since 2002; b. 30.5.50, Warrenpoint, Co Down; m., Florence Irwin; 2d. Educ. Portadown College; Queen's University, Belfast. Assistant Minister, Trinity Presbyterian Church, Bangor, 1974 - 77; Minister, 1st Dromore Presbyterian Church, 1977 - 83; Minister, Greystone Road, Presbyterian Church, Antrim, 1983 - 88; Minister, Finaghy Lowe Memorial Presbyterian Church, Belfast, 1988-2002. Former Member: Belfast Education and Library Board, Senate, Queen's Univ. Belfast. Recreations: reading; gardening; walking; history. Address: (h.) 82 Portglenone Road, Randalstown BT41 3EH. T.-028 9447 2277. e-mail: donald@wpatton.freeserve.co.uk

Pavlakos, Dr. George, LLB (Athens), LLM (Edin), PhD (Edin). Lecturer in Jurisprudence, Queen's University Belfast, since 2001; Member of The Athens Bar Association, since 1995; Partner of The Law Firm J. Pavlakos and Assoc., since 1996; b. 29.12.70, Athens, Greece. Educ. 2nd State School of N. Smirni, Athens; University of Athens; University of Edinburgh. Publications: various articles in journals. Recreations: reading; classical music; collecting books; cinema. Address: (b.) School of Law, Queen's University Belfast, 29 University Square, Belfast BT7 1NN. T.-028 9027 3602.

Pearce, Professor Jack, BSc, PhD, CChem, FRSC, FIFST. Former Head, Food Science Division and Agricultural and Environmental Science Division, Department of Agriculture; Emeritus Professor of Food Science, Queen's University, Belfast; b. 31.10.42, Yorkshire; m., Edith Alexandra Henning; 1s.; 1d. Educ. Wath-upon-Dearne Grammar School; University of Liverpool. Post Doctoral Fellowship, British Egg Marketing Board, 1967 - 69; Department of Agriculture for Northern Ireland: Scientific Officer, 1969 - 72; Senior Scientific Officer, 1972 - 74; Principal Scientific Officer, 1994 - 92; Senior Principal Scientific Officer, 1992 - 94; Deputy Chief Scientific Officer 1994-2002; Professor of Food Science, Queen's University, Belfast, 1994-2002. Consultant, United Nations International Atomic Energy Agency and Food and Drink Organisation, in a project to reduce radioactive contamination of milk and meat in the Republics of the former USSR following the Chernobyl accident, 1991 - 97. Publications: over 100 scientific papers; Assistant Editor, British Poultry Science; Editorial Advisor, British Journal of Nutrition. Recreations: gardening; painting; wine appreciation; music (especially jazz). Address: (h.) "Woodrow", 30 Gortin Park, Belfast BT5 7EP. T.-02890 419822.

Pearson, Professor Raymond, BA. PhD. Professor of Modern European History, University of Ulster, Emeritus Professor of History, 1995-2002; b. 13.10.42, Yeovil, Somerset; m., Margaret; 1d. Educ. Sir William Borlase's School, Marlow; University of Durham. Lecturer, History, New University of Ulster, 1968 - 80; University of Ulster: Senior Lecturer, History, 1980 - 90; Reader in History, 1990 - 95. Publications: The Rise and Fall of the Soviet Empire, 1997; European Nationalism, 1789 - 1920, 1993. Address: (b.) Department of History, University of Ulster, Cromore Road, Coleraine; BT52 1SA; T.- 028-703-24474. e-mail: r.pearson@ulster.ac.uk

Pentland, Heather G., BEd. Head, Rockport School since 1994; b. 13.7.55, Enniskillen; m., Tony; 2s. Educ. Collegiate Grammar School, Enniskillen; Queen's University, Belfast. Teacher, Sydenham Infants School, 1978 - 79; Rockport Preparatory School: Form Teacher 8 year olds, 1980 - 82; Head of Junior School, 1982 - 91; Deputy Head, 1991 - 94. First female and local Head of School; introduced Senior School in 1998. Recreations: music; drama; interior design; family. Address: (b.) Rockport School, Craigavad, Holywood, Co Down; T-028 9042 8372. e-mail: info@rockportschool.com

Percival, Robin George Edwin, MA (Oxon), MSc. Head of Department (Technology), North West Institute of Further and Higher Education, since 2001; b. 24.10.47. Educ. Kingswood School, Bath; St Peter's College, Oxford. Research Fellow, New University of Ulster, Coleraine, 1974 - 76; Secretary, Bogside Community Association, 1974 - 76; North West Institute of Further and Higher Education: Lecturer in Sociology, 1978 - 92, Staff Governor, 1982 - 90, Senior Lecturer, 1992-2001; Northern Ireland Regional Chair, NATFHE, 1986 - 87; Chair, Derry Trades Union Council, 1990 - 92; Co-Founder, Pat Finucane Centre, Derry, 1989; Chair, Bloody Sunday Trust since 1997; Chair, Cúnamh since 1998; occasional contributor to Irish News and Derry Journal. Recreations: fell walking; reading; classical music. Address: (h.) 38 Great James's Street, Derry, BT48 7BD; T.-02871 266298.

Perrott, Professor Ron, BSc, PhD, FBCS, FACM, FRSA, CEng. Professor of Software Engineering, Department of Computer Science, Queen's University, Belfast since 1984; b. 27.12.42; m., Valerie; 1s.; 2d. Educ. Portadown College; Queen's University, Belfast. University of Wisconsin, Madison USA; NASA Ames Research Center, California, USA; CERN, Geneva, Switzerland; Institute of Informatics, ETH, Zurich; Departement d'Informatique. EPFL, Lausanne. Director: Kainos Software Ltd; Institute of Software Engineering; Fellow: British Computer Society; US Association for Computing Machinery; Royal Society for the encouragement of Arts, Manufactures and Commerce; Member: IEEE Computer Society; Chartered Engineer; BCS Parallel Processing Group; SERC/DTI Information

Technology Advisory Board; Committee, Conference of Professors of Computer Science; EU Monitoring Panel; EC Supercomputer Initiative Working Group (Rubbia subcommittee); European Working Group on Parallel Computing; Industrial Working Group European Commission, Parallel Architectures; European Programme Chairman, ACM International Conference on Supercomputers. Assessor. HEFCE Teaching Quality Assessment Exercise; Chairman, Euro-Par, EPSRC Technology Watch Panel; Elected to IFIP WG 10.3 Concurrent Systems. British Computer Society, IT Professional of the Year, 1993. Editorial Board: Journal of Supercomputing; International Journal of High Speed Computing. Publications: Editor in Chief, Scientific Programming; Operating Systems Techniques (joint ed.), 1972; Software Engineering (ed.), 1978; Pascal for Fortan Programmers (with D C S Allison), 1983; Parallel Programming; 1987; Software for Parallel Computers (ed.), 1991. Address: (b.) Department of Computer Science, Queen's University, Belfast, BT7 1NN; T.- 028 90-335463. e-mail: r.perrott@qub.ac.uk

Peters, Dame Mary Elizabeth, DBE, CBE. Managing Director, Mary Peters Sports Ltd since 1977; b. 6.7.39, Liverpool. Educ Portadown College, Co Armagh; Belfast College of Domestic Science. Teacher, Graymount Girls' Secondary School, Belfast; Secretary McShane's Health Club; Represented Great Britain: Olympic Games: 4th Pentathlon, 1964; Ist Pentathlon (world record), 1972; Commonwealth Games, 2nd Shot, 1966; 1st Shot, Ist Pentathlon, 1970; Ist Pentathlon, 1974. Member: Sports Council, 1974 - 80 and 1987 - 94; Northern Ireland Sports Council, 1974 - 93 (Vice-Chairman, 1977 - 81); Ulster Games Foundation, 1984 - 93; Northern Ireland BBC Broadcasting Council, 1981 - 84; Northern Ireland Tourist Board 1993-2002; (Deputy Chairman since 1996). Director, Churchill Foundation Fellowship Scholarship, California, 1972; Assistant Secretary, Multiple Sclerosis Society, 1974 - 78; President: Northern Ireland WAAA, 1985 - 87; British Athletic Federation, 1996; Ulster Sports and Recreation Trust since 1996 (Trustee 1972); Member, womens' committee IAAF, 1995-99; Hon. Senior Athletic coach since 1975; BAAB Pentathlon coach, 1976; Team manager: GB women's athletics team, European Cup, 1979; GB women's athletic team, Moscow, 1980 and Los Angeles, 1984. Trustee, Outward Bound Trust; Lady Taverner's Northern Ireland; Vice-President: Association of Youth Clubs; Riding for the Disabled; Driving for the Disabled; Action Cancer; Patron: NIAAA since 1981; Intensive Care Unit of the Royal Victoria Hospital, Belfast, 1988 - 96; Member, RTE Authority. BBC Sports Personality of the Year, 1972; Athletics Writers' Award, 1972; Sports Writers' Award, 1972; Elizabeth Arden Visible Difference, 1976; Athletics, Dublin (Texaco), 1972; British Airways Tourist Endeavour, 1981; LinLiving Action, 1985; Evian Health, 1985; Lunn's Award of Excellence, 1996; Service to Sport Hall of Fame, 1998; Texico

Dublin Hall of Fame, 1998. Hon. DSc, New University of Ulster, 1974; Hon. Doctor, Queen's University Belfast, 1998; Freeman of the Borough of Lisburn, 1998; Hon. Doctor of Letters, Loughborough University. Publications: Mary P, an autobiography, 1974. Address: (h.) Willowtree Cottage, River Road, Dunmurry, Belfast, BT17 9DP; T.- 02890-618882.

Petrie, His Honour John, QC, BA. Crown and County Court Judge, 1985-2000; b. Belfast; m., Olive Jacqueline Houston; 1s.; 1d. Educ. Royal Belfast Academical Institution; Queen's University, Belfast. Called to the Bar of Northern Ireland, 1947; Reporter, Council of Law Reporting for Northern Ireland, 1950 - 69; Secretary and Treasurer, Council of Law Reporting for Northern Ireland, 1965 - 69; Chairman, Industrial Tribunals (NI), 1965 - 73; Resident Magistrate, 1973 - 85; Called to the Inner Bar, 1985; Bencher of the Inn of Court of Northern Ireland since 1995. Registrar, Chapter of St Anne's Cathedral, Belfast since 1984; Chairman, Trustees of the Percy French Society since 1994. Recreations: motoring especially vintage and classic cars. Address: (b.) c/o Bar Library, Royal Courts of Justice (Ulster), Chichester Street, Belfast BT1 3JQ.

Pettigrew, Geraldine. Principal, Our Lady's Grammar School, Newry, since 1997; b. Newry, Co Down; m., Raymond Mullan. Educ. Our Lady's Grammar School, Newry; Queen's University, Belfast. St Malachy's College, Belfast: Teacher of English, 1975-81, Head of Department, 1981-88, Senior Teacher, 1988-92, Vice Principal, 1992-97. Chairperson, Ministerial Working Group on English, 1987; Chief Moderator, GCSE English Literature, 1986-92; Panel Member, BBC English Committee; former Member, Irish Commission for Justice and Peace. Recreations: reading; cinema; far-flung travel. Address: (b.) Our Lady's Grammar School, Chequer Hill, Newry, Co Down; T.-028 302 63552.

Peyton, Lynne T.D., BSSc, MSc, CQSW. Child Care/Management Consultant; b. 5.3.53, Belfast; m., Rodney Peyton. Educ. Methodist College, Belfast; Queen's University, Belfast; University of Ulster at Coleraine. Social Worker, Team Leader and Assistant Principal, South Belfast Social Services, 1975-86; Principal Social Worker, North and West Belfast, 1986-91; Assistant Director, Child Care, Southern Health and Social Services Board, 1991-98; Chair, Northern Ireland Core Group for Joint Investigations into Child Abuse, 1996-98; Director (NI) NSPCC, 1998-2001. Publications: contributions to books and journals on commissioning and managing children's services. Recreations: badminton; swimming; walking. Address: (b.) 14 Ballynorthland Park, Dungannon BT71 6DY. T.-028 87727134. e-mail: lynnepeyton@aol.com

Philips, Professor Kenneth John Herbert, BSc, PhD. National Research Council Senior Research Associate, NASA Goddard Space Flight Center,

since 2002; Professor, Department of Physics, Queen's University, Belfast since 1997; b. 16.5.46, Isleworth Middlesex. Educ. Ashford County Grammar School, Ashford, Middlesex; University College, London. National Research Council (US) Post Doctoral Fellow, Goddard Space Flight Center, NASA, Greenbelt, USA, 1972 - 75; National Science Foundation (US) Post Doctoral Fellow, University of Hawaii, USA, 1975 - 76; Research Scientist, Rutherford Appleton Laboratory, 1977-2002; Research Scientist working in solar and stellar X-ray astronomy and solar flares. Fellow, Royal Astronomical Society; Member, International Astronomical Union. Huggins Prize, University College London, 1966; NRL (US) Publications Prize, 1994. Publications: Guide to the Sun, 1992 and 1995; Contributor: Oxford Dictionary of Astronomy, 1997, Encycl. of Astronomy and Astrophysics, 2000; over 200 papers to professional journals. Recreations: running; music; lecturing. Address: (b.) Code 682, NASA Goddard Space Flight Center, Greenbelt, MD20771, USA; T.-1-301-286-1758.

Pierce, Henry Edward, LLB. Retired Partner, L'Estrange and Brett; b. 18.2.24, Enniskillen; m., Mavis; 2s.; 1d. Educ. Portora Royal School, Enniskillen; Queen's University, Belfast. British Army, 1943 - 46; Partner, L'Estrange and Brett, 1955 - 89; President, Law Society of Northern Ireland, 1969 - 70 and Treasurer; Chairman, Mental Health Commission, 1989 - 94. Address: (h.) 24 Church Road, Helen's Bay, Bangor, Co. Down BT19 1TP. T.-028 91853696.

Pierce, T James. Deputy Chairman, R.W. Pierce Group Ltd; b. 20.4.44, Belfast; marr. diss.; 2s.; 1d. Educ. Royal Belfast Academical Institution. Works Manager, R. W. Pierce and Co; Director, R. W. Pierce and Co (Printers) Ltd. Recreations: golf; rugby. Address: (b.) R W Pierce Group Ltd. 17 Dargan Crescent, Belfast, BT3 9RP; T.- 028 9037 1010.

Piggot, Denis, BSc, Dip Arch, RIBA, RSUA Certificate in Conservation. Architect, Principal, D B Piggot; b. 25.4.47, Belfast; 1s.; 1d. Educ. Campbell College, Belfast; Queen's University, Belfast. Started own practice in 1984, specialising in restoration; former part-time inspector for the Environment Service (Historic Monuments and Buildings); over 30 restoration projects for the National Trust; work on over 50 listed buildings. Member: RIBA; RSUA; SPAB; UAHS; National Trust; Committee Member of Hearth Housing Association. Department of Environment Awards: Design a House in the Countryside, Houses in Harmony, 1988; commended by Department Of The Environment for two projects; co-authored 2 Department of Environment conservation area guides. Recreations: cars; planes; machines; history; sailing. Address: (b.) 78 Drumnaconagher Road, Crossgar, Co Down, BT30 9JH; T.-028 4483 0800.

Pilling, Sir Joseph Grant, KCB. Permanent Under-Secretary of State, Northern Ireland Office, since 1997; b. 8.7.45; m., Ann Cheetham; 2 s. Educ. Rochdale Grammar School; King's College, London; Harvard. Assistant Principal, 1966; Private Secretary to Minister of State, 1970; Assistant Private Secretary to Home Secretary, 1970-71; Northern Ireland Office, 1972; Harkness Fellow, Harvard University, and University of California at Berkeley, 1972-74; Home Office, 1974-78; Private Secretary to Secretary of State for Northern Ireland, 1978-79; Home Office, 1979-84; Under Secretary, DHSS, 1984-87; Director of Personnel and Finance, HM Prison Service, 1987-90; Deputy Under Secretary of State, Northern Ireland Office, 1990-91; Director-General, HM Prison Service, 1991-92; Principal Establishment and Finance Officer, DoH, 1993-97. Address: (b.) Northern Ireland Office, 11 Millbank, London SW1P 4PN.

Piper, Raymond Francis Richard Western, FLS, RUA, UWS (Hon.), HRHA, MUniv. Portrait Painter and Botanical Illustrator; b. 6.4.23, London. Educ. Belfast High School; Belfast College of Technology. Gallagher Ltd; Marine Engineering; Harland and Wolff; Art Master, Dungannon Royal School, 1948; Freelance Painter and Graphic Artist. Fellow, Linnean Society of London, 1974; Lindley Medal for Botanical Illustration and Research, Royal Horticultural Society, London, 1974; Becks Bursary for Art, 1988; Gold Medal for Portraiture, RUA, 1997; Kennedy Award for Portraiture, RHA, 1993. Publications: illustrated books on Ireland many by the late Richard Hayward: Leinster and the City of Belfast; Ulster and the City of Dublin; Connacht and the City of Galway (part 1); Connacht, Mayo, Leitrim, Sligo and Roscommon (part 2); Munster and the City of Cork; Old Belfast (Alfred S Moore); Richard Hayward: Belfast through the Ages; Border Foray; As I Roved Out (Cathal O'Byrne); The First of Trees (Robert Standish); Shakespeare Play by Play (Stephen Usherwood); The Experienced Huntsmen (James Fairley); An Irish Beast Book (James Fairley); Piper's Flowers (Charles Nelson); Three Orchids A Portfolio. Recreations: drawing; painting; botanising; archaeology. Address: (h.) 11c Nottinghill, Malone Road, Belfast, BT9 5NS; T.- 028 90 669095.

Place, Thomas L, MSc, BA, DPM, FCIPD, FRSA. Director and Chief Executive, East Down Institute of Further and Higher Education since 1994; b. 26.2.48, Co Fermanagh; m., Rita; 1s.; 1d. Educ. University of Ulster. Lecturer, North Down College, 1967 - 74; Senior Lecturer, North Down College, 1974 - 86; Head of Business Studies, Castlereagh College, 1986 - 90; Principal, Newcastle College, 1990 - 94. Chairman of the Association of Northern Ireland Colleges, since 2002. Address: (b.) East Down Institute of Further and Higher Education, Market Street, Downpatrick, Co Down, BT30 6ND; T.- 02844-611512. e-mail: director@edifhe.ac.uk

Pollock, Dr. Robert John Ivan, BSc, M Ed, PhD. Headmaster, Campbell College, Belfast since 1987; b. 12.4.48, Co Londonderry; m., Sara; 1s.; 1d. Educ. Royal School, Dungannon; Queen's University, Belfast. Research, Queen's University, Belfast, 1970 - 73; Campbell College: Assistant Chemistry Teacher, 1973 - 86; Head, General Studies, 1978 - 86; Housemaster, 1979 - 86; Head of Chemistry, 1986 - 87. Kilwaughter Medal for Chemistry, Queen's University, Belfast, 1969; Richardson Medal for Chemistry, Queen's University, Belfast, 1970. President, Secondary Heads' Association (NI), 1996 - 97. Recreations: reading; keep-fit; watching sport. Address: (b.) Headmaster's House, Campbell College, Belmont Road, Belfast, BT4 2ND; T.-028 9076 3076. e-mail: hmoffice@campbellcollege.co.uk

Poots, Edwin. Member (Lagan Valley), Democratic Unionist Party, Northern Ireland Assembly, since 1998. Educ. Wallace High School, Lisburn; Greenmount Agricultural College. Farmer; Member, Northern Ireland Forum, 1996-98. Address: (b.) Parliament Buildings, Stormont, Belfast, BT4 3SA; T.- 01232-520700.

Poots, Rev. Robert Frederick Shane, OBE, BA, BD, MA, DD. Deputy Clerk Emeritus, General Assembly of the Presbyterian Church in Ireland; b. 31.1.37, Lurgan; m., Catherine Mildred Thompson; 1s; 3d. Educ. Lurgan College; Queen's University, Belfast; Assembly's College, Belfast; Trinity College, Dublin. Student Assistant Minister; West Church, Ballymena; Student Assistant Minister, Dunmurry Presbyterian Church; Ordained Assistant Minister, Trinity Bangor; Minister, Trinity, Ballymoney; Deputy Clerk, General Assembly; Acting Clerk, General Assembly. Member, North Eastern Education and Library Board; Chairman, North Eastern Library Board. Recreations: music; reading; foreign travel; ornithology; sailing. Address: (b.) Ballymoney BT53 7HE. T.-028 2766 6331. e-mail: dpoots@presbyterianireland.org

Porter, Rt Hon. Sir Robert (Wilson), Kt, PC (NI), QC. b. 23.12.23, Londonderry; m., Margaret Adelaide Lynas; 1s.; 1d. Educ. Model School and Foyle College, Londonderry; Queen's University, Belfast. RAFVR, 1943 - 46; Royal Artillery (TA), 1950 - 56; Foundation Schol, Queen's University, Belfast, 1947 and 1948; LLB, 1949; Called to the Bar of Northern Ireland, 1950; Irish Bar, 1975; Middle Temple, 1988; Lecturer, Contract and Sale of Goods, Queen's University, Belfast, 1950 - 51; Junior Crown Counsel: Co Londonderry, 1960 - 63; Co Down, 1964 - 65; Counsel to Attorney General for Northern Ireland, 1963 - 64 and 1965. War Pensions Appeal Tribunal for Northern Ireland: Vice-Chairman, 1959 - 61; Chairman, 1961 - 66; MP (U) (Queen's University), 1966 - 69; (Lagan Valley), 1969 - 73 Parliament of Northern Ireland; Minister, Health and Social Services, Northern Ireland, 1969; Parliamentary Secretary, Ministry of Home Affairs, 1969; Minister for Home Affairs, 1969 - 70. County

Court Judge, 1978 - 95; Recorder of Londonderry, 1979 - 81; Recorder of Belfast, 1993 - 95. Recreations: gardening; golf. Address: (h.) Larch Hill, Church Close, Ballylesson, Belfast, BT8 8JX.

Poynor, Michael Howard, DipMgmt (Open), BSc (Econ), MBA, MCMI, ADA. General Manager, Belfast Festival at Queen's, since 2003; b. 29.9.42, Port Stanley, Falkland Islands; m., Anne-Marie Mathews; 1d. Educ. St George's College, Buenos Aires; Claysemore School, Dorset; Westminster College, University of London; LAMDA; Open University. Stage Manager/Lighting Designer, Castle Theatre, Farnham, 1970 - 72; Lighting Designer, Thorndyke Theatre, Leatherhead, 1972 - 73; Director of Productions, Lyric Theatre, Belfast, 1973 - 75; Resident Director, Overground Theatre, Kingston-upon-Thames, 1975 - 76; Artistic Director: Harrogate Theatre, 1977 - 79; Stage '80 Theatre Company, 1980 - 83; Ulster Youth Theatre Company, 1983 - 86; National Youth Theatre of Wales, 1987 - 90; Chief Executive, Millennium Forum, Derry/Londonderry, 1999-2002; Artistic Director, Ulster Theatre Company, since 1992. Bass (Ireland) Arts Award, 1981; 3 Peacock (Northern Ireland Arts) Awards, 1987; AIMS Lighting Award, 1993. Playwright, 17 plays/productions including eleven Christmas pantomimes. MENSA; Fight Director; British Academy of Dramatic Combat; Board Member, Ulster Association of Youth Drama; Board Member, Riverside Theatre, Coleraine; Advisory panel: Arts Council of Northern Ireland. Recreations: keep fit; chess; skiing; travel. Address: (b.) 17, Duncrun Road, Bellarena, Limavady, Co. Londonderry BT49 0JD. T.-028 77 750240.

Poyntz, Right Rev. Samuel Greenfield, BA, MA, BD, PhD, DLitt. (h.c University of Ulster) Retired Bishop of Connor; b. 4.3.26, Canada; m., Noreen Henrietta Armstrong; 1s.; 2d. Educ. Portora Royal School, Enniskillen; University of Dublin. Curate, St George's Church, Dublin, 1950 - 52; Curate, Bray, 1952 - 55; Curate, Parish of St Michan and St Paul, Dublin, 1955 - 59; Rector, St Stephen's Parish, Dublin, 1959 - 67; Vicar, St Ann's Parish, Dublin, 1967 - 78; Archdeacon of Dublin, 1974 - 78; Bishop of Cork, Cloyne and Ross, 1978 - 87; Bishop of Connor, 1987 - 95. Chairman, Irish Council of Churches, 1987 - 89; Vice President, British Council of Churches, 1986 - 90. Publications: Exaltation of the Blessed Virgin Mary, 1953; St Stephen's: One Hundred Years of Worship and Witness, 1974; St Ann's: The Church in the Heart of the City, 1976; Journey Towards Unity, 1975; Praying with our Church Family, 1983; co-editor and contributor to Mary for Earth and Heaven; article: Anglican and Roman Catholic ecumenical dialogue, 2002. Recreations: travel; walking; rugby football; stamp collecting. Address: (h.) 10 Harmony Hill, Lisburn, Co Antrim, BT27 4EP; T.-02892-679013.

Prenter, Stephen Philip, FCA, BSSc, MIMC. Managing Partner, BDO Stoy Hayward, Belfast; b.

3.8.53, Belfast; m., Patricia; 4s.; 1d. Educ. St Mary's Grammar School, Belfast; Queen's University Belfast. Established BDO Stoy Hayward, 1989. Fellow, Institute of Chartered Accountants; Member, Institute of Management Consultants; Licensed Insolvency Practitioner. Chairman, Ulster Society of Chartered Accountants, 1999; Chairman, Investment Belfast Limited; Director, Grand Opera House. Recreations: golf; tennis; handball; bridge; theatre. Address: (b.) Lindsay House, 10 Callender Street, Belfast BT1 5BN; T.- 028 9043 9009. e-mail: stephen.prenter@bdo.co.uk

Pringle, Hon. Sir John Kenneth, BSc (Hons), LLB (Hons). b. 23.6.29. Educ. Campbell College, Belfast; Queen's University, Belfast. Called to the Bar of Northern Ireland, 1953, Bencher, 1973; QC, 1970; Recorder of Belfast, 1984 - 93; Justice of the High Court of Justice in Northern Ireland, 1993-99; Member of the Parades Commission for Northern Ireland, 2000-2004. Address: (h.) Cottage Hill, 69 Ballinderry Road, Lisburn, Co. Antrim BT28 2NL.

Q

Quinn, Dr. Hugh, BSc, PhD, MCMI. Former Head of Social Education Department, North West Institute of Further and Higher Education; b. 21.6.43, Co Down; m., Elizabeth McCauley; 2s.; 2d. Educ. St Patrick's High School, Downpatrick; Queen's University, Belfast. Teacher, West Africa; Post Doctoral Fellow in Physical Chemistry, Queen's University, Belfast; Transport and Road Research Laboratory, BP; Industrial Liason/Marketing Officer, Londonderry College of Technology, 1973-78. Member, National Council, Institute of Management, 1992 - 98; Deputy Chairperson, Institute of Management Professional Practice Committee, 1994 - 97; Chairman, NI Regional Forum, Institute of Management, 1998-2002; Treasurer, NI Forum of Chartered Management Institute, 2003. Recreations: travel; literature; motor vehicle restoration. Address: (h.) 34 Hillview Avenue, Prehen, Londonderry; T.- 028 71346142.

Quinn, Jill (Nora Jillian), JP. Retired Company Director; b. 25.3.36, Dublin; separated; 1s.; 3d. Educ. Wesley College, Dublin. Children's wear designer for 15 years. Founder member, Lisburn, CAB; worker and member, Management Committee (including Chair), 1972 - 84; set up volunteer programme, NI Hopsice, 1984 - 93. Lay Panel Juvenile Court since 1991; Partner, Dreamcare specialist nightwear. Recreations: music; needlework; knitting; ballet; design. Address: (h.) 30 Pond Park Ave, Lisburn, Co Antrim. e-mail: jillquinn@utvinternet.com

Quinn, Sean Vincent, MA, DipEd, MSc. Principal, St Malachy's High School, Antrim, since 1998; b. 22.8.46, Coalisland; m., Janet McMurray; 1 s. Educ. St Patrick's College, Armagh; Trinity College, Dublin; St Joseph's Training College, Belfast; University of Ulster, Jordanstown. Teacher, St Patrick's College, Antrim Road, Belfastd, 1974-98. Vice Chair, Ballyclare Community Concerns; Secretary, Board of Governors, St Malachy's High School, Antrim. Recreations: sports. Address: (h.) 34 Grange Valley Avenue, Ballyclare. e-mail: svqi@hotmail.com

R

Rae, Prof. Gordon, BSc, MEd, PhD, AFBPsS. Professor of Psychology, University of Ulster, since 1995; b. 21.7.45, Rutherglen, Scotland. Educ. Rutherglen Academy; University of Glasgow; Aberdeen University. Physics Teacher, Aberdeen Grammar School, 1969-71; Lecturer in Educational Psychology, Aberdeen College of Education, 1971-78; Lecturer in Education, University of Ulster, 1978-85, Senior Lecturer in Education, 1985-91, Professor of Education, 1991-95, Dean of The Faculty of Education, 1991-94. Publication: co-author, Learning in the Primary School: A Systematic Approach, 1985. Recreations: playing the oboe; cooking. Address: (b.) School of Psychology, University of Ulster, Cromore Road, Coleraine, Co. Londonderry BT52 1SA. T.-028 70 324395.

Raghunathan, Professor Srinivasan Raghu, BEng, MTech, PhD, DSc, FRAeS, CEng. Professor and Head, School of Aeronautical Engineering, Queen's University, Belfast since 1995; Bombardier Aerospace Royal Academy Chair, 2001; b. 15.6.43, Akekal, India; m., Suman; 1s.; 1d. Educ. Fort High School, Bangalore, India; University College, Bangalore; I J T, Bombay. Lecturer, Mechanical Engineering, I J T, Bombay, 1967 - 70; Senior Research Associate, Loughborough University, 1970 - 74; Queen's University, Belfast: Lecturer, 1974 - 83; Senior Lecturer, 1983 - 86; Reader, 1986 - 95. Royal Society Esso Award, Gold Medal, 1994. Publications: 200 papers in technical journals. Recreations: cricket. Address: (b.) School of Aeronautical Engineering, Queen's University, Belfast, BT9 5AG; T.- 02890-335417.

Rainey, William Eric, MBE, DASE. Secretary for Northern Ireland, The Duke of Edinburgh's Award since 1980; b. 10.7.49, Strabane; m., June; 1s. 2d. Educ. Coleraine Academical Institution; Strannmillis College, Belfast; University of Ulster. Teacher, Aughnacloy Secondary School, 1970 - 72; Divisional Youth Officer, Western Education and Library Board, 1972 - 80. Methodist Local Preacher; wide involvement in voluntary sector, 1994 - 97. Recreations: walking; cycling; caravanning; family. Address: (b.) 28 Wellington Park, Belfast BT9 6DL; T.- 02890-509550. e-mail: nireland@theaward.org

Ramsay, John, JP. Farmer; b. 30.3.33; m., Margaret; 1s.; 1d. Educ. Coleraine Academical Institution. Address: (h.) 8 Culramoney Road, Ballymoney, Co Antrim BT53 8LL; T.-028 207 41265.

Ramsey, Sue. Member (West Belfast), Sinn Fein, Northern Ireland Assembly, 1998-2003. Address: (b.) Parliament Buildings, Stormont, Belfast, BT4 3ST; T.- 02890-520700.

Rankin, Alastair John, BA, TEP. Solicitor, Partner, Cleaver Fulton Rankin Solicitors since 1980; b. 5.9.51, Belfast; m. Gillian Elizabeth Susanne Dorrity; 2s. Educ. Royal Belfast Academical Institution; Trinity College, Dublin. Qualified as a solicitor, 1977. Elected Council, Law Society of Northern Ireland, 1985: Treasurer, 1991; Junior Vice-President, 1995; President, 1996; Senior Vice President, 1997. Member, Society of Trust and Estate Practitioners; Admitted Solicitor, Law Society of Ireland, 1997. Member, UK Delegation to the CCBE; Hon. Secretary, Ulster Architectural Heritage Society, 1984 - 95; General Commissioner, Income Tax; Part-time Chairman, Pensions Appeal Tribunal. Recreations: singing; listening to music. Address: (b.) 50 Bedford Street, Belfast, BT2 7FW; T.-028 9024 3141.

Rankin, David, BA (Hons) ModHist (QUB). Editor, Coleraine Times (Morton Newspapers), since 1998; b. Coleraine; partner: Sheena Kinney. Educ. St. Joseph's High, Coleraine; Dominican College, Portstewart; Queen's University Belfast. Reporter: Coleraine Chronicle, 1988-90, Coleraine Times, 1990-98; Correspondent: Sunday Express, Belfast Telegraph, Sunday Life, Irish Times, Radio and TV. Newspaper Society Best Weekly Newspaper in NI, 1998; IPR Best NI Weekly (Highly Commended), 1999. Recreations: sport; cinema; travelling; reading. Address: (h.) 35 Woodford Park, Coleraine, Co. Londonderry.

Rankin, Mervyn George, MCIEH. Chief Executive, Ballymena Borough Council since 1991; b. 29.11.48, Magherafelt, Co Londonderry; m., June; 2s. Educ. Rainey Endowed School; Belfast College of Technology; University of Ulster at Jordanstown. Environmental Health, Londonderry County Council, 1968 - 73; Environmental Health, Ballymena Borough Council, 1973 - 84; Cookstown District Council: Chief Evironmental Health, 1985 - 89; Chief Executive, 1989 - 91. Recreations: gardening; reading. Address: (b.) Ballymena Borough Council, Ardeevin, 80 Galgorm Road, Ballymena, Co Antrim, BT42 1AB; T.- 028 2566 0300.

Rathcavan, 3rd Baron, Hugh Detmar Torrens O'Neill. Director, Lamont Holdings, since 1973; b. 14.6.39.; m., Sylvie Marie-Therese Wichard Educ. Eton College. Army career, Captain, Irish Guards; Financial Journalism, Irish Times, Financial Times; Restaurant Owner, Brasserie St. Quentin, 1980 - 89, 2002-; Chairman: Northern Ireland Airports, 1986 - 92; Northern Ireland Tourist Board, 1988 - 96; Taste of Ulster, since 1996; Director: The Spectator, 1980 - 84; Savoy Hotel and Savoy Restaurants, 1989 - 96; Northern Bank Ltd, 1991 - 97; Old Bushmills Distillery Co, 1989 - 99. Member, British Tourist Authority, 1988 - 96; Member: House of Lords Select Committee, European Communities Sub-Committee D, 1997-99; British-Irish Interparliamentary Body, 1997-99. Deputy Lieutenant, Co Antrim since 1987. Recreations:

boating; travel; gardening; food. Address: (h.) Cleggan Lodge, Ballymena, Co Antrim, BT43 7JW. T.-02825-862222; Fax: 02825 86200. e-mail: lordrathcavan@btopenworld.com

Rea, Professor Desmond, OBE, MSc, (Econ), MBA, PhD. Chairman, Northern Ireland Policing Board; b. 4.3.37, Belfast; m., Dr. I Maeve Rea; 4d. Educ. Methodist College, Belfast; Queen's University, Belfast; University of California, Berkeley. 1969-75: Lecturer, then Senior Lecturer, Business Studies/Assistant Dean, Faculty of Economics and Social Sciences, Queen's University, Belfast; Professor Human Resource Management, University of Ulster until 1995; Emeritus Professor, 1995. Past Chairman: Northern Ireland Local Government Staff Commission; Northern Ireland Labour Relations Agency; Northern Ireland Curriculum, Examination and Assessment Council; Director, Allied Irish Bank Group (UK) Plc; Secretary, JIGSA Group. Editor, First Trust Bank's quarterly Economic Outlook and Business Review. Recreations: the Ulster Orchestra; watching rugby; reading; swimming. Address: (b.) Northern Ireland Policing Board, Waterside Tower, 31 Clarendon Road, Clarendon Dock, Belfast BT1 3BG. T.-028 9040 8500. Fax: 028 9040 8525.

Rea, Elsbeth Ann, OBE, BSc, MSW, MSc, AASW. Principal, Elsbeth Rea Associates, since 1993; b. 17.8.53, Belfast; m., Douglas H. Rea; 3 s. Educ. Glenlola Collegiate School, Bangor; University of Bristol; Queen's University, Belfast; University of Ulster. Probation Officer, 1978-82; Senior Probation Officer, 1982-85; Lecturer in Social Work, Queen's University, Belfast, 1985-93. Member, Police Authority for N. Ireland, 1994-2001; Non-Executive Director, Ulster Community and Hospitals Trust, 1999-2003; Member, British Board of Film Classification Advisory Panel on Children's Viewing; Life Sentence Review Commissioner. Address: (b.) 947 Upper Newtownards Road, Belfast BT16 0RL; T.-028 9041 0596.

Rea, Rev. James (Jim), MBE MTh (Oxon), Dip Theo. President, Methodist Church in Ireland, 2003/04; Methodist Minister, Superintendent, Portadown 1st since 1999; Chairman (Meth Ch), Belfast District, 1998 - 99; District Superintendent, Portadown District, 2001-03; b. 17.4.45, Belfast; m., Carol; 1s; 2d. Educ. Everton Secondary School; Edgehill College; Westminster College, Oxford. Probationary Minister, Cregagh Methodist, 1970 - 72; Superintendent Minister, Pettigo and Irvinestown Circuit, 1972 - 78; Superintendent, East Belfast Mission (Newtownards Road Methodist Church established as a Mission, 1985), 1978 - 99. Radio Presenter, Downtown Radio, 1977-2000; New World Missionary, United Methodist Church, USA; Preacher, International World Congress on Preaching, 1997; Visiting Lecturer: Princeton USA, Belfast Bible College, Cliff College, Sheffield, Edgehill Christian Education Centre;

Facilitator in cross community conflict with Stanford University Centre of Conflict and Negotiation USA; Twice Finalist, Times Preacher of the Year; Regular speaker at national and international events and conferences. Recreations: local cricket enthusiast; brass bands. Address: (h.) 35 Thomas Street, Portadown, BT62 3NU; T.-028 3833 3030.

Rea, Michael D.M., OBE, BSc, DipEd. Equality Commissioner and Member, Northern Ireland Council for Nursing and Midwifery; b. 2.1.41, Belfast; m., Margaret; 3 s.; 1 d. Educ. Bangor Grammar School; Queen's University Belfast. Formerly Senior Education Officer, Belfast Education and Library Board. Former International Rugby Referee.

Rea, Pamela, Dip Speech and Drama. Freelance Writer and Broadcaster; b. 24.10.43, Armagh; 1s.; 1d. Educ. Armagh College of Further Education; Queen's Outreach at Armagh. Freelance Broadcaster, Radio Ulster, Radio Foyle since 1980; Freelance Journalist, Ulster Tatler, Ulster Gazette and Times Group, 1980 - 97. Publications: Touching a Chord, cross community biographies, 1997; Armagh Voices, a Millennium Souvenir of the Century, 1999. Commended, Arts Council of England for Touching a Chord. Recreations: theatre; convivial restaurants. Address: (h.) 11 Grove Terrace, Armagh; T.- 028-37-528967.

Regan, Geraldine Rose, Cert Ed, Adv Cert Ed. Principal, St Columba's Primary School, Draperstown since 1991; b. 28.9.48, Belfast; m., Michael Niall; 1s.; 2d. Educ. Rathmore Grammar School, Belfast; St Mary's College, Belfast. St Oliver Plunkett Primary School, Belfast, 1970 - 71; Acting Principal, Lisamuck Primary School, 1972 - 73; Glenview Primary School, Maghera, 1973 - 91. Recreations: golf; bridge; antiques; reading. Address: (h.) 17 Hall Street, Maghera, Co Derry, BT46 5DA; T.- 028 796 42716.

Reid, Colin, BA (Hons), MSc. Chief Executive, Consilium Technologies, since 2000; b. 21.8.57, Killyleagh, Co Down; m., Joyce; 2d. Educ. St Patrick's Grammar School, Downpatrick; University of Ulster. Finance, IT and Internal Audit, Down District Council, 1977; Finance and IT Officer, Newry and Mourne District Council, 1982; Lecturer, Business Studies, 1984; Commercial Director, Task Software, 1986; Managing Director, 1995-2000. Board Member, Northern Ireland Growth Challenge; Software Cluster Team Leader, NI Growth Challenge; Board Member, Northern Ireland Software Federation (Past Chairman); Panel Member, Northern Ireland Technology Foresight. Past Chairman, Board of Governors, Down College. Northern Ireland IT Professional of the Year, 1996. Recreations: following Manchester United; golf.   T.-028 9480000.

Reid, Francesca, DipMan.   Partner, Portavoe Services, since 1995. Member, Probation Board for NI, since 2000; Director/Trustee, NI Police Fund, since 2001. Member, Lay Panel of Industrial Tribunals, since 1999; Governor, Dundonald High School, since 2002. Former member of the Police Authority for NI, 1997-2001. Former Member and Vice Chairman of South Eastern Education and Library Board, 1992-2001. Former Partner, Woodstock S.S., 1980-90; Former Partner, Woodstock Renault, 1980-95. Former Chairman, North Down Local Advisory Committee for Youth, 1996-98. Recreation: travel. Address: 6 Albany Road, Bangor BT19 6YW. T.-028 91 272561.

Reilly, Samuel Glenn, BEd, FRSA. Headmaster, Limavady High School, since 1998; b. 13.3.52, Limavady; m., Ivy; 1 s.; 2 d. Educ. Limavady Grammar School; Queen's University, Belfast. Limavady High School: Assistant Teacher, Head of English Department, Deputy Head; Headmaster, Faughan Valley High School, 1988-98; General Secondary Adviser, WELB (seconded), 1996-98. Certificate of Recognition for outstanding service to Duke of Edinburgh Award Scheme; Fellow, Royal Society of Arts. Recreations: rugby football supporter; reading; travel; family. Address: (h.) 21 Scroggy Road, Limavady, Co Londonderry BT49 0NA; T.-01504 764541.
e-mail: sgreilly@btopenworld.com

Ridley, Robert Michael, MA (Oxon), Cert Ed. Principal, Royal Belfast Academical Institution; b. 8.1.47, Oxford; m., Jennifer Mary Pearson; 2d. Educ. Clifton College, Bristol; St Edmund Hall, Oxford. Teacher, Wellington College, 1970 - 82 (Housemaster, 1975 - 82); Exchange Teacher, Sydney Church of England Grammar School, 1974; Head of English and Head of Drama, Merchiston Castle School, Edinburgh, 1982 - 86; Headmaster, Denstone College, Staffordshire, 1986 - 90. Cricket Blue, Oxford, 1968 - 70; played cricket for Ireland, 1968. Recreations: cricket; golf; theatre. Address: (b.) RBAI, College Square East, Belfast, BT1 6DL; 02890-240461.

Rima, Professor Bertus Karel, Ir PhD, CBiol, FIBiol, MRIA. Professor of Molecular Biology, Queen's University, Belfast since 1993; Assistant Director, Research and Development Office for Northern Ireland HPSS, 1998-2001; b. 3.6.45, The Hague; m., Dr B M R Harvey. Educ. Grotius Lyceum, The Hague; Delft University, McMaster University, Canada. Joined Queen's University, Belfast, 1974; Post Doctoral Research Fellow, 1974 - 78; Lecturer, Biochemistry, 1978 - 87; Reader in Biology, 1987 - 93. Ex Chairperson, Northern Ireland Federation of Housing Associations; Director, Ulidia Housing Association since 1979. Medal, National Committee for Biochemistry, Royal Irish Academy, 1994. Elected member of the Royal Irish Academy, 2002; Member, Medical Research Council Advisory Board and Grants Committee, 1993-2000; Member, UK Advisory Committee on Genetic Modification, since 2001; Member, Veterinary Products Committee of the Veterinary

Medicines Directorate, since 2002; Member, GM Science Review Panel, 2002-03. Publications: Vaccine Design; Editor, Journal of General Virology. Recreations: gardening; swimming. Address: (h.) 7 Cranmore Park, Belfast; T.-028 9066 5905 (b.) 028 9033 5858.
e-mail: b.rima@qub.ac.uk

Robb, James Arnold, MSc, FInstD. Proprietor, SPAVAK; b. 18.3.42, Portadown, Co Armagh; m., Marion; 1s.; 2d. Recreation: skiing. Address: (b.) 46 Broomhill Road, Ballynahinch, Co. Down BT24 8QH. T.-028 9756 2520.

Roberts, Dr. David, BA (IntRel and Pol), PhD (PolTrans). Lecturer in Politics, University of Ulster, since 1999; b. 10.8.62, London. Educ. King George Vth Grammar School, Southport; Staffordshire University. Lecturer in Politics and Development, Staffs, 1992-96; Lecturer in SE Asia Studies, School of Oriental and African Studies, London; Lecturer in Politics, King's College London, 1997-99. Publication: Political Transition in Cambodia, 1991-99: Power, Elitism and Democracy, 2001. Member of Political Studies Association. Recreations: motorcycling; portrait photography in SE Asia. Address: (b.) School of History and International Affairs, University of Ulster, Magee Campus, Londonderry BT48 7JL.

Robinson, Cora, BA (Hons) Education, M Med Sc. E-Learning and Training Consultancy; b. 2.11.67, Sligo; m., Brian Robinson. Educ. University of Limerick; The Queen's University of Belfast. Education Resource Development, 1994-99; Own business, since 1999. Publications: range of online and disc-based learning resources. Recreations: yoga; gym; walking; horse riding; dogs; music; reading. Address: (h.) Ormiston Lodge, 63 Hawthornden Way, Belfast BT4 3LA. T.-02890 672 100.
e-mail: cora@corarobinson.com

Robinson, David. Founder and Chairman, Northern Ireland Transplant Association; b. 18.8.33, Co Antrim; m., Beverly Joan Robinson; 2s.; 3d. Educ. Royal Belfast Academical Institution. Address: (b.) Northern Ireland Transplant Association, Eagle Lodge, 51 Circular Road, Belfast BT4 2GA; T.-028 9076 1394.

Robinson, Iris. Member, (Strangford), Democratic Unionist Party, Northern Ireland Assembly, since 1998; Member of Parliament, since 2001; b. 6.9.49, Belfast; m.; 2 s.; 1 d. Educ. Castlereagh Technical College. Elected to Castlereagh Borough Council, 1989; served as Mayor, 1992, 1995 and 2000; Member, Dundonald International Ice Bowl Board. Recreations: interior design; fund-raising for MS. Address: (b.) Parliament Buildings, Belfast BT4 3XX. T.-028 90 521990; (b.) 26 James Street, Newtownards BT23 4DY. T.-028 91 827701.

Robinson, Kenneth William, BEd, ACP. Member (East Antrim), Ulster Unionist Party,

Northern Ireland Assembly, since 1998; Former Education Spokesman, Ulster Unionist Party; Member of Education Committee; European Union Sub Committee; Committee of The Centre; Retired School Principal; Councillor, Newtownabbey Borough Council since 1985; b. 2.6.42, Belfast; m., Louisa Morrison; 3s. Educ. Ballyclare High School; Stranmillis College; Queen's University, Belfast. Assistant Teacher: Carr's Glen Primary School, 1969 - 1973; British Forces Education Service, Germany, Wolfenbüttel Primary School, 1969 - 73; Montgomery Primary School, Bergen-Hohne, 1974 - 75; Principal Teacher: Lisfearty Primary School, Co Tyrone, 1976 - 78; Argyle Primary School, Belfast, 1978 - 80; Cave Hill Primary School, Belfast, 1980 - 96; Retired, 1996. Deputy Mayor, Newtownabbey, 1986 - 87; 1987 - 88 and 1990 - 91; Mayor of Newtownabbey, 1991 - 92. Vice Chairman, Economic Development Committee; Member, North Eastern Education and Library Board, 1985 - 93 (Vice-Chairman, Education Committee); Board Member, Mallusk Enterprise Park. Contributor, historical articles for local magazines and booklets and travel articles for local newspapers. Recreations: swimming; soccer; music; continental travel; caravanning. Address: (h.) 5 Sycamore Close, Newtownabbey, Co Antrim, BT37 0PL; T.- 01232-866056. e-mail: ken.robinson@niassembly.gov.uk

Robinson, Peter David. MP. Democratic Unionist Member of Parliament, East Belfast, since 1979 (resigned seat, 1985 in protest against Anglo-Irish Agreement, re-elected 1986); Member (East Belfast), Democratic Unionist Party, Northern Ireland Assembly since 1998; b. 29.12.48, Belfast; m., Iris; 2s.; 1d. Educ. Annandale Grammar School; Castlereagh College of Further Education. Ulster Democratic Unionist Party: General Secretary, 1975 - 79; Deputy Leader since 1980; Member, East Belfast, Northern Ireland Assembly, 1982 - 86; Northern Ireland Forum, 1996-98. Councillor, Castlereagh Borough Council since 1977; Deputy Mayor, 1978; Mayor of Castlereagh, 1986. Member: Select Committee on Northern Ireland since 1994; All-party Committee on Shipbuilding. Northern Ireland Minister for Regional Development. Publications: Ulster the Facts (joint author), 1986; booklets: The North Answers Back, 1970; Capital Punishment for Capital Crime, 1978; Self-Inflicted, 1981; Ulster in Peril, 1981; Savagery and Suffering, 1981; Their Cry Was "No Surrender", 1989; The Union Under Fire, 1995. Recreations: golf; bowling. Address: (b.) Strandtown Hall, 96 Belmont Avenue, Belfast, BT4 3DE; T.-028 90473111.

Robinson, Robert M., BSc, MEd, PGCE. Headmaster, Rainey Endowed School, since 2002; b. 12.5.53; m., Sharon; 1 s.; 1 d. Educ. Methodist College Belfast; Queen's University Belfast. Teacher: Glastry High School, 1986-88, Cambridge House Boys Grammar School, 1988-90; Regent House, 1990-2002. Head of Year, ICT Development Officer. Recreations: reading;

keeping fit; playing guitar and mandolin. Address: (b.) Rainey Endowed School, 79 Rainey Street, Magherafelt, Co Londonderry BT45 5RA. T.-028 7963 2478.

Robinson, Simon Mark Peter. Member (South Belfast), Democratic Unionist Party, Northern Ireland Assembly, since 1998; b. 12.5.59, Belfast. Educ. Knockbreda High School; Castlereagh College of Further Education. Mechanical engineer, 1977-89; General Manager, 1989-95; Managing Director, 1995-98; Castlereagh Councillor, since 1997. Member, Loyal Orange Institution, Apprentice Boys of Derry; Member, Board of Governors, Belvoir Park Primary School. Recreations: golf; musical theatre. Address: (b.) 215A Lisburn Road, Belfast BT9 7EJ; T.-028 90 225969.

Roche, Patrick John. Deputy Leader, Northern Ireland Unionist Party; Member (Lagan Valley), Northern Ireland Assembly since 1998; m. Educ. Trinity College, Dublin; University of Durham. Early career in banking; Lecturer (retired), Economics, University of Ulster; Lecturer, Philosophy of Religion, Irish Baptist College. Publications: numerous publications on politics including most recently, The Northern Ireland Question: Nationalism, Unionism and Partition (co-editor) and The Appeasement of Terrorism and the Belfast Agreement; co-author of Defence of the Union, 2001. Address: (b.) Parliament Buildings, Stormont, Belfast, BT4 3XX; T.- 028 90521994.

Rodgers, Brid, BA. Deputy Leader, SDLP, since 2001; Minister for Agriculture and Rural Development, NI Executive, 1999-2002; Member (Upper Bann), Social Democratic and Labour Party, Northern Ireland Assembly, 1998-2003; Chairperson, SDLP Negotiating Team, Multi Party Talks since 1996; b. 20.2.35, Co Donegal; m., Antoin Rodgers; 3s.; 3d. Educ. St Louis Convent, Monaghan; University College, Dublin. Chairperson, SDLP, 1978 - 80; General Secretary, SDLP, 1981 - 83; Member, Irish Senate, 1983 - 87; Leader, SDLP Group, Craigavon District Council, 1985 - 93; SDLP Delegate, Brooke/Mayhew Talks, 1992; Elected, Upper Bann, to Multi Party Talks, 1996. Recreations: reading; swimming; golf. Address: (h.) 34 Kilmore Road, Lurgan, Co Armagh, BT67 9BP; T.- 028 38322140.

Rodgers, James Henry, BA. Her Majesty's Coroner Armagh and Craigavon since 1984; Deputy County Court Judge; Deputy District Judge since 1993; b. Newry, Co Down; m., Maralyn; 3s.; 1d. Educ. Portora Royal School; Trinity College, Dublin. Qualified as Solicitor, 1974; Senior partner in private practice; H M Deputy Coroner, Armagh and Craigavon. Past Chairman, Northern Ireland Coroner's Association, 1992; Past President, Rotary International, City of Armagh, 1993 - 94. Recreations: cricket; gardening; reading. Address: (b.) 15 Church Street, Portadown, County Armagh, BT62 3LN; T.-028 3833 7211.

Rodgers, Jim, BSc.   Former Lord Mayor of Belfast; b. 14.1.43, Belfast; m., Greta.   Educ. Mountpottinger Primary School; Annadale Grammar School; Stirling University.   Director of Several Companies; General Manager, Training Organisation in North West Belfast since 1984; Belfast City Councillor since 1993; Former Deputy Lord Mayor of Belfast.   Ex Member, Northern Ireland Forum for Political Dialogue; Deputy Chairman, Belfast Education and Library Board; Governor, several schools; Member, Northern Ireland Events Company; Chairman, Belfast District Police Partnership Board; Hon. Secretary, Ulster Unionist Party (UUP); serves on the committees of a number of community groups; Member of Sports Council for Northern Ireland; serves on the Board of The Grand Opera House in Belfast; Director of Glentoran Football Club. Recreations: reading; soccer; golf; bowls; cricket; athletics; walking. Address: (b.) City Hall, Belfast; T.- 028 90 320202.

Rodgers, Robert Frederick, LLB.   County Court Judge since 1997; b. 10.6.47, Belfast; m., Kathleen; 1s.; 1d. Educ. Royal Belfast Academical Institution; Queen's University, Belfast.   Solicitor, J C Taylor and Co, 1970 - 89; District Judge, 1989 - 97. Recreations: reading; music; walking; sailing. Address: (b.) Northern Ireland Court Service, Windsor House, Bedford Street, Belfast, BT2 7LT.

Rooney, Professor John Joseph, BSc, PhD, MRIA. Professor of Catalytic Chemistry, Queen's University, Belfast since 1980; b. 22.10.35, Downpatrick; m., Angela Keenan; 4s.; 3d. Educ. St Patrick's High School, Downpatrick; Queen's University, Belfast.   ICI Fellow, Queen's University, Belfast, 1960 - 62; Lecturer, University of Hull, 1962 - 65; Lecturer, Queen's University, Belfast, 1965.   Richardson's Medal and Prize, Queen's University, Belfast, 1957; Meldola Medal and Prize, 1965; Ciapetta Lectureship and Prize, USA and Canada Catalytic Societies, 1994; MRIA, 1990.   Publications: over 200 articles, papers and chapters in journals and books.   Recreations: playing bridge; walking. Address: (b.) Department of Chemistry, David Keir Building, Queen's University, Belfast, Belfast; T.- 02890-245133.

Rooney, Noel, BSc, MSc.   Chief Executive Officer, Probation Board for Northern Ireland, since 2003; b. 29.11.52, Belfast; m., Marie Rooney; 1s.; 3d. Educ. St Thomas's Secondary School; University of Ulster; Queen's University, Belfast.   Social Worker, 1977; Community Development Worker, 1979; Manager, Social Services, 1983; Assistant General Manager, Health and Social Services, 1987; Director, North and West Belfast Health and Social Services Trust 1993-2003. Graduate, Federal Executive Institute, Virginia America, 1997; Graduate, Top Management Programme, Kings Fund, London, 1994. Recreations: reading; walking; swimming. Address: (b.) 80-90 North Street, Belfast BT1 1LD. T.-028 90262437.

Rosborough, Robert John, BSc.   Station Director, Belfast City Beat, since 2000; b. 19.6.53, Cirencester, Glos.   Educ. Royal Belfast Academical Institution; Queen's University, Belfast. Downtown Radio: Sound Engineer, 1975 - 77; Production Manager, 1977-79; Head of Programming, 1979 - 2000. Member, Institution of Electrical Engineers; Member, Equity; Council Member, Radio Academy, 1989-2002; Member, Royal Television Society. Recreations: foreign travel; concert going. Address: (b.) Belfast City Beat, 46, Stranmillis Embankment, Belfast BT9 5FN. T.-028 9020 5967.
e-mail: john.rosborough@citybeat.co.uk

Ross, Hugh, BA, BD.   Minister, Carland and Newmills Presbyterian Churches since 1984; b. 12.11.43, Co Down; m., Evelyn; 4d.   Educ. Banbridge Intermediate School; Emmanuel Bible College, Birkenhead; College of Business Studies, Belfast; Union Theological College, Belfast; Queen's University Belfast. Lotus and Delta Down Shoes, 1958 - 64; Training for the ministry, 1964 - 67; Missionary Work, South Wales, Ireland and Northern Ireland, 1967 - 73; Assistant Minister, 1st Portadown Presbyterian Church, 1981 - 84. Founder and Leader, Ulster Independence Movement since 1988. Parliamentary Candidate, Upper Bann by election, 1990; Candidate European Election, 1994. Recreations: politics; reading; football. Address: (h.) The Manse, 69 Farlough Road, Newmills, Dungannon, Co Tyrone, Ulster, BT71 4DU; T.-028 8774 8643.

Ross, Oliver, BA, LLB. Solicitor, private practice; b. 30.4.54, Dungannon; m., Gwen; 3d.   Educ. Royal School, Dungannon; Trinity College, Dublin. Admitted as a Solicitor, 1978; Partner, Simmons Meglaughlin and Orr and associate firms J B and R H Twigg and Gordon Wallace and Company since 1982.   Non Executive Director, Armagh and Dungannon Health and Social Services Trust; Director, Dungannon and District Housing Association Ltd and Moygashel Community Development Association Ltd. Address: (b.) Simmons Meglaughlin and Orr, 20 Northland Row, Dungannon, Co Tyrone, BT71 6BL; T.- 028 87-722016.

Ross, Rev. Richard Samuel, MA.   Retired Presbyterian Minister; b. 16.11.23, Co Down; m., 1. Eileen Margaret Wadmore (dec); m., 2. Kathleen Maureen Bingham; 2s.; 1d.   Educ. Shaftesbury College; Magee University College; Trinity College, Dublin; Union Theological College. Assistant Minister, Rosemary Presbyterian Church, 1950 - 54; Harryville Presbyterian Church, 1955 - 81; Carnlough/Cushendall Presbyterian Churches, 1985 - 94. Deputy Chaplain, Waveney Hospital; Officiating Forces Chaplain, 1969 - 79; Moderator, Presbytery of Ballymena; Moderator, Synod of Ballymena and Coleraine. Symposium on Confession of Faith. Recreations: writing poetry; international travel. Address: (h) 23 Willowbrook, Kells, Ballymena, BT42 3JF; T.-028 25892668.

Ross, William. Former Member of Parliament, Londonderry East (1979-2001); b. 4.2.36, Co Londonderry; m., Christine; 3s.; 1d. Farmer, 1952 - 79. Recreations: shooting; angling. Address: (h) Turmeel, Dungiven, Co. Londonderry BT47 4SL. T.-02877 741428.

Rowan Hamilton, Lieut. Col. Denys Archibald, MVO, JP, DL; b. 26.4.21; m., Wanda Warburton; 1s.; 2d. Educ. Wellington College; Royal Military College, Sandhurst. 1st Battalion, Black Watch, North Africa, Sicily, Italy and North West Europe, 1939 - 45; ADC, Governor Southern Rhodesia, 1946; Served, West Africa Frontier Force, Black Watch; Staff College, 1953; Brigade Major, Korea, 1954; Oslo with NATO, Commanded 4th/5th Battalion, Black Watch; Defence Attaché, Damascus, Beirut, 1964 - 67; Farmer, 1967 - 87. Stood for Alliance Party in various elections; Councillor (and Chairman), Down District Council for 8 years. Recreations: shooting; fishing; golf; gardening; maintaining my home. Address: (h.) Tullymacnowes House, 120 Clay Road, Killyleagh BT30 9PN. T.-028 44828311.

Rowe, Esther Anne, CertEd, BEd, MEd. Principal, Strangford College, since 1997; b. 8.1.51, Narberth, Pembrokeshire. Educ. The Greenhill School, Tenby, Pembs; Birmingham University. Arden School, Knowle, 1973-75; Handsworth Wood Girls', 1975-79; Aston Manor, 1979-83; Boldmere School, Sutton Coldfield, 1983-86; Cockshut Hill, Yardley, 1987-89; Greenhill School, Tenby, 1989-94; Lagan College, 1994-97. These posts ranged from Teacher of English to Head of Dept., of English, Deputy Head, Tenby and Vice Principal of Lagan College. Served on PGCE Board of Studies Liaison Committee at Queen's University Belfast, since 1996; Member of The National Association of Teachers of English. Recreations: walking; travelling; cooking; game angling. Address: (b.) Strangford College, Abbey Road, Carrowdore, Co. Down BT22 2GB. T.-028 9186 1199.

Royle, Elizabeth Anne (Lisa), BSc. Secretary, Northern Ireland Blind Sports; b. 13.3.50, Birmingham; m., Stephen Arthur Royle (see Dr. Stephen Arthur Royle); 2s.; 1d. Educ. George Dixon Grammar School, Birmingham; University of Wales at Cardiff. Recreations: sailing; tandem cycling; reading; braille; ten pin bowling. Address: (b.) Northern Ireland Blind Sports, 12 Sandford Avenue, Belfast, BT5 5NW; T.- 028 90-657156. e-mail: elizabethroyle@utvinternet.com

Royle, Dr. Stephen Arthur, MA, PhD, ILTM, CGeog, FRGS. Reader in Geography, Queen's University, Belfast; b. 10.9.50, Prestwich, England; m., Elizabeth Anne Frame (qv); 2s; 1d. Educ. Palmer's Grammar School, Essex; George Dixon Grammar School, Birmingham; St John's College, Cambridge; Leicester University. Geography Lecturer, St Paul's College, Rugby, 1973 - 74; Tutorial Assistant, Geography, Leicester University, 1974 - 75; Visiting Professor of Geography, University of Iowa, USA, 1985; Visiting Professor, University of Prince Edward Island, Canada, 1991; President, Geographical Society of Ireland, 1998-2000; President, Ulster Society for Irish Historical Studies, 1997-2001; Co-Director, Queen's University Belfast Centre of Canadian Studies, 2001. Publications: over 170 academic publications including A Geography of Islands, 2001; Belfast to 1840, 2003. Recreations: travel especially to islands; classical music; theatre; sport. Address: (b.) School of Geography, Queen's University, Belfast, BT7 1NN; T.-028 9027 3355. e-mail: s.royle@qub.ac.uk

Rudge, Dr. Michael Ralph Howard, BSc, PhD. Reader in Applied Mathematics, Queen's University, Belfast since 1968; b. 17.3.37, Birmingham; m., Jean Dunn; 1s.; 2d. Educ. Moseley Grammar School; University College, London. Theoretical Physicist, GEC, Nuclear Power Division, 1958 - 59; Visiting Research fellow, Joint Institute for Laboratory Astrophysics, Boulder Colorado, USA, 1962 - 63; Temporary Lecturer, 1963 - 64; Lecturer, 1964 - 68. Publications: various articles in Journal of Physics, Physical Review, Reviews of Modern Physics. Recreations: golf; bridge. Address: (b.) Department of Applied Mathematics, Queen's University, Belfast, Belfast, BT7 1NN; T.-02890 273173. e-mail: mrh.rudge@btopenworld.com

Rushton, Brian Stanley, BSc, DPhil, PGCUT, FLS. Reader, University of Ulster since 1993; b. 8.5.47, West Bromwich, Staffs; m., Jennifer Mary Rushton; 1s. Educ. West Bromwich Grammar School; University of Birmingham; University of York. Lecturer, New University of Ulster, 1971; Senior Lecturer, University of Ulster, 1985. Distinguished Teaching Award, University of Ulster, 1991, Fellow, Linnean Society, 1986; Honorary member, Botanical Society of the British Isles, 2000. Publications: Editor, Watsonia, Journal of the Botanical Society of the British Isles; Editor, Irish Botanical News; Associate and Book Reviews Editor, Irish Naturalists' Journal; over 100 scientific papers, books and reviews. Recreations: listening to music; gardening; golf. Address: (b.) School of Environmental Science, University of Ulster, Coleraine; BT52 1SA; T.-028 7032 4452. e-mail: bs.rushton@ulster.ac.uk

Russ, Dr. Michael, PhD, MA, BMus, ARCM. Senior Lecturer in Music, University of Ulster, since 1990; Head of Music, University of Huddersfield; b. 28.2.52, Stevenage, Herts; m., Audrey; 1 s.; 1 d. Educ. Nobel Grammar School, Stevenage, Herts; Sheffield University; Royal Academy of Music. Lecturer in Music: Ulster Polytechnic, 1974, University of Ulster, 1984, then Senior Lecturer, 1990; Chairman, Drake Project Ireland (North and South), 1999; conductor, clarinettist and writer on music; Head of Media and Performing Arts, University of Ulster, 1998-2002. Jack Westrup Prize for Musicology, 1994; Distinguished Teaching Award, University of Ulster, 1995. Publications: book on Musorgsky;

numerous papers on late nineteenth and early twentieth century music and music analysis. Recreations: sailing; golf; walking; reading. Address: (h.) 1 Windslow Heights, Carrickfergus, Co. Antrim BT38 9AT. T.-02893 364210.

Russell, David George, BSc (Econ). Chairman: Eastern Health and Social Services Board, since 2001, Ulster Supported Employment Limited, since 2000; Commissioner, Belfast Harbour Commission, since 2002; b. 21.5.43, Belfast; m., Susan; 1 s.; 1 d. Educ. Royal Belfast Academical Institution; Queen's University Belfast. Financial Management Posts with Reckitt and Colman, ITT and Nabisco, 1964-70; Management Consultancy with MDS (NI) Ltd and Coopers and Lybrand (NI) Ltd, 1970-74; Finance Director, Masstock Systems Ltd, 1974-79; Finance Director, subsequently Chief Executive, Hampden Group Plc, 1979-2000. Member of Council, University of Ulster; Chairman, Save The Children N. Ireland; Trustee, Save The Children UK; Director and Hon. Treasurer, Portaferry Regeneration Ltd. Recreations: boating and (some) golf and tennis. Address: (h.) The Old Manse, 14 The Strand, Portaferry BT22 1PF. T.-028 427 28765. e-mail: david.g.russell@ukgateway.net

Russell, Ian, BA, MA, Adv Dip Ed. Principal, Banbridge High School since 1996; b. 17.3.47, Lurgan; m., Heather; 1s.; 3d. Educ. Lurgan Technical College; Stranmillis College; Open University. Physics Teacher, Newtownbreda High School, 1970; Head of Science, Newtownbreda High School; Vice-Principal, Drumglass High School, 1990; Principal, Drumglass High School, 1995. Recreations: ex soccer Glenavon and Newry Town "Sportsound" (now BBC) reporter. Address: (h.) 20 Kirkwood Park, Saintfield, Co Down, BT24 7DP; T.- 01238-510731.

Russell, Jacqueline Graham Simpson, BA (Hons). Solicitor; b. 21.2.55, Ballymena; m., James L. Russell (see James Russell); 2d. Educ. Cambridge House, Ballymena; Queen's University, Belfast; Institute of Professional Legal Studies. Recreations: family recreations; sports in general. Address: (b.) James L. Russell and Son, 55 High Street, Ballymena, Co Antrim; T.-028 25652154.

Russell, James Lockhart, BA (Hons), NP. Solicitor, James L. Russell and Son; b. 4.5.52, Ballymena; m., Jacqueline G S Simpson (see Jacqueline Russell); 2d. Educ. Ballymena Academy; University of Ulster at Coleraine; Queen's University, Belfast. Recreations: sport appreciation; family pursuits. Address: (b.) James L. Russell and Son, Maine Lea, 55 High Street, Ballymena, Co Antrim, BT43 6DT; T.- 028 25652154.

Russell, Noel, BA, MA, PGCE. Producer, Television Current Affairs, BBC Northern Ireland; Senior Broadcast Journalist, "Hearts and Minds", "Let's Talk"; b. 15.1.55, Belfast; m., Mary Kelly.

Educ. Christian Brothers Grammar School, Belfast; Queen's University, Belfast; University of Michigan. Reporter, Belfast Telegraph Newspapers, 1974 - 76; Reporter/Deputy News Editor/News Editor, Irish News, 1982 - 89; Joined BBC Northern Ireland, 1989: Producer, Radio Current Affairs; Assistant News Editor, BBC Newsroom, Belfast, Senior Press Officer, BBC Northern Ireland, 1999-2001. Literary Editor, Fortnight, mid eighties. Sony Award, Good Morning Ulster, 1993. Publications: Short story published. Recreations: reading; writing; music; sport. Address: (b.) Room 253, Broadcasting House, Ormeau Avenue, Belfast, BT2 8HQ; T.- 02890-338382.

Russell, Norman John, BA, MPhil, Dip Lib Stud. Director of Information Services, Queen's University, Belfast, since 2000; b. 18.4.44, Belfast; m., Dorothy Elizabeth; 1s.; 2d. Educ. Belfast High School; Queen's University of Belfast. Librarian: Queen's University, Belfast, 1966 - 68; McMaster University, Hamilton, Ontario, Canada, 1968 - 71; University of Ulster, 1971 - 1990; University Librarian, Queen's University, Belfast, 1990-2000. Address: (b.) Queen's University, Belfast, Belfast BT7 1NN; T.-028 90-335020. e-mail: n.russell@qub.ac.uk

Russell, Peter. Director General, Northern Ireland Prison Service. Address: Dundonald House, Upper Newtownards Road, Belfast BT4 3SU; T.-028 9052 2992. e-mail: info@niprisonservice.gov.uk

Ryan, Michael, MIME. Vice President and General Manager, Aerospace Operations, Bombardier Aerospace in Northern Ireland, since 2000; b. 1959, Belfast; m.; 3c. Educ. Queen's University Belfast (Hons. Degree in Aeronautical Engineering). Joined Short Brothers (Bombardier acquired Shorts in 1989), 1981; held various management positions in the company, including general manager of the advanced composites production unit and general manager of fabrications; Director of Procurement in Northern Ireland, 1997-99; General Manager, Procurement, Bombardier Aerospace, Montreal, 1999-2000. Member of the Institution of Mechanical Engineers; Board Member: Maydown Precision Engineer, Business in the Community, Centre for Competitiveness; Member: CBI Northern Ireland Council, the Aerospace Committee, Department of Trade and Industry, Council SBAC. Recreations: sports; reading; listening to music. Address: (b.) Bombardier Aerospace, Airport Road, Belfast BT3 9DZ. T.-028 90 458444.

S

Salisbury, Sir Robert (William), Kt. Educational Consultant, Northern Ireland; consultant to Department for Education and Skills, since 2001; Director of Partnerships, University of Nottingham, since 1999; b. 21.10.41; m., Rosemary D'Arcy; 3 s. Educ. Henry Mellish School, Nottingham; Kesteven Trng College, Lincs (Teacher's Cert); Nottingham University (CFPS); Loughborough University (MA). Geography Teacher, Holgate School, Hucknall, Notts, 1962-64; study in Europe, 1964-66; Second in English, Kimberley Comp. Sch., Notts, 1973-77; Head of Humanities and of 6th Form, Gedling Comp. Sch., Notts, 1977-83; Dep. Head, Alderman White Comp. Sch., Notts, 1983-89; Headteacher, Garibaldi Sch., Mansfield, 1989-99; Vis. Prof., Sch. of Education, Nottingham University, 1998. Chief Examiner, JMB/NEAB, 1979-90; tutor, Professional Qualification for Headship, since 2000; Formerly Ind. Chairman, NE Lincs Education Action Zone, 1998-99; Chairman, Sherwood Partnership, 1998-2002; Associate Adviser, Industrial Society, since 1992; Member, Adv. Council, Carlton Television, 2000-02; Education Adviser, Centre for British Teaching, since 1996; Regional Chairman, Teaching Awards Trust, since 1998; Chairman, Trustees: Fathers Direct, since 1998; Sherwood Coalfield Development Trust, since 1999; Patron, Drugs Abuse Resistance Education, since 2002; National and international speaker, since 1992. FRSA 1998. Publications: Series Ed., Humanities textbooks, 1988; Marketing for Schools Guide, 1993; contrib. numerous articles on educational issues, also on fishing and country matters; freelance articles for The Times and TES. Recreations: trout and salmon fishing; travel; gardening. Address: 9 Crevenagh Road, Omagh, Co. Tyrone BT79 0EW.

Salisbury, Lady Rosemary, BEd. Principal, Drumragh Integrated College, Omagh, since 2001; b. 3.1.50, Omagh, Co. Tyrone; m., Sir Robert Salisbury; 3 s. Educ. St. Brigit, Omagh; University of Nottingham; Mary Ward College, Nottingham. Career History: 16 secondary schools in England; Lowdham Borstal Institute; Deputy Head, Top Valley School, Nottingham; New College FE Institution, Nottingham; Principal, King Edward VI School, Retford. Speaker at national and international conferences; Member of the Regimental Council, Royal Irish Regiment. Recreations: walking; keep fit. Address: (b.) Drumragh College, 1 Donaghanie Road, Omagh, Co. Tyrone BT79 0NS. T.-028 82252440. e-mail: burntstump@aol.com

Saunders, Professor Eric D. Chairman, Sports Council for Northern Ireland, since 2000; b. 30.9.38; m., Christine (deceased); 1 s. Educ. Kirkcaldy High School; Strathclyde University; Loughborough University. Academic staff member, Loughborough College; University of Ulster (Professor 1982). Member, UK Sports Council and UK Sport Awards Panel, 2000. Recreations: watching sport and keeping fit. Address: (b.) Sports Council for Northern Ireland, House of Sport, Upper Malone Road, Belfast BT9 5LA.

Savage, George. Member (Upper Bann), Ulster Unionist Party, Northern Ireland Assembly, 1998-2003. Beef and dairy farmer; Member, European Committee of the Regions; Vice-Chairman, Agriculture and Rural Development Cttee; Councillor, Craigavon Borough Council. Address: (b.) Constituency Office, 22A Newry Street, Banbridge BT32 3HA. T.-/Fax: 028 406 24114.

Savage, Gwen, MBE, MIPnD, MIMGT. Chairman, Gwen Savage and Co Ltd; b. Northern Ireland; divorced; 2 s. Educ. Sullivan Upper School, Holywood. Founder Director, Gwen Savage and Company (Training and Recruitment) for over 20 years. MBE, 1994 for services to the training of young people. Member: Civic Forum, Transitional Objective 1 Programme; Director: Northern Ireland Management Council, RUC Athletic Association; Member, Fair Employment Tribunal. Address: (b.) Gwen Savage and Co Ltd, 6 Pinehill Road, Bangor, BT19 6SA; T.- 01247-456692.

Savage, Rev. Dr. James Ronald, BA, BD, ThM, DMin. Minister, Stormont Presbyterian Church since 1976; b. 4.5.42, Co Armagh; m., Margaret (Margie) McCullough; 2d. Educ. Belfast Royal Academy; Queen's University, Belfast; Trinity College, Dublin; Union Theological College, Belfast; Princeton Theological Seminary, USA. Assistant Minister, Fisherwick Presbyterian Church, Belfast, 1967 - 71; Minister, Drumachose and Derrymore Presbyterian Churches, Limavady, Co Londonderry, 1971 - 76. Address: (h.) 1 Knockdarragh Park, Belfast, BT4 2LE; T.-028 90 768155.

Savage, Prof. Joseph Maurice, MB, ChB, BAO, FRCP, FRCPCH, DCH. Consultant Paediatric Nephrologist; Professor of Paediatrics; Head, Medical Education, Queen's University, Belfast; b. 27.1.47, Belfast; m., Elizabeth Anne; 1s.; 2d. Educ. Belfast Royal Academy; Queen's University, Belfast. Medical Research Council Fellowship, Institute of Child Health and Great Ormond Street Children's Hospital, London; Lecturer, Child Health, University of Manchester. Publications: over 50 articles on renal disease and hypertension in children and on the genesis of coronary heart disease in children. Recreations: family; running; music. Address: (b.) Department of Child Health, Clinical Institute, Royal Victoria Hospital, Belfast BT12; T.- 01232-894743.

Savage, Rev. Robert Brian, BSc. Minister, Ballykeel Presbyterian Church since 1976; b. 21.4.43, Belfast; m., Phyllis Evelyn; 2s. Educ. Royal Belfast Academical Institution; Queen's

University, Belfast. Ordained, Assistant Minister, Newtown-breda, Belfast, 1970; Minister, Cavanleck and Aughentaine, 1972. Member of the NEELB (North Eastern Education and Library Board). Recreations: reading; walking; listening to music. Address: (h.) 25 Crebilly Road, Ballykeel, Ballymena, BT42 4DN; T.- 028 2564 2654. e-mail: bsavage@presbyterianireland.org

Scallon, William Michael, JP, DL. Retired Property Dealer; b. 29.9.30, Coolaness, Irvinestown, Co. Fermanagh; m., Anna Carolan; 3s.; 3d. Educ. Irvinestown Primary School; Dominican College, Newbridge, Co Kildare, Ireland. Appointed Lay Magistrate, 1963; Justice of the Peace since 1971; High Sheriff, Co Fermanagh, 1976; Chairman of Housing Benefit Review Board, 1984-87; Deputy Lieutenant for County Fermanagh, since 1985; Board Member, Enterprise Ulster, 1987-95. Treasurer of Irvinestown Health Centre Cardiac and Patient's Comforts Fund, 1966, 1988-89; Vice-Chairman for the Western Panel of LEDU, 1970-78; Member, Police Authority for Northern Ireland, 1988-94; Former President and Captain, Enniskillen Rugby Club; Founder Member of St. Molaise Accordion Band; Founder Member of Irvinestown Chamber of Commerce, Secretary, 1964-66, President, 1966-67; Member of Irvinestown Trustees, 1970-74. Recreations: walking; rugby; boating. Address: (h.) The Croft, 138 Kesh Road, Irvinestown, Co Fermanagh, BT94 1NS; T.- 028 686 21254.

Scholfield, Dr. C Norman, BSc, PhD. Senior Lecturer, Department of Physiology, Queen's University, Belfast since 1989; b. 22.4.45, Cambridge; 1s.; 2d. Educ. Duncan Hall School, Norfolk; University College, London. Technician, Imperial Cancer Research Fund, 1961 - 65; Research Assistant, Department of Pharmacology, St Bartholomew's Hospital Medical College, London, 1968 - 72; Research Associate, Department of Psychology, University of Iowa, Iowa City, USA, 1972 - 74; Research Associate, Department of Pharmacology, School of Pharmacy, London, 1974 - 76; Lecturer in Physiology, Queen's University, Belfast, 1976 - 89 (tenure granted, 1978); Efficiency bar passed, 1982. Publications: over 50 papers in various journals; research interests, refinal blood vessels, diabetes, membrane currents, smooth muscle; macula degeneration and microvessels, cerebral microvessels. Address: (b.) Department of Physiology, Queen's University, Belfast, 97 Lisburn Road, Belfast, BT9 7BL; T.- 01232-272082.

Scott, Prof. Norman Stanley, BSc (Hons) Maths, PhD. Professor, School of Computer Science, Queen's University Belfast, since 2001; b. 21.9.54, Belfast; m., Margaret Penelope Marshall; 2 d. Educ. Methodist College, Belfast; Queen's University Belfast. Higher Scientific Officer, Computer Science and Systems Division, Atomic Energy Research Establishment, Harwell, 1980-

81; Senior Computer Programmer, Department of Applied Mathematics and Theoretical Physics, The Queen's University of Belfast, 1981-84; Lecturer: Department of Computing Science, University of Ulster at Jordanstown, 1984-85, Department of Computer Science, The Queen's University of Belfast, 1985-91, Senior Lecturer, 1991-95, Reader, 1995-2000. Alexander von Humboldt Research Fellowship, 1994; Specialist Editor (Algorithms, Software and Architectures), Computer Physics Communications, since 1994; Director, Elsevier Science BV, Computer Physics Communications International Program Library, since 1995; Working Group Member, EPSRC Collaborative Computational Project 2, since 1995; Committee Member, UK Alexander von Humboldt Association, since 1997. Recreations: bell-ringing; cooking; reading; walking. Address: (b.) School of Computer Science, Queen's University Belfast, Belfast BT7 1NN. T.- +44 028 9027 4647. e-mail: ns.scott@qub.ac.uk

Scott, Richard, FInstD, DL. Non-Executive Chairman, Sperrin Lakeland Health and Social Services Trust since 1996; Non-Executive Chairman W and C Scott Ltd, 1996 - 98; b. 1.9.38, Omagh; m., Shirley M Scott; 3s.; 1d. Educ. Mourne Grange, Kilkeel; Loretto School, Edinburgh; Royal Agricultural College, Cirencester; Magee University College. W and C Scott: Apprentice, 1957; Chairman and Managing Director, 1981 - 96. Recreations: music; performing arts; country sports; hill walking. Address: (b.) Sperrin Lakeland Headquarters, Strathdene House, T and F Hospital, Omagh, Co Tyrone BT79 0NS; T.-028 8283 5285.

Scott, Robert Philip, B Ed (Hons), T Cert. Chief Commissioner, Scout Association in Northern Ireland since 1996; b. 20.11.47, Antrim; m., Anne Scott; 1s.; 2d. Educ. Ballyclare High School; Stranmillis College, Belfast; University of Ulster at Jordanstown. Physical Education and Geography Teacher, Randalstown High School, 1970 - 73; Head of Department, PE, Geography, Careers, Randalston High School, 1973 - 81; Vice-Principal, Gracehill Primary School, Ballymena, 1981 - 83; Principal, Fourtowns Primary School, 1984 - 89; Principal, Springfarm Primary School, Antrim since 1989. Scouting Career: Scout Leader, 1st Muckamore Scout Group, 1966 - 73; Assistant District Commissioner, Antrim, 1975 - 78; District Commissioner, Antrim, 1978 - 87; Northern Ireland Commissioner, Activities, 1985 - 90; Northern Ireland Commissioner, Scout Section, 1989 - 95; Group Scout Leader, 1st Randalstown, 1989 - 98; Scout Leader Awards, Medal Of Merit, 1982; Silver Acorn, 1989; Silver Wolf, 2002. Recreations: golf; tennis; sailing; canoeing; water colour painting. Address: (h.) 'Ramoan', 41a Glenkeen, Church Road, Randalstown, Co Antrim, BT41 3JX; T.- 02894 472986. e-mail: rphilipscott@hotmail.com

Scott, William Hartford, JP, BSc (Econ), FCA. Accountant, The Compensation Agency since

1988; b. 10.9.37, Armagh; m., Dorothy Hewitt; 1s.; 3d. Educ. The Royal School, Armagh; University of London. Assistant Clerk, Dungannon Rural District Council, 1960 - 67; Assistant Accountant, Armagh County Council, 1967 - 73; Finance Officer, Southern Education and Library Board, 1973 - 74; Managing Director, Hewitt's Menswear Ltd, 1974 - 88. Recreations: philately; gardening. Address: (h.) Mossview, 64 Ballygroobany Road, Richhill, Armagh, BT61 9NA; T.- 028 38871632.

Semple, Sir John, KCB. Director of Northern Ireland Affairs, Royal Mail Group, since 2001; b. 10.8.40, Belfast; m., Maureen; 3 c. Educ. Campbell College; Corpus Christi College, Cambridge. Joined Home Civil Service in 1961, later transferred to the Northern Ireland Civil Service: appointed Permanent Secretary to the Department of Finance and Personnel, 1988; 1997-2000: Head of the Northern Ireland Civil Service, Second Permanent Secretary in the Northern Ireland Office, became the first Secretary to the Executive Committee of the Northern Ireland Assembly, 1999, headed up the new Office of the First Minister and Deputy First Minister. Chairman of the Northern Ireland Police Fund; Governor, Campbell College. Recreations: golfing; tennis; skiing. Address: (b.) Royal Mail House, 20 Donegall Quay, Belfast BT1 1AA. T.- 028 9089 2334.

Semple, Dr. Samuel, MBE, JP, DUniv, FRSA, MFTCom. Director, Lisburn Enterprise Organisation Ltd; First Freeman of the City of Lisburn, 2003; Former Chairman, Board of Governors, Lisburn Institute of Further and Higher Education; b. 7.12.16, Newcastle-upon-Tyne; m., Edith Elizabeth Ritchie; 2s. Educ. Technical High School, Lisburn; Lisburn College; Belfast College of Technology; University of London; Further Education Staff College, Blagdon. Teacher/Lecturer/Senior Lecturer, Lisburn Technical College, 1943 - 58; Headmaster, Technical High School, Lisburn, 1958 - 63; Vice-Principal, Lisburn Technical College, 1963 - 66; Headmaster, Lisnagarvey High School, Lisburn, 1966 - 82. Officer of 817 (Lisburn) squadron Air Training Corps, 1943 - 56; Alderman, Borough of Lisburn, 1973 - 97; Deputy Mayor of Lisburn, 1977 - 79; Mayor of Lisburn, 1979 - 81. Association of Local Authorities of Northern Ireland: Member, 1977 - 87; Vice-President, 1981 - 83; President, 1983 - 86; Chairman, Joint Council (NI) For Local Authority Chief Executives, 1983 - 86; Co-Chairman, Local Government Consultative Committee (NI), 1983 - 86; Member, Local Government Bureau (UK) Steering Committee, 1985 - 87; Member, National Joint Council for Local Authorities (UK), 1987 - 88; Deputy Chairman, Council of European Municipalities and Regions, 1984 - 86; Member, Committee of Council Of Europe, 1983 - 86; Alternate Member, Local Government Consultative Council of the European Community, 1989 - 91; Member, European Seniors' Parliament (Luxembourg), 1993 - 95. Trustee, Ulster Museum, 1981 - 87;

Trustee, Ulster Folk and Transport Museum, 1987 - 98; Director, Northern Ireland Museums' Council, 1995 - 97; Vice-Chairman, Lisburn Arts Advisory Council, 1997 - 98. Chairman, Lisburn Historical Society, 1969 - 71; Lisburn Chamber of Commerce: President, 1977 - 78; Secretary, 1961 - 77 and 1978 - 96; Hon. Life Member since 1996; Secretary, Lisburn Civic Trust, 1963 - 67; Member, Fire Authority for Northern Ireland, 1981 - 89; Director, Northern Ireland Tourist Board, 1983 - 85; Director, Somme Advisory Council, 1988 - 98; Member, Lagan Valley Regional Park Advisory Committee, 1993 - 97; Member, Northern Ireland Training Council Committee, 1965 - 71; Member, Ministers Advisory Council for Education, 1965 - 68; South Eastern Education and Library Board: Member, 1973 - 97 (Vice-Chairman, 1989 - 91; Chairman, 1991 - 93); President, Association of Northern Ireland Education and Library Boards, 1990 - 91; Chairman, Chief Executive's Council of Staff Commission for Education, 1988 - 97; Member, Court of the University of Ulster, 1974 - 98; Member, Council of the University of Ulster, 1985 - 96. Hon. Doctorate, University of Ulster, 1997. Member: General Synod of the Church of Ireland, 1970 - 94; General Synod Board of Education, 1985 - 94; Connor Diocesan Synod, 1969 - 05; Diocesan Board of Education, 1978 - 98; Diocesan Council, 1997 - 05; Life Member, The Linenhall Library, Belfast, 1997. Publications: Commerce and Industry in the Lisburn District, 1964; Technical Education in Northern Ireland, 1964; An Historical Survey of Lisburn, 1964; Peripatetic Teachers in Primary Schools (with Malone), 1968; History of the Parish of Aghalee, 1971; The Age of Transfer from Primary School to Secondary School, 1972; A Headmaster's View of Education, 1975; The Christian in Public Life, 1977; Anglicanism, 1982; The Contribution of the Ulster Scot to the Creation and Development of the American Republic, 1983; The Family Semple; History of the Parish of Christ Church, Lisburn, 1984; Lisburn Borough Guide; History of Lisburn Borough and Its Noble Citizens, 1598 - 1973, Return of Functions and Powers to Local Government in Northern Ireland, 1982. Recreations: gardening; photography; travel; local history; writing. Address: (h.) Cedar Croft, 16 Belsize Road, Lisburn, Co Antrim, BT27 4AW; T.- 028 9266 3492.

Sha, Dr. Wei, BEng, DPhil. University Reader, The Queen's University of Belfast, since 1999; Visiting Professor at Harbin Institute of Technology, since 1997; Standing Committee member and Belfast Branch Coordinator of the Chinese Materials Association (UK), since 1996; b. 13.6.64, Beijing, China; m., Angela; 2 d. Educ. Beijing No.8 Middle School; Tsinghua University, Beijing; Oxford University. Post-doctoral Research Associate: Department of Materials, Imperial College, 1991-92, Department of Materials Science and Metallurgy, University of Cambridge, 1992-95; Seconded Consultant Engineer, Steel Construction Institute, Ascot, 1997; Research Scholar, Clemson University,

South Carolina, 2003-04; Lecturer, The Queen's University of Belfast, 1995-99, Leader of the Metals Research Group, School of Civil Engineering. Published over 180 scientific papers, edited one book and translated one book; award for Best Paper presented at the Institute of Materials Conference on Titanium Alloys at Elevated Temperature (2000); Session chairperson at international conferences; registered book reviewer; registered publishing referee; Member: Institute of Materials, Institute of Physics, Steel in Fire Forum, Editorial Board of book series "Progress in Materials Science and Engineering Research". Recreation: badminton. Address: (b.) Metals Research Group, School of Civil Engineering, The Queen's University of Belfast, Belfast BT7 1NN. T.-90274017.
e-mail: w.sha@qub.ac.uk

Shankey, Muriel, BA, MSc, CertEd, MCGLI. Principal/Chief Executive, Castlereagh College, since 1998; b. 11.1.47, Belfast; widowed; 2 s. Educ. Grosvenor Grammar School; Open University; University of Ulster. Rupert Stanley College (now Belfast Institute). Address: (b.) Castlereagh College, Montgomery Road, Belfast BT6 9JD. T.-02890 797144.
e-mail: m.shankey@castlereagh.ac.uk

Shanks, Professor Robin Gray, CBE, MD, DSc, FRCP, MRIA, FACP, LLD (Hon). Senior Pro-Vice Chancellor, Queen's University, Belfast, 1995 - 98; b. 4.4.34, Ballyclare; m. Denise Woods (dec.); 4d.; m., Mary Carson. Educ. Methodist College, Belfast; Queen's University, Belfast. Resident Medical Officer, Royal Victoria Hospital, Belfast, 1958; Research Fellow, Augusta , USA, 1959; Lecturer in Physiology, Queen's University, Belfast, 1960 - 62; Pharmaceuticals Division, ICI, 1962 - 66; Doctor of Medicine (Hons), 1963; Lecturer, Clinical Pharmacology, Queen's University, Belfast, 1967 - 72; Doctor of Science, 1969; Professor of Clinical Pharmacology, Queen's University, Belfast, 1972 - 77; Whitla Professor of Therapeutics and Pharmacology, Queen's University, Belfast, 1977 - 98; Dean, Faculty of Medicine, 1986 - 91; Pro-Vice-Chancellor, 1991 - 95; Acting Vice-Chancellor, 1997 (Oct - Dec). Recreations: golf; gardening; family. Address: (h.) Whitla Lodge, 15 Lenamore Park, Lisburn, Co Antrim BT28 3NJ.

Shannon, Randall Phillip, BMus.   Arts Management Consultant; b. 19.2.53, Holywood. Educ. Sullivan Upper School; University of Surrey. Orchestra Musician, London and Amsterdam, 1974 - 84; Manager, Irish Chamber Orchestra, 1984 - 87; Founder/Director, Opera Theatre Company, 1986; Managing Director, Opera Northern Ireland, 1987 - 97. Fellow, Institute of Directors; City and Guilds Gold Medal;. Recreations: music; theatre. Address: (h.) Redburn Lodge, 368 Old Holywood Road, Holywood, Co. Down BT18 9QH. T.-028 9042 5612.

Shannon, Richard James (Jim). Alderman, Ards Borough Council since 1997; Member (Strangford), Democratic Unionist Party, Northern Ireland Assembly, since 1998; b. 25.3.55, Omagh; m., Sandra; 3s. Educ. Coleraine Academical Institution. Served, Ulster Defence Regiment, 1974 - 75 and 1976 - 77; Served, Royal Artillery Regiment TA, 1977 - 88; Elected to Ards Borough Council, 1985; Mayor of Ards Borough, 1991 - 92; Elected to Northern Ireland Forum, 1996; Member, Democratic Unionist Party since 1977; Past Master, Kircubbin Lodge; Master, Royal Bank Perceptory, Ballywalter; President, Apprentice Boys of Derry - Comber Club; Royal British Legion - Greyabbey Branch; District Master, Royal Black Perceptors. Recreations: football; field sports; shooting; Ulster-Scots culture and language. Address: (h.) Strangford Lodge, 40 Portaferry Road, Kircubbin, Co Down, BT22 2RY.

Sharp, Prof. Alan, BA, PhD.   Professor of International Studies, University of Ulster, since 1994, Head of School of History and International Affairs, since 1998; b. 2.12.43, Farnborough, Kent; m., Jennifer; 1 s.; 1 d. Educ. Alleyn's School, Dulwich; University of Nottingham. Lecturer in History: University of Hull, 1969-70, University of Ulster, 1971-91, Senior Lecturer in History, 1991-94. Publications: The Versailles Settlement: Peacemaking Paris 1919, 1991; co-author, Anglo French Relations in the Twentieth Century, (ed) 2000. Recreations: bridge; wine; cricket. Address: (b.) University of Ulster, Coleraine Campus, Coleraine BT52 1SA. T.-028 7032 4651.

Shaw, Ann Forrest, CBE.   Director, Elmfield Farms Ltd., since 1973; Director, Shaws Farms, since 1988; m., J. Derek Shaw; 1 s.; 2 d. Chairman, Northern Ireland Division, Institute of Directors, 1998-2000; Trustee, Lloyds TSB Foundation N.I., since 1993; Chairman, Lloyds/TSB, since 2002; Hon. Vice-President, Institution of Occupational Safety and Health, since 1994; Director, N.I. Memorial Fund, 1999-2001. Trained as a physiotherapist; Chairman, Health and Safety Agency for Northern Ireland, 1993-99; Member, Senate of Queen's University Belfast, since 1999; Present Member, UK's Better Regulation Task Force, 1998-2001; Board Member, Co-operation Ireland, 1999-2002; Divisional Trustee, NSPCC N. Ireland, since 2002. Recreations: gardening; reading; bridge; tennis. Address: (b.) Elmfield, Gilford, Co. Down BT63 5JX; T.-028 38831253.
e mail: annshaw@elmfield.net

Shaw, Sir (Charles) Barry, Kt, CB, QC LLB, DL. Director of Public Prosecutions for Northern Ireland, 1972 - 89; b. 12.4.23. Educ. Inchmarlo House, Belfast; Pannal Ash College, Harrogate; Queen's University, Belfast. Called to the Bar of Northern Ireland, 1948, Bencher, 1968; Called to the Bar of the Middle Temple, 1970; Hon. Bencher, 1986. Deputy Lieutenant. Co Down,

1990. Address: c/o Royal Courts of Justice, Belfast BT1 3NX.

Shaw, Desmond Johnston, BA, FCA. Hon. President, Belfast City Mission; b. 24.1.33, Belfast. Educ. Campbell College, Belfast; Queen's University, Belfast. Joined firm of Chartered Accountants, 1953; Joined Electricity Board for Northern Ireland (now N I Electricity), 1960; retired from NI Electricity as Audit and Treasury Manager, 1990. Hon. Chairman, Northern Ireland Institute for the Disabled; Hon. Treasurer, Leprosy Mission; Hon. Treasurer, Belfast Music Festival. Recreations: music; amateur drama; swimming; walking. Address: (h.) 12 Osborne Drive, Belfast, BT9 6LG; T.- 028-90-668944.

Shaw, James Derek, NDA, FInstD, FRAgS. Managing Partner, Shaw Farms Partnership; Chairman, Shaws Farms Ltd., since 1979; Chairman, Linden Foods, 1994-2001, Vice Chairman, since 2001; Chairman, Armagh and Dungannon Health Trust, 1996-2003; Chairman, Ulster Farmers Investments Ltd, since 1992; Director, Slaney Foods, since 2000; b. 21.2.41, Belfast; m., Ann Forrest Shaw nee Stewart; 1 s.; 2 d. Educ. Friends School, Lisburn; Seale Hayne College, Newtownabbot. Managing Partner, Shaws Partnership, 1963-74; Managing Director, Elmfield Farms Ltd., since 1974; Managing Director, Colly Farms Ltd., Australia, 1979-84; Chairman and Chief Executive Officer, Colly Farms Cotton PLC, Australia, 1984-88; Chairman, Barbour Campbell Group, 1989-95; Vice Chairman, Lendu PLC, since 1989; Director: Industrial Development Board, N.I., 1997-2002, North Australian Pastoral Company, since 2000, Invest Northern Ireland, since 2001; Member, International Agribusiness Managers Association. Recreations: sport (former international hockey player); gardening. Address: (h.) Elmfield, Gilford, Co. Down BT63 5JX; T.-028 3883 1253.

Shaw, Rev. William Alexander, BD. Presbyterian Minister; Director, 174 Trust, Belfast; b. 25.5.56, Malta; m., Heather; 3s. Educ. Kelvin Secondary School; Queen's University, Belfast. Recreations: spectating and playing sport; reading; jogging. Address: (h.) 34 Kimberley Road, Carnmoney, Newtownabbey, BT36 6NZ; T.- 028 90-849700. e-mail: bill@174trust.org

Sheil, The Honourable Sir John Joseph, LLB, MA. Supreme Court Judge; b. 19.6.38, Belfast; m., Brenda Margaret Hale Patterson; 1s. Educ. Clongowes Wood College; Queen's University, Belfast; Trinity College, Dublin. Called to the Bar of Northern Ireland, 1964; QC, 1975; Bencher, 1988; Called to the English Bar, 1974; Hon. Bencher, 1996; Called to the Irish Bar, 1976. Senator, Queen's University, Belfast, 1987-99; British Council, since 2002. Recreations: golf; travel. Address: (b.) Royal Courts of Justice, Chichester Street, Belfast, BT1 3JP.

Shepherd, Geoff, BSc (Eng), MBA. Proprietor, Geoff Shepherd and Associates since 1994; b. 28.6.44, Birmingham; m., Clare; 1s.; 1d. Educ. King Edwards School, Birmingham; London University; University of Ulster. Service Manager, Lex Motor Co, 1975 - 77; General Manager, Codicote Motors Ltd, Hitchin, Herts, 1977 - 80; General Manager, Training Assessment, Road Transport Industry Training Board, 1980 - 83; Chief Executive, Construction Industry Training Board, Northern Ireland, 1984 - 94. Microsoft Certified Solution Developer. Recreations: video making. Address: (b.) 4 Meadowbank, Jordanstown, Newtownabbey, BT37 0UP; T.- 01232-862396.

Shillington, Colin John Graham, BA, CBE, JP, DL. Partner, Solutions Together since 1996; b. 6.2.39, Belfast; m., Melanie Ross; 3s. Educ. Stowe School, Buckingham; Trinity College, Dublin. Personnel Officer, Shellmex and BP Ltd, 1961 - 64; Personnel Officer/Staff Personnel Manager, British Enkagon Ltd, 1964 - 74; Personnel Dir/Managing Dir/Chairman, Dale Farm Dairies Ltd, 1974 - 96. Chief Executive, Northern Ireland Dairy Association; Chairman, Bryson House, 1993 - 98; President, Northern Ireland Commonwealth Games Council, 1989 - 99; Member of Northern Ireland Civic Forum; Member, Northern Ireland Committee of Institute of Directors; Former Director, Northern Ireland Partnership Board; Vice Chairman, Northern Ireland Sports Council; Chairman, Ulster Sports and Recreation Trust. Recreations: sport; gardening; travel. Address: (h.) 21, Dun-A-Mallaght Road, Ballycastle, Co. Antrim BT54 6PB. T.-028-2076-8211.

Sillery, William Moore, DL, OBE, MA. Retired Headmaster; b. 14.3.41. Educ. Methodist College, Belfast; St Catharine's College, Cambridge. Joined teaching staff, Belfast Royal Academy, 1962: Head of Modern Languages, 1968; Vice Principal, 1974 - 76; Deputy Headmaster, 1976 - 80, Headmaster, 1980-2000. Lay Member, Solicitors' Disciplinary Tribunal, NI, since 1999. Recreations: golf; bridge. Address: Ardmore, 15 Saintfield Road, Belfast BT8 7AE. T.-028 9064 5260.

Silvestri, Giuliana, MB, BCh, BAO, MD, FRCP, FRCS, FRCOphth. Senior Lecturer; Consultant Ophthalmic Surgeon; Head of Department of Ophthalmology; b. 24.9.59, Belfast; m., Mr Gordon Cushley; 1d.; 1 s. Educ. Dominican Convent; Queen's University, Belfast. Postgraduate Training in Ophthalmology, Royal Victoria Hospital, Belfast; Molecular Genetic Department, Queen's University, Belfast; Medical Retinal Fellowship, Moorfield's Eye Hospital, London. Young Career Woman, Northern Ireland, 1995; John Clarke BMA Award, 1994; Royal Victoria Hospital Fellowship Grant, 1994. Recreations: ballroom dancing at competitive level. Address: (b.) Royal Victoria Hospital, Eye and Ear Clinic, Grosvenor Road, Belfast, BT12

6BA; T.- 02890-240503 ext. 2342.
e-mail: g.silvestri@qub.ac.uk

Simms, Maurice Henry, BA. Principal, Wilson and Simms Solicitors; b. 9.12.41, Newtownstewart, Co Tyrone; m., Akke Leewering; 1d. Educ. Prior School, Lifford, Co Donegal, Ireland; Campbell College, Belfast; Trinity College, Dublin. Qualified as Solicitor, Northern Ireland, 1966; Qualified as Solicitor, Republic of Ireland, 1991. Recreations: hill walking; fishing; gardening; conjuring. Address: (b.) 35-37 Bowling Green, Strabane, Co Tyrone; T- 02871 882208/882622.
e-mail: msimms@btconnect.com

Slater, Dr G J. Chief Executive, Public Record Office. Address: (b.) 66 Balmoral Avenue, Belfast BT9 6NY; T.-028 90251318.

Sloan, Robert James, BEd, MSc, FRSA. Principal, Dunclug College, Ballymena since 1987; b. 31.7.46, Strabane, Co Tyrone. m., Anne, 2s. Educ. Masonic Boys' School; Stranmillis College, Belfast. Teacher: Mountcollyer Secondary School, 1968 - 72; Everton Girls' School, 1972 - 75; Rathcoole Secondary School, 1975 - 82; Deputy Principal, Balee Community High School, 1982 - 87. Member, North Eastern Education and Library Board, 1993-2001; Northern Ireland President, NASUWT, 1996. Fellow Royal Society of Arts since 1994. Recreations: reading; gardening; golf; rugby (chairman). Address: (b.) Dunclug College, Doury Road, Ballymena, BT43 6SU.

Smaczny, Professor Jan Albert, MA DPhil (Oxon). Hamilton Harty Professor of Music; Head, School of Music, Queen's University of Belfast since 1996, b. 21.12.54, Cambridge. Educ. Cambridgeshire High School for Boys; Magdalen College, Oxford; Charles University, Prague. Lecturer, Music, St Peter's College, Oxford, 1980 - 83; Lecturer, Music, University of Birmingham, 1983 - 95; Senior Lecturer, Music, University of Birmingham, 1995 - 96. Critic, Independent, Opera. Publications: Antonín Dvořák cello concerto in B minor, 1999. Recreations: reading; cooking; palaeoanthropology. Address: (b.) School of Music, Queen's University, Belfast, Belfast, BT7 1NN; T.- 028 90335201.
e-mail: j.smaczny@qub.ac.uk

Smallwoods, Thomas Albert, MBE, MIEI.ecI.E, IEng (CEI), KStJ. Northern Ireland Vice President, St John Ambulance; President, Northern Ireland Home Accident Prevention Council, b. 23.7.37, Londonderry; m., Vivian Anna Margaret; 2d. Educ. Londonderry/Belfast Technical College. Apprentice Electician, Londonderry Corporation, 1952; Coockeeragh Power Station: Switchboard Attendant, 1960; Junior Engineer, 1963; Assistant Charge Engineer, 1968; Charge Engineer, 1970 - Retired. Chairman, Londonderry Home Accident Prevention Committee; Press Officer, Londonderry Road Safety Committee;

Member, Foyle and Roe Valley Victim Support Committee; World Development Representative, Diocese of Derry and Raphoe Church of Ireland; Member, General Synod, Church of Ireland; Member of Church of Ireland Bishops' appeal Committee on World development. Recreations: working for road and home safety. Address: (h.) 'Shalom' 43 Deanfield, Londonderry, BT47 6HY; T.-028 71 342182.

Smart, Paul, LLB, CPLS. Partner, Stewarts Solicitors; b. Belfast; m., Anne O'Mullan; 3s.; 1d. Educ. St Mary's Grammar School; Queen's University Belfast. Recreations: music; member, Ardglen Golfing Society. Address: (b.) Stewarts, 3 Regent Street, Newtownards, 7a Greenvale Street, Ballymena. T.- (91) 826444, (25) 651414.

Smith, Prof. Alan, BSc (Hons), DPhil. UNESCO Chair, Professor of Education, University of Ulster, since 2000; Senior Research Fellow, Centre, Study Conflict, since 1985; Teacher, Zimbabwe, since 1981; b. 18.1.54, Belfast; m., Elaine; 2 d. Educ. Sullivan, Holywood, Co. Down; University of Ulster. Founder of the North Coast Charitable Trust for Integrated Education, 1986-96; Treasurer to the Board of Directors of Mill Strand Primary School, 1987-92; Chairman, Northern Ireland Council for Integrated Education (NICIE), 1987-89; Nominee of the Nuffield Foundation to the Integrated Education Fund, 1992-99; Member of the Northern Ireland Community Relations Council, 1995-97; UK representative to Council of Europe consultation Education for Democratic Citizenship, 1997; Consultant to the World Bank on education for social cohesion, Bosnia, 1999-2001; Consultant to UK Department for International Development, Sri Lanka, 2000-2001; Member of UNESCO Advisory Committee, Paris - Peace, Human Rights and Democracy (appointed by Director-General for a four-year term). Publications include: contributor, Education Together for a Change. Integrated Education in Northern Ireland, (ed) 1993; co-author, The Effects of the Selective System of Secondary Education in Northern Ireland, 2000; contributions to journals; papers presented. Address: (b.) School of Education, University of Ulster, Coleraine BT52 1SA. T.- 028 7032 4137. e-mail: a.smith@ulster.ac.uk

Smith, Professor Francis Jack, OBE, BSc, MA, PhD, FIMA, MRIA. Professor, Computer Science, Queen's University, Belfast, since 1977; b. 31.3.35, Belfast; m., Ann M. Dowling; 4 s.; 1 d. Educ. St Malachy's College; Queen's University, Belfast. Lecturer, Applied Mathematics, 1961-70; Reader; Director, Computer Centre, 1970-77; Head, Computer Science Department, 1977-87, 1990-93; Dean, Faculty of Science, 1986-89; Director, School of Electrical Engineering and Computer Science, 1993-98. Chairman of Alliance Party, 1975-76; OBE for services to Computer Science 2001. Recreations: archaeology; walking; bee-keeping. Address: (b.) Computer Science

Department, Queen's University, Belfast; T.-02890 274072.

Smith, Prof. Michael, BA, MA. Director, Institute of European Studies, Queen's University, Belfast; Jean Monnet Professor; b. 16.2.45, London; m., Lesley Milne; 2s. Educ. Christ's Hospital; Sidney Sussex College, Cambridge; London School of Economics. Harkness Fellow, Commonwealth Fund, 1970 - 72; Fellow, Sidney Sussex College, Cambridge, 1973 - 77; Lecturer/ Senior Lecturer/Head, Department of European Studies, University of Hull, 1977 - 92; Appointed, Queen's University, Belfast, 1993. Publications: numerous books and articles on the history of European Integration. Address: (b.) Institute of European Studies, Queen's University, Belfast BT7 1NN.

Smyth, Anthea Linda, JP, DL. Company Director/Horse Breeder; b. 15.1.54, Belfast; m., David William Smyth; 1s.; 2d. Educ. Richmond Lodge. Managing Director, Tullygowan Ltd; Member, Royal Belfast Hospital for Sick Children Ladies League Committee (Past Chairman); Serving sister, Order of St John; Committee Member, Irish Thoroughbred Breeders Association, Northern Ireland. Recreations: opera; horse racing; bridge; cycling. Address: (b.) Tullygowan, 32 Tullywest Road, Saintfield, BT24 7LX; T.-02897 511621.

Smyth, David William, QC, LLB. County Court Judge, Division of Antrim since 1997; b. 12.11.48, Belfast; m., Anthea Hall-Thompson DL; 1s.; 2d. Educ. Methodist College, Belfast; Queen's University, Belfast. Called to the Bar in Northern Ireland, 1972; Researcher, London, 1972 - 74; Called to the English Bar, Gray's Inn, 1978; Called to the Irish Bar, 1989; County Court Judge, Division of Fermanagh, 1990 - 97. President, Northern Ireland Community Addiction Services, 1994; Chairman, Lord Chancellor's Legal Aid Advisory Committee for Northern Ireland; Chairman of the Board of Advisors of the Institute of Criminology at Queen's University Belfast; Bencher, Inn of Court NI, 1998. Recreations: cycling; hill walking; history; opera; theatre. Address: (b.) Royal Courts of Justice, Chichester Street, Belfast, BT1 3JP; T.- 01232-235111.

Smyth, Professor Douglas Dempsey, OBE, Dip Ed, ADRC. Chairman, NI Ambulance Service, since 1999; b. 24.2.37, Belfast; m., Lillian McCartney; 2s.; 1d. Educ. Methodist College, Belfast; Stranmillis College; Loughborough College; University of Newcastle. School-master, Wellington Farm School, Penicuik, Scotland, 1961 - 65; Home Office, Childrens' Department Inspectorate, London, 1966 - 70; Director of Child Care, Barnardos UK, London, 1970 -73; Director of Social Services, Northern Health and Social Services Board, 1973 - 86; General Manager, NHSSB, 1986 - 96; Visiting Professor, University of Ulster at Jordanstown since 1998. OBE, 1996; Member, General Medical Council, since 1999;

Chairman, Royal Yachting Association, Sailing for the Disabled (NI) Committee. Recreations: music; sailing. Address: (b) Knockbracken Healthcare Park, Ambulance Headquarters, Saintfield Road, Belfast BT8 8SG. T.-02890 400999.

Smyth, Joan R, CBE, BSc (Econ), FIPD, LLD (Hon. University of Ulster 2000). Chairman, NI Transport Holding Company, since 1999; b, 29.12.46, Belfast; m., John V Smyth. Educ. Dalriada School, Ballymoney; Glenola Collegiate School, Bangor; Queen's University, Belfast. Equal Opportunities Manager, Gallaher Ltd, 1969 - 89; Personnel Consultant, Allen and Smyth, 1990 - 92; Chair, Equal Opportunities Commission for Northern Ireland, 1992 - 99. President, Soroptimist International of Great Britain and Ireland, 2002-03; Chair, British Council Northern Ireland Committee; Chair, Womens Regional Consultative Forum NI; Board Member, Progressive Building Society; Chairman, Chief Executives Forum NI. Recreations: golf; drama. Address: (b.) NITHCO, Chamber of Commerce House, 22 Great Victoria Street, Belfast, BT2 7LX; T.- 02890 243456.
e-mail: john.joansmyth@btclick.com

Smyth, Nigel P. E., Msc, CEng, MIMM. Regional Director, CBI Northern Ireland since 1991; b. 1956; m., Kay; 2s. Educ. University of Bristol; University of Leicester. Geologist, United Kingdom, Belgium, South America; Project management, AMEC Plc, late 1980's; joined CBI Northern Ireland, 1990; seconded, Director, Northern Ireland Growth Challenge, 1995 - 96. Member, Economic Research Institute of Northern Ireland. Recreations: outdoor activities; keen traveller. Address: (b.) CBI Northern Ireland, Scottish Amicable Building, 11 Donegall Square South, Belfast BT1 5JE. T.- 028 90-326658.

Smyth, Prof. William Franklin, CChem, BSc (Hons), PhD, DSc, FRSC, FICI. Professor of Bio-Analytical Chemistry, University of Ulster, Coleraine, since 1999; b. 17.9.45, Belfast; m., Jane Mary; 5 d. Educ. Coleraine Academical Institution; Queen's University Belfast. Career History: Lecturer in Chemistry: Chelsea College, University of London, University College Cork, Republic of Ireland; Quality Assurance Director, Norbrook Laboratories, Newry; Professor of Chemistry, University of Zambia. Publications in Bio-Analytical Chemistry: 115 papers and 20 reviews; edited 2 books and written 2 books. Recreations: tennis; jogging; snooker; classical music. Address: (b.) School of Biomedical Sciences, University of Ulster, Cromore Road, Coleraine BT52 1SA. T.-028 70 324425.
e-mail: wf.smyth@ulster.ac.uk

Smyth, Rev. William Martin, MP, BA, BD. Member of Parliament, Belfast South since 1982; President, Ulster Unionist Council, since 2001; m., Kathleen Jean Johnston; 3d. Educ. Methodist College, Belfast; Magee University College, Trinity College, Dublin; Assembly's College,

Belfast. Assistant, Lowe Memorial, 1955 - 57; Ordained, Raffrey Presbyterian Church, 1957; Minister, Alexandra Presbyterian Church, 1963. Member, Northern Ireland Constitutional Convention, 1975; Member, Northern Ireland Assembly, 1982 - 86; Chairman, Ulster Unionist Council Executive, 1972 - 75 (Vice President, 1974); Member, UK Executive Commonwealth Parliamentary Association since 1989; Member, UK Executive, Inter-Parliamentary Union since 1985; Grand Master, Orange Lodge of Ireland, 1972 - 96; Grand Master, Orange Lodge of World, 1974 - 82; Chairman, Belfast No1 School of Management, 1972 - 80; Governor, Belfast City Mission; Council Member, Belfast Bible College; Hon. Vice-President, Belfast Battalion Boys' Brigade. Publications: Faith For Today (ed.); various booklets, pamphlets and articles. Recreations: photography; reading; travel. Address (h.) 117 Cregagh Road, Belfast, BT6 0LA; T.- 01232-457009.

Smythe, Robin James, MSc, BEd, CertEd. Principal, Massereene Community College, Antrim, since 1998; b. 28.3.51, Belfast; m., Sheila Smythe (nee Gordon); 1 s.; 1 d. Educ. Annadale Grammar School, Belfast; Stranmillis College; Queen's University; University of Ulster, Jordanstown. Hopefield High School, 1973-79; Antrim High School: Head of English, 1980-89, Vice Principal, Sep. 1989-Dec. 1989, Acting Principal, then Principal, 1990-98. Trustee of the NI Special Olympics Committee; on the Council of Dunmurry Golf Club; Member of: Select Vestry of Christ Church, Lisburn, Lisburn Swimming Club; former Executive Member of the Ulster Region, Swim Ireland. Recreations: golf; walking; light weight training. Address: (b.) 6 Birch Hill Road, Antrim BT41 2QH. T.-028 9446 4034. e-mail: rjsmythe@massereenecommunitycollege. antrim.ni.sch.uk

Spence, Rev. George Leslie, MInst PS. Superintendent, Glenavy and Moira Circuit; Minister of Glenavy and Craigmore Methodist Churches, since 2001; b. 16.1.45, Belfast; m., Irene; 2s. Educ. Belfast Technical High School; Northern Ireland College; Ulster Polytechnic; Edgehill Theological College; Queen's University, Belfast. Office Assistant, Douglas and Green Ltd; Sales Assistant/Buyer, Brown Brothers Ltd; Radio/TV/Electrical Assistant, J C Holland Ltd; Radio/TV/Electrical Assistant, A W Gordon Ltd; Sales Assistant, Estimating and Purchasing, Walter S Mercer and Sons; Company Buyer, Richardsons Fertilisers Ltd; Ordained, 1984; Minister: Craigyhill Methodist Church, 1983 - 86; Magheragall Methodist Church, Trinity Methodist Church, Lisburn, 1986 - 89; Methodist Chaplain, H M Prison, Maze, 1987 - 89; Cookstown Methodist Church, 1989 - 97; Minister, Seymour Hill Methodist Church, 1997-2001; Methodist Chaplain, HM Prison, Maghaberry, since 2001. Formerly Council and Executive Member, Evangelical Alliance, Northern Ireland; Advisor, Aglow International (Ireland); Leader, Maranatha

Community and Ulster Project; Executive Member of the Northern Ireland Prison Chaplain's Association. Recreations: walking; soccer; bowls badminton. Address: (h.) Methodist Manse, 9 Belfast Road, Glenavy, Crumlin, Co Antrim BT29 4LL. T.-028 944 52494.

Spence, Professor Roy, OBE, MB, BCh, BaO, MA, MD. FRCS; FRCSI, FRCS (Ed), JP. Pro Chancellor, University of Ulster, since 2002; Hon. Professor, Queen's University Belfast, since 2001; Consultant Surgeon, Belfast City Hospital, since 1986; Hon. Lecturer, Surgery, Queen's University Belfast, since 1991; Hon. Lecturer in Oncology, Queen's University Belfast, since 1997; Hon. Professor, University of Ulster, since 1999; b. 15.7.52, Omagh; m., Dr. Diana Burns; 2s.; 1d. Educ. Annadale Grammar School; Queen's University, Belfast. Rotating surgical posts in Northern Ireland, 1977 - 84. Junior Consultant, Groote Schuur Hospital, Cape Town, 1984 - 86; Executive Director, Belfast City Hospital Trust, 1993 - 97; Chairman, Cancer PG since 1996; Lead Cancer Clinician, Belfast City Hospital, since 2000; Consultant General Surgeon with specialist interest in oncology, breast, head and neck and general abdominal surgery. Member, Board of Governors and Trustees, Wallace High School, 1993 - 99; Board Member, Crimestoppers, Northern Ireland since 1996; Member of Council of University of Ulster, since 2000; Member, Northern Ireland Growth Challenge; Member, Police Authority, Northern Ireland, 1994-2001; Chairman, Community Relations Committee, Police Authority, Northern Ireland, 1996 - 98; Member, Church Ireland Ethics Committee. Moynihan Medal Winner; ARIS/Gale Lectureship, College of Surgeons (England); Visiting Professor, The Cleveland Clinic, USA. Publications: over 180 papers and abstracts published; 10 text books. Recreation: history. Address: (h.) 7 Downshire Crescent, Hillsborough, BT26 6DD; T.- 028-92-682362. e-mail: roy.spence@bch.n-i.nhs.uk

Spiers, (Mary) Arlene (Anne), RGN, RM, RHV. Chief Executive, Ulster Cancer Foundation, since 2001; b. 7.4.46, Banbridge; m., David Whitehead (qv). Educ. Banbridge Academy; Royal Victoria Hospital, Belfast; Royal Maternity Hospital, Belfast; Royal College of Nursing, Belfast. Health Visitor, Southern Health and Social Services Board, 1972-78; Health Visitor and Acting Nursing Officer, Eastern Health and Social Services Board, 1978-80; Ulster Cancer Foundation: Education Officer, 1980-89, Senior Education Officer, 1989-95, Head of Community Services, 1995-99, Deputy Director, 1999-2000, Acting Chief Executive, 2000-2001. Board Member: No Smoking Day UK, European Cancer Leagues. Recreations: gardening; travel. Address: (h.) The Mill House, 54 Upper Mealough Road, Purdysburn, Belfast BT8 8LR. T.-028 9081 2741.

Steele, David James, LLB. Solicitor, Babington and Croasdale, Londonderry since 1993; b. 15.2.69, Larne. Educ. Larne Grammar School;

Queen's University, Belfast. Apprentice Solicitor, Babington and Croasdale, 1991 - 93. Address: (b.) 9 Limavady Road, Waterside, Londonderry; T.-02871-349531.

Steele, Ernest James Francis. Independent Liberal Unionist Councillor, North Down Borough Council; b. 12.3.43, Belfast; m., Claire; 1s. Educ. The Royal School, Armagh; Belfast College of Technology. Aircraft Engineer; Civil Engineer; Businessman (retired). Recreations: fly fishing; dog breeding. Address: (h.) 51 Donaghadee Road, Groomsport, Bangor Co Down; BT19 6LH; T.-02891-883118.

Stephens, Desmond, BA (Hons), Dip TP, MRTPI. Regional Policy Manager, Department for Regional Development, 2000-2003; b. 2.6.45, Belfast; m., Hilary Muriel Stephens; 2s.; 1d. Educ. Annadale Grammar School; Queen's University, Belfast; Leeds School of Town Planning. Planning Assistant, Planning Department, Belfast City Council, 1969 - 70; Assistant Planning Officer, Ministry of Development, 1970 - 73; Maingrade Planning Officer, Ministry of Development, 1973 - 74; Senior Planning Officer, Department of Housing, Local Government and Planning, 1974-75; Senior Planning Officer, Planning Services Headquarters, 1975 - 77; Senior Planning Officer, Divisional Planning Office, Downpatrick, 1977 - 86; Senior Planning Officer, Planning Service Headquarters, 1986 - 89; Principal Planning Officer, Divisional Planning Office, Ballymena, 1989 - 96; Principal Planning Officer, Planning Service Headquarters, 1996 - 98; Divisional Planning Manager, Craigavon, 1998-99. Chairman, Northern Ireland Branch, Royal Town Planning Institute, 1995 - 96. Publications: Road Design Guide, Layout of Residential Streets. 1989. Recreations: rugby; swimming; gardening; walking; travel and caravanning. Address: (h.) Stonecullen, 29 Old Belfast Road, Newtownards, Co Down, BT23 4SG. e-mail: desmond_stephens@lineone.net

Stephens, William Benjamin Synge, QC, LLB. Barrister-at-Law; b. 28.12.54, Dublin; m., Nicola Skrine; 1s.; 1d. Educ. Manchester University. Address: (b.) Bar Library, 91 Chichester Street, Belfast BT1 3JQ.

Stephenson, Jonathan, BA. b. 2.11.50, London; m., Marga Foley; 2s.; 1d. Educ. Stanbridge Earls' School, Romsey; Queen's University, Belfast. Deputy President, Queen's University, Belfast Students' Officer, 1974 - 75; Information Officer, Northern Ireland Council of Social Service, 1976 - 79; Press Officer, TUC, 1979 - 88; Press Officer, SDLP, 1989 - 91; Fundraiser, Northern Ireland Voluntary Trust, 1991 - 93; Press Officer, Northern Ireland Public Service Alliance since 1993. Executive Member, SDLP, 1991-2001; Chairman, 1995 - 98; Belfast City Councillor, 1993 - 97; Elected, Inter Party Negotiations, 1996. Part-time Editor, Fortnight Magazine, 1977 - 79; Director, Fortnight Magazine. Chairman, Ulster College of

Music, 1997-98. Recreations: current affairs; armchair sport. Address: (h.) 32b Windsor Park, Belfast, BT9 6FS; T.-02890-682682.

Stevenson, John Stewart, MA, BSc (Hons), DipASEd. Principal, Sullivan Upper School, Holywood, since 1998; b. 8.2.51, Belfast; m., Pamela Jane; 1 s.; 1 d. Educ. Annadale Grammar School; United World College of the Atlantic; University College, London. Volunteers Co-ordinator, Notting Hill Housing Trust, 1973; Biology, Chemistry and Mathematics Teacher, Dalriada School, Ballymoney, 1974-98. Chair, Northern Ireland United World Colleges Committee. Publication: GCSE Biology Questions (Co-author). Recreations: hill-walking; reading. Address: (b.) Sullivan Upper School, Belfast Road, Holywood, Co Down, BT18 9EP; T.-028 9042 8780.

Stevenson, William Bristow, MA (Oxon), DL. Semi-retired Solicitor/Farmer; b. 1.11.24, Knockan Feeny, Co Londonderry; m., 1. Barbara S B Iliff (m diss.) 2s.; m., 2. Julia H M Somerville; 2s.; 1d. Educ. Seafield Park, Lee-on-Solent; St Edward's School, Oxford; Trinity College, Oxford. Royal Navy, 1943 - 46; Qualified as a Solicitor, Northern Ireland, 1950. President, City of Londonderry Solicitors Association, 1984 - 92; Member, Londonderry Feis since 1950 (Chairman, 1985 - 90); Governor, Foyle and Londonderry College, 1971 - 88 (Vice-Chairman, 1983 - 88); President, Ulster Ram Breeders Association, 1975 - 88; Represented Northern Ireland, Hillfarming Committee, Westminster for nine years in the 1970's; High Sheriff, Co Londonderry, 1971; Deputy Lieutenant, Co Londonderry since 1977; Hon. Cases Secretary, NSPCC, Londonderry; President, Mental Health Review Tribunal for Northern Ireland, 1987 - 97; active in Church of Ireland Affairs: Chancellor Diocese of Derry and Raphoe since 1975; Member of many diocesan committees since 1955; member, General Synod (Lay Hon. Secretary, 1983 - 88); Member, Court of General Synod, Standing Committee; Representative Church Body, Priorities Fund (Chairman) and various other committees; Secretary and Treasurer, Banagher Parish Church since 1956; Parish reader since 1972; Member, Feeny Community Association. Recreations: shooting; golf; tennis; gardening; continuing to farm the family acres as has been done for 400 years. Address: (h.) Knockan, Feeny, Co Londonderry; T.-77 781265.

Stewart, Richard. Editor, Ulster Gazette and Armagh Standard; b. 6.9.63, Portadown, Co Armagh; m., Eileen Linda Gillespie; 1s.; 1d. Educ. Armagh Secondary School. Reporter, Ulster Gazette, 1980 - 89; Reporter/Deputy Editor/Editor, Morton Newspapers, 1989 - 97. Recreations: hockey; squash; swimming. Address: (h.) 6 Dobbin Manor, Armagh, Co Armagh, BT60 1AL; T.-028 37 526854.

Stout, Professor Robert William, MD, DSc, FRCP, FRCPEd, FRCPI, FRCPSGlas, FMedSci. Director of Research and Development, Northern Ireland HPSS, since 2001; Queen's University Belfast: Dean, Faculty of Medicine and Health Sciences, 1991-2001, Professor of Geriatric Medicine since 1976; b. 6.3.42, Belfast; m., Patricia Stout; 2s.; 1d. Educ. Campbell College, Belfast; Queen's University, Belfast. Visiting Scientist, University of Washington, School of Medicine, Seattle, USA (MRC Fellow), 1971 - 73; Senior Research Fellow, British Heart Foundation, 1974; Senior Lecturer, Department of Medicine, Queen's University of Belfast, 1975 - 76; Member: Royal Commission on Long Term Care, 1997-99, Southern Health and Social Services Board, 1982 - 90, Eastern Health and Social Services Board, 1992-2002, General Medical Council, 1992-2003, Health Research Board Ireland, since 2002; President, British Geriatrics Society, 2002-04. Publications: books and papers on atherosclerosis, geriatric medicine, medical education, seasonality of disease. Recreations: golf; gardening; reading. Address: (b.) Department of Geriatric Medicine, Queen's University, Belfast, Whitla Medical Building, 97 Lisburn Road, Belfast, BT9 7BL; T.- 028 9033 5777.

Strain, Professor Sean J J, BSc, BAgr, PhD, Dip Ed. Professor of Human Nutrition, University of Ulster since 1995; b. 17.2.50, Banbridge, Co Down; m., Brenda Eastwood, 3s. Educ. St Colman's College, Newry; Queen's University, Belfast. Lecturer/Senior Lecturer in Science, Newcastle College of Advance Education, Australia, 1977 - 81; Lecturer, Life Sciences, Ulster Polytechnic, 1981 - 84; University of Ulster: Lecturer, Human Nutrition, 1984 - 88; Senior Lecturer, 1988 - 91; Reader, 1991 - 94. Member, Royal Irish Academy (elected 2002); Non-Executive Director, Causeway Health and Social Services Trust; Member, Physiological Medicine and Infections Board of the MRC. Publications: over 250 research publications in journals and books; Editor, three books; Editor, award winning Encyclopedia of Human Nutrition. Recreations: keeping fit; horse-racing; bridge; chess; bird watching. Address: (b.) Northern Ireland Centre for Diet and Health, University of Ulster, Coleraine, BT52 1SA; T.- 01265-324795.

Stuart, John, BA, MSc, Dip Ed, DASE. Retired School Principal; b. 6.7.42, Belfast; m., Maíre McKeith; 3s.; 1d. Educ. St Malachy's College; St MacNissi's College; Queen's University, Belfast; University of Ulster at Coleraine. Assistant Teacher, St Malach's College, Belfast, 1965 - 70; Head, Geography Department, St Malachy's College, 1970 - 76; St Louis Grammar School: Assistant Teacher, 1976 - 77; Deputy Principal, 1977 - 87; Principal, 1987-2002. President, Ballymena and Antrim Athletic Club; Director, Ballymena Business Development Centre; Past President, Secondary Heads Association, N. Ireland; Member of Down and Connor Diocesan Ecumenical Commission; Member of Rotary International, Ballymena; Chairman, Translink's North Eastern Passenger Users' Group. Recreations: keep fit (running, cycling, swimming); travel; reading; environmental issues; railways; working for harmony in the community. Address: (h.) 34 Rathlin Drive, Ballymena, Co Antrim, BT43 6NH; T.- 02825-653052.

Sturdy, Professor David J., BA, PhD, FRHistS. Professor of Early Modern History, University of Ulster, Coleraine, since 1999; b. 23.2.40, Middlesbrough; m., Deirdre Mary Allbutt; 2 d. Educ. Sir William Turner's School, Redcar; Universities of Hull, London, Dublin. Lecturer in History, Trinity College, Dublin, 1965-70; Lecturer in History, New University of Ulster, 1970-79; Senior Lecturer in History, University of Ulster, 1979-99; author of several books. Recreation: music. Address: (b.) School of History and International Affairs, University of Ulster, Coleraine BT52 1SA; T.-028 703 44141.

Stutt, John Colin, MA (Cantab). Partner, Colin Stutt Consulting since 1994; b. 7.3.52, Carrickfergus; m., Jennifer Patricia; 1s.; 1d. Educ. Methodist College, Belfast; King's College, Cambridge. Variety of positions in Northern Ireland Civil Service in Department of Economic Development, finally Assistant Secretary in charge of Economic Development Policy, 1984 - 88; Director, Business and Economic Initiatives Ltd, 1988 - 91; Partner in charge of Consultancy Services, KPMG Peat Marwick, 1991 - 94; Director, International Business Initiatives Ltd, 1995 - 98; Chairman, Causeway Data Communications Ltd, since 1999; Chairman, Northern Ireland Centre in Europe, 1999-2003. Visiting Professor, University of Ulster, 1991 - 97. Publications: number of consultancy studies on economic policy in Northern Ireland and the Republic of Ireland. Recreations: reading; walking; music. Address: (b.) 15 Bridge Road, Helen's Bay, Co Down, BT19 1TW; T.- 02891-853710.
e-mail: cs@colinstutt.com
website: www.colinstutt.com

Swallow, Dr. Michael William, OBE, FRCP. Hon. Consultant Neurologist; b. 11.12.28, London; m., Barbara; 2d. Educ. Magdalen College School, Oxford; King's College; Westminster Hospital, London. Junior House Physician, Westminster Hospital; Registrar, St Stephen's Hospital, Fulham and Westminster Hospital; Senior Registrar, National Hospital for Nervous Diseases, London and University College Hospital, London; Consultant Neurologist, Royal Victoria Hospital, Belfast, 1964 - 90. Founder, Share Music; Founder and Secretary, Northern Ireland Music Therapy Trust; Vice President, British Society for Music Therapy. Recreations: music; wine; European travel. Address: (h.) 15 Deramore Drive, Belfast, BT9 5JQ; T.- 01232-669042.

Symington, Brian Norman, MBE, CQSW, CSWDP (PQ), Cert in Soc Wk with Deaf People,

Adv Cert Soc Wk (PG), RCCC, CRes Child Care
Cert. Director, Royal National Institute for Deaf
People (NI) since 1991; Member of Northern
Ireland Civic Forum, since 2000; b., Belfast; m.,
Edna Mary Simons; 2s.; 1d. Educ. Ashfield High
School;   Northern Ireland Polytechnic; North
London Polytechnic; Queen's University, Belfast;
Rupert Stanley College. Eastern Health and Social
Services Board: Social Worker with deaf people,
1971 - 76; Senior Social Worker, 1976 - 79;
Assistant Principal Social Worker, 1979 - 87;
Principal Social Worker, 1988 - 91.   Founder
Committee Member: Ulster Tinnitus Association;
Sense (NI); CACDP (NI); UK Council on
Deafness; Former Chairman, Ulster Institute for
the Deaf, 1980 - 91; Established first rehabilitation
unit for both deaf and blind people, Beechbank
House, Belfast, 1981; Chairman, Joint Universities
in Deaf Education since 1998; Former Executive
Member, Mobility International.   Former Irish
Schools, Youth and Universities International
footballer; professional footballer (Brighton &
Hove Albion). Publications: Communication
Matters,   1993;   Unfolding   Avenues   to
Communication (with A McGlade), 1994;
Breaking the Silence (with A McGlade), 1998
Recreations: all kinds of sport; reading; travel and
family. Address: (b.) RNID (NI) Wilton House, 5
College Square North, Belfast, BT1 6AR; T.-
02890-239619.

Symonds, Rev. Paul Edward, BA, BD. Parish of
Kirkinriola (Ballymena), since 2003; b. 27.10.44,
London. Educ. Windsor Grammar School; St
David's College, Lampeter, Heythrop College,
London.   Teacher and Assistant House Master,
Stonyhurst College, 1974 - 79; Director, Catholic
European Study and Information Centre, Brussels,
Strasbourg, 1980 - 86; Administration, Rome,
1986 - 89; Columbanus Community of
Reconciliation,   Belfast/Assistant   Priest,
Whitehouse Parish and in HM Prisons, 1989 - 92;
Curate, Parish of Drumbo, 1992 - 98; Spiritual
Director, St Malachy's College, 1998-2002; Parish
of Glenavy and Killead, 2002-03.   Secretary,
Ballynafeigh Clergy Fellowship; Chairman,
Diocesan Ecumenical Commission. Recreations:
classical music; reading; walking; home; cat.
Address: (b.) All Saints, 4 Broughshane Road,
Ballymena BT43 7DX.

T

Taggart, Dr. Allister James, MD, FRCP (London), FRCP (Edin). Consultant Rheumatologist, Musgrave Park and Belfast City Hospital since 1987; b. 7.3.52, Sheffield; m., Sandra Davis; 2s.; 1d. Educ. Campbell College, Belfast; Queen's University, Belfast. Junior hospital doctor posts, Belfast City Hospital/Royal Victoria Hospital, Belfast, 1975 - 82; Senior Registrar in Rheumatology, Rheumatism Research Unit, Leeds, 1982 - 84; Consultant Physician/Senior Lecturer, Clinical Pharmacology and Therapeutics, Queen's University, Belfast, 1984 - 87; Clinical Director, Rheumatology, Greenpark Healthcare Trust since 1991. Recreations: badminton; photography; family. Address: (b.) Department of Rheumatology, Musgrave Park Hospital, Stockmans Lane, Belfast. BT9 7JB; T.-028 90 669501.

Taggart, Hugh McAllister, MD, FRCP (Lond), FRCP (Glas). Consultant Physician in Elderly Care Medicine, City Hospital, Belfast, since 1980; Honorary Senior Lecturer in Geriatric Medicine, Queen's University, Belfast, since 1999; b. 29.11.49, Sheffield; m., Grace Campbell; 1 s.; 1 d. Educ. Campbell College, Belfast; Queen's University, Belfast. Senior Registrar, Geriatric Medicine, Belfast City Hospital, 1977-79; Senior Postdoctoral Research Fellow, University of Washington, Seattle, 1979-80; Senior Lecturer in Geriatric Medicine, Queen's University, Belfast, 1980-92; Member, Advisory Board, National Osteoporosis Society, since 1988. Publications: papers in osteoporosis and drug safety. Recreations: golf (handicap of 10); travel; bridge; badminton. Address: (h.) 1 Crawfordsburn Road, Crawfordsburn, Co Down BT19 1XB; T.-02891 852434. e-mail:hugh.taggart@nireland.com

Taggart, Rev. Norman Wilson, BA, BD, PhD. President, Methodist Church in Ireland, 1997 - 98; b. 31.10.35, Belfast; m., Margaret Adams; 2s.; 2d. Educ. Royal Belfast Academical Institution; Queen's University, Belfast; Edgehill Theological College, Belfast. Minister, Primitive Street Methodist Church, Belfast, 1961 - 62; Minister, Medak Diocese, Church of South India, 1962 - 66; Superintendent Minister, Sligo Methodist Circuit, 1966 - 68; Minister, Greenisland Methodist Church, 1968 - 72; Secretary, Irish Council of Churches, 1968 - 72; Home Secretary, Methodist Missionary Society, London, 1972 - 77; Superintendent Minister, Belfast Central Mission, 1979 - 87; Superintendent Minister, Cavehill Methodist Circuit, 1987 - 89; Minister, Methodist Church, Sri Lanka, 1989 - 94; Superintendent Minister, Coleraine Methodist Circuit,1994-2001. Publications: The Irish in World Methodism, 1760 - 1900, 1986; William Arthur, First Among Methodists, 1993; Entries in A Dictionary of Methodism in Britain and Ireland, 2000; Gideon Ouseley, Evangelist and the Irish Methodist Mission, 2001. Recreations: watching sport; Methodist history. Address: (h.) 5 Ashcroft Close, Lower Ballinderry, Lisburn BT28 2AZ; T.-028 9265 2200.

Tame, Dr. Peter David, BA (Hons), PhD. Reader in French, Queen's University, Belfast; b. 8.10.47, Kent; m., Barbara Anne Tame; 3s. Educ. Maidstone Grammar School, Kent; King's College, London; University College, London. French Teacher, Central Foundation Boys' Grammar School, London, 1971- 73; Assistant Lecturer, French, University College, London, 1973; French A Level Lecturer, City of London Polytechnic, 1973 - 77; Senior French Tutor, Eurolang College, Warwick, 1977 - 81; Postdoctoral Fellow in French Language and Literature, Massey University, New Zealand, 1981 - 82 Lecturer, French, Wakefield District College, West Yorkshire, 1982 - 83. Prix Robert Brasillach, 1980. Publications: La Mystique du Fascisme dans l'Oeuvre de Robert Brasillach, 1986; The Ideological Hero in the novels of Robert Brasillach, Roger Vailland and André Malraux, 1998; 'A Translation of Notre Avant-Guerre/Before the War by Robert Brasillach', translated and edited from the French original by Peter Tame, 2002. Recreations: piano playing; swimming; running. Address: (b.) French Studies, Queen's University, Belfast, Belfast BT7 1NN; T.-00 44 28 90 335363; Ext. 3875.

Tannahill, Elizabeth Anne, BA, MA. b. 14.6.42, Belfast; m., Brian Tannahill; 1s. Educ. Belfast High School; Queen's University, Belfast. Clerical Officer, Northern Ireland Civil Service, 1958 - 62; Clerical Officer, Northern Ireland Hospital Authority, 1962 - 65; Student, 1970 - 76; Lecturer, Further Education, 1975 - 76; Blackstaff Press: Editor, 1976 - 78, Director, 1978 - 80, Managing Director, 1980-2003. Fellow, Salzburg Seminar for American Studies, 1977; President, CLE, Irish Book Publishers Association, 1984 - 85; Governor, Linen Hall Library, Belfast, 1985 - 88; Member, Northern Ireland Cultural Tradition Group, 1989 - 93; Member, BBC Northern Ireland Broadcasting Council, 1989 - 94; Member, RTE Authority, Dublin, 1995 - 97. Recreations: reading; walking.

Taylor, Rev. Professor James Patton, TD, MA (Glasg), MA (Oxon), MA (QUB), MTh (QUB). Principal, Union Theological College, Belfast, since 2002, Professor, Old Testament Theology, since 1994; b. 10.5.51, Edinburgh; m., Rev. Margaret Taylor; 3s.; 2d. Educ. Methodist College, Belfast; Hutchesons' Boys' Grammar School, Glasgow; Glasgow University; Corpus Christi College, Oxford; Queen's University, Belfast. Ordained, Presbytery of Derry, 1975; Assistant Minister, Great James Street, 1975 - 76; Assistant Minister, Wellington Street, Ballymena, 1976 - 77; Minister: Duncairn, Belfast, 1977 - 94; Duncairn with St Enoch's 1983 - 94; Hon. Treasurer, Royal Life Saving Society (Ulster Branch). Recreations: squash; swimming; life saving; dinghy sailing. Address: (b.) Union College, 108 Botanic Avenue, Belfast, BT7 1JT; T.- 028 90205080.

Taylor, Rev. Margaret, BD. Associate Minister, Cooke Centenary Presbyterian Church, Belfast since 1985; b. 4.5.54, Ballymena; m., Rev. Professor J Patton Taylor; 3s.; 2d. Educ. Cambridge House School, Ballymena; Garnerville College; Union Theological College; Queen's University, Belfast. Teacher, Parkhall School, Antrim, 1975 - 77; training for the ministry, 1977 - 83; Ordained, 1985 (first mother to be ordained in Ireland). Recreations: dinghy sailing; swimming. Address: (h.) 694 Ravenhill Road, Belfast, BT6 0BZ; T.-02890 645275.

Taylor, Rev Richard Henry, BA. Retired Royal Air Force Chaplain; Retired Methodist Minister; b. 10.7.27, Belfast; m., Margaret Jean Magee; 1s.; 1d. Educ. Springfield Road PES (left school at 14); Belfast College of Technology (part-time); Edgehill Theological College; Open University. Message boy; Greaves Spinning Mill; Joined Merchant Navy, 1943 (at 15 years old), sailing in the North Atlantic; engineering apprentice; Merchant Navy rising to 4th Engineer; entered Methodist Church's ministry; Chaplain, Royal Air Force, 22 years; Assistant Principal Chaplain, Strike Command, 1980 - 83; Returned to Methodist Church in Ireland, 1983; President, Methodist Church in Ireland, 1993 - 94 Member: Boys' Brigade; Sea Cadets. Recreations: soccer – represented Irish and British universities and the RAF, played with Cliftonville Football Club for a short time; tennis. Address: (h.) 5 Knockdene Park, Ballynahinch, Co Down, BT24 8XH; T.- 02897 565720.

Temple, Rev. David John, BA, BD. Superintendent, Presbyterian Church's Irish Mission since 1989; b. 27.1.47, Belfast; 3s. Educ. Belfast Royal Academy; Magee University College; Trinity College, Dublin; University of Edinburgh. Ordained, 1975; Minister: Torry, Aberdeen, Church of Scotland, 1975 - 80; 3rd Portglenone Presbyterian Church, Co Antrim, 1980 - 86; Ballygomartin Presbyterian Church, Belfast, 1986 - 89. Editor, Christian Irishman (monthly magazine); Secretary, Board of Mission in Ireland; Hon. Secretary, Presbyterian Ministers Golfing Association; Hon. Secretary, Clandeboye Clerical Club. Publications: Truths to Transform Troubled Times; Though the Fig Tree Does Not Blossom; Elijah; Christian Baptism. Recreations: former soccer and badminton player gaining university colours; golf. Address: (b.) The Presbyterian Church in Ireland, Fisherwick Place, Belfast, BT1 6DW; T.-028 90322284.

Thomas, Nicholas, LLB, FCI Arb. Senior Partner, Kennedys Solicitors since 1997; b. 16.10.54; m., Jeanette; 1s.; 2d. Educ. Chesterfield School; Bristol University. Joined Kennedy's, 1977; qualified as Solicitor, England and Wales, 1980; Partner, 1981. Qualified to practise in Hong Kong,

Northern Ireland and the Republic of Ireland. School Governor. Publications: Professional Indemnity Claims – an Architects' Guide, 1981. Recreations: sports; travel; the arts. Address: (b.) Kennedys, Longbow House, 14-20 Chiswell Street, London, EC1Y 4TW; T.-020 7638 3688.

Thompson, Very Rev. Professor John, BA, BD, PhD, DD (Hon.). Emeritus Professor, Union Theological College, Belfast; b. 14.7.22, Bushmills, Co Antrim; m., Ingred V Barnes; 2s.; 1d. (pr. m.). Educ. Ballycastle High School; Magee University College; University of Edinburgh; Presbyterian College, Belfast; University of Basel, Switzerland. Assistant Minister, St Enoch's, Belfast, 1949 - 52; ordained, 1952; Minister, Sandymount, Dublin 1952 - 61; Minister, Fortwilliam Park, Belfast, 1961 - 76; Professor, Theology and Faculty Member, Queen's University, Belfast, 1976 - 94; Lecturer, Presbyterian Doctrine, Life and Worship in Relation to Ecumenics, Irish School of Ecumenics, Dublin since 1993. Moderator, General Assembly of the Presbyterian Church in Ireland, 1986 - 87; Convenor, Jewish Mission, 1956 - 69; Member and past Chairman, Doctrine Committee, Inter-Church Relations Board of Studies; Member, Senate, Queen's University, Belfast since 1985. Hon. DD, 1986. Publications: Shorter Catechism, Christ in Perspective, 1976; Holy Spirit in Theology of Karl Barth, 1991; Modern Trinitarian Perspectives, 1995; Theology Beyond Christendom (ed.), 1986; Biblical Theology (ed.); essays in various books and articles in magazines; honoured in 2002 (80th birthday) by three special editions of Irish Biblical Studies. Recreations: hockey (1944 - 45 and 1945 - 46), winning a blue for Edinburgh; soccer; tennis; walking; gardening. Address: (h.) 95 Malone Road, Belfast, BT9 6SP; T.- 02890-666662.

Thompson, (John) Daniel, CBE, MA, DL. Consultant Solicitor and Notary Public; HM Coroner for South Down; Part-time Chairman, The Appeals Service NI; b. Portadown; m., Joan Evelyn Elkin; 2s. Educ. Trinity College, Dublin. Member, Chartered Institute of Arbitrators; Fellow, Royal Society for the encouragement of Arts, Manufactures and Commerce; Board Member, Irish Association of Suicidology, since 2001 (Vice-Chairman, since 2003); Executive committee member, The Nexus Institute, since 2000; Senator, Queen's University Belfast, 1995-2000; Chairman, Eastern Health and Social Services Board, 1994-2000; Member, Historic Buildings Council NI, 1991-97; Chairman, Southern Health and Social Services Board, 1990 - 94; Member, Post Office Users' Council NI, 1989-2000; Member, NI Advisory Committee on Telecoms, 1989-97; Sheriff, Co. Armagh 1991. Publications: commentary on HPSS NI; guide to Greencastle, Co. Down. Recreations: The Armagh Club; cottage in South Down; sailing and playing pétanque. Address: (h.) Ardress Cottage, Annaghmore, Co. Armagh BT62 1SQ. T.-3885 1347.

Thompson, John Gilliland, BA (Hons), MSc. Head of Policy, North Down Borough Council; b. 22.2.49, Ballymena; m., Miriam; 1s.; 2d. Educ. Ballymena Academy; Queen's University, Belfast. Department of Housing, Local Government and Planning, 1973 - 74; Assistant Divisional Planning Officer, Kent County Council, 1974 - 82; Tourism Officer, Coleraine Borough Council, 1982 - 85; joined North Down Borough Council, 1985. Recreations: fishing; caravanning. Address: (b.) Town Hall, Castle Park Avenue, Bangor, Co Down. T.-028 91 270371. e-mail: john.thompson@northdown.gov.uk

Thompson, Prof. John J., BA, MA DPhil. Professor of English (English textual cultures), Queen's University Belfast, since 2001; b. 23.4.55. Educ. Omagh Academy; University of York; Queen's University, Belfast; University of Michigan, USA. English Teaching Instructor, University of Michigan, 1978 - 79; Lecturer in English, Queen's University, Belfast, 1981 - 95, Senior Lecturer, English, 1995-2001; Visiting Fellow, Beinecke Rare Book and Manuscript Library, Yale University, 1988 - 89; British Academy research leave, 1996 - 97; Visiting Scholar: Harvard University, 1998, Universities of Lodz and Krakow (Poland), 2001; British President (formerly Vice-President), International Courtly Literature Society; Office holder, New Chaucer Society; Early Book Society; Director, 'Imagining History' AHRB project, since 2002 (Queen's University Belfast); Member, national collaborative project on the lay urban household, 1300-1550 (University of York); also a research project on traditions of the book, 1000-1600 (Queen's University Belfast); project on reception (with University of Kent). Publications: three books on the history of the early book; 2 collections of essays, proceedings from an international conference of medievalists in Belfast; numerous articles in scholarly books and journals. Address: (b.) School of English, Queen's University Belfast, Belfast, BT7 1NN; T.- 02890 273781. e-mail: j.thompson@qub.ac.uk

Thompson, William John, Ulster Unionist MP (Tyrone West), 1997-2001; b. 26.10.39. Educ. Omagh Academy. Tyrone County Council, 1957 - 66; radio and TV retailer, 1966 - 97; Member, Northern Ireland Assembly, 1973 - 74 and 1982 - 85; Member, Northern Ireland Convention, 1975 - 76; Councillor, Omagh District Council, 1981 - 93. Address: (h.) 129 Donaghanie Road, Beragh, Co. Tyrone BT79 0XE.

Tierney, John. Member (Foyle), Social Democratic and Labour Party, Northern Ireland Assembly, since 1998; Assembly Group Whip, since 2002; b. 9.12.51, Derry; m., Bernadette; 2 s.; 1 d. Educ. St Joseph's, Derry. Elected to Derry City Council, 1981; Mayor of Derry, 1984-85; Leader, SDLP Group, City Council; elected to Northern Ireland Forum, 1996. Address: (b.) 1st Floor, 5 Bayview Terrace, Derry BT48 7EE. T.-028 7136 2631. Fax: 028 7136 2632.

Tierney, Roddy, MSc, BA. Headmaster, Christian Brothers Grammar School, Omagh, since 1993; Chairman, Omagh Boys' and Girls' Club, since 1980. Address: (b.) Christian Brothers Grammar School, Omagh, Co Tyrone, BT78 1LD; T.- 01662-243567.

Tilson, Nigel Paul, Business Editor, The Belfast Telegraph, since 2000; b. 29.9.65, Belfast. Educ. Portora Royal School, Enniskillen; Belfast College of Business Studies. Junior Reporter, The Outlook, Rathfriland, Co Down, 1985 - 86; Reporter, The Leader, Dromore, 1987; Senior Reporter/Sports Editor, The Ulster Star, Lisburn, 1988 - 89; Deputy Editor, Mid-Ulster Mail, Cookstown, Co Tyrone, 1990; Deputy Editor, Belfast Herald and Post Series, 1991 - 92; Editor, Belfast Community Telegraph Series, 1992-2000. Recreations: singer-songwriter; soccer coach; church activities. Address: (b.) The Belfast Telegraph, 124-144 Royal Avenue, Belfast BT1 1EB. T.-028 90264000.

Toal, John, BMus. Presenter, BBC Radio Ulster since 1989; b. 26.9.69, Newry, Co Down; m., Catriona Mullan. Educ. St Colman's College, Newry; Queen's University, Belfast. Presenter, Arts Extra, (Radio Ulster's Nightly Arts and Entertainment Show); has worked extensively on BBC Radio 3. Recreations: food; drink; music. Address: (b.) BBC Northern Ireland, Broadcasting House, Ormeau Avenue, Belfast, BT2 8HQ; T.-028 9033 8249.

Todd, Rev. John Andrew, BA. Retired Presbyterian Minister; b. 21.2.18; m., Margaret Philippa McQuoid; 1s.; 1d. Educ. Royal Belfast Academical Institution; Trinity College, Dublin; University of Edinburgh. Ordained, 1946; Garvaghy Presbyterian Church, Co Down, 1946 - 83; Anaghalone Presbyterian Church, Banbridge, Co Down, 1963 - 83. Publications: Livin' in Drumlister: poems by Rev. W F Marshall; History of Garvaghy Presbyterian Church (1800 - 1954). Recreations: rugby football; fly fishing. Address: (h.) 17 Orlock Road, Groomsport, Bangor, BT19 6LW; T.-028 9188 2985.

Todd, Nathan Wilson, BEd, MA, MSc, AdvDipEduc Man, Dip Man, MCIM. Assistant Senior Education Officer, Belfast Area LEA, since 1999; b. 17.7.50; m., Sandra; 2 s.; 1 d. Educ. Ballyclare High School; Queen's University Belfast; University of Ulster; Open University. Teacher of Geography, Orangefield Boys School, 1975-81; Senior Teacher: Ashleigh House School, 1981-87, Hunterhouse College, 1987-88; Support Officer, Belfast Education and Library Board, 1988-90; Secondary Education Adviser, 1990-99. Address: (b.) 40 Academy Street, Belfast BT1 2NQ. T.-028 90564036.

Toner, Michelle G., Certified Trainer NLP, Hons. Communication Arts. Director, Training Consultancy; b. 3.4.56, Calgary, Alberta, Canada. Educ. Western Canada High School; Southern

Alberta Institute of Technology. Motivational Speaker; radio and television broadcasting; sales and marketing; fitness coach; training and management consultant; executive coaching. Recreations: piano; singing; yoga; keep-fit; reading. Address: (h.) 89 The Park, Millars Forge, Dundonald; T.- 02890-484565.

Tonkin, Professor Jessica Elizabeth Ann, MA Dip Soc Anth, DPhil (Oxon), PGCE (London). Professor Emeritus of Social Anthropology; b. 11.2.34, Richmond, Surrey. Educ. Sidcot School; Lady Margaret Hall, Oxford. HM Inspector of Taxes; Education Officer, Kenya; Lecturer, English, Ahmadu Bello University, Nigeria; Lecturer/ Senior Lecturer, Social Anthropology, Centre of West African Studies, Birmingham University; Professor, Social Anthropology, Queen's University, Belfast. Publications: Narrating Our Pasts, 1992; many articles and book chapters. Recreations: gardening; walking. Address: (b.) School of Anthropological Studies, Queen's University, Belfast, Belfast, BT7 1NN.

Topping, Gordon, OBE, BA (Hons), MSc, MBA, DipEd, FRSA. Chief Executive, North Eastern Education and Library Board, Ballymena, since 1991; b. 25.4.47, Belfast; m., Carol; 1 s.; 1 d. Educ. Bangor Grammar School; Queen's University, Belfast; University of Ulster. Teacher, 1970-78; Educational Administrator, 1978-92. Member of Council, University of Ulster; Board of Governors, Stranmillis College of Education; Member, Northern Ireland Council for Curriculum Examinations and Assessment. Publications: various articles in educational journals. Recreations: painting; watching sport. Address: (b.) County Hall, 182 Galgorm Road, Ballymena, Co. Antrim BT42 1HN. T.-028 2566 2296/97. e-mail: gordon.topping@neelb.org.uk

Torrens, Samuel Henry, CBE, FIB. Chairman: Progressive Building Society, Linfield Properties Limited; b. 24.8.34, Coleraine; m., Marjorie Gillespie; 3s.; 1d. Educ. Coleraine Academical Institution. Clerk, Belfast Banking Company, 1951; Manager, Grafton Street Branch, Dublin, 76 - 79; Regional Director, Home Counties, Midland Bank (parent company), 1985 - 87; Director and Chief Executive, Northern Bank Group, 1988 - 93; retired, 1993. Recreations: foreign travel; gardening; reading. Address: (h.) Seahaven. 753 Shore Road, Newtownabbey, Co Antrim, BT37 0PZ; T.-028 9086 3388.

Trainor, Vincent Joseph, BA. Principal, Grange Primary School, Kilkeel since 1983; b. 20.3.50, Kilkeel; m., Anne, 2s. Educ. St Colman's College, Newry; Queen's University, Belfast. Teacher, St Patrick's Primary School, Ballynahinch, Co Down, 1972 - 83. Recreations: hill walking; music; reading. Address: (h.) 34 Grahamville Estate, Kilkeel, BT34 4DD; T.-028 417 63101.

Trimble, David, LLB, BL, MP, MLA. First Minister of Northern Ireland; Member (Upper Bann), Ulster Unionist Party, Northern Ireland Assembly, since 1998; Leader, Ulster Unionist Party since 1995; Member of Parliament, Upper Bann; b. 15.10.44; m., Daphne Elizabeth Orr; 2s.; 2d. Educ. Bangor Grammar School; Queen's University, Belfast. Barrister-at-Law, 1969; Lecturer, Law, Senior Lecturer, 1977; Head, Department, Commercial and Property Law, 1981 - 89; Vice-Chairman, Lagan Valley Unionist Association, 1983 - 85; Chairman, 1985 - 96; Hon. Secretary, Ulster Unionist Council, 1989 - 95; Founder Chairman, Ulster Society, 1985 - 90. Recreations: history; opera; reading. Address: (b.) Ulster Unionist Council, 429 Holywood Road, Belfast BT4 2LN. T.-02890 765500.

Trimble, Professor Elisabeth Ruth, CBE, MD, DCH, FRCP(Lond), FRCPath. Professor of Clinical Biochemistry and Metabolic Medicine, Queen's University, Belfast, since 1987; Consultant, Royal Group of Hospitals Trust, since 1987; b. 30.1.44, Kilkeel, Co Down. Educ. Kilkeel High School; Queen's University, Belfast. Vocational training in endocrinology/medicine, Belfast; Research Associate, Institut de Biochimie Clinique, University of Geneva, 1976-87, and Consultant Physician, Hopital Cantonal, Geneva, 1981-87. Recreations: art; reading. Address: (b.) Department of Clinical Biochemistry and Metabolic Medicine, Institute of Clinical Science, Royal Victoria Hospital, Grosvenor Road, Belfast BT12 6BA; T.-02890 263108.

Trinder, Charlotte, BA (Hons). Area Appeals Manager for NI with Arthritis Research Campaign, since 2001; b. 29.9.73, Oxford. Educ. Carrickfergus Grammar School; University of Luton. Spent last 6 years in the field of fundraising; NICOD, 1998-2000, then Marie Curie, NI Chest, Heart and Stroke Association, NSPCC; Concern Worldwide, 2000-2001. Vice-Chair of The Institute of Fundraising NI Committee. Recreations: swimming; keeping fit; cinema. Address: (h) 10 Abetta Parade, Belfast BT5 5EH. T.-028 90461529.

Trouton, Ronnie George, MBE, CertEd. President, Road Safety Council of Northern Ireland, 1997-2000; President, Association of Northern Ireland Car Clubs; b. 27.8.37, Portadown, Co Armagh; m., Fredé; 1s. Educ. Royal School, Dungannon; Stranmillis College of Education. Teacher, Armagh Technical College and Headmaster, Cabra Primary School, 1960 - 70; Senior Road Safety Education Officer, Southern Education Area, 1971 - 78; Chief Road Safety Education Officer for Northern Ireland, 1978 - 92. Early retirement, 1992. Member, Sports Council, Northern Ireland, 1994-2003; Non Executive Director, Royal Automobile Club Motor Sports Association, since 1996. Advanced Driving Instructor; Advanced Motorcycle Examiner. Recreations: motor sport; reading; walking; red wine. Address: (h.) 'Beaghmore', Cranagill, 27 Address Road, Portadown, Co Armagh, BT62 1SE; T.-028-38 851407.

Tumelty, Rev. Brian, BSc (Hons), PG Dip Schol Phil, BD, HDip Pas Stud. Catholic Curate, St Colmcille's Parish, Belfast, 1996-99; Larne parish, since 1999; b. 22.3.70, Lusaka. Educ. St Mary's Christian Brothers Grammar School, Belfast; Queen's University, Belfast; St Patrick's College, Maynooth. Ordained Deacon, Maynooth College, 1995; Ordained, Priest, St Brigid's Church, Belfast, 1996. Address: (h.) Larne Presbytery, 51 Victoria Road, Larne BT40 1LY. T.-028 2827 3053. e-mail: brian.tumelty@dnet.co.uk

Turkington, Trevor, OBE. Executive Director, Turkington Holdings Limited, since 1986; b. 3.10.54, Portadown; m., Mavis; 3s. Educ. Clounagh Junior High School; Portadown Technical College. Member: Institute of Directors; Upper Bann Institute. OBE, 1989. Recreations: interest in motor sports. Address: (b.) Turkington Holdings Limited, James Park, Mahon Road, Portadown, Co Armagh; T.- 02838 332807.

Turkington, William Andrew, MA, BA, PGCE, Adv Dip Ed. Headmaster, City of Armagh High School, since 2002; b. 8.7.51, Moira; m., Jennifer; 2d. Educ. Lurgan College; Queen's University, Belfast; Open University. History Teacher, Lisnagarvey High School, Lisburn, 1973 - 86; Field Officer, South Eastern Education and Library Board, 1986 - 90; Vice Principal, Markethill High School, 1990 - 94; Headmaster, Rathfriland High School, 1994-2002. Recreations: reading; sport. Address: (b.) City of Armagh High School, Alexander Road, Armagh BT61 7JH. T.-028 37522278.
e-mail: info@armaghhigh.armagh.ni.sch.uk

V

Vance, Hugh Thomas, NCTJ Dip. Editor: Larne Times, since 1974, Carrick Times, since 1974, Newtownabbey Times, since 1974; b. 9.11.50, Carrickfergus; m., Claire; 2 d. Educ. Belfast Royal Academy; Belfast College of Business Studies. Recreations: outdoors; photography;   music; computers; MP watching. Address: (b.) 8 Dunluce Street, Larne, Co. Antrim BT40 1JG. T.-028 28272303.

Vance, Lynda. Chief Executive, North Down Development Organisation Ltd since 1988; b. 31.10.50, Belfast; 1s.; 1d. Educ.   Bangor Technical College. Superintendent of Typists, Industrial Development Board, 1968 - 77. Recreations: theatre; reading.   Address: (b.) Enterprise House, 2-4 Balloo Avenue, Bangor, Co Down; T.-028 91 271525.
e-mail: lynne@nddo.co.uk

W

Walker, Dr. Graham Sinclair, MA, MA, PhD. Reader in Politics, Queen's University Belfast; b. 2.6.56, Glasgow; m., Elpida Nikolou. Educ. Hutchesons' Grammar School, Glasgow; University of Glasgow. History Lecturer: University of Bristol, 1986 - 87; Birkbeck College, University of London, 1987 - 89; University of Sussex, 1989 - 91; Lecturer in Politics, Queen's University Belfast since 1991. Publications: The Politics of Frustration: Harry Midgley and the Failure of Labour in Northern Ireland, 1985; Thomas Johnston, 1988; Intimate Strangers, Political and Cultural Interaction between Scotland and Ulster, 1995. Recreations: watching football of any kind, anywhere. Address: (b.) Department of Politics, Queen's University Belfast, Belfast, BT7 1PA; T.- 02890-245133.

Walker, Dr. Norman Jan Piet. OBE, JP, MB, BCh, BAO, MRCGP, MICGP. Principal in general practice since 1977; b. 15.3.48, Coleraine; m., Esme Sarah; 4 s. Educ. Coleraine Academical Institution; Queen's University Belfast. Junior House Officer, Ulster Hospital, Dundonald, 1972 - 73; Senior House Officer, Cardiology and Radiology, Royal Victoria Hospital, Belfast, 1973 - 74; Registrar, Radiology, Royal Victoria Hospital, Belfast, 1974 - 76; Senior House Officer, Obstetrics and Gynaecology, Royal Victoria Hospital, Belfast, 1976 - 77. Member, Royal College, General Practitioners, 1980; Member, Irish College of General Practitioners, 1988. Territorial Decoration, 1984; Officer Brother, Order of St John, 1980; OBE, 1989; Justice of the Peace since 1989; Chairman, The Association of JPs in NI, since 2001, Lay Panel Member. Recreations: walking; sailing; gardening. Address: (b.) Salisbury Medical Centre, 474 Antrim Road, Belfast, BT15 5GF; T.- 028 90 777905.

Wallace, Prof. William F. M., BSc, MD, FRCP, FRCA, FCARCSI, FRCSEd. Professor Emeritus; currently working part-time; Prof. of Applied Physiology, Queen's University Belfast, 1978-2001; Consultant Physiologist, 1969-2001; b. 5.7.36, Newry; m., Eleanor Bailey McComb; 3d. Educ. Newry Grammar School; Queen's University, Belfast. Department of Therapeutics, Queen's University, Belfast/Royal Victoria Hospital/Belfast City Hospital, 1961 - 66; Research Fellow, 1966; Senior Lecturer, 1969; formerly, Assistant Dean, Faculty of Medicine, Queen's University, Belfast; specialist assessor, Quality Assurance Agency for Higher Education. Currently Examiner, Royal College of Surgeons, Edinburgh, Dublin; Elected Fellow, Royal College of Anaesthetists, London; Honorary Fellow, College of Anaesthetists, Royal College of Surgeons in Ireland; Fellow ad hominem, Royal College of Surgeons, Edinburgh. Recreations: gardening; cycling. Address: (b.) Medical Biology Centre, 97 Lisburn Road, Belfast, BT9 7BL; T.- 02890-335796. e-mail: w.wallace@qub.ac.uk

Walmsley, Professor David George, BSc, MSc, PhD, DSc, FInstP, CPhys, MRIA, PPhys. Professor of Physics, Queen's University Belfast, since 1988; b. 3.2.38, Newtownstewart; m., Margaret Heather Edmonstone; 2s. Educ. Royal School, Armagh; Queen's University, Belfast; McMaster University, Hamilton, Ontario, Canada. Lecturer, Physics, McMaster University; Scientific Officer/Senior Scientific Officer, AERE, Harwell; Lecturer, Physics, New University of Ulster; Professor of Physics, University of Ulster; Queen's University Belfast: Director, School of Mathematics and Physics, 1993-98, Dean, Faculty of Science and Agriculture, 1998-2002. Visiting Professor at Iowa State University, University of Paris and Autonomous University of Madrid. Chairman, Northern Ireland Regional Medical Physics Agency; Fellow of the American Physical Society; Professional Physicist of the Canadian Association of Physicists. Publications: numerous on electron tunnelling and superconductivity in learned journals. Recreations: watching successive Secretaries of State for Education. Address: (b.) Department of Pure and Applied Physics, Queen's University Belfast, Belfast, BT7 1NN; T.- 028 90 273531.

Walsh, Most Rev. Bishop Patrick Joseph, MA, MA (Cantab), STL. Bishop of Down and Connor since 1991; b. 9.4.31, Cobh, Co Cork, Ireland. Educ. St Mary's Christian Brothers Grammar School, Belfast; Queen's University, Belfast; Cambridge University; Pontifical Lateran University, Rome. Teacher, St MacNissi's College, Garron Tower, 1958 - 64; Chaplain, Queen's University, Belfast, 1964 - 70; President, St Malachy's College, Belfast, 1970- 83; Auxiliary Bishop of Down and Connor, 1983 - 91. Recreations: walking; music; theatre. Address: (h.) Lisbreen, 73 Somerton Road, Belfast, BT15 4DE; T.- 028 9077 6185.

Walters, Ian, BSc, FIMechE, MIGasE, AMIEE, MIMgt. Chief Executive: Action Mental Health, since 2002, Training and Employment Agency, 1995-2002; b. 20.3.43, Stoke-on-Trent, m., Carol; 2s.; 1d. Educ. Moseley Hall Grammar School, Cheadle, Cheshire; University of Manchester. Positions rising to factory manager, Parkinson Cowan Measurement; Deputy Principal/Principal positions, Department of Commerce; Director/Senior Director, Industrial Development Board, North America, New York; Executive Director, International Representation Division/International Marketing Division/Food Division, Industrial Development Board; Senior Executive Director, Corporate Services Group, Industrial Development Board; Acting Deputy Chief Executive, Corporate Services Group, Industrial Development Board; Director, Training and Employment Agency, Business Support Division. Hon. Doctor of Public Services, Rocky Mountain College, Montana, USA, 1999.

Chairman, Board of Governors, Groomsport Primary School; Member of Governing Body, Belfast Institute of Further and Higher Education, 2002. Recreations: photography; swimming; gardening. Address: (b.) Action Mental Health, Mourne House, Knockbracken Health Care Park, Saintfield Road, Belfast BT8 8BH.
e-mail: ian.walters@actionmentalhealth.org.uk

Ward, Barbara Anne, BA (Hons), PGCE, MSc Ed Mgt. Principal, Cross and Passion College, since 1999; b. 25.10.55, Belfast; m., Hugh P. Ward; 3 d. Educ. St. Dominic's High School; Queen's University; University of Ulster. Teacher of Geography: St. Louis Grammar School, Ballymena, 1979-82, Dominican College Belfast, 1983-97; Principal, St. Mary's College, Portglenone, 1997-99. Winner of Geographical Association Silver Award for contribution to Geographical Education, 1996. Recreation: choral music. Address: (b.) 10, Moyle Road, Ballycastle BT54 6LA. T.-028 20762473.

Ward, Cecil, CBE, JP, MA (Hons). Retired, formerly Town Clerk of Belfast; b. 26.10.29, Belfast. Technical High School; College of Technology, Belfast. Belfast Corporation: Clerk, 1947 - 60; Committee Clerk, 1960 - 73; Belfast City Council: Chief Clerk, 1973 - 77; Assistant Town Clerk, 1977 - 79; Town Clerk and Chief Executive, 1979 - 89; Retired, 1989. Member: Board, Ulster Orchestra, 1981 - 94 (Chairman, 1990 - 94); Executive Council, Society of Local Authority Chief Executives, 1980 - 89; Arts Council of Northern Ireland, 1980 - 85, 1987 - 89; Board of Trustees, Ulster Museum, 1989 - 95; Senate, Queen's University, Belfast, 1990-2001; Board, Mater Hospital Trust, 1994-2002; Grand Opera House, Belfast, 1987 - 97 and 1998-99. Recreations: music; walking. Address: (h.) 24 Thornhill, Malone, Belfast, BT9 6SS; T.- 01232-668950.

Ward, Dr. Patrick Joshua, MBE, LRCPI, LRCSI, MRCGP, DPH, AFOM, JP, DL. Occupational Health Physician; Medical Advisor, Norbrook Laboratories, Newry; b. Dublin; m., Wendy Patricia Marsh; 2s.; 1d. Educ. Royal School, Armagh; Royal College of Surgeons (Ireland); Queen's University, Belfast; Royal College of Physicians (London). Assistant Medical Officer of Health, Belfast, 1956 - 58; general medical practice, 1959 - 95; Staff Medical Officer and Occupational Physician, Daisy Hill Hospital, Newry, 1963 - 96. Hon. Secretary, Southern Local Medical Committee, 1975 - 91 (Chairman, 1991 - 95); Member, Northern Ireland General Medical Services Committee, 1971 - 95 (Treasurer, 1981 - 95); Fellow, British Medical Association since 1996; Fellow, Ulster Medical Society, 1969; Fellow, Royal Academy of Medicine of Ireland, 1970; Fellow BMA, 1996; Chairman, British Medical Association (Southern Area), 1972, 1973, 1992 and 1993; Dep. Lt. Co Armagh, 1985. Editor, Ulster Doctor, 1993 - 96. Publications: several clinical trial reports in Ulster Medical Journal and Journal of Irish Medical Science. Recreations: fishing; golf; "the sport of kings"; medical politics. Address: (h.) Broomhill, Goragh Road, Newry, BT35 6PZ;

Wardlow, Michael Thomas, BD, MTh, FCII, FIPD. Chief Executive Officer, Northern Ireland Council for Integrated Education since 1995; b. 19.11.53, Belfast; m., Karen; 2s. Educ. Annadale Grammar School (now Wellington College); Queen's University, Belfast. Worked in commerce; worked with the Ugandan church in leadership training, youth work and famine relief, 1979 - 81; worked for voluntary organisation working with young people from the 32 counties of Ireland promoting opportunities for work abroad, 1981 - 88; Director of Training, National Council of YMCAs in Ireland, 1988 - 91; Project Director, Eastern and Central Europe, European Alliance of YMCAs, 1991 - 94; Consultant for voluntary organisations developing leadership training programmes, 1994 - 95. Fellow, Institute of Personnel and Development; Fellow (by examination), Chartered Insurance Institute. Involved with voluntary work including sitting on boards of non-governmental organisations. Speaker at national and international youth events; regular broadcaster and contributor to television and radio; written many articles for journals. Recreations: photography; walking; youth work; church activities. Address: (b.) Northern Ireland Council for Integrated Education, 44 University Street, Belfast BT7 1HB. T.-02890 236200.

Warke, Frederick John, BA, MSc, FRTPI. Chief Commissioner, Planning Appeals Commission since 1999; b. 9.10.45; m., Margaret Rosemary; 1s.; 1d. Educ. Limavady Grammar School; Queen's University, Belfast. Planning Assistant, Londonderry County Council, 1969 - 71; Planning Officer, Craigavon Development Commission, 1971 - 73; Planning Officer, Ministry of Development, 1973 - 76; Member, Planning Appeals Commission since 1976; Member, Water Appeals Commission since 1985. Occasional Lecturer on planning at Queen's University, Belfast and University of Ulster. Former Member, Editorial Board, The Property Journal; Former Committee Member, Environmental and Planning Law Association for Northern Ireland. Articles on planning published in local professional journals; regular speaker at local planning conferences and seminars. Recreations: gardening; reading; cricket. Address: (b.) Planning Appeals Commission, Park House, 87-91 Great Victoria Street, Belfast, BT2 7AG.
e mail: info@pacni.gov.uk

Warner, Dr. Julian Charles, BA, MA, MA (Lib), DPhil, FIInFSC. Lecturer, Queen's School of Management and Economics, since 1984; b. 4.3.55, London. Educ. St Albans School; University of Newcastle-upon-Tyne; Oxford University; University of Sheffield. Research Assistant, United Glass, 1973 - 74; Library Trainee, University of York, 1982 - 83. Visiting

Scholar, University of California at Berkeley, 1991 - 92, University of Illinois, 2000. Has held offices in Institute of Information Science, American Society for Information Scientists and Technology. Publications: From Writing to Computers, 1994; Information, Knowledge, Text, 2001; Humanizing Information Technology, 2004; articles in information science journals. Recreations: cycling; cinema; reading. Address: (b.) School of Management and Economics, Queen's University, Belfast, Belfast, BT7 1NN; T.-028 9027 3243.

Watson, Denis. Member (Upper Bann), United Unionist Assembly Party, Northern Ireland Assembly, 1998-2003. Financial consultant. Address: (b.) Parliament Buildings, Stormont, Belfast, BT4 3ST.

Watson, Prof. John David, BA, MB, BAO, LM, DRCOG, Dip Soc Med, FRCP, FFCM, FFPHM, MFPHM(I). Director of Public Health, Northern Health and Social Services Board since 1989; Visiting Professor of Public Health, University of Ulster, since 2000; b. 7.2.46, Belfast; m., Joyce Deirdre Alley; 2s.; 1d. Educ. The Academy, Omagh; Trinity College, Dublin; University of Edinburgh. Junior medical posts: Adelaide Hospital; Rotunda Hospital, Dublin; Eastern Health and Social Services Board; Edinburgh University; Queen's University, Belfast; Consultant, Eastern Health and Social Services Board. 1977 - 81; Chief Administrative Medical Officer, Northern Health and Social Services Board, 1981 - 89. Board Member, Faculty of Public Health Medicine, London; Chairman, Audit Committee, Northern Ireland Postgraduate Council, Medical and Dental Education. Publications: various learned papers. Recreations: sailing; reading; country pursuits; farming. Address: (b.) Northern Health and Social Services Board, County Hall, 182 Galgorm Road, Ballymena, Country Antrim, BT42 1QB; T.- 028 25662208. e-mail: john.watson@nhssb.n-i.nhs.uk

Watson, Tom (Thomas), BA. Secretary, Ulster Automobile Club Ltd since 1995; b. 30.1.55, Belfast; m., Heather McGreevy; 1s.; 2d. Educ. Royal Belfast Academical Institution; Stranmillis College, Belfast. Joined Ulster Automobile Club, 1977. Recreations: running; listening to popular music; football. Address: (b.) UAC Ltd, 29 Shore Road, Holywood, BT18 9HX; T.- 028 9042 6262; Fax: 028 9042 1818.
e-mail: office@ulsterac.dircon.co.uk

Watson, William Gardiner, BEd, Dip Ed, Cert Ed, DASE, FInstD. Chairman, Lisburn District Police Partnership Board; Director, Lisburn Enterprise Organisation Ltd; Chairman, Lisburn City Ecomomic Development Comm.; Chairman, Knocklofty Associates; Partner, G. & L. Developments; Councillor, Lisburn City Council, since 1977; Past President, Association of Northern Ireland Education and Library Boards; Member, Northern Ireland Education Forum; Governor, Lisburn Institute of Further and Higher

Education; Chairman of Governors, Laurelhill Community College; Governor of Armagh Observatory and Planetarium; b. 23.5.33, Lisburn; m., Doreen. Educ. Wallace High School, Lisburn; Queen's University, Belfast; Stranmillis College. Head, Science, Larkfield Secondary School, 1958 - 69; Director, Belfast Co-operative Society Ltd, 1976 - 83; Financial Director, Securafile and Company Ltd, 1981 - 85; Vice-Principal, Crumlin High School, 1969- 87; Development Officer, Northern Ireland Small Business Institute, 1987 - 88; Director, Hamwell Plc, 1989 - 97; Member, Youth Council for Northern Ireland, 1990 - 96; Member of Council, University of Ulster, 1996- 2000; Chairman, Travelcare (UK), 1996-2000; Director, Northern Ireland Museums Council, 1996-2001; Trustee, National Museums and Galleries of Northern Ireland. 1998-2002; Chairman, South Eastern Education and Library Board, 1999-2002; President, Lisburn Chamber of Commerce, 1987 - 88; Member, Sports Council for Northern Ireland, 1983 - 85. Recreations: golf; gardening. Address: (h.) Rosguil, 169 Ballynahinch Road, Lisburn, BT27 5LP; T.- 028 9266 3099.

Watterson, Maurice, MRICS. Director of Building Control Services, Ballymena Borough Council; b. 21.11.47, Ballymena; m., Martha Anne Watterson; 1s.; 1d. Educ. Ballymena Technical College; Jordanstown Polytechnic. Address: (b.) Ardeevin, 80 Galgorm Road, Ballymena, Co Antrim, BT42 1AB; T.- 028 25660410.

Waugh, Eric L, MA. Writer and Broadcaster; b. 1.7.29, Londonderry; m., Mattie McKane; 2d. Educ. Methodist College, Belfast; Trinity College, Dublin. Visiting Fellow in American History: Northwestern University, Illinois, USA, 1953; University of Chicago, USA, 1954; Radio Producer/Presenter Foreign News Features, Station WNMP, Chicago, 1954; Staff Writer, Belfast Telegraph/Commentator, BBC General Overseas service, 1955 - 62; BBC Industrial and Political Staff, 1962 - 87; freelance writer and broadcaster since 1988. Writer and presenter of numerous documentaries for BBC radio and television including, Living in Europe; Squaring the Triangle; radio biographies. Contributor to journals at home and abroad. Recreations: last month's newspapers; music. Address: (b.) Belfast Telegraph, 124-144 Royal Avenue, Belfast, BT1 1EB.

Weir, Brian, BA, DipBusAdmin. Local Government Officer, The Southern Education and Library Board, since 1968, Education Officer, since 1979; b. 1.3.46, Tobermore; m., Daphne Hempsall; 1 s.; 1 d. Educ. Rainey Endowed School, Magherafelt; The Queen's University of Belfast. Employed continuously in the local education authority in Armagh: Administrative Assistant, County of Armagh Education Committee, 1968-73; Professional Assistant, The Southern Education and Library Board, 1973-79. Board Member, Baptist Missions; Scorer, Armagh

Cricket Club; formerly Chairman, Baptist Missions (Ireland); Member, Armagh Baptist Church. Publications: Armagh City Football Club 1964-1989, 1989; Armagh Baptist Church: A History of God's Grace, 2003; numerous articles for magazines and newspapers. Recreations: collecting football programmes; watching Armagh City FC. Address: (h.) 30 Linsey's Hill, Armagh BT61 9HD. T.-3752 3378.
e-mail: b.weir@btinternet.com

Weir, Peter James, LLB, Cert Prof Legal Studies, MSSc. Barrister-at-Law. Member: NI Assembly, since 1998, Finance and Personnel Committee, since 1999, (North Down), Ulster Unionist Party, Northern Ireland Assembly, since 1998; b. 21.11.68. Educ. Bangor Grammar School; Queen's University, Belfast. Called to the Bar of Northern Ireland, 1992; Lecturer, Administrative and Constitutional Law. Member Ulster Unionist Party since 1987; Former Chairman, Queen's Ulster Unionists and Young Unionists; Member, Northern Ireland Forum since 1996; Member, Ulster Unionist Talks Team, 1996 - 98; Vice-Chairman, Forum's Education Committee, 1997 - 98; Member, Senate, Queen's University, Belfast, 1990 - 91 and since 1997; Member, Council for Legal Education since 1997. Publications: The Anglo-Irish Agreement – Three Years On (joint author); Unionism, The National Parties and Ulster; numerous articles. Recreations: cricket; football; snooker; music; reading. Address: (b.) Bar Library, Royal Courts of Justice, Chichester Street, Belfast, BT1 3JP; T.- 02890-662328.

Welch, Professor Robert Anthony, BA, MA, HDE, PhD. Professor of English Literature since 1984; Director, Centre for Irish Literature and Bibliography, University of Ulster since 1994; Dean, Faculty of Arts, since 2000; b. 25.11.47, Cork; m., Angela O'Riordan; 3s.; 1d. Educ. Coláiste Chríost Ri, Cork (by scholarship); University College, Cork (by scholarship); University of Leeds. Lecturer, School of English, University of Leeds, 1971 - 73; Lecturer, English, University of Ife, Nigeria, 1973 - 74; Lecturer, English, University of Leeds, 1974 - 84; Professor and Head of Department, University of Ulster, Coleraine, 1984 - 94; Dean, Faculty of Arts, since 2000. Publications: Irish Poetry from Moore to Yeats, 1980; A History of Verse Translation from the Irish, 1988; The Kilcolman Notebook (novel), 1992; Changing States, 1993; Muskerry (poems), 1993; Oxford Companion to Irish Literature, 1996; Tearmann (novel), 1997; Secret Societies (poems), 1997; Groundwork (novel), 1997; The Abbey Theatre 1899 - 1999, 1999; The Blue Formica Table (poems), 1999; The Kings Are Out (novel), 2003; The Evergreen Road (poems), 2004. Recreations: walking; gardening. Address: (b.) Faculty of Arts, University of Ulster, Cromore Road, Coleraine, BT52 1SA; T.- 028 7032 4517.

Wells, Andrew Edward, LLB, FCIArb. District Judge since 1996; b. 20.6.50, Co Monaghan, Ireland; m., Mary Elizabeth; 1s.; 1d. Educ.

Queen's University, Belfast. Solicitor, 1977 - 95; Judicial Studies Board, 1997-2003; Civil Justice Reform Group, 2001. Recreations: rowing; lunches. Address: (b.) Laganside Courts, 45 Oxford Street, Belfast BT1 3LL. T.-028 9072 4566.

Wells, James Henry, BA (Hons), DipTCP. Member (South Down), Democratic Unionist Party, Northern Ireland Assembly, since 1998; b. 27.4.57, Lurgan; m., Grace; 1 s.; 2 d. Educ. Lurgan College; Queen's University, Belfast. Assembly Member for South Down, 1982-86; Down District Council, 1981-85; Banbridge District Council, 1985-88; Assistant Regional Public Affairs Manager, National Trust, 1989-98. Recreations: hill-walking; wildlife conservation. Address: (b.) 2 Belfast Road, Ballynahinch BT24 7AP; T.-028-97-564200.

Wheeler, George Bomfforde, B Comm, LLB, MA. Retired District Judge; b. 8.4.32, Dublin; m., Rosalind Evangeline Merrick Dickson; 3s.; 1d. Educ. Mountjoy School, Dublin; Trinity College, Dublin. Administrative Officer, Southern Rhodesia Ministry of Native Affairs, 1957 - 62; Assistant Native Commissioner, Selukwe, 1962; Acting Assistant Magistrate, Salisbury, Southern Rhodesia, 1962 - 63; Magistrate, Salisbury, 1964; enrolled as Solicitor, Northern Ireland, 1968; Partner, J Murland and Co, Solicitors, 1968 - 79. Selected for Irish Universities hockey team 1954; selected Irish Universities Association football team, 1953 and 1954; Hon. Secretary, Dublin University Central Athletic Committee, 1954 - 55 and 1955 - 56, Commodore Quoile Yacht Club, 1988. Recreations: sailing; gardening; forestry; walking; travelling.

Wheeler, General Sir Roger (Neil), GCB, CBE, MA. Constable, HM Tower of London, since 2001; Chief of the General Staff, 1997-2000; b. 16.12.41; m., Felicity Hares; 3s.; 1d. (pr. m.). Educ. All Hallows School, Devon; Hertford College, Oxford. Early Army service in Borneo and Middle East, 1964 - 70; Bde Major, Cyprus Emergency, 1974; Member, Lord Carver's Staff, Rhodesia Talks, 1977; Battalion Commander, Belize, Gibraltar, Berlin and Canada, 1979 - 82; Chief of Staff, Falkland Islands, 1982; Bde Commander, BAOR, 1985 - 86; Director, Army Plans, 1987 - 89; Commander 1st Armoured Division, BAOR, 1989 - 90; ACGS, Ministry of Defence, 1990 - 92; GOC and Director of Military Operations, Northern Ireland, 1993 - 96; CinC, Land Command, 1996 - 97. Colonel, The Royal Irish Regiment, 1996-2001; Hon. Fellow, Hertford College, Oxford; Liveryman of the Worshipful Company of Painter-Stainers Company; Hon Col. Queen's University OTC; Hon. Col. Oxford University OTC; Hon. Col. London Irish Rifles; Chairman, Tank Museum, Bovington; President, Combat Stress. Recreations: fly fishing; cricket; shooting; ornithology.

Whitaker, Prof. M. Andrew B., MA, PhD, FIMA, CMath, FInstP CPhys. Professor in Physics, Queen's University, Belfast; b. 29.1.46, London; m., Joan Whitaker; 2s. Educ. Portsmouth Grammar School; Oxford University; Nottingham University. Lecturer/Senior Lecturer, Physics, New University of Ulster/University of Ulster, 1970 - 88; Senior Lecturer/Reader/Professor in Physics, Queen's University, Belfast since 1988; Sometime Visiting Scientist, Guildford; Madrid; Bangalore; Haifa. Publications: Einstein, Bohr and the Quantum Dilemma, 1996; Physicists of Ireland (co-editor), 2002. Recreation: walking. Address: (b.) Department of Physics, Queen's University, Belfast, BT7 1NN; T.- 01232-273576.

White, Brian, B Ed, MA. Principal, St Malachy's Primary School since 1989; b. 19.8.50, Belfast; m., Mary T Herdman; 4s.; 1d. Educ. Hardings Street Christian Brothers School; St Joseph's College of Education; Queen's University, Belfast; New University of Ulster. Teacher, St Patrick's Boys' Primary School, 1973 - 89. Address: (b.) St Malachy's Primary School, Eliza Street, Belfast, BT7 2BJ.

White, Rowan McMurray, MA (Cantab). Partner, Arthur Cox NI Solicitors since 1996; b. 9.4.53, Belfast; m., Pamela Joan Mack; 2s.; 1d. Educ. Campbell College, Belfast; Pembroke College, Cambridge. Admitted as solicitor, Northern Ireland, 1977; Partner, Norman Wilson and Co., Solicitors, 1985 (merged with Arthur Cox, 1996). Past Chairman, Belfast Solicitors Association. Recreations: cycling; family; reading; walking - but not necessarily in this order. Address: (b.) Arthur Cox NI, Stokes House, 17/25 College Square East, Belfast, BT1 6HD; T.-028 9023 0007.

Whitehead, Professor David, MA, PhD (Cantab), MRIA. Professor of Classics, Queen's University, Belfast since 1993; b. 9.10.49, Nottingham; m., 1. Mary Dainton (div.); 2d.; m., 2. Arlene Spiers (qv). Educ. Nottingham High School; Clare College, Cambridge. Research Fellow, Fitzwilliam Coll., Cambridge; Temporary Lecturer/Lecturer/Senior Lecturer/Reader in History, University of Manchester, 1975-92; Visiting Fellow, School of Historical Studies, Institute for Advanced Study, Princeton, New Jersey, USA; Visiting Fellow, Center for Hellenic Studies, Washington DC, USA; Co-Director, Copenhagen Polis Centre, 1993 - 97; Director, School of Greek Roman and Semitic Studies, Queen's University, Belfast, 1993 - 98; British Academy Research Reader, 1998 - 2000; Visiting Fellow, New College and All Souls College, Oxford. Editor, Clarendon Ancient History Series, Oxford University Press, since 1986; Senior Editor, Suda-On-Line Project (Kentucky), since 2001. Publications: The Ideology of the Athenian Metic, 1977; (with M. H. Crawford) Archaic and Classical Greece, 1983; The Demes of Attica, 1986; Aineias the Tactician, 1990; Hypereides: The Forensic Speeches, 2000; numerous articles and reviews. Recreations:

classical music; food and wine; cinema; horticulture. Address: (h.) The Mill House, 54 Upper Mealough Road, Purdysburn, Belfast, BT8 8LR; T.- 028 9081 2741.

Whitehouse, Prof. Harvey, BA (London), PhD (Cantab). Professor of Anthropology, Queen's University Belfast; b. 9.1.64, London; 1s. Educ. London School of Economics; Cambridge University. Research Fellow/Director of Studies in Archaeology and Anthropology, Trinity Hall, Cambridge, 1991 - 93. Publications: Inside the Cult: Religious Innovation and Transition in Papua New Guinea, 1995; Arguments and Icons: divergent modes of religiosity, 2000; The Debated Mind: evolutionary psychology versus ethnography, 2001. Address: (b.) School of Anthropological Studies, Queen's University Belfast, Belfast, BT7 1NN; T.- 02890-273706. e-mail: h.whitehouse@qub.ac.uk

Whittington, Prof. Dorothy Allan, MA. MEd, T Cert, AFBPsS, CPsychol. Professor of Health Psychology, University of Ulster since 1999; b. 14.12.41, Glasgow. Educ. Hutchesons' Girls' Grammar School; University of Glasgow. Infant School Teacher, Glasgow, 1962 - 67; Lecturer, Psychology, Callendar Park College, Falkirk, 1967 - 72; Ulster Polytechnic: Senior Lecturer, Education, 1972 - 73; Principal Lecturer, Psychology, 1973 - 81; Principal Lecturer, Communication, 1981 - 84; University of Ulster: Senior Lecturer, Psychology, 1984 - 94; Director, Centre for Health and Social Research, 1990 - 95; Head, School of Health Sciences, 1994 - 96; Director of Health Care Distance Learning, 1997-2002. Publications: 7 books and many other publications on quality assurance in health care, social skill and professional communication, patient satisfaction. Recreations: sailing; music. Address: (b.) Division of Public Health, Faculty of Life and Health Sciences, University of Ulster at Jordanstown, Shore Road, Newtownabbey, Co Antrim, BT37 0QB; T.- 028 90 366149.

Wichert, Sabine. Senior Lecturer, History, Queen's University, Belfast, since 1997; b. 8.6.42, Graudenz, Germany. Educ. Germany; London School of Economics; St Antony's College, Oxford. Lecturer, Modern History, Queen's University of Belfast, 1971 - 97. Past member, ACNI. Publications: Northern Ireland since 1945; several articles on Northern Ireland's history; Tin Drum Country (poems); Sharing Darwin (poems). Recreations: the arts; gardening; travel. Address: (b.) School of History, Queen's University, Belfast, Belfast, BT7 1NN; T.- 028-90 273431.

Wickstead, Professor Anthony William, MA (Cantab), PhD. Professor of Pure Mathematics, Queen's University, Belfast since 1992; b. 13.12.47, Plymouth. Educ. Devonport High School for Boys, Plymouth; St Catharine's College, Cambridge, Chelsea College, London. Lecturer, University of Ife, Nigeria, 1973 - 74; Temporary Assistant Lecturer, University College,

Cork, 1974 - 75; Queen's University, Belfast: Lecturer, 1975 - 85; Reader, 1985 - 89; Reader and Head, Pure Mathematics Teaching, 1989 - 92; Professor and Head, Pure Mathematics Research, 1992 - 95; Professor and Head, Pure Mathematics Teaching, 1998-2004. Recreations: cookery; wine making; coarse angling. Address: (b.) Department of Pure Mathematics, Queen's University, Belfast, BT7 1NN; T.- 028 9027 3673. e-mail: A. Wickstead@qub.ac.uk

Wilkinson, Alfred John, BSc, PhD, CEng, FIEE. Head of School of Electrical and Electronic Engineering, Queen's University Belfast, since 2000, Senior Lecturer, since 1979; b. 5.5.43, Randalstown; m., Gladys; 1 s.; 2 d. Educ. Randalstown Central PS; Ballymena Academy; Queen's University Belfast. Design Engineer, AEI Leicester, 1965-66; Engineering Assistant Lecturer, Electrical Engineering, Queen's University Belfast, 1966-70, Lecturer, 1970-79, Assistant Dean, Faculty of Engineering, 1987-90. Trustee and Treasurer for Eventide Home; Fellow of Institution of Electrical Engineers. Recreations: Bible study; Church activities; DIY. Address: (b.) School of Electrical and Electronic Engineering, Queen's University Belfast, Ashby Building, Stranmillis Road, Belfast BT9 5AH. T.-028 9027 4068. e-mail: aj.wilkinson@ee.qub.ac.uk

Wilkinson, Patricia Ellen, NCTJ qualifications. Presenter/Reporter/Producer, GMTV since 1995; b. Belfast; 1d. Educ. Bloomfield Collegiate Grammar School; College of Business Studies, Belfast. Freelance Writer/PR, 1982 - 84; Reporter, Newtownards Chronicle, 1984 - 85; Production/Current Affairs, Downtown Radio, 1985 - 88; News/Continuity, Ulster Television, 1988; Newscaster/Features Reporter, Cool FM/Downtown Radio; Freelance Writer/Broadcaster and partner in independent production company, Yellow Cactus Productions, 1994 - 98. Actress with many parts in films, plays and videos. National Radio Award, Best Regional Interview. Play, Bite Xmas, performed at the Lyric Theatre; films/shorts/videos produced. Publications: Annuals (novel). Recreations: writing; acting; music; the movies. Address: (b.) GMTV, 2nd Floor, Fanum House, 108 Great Victoria Street, Belfast, BT2 7BE; T.- 01232-234098/0421-598288..

Wilkinson, William John, MSc, BA, DASE, PCGE. Principal, Dromore High School since 1996; b. 21.3.53, Banbridge; m., Hazel Gamble; 1s.; 1d. Educ. Banbridge Academy; Queen's University, Belfast. Assistant Teacher, Ballynahinch, 1975 - 77; Dromore High School: Head of Department, 1977 - 83; Vice-Principal, 1983 - 93; Principal, Banbridge High School, 1993 - 96. Recreations: rugby; reading. Address: (b.) Dromore High School, 31 Banbridge Road, Dromore BT25 1ND.

Williams, Elizabeth (Betty) (Mrs J T Perkins). Working for peace since 1979; b. 22.5.43; m., 1,

Ralph Williams (m. diss.); 1s.; 1d. 2, James Perkins. Educ. St Dominic's Grammar School. Leader, NI Peace Movement, 1976 - 78. Hon. LLD, Yale University, 1977; Hon. HLD, College of Sienna Heights, Michigan, 1977; Nobel Prize for Peace (jointly with Mairead Corrigan Maguire, qv), 1976; Carl Von-Ossietsky-Medal for Courage, Berlin, 1976.

Williams, Prof. Ian David, BSc, PhD, FInstP. Professor of Physics, Queen's University, Belfast, since 1999 (Lecturer, 1985, Reader, 1996); b. 6.7.58, Bangor, Wales; m., Joanna; 3s.; 1d. Educ. Ysgol Dyffryn Nantlle; Queen's University, Belfast. Research Fellow, University of Sussex, 1983 - 84; NRC-NASA Research Associate, Jet Propulsion Laboratory, California Institute of Technology, Pasadena, California, USA, 1984 - 85. National Research Council (USA) Senior Research Associate, 1994. Publications: numerous in international scientific journals, in the field of atomic, molecular and optical physics. Recreations: spending time with family; reading; sailing. Address: (b.) Department of Physics, Queen's University, Belfast, Belfast BT7 1NN; T.-01232-273699.

Williams, Rev. Professor Stephen Nantlais, MA (Oxon), MA (Cantab), PhD (Yale). Professor of Systematic Theology, Union Theological College, Belfast, since 1994; b. 3.8.52, Cardiff; m., Susan Lecky Williams; 2s.; 1d. Educ. Ardwyn Grammar School, Aberystwyth; Queen's College, Oxford; Queen's College, Cambridge; Yale University. Professor of Theology, United Theological College, Aberystwyth, 1980 - 91; based at Whitefield Institute, Oxford, 1991 - 94. Address: (b.) Union Theological College, 108, Botanic Avenue, Belfast BT7 1JT; T.- 028 9020 5080.

Williamson, Janet Ann, MA (Oxon), NPQH. Principal, Antrim Grammar School, since 2001. Educ. Glenlola Collegiate, Bangor; Oxford University (Geography scholar). Senior Teacher and Head of Sixth Form, Aylesbury Grammar School, 1990-97; Deputy Head, Wilson's School, 1997-2001. Author with Oxford University Press. Recreations: travel; trekking; music. Address: (b.) Antrim Grammar School, Steeple Road, Antrim BT41 1AF.

Wilmont, Mary Bridget, CQSW. Director, Social Services, Northern Health and Social Services Board since 1994; b. Belfast; m., Colin; 2s.; 1d. Educ. Dominican College. Antrim County Welfare Committee: Social Worker, 1969 - 71; Senior Social Worker, 1971 - 73; Northern Health and Social Services Board: Assistant Principal Social Worker, 1973 - 74; Assistant Principal Social Worker, Training, 1979 - 90; Assistant Principal Social Worker, Loughside UOM, 1990 - 92; Assistant Director, Social Services, 1992 - 94. Chair, Dip. SW employment-based programme. Recreations: hill walking; music. Address: (b.) County Hall, Ballymena, BT42 1QB; T.-028 25 662218.

Wilson, Anne. Alliance Councillor, North Down Borough Council since 1995; Mayor of North Down, 2003-04; b. 13.2.47, Edinburgh; m., Brian Wilson (qv); 3s.; 1d. Educ. Leith Academy., Edinburgh; Dean College. Recreations: reading; charity work; family. Address: (h.) 1 Innisfayle Drive, Bangor, North Down, BT19 1DN; T.- 028 91455189. e-mail: councillorwilson@hotmail.com

Wilson, Councillor Brian Alfred Samuel, BA, MSc. Senior Lecturer, Economics, Belfast Institute of Further and Higher Education since 1979; Alderman, North Down Borough Council 1997-2001; b. 15.5.43, Belfast; m., Anne Wilson (qv.); 3s.; 1d. Educ. Bangor Grammar School; Open University; University of Strathclyde. Civil Servant, 1961 - 73; Lecturer, Omagh Technical College, 1976 - 79; Alliance Councillor, North Down Borough Council, 1981 - 97. Former Alliance Spokesman, Local Government, Housing and Health; Delegate, Atkins Talk, 1979 - 80; Mayor, North Down, 1993 - 94. Recreations: interested in all sport. Address: (h.) 1 Innisfayle Drive, Bangor, North Down, BT19 1DN; T.- 02891-455189. web: www.brianawilson.com

Wilson, Cedric. Member (Strangford), Northern Ireland Unionist Party, Northern Ireland Assembly, 1998-2003; Leader, Northern Ireland Unionist Party; m. Career: Castlereagh Borough Council: Councillor, 1981 - 89; Deputy Mayor; Mayor. Northern Ireland Forum, 1996-97; Chairman, Public Order Committee, Ballyhalbert and District Community Association. Address: (b.) Parliament Buildings, Stormont, Belfast, BT4 3XX; T.- 02890-521294; Fax: 02890-521293.

Wilson, Denis Henry, OBE, BSc, Dip Ed, JP. Administrative Secretary, Queen's University, Belfast, 1985-99; b. 25.10.39, Belfast; m, Betty; 2d. Educ. Methodist College, Belfast; Queen's University, Belfast. Assistant Master, Grosvenor High School, Belfast, 1962-66; Admin. Assistant/Admin. Officer/Senior Admin. Officer; Assistant Secretary/Senior Assistant Secretary, Queen's University, Belfast, 1966 - 85. Chairman, Mary Peters Track Committee; Deputy Chairman, Lloyds TSB Foundation for Northern Ireland; Governor, Wellington College, Belfast; Past President, Methodist College Old Boys' Association; Member, Belfast Rotary Club. Recreations: travel; walking. Address: (b.) c/o The Gatelodge, 73a Malone Road, Belfast BT9 6SB.

Wilson, Derek Geoffrey, BA, MSc. Principal, Drumglass High School since 1997; b. 24.8.42, Malawi; m., Elizabeth Agnes; 2d. Educ. Campbell College, Belfast; Stranmillis College. Teacher, Portadown College, 1968 - 84; Careers Adviser, Southern Education and Library Board, 1984 - 96. Recreations: golf; rugby (Ulster inter-provincial rugby, 1965 - 66); caravan. Address: (b.) Drumglass High School, Carland Road, Dungannon, Co Tyrone, BT71 4AA.

Wilson, James Elliott, OBE, JP, Commander Brother, O StJ. Lord-Lieutenant, County Borough of Belfast 1991-2000; b. 3.5.25, Belfast; m., Rosemary Clarke; 3d. Educ. Clifton College, Bristol. Royal Inniskilling Fusiliers, 1943 - 47; Ormeau Bakery, Belfast, 1948 - 80. Trustee, Belfast Savings Bank, 1974 - 82; Chairman, TSB Northern Ireland, 1974 - 82; Director, TSB Pension Trust, London, 1976 - 82; Director, TSB Trust Co, Andover, 1979 - 82; Deputy Chairman, TSB Central Board, London, 1979 - 82; retired as Director, TSB (NI), now First Trust Bank, 1996. Member, Management Committee, Northern Ireland Fever Hospital, 1968 - 73; Chairman, Association of Citizens' Advice Bureaux, Northern Ireland, 1985 - 88; Management Committee and Trustee, Somme Hospital, Belfast, now known as The Somme Nursing Home, 1965-2000; Management Committee, Glendhu Children's Hospital, 1971 - 85 (Chairman, 1981 - 85). OBE, 1978; Deputy Lieutenant, Belfast, 1982; Hon. Colonel, 40th Ulster Signal Regiment (V) 1982 - 90; JP since 1991. Recreations: golf; gardening; travel. Address: (h.) White Lodge, The Temple, Boardmills Lisburn, Co Antrim, BT27 6UQ; T.- 9263 8413.

Wilson, James Millar. Member (South Antrim), Ulster Unionist Party, Northern Ireland Assembly, since 1998; Deputy Speaker, Northern Ireland Assembly, since 2002; b. 15.12.41, Antrim; m., Muriel Roberta; Educ. Ballyclare High School; Belfast College of Technology. Engineer, Merchant Navy, 1961 - 65; Engineer, British Enkalon, 1965 - 73; Partner in retail business, 1972 - 88; Chief Whip, Ulster Unionist Assembly Party, 1998-2002; General Secretary, Ulster Unionist Party, 1987 - 98. Member, Ulster Unionist Council; Member, Party Executive Committee; Member, Newtownabbey Borough Council, 1975 - 88; Member, Northern Ireland Water Council. Recreations: angling; gardening. Address: (b.) 3a Rashee Road, Ballyclare, Co. Antrim BT39 9HJ. T.-028 9332 4461. e-mail: jim.wilson83@btopenworld.com web: www.jimwilsonuup.org.uk

Wilson, Prof. John, BEd, PhD, MIPR. Professor of Communication, University of Ulster, since 1995, Director of the Centre for English Language, 1992-2001; Director of the Institute for Ulster Scots, since 2001; b. 12.12.54, Belfast, NI; m., Linda Patricia; 2 d. Educ. Lisnasharragh; Ulster Polytechnic; Nottingham University; Queen's University Belfast. University of Ulster: Lecturer in Communications, 1982-92, Senior Lecturer and Head of School of Communications, 1992-95, Professor and Head of School of Psychology and Communications, 1995-2000, Dean, Faculty of Social and Health Sciences and Education. Founding Chairman, AFASCI. Recreation: golf. Address: (b.) School of Communication, University of Ulster, Co. Londonderry BT52 1SA. T.-028 90 366949.

Wilson, J W, QC (NI), MA, LLB. Master, Queen's Bench and Appeals, Supreme Court of Northern Ireland since 1993; Clerk of the Crown for Northern Ireland since 1993; Under Treasurer, Inn of Court of Northern Ireland since 1997; b. 4.9.33. Educ. Leys School; Magdalene College, Cambridge; Queen's University, Belfast. Called to the Bar of Northern Ireland, 1960; in practice, 1960 - 66; Private Secretary/Legal Secretary, Lord Chief Justice of Northern Ireland, 1966 - 80; Assistant Director, Northern Ireland Court Service, 1980 - 85; Master, High Court, Supreme Court, 1985 - 93. Address: (b.) Royal Courts of Justice, Chichester Street, Belfast, BT1 3JF.

Wilson, Martin Joseph, FCIBS, FIB, FCA. Group Chief Executive, Ulster Bank since 1998; b. 13.3.50, Dublin; m., Paulette; 1s.; 2d. Educ. Oatlands College, Mount Merrion, Dublin; University of Michigan. Fay McMahon Chartered Accountants, 1969 - 75; Senior Audit Manager, KPMG, 1975 - 78; Chief Accountant, Bell Lines Ltd, 1978 - 80; Financial Controller, UIB, 1980; Head of Treasury and Financial Control, UIB, 1984; Ulster Bank: Group Treasurer, 1989; Appointed to Board, 1991; Chief Executive, Ulster Bank Markets, 1995; Deputy Group Chief Executive, 1997. Recreations: golf; reading; music. Address: (b.) Ulster Bank Group Head Office, 11-16 Donegall Square East, Belfast BT1 5UB. T.-028-90-276000.

Wilson, Michael, LLB, Cert PLS, FSPI. Partner, Elliott Duffy Garrett Solicitors; b. 15.8.55, Belfast; m., Bronagh Carville; 2d. Educ. St Malachy's College, Belfast; Queen's University, Belfast. Admitted as Solicitor, 1978; former part-time Tutor, Institute of Professional Legal Studies, Belfast; former part-time Lecturer, Company Law, Belfast College of Business Studies. Fellow, Society of Practitioners of Insolvency, 1993; Member, Solicitors' Disciplinary Tribunal. Recreations: horse riding; golf; gardening. Address: (b.) Elliott Duffy Garrett, 7 Donegall Square East, Belfast, BT1 5HD; T.- 02890-245034.

Wilson, Patricia Doreen, BDS. Chief Dental Officer, Department of Health, Social Services & Public Safety, Northern Ireland, since 2000; b. 1947, Painswick, Glos. Educ. Edinburgh. General dental practitioner until joining NICS in 1995. Address: (b.) Castle Buildings, Belfast BT4 3SJ. T.-028 90 522940.
e-mail: doreen.wilson@dhsspsni.gov.uk

Wilson, Raymond James, LLB, MA. Partner in private law firm since 1986; b. 13.4.58, Larne; m., Jane; 1s.; 2d. Educ. Ballymena Academy; Queen's University, Belfast; City of London University. Lecturer, Law, City of London Polytechnic, 1982 - 86; In-house Counsel, Union Oil, 1986; Solicitor in private practice. Former Deputy Editor, Oil and Gas: Law and Taxation Review. Recreations: rugby; golf; reading. Address: (b.) Victoria House, 54-58 Chichester Street, Belfast, BT1 4HN; T.- 02890 323843.

Wilson, Robert W, OBE, JP, Dip DSc, FRAgS, FInstD, MGIM, MIBC. Retired; b. 22.3.24, Glenarm; m., Marie Reid; 4s.; 3d. Educ. Larne Grammar School; Queen's University, Belfast; University College, Cork. Dairy Manager, Fane Valley Co-op Agricultural and Dairy Society, 1951 - 71; General Manager, 1971 - 88; LEDU Counsellor/Advisor, SMES, 1990 - 97. Address: (h.) "Rozelle", 7 Dillon Heights, Armagh BT61 9HF. T.-028 3752 3320.

Wilson, Rosemary Helena, OBE, BA (Hons). Principal, Bloomfield Collegiate School, 1982 - 98; b. 14.7.39, Belfast. Educ. Ashleigh House School; Queen's University, Belfast. Assistant Teacher, Lowther College, North Wales, 1961 - 64; Assistant Teacher, Larne Grammar School, 1964 - 66; Head of Department, Ashleigh House School, 1966 - 73; Principal, Armagh Girls' High School, 1973 - 82. Retired 1998. Recreations: music; hill walking; reading. Address: (b.) Bloomfield Collegiate School; Astoria Gardens, Belfast, BT5 6HW; T.- 02890-471214.

Wilson, Sammy. Lord Mayor of Belfast, 2000/2001; Member (East Belfast), Democratic Unionist Party, Northern Ireland Assembly, since 1998. Teacher; elected to Belfast City Council, 1981; Lord Mayor, 1986-2000; Member, Northern Ireland Forum, 1996. Address: (b.) DUP Advice Centre, 13 Castlereagh Road, Belfast BT5 5FB. T.-028 9045 9500.

Wilson, Thomas Gordon, BA, DASE. Principal, Abbots Cross Primary School since 1979; b. 24.10.43, Portadown; m., E Louise Wilson; 2s.; 2d. Educ. Royal Belfast Academical Institution; Stranmillis College; University of London. VSO, Tanzania, East Africa, 1965 - 67; Teacher, King's Park Primary, Newtownabbey, 1967 - 75; Vice Principal, Whiteabbey Primary School, Newtownabbey, 1975 - 79. Methodist Local Preacher; Chairman, African Enterprise Ireland. Recreations: church activities; reading; swimming. Address: (b.) Abbots Cross Primary School, Doagh Road, Newtownabbey, BT37 9QW; T.-028 9086 4171.

Wilson, Thomas M., PhD, MA, MPhil, BA. Senior Lecturer in European Studies, Queen's University, Belfast, since 1998; b. 4.2.51, Brooklyn, New York; m., Dr Anahid Ordjanian-Wilson; 1 s. Educ. City University of New York. Publication: Borders – Frontiers of Identity, Nation and State (Co-author). Address: (b.) Institute of European Studies, Queen's University, Belfast BT7 1NN; T.-02890 335544.

Wilson, Trevor Hamilton, ACII, BD. Presbyterian Minister; b. Belfast; m., Elizabeth; 1d. Educ. Annadale Grammar School; Queen's University, Belfast; Assembly's College, Belfast. Insurance official, 1958 - 74; commenced assistantship, Megain Memorial Presbyterian Church, 1978; licensed, Bloomfield Presbyterian Church, 1980; Minister, Templepatrick

Presbyterian Church since 1981. Ordained Elder in Presbyterian Church, 1963; Member: North Eastern Education and Library Board, 1985-97, School Boards of Governors since 1985, General Assembly Education Board, 1985 - 97, General Assembly Home Board, 1989 - 98; Moderator, Templepatrick Presbytery, 1986 - 87; Captain, 24th Belfast Company, Boys' Brigade, 1963 - 77; President, Antrim and District Battalion, Boys' Brigade, 1989 - 92; Vice-President, Boys' Brigade in Ireland since 1988; National Vice-President, Boys' Brigade since 1996; Member, Curriculum Council for Examination and Assessment 1997-99. Associate of the Chartered Insurance Institute. Recreations: bowls; reading. Address: (h.) The Manse, 750 Antrim Road, Templepatrick, Co Antrim, BT39 0AP; T.-02894 432416.

Wolfenden-Orr, Eleanor Dorothy. Director of Antiques and Jewellery Business in Belfast, 1975-2003; similar business opened in Portrush, 1998; Auctioneer of Fine Quality Antiques, since 1975; b. 11.6.53, Ballymena; m., Sam Orr. Educ. Duneane Primary School; Ballymena Academy; Philippa Fawcett College, Streatham, London. Teacher training in London; opened up an auction room in Victoria Street, Belfast; continued in Lisburn Road, Belfast selling fine antiques and jewellery. Co-founder of "The Friends of Jessica" (charity). Recreations: reading; musicals; eating out. Address: (h.) 139 Church Road, Randalstown, Co. Antrim BT31 6JE. T.-07831 453038; 02870 822995.

Wolinski, Denis. Director for Northern Ireland, Ofcom. Address: (b.) Ofcom, Royston House, 34 Upper Queen Street, Belfast, BT1; T.- 02890-248733.

Wood, Michael Alexander, MBE, HonMSc. Chairman, Northern Health & Social Services Board, since 2000; b. 10.8.34, Brighton, Sussex; m., Grazyna; 2 s.; 1 d. Educ. Bangor Grammar; Sullivan Upper; University of Ulster. Royal Navy, 1952-64; Marketing Executive, Richardsons (Ulster) Ltd, 1964-71; Director/Chief Executive, Ulster Cancer Foundation, 1971-2000. Trustee/Director, NHS Confederation (UK), since 2003; Director, Action on Smoking and Health (UK), 1973-99; Chairman, International Union Against Cancer Anti-Tobacco Programme, 1991-98; World Health Organisation: Member and International Expert Panel on Smoking and Health, 1983-98, Consultant/Adviser on Tobacco Control. Recreations: travel; music; reading. Address: (h.) 5 Christine Avenue, Bangor BT20 4PF. T.-028 91 464817. e-mail: michael@mwood48.fsnet.co.uk

Woods, Brian, BA. PGEEM. Principal, Lead Hill Primary School since 1983; b. 28.7.47, Belfast; m., Patricia; 1s.; 1d. Educ. Annadale Grammar School; Stranmillis College; Open University; New University of Ulster. Assistant Teacher, Finiston Primary School, 1969 - 76; Vice-Principal, Edenbrook Primary School, 1976 - 82. Recreations: golf; rugby; reading; walking.

Address: (b.) Lead Hill Primary School, Casaeldona Park, Belfast, BT6 9RD; T.- 02890-401101.

Woods, Nigel Dermot, FRICS. Commissioner of Valuation and Chief Executive, Valuation and Lands Agency since 1998; b. 21.2.47, Bangor; m., Alison; 1s.; 2d. Educ. Bangor Grammar School; College of Estates Management. Joined Valuation and Lands Agency, 1967: Finance and Personnel Department; District Valuer, 1983; Assistant Commissioner, 1988. Recreations: golf; bridge. Address: (b.) Valuation and Lands Agency, Queen's Court, 56-66 Upper Queen Street, Belfast, BT1 6FD; T.- 02890-543923. e-mail: nigel.woods@dfpni.gov.uk

Woods, Dr. Roger Francis, BSc, PhD, CEng, SMIEE, FIEE. Senior Lecturer, School of Electrical and Electronic Engineering, Queen's University, Belfast since 1994; b. 21.8.63, New York, USA; m., Pauline Woods; 1s.; 3d. Educ. St Malachy's College, Belfast; Queen's University, Belfast. Holder of several patents, complex chips for image processing and digital TV. Chartered Engineer; Fellow, Institute of Electrical Engineers, Senior Member of Institute of Electrical and Electronic Engineers. Recreations: walking; swimming. Address: (b.) School of Electrical and Electronic Engineering, Queen's University, Belfast, Ashby Building, Stranmillis Road, Belfast BT9 5AH; T.-02890-274081. e-mail: r.woods@ee.qub.ac.uk

Woolley, Professor Tom, BArch, PhD, RSUA. Professor of Architecture, Queen's University, Belfast; b. 23.10.46, Stretford, England; m., Rachel Bevan; 3 d.; 1 s. Educ. University of Edinburgh. Environmental Officer, Glasgow; Lecturer, Architectural Association, London; Architect in private practice, London; Director of Housing Research Unit, University of Strathclyde; Head, School of Architecture, University of Humberside. Consultant on ecological design, straw bale building and community participation in architecture. Founder Member, Ecological Design Association and ACTAC, (Community Technical Aid Network); Chairman, Northern Ireland Building Regulations Advisory Committee. Publications: Rehumanising Housing; Green Building Handbook. Recreations: playing violin; gardening; building. Address: (b.) School of Architecture; Queen's University, Belfast, BT7 1NN; T.- 028 90 335466.

Wright, Christine Mary Arnott, DL, JP, NDD. b. 5.6.41, Market Harborough, England; m., 1, Bruce Rooken-Smith (m.diss.); 2d.; 2, Michael Wright (dec.); 1s.; 1d. Educ. Canterbury College of Art; Milliner, Madam Vernier, London, 1961 - 63; farmed Crossmaglen, 1969 - 79; opened The Kristyne Gallery, 1980; SSAFFA fund raising and caseworker since 1980. Member Banbridge Arts Committee since 1981 (Chairman, 1983 - 92); Member, Regional Board, Arts Council for Northern Ireland since 1984; Member, Conference

Committee for the Arts Council, 1985 - 88; Member Arts Council Association of Members since 1983; Member, Prince Philip Appeal for Commonwealth Veterans, 1985; National Year of the Blind Fundraising, 1991; Women Caring case worker and fund raiser since 1992; Board Member, ArtsCare since 1992; assisted with fundraising for Save the Children, Marie Curie Foundation and other charities; flower arranging at weddings and other functions; dress designing and teaching. Recreations: tennis; skiing; swimming; sewing; painting. Address: (h.) Gilford Castle, Gilford, Co Down, BT63 6DJ; T.- 01762 831866.

Wright, Kenneth S, BEd, DASE, MEd. Principal, Orritor Primary School, Cookstown; b. 25.3.61, Dungannon; m., Linda; 1s.; 1d. Educ. Royal School, Dungannon; Stranmillis College; Queen's University, Belfast. Principal, Queen Elizabeth (II) Primary School, Pomeroy, 1989 - 93. Recreations: sport; music. Address: (b.) Orritor Primary School, 249 Orritor Road, Cookstown Co Tyrone, T.-028 8675 1412.

Wylie, Thomas Michael, BA (Hons),   MSc. Financial Systems Manager, Queen's University Belfast; b. 18.4.60, Belfast. Educ. St Malachy's College, Belfast; University of Ulster. Prior to 1986 - Civil Service, 1986-95; Finance Officer, Royal Hospitals Trust, 1995-2000, Assistant Treasurer/Costing Manager. Recreations: hill walking; 5 a side soccer. Address: (h.) 66 Hydepark Manor, Newtownabbey.   T.-028 90841215.

Y

Yarnell, John William Gordon. Reader in Cardiovascular Epidemiology, Queen's University, Belfast, since 1993; Consultant, Health Promotion Agency of Northern Ireland, since 1993; b. 6.2.45, Folkestone; m., Gitanjali; 1 s.; 2 d. Educ. Dunstable Grammar School; Manchester University. Epidemiologist, Health Education Research Unit, Bristol, 1972-75; Member, Scientific Staff, MRC Epidemiology Unit (South Wales), 1975-93. Address: (b.) Department of Epidemiology and Public Health, Mulhouse Building, Grosvenor Road, Belfast BT12 6BJ; T.-028 90894614.

York, Professor Richard Anthony, BA, PhD. Professor of European Literature, University of Ulster; b. 8.1.41, Kettering, Northants; m., Rosemary Patricia Berridge. Educ. Kettering Grammar School; Emmanuel College, Cambridge; University College, London. Joined University of Ulster, 1969: Lecturer/Senior Lecturer/Professor. Publications: The Poem as Utterance, 1986; Strangers and Secrets, 1994; The Rule of Time, 1999; The Extension of Life, 2003. Recreations: music; cinema. Address: (b.) School of Languages and Literature, University of Ulster, Cromore Road, Coleraine, BT52 1SA; T.- 028 7032 4532.

Young, Prof. Ian Stuart, BSc, MD, FRCP, FRCPath, FRCPI. Professor, Medicine, Queen's University, Belfast, since 2001; Consultant Chemical Pathologist, Royal Group of Hospitals; b. 8.2.61, Belfast; m., Joanne Matthews; 1s.; 1d. Educ. Sullivan Upper School; Queen's University, Belfast. Training, Chemical Pathology, 1985 - 93; Senior Lecturer, Clinical Biochemistry, Queen's University, Belfast, 1993 - 99, Professor of Medical Biochemistry, 1999-2000. Publications: over 100 scientific papers and other publications. Recreations: books; fishing. Address: (b.) Department of Medicine, Mulhouse building, Royal Victoria Hospital, Belfast, BT12 6BJ; T.-02890-632743.

Young, John Andrew, LLB. Researcher (genetic material); b. 4.11.64, Belfast; m., Laura Naomi Taylor; 2 d. Educ. Gransha Boys' School; Southampton University. Taylor Joynson Garrett Solicitors, 1990 - 95. Recreations: alpaca breeding; farming; cross-country running; triathlons and skiing; Harley Davidson motorcycle touring; flying. Address: (h.) Ballyhenry House, 3 Loughshore Road, Portaferry, BT23 1PD; T.-01232-323864.

Young, Robin John Lawrence, National Union of Journalists, Society of Editors. Editor, Northern Constitution (Alpha Newspaper Group), since 2003; b. 8.2.53, Chester Castle (Army Barracks), England; m., Francesca Danila (nee Warner); 3 s.; 1 step d. Educ. Limavady Grammar School; Stamford School, Lincs; Warsash School of Navigation, Southampton University. Proof reader/copy holder, Peterborough Evening Telegraph, 1969-70; reporter: north-east Scotland, 1970-71, Oxford, south London, 1971-75; sub-editor, editor, Athens Daily Post, 1975-76; reporter, London, Folkestone Herald, 1977-82; sub-editor, Bristol Evening Post, 1982-83; sub-editor (and crossword editor), Yorkshire Post, 1984-86; chief sub-editor, Ulster News Letter, 1986-92; Freelance sub-editor, acting chief sub/night editor, features editor, Irish News, 1992-97; stone sub, Belfast Telegraph, 1997-98; design sub-editor, Sunday Life, 1998-2000; Community Telegraph Series Editor, 2000-03. Former Trades Councillor; Folkestone Labour Candidate, Kent County Council; NUJ Chairman, Bristol, Leeds; Member: National Union of Journalists, Newspapers Industrial Council, Society of Editors, (former) International Federation of Journalists. Recreations: walking; golf; cooking; sailing; reading; driving. Address: (h.) 5 Rossmara, Limavady, Co. Londonderry BT49 0UA. T.-028 777 68124.

Young, William S. F., MA. Headmaster, Belfast Royal Academy, since 2000; b. 15.8.44, Londonderry; m., Lorna Kathleen; 1 s.; 2 d. Educ. Foyle College, Londonderry; The Queen's University Belfast. Belfast Royal Academy, since 1968, Vice-Principal in 1980, Deputy Headmaster in 1990. Address: Belfast Royal Academy, Belfast BT14 6JL. T.-028 90 740423.